DARK ENCOUNTERS TRILOGY

THE CHILDREN OF THE GODS SERIES BOOKS 74-76

I. T. LUCAS

Published by Evening Star Press

EveningStarPress.com

ISBN: 978-1-962067-34-8

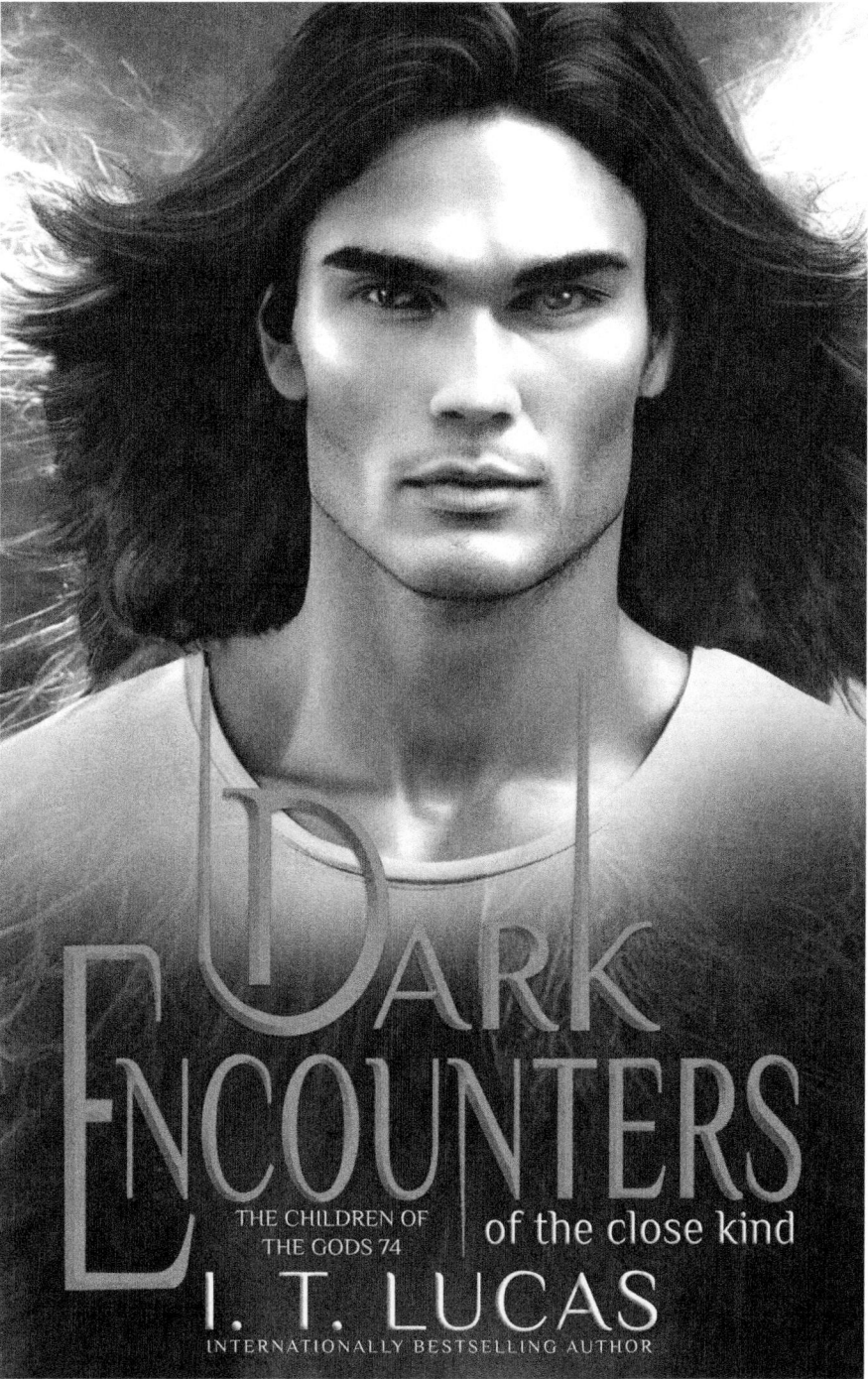

DARK ENCOUNTERS
of the close kind

THE CHILDREN OF
THE GODS 74

I. T. LUCAS

INTERNATIONALLY BESTSELLING AUTHOR

1

GABI

"I'm sorry, Ms. Emerson." The gate attendant assumed a fake apologetic smile. "The flight has been canceled due to technical issues."

They had been having those issues for the past two hours, and every time Gabi had approached the desk, the attendant's answer had been that the problem was being worked on and that boarding should start shortly.

She had been afraid to stray away from the gate to use the bathroom or grab a cup of coffee, but when she'd finally dared a dash to the nearest coffee shop, the announcement about her flight had finally come—not that boarding was starting but that the flight had been canceled and the passengers should head to the customer service desk to make other arrangements.

It had been such a bad idea to book a flight straight from the conference to Los Angeles. She should have gone home, rested for a few days, and then hazarded another flight.

Except, Gabi knew that she wouldn't have done that. She would have chickened out.

"I just heard the announcement about my flight being canceled, and that's why I'm here. Can you please check if a seat is available on another flight to Los Angeles today?"

The woman affected another one of her fake smiles, but this one also had a condescending slant to it. "We don't handle flight bookings at the gate. You should go to the customer service desk."

There was a separate desk for that?

Gabi stifled a biting retort that would have felt awesome passing her lips but would have probably resulted in airport security escorting her away.

Her temper and her big mouth had gotten her in trouble before.

Still, she couldn't just let it go. "You could have told us that the flight might be canceled two hours ago, when you first announced that there would be a delay. Now, I'm probably not going to find a seat on another flight leaving today."

"My apologies, but I can only convey the information I receive, and until fifteen minutes ago, I was told that they were working on the problem. The customer service desk can help you book another flight, and if none work for you today, they will provide vouchers for hotel accommodations and meals."

Realizing that she wouldn't get any help from the woman, Gabi forced down a cuss word and took a long breath instead. "Can you point me toward the customer service desk?"

The gate attendant looked relieved at the prospect of finally being rid of her. "It's located in Terminal D, next to gate 98. Good luck, Ms. Emerson. And I apologize again for the inconvenience."

Practiced, empty words.

"Thanks," Gabi murmured as she grabbed the carry-on handle and rolled it in the direction the attendant had indicated.

Terminal D was at least a twenty-minute walk, and Gabi, for some unfathomable reason, was still wearing the high heels she'd put on for the last event of the conference this morning. She should have gotten a pair of flats from her carry-on while getting coffee, but she'd been in a rush, and she hadn't expected to have to march across the airport. She couldn't stop and do it now either, because with every minute she delayed, there was less chance of her getting a seat on a flight leaving today.

Perhaps the malfunction was a sign that she shouldn't go to Los Angeles.

Good God, she hated flying.

It made no difference to her that her brother was a pilot who owned a couple of jets and, until recently, had flown them for a living, and it didn't help that she knew that flying was statistically safer than driving. Gabi still preferred ground transportation.

If people were meant to fly, they would have been born with wings.

She should just give up on the idea of visiting her brothers, rent a car, and drive back home to Cleveland. It was only a five-hour drive from Toronto, and she could listen to an audiobook to pass the time.

No, she couldn't do that.

She wouldn't have a decent night's sleep until she found out what was going on with her brothers and her honorary adopted niece, and it wasn't as if she could drive all the way to Los Angeles to check on them.

Something was very fishy about the stories they had been telling her lately.

Her niece was a prodigy who had earned her PhD in bioinformatics at nineteen, but instead of accepting the teaching job that she'd been offered at Stanford, Kaia had abandoned her dreams, gotten engaged to some dude she'd met while working on a top-secret project and moved in with him.

The girl might be a genius, but she had zero life experience, and the last thing she should do was move in with a guy who was more than a decade older than her.

What Gabi found even more suspicious than Kaia's sudden engagement was that Karen and Gilbert had not only approved of her questionable life choices but had also moved to Los Angeles to be close to her, uprooting their family and leaving behind their beautiful house in the Bay Area. On top of that, Eric had fallen in love with a woman who worked for Kaia's fiancé, and he had joined the rest of the family in Los Angeles, giving up his executive jets chartering business.

At first, Gabi had been curious, then worried, and now she was panicking.

It wasn't like her brothers to act so impulsively, and Gilbert was the last guy on the planet who would have been okay with his honorary adopted daughter giving up her dreams for a guy.

Well, that was a slight exaggeration. There were probably more protective fathers and stepfathers out there, but despite the fact that Gilbert and Karen had never bothered to get married, and he had never officially adopted Karen's two daughters from her previous marriage, he was definitely up there with the worst of them.

Or was it the best of them?

Gabi should know.

Gilbert had always been more of a father than a brother to her, and when she couldn't get him on the phone for three days straight, she'd even called Kaia and Cheryl and tried to get them to spill the beans, but they had been as evasive as their mother, telling her the same story about a wonderful new business opportunity that Kaia's fiancé had offered Gilbert and Eric, and how it was keeping them both insanely busy.

Gabi wasn't buying it, so she'd booked the flight to L.A. right after the Nutrition, Fitness, and Health Management conference in Toronto was over. If she could have gotten out of attending it, she would have, but her ticket had been paid for months in advance, and attending the conference was important for her business.

Staying on top of the latest trends and learning about all the new research and discoveries was what her clients expected from her.

When Gilbert had finally called her, echoing the same crappy excuse Karen had given her about him being swamped with work, it had reinforced her decision to pay them a visit without advance notice.

Did they think that she was dumb?

Gabi felt tears misting her eyes.

What if Gilbert had a terminal illness, and that was why everyone had moved to Los Angeles, and Kaia had given up on her dreams?

What if that was where he was being treated?

But why keep her out of the loop? And couldn't Gilbert have come to Cleveland instead of Los Angeles? After all, the Cleveland Clinic was there, mere minutes away from her home.

Except, Gilbert wouldn't have come to her hometown even if Cleveland was the better option.

Her brothers treated her like a delicate piece of china that would break from the slightest touch, but she was their sister, and if Gilbert didn't have long to live, she needed to be by his side.

Did they think she wouldn't be able to handle it? That she would fall apart and cry her eyes out instead of being helpful and supportive?

Gabi could be brave if she needed to be.

God, she prayed it wasn't what she was thinking, and that Gilbert had just had a hair transplant or some other cosmetic procedure, and that was why he hadn't called her back and had asked Karen and the girls to cover for him.

Yeah, that was probably it.

Gabi had already lost her parents. She couldn't lose anyone else.

She wouldn't survive it.

Taking a fortifying breath, she wiped away the tears welling in her eyes, blew her nose on a tissue, and joined the long line of airline customers waiting to be helped at the service desk.

2

KIAN

"Hello, Victor." Kian shook Turner's hand. "Thanks for coming."

The guy smiled. "I never say no to free food."

Next to him, Bridget chuckled. "Now look what you have done. You have given Kian the secret code." She lifted on her toes and kissed Kian's cheek. "If you want Victor's help, all you have to do is offer him a steak."

Kian doubted Turner would have enjoyed any steak Okidu had prepared. His butler sneered at anything produced on a grill, and if he cooked steak at all, it was in a pan or oven.

Turner, on the other hand, prided himself on being the best steak griller in the village, but his title was contested by Roni, who claimed that it belonged to him.

"I'm sorry to disappoint you, but Okidu is not serving steak for lunch."

Turner stopped and pretended to turn around. "Oh, well, I guess I have to go home and fire up the grill."

That was a rare display of humor for the guy, and Kian wondered whether Turner had been working on his people skills. It was also possible that he meant it literally.

"Don't be silly." Syssi gave Turner a brief hug. "Okidu made beef stroganoff. Wait until you taste it. You'll be licking your fingertips."

"I'm sure I will, but how would you know? Did you taste it?"

Yep. Turner was still as literal as usual.

Syssi shook her head. "I didn't have to. If the smells alone weren't mouth-watering enough to inform even a vegetarian like me, then Kalu-gal's frequent tasting and moaning were."

They needed to brainstorm the issue of the strange new signals that had popped up and immediately winked out twice so far, but Syssi hadn't wanted Kian to go to the office building on a Sunday, so she had invited everyone who could contribute to the brainstorming to lunch at their home.

Eighteen hours had passed since the last occurrence, so Kian's stress levels had decreased significantly, and he felt less urgency to send a team to investigate.

In fact, if not for Syssi's gut feeling about the importance of the occurrence, he might have been tempted to ignore the brief emergence of signals that had been supposedly emitted by alien trackers across the globe, but his wife's gut feelings were usually much more than a hunch, and ignoring them would be a mistake.

Ironically, what worried him the most about those new signals was that they were different from the ones emitted by the trackers that had been implanted in the Kra-ell settlers, meaning that they were not coming from the other assassins that Igor had told them about or the incredibly dangerous royal twins. Thankfully, it seemed that neither the assassins nor the twins had awakened from stasis. But the unknown source of the new signals was more concerning than a threat he'd already known about.

Okidu, who had deciphered the signals to identify their location, had said that they felt like an older model of those trackers, which probably meant that they belonged to earlier visitors to Earth.

Given that the settler ship had left Anumati seven thousand years ago, those trackers had to be even older than that. And since the signals were coming from Chengdu, the capital of China's Sichuan province and home to Lugu Lake and its Mosuo population, the assumption was

9

that they had belonged to the scouting team that had been sent ahead of the settler ship to verify that Earth was suitable for the Kra-ell.

The problem with that theory was that there was no way any members of the original scouting team were still alive. The Kra-ell were long-lived compared to humans, but they were not immortal, and those males should have died out millennia ago. Furthermore, the Kra-ell cremated their dead, so there were no bodies for anyone to dig out either, and no one could have gotten the trackers out of the remains.

Could it be that the human descendants of those original Kra-ell males had kept the trackers, and they were now trying to activate them for some reason?

But if William, a genius who knew a thing or two about alien technology, couldn't break the trackers apart without destroying them, how could some humans in China manage that?

On top of that, the devices only worked when inside a living organism, so even if the descendants of the Kra-ell had kept them throughout the generations, they would have to know that live hosts were needed.

The only other possible option was that the scouts had managed to prolong their lives somehow, perhaps by staying in their stasis pods for hundreds of years at a time, and they were now starting to wake up, but something wasn't working right.

In the dining room, Kian pulled out a chair next to William. "I have a theory about the scouts and want to run it by you."

"Shoot."

"Do you think that the Kra-ell scouts could have used the stasis pods to stay alive longer? We know those pods could sustain life for thousands of years, so that's not a far-fetched scenario."

William exchanged knowing looks with his mate before returning his gaze to Kian. "Kaia and I talked about that last night. If I were in the scouts' shoes, that was what I would have done, and that also explains the discrepancy in what we assumed about them. For them to influence the Mosuo society, they must have been around during the time the Mosuo settled around Lugu Lake, and if the scouts arrived more than seven thousand years ago, they must have found a way to survive or left descendants who took it upon themselves to continue the tradition of their forefathers, and they were the ones who influenced the Mosuo."

"I had a vision about a cremating ceremony for one of the scouts," Jacki said. "And the subterranean chamber in which the ceremony was held was no older than fifteen hundred years." She turned to Kalugal. "Am I right?"

"Give or take a few hundred years. It's sometimes difficult to ascertain whether the most ancient occupants we can date used preexisting caverns or dug them out themselves."

"Anyway," Jacki continued. "If they could use the stasis pods to prolong their lives, why did some still die? They could have stayed in the pod for centuries at a time, woken up for a few days or weeks to check what was going on and whether the settler ship had arrived, and then gone back into stasis. They could have survived to this day."

"I really need to get to that pod," Kalugal said. "It's extremely difficult, and my team is basically digging by hand an inch at a time. I don't want anyone dying there because the scouts booby-trapped the site."

"Perhaps there is no pod there." Kian got to his feet and walked over to sit next to Syssi. "You just assume that a pod is causing the alien transmissions, but it might be something else."

"Right. Maybe it's an alien aircraft." Kalugal grinned. "That would be an even more exciting discovery than a pod."

"Not if the pod has live people in it." Annani floated into the room and waited for Kian to pull out a chair for her before sitting down. "I am much more interested in those lives than in the technology that brought them here."

3

GABI

The customer service attendant looked like she'd been through the wringer, but she still managed a genuine apologetic expression for Gabi. "The only remaining direct flight to Los Angeles today is fully booked." She went back to her screen and kept typing. "Let me see if I can find you another way to get there."

Great. As if she needed two more takeoffs and landings.

"I hate flying," Gabi admitted. "I might not survive a flight with a stopover."

She should just give up.

No, she couldn't. She had to see Gilbert with her own eyes and hear him tell her he was okay.

"If you had gotten here fifteen minutes ago, I still had a couple of seats," the attendant murmured as she clicked on her keyboard. "Why did you wait so long?"

"I would have gotten here two hours earlier if the gate attendant at my original flight had told the truth about the flight being canceled and not delayed."

While waiting in line, Gabi had heard the other customers talking about how it was common practice. The airlines did it on purpose, so not everyone would storm the service desk at the same time, which explained why everyone else had gotten there ahead of her and she was the last one in line.

The woman's knowing smile confirmed the rumor. "I can put you on the first flight leaving for Los Angeles tomorrow morning and give you vouchers for a hotel and two meals."

"I don't want to stay overnight in the airport. I'm just going to rent a car and drive home to Cleveland."

She could go home, get some rest, and book a direct flight from there for the next day.

The attendant frowned at her screen. "It must be your lucky day, after all. I just had a cancellation in first class. I'm grabbing the seat for you." She typed furiously fast.

"Hold on." Gabi lifted her hand. "Do I have to pay for the upgrade?"

She rarely flew, so she didn't have any accumulated miles or preferred status or any of the other perks that airlines give to frequent travelers.

"It's a free special-circumstances upgrade." The woman lifted her head and gave her a conspiratorial smile. "I wrote down that it is an emergency. Your best friend is getting married tonight." She winked.

That was such an unexpected kindness that Gabi just gaped for a long moment. "Thank you," she finally croaked. "You're a miracle worker."

"Sometimes I am." The attendant handed Gabi the boarding pass. "Since you are flying first class, you also have access to the executive lounge. It's right across from here." She pointed at the opaque sliding doors across the aisle with the words Alliance Club engraved on them. "Enjoy."

"Thank you." Gabi snatched the pass. "You're the best airline employee I've ever encountered. If they send me a survey to fill in, I'm going to sing your praises."

"Thanks." The woman put up the closed sign on her desk. "Have a safe flight."

Gabi swallowed. The words safety and flight didn't belong together, not in her mind anyway, but since it was her lucky day, and she was flying first class and visiting the executive lounge for the first time, perhaps it was a sign that she was supposed to go to Los Angeles after all.

Rolling her carry-on, she sauntered over to the sliding doors and walked in as if she owned the place. The three-and-a-half-hour wait for the next flight didn't look so bad now when she could spend them having complimentary drinks at the bar.

The attendant took her boarding pass, scanned it, and handed it back, "Welcome to the club, Ms. Emerson."

"Thank you." Gabi rolled her carry-on straight to the bar and ordered a gin and tonic.

Since all the seats at the bar were taken, she took her drink to one of the round dining tables next to the buffet.

Come to think of it, she was a little peckish.

It had been a long time since she'd had breakfast, and she craved a salty snack along with her gin and tonic.

Hopefully, none of the conference attendees were in the club, or at least none of those who knew her, so she could indulge in peace.

A licensed nutritionist shouldn't consume alcohol and munch on pretzels in the middle of the day.

What kind of an example would she be setting?

Ugh, to hell with that.

She was a long way from home, and if anyone recognized her, she would pretend to be her own doppelgänger.

Putting the drink down, Gabi looked in the direction of the buffet, but her eyes didn't make it all the way to the food. They got snagged on three ridiculously good-looking men crowding one small table.

Had there been a model convention in Toronto she hadn't heard about?

Each of the guys could star in an ad for luxury cologne, cigars, whiskeys, watches, sports cars, or—

One of them must have felt her looking at him and turned toward her, taking her breath away.

The guy was unreal, with chiseled cheekbones that could cut granite and skin so smooth that it looked like his face was gold-plated. His eyes were dark, nearly black, but there was warmth in them as he looked at her.

He smiled, lifted his beer glass, and mouthed cheers.

Gabi swallowed. She couldn't take her eyes off him no matter how hard she tried, and she couldn't smile back or force her mouth to say cheers back to him either.

Damn, that was embarrassing.

It took a pinch to her inner arm to get her to stop staring, give him a slight nod of acknowledgment, and turn away.

Abandoning the idea of getting a snack because it meant passing by his table, Gabi sat down with her back to him, pulled out her phone, and pretended to read on it while sipping on her drink.

The book might have been written in Chinese for all she managed to read, and her stupid heart was racing as if she was a teenager with the hots for the most popular guy in the school cafeteria.

"Been there, done that, and I'm never doing that again," she murmured under her breath.

Gabi had married her prom king.

She'd snagged the hottest guy in school, married him after college, and divorced him five years later.

The problem with hot guys was that they were in high demand, and most didn't know how to say no, including her ex.

That had been eleven years ago, and she was still single, not because she lacked male attention but because she was a walking contradiction.

After divorcing Dylan, she'd vowed that if she got married again, it would be to a sweet nerd who attracted absolutely no female attention and would be hers and hers alone.

The problem with that was that she wasn't attracted to nice, nerdy men. She was drawn to the hot, bad boys who were bound to break her heart again.

4

KIAN

As Okidu collected the empty plates, Turner leaned back and looked at Jacki. "The guy you saw in your vision didn't necessarily die of old age. He might have been killed in battle. The Kra-ell are not as fast healing as we are, and they can die from injuries that we can heal."

"True." Jacki nibbled on her lower lip. "But I thought about it, and there could be another explanation. They might have devised the idea of using the life pods only after several hundred years had passed and the settlers hadn't arrived. So, they were already old when they started using the pods."

"I don't think so." Kalugal draped his arm over the back of Jacki's chair. "The settler ship was supposed to take three hundred years to get to Earth, and in the meantime, the scouts had nothing to do. I bet they came up with the idea of using the pods early on, and I think they took turns in them. If it was me and my men, I would have assigned at least two to stay awake at any time in case something unexpected happened while the rest slept. When they realized that the ship wasn't coming, they might have decided that there was no point in waiting, and all got into the pods, probably in the hopes that someone would collect them at some point."

"What about communications with Anumati?" Syssi asked. "The

scouts contacted the queen to tell her that Earth was habitable, so we know that they had the ability to communicate with home. But the question is how? Was there a god ship orbiting above the planet? Did they use the same satellites the exiled gods used before communications were severed? What were they told to do when it became clear that the ship wasn't coming?"

"Probably to go into the pods," Jacki said. "The queen would not have given up hope that her children were alive, and she would have told the scouts to sleep so they would be around when the twins finally arrived."

Kian had to admit that Jacki's assumption made sense. If Fates forbid his children were lost in space, he wouldn't have given up hope either and would have wanted the scouts to stay and wait for them.

The problem was that they were speculating, and by now they had so many ideas and possible scenarios that he had trouble keeping it all organized in his head.

"We should write down the sequence of events and all the good questions that are being raised. There are too many variables to keep track of."

Turner leaned down to pull his trusty yellow pad out of his satchel. "Let's do it now. What's our starting point?"

"Ahn and the Kra-ell queen have an affair," Syssi suggested. "The rebellion before that is less concerning to us. We need to determine the sequence of events from when the queen got pregnant with the twins."

"I agree." Turner wrote it down. "Next, the rebellion ends with a peace treaty, and Ahn and his cohorts are exiled to Earth. The queen is pregnant with his children, but we assume he doesn't know that. Does she know he's the father?"

Syssi pursed her lips. "The Kra-ell males know right away when a female is pregnant. The queen's consorts would have known it hadn't been one of them. How did she keep them from revealing her secret?"

"The vows," Kian said. "I'm sure the queen's consorts were bound by so many oaths of loyalty to her that they couldn't betray her even if they suspected that the father was a god, a big no-no in their society. Also, we know that the queen was a strong compeller. She might have compelled their silence."

"That wouldn't have been enough for her," Bridget said. "The Eternal

King was the strongest compeller on the planet, and he could have over-ridden her compulsion and forced the truth out of her consorts. That's why the queen would never have trusted her consorts or anyone else with crucial information about her children. She probably lied to them, saying the father was a lowly Kra-ell male who she didn't want anyone to know about. Or even better, she could have commanded one of her consorts to claim that the children were his."

"And then had him killed," Turner said. "So, he couldn't be forced to reveal the truth."

Annani laughed, the sound breaking the somber mood that Turner's words had brought about. "We do not know what actually happened, and we are getting carried away with *Game of Thrones* types of scenarios. It is very entertaining, but we should stick to what we know or can make an educated guess about."

Syssi nodded. "I agree. The next item on the timeline is the decommission of the Odus, but since the exiled gods knew about that, we can assume that it happened before they were sent to Earth or shortly after."

"Probably before." Turner wrote it down. "That's why I always leave several empty lines between each item. Otherwise, things get messy."

Kian stifled a chuckle. "We wouldn't want that." He continued, "The peace treaty also included a Kra-ell settlement on Earth, but that's where it gets muddy. If Ahn knew about the terms of the treaty, he would have said something about expecting the Kra-ell's arrival, but he and the others said nothing about it. They never even mentioned the Kra-ell. Why is that?"

His mother shrugged. "They also never said that they were exiled. They did not even tell us they were from somewhere else in the universe. Khiann's father told Khiann and me in confidence about an ugly war a long time ago, but he talked in general terms and never mentioned the Kra-ell either." She looked at Toven. "What about you? Did Ekin or Mortdh tell you anything or at least hint at it?"

"Ekin did not like to talk about politics, and he never talked about the home planet. Mortdh, on the other hand, threw a lot of hints around, but I did not take him seriously. Even our own father said that Mortdh was a lunatic and that I should not listen to his rants. Now I'm starting to think that maybe my brother was not as crazy as everyone thought. He was power-hungry and lacked scruples, but that did not make him insane. Those two character traits describe ninety-nine percent of the world's leaders."

Annani shifted in her chair. "Insanity comes in different forms. Mortdh was smart, but he was crazy. Navuh told Areana things that no one else knew about his father, and it confirmed what everyone suspected about Mortdh. He was prone to fits of rage, he was a megalo-maniac, he was violent, and he believed in patriarchy and the subjuga-tion of females." She sighed. "He also believed that he was doing good things for the population under his rule and that they had nothing to complain about."

"Was he right?" Jacki asked.

"They were not hungry, and no one dared attack his region, but they were all his to do with as he pleased. He treated everyone as mindless slaves, as cattle—the immortals in his army, the immortal and dormant females in his harem, and the humans serving him."

"That was common back then," Jacki said. "Not that it was right, but that was how those in power treated everyone else in the ancient world." She snorted. "Heck, they still do. They are just more circumspect about it now."

She should know. Kalugal had built an empire by manipulating people's herd mentality to his advantage.

With everything that had been going on, Kian hadn't had time to look into Kalugal's social media company. Hopefully, his cousin wasn't doing anything overly nefarious.

As Okidu walked in with a tray loaded with desserts, Annani's mood brightened. "Let us take a break and enjoy these lovely sweets with tea."

"That's a wonderful idea." Syssi pushed to her feet. "Does anyone want a cappuccino?"

5

GABI

Thankfully, the three hot guys hadn't stayed long in the club, or Gabi would have been starving by now.

Like a coward, she'd waited until they were gone to walk up to the buffet and load her plate with whatever junk food was offered. Well, most people would not call pasta with meatballs junk, but to a nutritionist, it was.

No one wanted advice about diet and fitness from an overweight or out-of-shape nutritionist. Heck, she would have no clients.

Nevertheless, it was free, and she was allowed to indulge once in a while. Just not too often. With a sigh, she put her fork down and pushed the plate away. It hadn't even been tasty.

What a waste of calories.

If she was sinning, she at least wanted to enjoy it.

Gabi softly chuckled as the impossibly gorgeous face of one of the three hunks popped into her mind's eye, the one she'd aptly nicknamed 'the devil.' The man was sin personified, and she wouldn't mind a tumble with either of his two buddies either.

No, that wasn't true.

They were just as gorgeous as her devil, but in a different way, and although they were nice to look at, she couldn't see herself naked with either of them.

Mr. Devil, however, was a different story. She could see herself doing a lot of naughty things with him.

Gabi sighed.

After the way she'd ignored his covert glances and his smiles when she'd caught him looking, it was pathetic of her to imagine herself doing anything with him. If she had given him the slightest indication that she was interested, he might have come over to her table and perhaps offered to buy her a drink.

He didn't seem like the shy type, but men these days were cautious about approaching women, and he was smart to stay away unless invited.

Not that she would have made a big deal of it if he had come over to talk to her uninvited, but she wouldn't have done anything more than talk, and if he wanted more, she would have politely declined.

Mr. Devil was too good-looking and too young for her.

Gabi knew that she looked incredible for a thirty-eight-year-old woman. She worked damn hard for it, and most people thought she was a decade younger, but she had experience and perspective that Mr. Devil most likely didn't have.

She shouldn't make assumptions based solely on his age and looks. Maybe he was a small business owner like her? With the muscles he was packing, he could be a personal trainer. But had he ever been an over-weight kid who the other kids made fun of?

Not likely.

Had he ever been cheated on by his girlfriend?

What woman in her right mind would replace that face and that body with another? Or what man, for that matter? Not that Gabi thought Mr. Devil swung that way. The looks he had given her had not been the platonic kind.

Whatever.

She should get going. The boarding for her flight had started several minutes ago, and although she had a first-class seat and could board without standing in line, she shouldn't delay too much.

With her luck, something would happen on the way to the gate, and she would miss her flight.

Gabi cleaned her table of the mess she'd made, pushed to her feet, and gripped the handle of her carry-on.

"Miss!" Someone called from behind her. "Miss!"

When she turned around, a man was pointing to the chair she had just vacated. "You forgot your purse."

"Thank you." She rushed back to retrieve it. "My passport and my boarding pass are in there." And her money and credit cards.

"You are welcome. Have a safe flight."

"You too." She smiled at him. "Thank you again. You are a lifesaver."

If the friendly man hadn't noticed the purse and called her, Gabi would have gotten all the way to the gate before realizing she'd left it behind. She would have been forced to run back to get it and would have missed her flight.

Was it lucky that the guy had noticed, though?

Or unlucky?

Was she supposed to be on that flight or not?

She was well aware that it wasn't smart to base her life decisions on what she thought was lucky or unlucky, and she shouldn't look for signs at every turn, but when someone was living in a state of constant fear, they clung to anything that could be a directional pointer in the chaos of life.

With panic seizing her lungs, Gabi forced her feet to keep moving. She was afraid of too many damn things, but her family needed her, and she needed to conquer these fears, at least for this one flight.

Hopefully, Gilbert and the rest of her family were fine, and she was panicking for nothing.

On the way back, though, she might rent a car and drive all the way home.

6

ANNANI

Ready to continue working on the timeline, Annani lifted her empty teacup, signaling to Okidu that she needed a refill.

"I hope Allegra is having fun at Amanda's," Syssi said. "I didn't want any distractions while we were brainstorming the signal issue, and Amanda volunteered to babysit, but it's not easy to take care of two babies at the same time."

As Okidu rushed over with the carafe and filled everyone's cups, starting with Annani's, she smiled at him. "Thank you, Okidu."

"It is my pleasure, Clan Mother."

He said that with so much conviction that there was no doubt in Annani's mind that he meant it, but she also had no doubt that it was part of his programming to enjoy serving his masters. Evidently, the gods had a way of programming even emotions, and she wondered whether that was part of their genetic manipulation. Could they make one person inherently happier than another? Or sadder?

She had read somewhere or heard from someone that people had a set point of happiness and that they always returned to that point no matter what happened in their lives, either good or bad.

It could have been wonderful if everyone was naturally happy, and if the gods were truly benevolent, they would have engineered people to be more cheerful. But maybe they had tried that, and it did not work.

Perhaps sadness was needed so that happiness could be appreciated.

Annani was the happiest when she was around her children and grandchildren, especially the little ones. There was no greater pleasure than holding a baby to her chest and kissing their little cheeks.

"Amanda has Onidu and Dalhu to help her," Jacki said. "I am sure Allegra is happy to spend some time with her aunt and uncle. What surprises me is that Amanda didn't want to join our discussion."

Kian huffed. "That's because she has nothing to say on the subject. We should have invited Jade." He cast his wife a look. "Somehow, it didn't occur to either of us."

Syssi's eyes widened. "Should I call her? We can wait for her to get here."

Kian shook his head. "She will be offended that we invited her as an afterthought. If we need to ask her anything, I'll text her."

"Good idea." Turner pulled out his yellow pad again. "Let me remind everyone where we were before the break. The last item on my timeline is Ahn's exile, and before that, the Odus's decommission." He cast a quick look at Okidu, but Kian's butler remained impassive. "Kian wondered why Ahn and the other gods had never mentioned the Kra-ell, and the Clan Mother hypothesized that they didn't want their descendants to know that they had been exiled from their home planet. The gods pretended they had always been on Earth—a divergent species." He looked at Annani. "Am I right so far?"

She nodded. "Yes. And since they wanted us to believe they were earthlings, they could not mention another species of intelligent humanoids."

Jacki looked like she was bristling to say something but did not want to interrupt.

Annani smiled at the young woman. "Go ahead, Jacki."

"Thank you. It has just occurred to me that the gods might have been spreading propaganda against the Kra-ell by telling stories about demons and vampires. I checked online, and both creatures were mentioned in the Sumerian myths. Isn't it suspicious that demons and vampires are often described as having forked tongues, fangs, and glowing red eyes? The resemblance to the Kra-ell is too much to be a coincidence."

"That does not make sense," Annani protested. "Ahn and the other gods were exiled because they supported the Kra-ell's emancipation. They would not have spread malicious stories about their friends."

Jacki's face fell. "Maybe some among them became disillusioned or bitter because of the price they'd been forced to pay."

"Or some of the so-called rebels might have been planted by the Eternal King," Kian said. "Although I don't know what he could have hoped to achieve by spreading those rumors. Did he want the humans to turn against the Kra-ell and eliminate them? Why did he care? He didn't want his children and the other gods to thrive on Earth. He wanted them all dead. The gods and the Kra-ell, and he wanted to blame their annihilation on the humans so their deaths couldn't be traced back to him."

Turner lifted his pencil. "That's your answer. He planned for Igor and the assassins to eliminate the gods and the twins and then for the humans to eliminate the Kra-ell."

"That's ironic," Bridget said. "Did he believe that the weak, easily-manipulated humans could get rid of a powerful compeller like Igor and many super-strong Kra-ell? There is strength in numbers, but still."

Syssi sighed. "The king had plans within plans, and all of them were meant to shield him from blame while accomplishing what he wanted. He only had to make it look like the humans eliminated the Kra-ell while sending others to do the job and then getting rid of them." She lifted her gaze to Kian. "Maybe the signals we picked up belong to another team of scouts or assassins that the king sent to deal with his problem. Maybe he still sends people to Earth occasionally to check whether the Kra-ell ship has arrived. A century or even a millennium is nothing for him and the other gods. The last team he sent might have paid Earth a visit hundreds of years ago and reported that there were no gods or Kra-ell to be found. This might be a new team that has just arrived."

Kian shook his head. "That's not likely given that the signals are coming from trackers that are an older technology than the ones implanted in the settlers. Also, it is too much of a coincidence that they started transmitting on the day we put Igor in stasis. I still think he had some kind of telepathic communication with Anumati. When they realized that Igor had found a descendant of Ahn, they might have activated a sleeper cell that had been in stasis on Earth all along."

Annani wanted to tell Kian that she had checked Igor's mind thoroughly and had not found a telepathic connection, but what if she had just not delved deep enough to find it?

Igor had been unaware of transmitting, but it could have happened subconsciously, and could have been buried too deep for her to discover.

Annani knew better than to let arrogance make her complacent.

Turning to her son, she nodded in acquiescence. "I wish I could tell you that you are getting carried away on the wings of imagination, but the truth is that what you said sounds logical to me. Igor might have been transmitting subconsciously, which was why I could not detect it. And a sleeper cell sounds like something the Eternal King would have done. A plot within a plot, a contingency within another contingency."

7

KIAN

Kian didn't know whether he should feel satisfied or worried that his mother had finally admitted that his suspicion about Igor transmitting information telepathically was valid. Not that he knew for a fact that Igor had done that, but he appreciated knowing that his speculation was no longer being dismissed.

Turner tapped his pen on his writing pad. "Our current working theory is that a sleeper team is waking up, and their trackers are malfunctioning. It's either the scouting team or one the gods subsequently sent to finish Igor's job."

"Gods would not have trackers," Bridget said. "Their bodies would have rejected them. The signals have to come from Kra-ell, which most likely means that they belong to the last surviving scouting team members. Since they are coming online and winking out, I assume they are coming out of stasis, but something is not working right, and they are slipping back in. That's the most logical explanation I can think of."

"I agree." Turner nodded at his mate and then looked at Kian. "What do you want to do about it? For obvious reasons, I advise against sending a local human team to investigate."

"Naturally." Kian leaned back in his chair. "We can't let humans discover a stasis pod. Especially not the Chinese."

Kalugal chuckled. "They would immediately reverse engineer it and make one for their Chairman so he could live forever."

Turner didn't even smile. "My recommendation is to send a team of Guardians with Kra-ell reinforcements. If Jade is willing, and if you trust her, she should lead the team."

Did he trust her?

Kian nodded. "That's a good suggestion, but I don't know whether Jade can leave her people at a critical time like this. Some of them are unhappy about the trial results, and they might stir things up in her absence."

"Can't her second-in-command hold the fort?" Syssi asked. "Kagra seems like a capable female."

"I doubt she's ready to take over full command." Kian lifted the delicate teacup and sipped the fragrant jasmine tea. "Kagra is full of swagger, but she's young and inexperienced. She can, however, join the team, not as its leader but as a second-in-command. I'll feel better with a Guardian in charge, but since none speak Chinese, Vrog could be a great asset to them because he speaks the language, knows the local customs, and can pass for a human. I will speak with him about joining the team and perhaps leading the Kra-ell portion."

"Good choice," Kalugal said. "Which Guardian do you want to put in charge of the team?"

"Yamanu is the obvious choice." Syssi turned to Kian. "Right? If there is a pod and shrouding is needed, he's the perfect Guardian for the job."

"You also need a doctor," Bridget said. "Merlin has experience treating Kra-ell, so he should go. The Kra-ell waking up from stasis might be in critical condition and in need of hospitalization. Yamanu's thralling and shrouding ability might come in handy in getting them into a hospital."

"I wish I could go." Syssi sighed. "I've never gone on any exciting missions."

Kian shuddered, just thinking about her in a dangerous situation. "You have a baby." He used the one argument that wouldn't make him sound like a chauvinist. "You can't leave Allegra, and you can't take her into a danger zone. She's still human."

"About that." Syssi turned to Annani. "Perhaps she should start spending time with you?"

Kian nearly choked on his tea. "It's too early. Usually, the girls turn at two years old. Right, Mother?"

Annani nodded. "The earliest was eighteen months. But I would be delighted to spend time with my granddaughter, and she will transition when she is ready."

They both knew it didn't work like that, and he was tired of hiding it from Syssi. Toven knew, and perhaps Mia did too, but Kian didn't want Syssi to be burdened with the knowledge. It had to remain a secret, and it was better that she didn't know. He hated keeping things from her, but to tell her would be selfish. He would unburden himself from the guilt but burden her with the knowledge.

"You know what has occurred to me?" Jacki said. "If those scouts were alive for much longer than we previously believed, and they took turns, with some staying awake and some going into stasis, then one of them must have fathered Mey and Jin. Perhaps the sisters should join the team going to China."

Bridget shook her head. "If Mey and Jin were fathered by a pureblood, they would have been born Kra-ell hybrids. But since they were Dormants and needed activation, we have to assume that their mother was a dormant immortal, and their father was either a hybrid Kra-ell or even a human with Kra-ell recessive genes like the children of the hybrid Kra-ell males."

"Right." Jacki pushed a lock of blond hair behind her ear. "It was a brain fart." She winced. "My apologies, Clan Mother. I shouldn't use such language in your presence."

"You are forgiven," Annani said magnanimously.

Turner cleared his throat. "We have a working assumption on what we expect to find and who we are going to send to find it. When do you want the team to leave?"

"Tomorrow is the earliest," Kian said. "I need to talk to Yamanu, Jade, Kagra, Merlin, and Vrog. If everyone is on board with the plan, we can make a flight plan and get the team to China on our jet."

"I'll make the flight arrangements," Bridget said.

"Is there anything else we need to discuss?" Turner asked.

"I think that's it." Kalugal turned to Kian. "I just hope we find them before it's too late. They can shed more light on what happened on Earth or what was supposed to happen."

Kian nodded. "I just hope our assumptions are correct and the signals came from the scouts and not some other unknown threat."

8

GABI

Gabi had never flown first class before, not because she couldn't afford it, but because she wouldn't spend money on something she hated no matter how comfortable and luxurious it was, and she had the same philosophy about food.

Why waste her allotment of daily calories on something that didn't taste great?

Well, the truth was that she didn't make as much money as she pretended to her brothers, and she couldn't afford first class if she flew often or overseas, but she did it so rarely that she could have indulged once in a blue moon if it was important to her.

Naturally, it wasn't.

"This way, Ms. Emerson." The flight attendant motioned for her to go around to the other row. "Your seat is in the middle."

Looking at her boarding pass, Gabi rechecked the seat number. It was row number three, seat D. The first class had lie-flat seats, two in the middle and one on each side by the window. She would have preferred to have a window seat so she wouldn't have to chat with the passenger seated next to her, but since she wasn't paying for this, she shouldn't complain.

Besides, having someone sitting next to her would force her to keep the panic at bay and pretend that she was okay, and pretending courage was sometimes the best way to overcome fear. Also, if she was busy chatting, she might not notice the takeoff, which for her was the scariest part of the flight. For some reason, it scared her even more than the landing, perhaps because it was the start of the torment and not the end of it.

"Let me help you with that." The older gentleman in the seat behind her got up and reached for her carry-on.

"Thank you." She gave him a smile and let him lift her luggage to the overhead bin even though she could have easily done so herself.

To decline the help would have been rude.

An hour of strength training three times a week ensured that Gabi had strong muscles and bones, and she even splurged on a personal trainer to instruct her on proper form and monitor her progress. Her trainer made the session bearable with her quirky humor and merciless teasing, and that alone was worth the price she was charging her, but the other benefit was the new clients Becky sent her way.

The seat beside hers was vacant, but Gabi knew it wouldn't stay that way. The flight was fully booked, so it was only a matter of time before she had company.

The attendant leaned toward her with a tray. "May I offer you champagne, orange juice, or water?"

"Champagne, please." Gabi smiled. "I need liquid courage."

The attendant smiled back. "I'll get you another one before takeoff."

"Thanks." Gabi cradled the flute in her palms, took a long sip, and closed her eyes.

Maybe the comfort and pampering would make flying less stressful. She could put on her headphones and watch a movie or listen to a book narration to take her mind off the fact that she was several thousand feet in the air. Getting a seat in the middle aisle and away from the window was also a stroke of good luck.

"What a happy coincidence," a deliciously male voice said on the other side of the aisle. "We meet again."

Thinking that he was talking to someone else, Gabi didn't bother to open her eyes, but then she felt the seat move and turned to see who was sitting next to her.

No way!

It was none other than Mr. Devil from the lounge, and he was smiling at her with those lips that were made for kissing.

How could it be?

He and his friends had left the lounge hours ago. She'd been certain that their departure meant their flight had been boarding.

"Hi," she croaked while eyeing the divider between the seats.

She hadn't pulled it across, and now it was too late. She couldn't just slam it in his face.

He rose on his knees, leaned over the wide center console, and offered her his hand. "Since we are going to be neighbors on this flight, we should get acquainted. I'm Uriel."

"The light of God." She put her hand in his, and as she'd expected, the contact was electrifying.

Smiling, he held on to her hand for longer than was necessary. "Is that your name? The light of God?"

She pulled her hand out of his gentle grip. "No, that's your name. My name is Gabi, short for Gabriella, which means heroine of God. We have that in common. Also, my last name is Emerson, which means brave, so basically, I'm a brave heroine of God, which is the least befitting name for me."

Her ex's last name would have been a better fit, but she hadn't taken it even when they'd been married. Perhaps it was a premonition that things between them were not going to last.

"Why is that?" Uriel asked.

"Why is what?"

"Why is the name not befitting?"

She snorted. "Because I'm terrified of flying, among many other things, so having a name that means brave is a joke."

"Fear is not the antonym of bravery. You are on a plane despite being afraid of flying, which means you are brave."

He had a point. He also hadn't told her his last name even though she'd revealed hers.

Oh well, maybe he was a famous movie star who wanted to fly incognito.

"Are your friends here with you?"

33

"They are in the first row." He pointed. "But I'm the lucky one. I get to sit next to you." His smile was so brilliant that it was blinding.

She tilted her head, the champagne finally doing its thing and loosening the tight muscles in her shoulders. "Do you believe in luck, Uriel?"

"Definitely." He leaned even closer, his dark, longish hair falling forward and framing his chiseled face. "I'm a big believer in fate."

9

JADE

Jade arched a brow. "You want me to go back to China?"

Kian shrugged. "You can send Kagra instead. But I'm sure you can understand why I need Kra-ell on the team."

When Kian had called for a meeting on a Sunday afternoon in the village square, Jade had assumed that he wanted to discuss the school Vrog was organizing. The last thing she could have imagined was a new complication in the form of signals from old trackers.

That sort of talk shouldn't be done out in the open where anyone could hear them, but it was Kian's business where and when he wanted to conduct his meetings, and apparently, he didn't want to be in his office on the weekend.

That reminded her that she needed to ask him for a space for Kra-ell headquarters. She couldn't continue having people show up at Phinas's home whenever they needed to talk to her. The space didn't have to be big or fancy, and she would even settle for a classroom in the underground structure. She hated being below ground, but beggars and choosers and all that.

She would take whatever he had.

"I'll gladly go," Vrog said. "Chengdu is a long way from my school, but it's still closer from there than from here. After we finish the investigation, I can book a flight to Beijing and visit." He rubbed his chin between his thumb and forefinger. "As part of the purchase contract, the new owners stipulated a certain number of hours I needed to dedicate to the school for the first two years. I've been doing that remotely via video meetings with the new management and Dr. Wang, but I really should visit in person. I'm curious to see how things are running under the new ownership."

"Can I go too?" Aliya asked Kian. "I mean to Chengdu. Vrog wants me to come with him to visit the school, but if I can't join the team, I can fly directly to Beijing and meet him there."

"You are welcome to join the team." Kian gave her an appraising look. "You don't blend in as easily as Vrog among humans. I wonder how the scouts' hybrid children went unnoticed in the human population. Or perhaps they were noticed, but back then, it was easier to keep things contained, especially when possessing the ability to thrall."

Aliya waved a hand over her face. "I don't blend in easily, but I managed to live among the Mosuo. If my mother hadn't died and I hadn't been so distraught after her death, I might have been able to hide my differences better. I would have just been the strange girl with eyes that were too big and who was too strong and too flat-chested."

Leaning over, Vrog wrapped his arm around her shoulders. "You are beautiful and perfect as you are."

She smiled. "You're sweet, and I might be perfect to you, but I definitely wasn't to the Mosuo boys."

"Their loss is my gain," Vrog said.

Kian turned to Jade. "So, what is it going to be? Are you going, or are you sending Kagra?"

"Why do you need either of us? I can assign a couple of the young pureblooded males to your team."

"I want someone with authority who can speak for your people. If the signals are coming from the scouts, and if they are in the process of emerging from their stasis pods, they will want to know what's going on, and they won't accept the word of a couple of young foot soldiers."

Jade sighed. "Kagra is young too, so even though she would be my representative, they might not accept someone who was born on Earth. Perhaps assigning one of the older females to the team is a better choice."

Kian hesitated for a moment. "Is there a way you can make the female your official spokesperson? Something that the scouts would recognize?"

Jade groaned. "The only thing I have is the dark triangle on my tongue to show my meager royal blood. The scouts would respond to that. But I don't want to go. I have a people to lead, and I can't leave them, especially not now that the tensions are high and threats have been issued."

The truth was that she didn't want to go because she wanted to stay with Phinas and Drova and enjoy the unit they had created. They were all still learning how to be a family, and it would be a mistake to press the pause button on that.

"I understand," Kian said. "Is there anyone else with royal blood among the settler females?"

"Yeah, with a very faint triangle and a combative attitude. Sheniya, who I personally don't like, but she will have to do." She drummed her fingers on the table. "On second thought, that could actually work to my advantage. Since Sheniya and Rishana are inseparable, they can both go, and I will get rid of two troublemakers."

They were instigators, and without them, the rest of her people would be much less antagonistic to the former prisoners, allowing them to acclimate to their new community faster.

Given his grimace, Kian was as unhappy about including Rishana and Sheniya in his team as Jade was happy about getting rid of them.

"Do you think they will want to go? I don't want them if they have to be forced. Yamanu doesn't need to babysit a pair of cantankerous females."

"Of course." Jade smiled. "I'll throw in Pavel as well. He's a charming guy, and he can be the peacekeeper. He's done a very good job of advocating for his father, and he might be able to talk some sense into them and change their minds about the former prisoners. Some additional compulsion from Toven would be helpful as well. He can compel them to be cooperative and do whatever Yamanu tells them. Naturally, I will command them to listen to him too, but they don't fully accept my authority either."

"Indeed." Kian gave her an assessing look. "But I think your motive

37

for sending Pavel on the mission has more to do with keeping him away from Drova than changing Sheniya and Rishana's minds."

She snorted. "Haven't you heard? Pavel is with Lusha now, but I wonder how long that will last. She's human, and he's a pureblood. Need I say more?"

Drova didn't seem upset about Pavel's interest in the attorney, so perhaps they were just friends.

"When are we supposed to leave?" Vrog asked. "And for how long?"

"Tomorrow," Kian said. "And I hope it will take no more than a couple of days in addition to travel time. We have the exact coordinates of the signals' origins, so there is no need to search, but if the pods are buried underground and booby-trapped like Kalugal's archeological excavation site in Lugu Lake, then digging them out might present a problem."

Jade shook her head. "I'll assign four young purebloods to your team. They can dig out whatever you need with shovels, and since they are nearly as strong as your Odus and don't need any heavy equipment to dig, it will be much safer all around. You can even send them later to help with Kalugal's site. "

"I like your idea." Kian regarded Vrog. "I'll put you in charge of the Kra-ell, including the two females. You know the language, you are the best diplomat of the bunch, and you know how to deal with the local authorities in China."

The color leached out of the guy's face. "I'm a hybrid. They will never listen to me."

He was correct, of course, but forcing the two females to answer to a hybrid would be one more way of putting Rishana and Sheniya in their place.

"They will do what I tell them," Jade said. "This is a new era for us, and blood purity will no longer determine one's status. It's going to be based purely on merit." She gave Vrog a smile. "Given your accomplishments in my absence, you've earned your place as my third alongside Kagra."

His eyes widened. "Thank you. It's a great honor, but I'm not interested in a leadership position. I'm not a politician."

"You don't need to be. You are a great administrator and educator, and you will be in charge of finances and education. Kagra can manage the more military and disciplinary aspects of our community."

That had been Valstar's job in Igor's compound, but she wasn't about to restore his former status. First, he had to earn redemption and prove himself to her and the rest of their combined community.

Vrog dipped his head. "In this case, I accept the nomination."

"Good." She pushed to her feet and turned to Kian. "I'll talk to Kagra and text you the list of names of the purebloods we choose for the mission."

10

GABI

By the time the captain asked the flight attendants to prepare for takeoff, Gabi had finished another two glasses of champagne, and her head was spinning, but she was still panicking despite the alcohol. The only thing it had managed to do was to make her speech a little slurred and the looks she was giving Uriel a little less guarded.

"Here, hold my hand." Uriel extended his arm over the center divider.

She hesitated only for a split second before taking his offer. Holding his hand would not make her any less fearful, but touching him would surely distract her.

Already, the warmth was spreading throughout her body, and it was the kind that was not calming in any way. She was feeling Uriel's innocent touch in the most un-innocent way possible.

Did he know the effect he had on her?

Uriel was surprisingly pleasant and unassuming for someone who looked like a god. Usually, people who were blessed with beauty either by birth or by scalpel were full of themselves and expected others to admire them.

Uriel was respectful and polite to a fault, and his flirting was so gentle that she wasn't sure he was actually flirting with her.

Maybe he was just being nice.

Mr. Devil had turned out to be a very nice guy who was just devilishly handsome.

"How come you and your friends are so good-looking?" she blurted out. "Did you all just come from Korea and have a layover in Toronto?"

He glanced at his arm, frowned, and then looked back at her with confusion in his eyes. "What made you think that we came from Korea?"

Had he had surgery on his arm?

Gabi hadn't heard about bicep implants, but who knew? If women had breast implants because guys liked buxom ladies, men could have bicep implants because women liked buff guys.

She laughed. "Everyone is raving about the plastic surgery in Korea. Supposedly, it is so popular that they have great surgeons with a lots of experience, and it's much less expensive to have it done there than in the States. They also have the best cosmetic products. My cosmetologist only carries stuff from Korea."

For a long moment, he stared at her with his dark, intense eyes. "Did you have plastic surgery on your face?"

That was a rude question, but she'd started it, so she'd earned it. "No. Did you?"

"I did not. I was just born with the right genes." He smiled his brilliant smile. "My father was a weatherman, and my mother was a supermodel."

For a moment she took him seriously, but the way his lips were quirking at the corners betrayed him.

"That's a line from a movie. At least the first part about your father being a weatherman is. That's what Brad Pitt said to Sandra Bullock in *The Lost City* when she asked him why he was so handsome."

As he laughed, the masculine sound went straight to her feminine center, making her tingly and needy.

Damn.

"I watched that movie on the way to Toronto," he admitted. "It was very funny."

"So, you did come from Korea."

"My friends and I toured the area."

"What were you doing there?"

41

He leaned over and whispered, "We were looking for a lost treasure."

His closeness was making her literally swoon like some heroine from a historical romance novel, but her mind was still working just fine. "I'm serious." She gave him a mock hard stare. "Don't quote that movie again."

"I wasn't." He returned to leaning against the back of his seat. "Why would I do that?"

Uriel had an annoying habit of answering her questions with his own.

"If you don't want to tell me what you were doing in Korea or can't, just say so."

He could at least make up a better story than looking for a lost treasure, especially after just quoting a line from a movie on the same subject.

Leaning over, she regarded his handsome face.

Uriel could have some Asian genes in him. Maybe one of his parents was half-Asian, and he'd been visiting family? But then his friends looked nothing like him, and she doubted they had gone with him to visit his relatives.

"We deal in antiques," he said. "Finding lost treasures in flea markets and secondhand shops is what we do."

Why did Gabi have a feeling that Uriel was once again basing his answers on something he'd seen on television?

She'd watched *Flea Market Flip*, and some of the contestants were hot, so that might have given Uriel the idea. He and his friends were probably actors, and all three had gotten enhancements in Korea. Those cheekbones couldn't be real.

"Right. And I'm the Queen of England." Gabi leaned away. "But whatever." She waved a dismissive hand. "Keep your secrets."

He frowned. "The queen died. England has a king now."

"It's an expression."

"I know. But maybe it should be modified now that there is a king."

Gabi's brain was hazy from too much champagne, but she was starting to notice more and more anomalies about Uriel.

His English was perfect, maybe even too perfect, because his accent was all American and not regional, but there was a hint of something else in it.

Children of immigrants who spoke a different language at home sometimes had a slight accent even though they had been born and raised as Americans, and Uriel had such an accent, but Gabi couldn't identify the language of origin.

"Where are your parents from?"

He chuckled. "They are not from Korea."

"But they are immigrants, right?"

"Why would you think that?"

Again with a question instead of an answer. "You have a slight accent. I assume that you spoke another language as a child."

"I did. You guessed correctly."

Uriel still hadn't told her where his parents were from, but she was tired of trying to get him to tell her things about himself.

He had told her about being a flea market flipper, though, so maybe he would answer questions about that. Not that she thought that was really what he did for a living.

"Did you find what you were looking for on your trip?"

"We did."

"So, are you rich now?"

"It wasn't that kind of treasure." He pulled out the remote and turned on the screen with the flight information showing. "Look, Gabi. We are at cruising altitude, and you haven't panicked."

"You distracted me." She pretended an accusatory tone. "Thank you."

"It was my pleasure." He released his seatbelt and got to his feet. "I'm going to talk to my friends. Will you be okay here without me for a few minutes?"

That was such a sweet thing for a stranger to say.

"I managed thirty-eight years without you. I think I can manage a few moments longer."

Better get her age out in the open before he asked for her phone number, they went on a date, and then he discovered that she was at least a decade older than he was.

Uriel didn't seem to care one bit about her age, though, and he also didn't seem to know how to respond to what she'd just said and smiled instead. "I'll be back in a few minutes."

The flight attendant came down the aisle with her notepad. "What would you like for dinner, Ms. Emerson? We have chicken with potatoes or pasta with vegetables."

"The chicken, please."

"Of course. And what would you like to drink?"

"Water, please."

"Naturally. If you would like a cocktail after dinner, you can browse the selection on the flight menu."

"Thank you. I will."

Gabi turned on the screen and started browsing. There was a large selection of movies, and she also discovered that satellite internet was complimentary in first class and that she could text if she wanted to.

Perhaps she should text Gilbert and let him know that she was coming?

After all, he couldn't tell her not to come when she was in the air, right?

She pulled out her phone and typed.

Hi, Gilbert. Believe it or not, I'm sitting in the first-class cabin of a Dream Liner on my way to Los Angeles. My ETA is five fifteen in the afternoon your time. I didn't book a hotel, and I hope I can stay with you and Karen or Eric and Darlene, but if it's inconvenient, I'll get a room in a hotel. I want to see all of you as soon as possible, though, preferably at your new place, and I hope you're not going to stonewall me again. I need to know what's happening with you, Eric, and Kaia.

His answer came a couple of minutes later.

I'm in the middle of something right now. I'll text you as soon as I can.

11

GILBERT

Gilbert threw the phone on the couch and groaned. "Gabi is on her way, and we are not ready for her."

His sister must be really freaking out to be on a transcontinental flight, and it was his fault. He hadn't come up with a convincing enough story for why they had all moved to Los Angeles, and she was worried.

Karen put down her book. "What do you mean she is on her way? When is she coming?"

He lifted his phone and checked the time. "She lands in four and a half hours. How the hell are we going to be ready for her by then? We can't just bring her to the village."

"Why not? We can ask Kalugal to compel her after she's here."

"No, we can't. It's against clan rules to compel people without their consent. We need to meet her in a neutral place, explain that we can't tell her anything without her agreeing to be hypnotized to keep it a secret, and only when she agrees can we tell her what's going on."

"Right." Karen reached for her phone. "I'm calling Darlene. I'll ask her to talk with Orion. I hope he's willing to help."

Gilbert nodded. "I'll call Eric."

About half an hour later, the family was gathered in their living room, including Orion and Alena, Kaia and William, Eric and Darlene, Cheryl, and the little ones.

Gilbert had wanted Cheryl to take them to the playground, but she'd refused. She wanted to be part of the conversation about her Aunt Gabi, and that was sweet, so he hadn't argued with her about staying.

Eric handed Gilbert a beer, and he took it even though he wasn't sure he should drink alcohol so soon after his transition. He was still weak, but he was getting stronger by the day. Regrettably, there was no change in his hair or wrinkles situation yet, but maybe it was for the best. Gabi wouldn't be shocked when she saw him.

"We need to give Kian a heads up that we might be bringing Gabi to the village," Eric said.

"Might?" Cheryl arched a brow. "Do you expect her to say no to the hypnotism, aka compulsion?"

He shrugged. "I never know with Gabi. She's afraid of so many things, but then she's so brave too. She might be terrified of letting someone take over her free will, even if it's for something as innocuous as ensuring that she keeps a secret."

"I'll come with you and convince her," Cheryl said. "She will believe me more readily than the two of you."

Gilbert frowned at the girl. "We are her brothers. Why would she believe a teenager over us?"

Cheryl rolled her eyes. "Because she knows you, and she knows me. You and Eric keep things from her because you think of her as your baby sister who can't handle anything. I'm a straight shooter."

"She is right," Karen said. "Gabi doesn't believe you two. She always double-checks with me, and I'm a terrible liar. That's probably why she's on a plane despite how much she hates flying. She thinks something is wrong with you, and we are not telling her."

"Yeah." Gilbert ran a hand over his thinning hair. "She's probably freaking out."

Ever since they had lost their parents, Gabi had been anxious about losing him and Eric. She'd begged Eric not to join the Air Force, and when he did that anyway, she hadn't spoken to him for a whole year.

"You can leave the kids with me," Kaia offered.

Gilbert shook his head. "We should all go, including the little ones, so Gabi doesn't think something is wrong with one of them. You know how she is. When she sees that I'm fine and not dying, she will immediately assume that someone else in the family is."

Karen didn't look happy about that. "I don't want the kids to witness Gabi losing it or making you lose it. They should stay here, but Kaia should come with us."

"My mom could babysit," Darlene said. "And I can ask Cassandra to help her out."

"I'll help as well." Alena rubbed her rounded tummy. "I have plenty of practice caring for children, but more importantly, I love doing it."

"Thank you." Gilbert dipped his head. "If Gabi wants to see them, she can agree to the compulsion and come with us to the village."

"Do you need me to come too?" William asked.

"If you can." Gilbert gave him an apologetic smile. "I know how busy you are, but part of my sister's anxiety is over Kaia's decision to get engaged so young and move in with an older guy."

"She can also meet William in the village," Eric said. "As always, Gabi's theatrics are making everyone jump through hoops to accommodate her."

His brother wasn't wrong, but Gabi deserved some coddling. Life hadn't been kind to her. She'd lost her parents at fourteen, had gained nearly a hundred pounds trying to eat her grief away, and then had worked her butt off to get rid of the excess. Her trouble with regulating her eating habits had led her to study nutrition and fitness, and for a while, it seemed like her life finally had been going well. She'd had her own practice that was steadily growing and gaining clientele and a marriage that had seemed stable.

Then she'd discovered that her bastard of a husband had had multiple affairs behind her back, had gotten divorced, and had gained back all the weight that she'd lost as a teenager. Her practice had gone down the drain along with her weight gain, and for nearly a year, she'd lived in Gilbert's house and grieved the death of her marriage and her professional career.

It had taken a lot of effort and courage to pull herself back up and start over in a new place. She'd chosen Cleveland because it was far from her ex-husband and her brothers, and no one had known her there.

Her practice was thriving again, but her personal life hadn't improved. She dated many guys but never stuck with anyone for more than two weeks. To her, everyone looked like a cheater who was bound to break her heart.

Sighing, Gilbert looked at his younger brother. "Gabi has her faults, but she has a heart of gold, and she loves us as much as we love her. I don't mind jumping through hoops for her. If you do, you can walk away and leave her to me. She won't hold it against you."

1 2

GABI

From the moment the pilot had asked the flight attendants to prepare the cabin for landing, Gabi had been clutching Uriel's hand in a death grip, and she didn't let go until the plane was on the ground and taxiing.

The poor guy had probably lost circulation in his hand, but he hadn't complained, and he'd even tried to amuse her with a string of bad jokes that Gabi would have laughed at if she hadn't been fighting nausea.

After such a display of mental instability, there was no chance he would want to see her again or ask for her phone number. She'd told him her full name so he could find her on social media, but would he bother?

Was that the reason he hadn't given her his last name?

Nah, Uriel definitely had been flirting with her throughout the flight, and she doubted he had done it only to help a fellow passenger and keep her from panicking.

Should she initiate and ask for his number?

He could make up a girlfriend or give her a fake phone number if he didn't want to see her again.

Gabi had been guilty of such tactics herself, so she wouldn't hold it against him, but it would be humiliating, nonetheless.

How to do that, though?

She had no practice initiating things, not because she was shy but because she'd never had to do that. When she was a depressed, overweight teenager, she hadn't dared to even look at the hot boys, let alone flirt with them, and once she'd gotten in shape, all she'd had to do was give a guy an encouraging smile, and he would do the rest. After discovering Dylan's infidelity, she'd gone down the rabbit hole again and had gained a ton of weight back. She hadn't been interested in dating anyone back then, but once she'd pulled herself together, she again had plenty of offers.

Regrettably, people judged one another based on looks, and when she looked good, the fish were plentiful.

In fact, usually her problem was keeping men from asking her out when she didn't want them to. She hated saying no and seeing the disappointment in their eyes, but she wasn't willing to go out with a guy just because she felt bad about declining. It required some finesse, but she usually managed to do it in a way that didn't hurt their feelings too much.

On more than one occasion, she'd pretended to be in a long-term relationship to stave off advances without offending the guy, but things were more complicated when she didn't want to go out again with someone she had already seen once or twice. That was one of the reasons Gabi didn't date much.

Who had the patience for all that drama?

If only a magic wand could conjure Mr. Perfect out of thin air and end the search so she would never have to go out on first dates again.

Uriel was the closest to the perfect guy Gabi had ever met. He was gorgeous, funny, not full of himself, and kind, but then every woman who met him would think the same thing and do everything in her power to get him, and that was less than perfect.

Ugh. If only he was a nerd. Some adult acne and thick glasses would have been nice.

A Clark Kent to the world and Superman to her.

Gabi sighed. A girl could dream.

As if acne and glasses could have diminished his appeal.

How was Uriel even single?

He hadn't mentioned a significant other, but he might have chosen not to mention her. Dylan surely hadn't told the women he'd been cheating with that he was married.

To this day, Gabi couldn't understand what made him cheat on her.

She had been a good wife, the sex had been above average and plentiful, and they had been comfortable with each other. Had he done it for the simple reason that he could? That the opportunity presented itself?

His excuse had been that she'd never really loved him and that he'd felt lonely even when he'd been with her, but that was a load of crap. He'd been her first boyfriend, her first lover, and she'd thought herself the luckiest girl in school for snagging the hot basketball star all the girls had drooled over.

She'd even enrolled in the same college he got into so she could be close to him, when she could have gone to a better one.

"We've arrived at the gate," the flight attendant announced over the speakers. "Please check the pockets of the seat in front of you to ensure you haven't forgotten anything. Once you deplane, you won't be allowed back to retrieve your item. If you find that you've left something behind, please ask an airline representative for assistance."

Gabi checked the pocket even though she was certain her phone and tablet were in her purse, and she verified that she had the purse with her before getting up.

As she reached for her carry-on, the older gentleman who had offered to help her at the beginning of the flight pulled it down for her.

"Thank you." Gabi smiled. "I appreciate your help."

"It's my pleasure."

Holding the handle, she glanced at Uriel, who was standing in the other aisle and talking with his friend, who was behind him. They were both so strikingly handsome that everyone was looking at them, including the gentleman who had helped her before.

The third member of their party was behind her, and since he was a head taller than the woman standing between them, Gabi was treated once again to the full beauty of his face.

She wondered which show they were playing in.

She would definitely watch it.

There was no way those three were flea market treasure hunters. Maybe they were method actors starring in a movie that had flea market treasure hunting as its theme, and the three had to stay in character throughout the production.

Uriel had told her a few anecdotes about his bargain hunting, but they had sounded like a combination of something he had seen on television and some real-life experiences. He had evaded every question she asked him about his family or where he lived, answering with another question, an evasive comment, or a change of subject.

On the other hand, she had told him about Gilbert and Kaia, her young niece's engagement to an older guy, and every other suspicion she had about what her brothers might be hiding.

It was the alcohol's fault. She'd had too much of it, partly because she was anxious about being thousands of feet above the earth and partly because of Uriel's presence, which had been curiously comforting and nerve-racking at the same time.

She wouldn't have made it throughout the five-hour flight without him constantly distracting her, and she would have gladly continued spending time with him and having him distract her some more.

Surprisingly, she found him waiting for her just outside the door. "I forgot to ask. Did your brother answer your text?"

"Yes." She grimaced. "My brothers are meeting me in a hotel, and Gilbert said everything was fine and that I should stop imagining terminal diseases and other catastrophes. He promised to explain everything when we meet."

"Did you believe him?"

"I don't know." Gabi let out a breath. "Gilbert likes exaggerating and telling tall tales, but he's not a liar. Then again, he's very protective of me, so if he or Eric have a major health issue, they are not going to tell me about it unless I wring it out of them. I guess I'll find out soon enough whether my suspicions were right."

"In which hotel are you meeting your brothers?"

Hope surged in her chest. Was he going to ask to see her again?

"It's downtown. I have the information on my phone. Why?"

"My friends and I are also staying downtown, so maybe we can meet for breakfast tomorrow?"

Gabi's heart did a happy flip.

One of his friends cleared his throat. "We are leaving very early for that appointment we came here for. We won't have time for breakfast."

"Yes." Uriel pushed his long dark hair back. "We have some meetings scheduled for tomorrow and some more that we hope to schedule for the rest of the day, so I don't know when I will be free. Can I call you once we both get settled?"

"Sure." She pulled out her phone. "What's your number? I'll call you so you'll also have mine."

After he gave her his number and she called him, he entered her information and then looked into her eyes. "Until we meet again, Gabriella Emerson, the courageous defender of god."

13

GILBERT

"Learning about your world was so much simpler for us," Gilbert said as they entered the hotel's top-floor restaurant. "We were already in Safe Haven, visiting Kaia, and there were two compellers on site."

"Shhh." Onegus put his hand on Gilbert's shoulder. "You need to watch what you say here." He pointed with his chin at the hostess.

After they had informed Kian about Gabi's arrival, he'd insisted on Onegus accompanying them to the meeting to ensure everything was handled correctly.

What had he thought, that Orion would compel Gabi without getting her consent first and that they would approve?

Well, to be honest, Gilbert would have considered that if Gabi proved to be as stubborn and as contrary as ever. Her not turning immortal was not an option.

"I love running script ideas by you." He clapped Onegus on the back. "You always think I'm talking about real stuff."

Karen chuckled. "We are all very talented screenwriters. I wonder what Gabi will think about our latest movie idea."

Orion looked amused, but he didn't say anything. Alena had stayed behind to help Geraldine and Cassandra babysit the kids, and he obviously didn't like going anywhere without her.

Gilbert could empathize.

Now that he was immortal, everything felt much more acute, and it wasn't just his hearing and eyesight that had gotten sharper. His feelings for Karen and the kids had intensified tenfold. He'd thought that he was an overprotective partner and father before, but it was nothing compared to what he was experiencing now. That included love so intense for his mate that he couldn't imagine continuing to go on business trips without her.

"McBain party of ten," Onegus told the hostess. "We reserved the private room."

"Of course, sir." She collected ten menus and walked around her station. "Please, follow me."

If the hostess had counted heads, she would have realized that there were only nine of them and one was missing, but she hadn't.

Gilbert fell in step with the woman. "My sister will be here shortly, and she'll be looking for the Emerson party. Can you make a note of it?"

Gabi had taken an Uber over an hour ago, but traffic was heavy this time of day, so it was anyone's guess when she would get there. Onegus had made the reservation for six in the evening, and they were a few minutes early.

"Naturally," the hostess smiled. "Mr. McBain had already asked me to note that the party would include the Emersons when he made the reservation."

"That's right," Kaia said. "The Emersons and the McBains."

Gilbert wondered how many clan members were using the same fake last name. Kian wanted him and Eric to get fake documents as well, but since they still had business interests outside of the clan, it was more challenging for them to just disappear as the Emersons and emerge as McBains. Besides, he wasn't rushing to give up his family name.

"I hope the kids are okay," Karen said. "That's the first time they have had Geraldine, Cassandra, and Alena babysit them."

Idina had looked delighted to spend time with three fancy ladies, as she had called them, and the boys were fascinated with Cassandra after she'd shown them a mini explosion.

Gilbert had no doubt that his kids were having a good time, he just hoped it wouldn't be too big of a blast, given what Cassandra could do.

Orion chuckled. "Don't worry. My sister is forgetful, but she never forgot to take care of Cassandra when she was little."

As the hostess opened the door to the private room they had reserved, Darlene let out a breath. "This brings back memories. Not too long ago, it was my turn to read the new script. I had Roni to help me absorb it all, and Gabi has you." She put her arm around Cheryl's shoulders. "It's nice of you to do this for your aunt."

"Gabi is not really my aunt." She cast Gilbert a reproachful look. "Not yet, anyway. She will be my step-aunt when he finally marries my mother."

"Don't look at me." Gilbert tilted his head in Karen's direction. "It's your mother who is putting on the brakes. I'm ready to have the ceremony tomorrow."

Karen shook her head. "You know what I'm waiting for."

Yeah, he did. She wanted them both to be immortal when they finally tied the knot, and he couldn't wait for her to turn immortal, but he wasn't looking forward to what was required to achieve that.

The hostess waited until everyone was seated before distributing the menus. "Your waiter will be with you shortly. In the meantime, can I get you a bottle of wine?"

"That's a splendid idea," Gilbert said. "What do you have?"

"We have a large selection." The hostess lifted the wine menu and offered it to him.

As he chose three of the most expensive bottles, Karen regarded him with an amused smirk. "Are you hoping to get Gabi to relax with a good wine?"

"That's my plan."

"Can I have some?" Cheryl asked after the hostess closed the door behind her. "I know I'm not supposed to have wine in restaurants, but we are in a private room."

The girls had been allowed to have a small amount of wine with dinner since they were twelve, but only at home.

"I'll let you drink from mine." Kaia patted her sister's arm. "My ID says that I'm twenty-two."

"You don't look it," Darlene said.

Kaia shrugged. "The ID is as legit as the clan's forger can make it.

Besides, having an older man by my side helps." She leaned her head on William's shoulder. "So, who is going to tell Gabi about us all being immortal?"

Cheryl grimaced. "I think it's going to be most believable coming from me. She knows that I'm too cynical to get brainwashed into believing something that's not true."

"I can show her illusions," Orion suggested.

"Don't show Gabi anything scary," Eric said. "Go for something like a rainbow unicorn or a tiny fairy with wings, and don't spring it on her. Tell her what you are about to do before you do it. She gets scared easily, and if she gets agitated, there will be no way to reason with her until she calms down."

Gilbert hated how it made Gabi sound, but Eric was right. Their sister needed to be approached carefully and with kid gloves.

Orion nodded. "Thanks for the warning. I'll keep that in mind."

14

GABI

As the Uber driver stopped in front of what looked like an office building and not a hotel, Gabi checked the address to make sure she was at the right place.

The number on the building matched the one Gilbert had texted her, and the name of the street matched as well.

"The restaurant is on the top floor," the Uber driver said as he opened the door for her. "It's called the Seventy-Second because it's the number of the floor it is on. I've heard that it has a great view."

"I'm sure it does. How about the food?"

The guy made a face that indicated it wasn't the best.

She laughed. "You can't have everything, right? A beautiful view and a good meal? That's asking for too much."

"Yeah. It's like what they say about translations. If it's beautiful, it's not faithful, and if it's faithful, it's not beautiful."

The saying actually compared a translation to a woman, but in her experience, it was no less true about men. Dylan was handsome, and he had been unfaithful.

"Regrettably, that's true." Gabi got out, checked that she had her purse on her, and took the carry-on he'd pulled out of the trunk. "Thank you. Have a great evening."

"You too. Enjoy your meal. I'm sure it's going to be great." He got in his car and drove away.

There was no one on the sidewalk on either side of the street, and as she walked toward the front door, she was relieved to see a reception desk with an actual person behind it.

The guy saw her and buzzed the door open.

It certainly didn't feel like any hotel she'd stayed in before.

"Good evening," she said as she stopped in front of the desk. "I don't know if I am at the right place. Is this the—"

"It is." He smiled. "The hotel occupies the top ten floors, and its lobby and reception are on the sixtieth floor. The elevator marked hotel lobby will take you directly there."

That explained it, but they could have placed a sign so guests wouldn't get anxious about being at the wrong place.

Not that she was sure she was going to be a guest. Gilbert hadn't given her an answer about where she was staying tonight, and she hadn't wanted to push. Perhaps there was a reason they didn't want her to stay with them.

"Actually, I'm meeting my family in the restaurant first."

"Not a problem." He clicked on his keyboard. "What's the last name on the reservation?"

"Emerson."

"Excellent. Your party is already there. Take the elevator that has the Seventy-Second logo on it. It will take you straight to the restaurant without stopping at any of the other floors."

"Thanks." She gave him a polite smile. "Have a great evening."

"You too."

Gabi wasn't looking forward to riding the elevator alone. It was one more phobia on a long list of them, but it wasn't as bad as flying. She wouldn't be comfortable, but she wouldn't panic either.

Yeah, well.

Live and learn.

There were always new experiences to scare the crap out of her, and the guy at the reception counter hadn't warned her that the elevator would take off like a rocket.

Holding on to the rail, Gabi closed her eyes tightly and counted, hoping she wouldn't get ejected into space. On the count of twelve, the elevator slowed down, and on the count of fourteen, it stopped so smoothly that it was almost as shocking as the speed of going up.

As the doors slid open, Gabi exhaled, stepped out on shaky legs, and approached the hostess. "Hello. I'm with the Emerson party. Can you point me in their direction?"

The hostess smiled a well-practiced, professional smile. "Good evening, Ms. Emerson. I will be more than happy to escort you to the private room your party has reserved."

A private room?

Had she forgotten someone's birthday? Anniversary?

Gilbert was a big spender who enjoyed grand gestures, but even he wouldn't have splurged on a private dinner in a fancy place like this for no special reason.

Then again, reserving a private room might not cost more than dining in the main one.

Walking behind the hostess, Gabi looked through the restaurant's windows at the cityscape. Thankfully, fear of heights was not on her list of phobias, so she could enjoy the view without choking from fear.

As the hostess opened the door to the private room, Gabi's eyes misted with tears to see her family's smiling faces, and as her brothers rose to their feet, she left the carry-on by the door and ran into Gilbert's open arms.

"I was so worried." She hugged him fiercely and then stepped back and slugged his arm. "That's for being an evasive bastard and keeping secrets from me."

He just kept grinning as if her punch was no more than a pat when it had been hard enough to leave a bruise.

"I missed you too," he said.

"Come here." Eric pulled her into his arms. "Are you okay? I mean, after the long flight."

"I'm fine." She pushed out of his arms and gave him an appraising look. "When I couldn't get ahold of Gilbert, and everyone was giving me lame excuses why he couldn't call me back, I suspected that he had a hair transplant or plastic surgery, and that's why he was hiding in Los Angeles, but I was wrong. It was you. What possessed you to do that?"

Eric smiled. "Do I look good?"

"You look fantastic, but you are too young to do stuff like that."

"And I'm not?" Gilbert asked.

She huffed out a breath. "You are much vainer than Eric, and you've been talking about a hair transplant for years."

"That's true." He ran a hand over his balding head. "I might still have to do that. I hoped I wouldn't."

"Hi, Gabi," Kaia said. "Let me introduce my fiancé, William."

By his looks alone, the guy was perfect for Kaia. He was handsome, tall, and with gorgeous, smart eyes, and he seemed like a sweet nerd. No wonder Kaia had snagged him quickly before anyone else had a chance to discover such a rare diamond.

"Hi, sweetie." Gabi hugged her adopted niece and then offered her hand to William. "It's a pleasure to meet you. I wondered about Kaia's rush to get engaged, but now I understand why she did it."

William looked confused, which further endeared him to her. "Thank you. I'm glad to finally meet the famous Gabriella Emerson."

She tilted her head. "Famous? How?"

His cheeks reddened. "Your brothers talk about you a lot."

"They do, do they?" She cast them both hard looks. "What have you two been saying about me?"

15

GILBERT

"Only good things." Gilbert made room for Cheryl to get to her favorite almost step-aunt.

"Oh dear, you've grown at least two inches taller since the last time I saw you." Gabi kissed Cheryl on both cheeks. "And your hair got longer. You are so pretty!"

"Thanks." Cheryl took the compliments in stride. "You look good, too, Gabi. I've missed you." She kissed her and gave her another hug. "It's been too long since I last saw you."

Gabi hadn't visited since right after the twins were born, and that time, Eric had had to fly her in because she'd been too terrified to get on a commercial jetliner.

Gilbert hadn't wanted to tell her that commercial airliners were safer than private jets because then she would have been obsessing about Eric flying them. She'd either learned that on her own or had made some progress with her phobias.

He wondered if she'd started seeing a therapist.

Next came Darlene, who didn't wait for Eric to introduce her and pulled Gabi into her arms for a fierce hug. "If you haven't guessed already, I'm Darlene, Eric's fiancée."

"Hi." Gabi laughed. "You are stronger than you look."

Darlene let go of her. "Sorry about that. I've been working out, and I underestimate how strong I've gotten."

Gabi was still smiling. "You must show me your routine. I lift weights thrice a week with a personal trainer and don't have half your upper body strength."

"It's also genetic," Darlene murmured as she stepped away to let others welcome Gabi.

The last ones were Onegus and Orion.

Gabi's eyes widened as she took a gander at them. "What's going on in this town? Is there a hunk conference in Los Angeles?"

Onegus chuckled or coughed. Since the chief was covering his mouth with his fist, Gilbert couldn't tell which one it was.

Orion laughed. "Thank you, I think."

Hopefully, Gabi hadn't gotten the wrong impression, thinking he had brought two single men to the family dinner as potential dates.

"No, I'm serious," Gabi said. "Three gorgeous guys were flying in first class with me, and one of them was even seated right next to me. He said that they were flea market bargain hunters and flippers, but I suspect that they were actors who were playing characters who flipped flea market finds, and they were staying in character. The guy sitting next to me was super polite, like someone from the forties, so maybe the movie was about that era. An Indiana Jones style action thing. Now that I think of it, that makes perfect sense. If I were a casting director, I would have cast all three as action heroes."

Poor Gabi tended to talk fast when nervous, and they hadn't even told her anything yet.

Onegus and Orion exchanged loaded looks, but then Onegus shook his head. "They wouldn't have been flying first class. Navuh is not that generous. Also, they are typically not as good-looking and definitely not as polite as Gabriella described the one sitting next to her."

"The ones Navuh claims as his sons might be flying first class," Orion said. "You told me that they are closer to the source because of who their mothers are, so they are good-looking, and because he claims them as his they are also well-educated, which in turn could make them better mannered than the rank and file."

Onegus shook his head. "There wouldn't be three of them on the same flight. Navuh believes in the method of divide and conquer."

"Who is Navuh?" Gabi asked. "And what's the deal with his sons, who he claims are his but aren't?"

"We'd better sit down first." Karen hugged Gabi briefly and then led her to a chair. "So, how have you been, Gabi? Anyone interesting you've been dating lately?"

Gabi shook her head. "The only interesting guy I've met in a long while was the handsome dude sitting next to me during the flight from Toronto." She looked at Onegus. "The one who may or may not be one of Navuh's sons, whoever Navuh is. The name sounds biblical. Is that the nickname of some cartel boss?"

Gabi had always been sharp, and Onegus shouldn't have spoken so freely about Navuh before Orion ensured her silence. Then again, if she refused, he could thrall the memory from her mind.

"Good guess," Orion said. "The name is biblical, and the guy is the boss of a nefarious organization, but the name was given to him at birth."

When he didn't continue, Gabi arched a brow. "And? Now that you got me curious, you have to tell me more. By the way, we haven't been introduced yet."

"My name is Orion. I'm Darlene's cousin."

He was her uncle, but cousin would be more appropriate for now, given how young he looked.

"I'm Onegus," the chief said. "I'm mated to Darlene's sister, who apologizes for not joining us. She's helping Darlene's mother babysit Karen and Gilbert's kids."

Gabi's relieved expression confirmed Gilbert's suspicion that she'd thought the two men were there as potential dating material.

"That's so nice of her." She cast a quick glance at Darlene. "Eric and Gilbert are terrible at keeping me in the know. They didn't tell me anything about your family. I didn't even know that you have a sister."

"Her name is Cassandra, and she's much younger than me." Darlene pulled out her phone, probably intending to show Gabi Cassandra's picture, but Onegus put a hand on her shoulder. "Let's save family photos for later."

Understanding dawning, she nodded. Darlene no longer looked like Cassandra's older sister, and Geraldine definitely didn't look like the mother of two adult women.

As the door opened, two waiters came in with the wine Gilbert had ordered and baskets of assorted slices of bread.

"I didn't even look at the menu yet." Gabi started leafing through the pages. "There is so much to choose from." She turned to Gilbert. "Have any of you eaten here before? I need recommendations."

Gilbert shook his head. "Onegus and Darlene recommended the place. It's the first time here for the rest of us."

"Everything here is excellent." Darlene reached for the bread. "But this is my Achilles heel. I can't say no to a freshly baked baguette smothered with butter." She grimaced. "As a nutritionist, you probably think that's terrible."

Gabi laughed. "I love a baguette with butter as much as anyone, but I allow myself to indulge only on special occasions." She snatched a piece. "Today qualifies as such. I've flown over the entire continent today. I deserve a treat."

16

GABI

As one waiter poured the wine and the other took the orders, Gabi looked at Eric again and was stunned at his transformation. He wasn't that much older than her, and he'd been in good shape before, but he looked a decade younger now.

Was it love that made his skin glow with health and his hair look thicker, or was it the cosmetic procedures for which Los Angeles was known? Not that it was difficult to get Botox and fillers in Cleveland, but it wasn't as prevalent.

Heck, maybe she should book an appointment at a clinic while she was in Los Angeles.

So far, she'd managed to keep her youthful looks with careful adherence to a nutritional plan and a rigorous fitness schedule, but soon it wouldn't be enough. The feathering of barely-there wrinkles around her eyes didn't bother her, but she had dark circles under her eyes that she masked with concealer and foundation, and it would be nice to look good without anything on her face.

"What's your secret, Eric?" she asked as soon as the waiters left with their orders. "Love or cosmetic procedures?"

Smiling, he draped his arm over the back of Darlene's chair. "It's definitely love."

"Gabriella," Orion said. "I want to ask you something."

"Yes?" She looked at him.

Really looked at him.

If she hadn't met Uriel, she would have thought him the most gorgeous man she'd ever seen.

It was hard to look away.

"What did you want to ask me?"

"Remember the nefarious organization Onegus and I mentioned?"

"I do."

"Do you remember the name of its boss?"

Gabi frowned. She remembered thinking that the name sounded biblical and that she'd asked whether it was a cartel boss's nickname, but she couldn't remember what it was.

What the hell?

She was too young to have memory issues.

"I'm sorry." She looked at her wine glass. "I must have drunk too much today. Usually, I restrict my alcohol consumption to one glass of wine a week, but today was a stressful day, and I overindulged. It must have affected my memory."

For some reason, Orion seemed very happy with her answer. "It didn't. I made you forget the name. It was a test to see whether you were susceptible to hypnosis."

She frowned. "You didn't do anything. You didn't swing a watch in front of my eyes or tell me to count back from ten or any of those things. How could you have hypnotized me without me knowing you were doing that?"

It was scary to think it was possible to hypnotize people without their knowledge or consent, but she was sure Orion was just pulling her leg.

"I have my subtle ways, and I apologize for not asking your permission first, but I had to know that you can be hypnotized before we can tell you more about Eric's marvelous transformation."

That got her curious.

Stress was a major cause of premature aging, which she tried to combat with exercise, but perhaps hypnosis was the secret?

"Was it relaxation that did it?" she asked.

"No." Looking frustrated, Orion pushed his long bangs back. "I don't really know how to approach this without sounding creepy."

"Let me explain," Cheryl said. "Eric, Gilbert, and Kaia have the secret to immortality. You can have it too, but it's a big secret, and the only way they are going to tell you about it is if you allow Orion to hypnotize you so you can't tell anyone on the outside about it."

"What?" Gabi gaped at her niece.

That sounded insane, but Cheryl was as sane as a person can get, and she was also cynical and questioned everything. She wouldn't have said what she just had if she didn't believe it was true.

Perhaps she was referring to some new method of prolonging life.

Except, Cheryl hadn't included herself among those who had the longevity secret, and that bothered Gabi.

"Why don't you have it?"

Cheryl chuckled. "I have it. I just can't implement it yet because sex is involved, and I'm too young."

That was completely bonkers.

Sex was good and healthy, but it wasn't the secret to longevity. What had all of them gotten into? Had they been brainwashed by some guru to part with all their money in exchange for some bogus claims about long life that involved sex?

Was it some crazy sex cult?

It was fortunate that she'd overcome her fear when she had and came to see them.

She had to save them.

Turning to Gilbert, Gabi glared at him. "Have you all joined some crazy cult and gotten even poor Cheryl brainwashed?" She turned her gaze to William. "It must have started with you. You brainwashed Kaia first and then the rest of her family." She shook her head. "Un-freaking-believable. You look like such a sweet nerd, I would have never suspected you of such powers."

Hell, maybe it wasn't his power but Orion's?

After all, he was the hypnotist who didn't need to swing watches or do anything overt to get someone's mind enslaved to his will. That was one hell of a talent to have.

"You got it all wrong," Kaia said. "No one brainwashed anyone. Orion can show you proof."

Gabi lifted her hands in the air. "No, thank you. I don't want him to use his mind tricks on me."

"It's not mind tricks." Eric leaned over to Darlene and did the last thing Gabi had expected. He lifted her off her chair as if she weighed nothing, pulled her onto his lap, and kissed her like his underage niece and other members of his family weren't watching.

"What the heck, Eric? If you are so desperate for your fiancée, get a room. There are kids watching."

"I'm not a kid," Cheryl grumbled. "In some countries, girls my age are already mothers."

"We are not in those countries," Gabi spat. "If this is not some alternate reality I somehow stumbled into, we are still in the United States of America."

Finally, Eric let go of Darlene's mouth, turned toward her, and smiled with a pair of small fangs that were, nevertheless, definitely not the canines he'd had moments ago.

"This is not real." Gabi felt faint. "The plane must have crashed, I must be dead, and I'm in hell."

ERIC

As Gabi's eyes rolled back in her head, Gilbert leaped from his chair to catch her before she fell.

"Way to go, Eric," Kaia said sarcastically. "You've literally scared her half to death."

"What else was I supposed to do? You know Gabi. She's contrary on a good day and impossible to talk to on a bad one. She wouldn't have believed anything other than the hard facts, and it's difficult to argue with the sharp points of my fangs. I had to convince her to let Orion compel her."

Karen chuckled. "Your baby fangs are not much to show, but you managed to scare her with them anyway."

"It's not going to work," Cheryl said. "Gabi is too scared to let Orion manipulate her mind, but since she's obviously susceptible to thralling, you can tell her everything without compelling her first, and if she still doesn't want Orion to get into her head, Onegus can thrall the memories away, or suppress them, or whatever it is that thralling does. I'm still not sure what the difference is between thralling and compulsion."

"A person is aware of compulsion," Onegus explained. "They are not aware of thralling. It feels like their own thoughts and decisions."

Eric waited until Onegus was done explaining. "Is that okay with you if we tell Gabi first?"

The chief nodded. "That's how we traditionally did that before we had compellers, but that was when the Dormant was already in a relationship with a clan member and was willing to stay in the village until she or he transitioned or failed to do so. So far, we've been lucky that all the suspected Dormants eventually transitioned. Once we had compellers join the clan, things got much easier." He looked at Darlene. "Like in your case. There was no doubt that you were a Dormant, but you were hesitant about leaving your husband."

"I was so stupid." She looked at Gabi, and her eyes softened. "No, I take it back. It wasn't stupidity. It was fear. I was scared like Gabi is now, just for different reasons."

"What happened?" Gabi murmured in Gilbert's arms.

"You got overexcited and passed out." He took the glass of water Karen handed him and brought it to Gabi's lips. "Here, take a sip, and no more alcohol for you today."

She took a couple of sips, sat up, and realizing that she was sitting in Gilbert's lap, pushed to her feet. "Get out of my chair. I'm not a little kid anymore."

He rolled his eyes. "Could have fooled me with that tantrum."

"He had fangs in his mouth!" She pointed at Eric without looking at him. "I thought that they were real. Which one of you morons came up with such an idiotic stunt?"

"It was me." Eric lifted his hand. "But it was not a stunt. I'm immortal now, and I have fangs."

By now, his fangs were back to normal size, so he had nothing to show her. He also couldn't produce illusions like other immortals because, supposedly, that could be learned only at a young age, but he was going to prove them all wrong and master the skill.

Plopping down on the chair, Gabi groaned. "Do me a favor and stop with all this nonsense. My nerves are already frayed after having flown for over five hours. I need a couple of days to relax."

"It's not nonsense," Kaia said. "And regrettably, we can't wait a couple of days. It has to be done today. There is nothing magical or supernatural about immortality or Eric's fangs. It's genetics, and I can explain how it works. But you need to stop arguing and start listening."

That finally pierced through Gabi's stubborn shields. "Okay, Ms. Genius Prodigy. Enlighten your dumb step-aunt."

"You're not dumb, Gabi," Gilbert grumbled. "You're just as stubborn as a mule and closed-minded."

"I'm not closed-minded," she bristled. "Any normal person would have reacted the same way I did. Perhaps minus the fainting, but I blame that on excess alcohol."

"I'll make it short and simple," Kaia said. "And if you have questions, keep them until I'm done. But before I start, I want you to know that if you don't let Orion compel you to keep everything that I tell you a secret, all that knowledge will be erased from your memory the same way the name of the nefarious leader was. If this information falls into the wrong hands, our lives will be in danger." She waved a hand at everyone sitting around the table. "As you can imagine, there is nothing people won't do to get their hands on the secret to immortality."

Gabi swallowed. "I will never do anything to endanger my family. If this is for real, I'd rather die than reveal your secret."

Eric chuckled. "It would be easier and less traumatic to just let Orion compel you to keep the secret so you can't reveal it even if you try, but that can wait until after Kaia is done explaining. Although I suggest we wait with that as well because I can see a bunch of waiters heading this way with loaded trays." He waved a hand at the glass doors.

18

GABI

As Gabi waited impatiently for the waiters to be done distributing the appetizers and the main dishes, she was glad that Gilbert had asked for everything to be delivered at once so they wouldn't be disturbed again.

When it was finally done, she didn't even look at what was on her plate.

Who could think of food at a time like this?

Kaia, on the other hand, cut off a big piece of the roasted chicken she'd ordered and put it in her mouth.

"Am I supposed to wait until after everyone is done eating?" Gabi asked.

Kaia lifted a finger and chewed faster. When she was done, she wiped her mouth with a napkin and took a sip from her Coke. "I'm sorry, but this smelled so good I couldn't wait. So here is the story in a nutshell. The myths about the gods were not really myths. They were history. The gods were aliens who had been exiled from their home planet for their part in a rebellion. There weren't enough of them to provide genetic variety, so they took human mates. The children born from those unions were immortal, with some of the powers of their ancestors but not all. When the immortals took human partners, though, their children were born seemingly human, but the girls carried the dormant godly genes and transferred them to their offspring because they are transferred only through the mother. The gods and immortals discovered that it was possible to activate those dormant genes, and when the gods were still around, it was done when those carriers reached puberty. After most gods and immortals perished, what was left of their population got dispersed, and many of the Dormants born after the destruction didn't even know that they were carriers. Our mother and her children happen to be such carriers, and the fantastic coincidence is that your family has those genes as well, a gift from your mother and before that her mother and so on. Gilbert, Eric and I went through the process and transitioned already. Cheryl and the younger kids have to wait a little longer before they can attempt it."

With that, Kaia smiled, cut off another piece of the chicken, and put it in her mouth.

Apparently, she was done, so Gabi was allowed to ask questions.

It all sounded like science fiction, not science, but she knew better than to doubt Kaia.

"What about Eric's fangs? Do you have fangs, too? And what about Karen?" She looked at her brother's partner. "Did you turn immortal?"

"Not yet." Karen winced. "Gilbert is a baby immortal, and he's still growing his fangs. So is Eric, which is why his fangs are still so small. They are going to get much larger before they are operational."

Those were small baby fangs?

She turned to Onegus and Orion. "You are not baby immortals, right? Can you show me how long those fangs can become?"

Onegus shook his head. "Some of us can do it at will, but most of us need aggression or arousal for our venom glands to activate and our fangs to drop. I can probably do that if I concentrate, but I prefer not to if you don't mind."

Orion chuckled softly. "For most of us, it's a struggle not to let them elongate at inappropriate moments. Regulating aggression is one of the first skills a newly turned male immortal must learn."

"Yeah," Kaia said. "I forgot to mention that females don't have elongating fangs or venom glands, so you don't have to worry about that."

"Awesome." Gabi gestured as if erasing an item from a list.

If any of this was real, which it seemed to be unless she was dreaming, the last thing she needed was a pair of fangs that made an appearance every time she got angry or horny. She would have been flashing fangs nonstop.

Except, she knew better than to hope there would be no other weird side effect to gaining immortality.

"What do I need to worry about?" she asked. "How are those genes activated?"

"I told you," Cheryl said. "Sex. You need to find a male immortal to bond with, and when he bites you during sex, his venom will induce your transition, and it usually takes more than one time to do that."

Having her sixteen-year-old niece explain the immortal birds and bees to her was extremely awkward. It should have been done by Karen, Darlene, or even Kaia. Not Cheryl.

"What do you mean by bonding?" She looked pointedly at Darlene. "Is it another term for sex?"

"No, it's precisely what you think it is. You need to fall in love and create a bond. Supposedly, it makes the induction process easier. But in my case, I was bitten by a friend who did Eric and me a favor, so I obviously wasn't bonded with him. I was bonded with Eric, but his fangs and venom weren't operational yet. They still aren't."

Confused, Gabi shook her head. "So, you were a Dormant when you met Eric? Not an immortal?"

"Correct." Darlene nodded. "I was a confirmed Dormant because my mother and sister were immortal, but I couldn't find an immortal male I was drawn to. Then Eric showed up when he flew the family in to visit Kaia, where she was working on a secret project with William, and when I saw him, I knew he was the one for me." She smiled at Eric. "Well, I knew I wanted him, but I had no idea he was a Dormant like me. I thought that I was just attracted to a very handsome human."

Eric lifted Darlene's hand to his lips and brushed them over her knuckles. "I felt the connection right away. I couldn't keep away from Darlene, and I reorganized my schedule so I could see her again."

"It was the Fates' work," Karen said. "You were destined to be together."

Gabi knew Karen well, and she wasn't the type who believed in divine intervention or any other supernatural force. After losing her first husband when Kaia and Cheryl were practically babies, Karen had become an atheist, and Gabi could understand why.

"I'm surprised to hear you say that. You didn't use to believe in anything."

Karen let out a breath. "I still struggle with that, but I can't deny the facts. There aren't many immortals left, or Dormants, although I suspect there are many more Dormants than immortals. Still, Gilbert and me finding each other was too much of a coincidence. The same is true for William and Kaia and many other immortal/Dormant or two Dormant couples. The clan believes in the three Fates, and it's easier for me to accept three capricious female entities as the supernatural power in charge of pairings than a benevolent creator who doesn't seem benevolent at all."

19

KAREN

Karen had lost too many people she loved—good people who deserved a long, happy life—to still believe in divinity, and although she shouldn't base her beliefs solely on her life experience, there was so much ugliness in the world that it almost seemed as if the devil was in charge and not the supposedly good creator. But since she didn't believe in the devil either, she chose to believe in chaos.

Nothing was predetermined, and things just happened for no good reason.

Except for immortal pairings that were orchestrated by the Fates.

The irony of her conflicting beliefs wasn't lost on her, but Karen was both experienced and humble enough to realize that neither she nor the greatest human minds had all the answers. What had been held as the absolute truth yesterday was proven just as absolutely false today, and the same would happen to the accepted truths of today. In fact, the cycling of scientific dogmas was becoming much faster because the power of computation was increasing exponentially, and the dawn of the artificial intelligence age would accelerate that process by an order of magnitude.

"So let me understand," Gabi said. "I am the descendant of gods, and I can turn immortal if I have sex with an immortal male, preferably one

I can bond with, but that's not absolutely necessary. Falling in love is optional, but hooking up is not."

"Correct," Karen said. "You are the youngest sibling of the three, and you're in excellent physical shape, so you don't have to rush to find an inducer. You can take your time and check out the selection."

Darlene chuckled. "The selection is impressive, but those pesky Fates won't let you lust after just anyone. I was surrounded by hot males, but none of them stirred anything in me. I thought I was damaged goods after being married to a jerk for so long, but then I met Eric, and the rest is history. Regrettably, I'm much older than you, so I didn't have the luxury of waiting until Eric was done growing his fangs and venom so he could induce me, and we had a friend provide the biting services."

Karen cleared her throat. "This isn't the place or time to get into the particulars." She quickly glanced at her daughters and then turned her gaze to Gabi. "What you need to decide now is whether you want to forget everything we've just told you and go back to being oblivious, or agree to Orion compelling you to keep everything a secret."

"Can't I just promise not to tell anyone? As I said, I will never do anything to endanger my family."

"You might do it unintentionally," Onegus said. "Or, Fates forbid, you fall into the hands of someone who wants to torture the information out of you. Wouldn't you feel better knowing that no one can force you to reveal the secret that keeps your family safe?"

Gabi's eyes widened. "Is that just hypothetical, or is it a real possibility?"

"It's hypothetical." Karen rushed to answer before Onegus could scare Gabi even more. "But too much is at stake to take unnecessary risks, and that's why these rules are in place. It's either forgetting everything you were told or compulsion."

"There is a third choice," Onegus said. "You can come with us to our village, stay for a bit, and then decide what you want to do. You won't be allowed to leave the village without choosing either thralling or compulsion, but you will be able to see for yourself that everything we told you is true."

Karen hadn't known that was an option, and given Gilbert's surprised expression, he hadn't known either. Their entire family had been compelled to secrecy before ever setting foot in the village, so it hadn't occurred to them.

"How long is a little bit?" Gabi asked.

"Two weeks, more or less. The longer the duration and the number of memories accumulated, the harder it becomes to thrall them away, and if forced, it could cause damage to your mind. Two weeks is the Goldilocks zone."

"That actually makes sense." Gabi turned to Gilbert. "I would love to see your village. Can I stay with you and Karen?"

"Our house is really small, and you'll have to sleep on the living room couch. Darlene and Eric have a spare bedroom, so you'll be more comfortable with them."

Onegus lifted his hand. "One more thing. You have to leave your phone behind. I will put it in a locker downstairs, and you can get it back when you are ready to go home." He smiled. "Either compelled to keep a secret or minus your memories of immortals and everything else you have learned and will continue to learn during your stay in the village."

20

GABI

"Why do I need to leave my phone behind?"

Gabi couldn't leave her phone. What if Uriel called her?

What if she wanted to call him?

Onegus smiled indulgently. "We don't want anyone to be able to track you to our village by your phone."

"Who is going to track me? I'm a nobody."

"We can give her a clan phone," Gilbert said. "William even brought one with him. She can forward her calls to the new number."

Onegus shook his head. "I can't allow Gabi to talk to anyone outside the village unless she's under Orion's compulsion."

Crap. Unless she agreed to let the immortal compel her, she couldn't talk with Uriel, and if he called her, got her voicemail, and didn't hear from her within a reasonable timeframe, he would assume she was ghosting him.

But wait, hadn't she decided that he was too good-looking and too young for her?

Maybe it was for the best if the decision was taken out of her hands?

"You look conflicted," Darlene said. "Are your clients expecting you to always be reachable? Or is it personal?"

"Both." Gabi reached for the glass of wine and then changed her mind. "My clients always text me with questions about food substitutions, cheat days, and the like. I usually respond within an hour or so. My friends are used to me taking a little longer to get back to them, so that's not a problem."

Except for Uriel, who was neither a client nor a friend.

What was he?

A potential hookup?

Yeah. That was the extent of what she should expect from him, and now that she had come to that realization, she knew that she had to have him either tonight or the next or never.

If what her family had told her was true, and she had no reason to think it wasn't, even though it sounded like a delusional fantasy, then she would have to go to their village and choose an immortal male to induce her into immortality.

If she wanted a tumble in bed with Uriel, this might be her last chance.

God. How could they expect her to make life-changing decisions on the spot like that?

Besides, she couldn't stay in their village for more than a few days. She had a flight booked back to Cleveland on Wednesday, and she had a full day of appointments with clients on Thursday. Was she expected to drop everything she'd worked so hard for and concentrate on finding a guy?

It sounded like something that belonged in the fifties.

"Let me ask you a question." She looked at Onegus, who seemed to be the authority figure in the group. "If I move to your village, what am I supposed to do for a living? Do immortals require a nutritionist or a lifestyle coach?"

William cleared his throat. "I used to be significantly overweight, but I was the exception. It's rare for immortals to have problems regulating their appetites. Our bodies are very efficient machines, and it takes a lot of abuse to get them out of equilibrium."

"That's what I thought. What the heck am I going to do after I turn immortal? Can I go back to Cleveland after I become one?"

Given the looks everyone was giving her, that was a no.

"You can open a new clinic in Los Angeles," Karen said. "Some of the village residents commute to the city every day."

That was good to know, but the thought of starting from scratch was still disheartening. She had a business she'd worked hard on building, a group of friends she would miss, and a two-story condominium that she'd furnished and decorated exactly how she wanted it.

Gabi needed time to process everything, and she needed to have at least one night with Uriel, or she would forever regret missing the opportunity.

There wasn't much she could do about the changes looming on the horizon, but she could do something about tonight.

Even if he ended up declining her offer, she would at least know that she'd given it a try.

One night.

That was all she wanted.

Well, maybe two.

Three at the most.

Gabi shook her head. She'd just decided that Uriel would be a one-time hookup, and by definition, that meant that she would give him only one night.

"If you don't mind, I would like to stay in the hotel tonight and think everything over." She looked at Orion. "I guess what I'm saying is that I agree to your offer to compel me to keep everything I learned today a secret."

Gilbert frowned at her. "Why? Is it because I said we don't have room? It wasn't an excuse. We really don't. I would love to have you stay with us."

"You can have my cabana," Cheryl said. "I'll sleep in Idina's room."

Gabi smiled at her niece. "Thank you for your generous offer. It's very sweet of you. But it's not about the sleeping accommodations. I just need one night by myself to process everything I've learned today and everything in my future. It's a lot to take in."

"That's understandable," Onegus said. "I can get you a room in this hotel." He pulled out his phone and started texting.

Gabi turned to Orion. "So, how are you going to do it?"

"It's very simple. Look into my eyes and focus on the sound of my voice."

"Hold on." Kaia stopped him. "Compulsion doesn't erase memories; someone with thralling ability can pluck them from Gabi's mind. Those three hunks on the plane worry me. What if they are Doomers?"

What the hell were Doomers?

Onegus stopped texting and leveled his gaze on Gabi. "Did you exchange phone numbers with any of them?"

She swallowed. "I did."

"Don't call him." He turned to Orion. "Make sure that she doesn't. I don't want to take any chances."

Damn. That was the whole reason for her staying in the hotel.

"Come on, he was just a good-looking guy. A human. You can't compel me not to have contact with whomever I choose just because I made a stupid comment about how handsome he was."

Orion regarded her with his shrewd eyes. "I can compel you to forget what you were told until one of your brothers picks you up from the hotel tomorrow afternoon. That way, your guy won't be able to peek into your mind even if he is one of us."

"That's fine. Well, maybe—"

What if Uriel couldn't make it tonight?

Damn. Why was she so obsessed about hooking up with him?

So, he was hot, so what?

It wasn't just about the hookup. She felt as if the old Gabi was about to disappear, and she had to treat herself before it happened. Except, she hadn't decided yet whether she was going to leave everything behind and join her family as an immortal.

Ugh, who was she kidding?

As if that was a choice. Of course, she would do that, but maybe not right away. She had to go back to Cleveland, transfer her clients to a colleague, sell her condo or rent it out, and tell her friends a very convincing story about why she was moving away and couldn't give them her new address.

"What do you mean by maybe?" Orion asked.

"I might not be ready tomorrow either."

"Gabi," Gilbert said in the same tone he'd used when she'd done something he'd disapproved of when she was a teenager. "You came here because you were concerned about your family, you wanted to know what's going on and see where we live, and now you are willing to put everything on ice because of a guy? What kind of an example are you setting for your nieces?"

"A very good one," Cheryl grumbled. "Gabi is an independent woman who doesn't let her older brothers dictate who she has fun with and when."

Gabi shook her head. "I've just learned that I'm not fully human, that I will have to leave behind my friends and everything I've worked for and move across the country to live in a hidden immortal village. I will also have to find an immortal lover to hook up with and hope my godly genes get activated. Forgive me for wanting to get a breather and cling to normalcy for a little longer than eighteen hours."

21

ORION

Orion felt for Gabriella. Gilbert loved his sister and wanted the best for her, but he was also a prick to her, allowing his frustration to get the better of him and taking it out in the form of scolding that wasn't helpful.

Compared to Orion's own sister, Gabi had taken the news about her alien genetics remarkably well.

He still remembered the first time he'd told Geraldine that she was the daughter of a god and, therefore, immortal. Suffice it to say that she hadn't been nearly as calm and accepting as Gabi.

Then again, the circumstances had been different. He'd been a stranger who had shown up out of the blue, and he hadn't had an entire family of immortals to back up his claim. Geraldine, or Sabina as she'd been named by her adoptive parents, simply couldn't believe him.

Nevertheless, it wasn't his place to correct Gilbert. The guy had been the de facto parent for his younger siblings for a long time, and they had their own family dynamic.

Gabi turned a pair of pleading blue eyes at him. "Is there a way you can leave my memories of today intact so I can think about them and plan for the future, but so no one else can see them if they peek into my mind?"

Gilbert snorted. "As always, you want to have your cake and eat it too. You can't have both. If you want to think about what you've learned and discuss plans for the future with your family, you should come with us to the village. If that guy is so interested in you, he can meet you when you return to Cleveland to settle your affairs there."

Gabriella cast him an incredulous look. "How is that going to be any different? I will still have memories that Uriel can supposedly see if he's one of you, which I doubt. Seriously, what are the chances of me sitting on a plane next to an immortal? How many of those guys are there?"

"Counting our enemies, many thousands," Onegus said. "Although I don't know what three of them would be doing in Toronto. Were there reports of attractive young women disappearing in the area?"

Gabriella blanched. "Why? What do they do to those women?"

"They finance their operation by dabbling in trafficking." Onegus shook his head. "But that's a topic for a whole different conversation. For now, I just want to rule out some variables."

She shrugged. "I was in Toronto for a three-day conference on nutrition and fitness, and I didn't watch the news. Besides, Toronto was just a layover for Uriel and his friends. They'd come from Korea, where they probably had their faces perfected. It's a popular destination for people looking to have plastic surgery on a budget."

Gilbert pursed his lips. "People flying first class are not concerned with saving a few bucks on surgery. The difference in cost between first class and coach would eat up whatever they saved on the procedures."

"They could have gotten a free upgrade like I did."

"What kind of luggage did they have?" Cheryl asked. "You can tell a lot by that. All the rich guys have Tumi backpacks."

"Not only Tumi," Karen said, "there is also that other brand." She waved a hand at Gilbert. "You know. You ordered one and then returned it. What was the name?"

"Briggs & Riley. But they are not that expensive. There are more luxurious brands out there." He looked at Gabriella. "Did you notice what kind of luggage your hunk had? Or were you too busy ogling his body?"

The small smile lifting her lips confirmed Gilbert's assertion, but she didn't seem at all embarrassed or upset about it, which Orion applauded her for. She had every right to admire a male's physique.

"He had a backpack, but I wasn't paying attention to the kind it was. He had a simple white T-shirt on and a pair of jeans. I didn't notice the brand of the jeans either."

"Of course not." Cheryl smirked. "Who cares about the clothes? It's what's under them that's interesting."

Gilbert groaned. "Why can't little girls stay little forever?"

"Wait until Idina is Cheryl's age," Kaia said. "You will miss how tame we were as teenagers."

Gilbert grimaced. "I have no doubt."

As entertaining as it was to watch the family dynamics, Orion wanted to be done so he could go home to Alena.

"I have a solution that will satisfy everyone. I can compel you not to think about what you've learned when you are around other people. You'll only be able to think about it when you are alone."

Gabriella's smile was brilliant enough to illuminate the room. "Perfect."

Gilbert, on the other hand, didn't look happy with Orion's solution. "What if he can get into her head from afar?"

"Thankfully, it's not possible," Onegus said. "A very strong thraller can plant suggestions and illusions in people's minds from a distance, and a strong empath can feel what others are feeling in a wide area. But neither can pinpoint which thoughts are emanating from whom unless they are right next to that person. "

"What about Vivian and Ella?" Karen asked. "They can communicate telepathically from wherever regardless of distance."

"That's a very different paranormal talent," Onegus said. "And it is also extremely rare. I doubt any of the Doomers have this kind of telepathic ability. At most, some of them might be weak telepaths who won't be able to pinpoint which thought is coming from whom."

Gabi groaned. "You're giving me a headache. Do all immortals have paranormal abilities?"

"Not all," Kaia said. "I'm still trying to figure out mine."

William looked at her with adoring eyes. "Your talent is solving scientific puzzles."

"Maybe." Kaia let out a breath. "I'm still transitioning, so maybe something cooler than that will emerge."

Gabriella turned to Onegus. "Will I also develop a paranormal talent once I'm immortal?"

He shook his head. "If you don't have any special talents now, you probably won't get any after. Usually, existing talents intensify after the transition." He smiled. "My mate can blow things up with her mind. She could do that before her transition but had difficulty controlling it, and her explosions were small. After the transition, she started practicing, and now she has full control over her power and can blow up a car."

Eyes wide, Gabriella turned to Darlene. "Can you blow things up like your sister?"

"Regrettably, I can't. Cassandra is a badass, and she has a badass talent."

"What is your talent?" Gabi asked.

Orion lifted his hand. "If you don't mind, I would like to commence with the compulsion, and I need a few quiet moments with no distractions to do so. I don't want to leave any wiggle room in my phrasing."

22

JADE

Kagra strode into Phinas's home as if it was her own. "You're going to love me for this." She pulled out one of the dining table chairs, turned it around, and straddled it. "Ask me why."

Phinas arched a brow. "I'm almost afraid to, especially when you use the word love in the sentence, but why?"

She waved a hand dismissively. "It's just an expression." Mischief danced in her eyes as she winked at Jade. "I know that you love me no matter what. I'm just so lovable." She batted her eyelashes.

"Can you get to the point?" Jade pulled out a chair next to her second-in-command. "We have a lot to talk about."

"I've got us an office, and it's not in the underground. It has a nice big window that overlooks the ravine."

The office building overlooked the village square, as did the building that housed the clinic and Bridget's research facilities, so she wasn't talking about a room there.

"Where is this lovely office?" Phinas asked.

"In Ingrid's design center. Kian gave her an entire house to use as her base of operations, and it has a living room and two bedrooms. She only uses the living room as her showroom and one of the bedrooms as an office. She has no problem with you using the other bedroom as the Kra-ell headquarters. You can use the sliding door to the backyard to come and go without going through the center, and if you need to have meetings with several people, you can do that in the backyard."

That sounded like a great solution, but in Jade's experience, nothing was ever given out for free. "What's the catch?"

Kagra shrugged. "Ingrid said that she needs help with deliveries from time to time, and the Guardians are not always available. She will collect the favor by asking us to help carry things."

"I'd rather pay rent," Jade grumbled.

It wasn't because she was averse to using her people as pack mules but because she had the money, and she didn't like to feel like a beggar.

Phinas pushed to his feet. "You can't pay rent because the house does not belong to Ingrid, and she doesn't pay rent either." He stopped next to the bar cabinet. "Can I offer you ladies something to drink?"

"Sure," Kagra said. "I'll take a vodka with cranberry juice."

"Coming up." He glanced at Jade. "I assume that you want one too?"

"Since you are already making a cocktail for Kagra, sure."

Taking Ingrid up on her offer would at least give Phinas his house back. Jade tried to hold as many of her meetings as possible in the café, but not everything could or should be discussed in public, and her place of residence was the only other option. During the week, Phinas spent time at Kalugal's office building in the city, so she could see people while he wasn't home, but some always showed up after hours, and it wasn't fair to him.

As for Drova, she was rarely home, and when she was, it wouldn't be a bad idea for her to witness what was involved in leading a community. One day she might become a leader herself, and the experience she could gain by watching Jade would be invaluable.

The problem was that she had trouble getting through to the girl, and most of her suggestions were met with such opposition that she kept them to a minimum. Drova was still struggling with her father's fate, and she needed time but, at some point, Jade would have to stop coddling her and start enforcing more rigid rules.

"When can I start using that other room in Ingrid's design center?" she asked.

"Right now, it is furnished as a bedroom." Kagra pulled out her phone. "I took a picture if you want to take a look." She handed the phone to Jade.

It was identical to Drova's room, with a sliding glass door leading to the backyard.

"It will do." She handed Kagra back her phone.

"Ingrid said that as soon as you give her the okay, she'll order proper office furniture to replace what is there now. She suggested that you drop by during business hours and look through some catalogs so you can choose what you like."

Jade didn't really care. A dining room table could serve as a conference table, and she could also use it as her desk.

"I'll go to see the place tomorrow."

Kagra grimaced. "So, I assume you decided not to go to China after all, and you want me to go instead."

"I can't leave the village right now, and frankly, I'm not happy about you going either. I wanted Vrog to lead the Kra-ell portion of the team. Kian even seemed like he was okay with that, but then he called me and said that he wanted either you or me to co-lead the team with Yamanu because Vrog wouldn't be able to handle Rishana and Sheniya. Even with Toven's compulsion and my direct orders to follow Vrog's lead, they would find ways to make his life miserable."

Kagra sighed. "If Yamanu were single, I would jump on the opportunity to co-lead with him, but he's happily mated, and immortals are obsessively loyal to their mates. I think you should go. I can hold the fort in your absence."

That was probably true, but Jade didn't want to go.

"It'll be good practice for you. Did you speak with the males on the list?"

Kagra nodded. "They are all eager to go, including Pavel. They regard it as an honor to be chosen and trusted to leave the village, and an opportunity for an adventure."

"I bet." Jade took the glass Phinas handed her. "I wish at least one person on the team was a compeller. I don't trust Sheniya and Rishana."

Kagra looked offended. "Don't you trust me to keep them in check? They won't dare do anything with me in charge."

Jade wasn't sure about that at all.

91

Kagra was a great fighter and in much better shape than the two older females. But she was too young and cheerful to be taken seriously by them. She also had a temper, which she sometimes failed to control.

In short, she suffered from the maladies of youth and temperament, but the mission was a perfect test to see how she handled leading a team.

"I'm sure you'll do your best, but you are young and Earthborn, which might diminish your authority in their minds. It will be a good test, though."

Kagra took a sip from the drink and put it down. "Don't worry. I can handle them, and if they underestimate me, they will learn never to repeat that mistake."

23

GABI

The hotel room was much more luxurious than Gabi had expected. She wondered how much it would cost her. Onegus had made the reservations, but she had no doubt that she would have to pay upon checkout.

Just one more thing to fuel her anxiety.

Perhaps she should just call the front desk and ask?

The truth was that her business was not as profitable as she'd made her brothers believe it was, and she had to be very calculated with how she spent her money.

Oh well, soon none of that would matter because she would again have to give it all up and live with Eric and Darlene until she got a new clinic running in Los Angeles.

Renting office space in the city would be much more expensive than what she was paying in Cleveland, but she could probably charge more for her services. Except, she would have to build up a client base from scratch, which would take time. Perhaps she could keep helping her Cleveland clients remotely? They might not object if she lowered her fees, but would they keep recommending her to their family and friends?

In the meantime, she could probably get by on the money she would collect for renting out her condo. She'd bought it twelve years ago and had taken out a fifteen-year mortgage, so in three years it would be free and clear, and since it had tripled in value, she could charge much more for rent than what she was still paying on the mortgage and all the other expenses associated with homeownership.

Gabi was very well aware that those thoughts about mortgage, rent, and other mundane things were nothing more than a delaying tactic. Sitting on the couch in her hotel room and clutching her phone, she hoped Uriel would call her first so she wouldn't have to call him and risk rejection.

Perhaps she could wait a little longer and, in the meantime, ponder the bigger issues of immortality and the pending changes in her life. After all, she wouldn't be able to do that with Uriel around.

Orion's compulsion worked so well that it was disturbing.

When Gabi had collected her room key from the front desk, she couldn't remember anything she had talked about with her family, and she'd thought that she wanted to stay in the hotel so she could meet with Uriel. That was true, but there was so much more to it that she remembered as soon as she entered the elevator and the doors closed behind her.

It was the weirdest feeling. It was like trying to remember a word or a name or something important that she needed to do and struggling with it for hours, and then it suddenly popped into her mind when she was least expecting it.

Perhaps she should write it down somewhere so it wouldn't be as jarring the next time?

She could make a note in the application she used for monitoring her clients. She checked it frequently, especially when she was anxious, so when she felt like she was forgetting something, she would open the application and check her notes.

"Quit stalling," she murmured. "Call him and get it over with."

What was the worst that could happen? Uriel would come up with some polite excuse for why he couldn't see her, she would be hurt, and she'd get over it.

Case closed.

Would she still remember everything she'd been told about immortals while talking on the phone with him? Or would she forget the moment he answered?

Perhaps she should start with a text.

If he rejected her via text, it would feel less personal. It would also be a good test to see whether her memories were affected by texting.

"You are such a damn coward," Gabi murmured as she opened the text application.

Hi, Uriel, it's Gabi. I'm spending the night in a hotel after all, and I'm wondering whether we could meet for drinks. The hotel I am staying in is in downtown Los Angeles. It's called the 72nd like the restaurant on top of the building. If you want to come over, I'll text you the address. I can also take an Uber and meet you in a bar or come to your hotel.

She read over the text twice, corrected a couple of typos, and then hesitated with her finger hovering over the send button.

"I'm not a coward." She tapped the screen and sent the text.

Her heart was racing like crazy until the three dots appeared, indicating that he was typing an answer, and when they kept blinking for long moments, it went into hyperdrive, threatening to burst out of her ribcage and commit suicide by jumping off the window of her room on the sixty-ninth floor.

Good thing that the windows couldn't be opened and there was no balcony.

Uriel's reply was taking so long that he was either typing a very long text, someone was interrupting him, or he was writing and erasing and writing it again.

Finally, when the words appeared on her screen, she felt faint with relief.

I can be there in an hour. Do you want to meet in the lobby?

Gabi let out a breath. It wasn't a polite letdown, and he was willing to come to her.

Feeling emboldened, she typed, *you can come up to my room, and we can order room service. I'm on the sixty-ninth floor, room 6914. I'll check the exact address and send it to you in a moment.*

This time the three dots blinked for only a few seconds. *No need to send me the address. I know where your hotel is. I'll bring a bottle of wine.*

Smiling, Gabi typed back, *I can't wait to see you again.*

The three dots danced for a couple of seconds. *I'm eager to see you again too.*

24

VROG

"It's so nice in the café in the evenings." Aliya stretched her long legs in front of her. "Especially since it is closed, and I don't have to serve customers." She cast Vrog a sidelong smile. "Don't get me wrong. I love working in the café, and I love the village, but I'm excited about visiting China. I haven't been back since I left."

Vrog reached for her hand. "It will be like a honeymoon for us."

Aliya was allowed to leave the village now, but they hadn't done it often. She worked long hours at the café, and in the evenings, she worked on supplementing her education. That didn't leave much time for leisure, and he was glad she was finally willing to take a vacation.

He was also glad that Kian had convinced Jade to send Kagra as the Kra-ell team leader, and Vrog's job description had been reduced to an advisor.

Wendy sighed. "Yeah, except you are not married, and neither are Vlad and I. We don't even know if the wedding cruise is still happening. Did anyone hear any updates about that?"

Vrog shook his head. "Maybe now that the trial is over and things are back to normal, Kian will announce when the cruise will take place."

Vlad chuckled. "Things are never back to normal for long. I bet that those signals you are going to investigate are another crisis that's brewing." He leaned toward Wendy and planted a kiss on her cheek. "We should just elope. How does a Vegas wedding sound to you?"

Vrog didn't know whether his son was jesting, but given Wendy's laugh, she seemed to think it was a joke. "I have a gorgeous wedding dress that's fit for a grand wedding. I'm not wasting it on a ceremony in a stinky chapel in Vegas."

"Why is the chapel stinky?" Aliya asked.

"It's just an expression to describe something that's not up to par," Wendy explained. "On another subject, this trip to China means that Wonder and I will have to hire one of the hybrids to take your place while you are gone." She affected a pout. "We've gotten spoiled having you around, and now we can't manage without you."

"About that." Aliya straightened in her chair. "The timing is actually good. I wanted to talk to you about cutting down my shifts. I want to speed up my online studies so I can finally get my high school equivalency diploma and apply to colleges."

"Did you decide what you want to study?" Vlad asked.

She smiled shyly. "Until recently, I thought about becoming a teacher, but after seeing Lusha handling the trial, I want to study law. I'll start with an English major, maybe with a minor in education, and then go to law school."

Vrog still hoped she would change her mind about that, but she was enamored with the idea of becoming a lawyer.

"I don't know if that's a good idea," Wendy said. "Does the village need another attorney? You should ask Kian whether he needs legal services for the clan's many businesses. If he doesn't, you will have to find a job in the human world, and with your looks, it's not really practical."

Vrog could kiss the girl for saying all the things he'd been trying to tell Aliya without offending her. Wendy had just said them without trying to sugarcoat a thing.

Shrugging, Aliya lifted her coffee cup and took a sip. "Maybe I will study international law and write books about it. Or maybe I will write courtroom drama stories. I don't have to become an actual lawyer."

"Then why bother?" Vlad asked. "It doesn't make sense to invest the time and effort. You can easily learn everything you need from reading books on the subject."

"Well, I'll start with the English major and decide what to do with it later. I can always teach English in the village school."

Vrog stifled a relieved breath.

That was precisely what he wished Aliya would choose, but he didn't want to appear to be dictating her future to her.

"How is the school coming along?" Wendy asked. "Any progress?"

"It's progressing well, given the limitations." Vrog leaned back in his chair. "The older kids are set up with laptops and self-learning programs, but they need a lot of help from me to get going. They are less proficient with computers than other kids their age, and many struggle with the language. Jade initially agreed to teach the little ones, but she doesn't have time, so I will have to find someone else to do that."

Wendy's eyes brightened. "I can teach a preschool class. I can do arts and crafts with the little ones."

Vrog smiled apologetically. "That would be lovely if you spoke Kra-ell. Regrettably, none of the little ones speak English, and I need a Kra-ell to teach them."

"Oh." Wendy's face fell. "Well, I'm sure you will find a volunteer. It's not like there is much for the Kra-ell to do in the village."

"It will have to wait for when I get back." Vrog glanced at Vlad. "I had an idea I wanted to run by you. What do you think about teaching the older kids and some of the young adults graphic design as an after-school class? They weren't exposed to any art in Igor's compound, and they could benefit from an introduction."

What Vrog really had in mind was getting Vlad more involved with the Kra-ell community.

So far, his son was like an outsider looking in. Even after the impromptu band performance Jackson had organized with his old band members and his new stepbrothers, Vlad was still too reserved to pursue friendships with the young Kra-ell, hybrids or purebloods. Teaching a class would give him an opportunity to get to know them better and for them to get to know him.

"I can spare an hour a week if you think they would be interested. I can also teach guitar playing. I think music will be even more appealing to them than art."

"That's a wonderful idea," Wendy said. "I wish I had an artistic skill I could teach, but even though I'm studying to become an art therapist, I can't do more than basic arts and crafts that are only good for little kids."

"Not necessarily," Vrog said as an idea started coalescing in his mind. "The Kra-ell carry a lot of emotional issues that they have no tools to express or deal with. I think that even the adults could benefit from a therapeutic arts and crafts class."

"I'm not licensed yet." Wendy chewed on her lower lip. "But since outside human world rules don't apply in the village, I can lead a class and see if I can help guide a discussion." She looked at Vrog. "What do you think?"

"I think it will not be easy to convince the Kra-ell that arts and crafts are a suitable way to pass the time, but I will find a way to market it. Perhaps we can call it conversational English practice. They all want to get proficient, and you can correct them when they make a mistake."

"That's an awesome idea." Wendy rubbed her hands together. "I'll have a curriculum ready when you get back."

25

GABI

G abi searched her carry-on for something sexy to wear, but she hadn't packed anything that fit the bill. Traveling with only a carry-on as her luggage, she could only pack the bare necessities, which were six light dresses that didn't wrinkle, didn't take up much space, and were more professional in appearance than sexy.

She had one pair of pumps, which she was now wearing, flip-flops that served as slippers at the end of the day, one black cardigan that matched all six dresses, a nightshirt, two simple bras, and ten pairs of underwear that took nearly no space at all.

The fact that she hated flying didn't mean she didn't travel or didn't know how to pack light. People could use other modes of transportation, like trains and buses, cruise ships, and her old trusty car.

The problem was that she hadn't planned on hooking up with anyone during the conference or her family visit, and now she had none of her single-girl weapons with her. No sexy lingerie and no tight-fitting skirts or leggings. All she had to work with was a hairbrush and some makeup.

After showering, she put on the sexiest of her six dresses, a black off-the-shoulder stretchy number that flared around her hips and reached below her knees. There was no time to do anything elaborate with her long hair, so she didn't even wash it to save on blow-drying time.

Instead, she teased it to give it some volume and tied the ends in a loose braid. She then applied a little makeup, just a concealer under her eyes, some eyeliner, and a touch of gloss.

She didn't want to look as if she was trying too hard.

After all, they weren't meeting in the hotel bar, so she had no excuse to put on the glossy red lipstick that would have made her entire face pop with color and provide a contrast to the simple black dress.

Oh, fine. Red lipstick it is.

A girl needed her armor, and if all she had was red lipstick, then that was what she would use.

After applying the bright cherry color, she smacked her lips and batted her eyelashes at her reflection. "Sweet and sexy. An irresistible combination."

Or so she hoped.

When the knock on the door sounded a little earlier than she'd expected, Gabi walked over and looked through the peephole to make sure it was indeed Uriel.

Looking even more gorgeous than she'd remembered, he was smiling as if he knew she was looking at him, and as she opened the door, his smile got even wider.

"Hello, Gabi." He leaned and kissed her cheek as if they were long-time acquaintances.

Her heart was beating like a marching band possessed by demons, but her brain still functioned well enough to find it odd that no one had called her from the reception desk to ask whether it was okay for Uriel to come to her room.

"Hi." She smiled back. "Did you have trouble getting up here?"

"Not at all." He put a large paper bag on the coffee table. "The reception guy was busy checking in a family of six, so when I told him I had a delivery for Gabriella Emerson in room 6914, he just let me through."

She chuckled. "He should have called and asked if I was expecting a delivery. Anyone can claim to be a delivery person and do unmentionable things to the hotel guests, who could then sue the hotel."

He frowned. "You said that you were a nutritionist. Are you also an attorney?"

Was he serious, or was he teasing her?

He looked serious.

"I'm not a lawyer, but that's common knowledge. People sue over things like a cup of coffee being too hot. Do you think they wouldn't sue for something like that?"

"I guess you are right."

Realizing he was still standing because she hadn't invited him to sit, she pointed to the couch. "Let's sit down so you can show me what you've got in that bag."

As he sat right next to her, so close that their thighs were nearly touching, his scent permeated her senses, and her eyes threatened to roll back in her head. Forcing them to stay focused, she leaned closer to sniff him better. "What's the name of the cologne you're wearing? It's amazing."

He looked embarrassed. "I don't know. My friends and I went shopping in a department store earlier, and a lady sprayed it all over me. I don't know what it's called."

Was it her imagination, or was Uriel kind of nerdy for the hottest guy she'd ever met?

He wasn't full of himself, and he wasn't boastful about anything. He was like the boy next door, just on steroids and with lots of plastic surgery.

"What were you and your friends looking for at the department store?"

She didn't really care about his shopping excursion, but it was a good conversation starter.

"Oh, this and that. Clothing mostly. I got a new wallet." He pulled it from his pocket, but regrettably he didn't open it to show her what was inside.

She didn't care about the credit cards he carried or how much cash he had in there, but she would have liked to know his last name, and so far, he'd managed to wiggle out of telling her every time she'd asked.

26

ONEGUS

"Thank you so much for babysitting." Karen held one of her sleeping boys over her shoulder. "Did they give you any trouble?"

Geraldine smiled. "None at all. They were three little angels. Anytime you need someone to babysit for you, I'm here."

Looking a little doubtful, Karen glanced at Cassandra and then Alena, but both nodded their agreement.

"Idina is such a smart girl," Alena said. "It's hard to believe that she's only three and a half years old."

Karen's expression was filled with pride. "I think kids grow up faster these days. They are exposed to so much more information than we were as kids."

Onegus didn't want to point out that she shouldn't include the immortals in her collective we. The world was different for each of them growing up.

"We need to go, Mom," Kaia said. "Idina is tired."

The girl was in William's arms, making grumbling noises about wanting to sleep.

"Yes. We should go." Gilbert adjusted the other sleeping boy on his shoulder. "Thanks again for babysitting. Have a good night."

When the door closed behind them, Onegus turned to Cassandra. "We should go too."

"No way. I want to hear all about Gabi and why she didn't come back with you as planned."

"Yeah," Alena said. "I want to hear that too."

Geraldine pushed to her feet. "I'll brew a fresh pot of coffee." She smiled. "You can't have juicy gossip without coffee and cake, right?"

Darlene laughed. "Absolutely."

After coffee was served, Darlene and Eric took turns recounting Gabriella's curious response to learning that her brothers and niece were immortal and that she could turn immortal as well.

"All because of a guy?" Cassandra asked. "He must have left one hell of an impression on her."

"Evidently." Darlene smirked. "She had it bad for him. I could see it in her eyes. When Onegus said that she would have to leave her phone behind, her entire attitude changed. Suddenly, she no longer wanted to go to the village with us and was okay with Orion compelling her to keep immortals a secret. It was a complete one-eighty."

"I need to find out more about that Uriel guy." Onegus took the coffee cup Geraldine handed him.

Orion eyed him with a doubtful expression. "How? Gabriella didn't tell us his last name. I don't think she even knows it."

"Roni can hack into the airline servers and easily find out who flew first class from Toronto to Los Angeles today."

"Do you know which airline she flew on?" Shai asked.

"No, but Roni can find that out in seconds. Gabi didn't use a fake name to book her flight, so that should be a piece of cake for him."

The guy who claimed his name was Uriel had probably lied about it. Uriel wasn't a common name, though, so maybe Onegus was seeing shadows where there were none. When people faked their identities, they usually used common names like Tom, Michael, or David and last names like Smith or Baker. The more common the name, the better.

It also wasn't a Doomer's name, but it would be a mistake to base his assumption on that alone.

Orion looked amused. "If you were so suspicious, you should have just asked Gabriella which airline she flew on and what her flight number was. She probably called that guy up as soon as she got settled in her hotel room, and he's probably already there. Gabriella is a looker, and any single man would jump to attention when getting an invitation from a beautiful lady."

"Guys." Cassandra lifted her hand. "Give the girl a break, will you? All she wants is a night of passion with a hot stranger. You are all jumping to conclusions about Uriel's identity just because of Gabi's stupid remark about him and his friends being as good-looking as you are." She waved her hand over the immortal males in the room. "Is it really so hard to believe that there are gorgeous male specimens among humans? And especially on a flight to Los Angeles—the mecca of actors and other performers worldwide?"

"It's also where the Brotherhood likes to hunt for unsuspecting females," Onegus said. "Although I have to admit that Gabi doesn't fit the profile of their typical victim. For starters, even though she's a beautiful woman, she's too old. Secondly, she has family that will notice immediately if she goes missing. Also, Doomers don't typically fly first class or travel in threes. That being said, Roni can do a quick search, find out who the guy is, and assuage my fears."

"What fears?" Cassandra asked. "You put Gabi in the clan's hotel, and knowing you, you've asked the front desk to notify you when someone visits her."

Onegus smirked. "Of course. That's why I offered to book her a room in our hotel."

Orion leaned back with his coffee cup. "Was I right? Is the guy already there?"

Onegus shook his head. "She ordered some stuff from a nearby liquor store, which was delivered to her room. Other than that, she hasn't had any other visitors."

"She probably ordered stuff in preparation for the visit," Darlene said. "Can we please stop talking about Gabi's love life?"

Cassandra snorted. "Says the woman who was making a list of possible suitors for Gabriella, with Max topping the list."

"That's different." Darlene pouted. "She needs an inducer, and I was looking out for her interests."

As the sisters argued about Gabriella and her future guy, Onegus pulled out his phone and texted Roni.

I need a quick favor. If you can do it tonight, great, and if not, tomorrow works as well.

The return text came in a few minutes later. *I'm hanging out with some new friends. If it's not urgent, I'll do it tomorrow morning. Send me the info.*

The new friends were probably some of the young Kra-ell pure-bloods and hybrids, and Onegus was glad that they were hanging out together.

Gabi's mystery man could wait.

2 7

GABI

" I didn't know what you liked." Uriel started pulling things out of the paper bag. "I got a chocolate liqueur that the guy at the store said was a ladies' favorite and two bottles of wine, one red and one white. I also got mixed nuts in case you like salty things and a box of chocolates in case you like sweets."

With him sitting so close and smelling divine, it was hard to concentrate on what he was showing her.

He'd showered and changed, exchanging the white T-shirt for a gray one and the blue jeans for a pair of black ones, and Gabi couldn't decide which outfit looked better on him.

Easy, he was delicious in both, and she couldn't wait to see him in nothing at all.

"I like both sweet and salty," she murmured absentmindedly. "But that doesn't mean that I can indulge in either. They are both unhealthy for different reasons."

When Uriel's face fell, Gabi quickly added, "I don't need to be a good girl all the time. I can be naughty once in a while and snack on unhealthy things." She gave him a loaded look that left little room for misinterpretation.

Uriel seemed surprisingly unpracticed in the art of flirting, but perhaps he had never needed to develop the skill because women had just fallen into his lap.

Heck, she was a case in point. She'd called him up and invited him to her hotel room, and she'd done that with only the slightest indication that he even wanted to see her again.

Thankfully, Uriel had no problem understanding her double entendre if the gleam in his dark eyes was any indication.

"Snacking on me can be very healthy for you." He reached for her hand and brought it to his lips. "But I need to hear you ask for what you want."

Was this a sex game? Or was it just an insurance policy against later possible accusations of rape?

In today's litigious world, a guy couldn't be too careful, especially since he had snuck up to her room under false pretenses.

Given the devilish expression on Uriel's face, though, it was her first guess and not the second.

Well, if he wanted to play games, she was not going to refuse.

Gabi swallowed.

She wasn't shy about what she wanted, but she wasn't used to actually verbalizing her desires.

"I want you to kiss me." That should do it if he was after her consent. If he wanted to play dominance games, she wasn't sure how to proceed.

Gabi had no experience with that, and all she knew about the alternative lifestyle was from romance novels that probably got it all wrong, but if she was ever tempted to experiment, it was now with Uriel.

Just not anything that involved being tied up. She wasn't that dumb or horny. Although, with those muscles, Uriel didn't need ropes to immobilize her.

Strike the not-that-horny. She had never been so aroused just by talking to a guy and imagining what he was about to do to her.

"Where do you want me to kiss you?" he asked with that velvety smooth, sexy-as-sin voice of his.

"Right here." She tapped her lips with her pointer finger.

As a groan rose in his throat, the sound traveled right to where she was already tingling with need.

"Close your eyes," he commanded.

It was a shame to lose the magnificent view of his incredible face, but Gabi was all up for playing Uriel's game.

Despite him being a stranger, despite the sheer size of him and his muscles, and despite his evasiveness, she felt safe with him.

A small voice in the back of her head whispered that victims of serial killers had probably felt safe with them before they did not. Sociopaths were known to be great mimickers, and they could pretend to be very charming, fooling their victims into a false sense of security.

Despite the sinister whispers, though, Gabi trusted her instincts.

Uriel wasn't a serial killer.

He was keeping secrets, and there was probably no future for them beyond this one night, but she would be damned if she didn't enjoy it to the fullest for as long as it lasted.

When his large hand closed over the nape of her neck, she couldn't help the shiver that ran through her, and her lips parted of their own volition, but Uriel didn't immediately close the distance as she'd expected.

Instead, she felt him looking at her.

Did he need another invitation?

"You're so beautiful," he whispered.

A smile curved her lips. Men had called her beautiful before, but when coming from Uriel and spoken with such sincerity, it meant more to her.

"Kiss me," she murmured.

Instead of his lips, she felt his finger on her lips, wiping at her lipstick.

So that was his problem. He didn't want to taste lipstick.

"It's not going to come off, and you're not going to taste it." She was tempted to open her eyes but couldn't bring herself to disobey his command for some reason.

If she did, the magic would be broken, and that was the last thing she wanted.

He chuckled softly. "I wondered what it would taste like. I was hoping for cherries." He brushed his lips against hers ever so softly. "But you are right. It doesn't taste like anything. Maybe I need to give it another try." He swiped his tongue over the seam of her lips, demanding access which she gladly granted.

As he swooped inside, taking possession of her mouth, Gabi's eyes rolled back in her head behind her closed lids, and as his hold on her nape tightened, she moaned into his mouth, but it sounded more like a whimper.

His hold immediately relaxed, and he pulled back. "Did I hurt you?"

Was he kidding her?

Once again, she wanted to open her eyes and look at his face, but something prevented her from doing so. Was it her stubbornness to see this game play out as she'd expected?

"You didn't. That's the kind of sound I make when I'm turned on. Can you go back to kissing and stop worrying about hurting me?"

He cupped her cheek. "Only if you promise to tell me to stop the moment something feels uncomfortable."

Damn, Gabi wanted to open her eyes so badly that it hurt. "I promise. But I'm not as fragile as I seem."

"To me, you are." He took her lips, applying just the barest of pressure. "I don't want to accidentally cause you harm."

"Don't worry about hurting me," she murmured against his lips. "If I don't like what you're doing, I'll say the word cease."

He chuckled. "Why not just a simple stop?"

"Because I fully expect to tell you 'don't stop,' and I don't want any misunderstandings."

28

KAREN

"Goodnight, sweetie." Karen kissed Idina's forehead.

"Goodnight, Mommy."

Karen tucked in the blanket again, looked at her daughter's angelic face, and smiled. Idina looked angelic only when she was asleep. When awake, she had a mischievous streak that bordered on mean, and the look she sometimes got in her eyes was a little devilish.

Tiptoeing out of the room, Karen didn't close the door all the way behind her and headed to the living room.

She found Gilbert brooding over a glass of whiskey that he seemed to be holding but not drinking from.

"What's the matter? Are you still upset about Gabi?"

"Yeah. I'm thinking back to how I was with her after our parents died, and I realize I let her get away with everything. I didn't hold her accountable for anything other than keeping up her grades in school."

"Oh, sweetheart." She sat on his lap and leaned her head on his shoulder. "You were just a kid yourself when you were tasked with raising your brother and sister. You've done amazingly well."

He shrugged. "I could have done better. I should have expected more of the two of them. But to be frank, Gabi did her share. She took on cooking for the three of us, which was a great help. She also helped with cleaning and the laundry. But emotionally, well, I didn't know how to handle her. She had temper tantrums and crying fits, and I humored her because I felt sorry for her. I feel like she hasn't grown up emotionally because of that."

Karen sighed.

It was so like Gilbert to take responsibility for everything, including things he had no control over. It was the eldest child syndrome taken to the umpteenth degree.

"Gabi has a certain personality, and I'm sure it was volatile even before your parents' deaths. You just didn't pay that much attention to her before. It's like Idina. Is her mean streak our fault? Do we encourage it in any way? We don't, and I hope she will grow out of it, but if she doesn't, I'm not going to blame myself or you for it. She was born a certain way, and all we can do is encourage the good and discourage the bad. The rest is up to her."

Being the stubborn ox that he was, Gilbert only pretended to accept what she was saying, but given his expression, he wasn't internalizing any of it.

"I shouldn't have let her marry that jerk. That was another mistake I made. It destroyed her self-confidence."

Gabi was confident in some ways and not so much in others, but that was true of most people.

"Would she have listened to you if you had told her not to marry her ex?"

Karen couldn't remember his name, and she didn't want to. The idiot did not deserve to be remembered.

"Probably not. I knew the type, and I warned her, but she said that I was generalizing and that her guy was not like the other basketball or football stars who slept with half the school. She thought he loved her."

"Did he?" Karen asked rhetorically. "You don't cheat on someone you love. But maybe he thought that he loved Gabi when he married her?"

"Probably." Gilbert sighed. "I've made my share of relationship mistakes, so I'm not one to talk. I thought my ex loved me, and I think she thought so for a while too. But then she started screwing her CFO, and when I confronted her, she didn't even deny it. She said she didn't love me anymore."

Karen had heard all of it before, but it was no less painful to hear again. Regrettably, the transition couldn't heal the scars that the woman had left on Gilbert's soul. But maybe plenty of time eventually would.

Cupping his cheeks, she lifted his face so he had to look at her. "I love you, and I will never stop loving you. Do you know why?"

"Why?" He seemed truly perplexed by that.

"Because I see you, every part of you, the good, the not-so-good, and everything in between, and there is not a single piece of you that I don't love. That's why my love for you is eternal. And that's even before the bond. I can't imagine our connection getting even stronger than that, but everyone says that it will."

He grimaced. "Yeah. I just hope our love can survive getting in bed with another couple. The idea repulses me. Perhaps I should ask Bridget to give me a tranquilizer so when the time comes for the other guy to bite you, someone can put me out of my misery."

"Don't be silly. You'll be fine. Would you prefer to wait until your fangs and venom glands are functional? Because I don't mind waiting. You were the one pushing to do it as soon as possible."

"I don't want to risk you." He put the full glass of whiskey aside and wrapped his arms around her. "I'm just in a bad mood, and everything seems bleak. I will do anything to keep you safe, even if that involves having another couple with us in bed and someone else biting you. I'm terrified of anything happening to you before or during the transition. I want all this to be behind us."

29

GABI

The kiss must have been the longest Gabi had ever shared with a guy, and Uriel didn't seem like he was about to be done any time soon. Twice he'd released her mouth for a split second to allow her to take a breath, and then he'd gone back to ravishing it with such fervor that she was on the cusp of orgasm even though his hands still hadn't found her breasts or reached beneath her dress to touch her where she needed him to touch her the most.

If not for the sounds he was making in the back of his throat and his tight grip on her nape, she would have thought that he wasn't going to take it any further than kissing, but he was clearly as affected as she was.

Besides, they were not teenagers, and she'd made her expectations clear.

Suddenly, he released her mouth and her nape, gripped her hips, and flipped her around so her front was pressed against the rounded armrest, and he was behind her with his hands on her hips.

Goodness, that display of strength was hot, and so was the pose he'd put her in.

All he had to do now was to flip her dress up and expose her bottom that was barely covered and thong-style panties that by now were soaking wet.

When nothing happened, she wanted to turn her head and look over her shoulder to see what was keeping him, but as before, her eyes remained tightly closed.

When she felt his hands on the back of her thighs, she nearly moaned in relief, and as he smoothed them up toward her ass, pushing the skirt of her dress along the way, she sagged against the armrest and surrendered to the sensations.

"Perfection," he murmured as he exposed her bottom, which was bare save for the thin strip of fabric scarcely covering the center. "I hope you are not too attached to these." She felt his fingers pushing under the elastic, and a moment later, there was a tearing sound, and her panties were gone.

How had he done that so effortlessly?

And why did he want her with her back to him?

Was it part of the game?

Between commanding her to keep her eyes closed and turning her around, it seemed as if he didn't want her to see him.

Or maybe, maybe he wanted to keep it impersonal so she wouldn't get any ideas about this being anything more than a hookup.

The thought shouldn't be painful. After all, that was what she'd wanted, what she'd planned. It was supposed to be a one-time adventure before she embarked on—on what?

Her mind went blank, and a headache started pulsing at her temples. There was something she'd been planning to do, but she couldn't remember what it was. Something about moving to Los Angeles to be near her family, something she'd discussed with Gilbert and Eric during dinner, but she couldn't remember any of the particulars or why she'd promised them to think about it.

"You have a gorgeous ass." Uriel pulled her from her rambling thoughts, centering her on the here and now.

With his large hands closing over the sides of her butt cheeks, he pressed a kiss to each globe, and then he nipped her, once, twice, eliciting a yelp each time. The sting was a little uncomfortable but also arousing, and certainly nothing that required the word she'd promised him if it got too much for her.

The small bites had been playful, but Gabi had a feeling that Uriel was testing her with them to see whether she was averse to some sexual pain.

Evidently, she wasn't because those little nips had just gotten her wetter and needier. If he asked her now what she wanted him to do, she would tell him to get naked and feed her that hard length she'd spied before he'd ordered her to close her eyes.

It had been far too long for her, and she hadn't even realized how much she craved the touch of another instead of her own fingers or her trusty BOB.

Leaning over her, he kissed her neck, pulled her dress down, and then yanked it from under her knees, leaving her naked save for her bra, but not for long.

As his deft fingers did away with the clasp in a practiced move, she wondered how many women he had undressed during his young life to learn to do that so skillfully.

Most men, including her ex, fumbled around a bra clasp as if it was a bomb in need of defusing.

Whatever. Don't go there. He's not yours. Never was and never will be.

"What's wrong?" Uriel leaned over her again, palmed both of her breasts and then tugged on her nipples, scrambling her thoughts.

She stifled a moan. "You've gotten me naked, but you are still dressed."

"That's true. Do you prefer me unclothed?"

"Oh, yes, definitely, please, and thank you."

Uriel chuckled. "So polite." He rewarded her with a nip to her shoulder and then a lick to soothe the little hurt away. "And such a beautiful little liar."

30

GABI

Uriel was reading her like an open book, which should have flattered her but instead alarmed her for some reason.

Men were normally not that perceptive, and Gabi preferred it that way. Her thoughts were not always kind or sane, and she didn't need anyone inside her head, especially not a guy she'd just met.

Except, this was only a one-night stand, and she shouldn't worry about his ability to guess her thoughts and her moods so easily.

What was the worst that could happen? Uriel would tell his friends that he'd banged the crazy chick from the flight?

Who cared. They probably already thought that about her.

"You're still dressed." She wiggled her bottom, rubbing it against his erection.

"Patience, beautiful. First, I want to pleasure you so thoroughly that you will forget whatever is troubling you."

She smiled even though he couldn't see her. "I like your plan."

It would be nice to have a guy focused on her pleasure for a change, someone who actually knew what he was doing.

"Keep your eyes closed until I tell you that you can open them."

"Yes, sir."

Gabi was barely done saying the words when Uriel flipped her around, landing her flat on her back.

Lifting her arms, she found his neck and twined them around it, pulling him down for a kiss, but he kept the kiss light and continued down her throat, kissing and nipping his way to her aching breasts.

When he took her nipple between his lips, she arched up and moaned. "Goodness, Uriel. I wanted you to do this for so long."

He chuckled around her nipple and then bit it lightly before moving to the other one. It hurt, but in a good way, and as she threaded her fingers in his long hair, he bit the other one. This time it hurt even more, and she was sure he'd drawn blood, and as he started sucking on it, she had the crazy thought that her one-night stand was a vampire.

It was silly, but the idea of hooking up with a vampire fueled her desire to a whole new level.

I'm certifiable.

There was a difference between having a vivid imagination and actually convincing herself that what she was imagining was true.

When he slid lower, his intention was clear, and Gabi wantonly spread her knees wider to give him better access, and as his mouth made contact, she gripped his hair and arched off the couch.

It was so hard to keep her eyes closed.

She could feel his lips on her, his tongue lapping at her juices as if it was the best nectar he'd ever tasted. His growls and groans of approval reverberated through her body while providing a lewd soundtrack.

Gabi wanted to watch, but she didn't dare open her eyes.

What if she did, and he disappeared?

It was one more crazy thought, but she kept her eyes closed, nonetheless.

Not wanting to pull out his hair, she let go and gripped the couch instead, her fingernails digging into the soft velvet. "What are you doing to me?"

Instead of answering, he reached for her nipple and pinched it as he stabbed his tongue into her entrance and fucked her with it.

"Oh, my God," she croaked, her hips undulating with his lapping.

She'd never been eaten out and tongued like that before, and it was exquisite.

Pulling his tongue out, he replaced it with two fingers and then used it on the bundle of nerves at the top of her entrance.

Gabi was a hair away from climaxing, everything inside her coiling upon itself until it was so tight that she couldn't breathe.

When he pushed his fingers even deeper and hooked them inside of her while swiping his tongue just right over her clit, the coil sprang free, exploding from her with a moan that must have been incredibly loud, but she couldn't hear it because her climax was still roaring in her ears.

When Gabi's butt finally touched the couch again, her legs were shaky, and her throat felt hoarse as if she'd shouted her climax all over the hotel's sixty-ninth floor, which she probably had.

"Wow," she murmured. "Can I open my eyes now?"

"Not yet."

The sound of clothing being removed brought a smile to her lips.

"Finally."

When he climbed on top of her, the feel of his hard length against her entrance was a temptation she didn't want to resist. Putting her hands on his shoulders, she pulled him down for a kiss.

They kissed softly, like lovers who had known each other forever, their lips and tongues practiced in the dance of seduction they had perfected over the years.

But it was just an illusion, and tomorrow, Uriel would be gone, and she would move on.

As a tear slipped from her eye, he swiped it with his lips. "Why are you sad?"

"I'm not," she lied. "It's what I do after I orgasm so hard that I can't breathe."

He chuckled. "Such a pretty little liar."

Nevertheless, his erection twitched against her entrance as if in gratitude for her compliment.

Claiming her mouth with another kiss, he thrust his hips in one brutal move and seated himself deep inside her.

"Uriel!" She threw her head back.

"Did I hurt you?" he murmured against her throat.

Yes, he did, but she didn't want to tell him that, or he would stop. He was larger than anyone she'd been with before, but she was already getting used to the sensation, and the initial shock of his penetration was turning into pleasure.

"Don't stop," she whispered.

"I wouldn't dream of it." He gripped her hip and started thrusting slowly and deliberately inside her.

Gabi had a feeling that he was watching her face to gauge her reaction, and only when he was convinced that all she was experiencing was pleasure did he start going faster and deeper.

Her fingernails must have left grooves on his back, but that didn't slow him down one bit, and his groans of pleasure were turning more and more animalistic.

Just when she thought he was about to climax, he pulled out, flipped her around, yanked her ass up, and entered her from behind.

Wow, the guy couldn't make up his mind about how he wanted her—front or back or even sideways, but they hadn't done that yet.

Gabi had no problem with any of that.

It was refreshing.

Exciting.

Exhilarating.

From this angle, he was impossibly deep inside of her, and she wondered at her body's ability to accommodate him, but it was as if they were made for each other.

Except for that first shocking moment of penetration, they were a perfect fit.

Reaching around her, he feathered his fingers over her sensitive nub, applying just the right amount of pressure to heighten her pleasure without overstimulating her, and when she was about to explode again, she heard him hiss, and then he bit her shoulder so hard that she screamed.

The pain was gone almost immediately, the burn replaced by a cooling sensation, and Gabi wondered whether she'd imagined it, but her thoughts were obliterated as a climax exploded over her like a tornado, and it didn't end with just one. She wasn't sure whether it was a string of orgasms or the same one that came in waves, but with each new surge, she was catapulted higher to the clouds and beyond—the euphoric bliss indescribable.

ONEGUS

Onegus strode into the lab and headed straight for Roni's station. "Good morning." He pulled a rolling stool from the nearest desk and sat next to the young hacker. "Show me what you got."

"Nothing exciting." Roni clicked on his keyboard, and a grainy black-and-white passport photo appeared. "Uriel Delgado, age thirty-one, born in the USA to Portuguese parents, currently resides in Portugal and has Portuguese citizenship in addition to his American one."

"Can you make the picture sharper?"

"Sure." Roni clicked on his keyboard, and the passport picture filled the screen in moments.

"I'll admit he's a good-looking fellow, but Gabi's description was grossly exaggerated."

Roni arched a brow. "How did she describe him? Does it match the picture?"

"She didn't actually mention any particular features. Gabriella said that he was as good-looking as Orion and me, which naturally made us think that he might be an immortal, potentially a Doomer, although members of the Brotherhood are usually not as striking as Orion." Onegus felt awkward talking about himself as handsome, and the truth was that he wasn't in the same league as Orion's godly perfection, so it was okay for him to exclude himself from the comparison. "Their mothers don't have the luxury of being discriminating about the men who father them, and Navuh doesn't care about how his warriors look. In the past, it was all about brawn and cruelty; now, it's about brains."

Roni snorted. "The next generation of Doomers will probably look like me. I don't look like a descendant of the gods, and that's really annoying since I'm the great-grandson of a god, and I'm damn close to the source. I probably resemble my human father, and he must have been a very average-looking guy for me to come out like this." He waved a hand over his face. "He's still around, so theoretically I could track him down, but my mother doesn't want me to do that. She says it wouldn't do me any good to see him as he's old now and most likely married with several kids."

"True." Onegus nodded. "Most of us never knew who our fathers were. That's how it was for us until we started finding Dormants. At least you know you got your brains from your human father, and that's much more valuable than looks. You should be thankful for that."

Onegus would have loved to tell the kid that he was handsome, but the truth was that Roni was average looking, which must have rankled in a village full of gorgeous immortals.

"I agree." Roni smirked. "It's a great trade-off." The smirk turned into a frown. "But why couldn't I have gotten both? Just look at Kaia. She's brilliant and gorgeous, despite being a weak immortal who is far removed from the source, and she took a long time to transition despite being so young. I was the same age as she is now when I transitioned."

"I guess it's up to the Fates." Onegus really didn't want to get into a discussion about genetics. First of all, he didn't know much about it, and secondly, he was pressed for time. "What else did you discover about Uriel Delgado?"

"That's it. He left the States with his parents when he was six and hadn't been back for over twenty years. The first time he came for a visit was five years ago, and since then, he's been visiting quite frequently. If you want, I can find out which hotel he's staying at, and if he rented a car, I can find out the license plate number so we can track it."

Onegus looked at the photograph again. The guy could be an immortal, but he was most likely human.

"Does he have social media?"

Roni shook his head. "Nothing. But before you get your panties in a wad, that doesn't mean he's a fake. We create fake social media accounts for all clan members' assumed identities, and everyone who knows what they are doing does the same. If this passport and his other information is a counterfeit, someone has done an excellent job of it, and those kinds of people would have included a social media profile as well."

Onegus pushed to his feet. "So, what you are basically telling me is that if someone's info looks too complete, it's more suspicious than if it's lacking?"

"It depends. If it's a bad fakery, then less is less. But if it's a good one, then sometimes less means more, and more means less."

Onegus shook his head. "Now I'm even more confused. Is there any way you can hack into the Portuguese database to find out more about him? Tax returns, marriage certificates, etc?"

Roni grimaced. "I don't speak the language, and it will take time I don't have, but I can search for a local hacker to do the job for us. Do you want to spend time and money on this?"

Onegus glanced at the picture again. The guy looked like a typical Southern European, with dark hair, eyes, and olive-toned skin. He was good-looking, but that didn't mean he was an immortal. Human males could be just as handsome, especially since the advent of plastic surgery that could correct small imperfections. Should he spend any more time investigating a guy who seemed legit?

Gabi might see him once or twice, get her itch scratched, and then move into the village and start looking for an immortal to induce her. When she saw the selection available to her, Uriel Delgado would be of no more interest to her or anyone else in the clan.

"Nah. You're right. It's probably a waste of time."

32

GABI

Gabi wasn't surprised to wake up alone in bed. Uriel hadn't made any promises about staying the night, and she remembered his friend's comment about an early morning meeting. Had he left a note, though?

Snatching her phone off the nightstand, it dawned on her that she'd passed out on the couch last night, which meant that Uriel had carried her to bed and tucked her in.

He'd also collected her phone from the coffee table and connected it to the charging cable on the nightstand.

That was so thoughtful of him.

Releasing a contented sigh, Gabi turned her phone on and checked her messages. As usual, there were several from her clients, probably asking about food substitutions and confessing to not following their prescribed diet, but before she read any of them, she scrolled until she saw the one she was looking for.

Last night was incredible. I wish I could have stayed in bed with you, but I had an early morning meeting. I'll get in touch later today, probably in the evening. Have a wonderful day, and thank you for the smile you put on my face. It's going to stay with me throughout the day.

"Oh, that's so sweet." Gabi hugged the phone to her chest and then reread the message two more times before typing a reply.

Ditto. I'll be smiling all day long too.

The rest of the messages could wait for after she'd used the bathroom.

Surprisingly, she wasn't sore. It had been a while since she'd been with anyone other than her battery-operated boyfriend, and her BOB was modestly sized and gently used.

Neither could describe Uriel.

It had been pretty intense with him, and she'd fully expected to pay the price for last night's fun today, but there was no discomfort whatsoever, which meant that in addition to carrying her to bed, he'd also cleaned her up before tucking the blanket around her.

It was so damn sweet that it brought tears to her eyes.

A glance around the bathroom confirmed her suspicions. There was a pile of used washcloths in the corner that hadn't been there before.

What a considerate guy—

Wait a minute.

She'd expected to be itchy and sticky because they hadn't used a condom.

Oh, hell. How stupid could she get?

She'd invited a stranger to her hotel room and had unprotected sex with him?

It was his fault.

Every man she'd been with after her divorce had taken care of the condom part. She couldn't remember even one instance of having to remind a guy to put one on. Everyone knew that it wasn't safe otherwise. That was why it hadn't occurred to her to check whether Uriel was using protection.

She wasn't even on the pill!

"Way to go, Gabi. You might have gotten knocked up by a stranger."

But wait, her period had ended the first day of the conference, so there was no way she was ovulating.

"That's a relief." She put her hands on the vanity and made a disapproving face. "Dumb luck, Gabi. You were saved by sheer dumb luck."

Looking closer, she lifted her shoulder, expecting to see a bite mark, but her skin was as smooth and blemish-free as always.

"That's weird."

She could have sworn that Uriel had bitten her pretty hard, but she must have imagined it.

"Or maybe he got into my head and made me experience a phantom bite." She laughed at her reflection.

After what she'd learned yesterday evening, that wasn't such a crazy idea. Or maybe her mind had finally snapped, and she had imagined everything, including the sex god who'd made her black out from pleasure.

What the hell was that about, though?

She'd never blacked out from sex before, but it had been such a traumatic day that her brain might have short-circuited. It had started with the stress of anticipating the long flight, then its cancellation, then flying first class and drinking too much champagne while flirting with Uriel, and then Eric had pulled that fang stunt, and she'd fainted.

It was a miracle that she hadn't passed out before Uriel had even gotten to her room. She should have been exhausted. Heck, after the day she'd had, she should still be tired but felt great instead.

Well, except for the anxiety over contracting an STD, or the less likely but not entirely impossible pregnancy.

After a quick shower Gabi put on the hotel bathrobe, made herself a cup of coffee, and sat on the couch with her phone clutched in her hand.

She should answer her clients first, but she was too anxious to concentrate on them and typed a text to Uriel instead.

I had a great time with you last night, but this morning I realized that you didn't use protection. How could you have been so irresponsible? I blame myself, too. I should have paid attention, but I expected you to take care of it. I hope you didn't give me any sexually transmitted diseases or get me pregnant.

Gabi hesitated a moment before sending the text. There was a very slim chance Uriel could have gotten her pregnant, and she should have mentioned that pregnancy wasn't likely, but she was mad, and she wanted him to freak out the same as she had.

Then again, she was also at fault for not verifying that he used protection, but that only made her angrier.

Nevertheless, she hit send, lifted her coffee mug, and leaned back.

JADE

"Good morning, Ingrid." Jade offered the designer her hand. "This is a very nice showroom you have here."

Photographs of interiors done in different styles hung on the walls, some from private residences and some from hotel rooms, and it was easy to see that the same person had been in charge of designing them all, whether the style was contemporary or traditional. Ingrid liked warm woods and light flooring, and the accessories provided colorful accents. Pictures, pillows, blankets, vases, and potted plants were strategically scattered throughout the rooms.

"Thank you." Ingrid smiled. "For the longest time, I worked from my place, and it was a pain having people come over to choose furniture or ask to be teamed with a different roommate. That's why I understand your pain, and it must be even more difficult for you because you live with a mate and a daughter. I only had a roommate who didn't mind the constant flow of people."

Jade nodded. "I feel like I've taken over Phinas's home."

"Let me show you the spare room." Ingrid led her down the hallway and opened the door. "I've already had the bed taken out, and I asked Onegus to send a desk and a chair from one of the classrooms. So, if you want, you can start using it right away."

The room was clean, and the wall art was probably there when it was still a bedroom, but it was more than she'd expected. All she needed to add were a few more chairs, or if she wanted to keep it more traditionally Kra-ell, she could get a few floor pillows.

"It's perfect. Thank you."

"I'm glad. Do you want to return to the showroom and look through furniture catalogs? I'm sure that in the long run, you will need more than a chair and a small desk. A conference table, perhaps?"

"I was actually thinking about floor pillows. That's how I traditionally conducted meetings before my compound was attacked."

"Of course." Ingrid looked slightly offended or maybe disappointed that Jade didn't want to invest time and effort into decorating. "Do you want me to take the desk out?"

"No, I'll use it when I need to do administrative work. The floor pillows are for meetings. I don't have time to look through catalogs. Can you pick something for me and tell me how much it will cost?"

Ingrid frowned. "I'd rather not. Floor pillows can be done in countless combinations of fabrics with different textures, patterns, and colors. I have several books with samples that you can flip through."

Evidently the designer didn't want to decide for her.

Perhaps some flattery was needed. "You have great taste and a lot of experience, Ingrid." Jade waved a hand over her outfit and smiled. "As you can see, I don't. There is a reason all my clothes are either black, gray, or olive. That way, I don't need to think about what I'm going to put on in the morning. Can you please decorate my office for me? I'm positive that it will come out a hundred percent better than anything I can come up with."

Ingrid let out a breath. "Can you at least give me some clues? What are your color preferences?"

"I like bold colors and comfortable, durable fabrics."

Ingrid tilted her head. "Do you like Moroccan decor?"

"I like the colors but not how busy the patterns are. Can you marry Japanese minimalism with a Moroccan color palette?"

The designer's eyes brightened. "Now I know precisely what you want. I'll have a design ready for you by tomorrow."

Jade hadn't wanted to make a big production out of it and hoped that Ingrid would just order a few items to make the room fit the way Kra-ell traditionally conducted meetings, but apparently, that was not how things worked with the designer, and Jade didn't want to start their relationship on the wrong foot.

"Thank you. I know how busy you are, and I truly appreciate you taking the time to help me furnish my new office."

Ingrid's smile grew wider. "You've given me a challenge, a new style that I haven't seen anyone attempt before. I will enjoy playing around with it."

As the front door chimed, announcing a new visitor to the design center, Ingrid offered Jade her hand. "Welcome aboard, partner. I'll see you here tomorrow."

"Thank you."

As Ingrid went to take care of her customer, Jade took another look at her new office and then slipped out through the sliding door to the backyard and out through the side gate.

Security was not an issue in the village, and no one locked their doors. The fences around the backyards were for privacy, not security.

Glancing at her watch, Jade quickened her step. Talking with Ingrid had taken longer than expected, and she was late. Kagra would keep Rishana and Sheniya and the rest of the Kra-ell team busy, but that wasn't how Jade liked to run things. When she called a meeting, she always planned to be the first one there.

That was why Ingrid's offer was such a timely gift. Once the place was set up, Jade wouldn't need to rush from place to place to meet with people. It was far from perfect, and having a private area for her people to train and to gather in would have been better, but she'd promised herself to take things one step at a time and not obsess about the long list of items still pending on her to-do list.

GABI

As the minutes ticked away, and there was still no response from Uriel, Gabi's chest tightened with anxiety.

Had she gone too far?

Had her text been too accusatory?

After all, it was her responsibility to protect herself, and she shouldn't delegate it to anyone else.

Letting out an exasperated breath, she closed her eyes and dropped her head back on the overstuffed cushions of the couch.

It would be a shame if this was how things ended between them.

Uriel was supposed to be a one-night stand, but last night had just whetted her appetite, and she wanted one more taste. Not that it would be enough, but given that there was no future for them, perhaps it was better to pull the Band-Aid off sooner rather than later.

Regrettably, Uriel wasn't immortal, and it was a shame because she really liked him.

It wasn't just because of his gorgeous face and great body. He was sweet and considerate and didn't fit the stereotype of the hot bad boy. So, he was a little bit of an airhead and had forgotten to put a condom on, but she was guilty of the same thing, so she couldn't hold that against him.

When her phone pinged with an incoming text, Gabi was so startled that the device almost flew out of her hands. She fumbled to hold on to it but then couldn't focus her eyes to read the text.

She had to squint to make out the words.

I'm sorry. It didn't occur to me that I would need one. I'm clean and can't get you pregnant, so you have nothing to worry about.

Gabi reread the short text to make sure she hadn't misunderstood anything.

Why couldn't he get her pregnant?

Was there something wrong with him?

And why hadn't it occurred to him that he would need protection?

Had he thought she'd invited him to her hotel room to chat?

No one was that naive. He was probably lying to avoid taking responsibility for his mistake. He'd gotten carried away the same way she had and had forgotten the condom, and he might be clean or not, but he was probably just making up the stuff about being infertile.

Damn, she hated liars.

She'd had enough of that with Dylan, who had lied to her about everything and denied having affairs until she'd shown him the proof.

When she'd started suspecting him and confided her suspicions to her brother, Gilbert had hired a private investigator to follow Dylan around. It had been shocking to discover how many women her ex had been screwing on the side, especially given that, at the same time, he had also been having plenty of sex with her.

It was a wonder that he'd managed to hold on to a job and an even greater wonder that he hadn't given her an STD.

Dylan was a sex addict, which was one of the things he had said in his defense, explaining his addiction as an unquenchable thirst for love.

Gabi groaned.

If Uriel was a liar, it was best she'd discovered it sooner rather than later. She had no room in her life for liars.

"Focus, Gabriella, and repeat until you get it through your thick skull —Uriel is just a hookup, not boyfriend material, and not future husband material."

It was her rotten luck to find a man who was a nice guy in addition to being a sex god, but who she couldn't have even if he was honest because she was about to jump down the rabbit hole.

He could, however, be a hookup for one more night.

Taking a deep breath, she typed a message back.

I'm glad you are clean, and I'm sorry about your fertility issues, but if we meet again, please bring a condom with you. I don't think I can order them from room service.

Hopefully, the humor would take the sting out of her demand.

The three dots appeared immediately, and she didn't have to wait long for his reply.

I wish I could call you instead of answering with a text, but I'm in the middle of a meeting, and my friends are giving me dirty looks. I'm so glad you want to see me again, and I didn't blow my chances with you by admitting to being a moron with a low sperm count.

"Oh, my goodness. He really is infertile."

Or he could be perpetuating the lie.

In either case, his answer was so sweet that it was moving. What hunk in the history of hunks would have admitted those things to a woman he'd just met?

None that Gabi had ever met, and she'd met many in her personal life as well as in her practice. Cleveland wasn't Los Angeles, but it still had actors and models, and some of them needed help maintaining their ideal weight, so they came to her for help.

Gabi texted back.

Call me when you are done with your meetings. I want to see you one more time tonight before I leave tomorrow.

She had a flight back home on Wednesday, which meant that she had only one day left to visit her family in their village. She had to check out of the hotel tomorrow morning and spend the rest of her short vacation with them. After all, they had been the reason for her braving the flight over.

133

35

JADE

P hinas's dining room had never been as full of people as it
was now.

Jade was grateful he was at the downtown office and didn't
have to witness the Kra-ell invasion of his home. He'd told her a
hundred times, if not more, that she should think of the house as theirs,
not his, but she had trouble doing that. She hadn't chosen a single item
of decor, hadn't changed the location of any of the plants, and hadn't
even taken more than a tiny section of his closet.

Phinas was not a fancy dresser by any stretch of the imagination, but
he had at least four times as many articles of clothing as she did.

"Anyone want any more?" Kagra lifted her empty glass of vodka with
cranberry. She was handing it out as if this was her house, but Jade
didn't say a thing.

Her second-in-command had a way with people that Jade lacked,
and if a bottle of vodka smoothed things over, it was well worth it. The
problem was that Jade couldn't order it online and would have to ask
someone to get it for her.

None of the Kra-ell had cars, which was probably why the four
young males Kagra had recruited for the mission were so eager to go.

Vrog and Aliya had their own reason for being excited about the mission, but it probably had more to do with visiting Vrog's former school than curiosity about the scouts. Even though it was no longer his, Vrog was proud of it, and he wanted Aliya to see what he had managed to build.

Sheniya and Rishana looked suspicious and sour as usual. They had both arrived on Igor's pod, which made them the oldest members of the community, and that might have been the source of their animosity, especially Sheniya, who thought that the faint traces of royal blood she carried entitled her to special treatment.

She had begrudgingly accepted Jade's position as Igor's prime and later the new community's leader only because Jade's triangle was darker than hers. That alone was enough for Jade to doubt the female's intelligence. Having faint traces of royal blood was meaningless, and it wasn't what made Jade a good leader.

Still, Sheniya's dark triangle, however faint, might convince the scouts that they were dealing with someone who was in charge.

Sheniya leaned back with the fresh drink Kagra had handed her. "Finally, you realize how important blood is." She turned her eyes to Jade. "All that talk about meritocracy becomes nonsense when proof of royalty is stamped on one's tongue." She extended the appendage and flipped the tip in a show of agility.

Rishana laughed. "Is that how you are going to greet the scouts? You're going to waggle your tongue at them and say, I have royal blood, therefore you must obey me?"

The males and Kagra chuckled, but Jade kept a straight face.

Sheniya turned to her. "That's a good question. What am I supposed to tell them?"

Jade hadn't thought it through yet. "That depends on the last time they were awake and what they knew. I have to assume they didn't know about the ship's arrival or would have looked for us. You can tell them what happened to the ship but don't tell them about Igor. It will be interesting to find out whether they knew about the assassins hidden among the settlers."

"Why would they?" Rishana asked. "They were sent by our queen, and the assassins were planted by the Eternal King. The scouts could only know what she knew."

Jade shrugged. "I'm no longer sure of anything. For all we know, the Eternal King could have also planted spies among the scouts."

"Not possible," Sheniya said. "The scouts were handpicked by the queen. She knew each of them in person."

That was true. They had been selected from the queen's guard, so unless the Eternal King had created clones of those guards, the scouts were bound by vows of loyalty to the queen.

The question was how Sheniya knew that. The scouts' identities hadn't been public knowledge, and Sheniya shouldn't have known they had been selected from the queen's guard unless she knew one of them personally.

"How do you know who the scouts were?"

"One of them was my uncle. My mother told me to look for him when I got to Earth." Sheniya lifted her drink and threw it down her throat. "Not many Kra-ell warriors reach old age, but if they do, it's their family's responsibility to take care of them. It was up to me since I was the only family my uncle would have on Earth. Maybe I will still get to fulfill my duty."

That had sounded reasonable enough.

The queen's guard was usually selected from those who had some traces of royal blood in them, and Sheniya's uncle fit the profile.

"That's very honorable of you," Vrog said.

Sheniya shrugged. "It's my duty. We are all bound by it."

Pavel raised his hand. "I have a question."

"Go ahead."

"What are the four of us supposed to do?" He waved a hand over himself and the other three males. "Are we there to protect Sheniya and Rishana? And who are we supposed to take orders from, the Guardians or Kagra?"

Jade thought that Kagra had explained their duties, but evidently, she hadn't.

"We know the location of the signals, but for all we know, the pods could be buried deep underground, and you will have to dig them out. Also, we don't know what state the scouts are in. They might need to be transported to a hospital."

"We might also search for another pod in Lugu Lake," Vrog said.

"That's where Aliya grew up, and it seems like there might be a pod there as well, but the excavation site is booby-trapped, and the humans digging there are being very careful. We can do a better job, but whether we get to do that or not is up to the guy with the digging permit."

"Who's that?" Pavel asked.

"Kalugal," Kagra said. "But let's not get carried away. The excavation site in Lugu Lake will probably mean another mission for us."

"Hold on." Pavel lifted a hand. "How large was the scouting team? Did they arrive in two pods? And why would the pods land in two different places? They didn't crash land."

Those were valid questions, but again, Jade didn't have the answers. "We weren't told how large the scouting team was and what exactly their mission was. I find it odd that they didn't make any effort to find the gods, who had already been settled on Earth by then. But this is not the time for speculation." She glanced at her watch. "You are departing for the clan's landing strip in five hours, and we need to go over the chain of command and the conduct I expect from you." She looked pointedly at Sheniya and Rishana. "If you screw up this mission, it will be a long time before the immortals let us join forces with them again, and that includes the war on trafficking, which many of our people wish to take part in. I want your behavior to be exemplary and leave an impression of professionalism, courtesy, and dedication. I don't want to hear about any immature squabbles or temper tantrums. Am I clear?"

"Yes, Mistress." Vrog bowed his head.

"It's yes, Jade, and I'm not worried about you." She kept her eyes on the two females. "Vow it, or you are not going."

GABI

G abi got dressed in a state of funk.

The excitement over meeting Uriel again was tinged with sadness because it would be their last time together, and that confused and alarmed her.

Why was she mourning the end of what was basically a pleasant hookup?

Ugh, who was she kidding?

Uriel had rocked her world, which hadn't happened with any of the men she'd dated since her divorce. Thinking back to her dating history over the last eleven years, she couldn't bring up even one that she would have wanted to see again, and it wasn't because they had all been so terrible.

Some were nice men who could have been great for someone else, just not for her. A lot of it had to do with how broken she'd felt after the divorce and her trust issues. Even though she was fully aware of her faulty reasoning, Gabi had deemed every guy she'd gone out with guilty of duplicity until proven innocent.

Yeah, that hadn't worked out great for her, which was why she was still single.

Perhaps she should go shopping to lift her mood.

She needed some sexy lingerie, and perhaps also a pair of slim-fitting pants and a nice loose blouse, or maybe a tight skirt that showed off her legs. None of the dresses she'd packed for this trip were designed to entice or make her look sexy. Their purpose was to make her look professional, which was also fine for visiting family but not for going out with a hot guy, even if they never left her hotel room.

On the other hand, wearing a dress last night had proven expeditious. It had been very easy to take off. So maybe she should go for a casual dress that was sexier than what she had brought with her but still comfortable and easily discarded.

The problem was that she couldn't fit any additional clothing in her carry-on, so if she bought more clothes, she would have to leave them in Gilbert or Eric's home. Except, once she was in the mall, she would not remember that she was planning on moving in with her brother in the near future, and she would either not buy anything or get a suitcase.

Whatever. She could use the new suitcase to store her purchases.

When her phone rang, her heart accelerated, hoping it was Uriel, but then she realized it wasn't her regular phone ringing, but the one Gilbert had given her yesterday.

She pulled it out of her purse and smiled at her brother's photo on the screen. "Good morning, Gilbert."

"Good morning, Gabi. How was your night?"

"It was great." She affected a sugary tone. "Thanks for asking."

"Did he show up?"

She chuckled. "A lady doesn't kiss and tell."

"So, the answer is yes. You're a big girl, Gabi, and you deserve to have fun, but I hope you are being careful. Safety first."

Gabi winced. She hadn't been careful, but Gilbert didn't need to know that.

"Of course."

"Good. I'm glad that you are cautious. So, are you ready to visit your family in our new home?"

Realizing she remembered everything she'd learned about immortals was a relief. "I was afraid that Orion's mind trick would make it impossible to talk about you-know-what over the phone."

"He excluded everyone who was with you in the restaurant from the prohibition, but it's never a good idea to speak about those matters on a device that is not secure or a place that might not be safe. As it happens, the hotel you are staying in belongs to the clan, and your room is free of listening devices and surveillance cameras, but you need to be careful when you do so from anywhere else. Always use the clan-issued phone."

"Got it."

The thing looked like a standard iPhone, just without the logo, and was programmed to respond only to her. It only unlocked after scanning her face and locked the moment her face wasn't in front of it. The immortals took security seriously, and rightfully so.

If the secret ever got out, they would be hunted and experimented on to discover the secret of their immortality.

"We've gotten distracted," Gilbert said. "You still didn't answer whether you want me to come to pick you up?"

She felt a little guilty about postponing her visit by one more day, but then she was about to move in with her family in the near future and would get to see them all of the time, so it wasn't a big deal.

"I want to stay in the hotel for one more night, but I'm coming to your place Tuesday morning and staying overnight. My return flight is Wednesday afternoon."

"Are you spending the day with that guy?"

"No, I'm only seeing him in the evening, but I want to do some shopping. Do you think Karen would like to join me?"

"She's at work, but maybe she can meet you for lunch. Call her. And use the new phone. Her number is already in your contacts list, and so are the phone numbers of everyone else in the family."

"Awesome. I'll give her a call right now."

"I wish you could stay longer," Gilbert said. "You finally get up the courage to come, but it's only for three days, and you spend two of them away from us."

Got guilt?

"I know, but I'm about to move in with Eric and Darlene and spend so much time with you that you will get sick of seeing me all the time."

"Never. You have no idea how excited I am about you joining us here. Our family wasn't complete without you."

"Oh, that's so sweet. How about you, Eric, and Darlene join Karen and me for lunch? We can meet somewhere in the middle so it's convenient for everyone. I'll call Kaia too. Cheryl is at school, right?"

"No, she's actually on her summer break."

Gabi winced. "I forgot. Is she doing anything interesting over the summer?"

"Yeah, she's working on her Instatock account."

Gabi was the worst aunt ever. She knew how important that app was to Cheryl, and she hadn't even asked about it.

Talk about self-absorbed.

All she could think about was how difficult it was to wrap her head around what they were telling her and about her infatuation with Uriel.

She should have asked her nieces how they were doing, Kaia about the project she was working on and Cheryl about school, and she should have asked Karen about her new job. And what was Gilbert doing with his properties? And Eric with his jets?

"I'll call Cheryl too. Maybe she'd like to take a break from building her social media empire and hang out with us for a little bit."

"Call Karen first and see if she's available."

"I'll do that. Talk to you later, Gilbert. I love you," she tacked on at the end.

"I love you too, Gabi."

KIAN

After a quick stop at the lab and a chat with William and Roni, Kian joined Onegus in the conference room. "The good news is that there were no more signals. If the team doesn't find anything at Chengdu, which is likely, I want them to continue to Lugu Lake and help Kalugal with the excavations over there. He's actually planning to take Jacki and Darius and several of his men and fly directly there."

"I don't know whether to hope that they find something or that they don't." Onegus pulled a bottle of water from the fridge and opened it. "In any case, it will be an interesting experiment to see how well the Kra-ell get along with the Guardians."

"Indeed." Kian pulled out a chair and sat down. "Especially since Jade regards the two females as troublemakers. If they can behave and follow orders, then working with the Kra-ell should be a viable option."

"Yeah, well. I have a problem with including warriors that haven't gone through Guardian training in combined missions. I have the same misgiving about Kalugal's men."

Kian arched a brow. "They did remarkably well in Karelia and on the decoy ship. I think that they have proven their worth."

"They did, and I appreciated the help, but I would like them to train with our men. I brought it up with Kalugal, and he said that they don't have time. That's nonsense. All I asked for was one weekend a month. I'm sure they can spare the time."

"They probably don't want to." Kian glanced at his watch to check how much time he had left before his next meeting. "They are not eager to join missions. The only reason Kalugal volunteered their help in Karelia was that he didn't want to be left out of the loop. Now that he's a council member, he probably won't be as quick to volunteer his men."

Onegus chuckled. "Yeah, most likely. Kalugal views them as a resource, and he's not the sharing type."

"Right." Kian leaned back. "I spoke to Roni, and he told me about the snooping he did on the guy Gilbert's sister had met on the plane. Why did you consider him worthy of investigation?"

Kian was surprised that Onegus had even requested that of Roni based on a remark she'd made about the guy's looks. The chief had good instincts, and if he felt the need to investigate, then he had a good reason to do that.

Onegus shrugged. "She gushed about how incredibly good-looking he was and compared him to Orion and me, so naturally, I got suspicious. Doomers are usually not that striking, but there could be exceptions. I should have known that she was exaggerating. I've seen his passport photo, and the guy is handsome, but he's not in Orion's league. He also seems to be who he claims to be. They spent half the night together, and he left early in the morning. When he visited her, he pretended to be the delivery guy, but that's not a big deal. He stopped by the front desk on his way out and apologized, saying that he didn't want to get the receptionist in trouble. That's not something a Doomer would have done."

"Did you have him followed?"

"Why would I? If we follow every human a clan member hooks up with, we would need triple the number of Guardians we have. Gabi's fling is not a priority."

"Yeah, I guess you are right. When is she coming to the village?"

"She told Gilbert she would come tomorrow morning. I guess she wants to spend another night with her guy. But then she's flying back to Cleveland to finalize her affairs there. When she's ready to move into the village, Eric and Darlene are going to host her for as long as she needs." Onegus smiled. "I don't think it's going to be long at all. Gabriella Emerson is a looker, and she has a fiery personality. There will be plenty of suitors for her to choose from."

"It's up to the Fates and what they have planned for her." Kian turned his gaze to the door, which he had left open. "Who did Yamanu choose for his team?"

"He's taking Peter, Franco, and Jason."

"Is Mey going?"

Onegus shook his head. "Not this time. But if they don't find anything in Chengdu and the team continues to Lugu Lake, they are going to do so without Yamanu. He will book a commercial flight from Chengdu and come home."

"I can understand that. Who will take over leading the team in his absence?"

"Peter. He needs to gain experience as a team leader, and the Lugu Lake excavation is a low-risk mission that's a perfect learning opportunity."

38

GABI

As the Uber driver stopped in front of Gino's, Gabi thanked the lady and stepped out.

The place was packed, but Karen had told her that they had a private room reserved on the second floor for special customers, and that was where they were meeting.

Two of Karen's friends from the university were joining them for lunch, but Gabi couldn't remember why. Did they work in the same department as Karen?

Karen was a system administrator, and she used to work for a large defense contractor, but she'd taken a pay cut to work at the university because they offered in-house daycare, and she preferred to have Ryan and Evan close by.

Despite never having kids, Gabi could understand that, and she was super excited to see her nephews. They must have grown so much since she'd last seen them.

Regrettably, Idina was in preschool, Kaia was too busy at work and couldn't get away, and Cheryl had made prior plans to hang out with friends.

Darlene was coming, though, and Gilbert had said that he and Eric might stop by after lunch and join the ladies for coffee.

"Hello." She smiled at the host. "My name is Gabriella Emerson, and I'm here for the private party on the second floor."

"Oh, yes, Signora Emerson." The guy grinned as if she was his favorite person in the world. "Follow me, *per favore*." He grabbed a menu and gestured with his hand toward the stairs.

If he wanted her to follow him, he should have gone ahead of her, but whatever. Given his lascivious smile, he wanted to look at her ass while she climbed the stairs.

Men lived for those small thrills, and she didn't begrudge them.

Well, to be fair, women did the same thing. If she was a restaurant hostess and Uriel was a client, she would have followed his fine ass up the stairs and admired it all the way.

The rickety stairs groaned under her feet as if she were still a hundred pounds overweight, or rather like a two-hundred-pound guy was climbing them behind her.

The host looked like someone who enjoyed food.

When they got to the second floor without the staircase collapsing under their combined weight, Gabi released a relieved breath and scanned the room for familiar faces. Her gaze got snagged on a stunning brunette holding a baby and grinning with a set of teeth that belonged in a commercial for dental work.

In fact, everything about the woman was commercial-worthy.

Gabi wasn't a fashionista, but she could recognize luxury brands when she saw them, and what the woman was wearing was head-to-toe Prada. She'd seen that exact same outfit of olive blouse and black trousers in a fashion magazine she'd bought for the clinic a couple of weeks ago.

Was the gorgeous brunette a famous actress? Or maybe the trophy wife of a famous Hollywood producer? But then, what was she doing with Karen?

"Gabi." Karen pushed to her feet and came over to give her a hug. "Let me introduce my friends." She walked over to a pretty blonde woman who was feeding an adorable baby girl with a spoon. "This is Syssi. Syssi, this is my sister-in-law, Gabriella."

Karen and Gilbert weren't officially married, but Gabi and Karen had always introduced one another as sisters-in-law. It was easier than getting into an explanation for why Karen and Gilbert had three kids together but hadn't gotten married yet.

The woman smiled and offered Gabi her hand. "It's so nice to finally meet you. I've heard a lot about you."

Gabi arched a brow. "You did? From Karen?"

What reason did Karen have to mention her to her coworkers? Neither of them looked like they needed a nutritionist.

Syssi glanced at Karen. "I thought Gabi was told."

"She was." Karen looked at the waiter. "It must be the effect of what Orion did to her."

The name sounded familiar, but Gabi couldn't remember where she'd heard it. A handsome face popped into her mind, dark hair, intelligent blue eyes—

"Alfonso," the brunette said. "Can you please tell Gino to get my favorite wine and bring it up? I'm in the mood to celebrate."

"Of course, Signora Amanda." He bowed, folding nearly in half and confirming Gabi's suspicion that the brunette was someone famous.

Karen waited until his footsteps faded before walking up to the woman. "This is Dr. Amanda Dokani. She heads the neuroscience lab in the university, and Syssi is her research assistant."

That was odd. How had Karen become friends with the two ladies if they didn't work in the same office as she did?

"It's a pleasure to meet you, Gabi." The professor smiled again. "This is my daughter, Evie, and the sweetie in the highchair is my niece, Allegra."

"The pleasure is all mine." Gabi waved at the older baby, who was watching her with eyes that seemed too old for the young child they belonged to.

"Oh, now I get the connection. You all have kids in Evan and Ryan's daycare." She looked for her nephews. "Where are they?"

"Over here." Karen pointed behind the table. "On the floor."

Gabi rushed around and gasped. "Oh, my goodness. Look at you! You are so big!" She crouched next to the boys, who were eyeing her with curiosity. "You don't remember me, but I'm your Aunt Gabi, and I'm so sorry I didn't visit you more often."

"Ga?" One of them lifted a toy truck and offered it to her.

"Thank you." She took it and glanced at Karen. "What am I supposed to do with it?"

39

KAREN

Karen laughed. "You can make *vroom-vroom* sounds." She demonstrated. "Or you can admire the truck for a moment, say it's very cool, and return it."

To Evan's great delight, Gabi did both.

"We need to do something about the block," Amanda said. "Otherwise, it's not going to be any fun." She pulled out her phone and scrolled through the contacts with a manicured long fingernail. "Here you are." She chose the number. "Hello, Orion. I'm sorry to bother you, but Gabi is here, and she's confused. Can you please modify your phrasing so she can remember everything around us?"

As footsteps sounded on the stairs, they all turned toward the landing, but it wasn't Gino or one of the waiters. It was Darlene.

"Sorry for being late. Traffic was a bitch."

"Can you guard the entrance for a moment?" Karen motioned for her to stay where she was. "We need Orion to modify his instructions. Gabi doesn't remember what we told her because Amanda and Syssi are strangers to her."

"Right." Darlene nodded. "Go ahead. I'll tell you if anyone comes up."

"Here you go." Amanda handed the phone to Gabi. "Talk with Orion."

Eyebrows arched, she took the phone. "Why?"

Amanda waved her hand. "Just humor me."

Gabi put the phone against her ear. "Hi, Orion. Do I know you?"

Karen was the only adult in the room who couldn't hear what Orion was telling Gabi, but watching the woman's facial expression, she could see exactly when the memories resurfaced.

"Damn, this is confusing," Gabi told Orion. "How long will I have to live with this dual existence? It's like I have a split personality, and one half does not know what the other half knows. I can't go on like that."

A couple of seconds later, she nodded. "Tonight, I'm going to say goodbye to him, and tomorrow morning I'm coming to the village. Once that's done, I hope I can keep the memories whether I'm in company or alone."

A few moments later, Gabi nodded again. "Awesome. Thank you." She handed the phone back to Amanda. "I feel sorry for people who suffer from a split personality disorder. It's so confusing."

Amanda took the phone and put it on the table beside her bread plate. "It's no longer called multiple personality disorder. We now call it a dissociative disorder." She smiled. "It's not my field of expertise, so I can't really say much more about it, but I get how disorienting it must be for you."

Darlene abandoned her station by the door and came over to give Gabi a hug. "What I want to know is how it went with your mystery man last night."

"Oooh." Amanda clapped her hands. "A mystery man. That sounds exciting. Do tell, darling."

Karen took pity on Gabi, who looked like a deer caught in the headlights. "Before we get Gabi to entertain us with all the juicy details, let's introduce you properly." She waited for Gabi to sit down. "Syssi is the wife of the clan's leader, and Amanda is his sister, and she's also a council member."

Not sure whether she was allowed to tell Gabi about Annani, Karen looked at Amanda. "Should I continue?"

Amanda shook her head. "Let's keep some of the details for later. Poor Gabi looks like she's been hit over the head with a frying pan."

Gabi patted her head. "Is my hair that flat?"

As Amanda started to apologize for her comment, Gabi laughed. "I was just joking. I know what you meant, and the truth is that I have a headache." She rubbed her temples. "I get it every time I try to remember things I'm not supposed to remember around strangers. Since you are a neuroscientist, can you tell me whether I should worry about brain damage?"

Amanda looked unsure. "If it was to last much longer, I would have said that it was potentially harmful, but since it's only until tomorrow, you're probably safe. What I don't understand is why Orion felt the need to make you forget what you learned when you were around strangers and remember it when you were alone or with your family."

Gabi let out a long-suffering sigh. "It's because of a stupid comment I made about the guy I met on the flight being good-looking enough to be an immortal. They right away jumped to the conclusion that he was indeed an immortal, and perhaps even one of the enemy immortals." She scrunched her nose. "Dumbers? Is that what they are called?"

"Doomers," Darlene corrected. "It's an acronym for the Brotherhood of the Devout followers of Mortdh."

Gabi tilted her head. "That doesn't make Doom. It spells BDFOM." She chuckled. "It sounds like something kinky."

"The name is actually the Brotherhood of the Devout Order of Mortdh," Syssi said. "And there is nothing funny about them, but it's kind of funny that the first letter of the last four words of their bombastic name spells doom in English."

40

GABI

Gabi was about to ask about those Doomers, the clan's enemies that Syssi seemed very concerned about, but as the waiter came up with two bottles of Amanda's wine and two baskets of bread, she forgot what she was about to ask.

Once their server was done taking everyone's order and departed, she suddenly remembered what Onegus and Orion had said about them.

They were led by a guy named Navuh, who was up to no good. Trafficking was one of the things mentioned. They also had said that he wasn't generous and wouldn't have paid for his men to travel in first class. He also had sons who weren't actually his but who he claimed as his, and those sons might fly first class, but not all three at the same time.

Or were there more than three?

The sons were good-looking because their mothers were close to the source, whatever that meant, and they were also well-educated and therefore polite.

Uriel could very loosely fit that description.

He was good-looking and had a good vocabulary, so perhaps he was well-educated and polite. He was also a wonderfully generous lover, and she doubted the son of a misogynist would be into giving more pleasure to their female partners than receiving.

Navuh had to be a misogynist to deal in trafficking, right?

It wasn't possible to be one way in public and another in private. Of course, people could pretend, but that didn't change who they were at their core. She couldn't imagine a cheater like Dylan being honest in his business dealings, or someone that was a hundred percent loyal to his wife cheating on his business partners.

So yeah, she might be seeing the world in black and white while it was many shades of gray, but that only meant she was right most of the time and not all of the time, and that was good enough.

Amanda trained her impossibly blue eyes on her. "Fess up, sister. I want to hear all about the yummy hottie you met on the plane."

Gabi glanced at the baby girl who was chewing on a piece of baguette while watching them with her smart eyes and listening as if she could understand every word.

"It's okay." Her mother winked. "Allegra is good at keeping secrets."

The girl nodded, pulled the chewed-up piece of bread out of her mouth, and offered it to Gabi. "Yum."

Amanda laughed. "Yes, sweetie. The baguette is so very yummy."

Allegra gave her aunt a cute smile, shoved the bread back into her mouth, and resumed chewing.

Babies were fascinating, adorable, and very kissable, but they were also a lot of work. At some moments, Gabi craved a baby with excruciating intensity, and at others, she was glad to be single and childless and to have all the freedom to do what she pleased whenever she pleased.

Choices, choices. Life was all about making choices and hoping not to make the wrong ones.

"We are waiting." Amanda tapped the perfectly manicured fingernails of one hand on her opposite arm.

"There isn't much to tell. Uriel is gorgeous, sweet, polite, accommodating, and great between the sheets, but I'm probably not going to see him again after tonight." The thought brought tears to her eyes, but she managed to keep them at bay. "Although he looks like a god, he's human, and from what I was told, I need to find an immortal male to induce me. I don't suppose I can keep a human lover on the side, can I?"

Amanda shook her head. "If you don't bond with your inducer, which might happen, you can keep having hookups with humans after you turn immortal, but you can't have a long-term relationship with them. You will become stronger, your hearing and eyesight will improve dramatically, and you will heal from scrapes and bruises in moments instead of days. It's possible to hide all those things from a casual lover, but it's nearly impossible to hide them from someone you live with or even see on a regular basis."

Gabi hadn't known about all the perks that came with immortality that Amanda had just mentioned, and they sounded exciting, but would they help alleviate the heartbreak of saying goodbye to Uriel forever?

Get a grip, Gabi. You've known the guy for less than twenty-four hours and had sex with him once. You are not saying goodbye to the love of your life.

So why the hell did it feel like she was?

Syssi cleared her throat. "Did you ask him what he does for a living?"

It was an obvious attempt to steer the conversation in a less depressing direction, and Gabi was grateful for it.

"Uriel said that he and his friends are flea market flippers and were hunting for treasures in Korea and other countries in the area, but somehow I doubt it. I think the three of them are starring in a movie or a show about flea market finds, and Uriel was staying in character."

"Why do you think that?" Amanda asked.

"Well, for starters, they came from South Korea, which everyone knows is where people go to get plastic surgery, especially men who don't want people to find out that they had chin implants to make their jaws look like they can cut stone, or hair transplants, or nose jobs, and whatever else. Secondly, flea market treasure hunting is not so lucrative that they could fly first class. And thirdly, they were flying to Los Angeles, the world capital of movie making."

Perhaps the story she'd painted in her mind had lost some of its vividness with each retelling because it sounded flimsy to her now. She knew nothing about the real business of flea market treasure hunting, and the fact that Uriel and his buddies were gorgeous and had just returned from South Korea didn't necessarily mean that they had undergone procedures there.

"It could be true," Amanda said. "Orion deals in antiques, and he finds undervalued treasures all over the world. He says that the Orient has recently emerged as a fertile hunting ground for great finds, so it's entirely possible for Uriel and his friends to find undervalued bargains that they can sell for a nice profit in the West."

41

DARLENE

As Darlene listened to the exchange, she debated whether to tell Gabi about Roni's investigation and what he had discovered about Uriel.

Gabi would probably get upset that Onegus had asked Roni to do that, and there wasn't much to tell because none of the things Roni had discovered were incriminating in any way. But perhaps she would find it interesting that Uriel lived in Portugal, and it would ease her mind that he wasn't an actor.

Perhaps he was a wannabe actor, but he wasn't yet, and it wasn't likely that a movie studio was paying for his first-class ticket. Uriel was either making good money flipping flea market finds, or his parents were rich and were paying for him to travel in style.

"I have some information on Uriel," Darlene said. "But all of you must swear you won't tell anyone I spilled the beans."

Syssi grimaced. "You know how hard it is to keep secrets from our mates. Can I tell Kian?"

"He probably already knows what I'm going to tell you. It's just that Roni wasn't supposed to tell me, and if I tell Gabi, and Onegus finds out, he will be furious, and I don't want him to get mad at Roni."

Gabi lifted her hand. "Wait a minute. Are we talking about the same

Roni, who is your son from a previous marriage? How did he find out information about Uriel?"

There was still so much that Gabi didn't know, and there hadn't been time to tell her.

"Yes, it's the same Roni, and he's the clan's hacker. Whenever they need to dig out information about someone, he's the guy they turn to."

Gabi pursed her lips and nodded. "Impressive. He must be really smart."

"He is, and it's not thanks to my ex. His father was a fling I had while temporarily separated from my husband." Darlene snorted. "For long years, I regretted returning to my husband and not pursuing a relationship with Roni's father, but it was all decreed by the Fates. I was supposed to meet Eric."

"Well." Amanda waved a hand. "Don't keep us in suspense. What did Roni find out about our mystery hunk?"

"His name is Uriel Delgado. He's thirty-one, was born in the US to Portuguese parents who returned to Portugal when he was a young boy. He hasn't been back to the States until about five years ago and has been visiting frequently since. He doesn't own or rent a residence in the States, and he doesn't have a car registered to his name."

Gabi's lips were still pursed. "How old was he when his parents took him to Portugal?"

"I think he was six. Why?"

"His English is perfect, but I could tell he was the child of immigrant parents. There was only a shadow of an accent in his English, and I couldn't tell which language contributed to it. Now I know why. Portuguese is so strange. It doesn't sound like Spanish."

"It's part of the Ibero-Romance group of dialects that evolved from colloquial Latin," Amanda said. "It has common roots with Spanish, but they are two separate languages."

Syssi frowned at her. "It never ceases to amaze me how much you know about so many topics."

Amanda laughed. "I had a long time to learn all those tidbits of information. Compared to you, I'm ancient."

"How old are you?" Gabi asked. "Or is it a rude question to ask an immortal?"

"It's not rude. I'm a young immortal. I'm only two hundred and fifty years old."

Gabi's eyes widened. "That's young? How old is the oldest member of your community?"

"That would be my grandfather," Darlene said. "He's over seven thousand years old."

"Wow." Gabi shook her head. "That's older than human civilization."

Amanda smiled. "That's because our ancestors were responsible for the creation of human civilization. Humanity would have eventually gotten there, but without their help, it would have taken much longer."

While the gods had been discussed extensively over dinner the day before, no one had told Gabi that some of the gods were still around. Gabi was under the impression that only their immortal descendants remained, and she was under compulsion to keep it all a secret. Nevertheless, they all seemed to share the same feeling that she shouldn't be told more while she was still hanging out with Uriel.

Logically, it didn't make sense to keep suspecting him of being an immortal after Roni had found his birth certificate, his parents' identities, and where he lived—the guy seemed to be legitimately human, and even Onegus didn't feel the need to investigate him any further. And yet, Darlene's gut feeling to exercise caution persisted.

"Well, at least I now know Uriel's last name." Gabi reached for the wine bottle and refilled her glass. "For some reason, he didn't want to tell me what it was." She took a sip. "Did Roni find out whether he was married?"

Darlene shook her head. "Roni doesn't speak Portuguese and is unfamiliar with their bureaucracy. He asked Onegus whether he wanted to hire a local hacker to find out more about Uriel, but Onegus didn't deem it a priority."

42

GABI

Darlene threaded her arm through Gabi's. "I haven't been shopping in so long. Thanks for inviting me."

After lunch, the others had returned to work, but Darlene had taken the rest of the afternoon off to accompany her to the mall.

Gabi smiled. "Thank you for driving me."

"It's my pleasure. Let's check out the sale at Nordstrom." Darlene leaned closer to whisper in her ear, "They have a very nice lingerie department, but if you prefer a specialty store, I think they have a Frederick's in this mall."

The stuff they sold at that store looked like it was made for strippers or porn stars, and Gabi's tastes were demurer.

"Nordstrom is good enough."

"It is." Darlene nodded sagely, but the corner of her lips twitched in a suppressed smile. "To quote Eric, sexy lingerie is a waste of money because all he wants to do is take it off as fast as he can."

Gabi winced. "Please. I don't want to think about my brothers and sex."

"Pish posh. We are all grownups. When you come to live in the village, you will discover that immortals don't have human hang-ups about it."

What village and what immortals? Was the village a movie theater name, and there was a new movie about immortals Gabi had agreed to watch but had forgotten about?

As a headache pounded against her temples, she pulled her arm from Darlene's and rubbed at it. "What are you talking about?"

"Oh, right. Sorry about that. Forget I said anything."

Gabi was more than happy to do that. The headache was making her nauseous, and she needed to sit down.

"Do you mind if we take a break for coffee? I've gotten a sudden headache."

"Sure, no problem. Nordstrom has a great coffee shop." Darlene guided her back toward the entrance. "Sit down, and I'll get us coffees. How do you like yours?"

"Non-fat small cappuccino, please." Gabi scanned the small sitting area, but all the tables were taken.

"Sugar?"

Gabi shook her head and immediately regretted it as her headache had worsened. "No sugar and no artificial sweetener either." She spotted a couple getting up and rushed over to secure the table.

She heard Darlene chuckling and murmuring something under her breath, but with how noisy it was in the mall, she couldn't hear what it was.

Whatever.

It was probably something along the lines of how miserable a nutritionist's life was because of all the dietary restrictions. Her friends who didn't work in nutrition and fitness made similar comments, but Gabi no longer bothered to explain that it was a state of mind. Everyone made their own choices about how they wanted to live their lives and what they wanted to put in their mouths.

To her, coffee tasted great without any sugar, and it wasn't even a question of sacrificing anything. The hardest part wasn't the restrictions. It was always being mindful of portion size and nutritional value.

But people were judgmental, and they either thought that everyone who didn't make the same choices as them was doing things wrong or that she was trying to preach to them to adopt her ways.

Heck, no.

People paid her good money for that advice, and the only ones she'd tried to convert for free had been her brothers, but they had ignored her and continued eating like they were immortal.

Damn, the headache had just gotten worse.

Was it because it always made her angry when her brothers dismissed her on account of her being the youngest?

No, the cause of the headache couldn't be anger because she hadn't been mad at anything that Darlene had said. Strangely, the trigger seemed to be the word immortal.

As a piercing pain shot through her eyes, Gabi winced.

Evidently, she was allergic to that word even when she was just thinking it. Reaching into her purse, Gabi searched for the small container of Motrin she kept for emergencies, and when she found it, she glanced at Darlene to see if she was any closer in line to getting coffee so she would have something to wash the pills down.

It looked like it would be a while, so she pulled out her phone to check her messages.

As usual, most were from her clients, and as she scrolled through them, she tried to convince herself that she wasn't disappointed that there were none from Uriel.

It was after four in the afternoon, and if he wanted to make plans for later, he should have called her already or at least texted her.

She was replying to a client's text when the message she'd been waiting for came in. Abandoning the half-finished text, she switched to his contact to read what he wrote her.

I'm still in meetings, which is why I didn't call. Can you go out to dinner with me at seven?

Gabi forced herself to count to twenty before replying so he wouldn't think she had been so anxious to hear from him that she was constantly checking her messages.

My hotel has a restaurant with a great view of the city, and the food is good.

His reply arrived a moment later. *I'll meet you there at seven.*

"Someone looks in a much better mood." Darlene put a paper coffee cup in front of her. "Got some good news?"

Gabi smiled. "Uriel texted me. He's meeting me in the hotel's restaurant."

Darlene sat down and removed the lid from her coffee. "Who suggested the hotel? Was it Uriel or you?"

"I did." Gabi smiled sheepishly. "The distance to my room was a deciding factor."

43

ANNANI

Annani looked around the living room of her modest village house and sighed.

It was a nice room, but it was too quiet, and she missed Kian and Syssi's place. However, she would have been alone there this time of day as well, so feeling down made little sense. Her son and his wife were at work, and Syssi took Allegra with her to the university, but in the evenings the house filled up with baby sounds and cooking smells, and later with Kian's gruff voice that turned softer the longer he was home.

Staying with them had been very enjoyable, but it was time for her to resume her duties.

"I need to organize my schedule," she said aloud, even though she had only the Odus for company. "I need to make new appointments with clan members and also start meeting with the Kra-ell."

Oshidu walked over to her and bowed. "Should I retrieve your appointment book, Clan Mother?"

"No, thank you. I need to think of what I want to do first."

"As you wish, Clan Mother." He bowed again. "May I offer you a fresh cup of tea?"

"Yes, that would be lovely. Also, if you do not mind, put on some music for me. It is too quiet in this house."

"Of course, Clan Mother."

She did not need to specify which music she liked. Her Odus had stored every selection she had ever made in their memory banks, including what she liked to listen to with different activities.

When she needed to think, classical or instrumental music was best. Lyrics tended to distract her because she always pondered whether there was meaning behind them or if they were just a selection of words that went well with the melody and rhymed at the appropriate places.

With Tchaikovsky's Violin Concerto playing in the background, Annani started a mental list of people she needed to see.

Kaia still needed some help with the ghost of her previous incarnation, but it was not urgent. Nathalie and Andrew were taking fertility potions in the hopes of conceiving again, and she wondered how that was going, but it was not polite to inquire on matters of that kind over the phone.

Then there were the new immortal and Kra-ell couples that she wanted to meet for an afternoon tea and learn about the difficulties they were facing. She was very curious about how those pairings were working out.

The Fates' touch was evident in Jade and Phinas's union and Vanessa and Mo-red's.

On the face of things, the Fates' agenda was clear.

It seemed they wanted the immortal descendants of the gods and their old enemies to get along and show their ancestors that they had been wrong about the strict prohibition on such pairings.

Annani suspected that the Fates' tapestry had a much deeper and more intricate design than any god or mortal could discern. What if their intent was a new super race of people who exceeded the best genetic design the gods could master?

Was it possible that the Fates were behind keeping the twins in stasis long enough for the new pairings to produce offspring powerful enough to stand in their way?

Except, if that was the case, they would have paired Toven with a pureblooded Kra-ell female to achieve maximum results, or perhaps even paired Annani with a Kra-ell male.

Could one of these Kra-ell be the reincarnation of her Khiann?

Annani hoped that was not the case.

It was not that she thought them unattractive, but they just did not look like her Khiann.

Ever since she had been given the prophecy about Khiann's reincarnations fathering her seven children, she had always searched for men who resembled him. Tall, broad-shouldered, blue-eyed, and with a charming smile.

The Kra-ell were just too different.

Did she truly believe that each of her five children had been fathered by a reincarnation of Khiann, though?

Annani let out a sigh. The mortal males had all shared physical characteristics with him, and also some of his other attributes like innate leadership, intelligence, and moral decency, but none had been even a fraction of the whole that was Khiann.

They had not been together long, and since his death he might have grown to mythical proportions in her mind, but he was still her one true love, and she doubted she could fall in love again, even with his reincarnation, unless the new Khiann was an exact replica of the old one.

Getting to know David and realizing how little he had in common with the prior incarnation of himself, whom she had personally known, had driven the point home.

The entire purpose of reincarnation was to allow the soul to grow and change. Even if she found her Khiann as a new incarnation, he would not be the same male she still loved with every fiber of her being.

Had she given up hope of ever finding the perfect replica of him?

No. She could not do that. That sliver of hope was what kept her going.

Still, even though she did not expect to find Khiann among the Kra-ell, it was time she met with them. The question was whether to organize a big event with all of them gathered in the large assembly hall or invite them to her place in small groups of two or three.

Pulling out her phone, she called Kian.

"Mother, good afternoon."

"Good afternoon, Kian. Do you have a moment?"

"For you, always. But it will have to be quick. The team I'm sending to China is about to leave, and I'm giving them last-minute instructions."

"Then please call me when you are done. I want to discuss my introduction to the Kra-ell with you."

44

PETER

It had been two weeks since the day Peter had flirted with Kagra in the training center, but nothing had come of it. She'd been busy helping Jade prepare for the trial and training the females wishing to join the war on trafficking, and it was also possible that she was avoiding him intentionally, although he had no idea why she'd want to do that.

He'd been polite, not too pushy, and she'd seemed interested. She also hadn't been hanging out with anyone else or inviting males to her house.

Yeah, he'd been checking.

Was he a little obsessed with Jade's second-in-command?

Maybe a little was describing it too mildly. Something about her drew him to her like a moth to a flame, and it could very possibly be a sense of danger that he had never felt with any other female.

It was exciting, it was new, and Peter wasn't going to give up just because she was playing hard to get.

When he'd heard that Yamanu was seeking volunteers to join the team investigating the signals in China and that Kagra was going to lead the Kra-ell portion of the team, he jumped at the opportunity.

During the orientation Kagra merely acknowledged him with a nod, but he was a patient guy, and as the team members boarded the bus, he lingered by the stairs, waiting for Kagra to finish her conversation with Jade.

When she turned around and caught his gaze, he waved at the open bus door. "Ladies first," he said.

That earned him a crooked smile. "Who said I'm a lady?"

"Is mistress better?"

Her smile widened, and after giving him a sultry look, she started up the stairs.

Following, Peter enjoyed the captivating sway of her hips. Was it his imagination, or was she deliberately exaggerating her movements?

As he scanned the bus, he was happy to see that everyone had already paired up, leaving Kagra with no choice but to select a seat that left the one next to her vacant, seemingly reserved for Peter.

The Fates must have been smiling upon him.

Settling beside her, he respected her personal space, ensuring his thigh wasn't touching hers.

From everything he'd heard about the Kra-ell, he knew that the females expected the males to wait for an invitation, much as it had been in Safe Haven, and he had to wait for Kagra to initiate. He'd given her enough not-so-subtle hints that he was interested, so if she found him attractive, she should feel free to do so.

Heck, he was more than interested. At this point, he was obsessed and guilty of stalking.

Had she noticed he'd been hanging around the café when she was? Or that his training schedule had somehow coincided with hers? Or that his nightly walks just happened to include the path near her house?

"This must be my lucky day," he said to start a conversation. "I get to sit next to you."

"You think?" She gave him the half smile that always made him think she was hiding a secret.

"Yeah, I do."

He loved Kagra's snarky attitude. She was so different from every woman he had ever dated. Eleanor was the only other female he'd been interested in, whose assertive character and no-nonsense attitude were similar to Kagra's, but Eleanor lacked Kagra's charm and sense of humor.

There was a lightness to Kagra that belied the hard life she'd had in Igor's compound.

As the bus door closed and the engine engaged, Peter experienced an unexpected surge of excitement mixed with nervous anticipation, making him wonder whether it was about the mission or the female sitting next to him.

The clan's airstrip was forty-five minutes away, and Kagra was his captive for the duration. A lot could be achieved in that span of time, and he intended to take advantage of every moment.

As the bus windows turned clear again, revealing the scenic route they were traveling, Peter affected a dramatic sigh. "We never got to dance, after all."

She turned to look at him. "I expected you to invite me to a party in your house, but you never did."

That was true, but only because she hadn't shown the slightest interest in him. What was the point of organizing a party and going to all that effort if she didn't show up?

"Would you have come?"

She shrugged. "If I had nothing better to do. Jade keeps me very busy these days."

"I know. All the preparations for the trial and Igor's interrogations kept her busy, so she had to lean more heavily on you to keep your people occupied and out of trouble."

Kagra seemed surprised that he knew that. "Yeah, I'm glad that's over. By the way, your psychologist marrying Mo-red was a gutsy move. She looks like such a straight shooter, a goody two-shoes as you say, and I didn't expect her to do something so underhanded to save him."

"Vanessa is a straight shooter, but she also loves Mo-red. Wouldn't you have done the same if you were in her goody shoes?"

Her lips curved in that half smile that he adored. "Love is a foreign concept to me, but I would have used every loophole to save one of my consorts. It would have been expected of me to protect them, but even if it wasn't, I cared for them."

The mention of Kagra's paramours soured Peter's gut. But maybe she was referring to the males of her tribe who Igor had murdered?

"What is a consort? Is that like a lover?"

"It's more than that." She sighed. "The way we live here on Earth is not the traditional Kra-ell way. If I were back home, I would have a group of three to five consorts that would be my personal harem, for lack of a better word. It would be my responsibility to ensure they each had a chance to father a child with me, but I could have a favorite if I chose to. In Jade's compound, the lines were blurred. The males were allowed to have sex with humans and father hybrid children, and the pureblooded males were shared among the adult females. But Jade and I agreed not to engage with the same males."

That was interesting. "Why?"

She shrugged. "We are both very competitive females, and it wouldn't have been healthy for our relationship to squabble over the males. It was better to keep our harems separate." When he cringed, she lifted her hands. "I only use that word because there is nothing better to describe the relationship. I could call them my boyfriends or husbands, but that wouldn't be accurate either."

"What about Igor's compound? Did you have consorts there?"

She shook her head. "The males I engaged with weren't my consorts because I didn't select them to be mine." She closed her eyes. "We didn't have much choice. None of us did. We did what we had to in order to survive, and I tried to find joy in it despite the tragedy of the past and the sad circumstances of the present."

He regarded her with even more appreciation than before. "You are an incredible female, Kagra. I admire your strength."

A flicker of surprise danced across her face as if she hadn't expected praise from him. "Thanks." She arched a brow. "That's what I'm supposed to say when someone compliments me, right? I should just thank them?"

"Yes. You are catching on quickly." He needed to change the subject and move to more pleasant topics. "So, tell me. What do you do for fun?"

Again, she looked surprised, and after a brief pause, she waved her hand at the window. "I love nature. In Karelia, I escaped into the wilderness whenever I could. We were allowed to hunt, and Jade and I used hunting as an excuse to let off steam and run like the wind. It rejuvenated my spirit and reminded me of the beauty outside the compound walls."

He wasn't sure whether she meant it seriously or was being sarcastic. "You must feel stifled in the village. I mean, since you have livestock to feed off, you don't need to run to hunt."

She shrugged. "I also don't have excess steam to release. Life is good in your village, and I'm excited about building a new Kra-ell society free from the traditional rules of conduct. We are making new rules as we go along, and it's fun. Instead of letting the past shape our future, we are building a new one as we want it to be." As her eyes sparkled with excitement, their color flickered between blue, green, and purple. "It's like the difference between remodeling an old house and building a new one. You are not constricted by the preexisting foundation."

"That's actually an excellent analogy. But I have to wonder—what do you know about remodeling?"

She laughed. "I have a new addiction. Do you know the show *Fix that Dump?*"

"I've never heard of it."

"It's about remodeling versus rebuilding. A team of five experts evaluates old run-down houses and decides whether something is salvageable or if it's better to demolish and start from scratch." A smile lifted one corner of her mouth. "If you want, we can watch an episode together. Do you have Netflix on your phone? Mine is useless outside the village."

Peter would have preferred to keep talking, but if he showed interest in the show she liked, it could lead to many more shared viewings that might then lead to other things.

Like dancing.

"I sure do." He pulled out his phone. "What is the name of that show again?"

"*Fix That Dump!*"

45

GABI

"Come on." Gabi yanked on the hairbrush. Once again, it got snagged as she pulled it down, trying to smooth the flyaways that refused to be tamed.

The hairdryer supplied by the hotel just wasn't strong enough for her stubborn hair, and she was impatient because she was running out of time. Maybe she should just braid it. Uriel had no problem with how she looked the day before, so there was that.

She had a sexy new outfit and even sexier lingerie underneath. This time, however, she decided not to put on the red lipstick. For some reason, it had bothered Uriel yesterday, so today, she was going for the nude look.

Well, her lips were nude, but she'd used plenty of makeup on the rest of her face.

Would she still need as much when she turned immortal? Amanda was the most beautiful woman Gabi had ever seen, and she'd had makeup on. That was probably due to the perfect canvas it had been applied on and many years of practice. The woman, or rather female, was two hundred and fifty years old, which was considered young for an immortal.

"That's what your future holds." Gabi smiled sadly at her reflection. "You should be grateful and happy instead of moping over a guy." She braided the ends of her frizzy hair and secured the small braid with an elastic hair tie. "You should also hurry up and finish getting ready. You don't want to keep him waiting."

She also should get a pet so people would not wonder about her sanity when she talked to herself. Gabi did that often, and it wasn't because she lived alone. She'd been doing that ever since she could remember.

"What can I do?" She smiled at her reflection. "I'm such a great conversationalist."

Perhaps she should tell Uriel about it tonight, so he wouldn't feel as bad when she told him she wouldn't be seeing him again.

Gabi didn't want to do that, in fact, she hated it, but it was the right thing to do.

He was thirty-one, seven years younger than her, and lived in Portugal. So even if she wasn't about to turn immortal and was returning to her normal life in Cleveland, a relationship wasn't an option.

Regrettably, there was no alternative, and tonight would be the last.

Hey, maybe she could ask Orion to make her forget Uriel?

Should she?

The idea of forgetting him and their time together seemed even worse than the pain of remembering him and wondering about what could have been if the universe wasn't against them becoming a couple.

With a sigh, Gabi stepped into her new shoes, took her purse, checked that she had the room key in her wallet, and headed out the door.

To get to the restaurant, she had to take the elevator to the lobby downstairs first and then take the rocket elevator up to the top floor where the restaurant was located.

At least this time she was ready for it and held on to the side rail throughout the ear-popping fast ride.

Her legs were surprisingly steady as she approached the hostess's desk.

"Hi, I have a reservation for two under Gabriella Emerson."

The hostess smiled. "Your party is already here." She walked around the station. "I'll take you to your table."

"Thank you."

Excitement thrumming through her ribcage, Gabi scanned the restaurant for dark, longish hair, cheekbones chiseled from granite, and a radiant smile. She didn't have to look for long.

As soon as Uriel saw her, he rose to his feet and pulled out a chair, waiting for her to reach him.

He looked even more stunning in a gray suit, a black dress shirt, and no tie. A movie star if ever she saw one.

It seemed like it took her forever to cross the twenty feet or so between them.

"Hello, Gabriella." He leaned and kissed her cheek. "You look stunning tonight."

"Ditto." She sat down and let him push her chair in. "It should be illegal to look that good," she murmured.

Behind her, the forgotten hostess chuckled. "Can I get you some wine or a cocktail while you look over the menu?"

"Yes, please." Gabi looked up at her and would have smiled if the girl's eyes weren't eating Uriel up. "I would like a Southside, please."

"Of course." The girl was still staring at Uriel. "And for you?"

"I'll have what she's having."

Gabi stifled a chuckle. "Good choice," she croaked. "We would also like a basket of bread, please."

Not for her, but Uriel would probably love to have some.

"Naturally." The hostess finally took the hint and walked away.

Uriel's smile was just as brilliant as Gabi remembered. "What's a Southside?" he asked. "I've never had it."

"It's made with gin, simple syrup, lime juice, and mint leaves. It's like a Mojito just with gin instead of rum. It's on the sweet side, so it's considered a girly drink, but look on the bright side, it's not going to grow unwanted hair on your chest."

Uriel looked confused. "What kinds of drinks do that?"

Was he teasing, or had he really not gotten the joke?

"The manly kind, of course. Straight vodka, whiskey, tequila. Manly men drinks."

He laughed. "Oh, now I get it."

It was strange that he hadn't gotten the reference right away, and there was something in the back of her mind that knew why he hadn't, but when she tried to tug on the misty string and pull the thought through the hazy curtain, her head started aching so badly that she let go of it.

Uriel frowned. "What's the matter?"

"Oh, it's nothing. I get these headaches from time to time. They suddenly come out of nowhere and then disappear just as fast."

The crease between his eyes deepened. "You should get it checked out."

"Yeah." She rubbed her temple. "I'll call my doctor when I get home."

"When is that?"

Gabi thought she'd told him she was leaving the next day. "I'm flying back Wednesday afternoon, but I promised my brothers to spend time with them tomorrow, so I don't know if I'll be able to get away, but I'll definitely try."

Uriel looked sad. "Then we have to make the most of today."

She had a feeling that there was something she was forgetting, but as the headache assaulted her again, she relinquished the thought.

46

ERIC

"Catch." Darlene tossed a pillowcase at Eric, which he caught with ease.

In preparation for Gabi's one-night stay in their guest room, Darlene had insisted on washing all the linens even though no one had ever slept in that bed, and they were clean. But Eric was a smart man and knew not to get into arguments he had no chance of winning.

"I'm excited about Gabi staying with us, but I want to give you fair warning." He stuffed the pillow inside the case. "She is a sweetheart ninety percent of the time, but the remaining ten she can be a handful, especially when she gets in a mood."

Darlene smiled. "I think a ninety-to-ten ratio is better than most."

"Yeah, that's true. But Gabi's ten can get intense. It's like she's holding things in until she can't anymore, and the smallest thing can trigger an explosion."

Darlene put down the pillow she was trying to force into a too-tight pillowcase.

"First of all, Gabi is only going to be with us for one day, and most of it is going to be spent touring the village and visiting people. She will have no reason to get upset. Secondly, what do you mean by her getting in a mood? Does she get depressed? Angry?"

"Both." He took the pillow she'd been wrestling with and slowly forced it into the case, careful not to tear it. "It's hard to explain. Gabi has a heart of gold. She will never say no to a friend who needs help, and she is generous to a fault with money she doesn't have." He smiled. "She pretends to make a fortune, but I know she doesn't. It's not easy to make a lot of money as a nutritionist unless you have movie stars singing your praise to the press. But I digress. She's not the mellow type. She's emotional and assertive, and when you combine the two, they sometimes become explosive. Like vinegar and baking soda."

"They foam up, not explode, but I get what you mean. Is it really that bad, though? No one is perfect, and we all have our pet peeves and character flaws. I'm not assertive enough, and I hate thinking about all the years I let people walk all over me because I wanted to avoid conflict. I admire Gabi for fighting for what she wants."

Eric walked back to the other side of the bed and fluffed the pillows. "It gets her in trouble. There is a good reason she chose to have her own business and stay small with no additional employees. Eventually, she would have picked fights with them and either fired them or just lived with the bad dynamics."

"Is that why she got divorced? Was she fighting a lot with her ex?"

"No." Eric walked around the bed and put his arm around Darlene's middle. "The bastard was a serial cheater and a liar. The thing is, Gabi divorced him eleven years ago, and she's still single despite being beautiful and smart, having her own condominium that is almost free and clear, and a small business that supports her perhaps not lavishly but well enough. I don't pry into her love life, but I assume that she has no shortage of men to choose from, and yet she hasn't had even one serious boyfriend since she got divorced. She sees a guy once, twice, and that's it. She moves to the next one. That's no way to live."

Darlene chuckled. "You lived like that for a long time, and until you met me, you were perfectly happy with your player ways."

"I wasn't happy." He pulled her into his arms. "I was getting by." He kissed her on the tip of her nose. "What say you we go to our bedroom and test how fresh the bedding is?"

"I washed it last Thursday." She affected a frown. "But we've been very active in that bed, so perhaps we should change the linens before Gabi gets here. I don't want your sister to think that we are slobs."

"Fates forbid." He stifled a smile. "Not to be wasteful, though, first we need to mess up the bedding some more, so it will need washing for sure."

"Absolutely." Darlene nodded sagely, took his hand, and led him toward their bedroom.

47

GABI

Somehow, Uriel had managed to pass the entire evening without telling Gabi even one fact about his childhood or his parents, or where he lived when he wasn't traveling.

He'd kept her entertained with anecdotes of his bargain hunting all over the world, which Gabi doubted were real and not part of a script he'd memorized for a movie, but she didn't want to spoil their last evening together by poking holes in his stories or challenging their veracity. Besides, just hearing him talk and looking at those perfect lips of his was making it difficult for her to think about anything other than taking him to her room and having her way with him.

She was on her third Southside, which was one of the best she'd ever had, and Uriel had been matching her glass for glass, but the difference was that she was woozy while he was not.

Well, he had at least a hundred pounds on her, if not more, so he was obviously not as affected.

Still, despite the alcohol overindulgence, her brain remained as sharp as ever, and when Uriel finally overdid it, telling her a story about a pair of shoes he'd found in a secondhand clothing store that had belonged to a Korean princess and was worth tens of thousands of dollars, Gabi found it so unbelievable that she could no longer hold her tongue.

"You know what I think?" She lifted her glass and took a sip.

"What?" He held his glass up but didn't bring it to his lips.

"I don't think that you are really a flea market bargain flipper. I think that you are an actor, and so are your friends, and that you've been cast in a show about bargain flipping, and because the three of you are method actors, you stay in character and pretend that you are flippers in real life."

Leaning forward, he gave her a panty-melting smile. "All of us are actors on the stage of life. Perhaps you are not really a nutritionist from Cleveland who is visiting her family in Los Angeles but an actress playing the role of Gabriella Emerson, the brave hero of God, galloping to the rescue of her eldest brother? Maybe your method acting is so immersive that you can't remember who you really are?"

"Galloping?" She laughed. "I flew over, and as you've witnessed first-hand, it required a lot of bravery on my part." She shook her head. "You are doing it again. You're answering my question with another question."

He frowned. "Was there a question in there? You asked if I wanted to know your thoughts, and I asked what? Then you told me what you thought, and I answered with what I thought about what you thought."

Gabi laughed again. "Goodness gracious, you are giving me a headache." She drank the rest of the Southside. "I need another one." She lifted the glass to signal the waitress.

Uriel arched one dark brow that was so perfectly shaped that it had to be painted on or plucked to perfection. "Are you sure you want another one?" He leaned forward. "I have an early morning meeting tomorrow, and I was hoping we could retire to your room and spend the next few hours enjoying each other. After tonight, we might not see each other again for a while."

"Just for a while?"

This was the end of their time together. She would never see him again, and it hurt more than it should.

"Don't be sad." He reached over the table and wiped a tear that had slid down her cheek. "I'll come visit you in Cleveland."

"Promise?"

She should feel lighter, but she didn't. There was something she was forgetting that would make it impossible for Uriel to find her, but she couldn't remember what it was.

What the hell was wrong with her?

Was this a dream? Was that why she felt like there were gaps in her memory?

"I promise. I'm just not sure when I will be able to get away. My friends and I are working on an important deal, and I don't know how long it will take to finalize it."

"Is that what your early morning meeting is about?"

He nodded. "I wanted it to happen later in the day, but my friends are impatient and want to proceed as soon as possible."

When he lifted his hand to signal to the waitress, she arrived immediately. "Would you like another drink?" she asked Uriel, whose glass was still half full, while ignoring Gabi's empty one.

"No, thank you. We are ready for the check," he said.

"Of course." She pulled out a leather folder and put it on the table. "Whenever you are ready."

Uriel snatched the thing, opened it, and put three one-hundred-dollar bills inside. "No change."

When had he pulled out his wallet?

Gabi hadn't seen him opening it.

Had he been holding the money in his pocket?

And who paid with cash these days?

People with shady deals, that's who. Flipping flea market finds, my ass.

"Thank you." The waitress smiled sweetly at Uriel. "I hope to see you at the Seventy-Second again soon."

"I hope so too." He rose to his feet and offered Gabi a hand up.

Forcing a smile, she took it.

This was not the time nor place to let nasty Gabi out to play. Usually, she kept her temper on a tight leash, but sometimes the trigger just flipped the switch on, and she had to react even though she was aware that the impetus might exist only in her head.

Uriel could have a thousand legitimate reasons for paying cash, and she shouldn't jump to conclusions and accuse him of imaginary crimes. He traveled all over the world, and many places still didn't accept credit cards. He had to have cash on him.

181

"Did she annoy you?" he whispered in her ear as he pressed the button for the elevator.

"Who?"

"The waitress who was trying to flirt with me. I didn't encourage her, but it probably still angered you. If the roles were reversed, I would have been growling at the waiter, if not worse. And then I left her a big tip, which must have made you really mad."

Gabi hadn't seen the bill, so she didn't know how big the tip was, and if he hadn't mentioned it, she wouldn't have cared.

"How big was the tip?"

"More than twenty-five percent." Uriel pulled her into his arms as soon as the elevator door closed behind them. "I just didn't want to wait for the change."

Well, that was actually a very good reason to leave a big tip.

"I don't care about that, and I didn't care about her flirting with you. What got me angry was—"

He kissed her, and Gabi forgot what she'd gotten upset about.

KAGRA

Peter was persistent, but surprisingly, Kagra wasn't annoyed with him, perhaps because he didn't strut and posture to get her attention like the Kra-ell males would.

Rishana and Sheniya had been casting her dirty looks, but their disapproval had only prompted her to respond to Peter's flirting with more enthusiasm.

She was finally free, and no one was going to dictate to her who she could hang out with or who she invited to her bed.

"Kagra," Pavel called from the last row on the plane. "They have Russian dubbing for the movies." He lifted the earphones. "Every seat has one."

"Awesome," she answered in English. "But I suggest that everyone watch in English. Most of you need to work on your language skills." She frowned at Rishana. "Are you watching the movie with Russian dubbing?"

"*Chto?*"

Kagra motioned for her to remove the earphones. "You need to learn English. Don't listen to the movie in Russian."

Rishana shrugged and put the earphones back on. She probably was still listening in Russian, and Kagra didn't want to make a scene in front of Peter and the other Guardians. She would deal with her later.

"How come you speak such good English?" Peter asked.

"I wasn't as fluent before your people liberated us. But I have a good ear, and I learn fast."

For some reason, her answer made him happy. "Immortals learn languages quickly too. Evidently, we are genetically similar."

"Of course, we are. Otherwise, we wouldn't be able to produce children together."

"True that." Peter's sultry look invited a comeback, but Kagra had to be careful about what she said in front of her people.

She cast a quick glance around to make sure no one was eavesdropping on their conversation.

Aliya and Vrog were cuddled under a blanket and talking in hushed voices, which was kind of cute but also disturbing. Her people didn't cuddle, and although Vrog looked human, Aliya didn't, and it was just odd.

Thankfully, Jade was more circumspect about touching Phinas in public or even in the house they shared while Kagra or other Kra-ell were there.

Pavel and the other three purebloods were all watching movies on the monitors mounted on each seat, Rishana and Sheniya did the same, and the Guardians were mostly doing stuff on their phones and tablets.

Yamanu was humming quietly, and although she could barely hear him, there was something soothing about the faint melody. Maybe it was one of his many talents.

The guy was incredible, and it was a shame he was taken. She would have liked a tumble in bed with him. She also liked Dalhu, the former Doomer, but he was also taken.

That was the trouble with the immortals. They didn't share.

Peter was single, and he was obviously interested, but he was too interested, and she wasn't looking to repeat Jade's mistake. All she wanted was good sex with a male who knew what he was doing and wouldn't expect her to fall in love with him.

Peter shifted in his seat, making her wonder whether he had to change positions because he was aroused. "So far, there is only one kid who was born to an immortal female and a hybrid Kra-ell father, which means that both parents are part human. We don't know whether purebloods and immortals are compatible." He smiled devilishly. "But I would sure like to try."

Damn, it was difficult to keep him at arm's length without offending him, especially since she really liked him. Just not as much as he liked her.

"Do you have children?" Kagra asked, pretending not to get the sexual innuendo.

"Not that I know of. I hope I don't. If I ever have children, I want to be part of their lives, not just the sperm donor."

She nodded. "That's what the fathers of my sons were. The difference is that they knew they were the fathers, but I wish they hadn't."

"Why?"

"Because we are connected through the sons we share, and I don't want to be connected to them. They didn't do anything to help raise my sons, and they don't deserve to be part of their lives."

Peter regarded her with his smart, dark eyes. "I thought that was the Kra-ell way—the tribe raised the kids, not their individual parents."

"I was born on Earth, but Jade was pretty traditional in how she ran her compound. The children belonged to the mothers, and the fathers' role in raising the children was limited. Some were better than others, though." She didn't want to talk about it. The loss felt less acute now, but it still pained her to think about all the people she'd lost— her father, her brother, and the other males. It was better to feel angry. "Igor spat on the Kra-ell traditions, and he didn't want the males to be involved in raising the children at all. He embraced human patriarchal attitudes."

"I'm sorry." Peter put a hand on her arm. "Would you like to watch another episode of *Fix That Dump*?"

She would have watched a show about the lives of ants just to take her mind off the past.

"Do you get Netflix up here?"

They'd watched one episode on the bus, but now they were several thousand feet in the air and flying over the ocean.

He grinned. "Yes, I do." He lifted his phone to show her that he had reception.

"Then what are you waiting for? Let's watch."

49

GABI

The short walk from the elevator to Gabi's room could have gotten them in trouble if any of the other guests had stepped out into the hallway.

Uriel was holding her up by her ass, her legs were wrapped around his narrow waist, and the skirt of her dress was hitched all the way up her hips, so she was practically exposed, and they were kissing.

Somehow, he'd managed to get them to her door and leaned her against it, holding her up with one hand while reaching his other hand out. "Give me the key."

"It's in my purse," she murmured. "Where the credit cards are."

"Got it." He pulled out her wallet and handed it to her.

She found the key and touched it to the reader while he got the handle and pushed the door open.

Uriel didn't bother turning the lights on as he carried her to the bed and laid her on top of the cover.

"I want you so much." She held up her arms.

She must have been really drunk because it looked as if he was moving too fast for her to catch his movements, and when he was done, his suit jacket, dress shirt, and pants were draped over the desk chair, and his magnificent body was clad only in a pair of tight-fitting boxer shorts that left very little to the imagination.

His bulge was just as massive as she'd remembered, and she had a flicker of apprehension before also remembering how perfectly they had ended up fitting and that, in the morning, she hadn't been sore at all.

As he came into her arms, his incredible body moving with the powerful fluidity of a puma, he didn't climb on top of her but rather lay beside her and pulled her to him. Her breasts were pressing into his bare chest through the fabrics of her dress and bra, but her hips were exposed, and it was skin-to-skin below the waist except for their underwear.

Impatient, she wrapped her arms around him and tried to roll on her back, but trying to move Uriel was like trying to move a boulder, and he wouldn't budge until he was good and ready.

"Patience," he murmured against her lips and then proceeded to kiss her softly as if they were just starting their sensual dance and not ready for the main act to commence.

The two elevator rides, one from the restaurant down to the lobby and then the second one from the lobby up to her room, had provided enough of an opening act, and Gabi was primed and ready to go.

When she groaned, he rolled her onto her back and propped himself on his elbows. Hovering only inches above her, with his hair falling like two black curtains on both sides of his impossibly gorgeous face, he was distorting her reality.

She cupped his cheek, which was covered in a five-o'clock shadow. "How can you be so beautiful?"

"Beauty is in the eye of the beholder." He leaned down and kissed her eyelids, forcing her to close her eyes.

Feeling the hard length that was still trapped inside his boxer shorts pressed against her inner thigh, Gabi spread her legs to make room for him.

He shifted, letting some of his weight press her into the mattress, but she knew he was still bracing most of it on his forearms, or he would have squashed her.

Running her hands from his shoulders down to his arms, she tried to memorize the feel of his smooth skin, the powerful muscles underneath it, the way he felt on top of her, and as she opened her eyes and looked up at him, she was in awe of the creator's scalpel and the magnificent male animal it had crafted.

"Uriel," she whispered his name as if it was a prayer, and with a name like his, perhaps it was.

Names had power, and Uriel was the light of God.

He took her lips in another kiss, and as she surrendered to it, she was acutely aware of the fact that they were running out of time and that they had to make every second count.

Perhaps the same thought had run through his mind because his kiss got harder, more demanding, his tongue dueling with hers, probing and licking.

When he let go of her mouth, it was only to pull her dress off, free her breasts from the bra, and yank her panties off.

Fully bared before his eyes, the cool air from the air conditioning vent tightening her nipples into hard points, she undulated her hips in blatant invitation.

His nostrils flared, and she could have sworn that a glow was coming from his dark eyes, but it must have been the reflection of the moonlight shining through the expansive windows of the hotel room.

"I want you," she said in case her previous hint wasn't clear enough. "All of you."

He blinked, and the glow was gone, and then he lowered himself on top of her in slow motion, his arms bowing as he suspended his mouth over her aching nipples.

Remembering the night before and how he'd demanded that she ask for what she wanted him to do to her, she groaned. "Don't tease me. Kiss them."

Smiling like the devil he was, Uriel didn't do what she asked. Instead, he feathered kisses over her collarbones and sternum, teasing her mercilessly before finally swiping his tongue over one turgid peak.

"God, yes." She pitched her head back, and as she churned her hips under him, she was annoyed that he still had his boxer shorts on.

That thought didn't last long.

As he latched onto her nipple, sucking and licking it, she lifted her legs and wrapped them around his hips for better friction.

Uriel let go of her nipple with a pop, but instead of giving its twin the same agonizingly pleasurable treatment, he slid his mouth down her body, kissing and licking along the way.

"Oh, yeah," she breathed. "I definitely want that."

His growl of approval was delicious, the vibrations going straight to her core.

PETER

Peter had watched the episode of *Fix That Dump* with just enough focus to make occasional remarks and to be able to talk about it later.

Running a parallel script in his mind, he wondered whether Kagra's charm and playfulness were just a cover and that underneath, she was hurt and damaged like the other Kra-ell. She hadn't lost children like Jade had, but she must have lost her father and other males she cared about.

He should avoid asking her questions about her life before coming to the village.

But then, how would he get to know her?

He didn't even know how old she was or how she'd become Jade's second-in-command despite being Earthborn.

The other thing he needed to figure out was the mixed signals she was sending him. When he was teasing and playful, she was teasing and playful back, but when he expressed more serious interest in her, she backed away.

Well, that should have been as obvious as a new day, but he hadn't been thinking in Kra-ell terms. He'd been thinking in immortal terms.

He needed to approach Kagra as someone who was looking for some fun but didn't want to commit. Or he should just treat her as he had treated any of the human females he had hooked up with over the years. He'd never pretended to want more than one night of pleasure with them, and if the lady wasn't okay with that, they'd parted with no hard feelings.

But if he did that with Kagra, he would be pretending in the other direction. He wanted more than one night of passion with her, but he would be fine starting with that.

Perhaps that was how he should approach it.

One step at a time.

"This is amazing." Kagra waved a hand at the screen. "How do people come up with such pretty combinations? I would have never thought a pink fluffy pillow could liven up a space like that." She turned and smiled. "Can I tell you a secret?"

"Always." He leaned closer, excitement bubbling in his chest.

"I love this shit. I love decorating, and that's why I was finding excuses to hang around Ingrid's design center and chat with her. When she offered us the spare room in the center for our headquarters, I jumped at the opportunity and convinced Jade to take it. Now I will get to hang around there whenever I want."

This was the last thing Peter had expected from Kagra, which was an excellent lesson to be learned. People were multilayered, and it was a mistake to assume that the face they showed the world was the only one they had.

"Did you decorate your new home?"

She shook her head. "Jade has just gotten access to our money, and we are in the process of getting fake documents and opening bank accounts for everyone. Bottom line, I don't have the money to spend." She leaned forward to glance at the other Kra-ell on the flight and then leaned back and sighed. "Even when I have the money, I doubt I will use it to redecorate the house I'm staying in. Ingrid did a great job with it, and I would just mess it up. Besides, decorating doesn't go with my persona." She waved a hand over herself. "I'm a tough warrior, not a designer."

"Can't you be both?"

She arched a brow. "Do any of your Guardian friends have artistic hobbies?"

"Yeah. You know Magnus, right?"

She nodded.

"So, he retired from the force a long time ago, and for many years he was into men's fashion and other things that most of the Guardians wouldn't have considered very manly. But he didn't care about their opinions and did what he loved doing."

"Why did he get out of the fashion business?"

"He answered a call like the rest of us." Peter smoothed his hand over his goatee. "I was retired as well. When the world had become a more peaceful place, there was no more use for a large Guardian force, and many of us retired and turned to different occupations. But then Bridget summoned us back and offered us a worthy reason to join the force again. The clan decided to wage war on trafficking, and we were needed."

There was understanding in her big eyes that only a fellow warrior could have. "I bet you and your friends were thrilled to be needed again. It's no fun to feel like the skills you've honed over years and years of sweat and blood are suddenly obsolete. It would have been devastating to me."

"Really? Even if you could attend a design school and become an interior designer or even an architect?"

"I would love to do that as a hobby, not a job. My ultimate goal is to one day lead a tribe of my own."

That was another surprise. "You would leave the village?"

She winced. "No, I love it in the village. But maybe we could organize our community as smaller tribes." Leaning back, she closed her eyes. "I don't know. Branching off on my own used to be all I wanted, all I dreamt about, and then our compound got sacked, and my dreams and aspirations were put on hold. But now that I think about it, they are not really what I should aspire to. I need to find a different goal."

He leaned closer to her and whispered conspiratorially, "It could be designing homes."

"I don't even know whether I have any talent."

"I have an idea." He smiled. "How would you like to decorate my house? I'm tired of it looking exactly like all the other houses in the village. I want something different, and I have the money to get it done. I just need someone with a vision."

She slanted him a look. "Is that a ploy to get me into your bed?"

"No, it's a genuine offer, but if you happen to find yourself in my bed, I won't throw you out."

She laughed. "Good to know."

GABI

G abi lay panting, spent from the string of orgasms Uriel had wrought out of her, but as he brought his fingers to his mouth and sucked on them, her arousal flared again.

How could one man be so damn sexy?

A satisfied smirk lifting one corner of his lips, he put his fingers back where they'd been a moment ago and started stroking her again.

She wanted to tell him that she was too sensitive and couldn't take it anymore, but then he lowered his head and teased her nipple with the tip of his tongue, and when her hips arched off the bed to meet his fingers instead of pulling away, he took her mouth in a scorching kiss, and she came again.

Leaning away, he grinned. "Was there something you wanted to say?"

Was the guy made of granite?

How come he wasn't inside her already? His erection was sticking over the elastic of his boxer shorts, and the tip was beaded with pre-cum. Which reminded her that they needed a condom.

Maybe that was why he wasn't inside her yet?

She'd demanded that he bring them, but perhaps he'd forgotten? Or maybe he hated using them?

Well, tough. It was a mood spoiler to remind him to put it on, but even if he was as clean as he claimed, she didn't want to get pregnant—

Or did she?

Gabi was thirty-eight, and her biological clock was ticking. Once it had become clear to her that she wasn't going to find the man of her dreams because she couldn't bring herself to trust any guy she dated, she'd considered using donor sperm to have a baby on her own. Then she'd realized that, without a support system, she couldn't raise a child and also run her business, and she had given up on the idea.

But perhaps she could move to Los Angeles to be near her family and let her brothers help her. She really shouldn't wait much longer, and she couldn't have asked for a more magnificent sperm donor than Uriel.

He'd claimed he couldn't get her pregnant because of his low sperm count but, somehow, she doubted that was true. He was too virile and too masculine to have such a problem.

The logical part of her brain knew that it was nonsense and that one had nothing to do with the other, but her hormone-saturated brain had its own ideas, and they were more appropriate for a cavewoman than a twenty-first-century college graduate.

All it perceived was—a big, healthy man with big muscles—strong, healthy babies.

Gabi put a hand on Uriel's wrist. "I want you inside of me without any barrier between us. I'm willing to take the risk if you are."

"Are you sure? I brought a big pack of condoms."

It gladdened her that he hadn't forgotten and that he had considered her wishes, but she was still convinced that taking a risk on him was the right thing to do.

She had no illusions about him being a part of the baby's life, but she'd given up on having a partner she could trust enough to commit to a long time ago.

"I'm sure," she breathed.

As his expression turned feral, she had a moment of trepidation, but when he got rid of his boxer shorts between one blink of an eye and the next and gripped his erection, she was glad of issuing the invitation.

She wanted to feel that velvety length inside her, and without a trench coat taking away even an iota of the experience.

Supporting his weight with one arm, he positioned himself at her entrance and stroked the tip of his erection up and down.

She held her breath, waiting for the moment he would push inside her, and when he surged in with one brutal thrust, she gasped, not from discomfort, but from bliss.

As Uriel let loose, going hard and fast, Gabi's body greedily absorbed his thrusting, relishing the clapping and grinding of their bodies, and she didn't want it to end.

But then he pulled out, flipped her around, pulled her hips up, and surged in again. She felt owned and possessed, but it didn't bother her in the slightest. In fact, being aware of how temporary it was and that soon she would regain full ownership of her body made her sad and took away from the incredible experience.

His hands clamping her hips, he was shafting into her with such force that the bed was banging against the wall with each thrust, and as the coil winding inside her sprang free, it released a climax and a torrent of sensations that was so overwhelming she was gasping for air.

Behind her, Uriel stilled, and as his erection kicked inside her, she heard him hiss, and then he bit into her shoulder, and she orgasmed again.

KIAN

A sense of unease had kept Kian awake long into the night, and as he wondered about its source, he wasn't sure whether it was connected to his mother's wish to start introductory meetings with the Kra-ell or to the team flying to China.

His mother hadn't decided yet whether she wanted to organize a grand appearance and a speech in the assembly hall first, and then start meeting small groups of Kra-ell to create a more personal connection, or the other way around. In either case, he shouldn't be worried because they were all under Toven's compulsion to do no harm and wore cuffs that would immobilize them with a neurotoxin if they dared anything.

Was he still wary of them because of the residual effect of Igor's attack?

It wasn't only about being under the guy's compulsion. The pure-blood's physical strength alone was enough to give Kian nightmares. As someone who had felt physically superior to nearly everyone around him throughout his long life, it was a hard pill to swallow.

Still, the unease was more likely about the mission than his mother's plans.

He had been checking his phone for messages and had even called Morris a couple of times to make sure that the team was okay and that the jet was in the air.

Perhaps it was time to make another call?

Syssi was sleeping peacefully beside him, and he could hear Allegra's breathing through the baby monitor, and whenever he wanted, he could watch her sleep through the camera mounted in her room, but with that strange unease churning in his stomach, it wasn't good enough. He needed to check on her in person.

With a sigh, he glanced at his mate. Somehow, she'd managed to sleep through his tossing and turning. Not wishing to disturb her, he'd called Morris from the bathroom, but this time he was going to make the call from his office and call village security as well.

After that, he could make a couple of cappuccinos and surprise Syssi with coffee in bed. It had been a long time since he had done anything to spoil her, and Kian felt guilty for neglecting her.

His plan had been to be all hers during the wedding cruise, but with everything that had happened since the idea had been originally hatched, he doubted they were going to sail anytime soon, and certainly not with the entire clan. They would have to break it up, which defied the whole purpose of having Alena's wedding on a cruise ship.

They wanted the entire family to be there, and since Alena was the de facto Mother of the Clan, that was the whole clan.

After carefully slipping out of bed, he tiptoed into Allegra's room to check on her.

His daughter's sweet little face tempted him to kiss her rosy cheeks, but she was a light sleeper, and if he touched her or made a noise, she would wake up and would be cranky the rest of the day.

After tiptoeing out of her room, he walked over to his office to call Morris again to confirm that everything was fine on that front.

The jet had taken off at six in the evening the day before, and it should land at about eight in the morning, but that was three hours from now, and Kian knew that he wouldn't be able to sleep until it landed safely.

He was turning into a damn mother hen.

What if the sense of impending danger had nothing to do with the flight but with the mission itself?

Nah, that wasn't likely.

Even if they found the scouts, and even if they were hostile, the team could handle them. The Kra-ell settlers hadn't arrived with any advanced weapons, and Kian had no reason to think that the scouts who had arrived before them had anything better.

From what he had gathered so far, the gods' mode of operation was not to land a craft on Earth but rather to dispatch pods from a large spaceship that didn't enter Earth's atmosphere, and those pods didn't have room for much more than their occupants. Then again, a pod loaded with supplies might have been dropped along with the settlers.

However, he wondered how they were supposed to get picked up. The large spaceship had to have a smaller vessel capable of passing through Earth's atmosphere, landing, and taking off to reach the mother ship.

Kian wasn't a rocket engineer, but he knew that was not an easy feat to pull off. The amount of fuel required was staggering, but even though the gods probably had a very different way of fueling their vessels, it still had to be costly or dangerous to land on Earth and take off. Otherwise, they wouldn't have bothered with pods to drop off their people.

He pulled a bottle of water from the minibar fridge, removed the cap, and took a long swig before calling Morris.

"Good morning, boss. Everything is fine, and we are still in the air."

Thankfully, Kian's anxiety hadn't influenced the veteran pilot, and he sounded as calm and collected as ever.

"Good to know. Call me when you land."

"I will. Morris out."

Next, Kian called the security office. "Good morning. How are you guys doing?"

"Good morning, Kian. Jarmo and his crew are at the barn, tending to the animals, but other than that, there is nothing to report. Everything is still quiet."

"Excellent. No news is good news. Let me know if anything seems out of order, and I mean anything."

"Are we expecting trouble?" the Guardian asked.

"No, but I have an uneasy feeling."

"Got it. Do you want us to raise the alert level?"

"No, just stay vigilant."

"Always, boss."

After ending the call, Kian leaned back in his chair, took another big gulp from the water, and turned to look at the rising sun through the sliding doors of his home office.

"What is it going to be this time?"

53

GABI

Gabi opened her eyes, turned on her side, and put her hand on the pillow beside her.

It was cold, which meant that Uriel had left right after she'd passed out from bliss. This time, they had done it on the bed, so he hadn't needed to carry her from the couch, but she wasn't sticky, meaning he'd cleaned her before leaving.

Strangely, she didn't feel embarrassed. If their roles were reversed and he passed out from bliss while she remained awake, she would lovingly clean him up too.

Lovingly was the wrong qualifier, though. She was in lust with Uriel, not in love. She didn't know enough about him to be in love with him. Perhaps tenderly was a better word.

The memory of the evening they had spent together was bittersweet.

She'd had a great time. Both in and out of bed, and now that she remembered what her subconscious had been trying to tell her, she had even less reason to regret the decision not to use a condom.

While Uriel had been with her, she hadn't remembered that she was about to close or sell her business in Cleveland and move into the immortals' village with her family. She was supposed to find an immortal to induce her transition, but she didn't need to hurry because she was relatively young and in great shape. During lunch, Karen, Darlene, and the other immortal ladies had told her about how low fertility was for immortals and that she should mentally prepare to wait decades to have a baby. They had a doctor in the village who gave out potions that were supposed to help with conception, but no one knew whether they worked. So far, Syssi and her husband were the only success story, and the others were still waiting to conceive.

If by some miracle she'd gotten pregnant, which was almost as unlikely as her winning the lottery, she could raise the child in the village, surrounded by aunts and uncles and cousins, and in the meantime, she could find a nice immortal nerd to bond with and to induce her transition.

It was a fantastic plan, but the one thing missing in the beautiful picture she'd painted was Uriel.

With a groan, Gabi turned on her back and draped her arm over her eyes to stop them from tearing up.

She was going to miss him.

He'd promised to visit her in Cleveland, and he might have even meant it, but life would come up with ways of keeping them apart, and if he ever ended up visiting the city that had been her home for so long, he wouldn't find her there because she would be in the hidden immortal village in California.

Reaching blindly for her phone, Gabi patted the nightstand until her hand landed on it and brought the device in front of her eyes.

There was no message from Uriel, which was so disappointing that annoying tears leaked out of her eyes. There were two messages from the same client asking if it was okay to substitute Eggs Benedict with Canadian bacon for her prescribed morning omelet of two eggs and a cup of spinach.

What did Melinda expect the answer to be? *Go ahead, honey. Enjoy your Eggs Benedict?*

"People are so dumb," Gabi groaned. "Actually, they just like playing dumb."

Melinda Ratcliffe was an attorney, and to become one, she'd had to pass the bar, so she couldn't be stupid. She just wanted Gabi to allow her to cheat on her diet, and later she would blame her for not losing any inches from her hips.

Talk about wanting to have your cake and eat it too.

If that was an option, Gabi would have no business and no income, but she could also turn immortal and keep Uriel as her lover.

Except, he hadn't even left her a message, which was a message in itself. It was over, and there was no reason to drag the pain out.

Then again, he might have been in a rush and forgotten.

Ugh, she needed to talk to someone about this, someone who could help her get her emotions together and who wasn't a member of her family.

Was it too early to call Becky?

Her trainer should be in her gym already, but if she was coaching a client, she might be unable to talk. Perhaps calling Suzi or Mira would be better?

Nah, they were both good friends, but they wouldn't tell her what they really thought, like Becky would. They were too nice and wouldn't want to hurt her feelings. She also didn't want to tell them she was moving to Los Angeles. Not yet, anyway.

She would have to tell them eventually.

Becky was a straight shooter, and she had no qualms about hurting someone's feelings if it was for their own good.

The problem with that plan was that as soon as Becky got on the line, Orion's compulsion might cause Gabi to forget about moving to Los Angeles and why she couldn't be with Uriel. Not that she could tell her friend anything about immortals and how they affected her future plans, but at least she wouldn't have big gaps in her memories.

When she'd spoken with Gilbert on the phone before, she'd remembered everything, but when she'd met Karen and Darlene in the restaurant, she'd forgotten again, but that could have been because of Syssi and Amanda who had been strangers to her at that point.

Oh well, she wouldn't know until she tried.

After a visit to the bathroom and a cup of coffee from the coffee maker, Gabi sat on the couch and called Becky.

The phone rang for so long that she was about to end the call, but then Becky's voice came on. "Gabi? Are you back in town?"

"I'm in Los Angeles, visiting my brothers."

"Oh, right. I forgot that you were going there straight from the conference. How did it go with the flight?"

"Better than I expected. My flight was canceled, and I got a free upgrade to first-class another flight."

"That's amazing. Those tickets are three times more expensive than coach. Did you get gourmet meals and free booze?"

Gabi chuckled. "The meal was far from gourmet, but I got plenty of free champagne. I also got to sit next to the most gorgeous guy I've ever seen, and I mean ever. You know how crazy I am about Henry Cavill, and he has nothing on Uriel."

"Really?" Becky sounded skeptical. "Did Uriel also have a jaw implant?"

They had joked about the actor's jaw being impossibly big and square, but none of the gossip magazines confirmed that he'd had anything done. Supposedly, it was the result of weightlifting.

Becky had even joked that she needed to up the weights in her routine.

"I suspect that he did. He and his friends came from a trip that included South Korea, and all three looked like a walking commercial for some luxury brand for men."

Gabi continued to tell Becky about the two nights she'd spent with Uriel, how he had been so intently focused on her but had left each time in the middle of the night because of early morning meetings.

She didn't tell her about moving to Los Angeles, even though her memory of immortals had thankfully remained intact. It was premature, and she hadn't come up with a good enough reason to explain her move to her friends and clients.

"The guy is a beautiful butterfly," Becky said. "Nice to look at but not lasting. You had your fun, and whether you want to move on or not, you have no choice. Neither of you lives in Los Angeles, and from what you've told me, the guy evaded answering personal questions. For all you know, he might be married."

"He's not."

Darlene's son hadn't found evidence of Uriel having a wife, but he'd also admitted to having limited access to government records in Portugal.

"Why, because he didn't have a wedding ring?" Becky asked sarcastically. "Lots of guys don't wear them. Also, he might not have a wife, but he could have a steady girlfriend he's cheating on, and that's just as bad."

"Yeah. I didn't consider that." Roni wouldn't have been able to find out about a girlfriend even if he could easily hack into Uriel's official records.

"Keep your fun memories of him and move on," Becky said. "That's my advice, but you will do as you please." She chuckled. "I don't think you've ever followed my advice. You only use me as your sounding board."

"I ask for your advice because you will not try to sugarcoat anything for me. You are always the voice of reason." She laughed. "I'm the unreasonable one who sometimes chooses the wrong thing to do."

"At least you admit it. That's the first step in recovery. When are you coming back?"

"Wednesday night."

"Should I pencil you in for Thursday morning?"

"No, I have a full day of consultations. But you can pencil me in for Friday morning. Our usual time."

"Will do. I thought you would like a make-up session for the ones you missed."

"No, thanks." Gabi chuckled. "I had plenty of exercise the last two nights."

"Yeah, well, but not for the right muscle groups," Becky said. "Be strong, Gabi," she continued in a more serious tone. "Don't call him, don't message him, just let him go."

"Yeah, you're right. Bye, Becky. I'll see you Friday at eight."

As she ended the call, Gabi leaned back and released a long breath. Was she going to take Becky's advice?

Probably not.

It just didn't feel right.

KIAN

K ian finished making the cappuccinos and was ready to go back to bed when his phone pinged with an incoming message.

Putting the cups on the counter, he reached into the pocket of his robe to retrieve the phone and frowned at William's picture on the screen.

As he read the message, alarm bells went off in his head. *Call me as soon as you can.*

It wasn't about the plane crashing because William wouldn't have known about that before him, and the only other thing that came to mind was the damn signals.

Were they broadcasting again?

Choosing William's contact from the list, he held the device to his ear, and the moment the call was answered, he barked, "Report."

"The signals are on again, and they are broadcasting steadily. No more winking in and out. We need the Odus to decipher the location, and I really hope the signals are still coming from Chengdu."

So that was what the uneasy feeling had been about.

In a way, it was a relief. He could deal with whoever was broadcasting those signals and what they represented, but he couldn't control weather conditions in China and ensure the safe landing of the jet carrying his team.

"I'll get the Odus. Meet me at my office in half an hour."

William let out a breath. "Here we go again."

"Indeed."

By the time Kian got to his office accompanied by Okidu, Onidu was already there and coffee was brewing.

William looked exactly the same way he had Monday morning when they had met for the same reason—his hair was disheveled, his billowing T-shirt was a remnant from the days he'd been much larger, and his feet were in the same pair of blue Crocs.

"Good morning, boss." He opened his laptop. "I recorded the signals, but since they are still broadcasting, I will just run the live feed." His fingers flew over the keyboard.

As before, Kian couldn't hear anything, but he knew the Odus heard it just fine, given their trance-like frozen mode.

It was spooky to see them like that, their robotic nature suddenly so evident and disturbing. He much preferred seeing them animated and displaying signs of sentience. Thinking of them as constructs was disturbing, and if he cared to be honest with himself, it had been one of the reasons he hadn't pushed for faster deciphering of the journals.

Humanity hadn't yet developed the materials necessary to build Odus as lifelike as Okidu and his brothers, and what the clan could accomplish with what was available were either robotic creations that looked like machines or mannequin-like at best. Despite having the same neural network as the original Odus and the same capacity for sentience, they would be regarded as less because of their appearance.

"Should I write down the coordinates?" Okidu asked.

"Please do." William handed him a sheet of paper and a mechanical pencil.

"Thank you, master." Okidu scribbled a list of numbers in his neat handwriting. "Here you go, master." He handed William the page.

William looked at the numbers and frowned. "This is not good." He typed in the coordinates and turned the screen toward Kian so he could see the location on the map. "All three signals are coming from the same place, and it's not from Chengdu."

"Indeed." Kian pulled out his phone and called the chief.

Onegus answered immediately. "Good morning, Kian. What's up?"

"The three signals are back, and they are not coming from China this time. They are right here in our backyard. The implications are obvious, and as much as I hate to do it, we have to implement the lockdown protocols here and in the keep. Once that's done, please come to my office."

The signals were not originating from the scouts who had been sent thousands of years before, and this was a new threat.

There could be only one reason the signals were that close. Whoever was emitting them must have followed Igor's signal to the keep, and for some reason, they wanted that to be known.

Otherwise, why hadn't the signals been broadcasting continuously?

Why had they been activated in China, deactivated, and then activated again right here under his nose?

Locking down the keep wasn't optional, but locking down the village as well was an extreme measure. Until they figured out what and who they were dealing with, Kian wasn't taking any chances.

"Roger that," Onegus said. "I'll implement the protocol and head to your office."

Ending the call, Kian turned to William. "Can you please zoom in on the precise location?

He nodded and did as Kian had requested. "They are about ninety miles due east from us, located in a wilderness area at the foothills of Mount Baldy."

"It's like they are taunting us." Kian raked his fingers through his hair. "Obviously, they know how to turn the signals on and off, and they kept them off until they got in position. They turned them on to let us know that they are here."

As the door opened and the chief walked in, his eyes zeroed in on the screen. "I know the area." He walked up to the laptop and leaned closer for a better look. "The actual location is very hard to access. It's a mountainous canyon surrounded by sheer cliffs and accessible only through a very narrow dirt road."

Kian wondered why Onegus was familiar with the Mount Baldy area, but that was immaterial at the moment.

"Would you like some coffee, master?" Okidu asked the chief.

"I would love some, thank you."

"We need to find out what is out there and who we are dealing with," Kian said, "But we need to do that cautiously. I think those signals are meant to draw us out. Whoever was emitting them followed the signals from the Kra-ell, and since we failed to remove Igor's tracker before bringing him to the keep, they discovered that location. I'm just glad that the village wasn't compromised."

Onegus nodded. "I agree that it's a trap and with your decision to initiate the lockdowns. I alerted Anandur and Brundar, and they will be here any moment now. You know the protocol. If the alert level is raised to red, you need to have them by your side at all times."

That reminded Kian that Syssi and Allegra were alone and unprotected in the house. Not that anyone or anything could get into the village, and even an aerial attack would be difficult to pull off with all the safety precautions William had incorporated. Nevertheless, he would feel better knowing that Okidu was there to shield them.

Onidu needed to go home as well.

He turned to the Odus. "Thank you for your help, but you should return home and resume your duties." He looked at Okidu. "The village might be in danger, and I count on you to defend Syssi and Allegra." He shifted his eyes to Onidu. "Same goes for you. Your job is to defend Amanda and Evie."

"Yes, master." Both the Odus bowed and headed for the door.

"Don't leave their sides for any reason," he added.

Okidu hesitated by the door. "What should I tell Mistress Syssi?" he asked.

It was early, and Syssi was probably still sleeping, but she would wake up soon and prepare to leave for the university.

He needed to notify everyone about the lockdown without creating panic.

They had an alert system, but sounding the alarm would freak everyone out.

"I'll call Syssi shortly," he told the Odu.

"Thank you, master." Okidu dipped his head and walked out the door.

Kian turned to Onegus. "We need to alert everyone without creating panic. Any suggestions as to how we should handle that?"

"I'll send a broadcast text to everyone," William offered. "They will see it when they wake up."

"Try to make it sound like locking the village down is only a precaution because the keep's location was compromised."

Kian wasn't sure that William was the best person for the task, but he didn't have time to compose the text himself, and he would probably do a much worse job than William.

"We can use our high-altitude surveillance drone," Onegus suggested. "Although it has the range, we shouldn't fly it from here because it will have to go through the airspace of three international airports. I suggest dispatching a team to drive it closer to the area and fly it from there."

"That's an excellent idea." Kian tapped his fingers on the conference table. "Make it so. Also, wake Roni up and have him hack into the FAA's global tracking system so our drone remains undetected. If whoever sends the signals can access the network, I don't want them to know we are flying a drone to spy on them."

Onegus looked as if he wanted to say something but decided not to. "I'll wake Charlie up. He's the best at flying drones."

The chief probably thought hacking into the FAA's global tracking system was taking it too far, but Kian had just gotten confirmation that his paranoia was not only entirely justified but not far-reaching enough to think up all the possible doomsday scenarios reality was throwing at him.

As Onegus got busy, Kian turned to William. "Do you have a backup for the specialty monitors and receivers in case they malfunction?"

"I do."

"Good. I know you have alerts on your phone and laptop whenever a signal goes on, but I also want someone in the lab babysitting the equipment twenty-four-seven."

William nodded. "I'll put Marcel in charge of assigning people to the job."

"Good choice. Can you reroute the signals to the war room?"

"Of course."

"Excellent. Make it so. I want to hold an emergency meeting in there."

It was time to assemble the troops, so to speak.

Onegus paused his phone conversation with Charlie and turned to Kian. "What do you want to do with the team when they land in China? Do you want them to refuel and turn around? We might need Yamanu here."

By the time they were back, the crisis might be over. "Not yet. Have them investigate the location the signals came from before. Maybe they will find clues to help us figure out what and who we are dealing with."

Kian typed a message and sent it to Turner, Kalugal, and Jade to come to the war room at their earliest convenience.

Onegus ended the call and lifted his hand to get Kian's attention. "I suggest alerting security in Alaska and Scotland as well. They don't need to go into lockdown mode, but they should take precautions just in case."

"I'll call them." Evidently, Kian's paranoia didn't go deep enough because he should have thought of that before Onegus brought it up.

After Igor's capture, Kian had hoped for peaceful times ahead, but he should have known better. Igor-caliber assassins were waiting to be revived from stasis, and now three mysterious signals had appeared within days of them bringing Igor to the keep.

55

GABI

After talking to Becky, Gabi's mind had been too busy running in circles to go back to sleep, but it was still too early to call Gilbert to get her.

She'd tried watching television, but nothing could hold her focus, especially since she kept glancing at her phone, hoping to see a message from Uriel.

Perhaps Becky was right, and she should at least try to forget about him.

Yeah, good luck with that.

Running always helped clear her mind, and the hotel probably had a gym with some treadmills she could use, but she didn't have gym clothes or running shoes. Also, she wouldn't be alone in the gym, which would make her memories of immortals disappear again, so that wouldn't be very helpful anyway.

If the hotel had a pool, though, she could go for a swim. She'd gotten a new bikini on her shopping trip with Darlene, along with a matching cover-up, and her flip-flops would do just fine as footwear.

Picking up the receiver, she called the front desk.

"Good morning, Ms. Emerson," a cheerful lady answered. "How can I help you?"

"Good morning. I was wondering whether you have a pool in the hotel?"

"We have an exercise pool in the gym."

Gabi had seen commercials for those pools but never used one.

"Is that like a small pool with jets you're supposed to swim against?"

"It's more like a current than a jet. It allows you to work on your strokes without moving forward."

"Have you tried it?"

The woman laughed. "I have not. It scares me. But many of the hotel's guests enjoy it. You should give it a try."

"I think I will. Where is the gym?"

"It's on the sixty-second floor next to the spa."

"Thank you. I'll tell you how it was after I'm done."

"That would be great. Enjoy your swim, Ms. Emerson."

"Thanks."

After ending the call, Gabi walked over to the closet, took the bikini and the matching cover-up out of the shopping bag, removed the tags, and put everything on.

"Not bad." She admired herself in the mirror from several angles.

The bikini was dark blue with a slim golden line on the edges that made it look sporty and elegant at the same time. The bottoms provided adequate coverage for her ass without looking like it belonged on a grandma, and the top was like a good bra, giving her breasts the slight push-up they needed.

Good nutrition and exercise could only go so far, and some signs of aging could only be addressed by plastic surgery. Luckily, Gabi's plan to get breast implants for her fortieth birthday was obsolete. After her transition, her breasts would go back to being as perky and as lovely as they had been in her early twenties.

Hopefully.

She was still thinking about all the things that would improve after her transition when she got to the gym, but as soon as she stepped inside, she couldn't remember what she'd been thinking about on her way there.

The place was packed, and every treadmill was taken, and so was the exercise pool.

The attendant smiled politely. "The current session is about to end in a few minutes, and the next reservation is for half an hour from now. Should I put your name down for the one in between? They run twenty-five minutes each."

"Please do. My name is Gabriella Emerson. I would have called ahead if I had known that reservations were needed."

The guy smiled politely again. "The gym is small, so reservations are a must even for treadmill time. They should have told you that at the front desk when you checked in."

She hadn't done the checking in because Gilbert's friend had done it for her. He'd even handed her the key.

Why had Gilbert brought him to the family dinner?

As a headache pierced her temples, Gabi rubbed at them with her thumbs.

"Are you okay?" the guy asked.

"Yeah, it's just a headache. It will clear up as soon as I start moving."

"You can wait over there." He pointed at a row of three chairs next to the pool. "Mr. Clark's session will be over in four minutes."

"Thank you." Gabi walked over to where he had pointed and sat down.

Watching the guy in the pool battling the current, she wasn't sure she could manage it unless the force of the jets was adjustable. His muscular arms powered through the stream, and as his torso lifted from side to side, she got a good view of his chest muscles as well. It was a nice view, but it wasn't nearly as magnificent as Uriel's.

You need to forget about him.

As the session ended and the guy climbed out of the pool, his powerful body dripping water, Gabi waited for that spark of attraction she should have felt for such a fine male specimen, but there was nothing. It was like looking at a store mannequin and admiring how well it was made.

I'm so screwed.

Gabi lifted her phone to check if a message had come in without her noticing it, even though it wasn't likely given that the device had been clutched in her hand the entire time, and she would have felt the vibrations.

There was nothing.

Yep, I'm royally screwed.

JADE

awn had barely broken over the horizon, the darkness slowly giving way to light, but it was still cold, and Jade zipped up her light jacket before breaking into a light jog.

It was funny how quickly she'd gotten used to the balmy weather of Southern California. Compared to how cold it was in Karelia, this was a warm summer day, but good things were easy to get used to.

They were also worth protecting.

The team should be landing in Chengdu soon, and she hoped they would proceed straight to the location of the signals instead of checking into a hotel first. She had to know whether the signals had originated with the scouts and if they were still alive or could be awoken from stasis. Talking to them might shed more light on the real purpose of the settler expedition, because Jade doubted it had been about the Kra-ell establishing a colony on Earth.

The Eternal King hadn't been the only one with plots within plots. The Kra-ell queen had been a shrewd manipulator as well.

When her phone buzzed in her jacket pocket, she pulled it out and wasn't surprised to see that it was from Kian. He was probably letting her know that the team had landed safely.

Instead, the text was an urgent summons to his office.

Jade slowed down to reread it. It didn't say why he wanted her to come as soon as she could, only that her presence was required.

Putting the phone back in the pocket, Jade changed direction and jogged the other way.

The team couldn't have discovered anything yet, so it had to be about something else, and since the biggest troublemakers were away on the mission, it wasn't about her people causing problems in the village either.

Could it be about more signals coming online?

Or maybe Syssi had had a vision about the twins?

Jade had heard the rumors about Kian's mate predicting the Kra-ell years before the first contact was made with Emmett.

Well, that wasn't accurate. The first contact had been between Stella and Vrog, and the result was Vlad, but Stella hadn't told anyone that her son's father was a hybrid alien she'd hooked up with while traveling the world.

Still, Syssi hadn't known that the Kra-ell were real until the clan found Veskar aka Emmett, but she'd written scripts about them for that Perfect Match thing.

Jade hadn't tried it out yet, and she probably wouldn't unless Phinas wanted to. She wasn't a fan of living out fantasies but would do it for him.

Love was a great motivator for doing things a sane person wouldn't have done otherwise. The queen must have loved Ahn to have a forbidden affair with him, and then she was saddled with hybrid twins she had to hide from the world because both the gods and the Kra-ell would have wanted to kill them if they found out about their mixed parentage.

The thing was, they'd looked perfectly Kra-ell when Jade had seen them entering their pods. Perhaps they were so powerful that they could use a shroud that even Kra-ell were not immune to. But if they could do that, why hide behind veils?

Maybe they couldn't maintain the illusion for long.

Yeah, that made sense. It also meant they were probably not as powerful as their grandfather feared.

As Jade rounded the bend and the café came into view, she was surprised to see several males sitting at the tables and drinking coffee in paper cups that came from the vending machines and eating prepackaged pastries. Usually, this early in the morning, the place was deserted.

She recognized some of them from the ship, which meant that they were Guardians, which also meant that village security had been beefed up.

Something was definitely going on.

With a sense of foreboding adding urgency to the summons, Jade took the stairs to the second floor of the office building two at a time and then strode down the hallway to Kian's office.

The door was open, and as she walked in and saw who else had been summoned, her sense of foreboding was confirmed.

If Kian had called her, William, Kalugal, Onegus, and Turner for a meeting at six in the morning, it wasn't to discuss trivial matters.

Most ominous of all was the presence of Brundar and Anandur. She had never seen Kian shadowed by his personal bodyguards while in the village before.

"Good morning, Jade," Kian greeted her as the others nodded. "Grab a seat. Would you like some coffee or water before we begin?"

"Thanks, but I'd rather get right to business." She sat down.

"My apologies for dragging all of you out of bed so early, but this couldn't wait. The signals are back, and this time they are coming from our backyard, so to speak—a canyon near Mount Baldy. We initiated lockdown protocols here and in the keep, and we alerted all other clan members currently residing in Scotland, Alaska, and elsewhere. Until we identify the source of these signals, we have to assume that this is an assassins' force that was somehow activated as a result of moving the Kra-ell here or because of Igor's capture and that, for some reason, their trackers are an older technology, or that the Odus misinterpreted the difference in the signals. They appear to have the ability to turn the trackers on and off at will, which means that they are not the same type as the ones the settlers and even Igor had."

"Let me recap," Turner said. "Sunday, the signals came from China, winked out, came back on again, and winked out again. The assumption was that they originated from the scouting team that had been dispatched ahead of the settler ship. Now the signals are coming from the Mount Baldy area, and they just popped up here with nothing between here and Chengdu. We assume that they belong to the other assassins that were smuggled among the settlers and that they are a slightly different technology with the ability to be turned on and off. Did I get it right so far?"

When Kian nodded, Turner looked at William. "Have they moved since they were first located in the Mount Baldy area?"

William cleared his throat. "They haven't. After the system pinged my phone, activating the alarm I'd set up, I identified the signals, but I needed the Odus's help to locate where the signals were coming from. After the Odus provided us with the coordinates, and those trackers kept broadcasting, I was able to triangulate the signals with our other receivers and keep track of them. They haven't moved. But just to confirm, we can have the Odus do another round of deciphering."

"How far from here is Mount Baldy?" Jade asked.

"It's about seventy miles from the village," Onegus said. "We are sending a drone to investigate the area before we dispatch Guardians."

Kian nodded. "It might be a trap, and I won't send our people without utilizing every precaution available to us. We are dispatching a small team with a van to launch a high-altitude surveillance drone. Charlie will remotely pilot the drone, and Roni will tend to the FAA's tracking system while we are at it."

Jade tilted her head. "Why can't you just send a small drone that flies under the radar and doesn't register on the FAA tracking system?"

"I don't want the assassins, or whoever these people are, to realize they are being watched. A small, low-altitude drone in a remote area will be clearly visible to humans, let alone Kra-ell, who possess superior vision and hearing."

Leaning back in his chair, Kalugal braced his elbow on his other arm and leaned his chin on it. "If these are the assassins from the ill-fated settlers' spaceship, where are the rest of their pod members? In my opinion, we are dealing with something or someone entirely different but somehow connected to the Kra-ell or to Igor or both."

"Like who?" William asked. "Who else could it be?"

Jade had no clue. It didn't make sense for the assassins to have a different kind of tracker than the settlers, especially given the fact that

Igor's tracker was the same as everyone else's on the ship. No one from Anumati could have arrived so quickly, either. The scouts were still the best candidates for the signal origins, but then how did they get from China to Los Angeles without their trackers transmitting in the interim?

Unless...

Unless some of the survivors had woken up a long time ago, removed their trackers so they would stop broadcasting, and then put them in again to send a message. But then, how had they known where Igor and the people he had held captive in his compound had been taken?

"It might be related to what I suspect was Igor's ability to communicate telepathically," Kian said. "And to his so-called tasting of my blood. If his primary objective was the assassination of all the legitimate heirs to the throne, and if he was somehow able to broadcast telepathically across space and time, his handlers now know that he found a direct descendant. I have human blood mixed in, but they might assume that Ahn has other descendants who are purely gods."

"They couldn't have gotten here so fast," Jade said.

"Probably not," Kian agreed. "But for all we know, the gods could have activated resources that they already had on Earth. Igor might not have been aware of being watched."

Leaning forward, Turner lifted his coffee mug. "The how of the signals' sudden appearance is certainly interesting, but for now, we need to focus on the who and what and neutralize the threat. Unless we get proof to the contrary, we must assume that each signal point is at least as dangerous to us as Igor, and since we could barely handle one, we need to figure out how to deal with three Igor-caliber adversaries at once."

KIAN

"My thoughts exactly," Onegus said. "My guys are mapping out all the locations the Kra-ell passed through while their trackers were still active, and the same goes for the gerbils that hosted them after we removed them from the Kra-ell. If we assume that the originators of the new signals can trace the trackers, and that's why they are here, all the locations those trackers passed through need to be either fortified, evacuated, or used as honey traps to draw them in. Fortunately, we made sure that no trackers made it to the village. But that still leaves the keep, our warehouse downtown, and Safe Haven."

"We are assuming that the three signals represent three people," William said. "But if the signals were turned on deliberately to flush us out, there might be many more of them who don't have trackers and are not broadcasting. The assassins might have followed the Kra-ell trackers until they were all deactivated, so they know the general location of where that was done, but they don't know who did it and where they are now. They most likely figured out that we can trace the trackers, and that's how we found Igor's compound and the Kra-ell, and since they don't know where to find us now, they are luring us in with a limited number of signals, hoping we will assume that we are missing a few Kra-ell settlers and want to collect them as well. "

William wasn't a strategist, but he was a smart guy, and his assumptions made sense, but they were incomplete. "If they saw the damage we did to the compound, they probably assumed that we took the Kra-ell by force, and to do that, we needed to have a large force with advanced weapons." Kian pushed to his feet and took his nearly empty coffee mug with him. "If they suspect the truth, that the Kra-ell rebelled and we only assisted in their liberation, they would also suspect that we have a strong compeller to free them from Igor's compulsion. But in either case, the fact that we found the Kra-ell and freed them from their trackers indicates that we are familiar with the technology and that we are capable of identifying the signals and deciphering their location."

Merlin along with Hildegard had flown to Helsinki to remove the trackers from the students who had been away at the university at the time of the attack, but unlike Sofia, the others hadn't been deemed important enough to receive the alien trackers. They had been implanted with man-made ones.

Kian refilled the mug with coffee from the carafe and returned to the table. "Also, they must assume that three signals are not going to get our panties in a wad and that we will not think twice about sending a team to investigate."

Onegus chuckled. "That's exactly what we have done. To achieve their goal, they should have remained in China instead of coming here."

"They couldn't be sure we would take the bait when the signals were far away." Kian put the mug on the table. "In fact, I was inclined to let it go. Still, they might have split forces, and some are still in China. We've alerted the team in Chengdu, and they know that the signals have moved here, but we also need to let them know we suspect there could be more than three people behind the signals."

"Right." Onegus pulled out his phone. "They should be landing shortly, and I don't want them to proceed to the location. I'm putting Yamanu on the line so he can participate in this discussion."

Kian nodded. "Good idea."

Jade's doubtful expression indicated that she disagreed. "That only makes sense if those other assassins figured out that they have trackers implanted in their bodies and removed them before the technology to build the receivers became available. Otherwise, Igor would have found them. He went after any signal he detected, and I believe he was telling the truth when he said that he collected all that had come online."

Kalugal tilted his head. "I'll tell you why that's not likely. If those were indeed other assassins from the ship, who knew how to track the signals and decipher them, they would have joined forces with Igor as soon as they found him. They wouldn't have been watching from afar to see what he was up to. They had their orders the same way he did, and given that the gods bred them for that purpose and programmed them for a specific task, they wouldn't have been able to resist contacting Igor. But if those are not the assassins, then who could they be?"

Frowning, Jade turned to Kian. "You said something before that got me thinking. What if you are right, and the gods have hidden assets on Earth that they can deploy quickly? I don't understand what purpose a hidden cell of gods could serve after determining that the exiled gods were gone, and if they were sent to observe Igor, why didn't they intervene with what he was doing?"

"We can speculate all we want," Kian said. "But without collecting more intel, we won't get any smarter. Let's take a short break and continue this in the war room.

58

SYSSI

As soon as the cobwebs of sleep receded, or maybe even before, Syssi sensed that Kian wasn't with her in bed, which worried her.

Not too long after they had gotten married, he had promised not to leave their bed before she was awake, because she hated waking up alone, and also so they could spend their mornings together. They were a bonded immortal couple, so on the face of things, they didn't need to work on keeping their marriage healthy because it was a given, but she thought it was important to grant their union a priority status.

It was so easy to get all bogged down with work, especially for Kian, and to neglect all the things that brought him pleasure, like spending time with his wife and daughter. As an immortal, he lived with the sense that there would always be time for that later, but it was an illusion, and it wasn't good for him.

First of all, Allegra wouldn't stay a baby for long, and that window of opportunity for father and daughter to bond would be missed if Kian didn't prioritize spending time with her. Secondly, the more Kian allowed himself to get sucked into the vortex of the never-ending issues and problems facing the clan, and the less quality time he spent with his family, the more agitated and dejected he became.

For the sake of everyone in the village, it was important to keep Kian's life balanced.

Touching his pillow confirmed that he had gotten up a long time ago. Sometimes he got up to check on Allegra and returned within seconds, but that wasn't the case today.

He might have thought that she hadn't noticed he couldn't fall asleep for hours or that he'd left the bed a few times and returned a few minutes later, but not from Allegra's room. She'd heard him talking in a hushed voice from the bathroom and had figured out that he'd been checking up on the team he'd sent to China.

They were still en route, and it wasn't like Kian to be so worried about the flight. Morris was a capable pilot, and the clan maintained its jets expertly, so a malfunction wasn't likely.

Perhaps he'd gotten more information about the signals at night?

He was probably in his office, and she could make them both cappuccinos and bring them there so they could at least salvage that part of their morning routine.

After a much-needed visit to the bathroom, Syssi checked Allegra's room first. Finding her daughter peacefully asleep, she walked down the hallway to Kian's office.

When she didn't find him there, she sat behind his desk, picked up the receiver, and called him.

"Good morning, my love," Kian answered. "What are you doing awake this early?"

"That's what I want to know. Where are you?"

"I'm on my way to the war room from an emergency meeting in my office."

Her stomach twisted in knots. "What happened?"

"The signals are back, and this time they are broadcasting from an area about an hour away from the village. Right now, that's all I know. I'll call you as soon as I know more. In the meantime, the village is in lockdown, so you can stay in bed longer because no one is leaving."

"Does Amanda know?"

"She will when she wakes up and checks her messages. I have to go, love. I'll call you later."

As the call ended, Syssi put the receiver down and leaned back in Kian's chair.

Why had he ordered a lockdown?

Three signals meant three people. Even if they were assassins, the Guardians could deal with them.

What wasn't Kian telling her?

Could the Doomers be involved somehow? Was it possible that they had discovered one of the missing pods?

She wouldn't put it past them to kill the twenty Kra-ell in the pod, dig out the trackers from the bodies, and then use them to lure Guardians into a trap.

Navuh hadn't launched a direct attack on the clan in far too long, and he was overdue.

No, that wasn't a likely scenario.

Lokan would have warned them of an impending attack, and even if he didn't know about it, Andrew would have known if a large group of foreign nationals had entered the city and would have checked them out.

But that was provided they had arrived at one of the major airports. If they had landed somewhere else and had used ground transportation to get to Los Angeles, Andrew wouldn't know about them.

Fates, Syssi hoped it wasn't the Doomers.

Even with all their genetically enhanced features, a few Kra-ell assassins worried her much less than Navuh and his legions of vicious warriors.

5 9

KIAN

The call from Syssi had kept Kian out of the war room for a couple of minutes, and as he entered, the others were already seated around the table.

He'd hoped not to see that room for a long time, but he should have known better. It was like a game of whack-a-mole. He would barely get one crisis under control when a new one popped up.

As Anandur distributed water bottles, Kian sat down next to Kalugal.

Given the situation, he would have preferred a few shots of whiskey, but it was too early in the morning even for an immortal who had been born and raised in Scotland.

Kalugal removed the cap from the bottle Anandur handed him. "Since my men are stuck in the village along with everyone else, they might as well help out. I'm placing them under Onegus's command."

"Thank you." Kian gave him a nod of approval. "I appreciate the offer, but I hope we won't need the reinforcements. Can't your guys work from home? You have everything you need in your house to run your empire from here."

"True, true." Kalugal's lips lifted in a barely-there smirk. "But someone told me that my men have gotten soft and need more training.

Not that I accept the unflattering assessment. They made me proud in Karelia."

Kian sincerely doubted that Kalugal's reason for volunteering his men was that he wanted them to train. That could have been achieved by talking to Bhathian, who was in charge of the training, and coming up with a schedule of classes for the men.

"A skill is like a knife." Kian removed the cap from his bottle. "If it's not regularly honed and sharpened, it becomes dull."

"I agree," Jade said. "My people train regularly, and a group of pure-blooded females has joined the Guardians to train for the rescue operations. Other than the former prisoners, every adult member of the Kra-ell community is at your disposal."

Considering, Kian nodded. "Thank you, but don't share the particulars with them yet. Not before we know more." He turned to Kalugal. "Same goes for your men. I'm keeping it on the down low with my people as well. We don't want the civilians to panic."

Behind them, Turner chuckled. "With the village in lockdown, and all the able fighters on alert, that ship has sailed. Not knowing the nature of the threat, they will assume the worst, and you'll have the entire village banked up outside your office window, waiting to hear what's going on. I recommend bringing everyone up to speed and posting updates on the clan's virtual bulletin board."

That was atypical of Turner, who was always security first, but he had a point.

Kian glanced at William. "Did you send the group text already?"

William shook his head. "When? I haven't had time to do it yet, but I planned to follow your suggestion and keep it as vague as possible. I will only mention the keep's location being compromised and this being a safety precaution, without providing more details." He looked at Turner. "Should I say more?"

"No, that's good. Keep it vague, but not so much that people will imagine the worst." Turner pulled out his phone. "I need to alert my office that I cannot come in until further notice."

"Can't you work remotely?" Kian asked. "Your work involves saving lives, and I don't want them on my conscience. If your presence is essential at your office, I will make an exception for you and let you leave."

"It's fine." Turner waved a dismissive hand. "I can work from here. It will put more strain on my office staff, but they can handle it. Fortunately, I don't have anything urgent right now. My current mission is in the initial planning stages, and it's not a life-or-death situation, so I can make this my priority and start working on contingencies and strategies."

"That's good." Kian let out a breath. "I need your brain working on this, especially once we have more information."

Turner nodded. "On the way here, I thought about Jade's suggestion to fly a small surveillance drone, and I think that's a good idea."

Kian thought it was a terrible idea. "Why? That would alert them to our presence."

"Precisely." Turner tapped his pen on his yellow pad. "Think of it as a chess game. They made their first move, moving a pawn on the board, meaning the signals. We will respond in kind, sending a pawn of our own to signal that we are ready to play the game, meaning the small drone they will have no problem seeing. It's much better than sending in a knight or a bishop, don't you think?"

60

SYSSI

After getting dressed, Syssi walked into the kitchen, where Okidu was expertly flipping an omelet.

"Good morning, Okidu." She walked up to the stove. "That smells good." Usually, he made her omelet from real eggs and Kian's from an egg substitute, but since Kian wasn't home, it was only real eggs.

"Good morning, mistress." He bowed. "Your breakfast is almost ready. I added plenty of spinach and feta cheese, just as you like."

"Thank you. I'm sure it's delicious, but I'm not hungry yet." When he looked mortified, she amended, "I need to check on Allegra, and when she wakes up, I will eat breakfast with her. Can you put it in the warming drawer for me?"

That brought a smile to his face. "Of course, mistress."

When he turned his attention back to the skillet, it dawned on Syssi that she wouldn't be heading to work this morning and that Amanda probably didn't know about the lockdown yet. Her sister-in-law was probably still asleep.

Pulling her phone from her pocket, she typed a message to her sister-in-law.

Good morning. I don't want to alarm you, but in case you don't know yet, the village is locked down, and we can't go to the university today. Do you want me to call the lab and let our team know?

There was no reason to expect Amanda to respond anytime soon, so Syssi placed her phone on the counter and replayed what Kian had told her. The three signals were now coming from a nearby location, and it could be a trap.

He hadn't said that, but he hadn't needed to. Obviously, those people had gotten nearer to lure the clan into a trap. Hopefully, it was as clear to Kian and his team as it was to her, and they were being careful and not sending Guardians to investigate without doing an aerial sweep of the area first.

Should she call him? Or maybe text him?

Would he be upset that she was telling him how to do his job?

Kian was usually good about taking advice from her. Still, when he was stressed, especially about the clan's safety, he turned into a caveman, listening only to people he considered experts on security and strategy, meaning Onegus and Turner and sometimes Andrew.

He'd promised to call her as soon as he knew more, but he'd either forgotten or there was no new information, and she was so anxious that she was starting to hyperventilate.

Perhaps she should take a few minutes to relax before Allegra woke up to a stressed-out mom. A cappuccino would be a step in the right direction. Unlike most people, Syssi found caffeine relaxing rather than stimulating, and the ritual of preparing the perfect cup was calming in itself.

The familiar movements, the thumping sounds of the machine, the aroma permeating the room.

As she'd expected, preparing the cup had reduced her stress level by at least twenty percent, and as she took it with her to the family room and sat on the comfortable couch, she closed her eyes and imagined a placid lake bathed in moonlight. Usually, that was enough to calm her down, but not today.

Ravenous sharks lurked beneath the deceptively tranquil waters, and owls hooted ominously from the trees swaying prettily in the breeze.

Having a vivid imagination was a double-edged sword.

To achieve calmness, she needed to clear her mind from all thoughts, which was incredibly difficult, and she still struggled with it even after all the lessons she'd had with Madame Salinka and the many hours of practice since.

Setting the coffee down, Syssi started the slow, practiced breathing and repeated the meditative sound in her mind. After a while, she found herself floating aimlessly among the clouds with little or no thoughts at all.

Peace.

As the clouds thinned and the view below came into focus, some part of Syssi was aware that she wasn't meditating. This was a vision, but it lacked the ominous nature of most of her doomsday predictions.

She felt light as a feather and without a care in the world.

The canyon below wasn't pretty. The vegetation was sparse, the creek at its bottom was dry, and the soil looked parched, with cracked veins running through its dusty, yellow surface, but there was nothing unusual about it. This was Southern California on the cusp of summer. It hadn't rained in a while, and things had dried out pretty quickly despite the heavy rainfall of the preceding months.

As movement ahead drew her attention, she floated forward.

Below, three men were arguing, gesticulating with their hands, and getting in each other's faces like three bucks competing for the favors of one doe. She couldn't hear what they were arguing about, but it seemed important.

As she drew nearer, the men raised their heads and seemed to stare straight at her.

Even in the hazy dream-like world of a vision, Syssi knew they couldn't see or even sense her, but the impulse to fly away and hide was strong. They must be looking at something behind her, but she couldn't see it. She could only see them and the canyon they were in.

It wasn't the first time Syssi realized that she was being shown only a fraction of the experience, and that some things remained outside her perception without any rhyme or reason. Sometimes it was sounds, other times it was part of the scenery, and in still others it was any identifying features of the main players.

When one of the men lifted a strange-looking cylinder and pointed it at her, Syssi gasped and recoiled, thinking it was a monocular and that he was trying to get a better look at her, but then the one standing next to him grabbed his wrist and pushed his arm down.

At that instant, Syssi realized that the cylindrical tool was a weapon of some sort, and that the man who had pointed it at her was about to shoot something that was flying either behind or above her.

The third realization was that the weapon was not from Earth, and neither were the three males.

61

GABI

When Gabi returned to her room, every muscle in her body was aching. Swimming against the current had been difficult, requiring the use of muscles she must have neglected during her workouts with Becky. Usually, she would have welcomed the ache because it meant that her muscles were getting stronger, but today it just added to the feeling of exhaustion that had nothing to do with physical activity and everything to do with the lack of a message from Uriel.

Even Gilbert hadn't called her yet, and there was no way he was still sleeping.

Leaving both her regular phone and the clan phone on the bathroom vanity, she stepped into the shower and made quick work of shampooing and conditioning her hair, washing the pool chlorine off, all while listening intently so she wouldn't miss an incoming call or message.

Except, none came during the shower or while she toweled off and blow-dried her hair.

It was after nine in the morning, and the day was wasted.

After making herself another cup of coffee, Gabi sat on the couch and looked at both phones, contemplating Becky's advice and whether she was going to listen to it or ignore it.

If life had taught her anything, it was that leaving the initiative to others was never a good plan. If she wanted Uriel or just wanted to hear from him, she should contact him and not wait for him to do it first.

On the other hand, what was the point of dragging this out when she would have to disappear soon?

Perhaps she should just say goodbye one last time?

Well, first she needed to call Gilbert and find out when he was coming to pick her up. Perhaps Uriel was done with his first meeting of the day and had time to meet her for breakfast?

But even if he could, it was such a bad idea. She was just prolonging their parting and making it more difficult for herself, but she couldn't help it.

She just needed to see him one last time, or at least try to.

Damn, why was it so hard?

He was supposed to be just a hookup, and he'd been a wonderful one. Why did she have to ruin it by wanting more?

Grabbing the white not-iPhone, she lifted it to her face to unlock it, found Gilbert's contact, and called him.

"Hi, Gabi," he answered right away. "How are you doing?"

"Great," she affected a cheerful tone. "I went for a swim in the exercise pool they have here in the hotel. I didn't know how hard it was to swim against a current. I'm aching all over. Anyway, when are you picking me up?"

He groaned. "I'm not. The village is in lockdown, and no one is coming or going."

Anxiety tightening a vise around her heart, Gabi forced herself to take a deep breath. "Please tell me it's a drill, and nothing terrible is happening."

The clan had enemies. The Doomers. What if they had launched an attack? What would happen to her family?

"It's nothing to worry about," Gilbert said. "A different clan location was potentially compromised, and Kian is not taking any chances with security, so he ordered both locations locked down. He's known to be a little paranoid, or a lot, so he's probably overreacting. I expect the village will open up in a few hours, but it sucks that we are missing out

235

on the one day you had for us. Is there any way you can postpone your return flight? Can you at least stay over the weekend?"

His explanation alleviated some of her anxiety, but was he telling her the truth? Gilbert and Eric thought they were shielding her from worry by not telling her stuff, but it only made her worry more because she expected them to hide things from her.

"Tell me the truth, Gilbert. Are you really in no danger?"

"I told you everything I know. Do you think I would be asking you to stay longer if I thought I might be putting you in danger?"

He had a point.

It would take some maneuvering to reschedule the sessions she had arranged for Thursday and Friday, or she could turn them into virtual meetings. After all, she'd flown across the country to visit her family, and if she didn't get to do that, it would be such a waste of money and effort. So yeah, she'd seen most of them already, but it had been only a few hours, and she hadn't seen Idina yet.

Besides, if she stayed longer, she could see Uriel again.

"I'll check what can be done about the return flight. I can't go back without visiting the village, and seeing your new homes, and meeting the rest of Darlene's family. I didn't even get to see Idina."

"What about your clients?"

"I'll have to make up a good excuse for why I have to meet with them virtually and not in person and give them some sort of bonus in exchange for the inconvenience."

"That's great. We will have the entire weekend to spend together. Karen and the kids are going to be so happy."

"Don't tell them yet. I don't know if I can get a return flight Sunday evening or Monday morning at the same price, and secondly, what if your village remains in lockdown for more than a day or two?"

"All we can do is hope for the best. Check the flight situation and get back to me. Perhaps the lockdown will be canceled by the time you call."

"I hope so."

Well, at this point, she hoped the lockdown would remain in effect for a little longer. Otherwise, she would have no reason to postpone her return flight and wouldn't get to see Uriel again.

236

KALUGAL

Kalugal stared at the large screen mounted on the war room's east wall and the images the drone was broadcasting—rocks, dry soil, and a few scattered bushes.

"What are we looking at?" he asked.

"A lot of nothing." Kian groaned and leaned back. "I don't understand. The trackers are still sending signals, the Odus gave us the precise coordinates, and they are supposed to be right there, but there is nothing alive in that spot, not even gerbils."

"We can't be sure of that," Onegus said. "The resolution is insufficient to show very small animals, especially if they have the same coloring as the surroundings." He looked at William. "Could it be that some of the gerbils got away from our downtown warehouse before you removed the trackers from them?"

William shook his head. "All the trackers are accounted for. Merlin kept meticulous records, noting each tracker and who it had belonged to before taking it out. I compared our records, and they match. Well, we have four more trackers because we also removed them from Igor, Sofia, and the two hybrids that had been following her when she was at Safe Haven."

"Is there a way to enhance the resolution?" Kian asked.

"I'm running it through AI." William turned his laptop around so they could all see his screen. "There is nothing there."

The drone had spent over an hour in the air filming, and then it had to go back to change batteries.

"We should have sent two drones," Kalugal grumbled. "While one was recharging, the other one could have been filming."

"So we could stare at more rocks?" Kian rose to his feet. "They must have a way to activate the trackers without using a live host, and they buried them in the ground to set a trap for us while they are hiding and waiting to see who will show up. I wouldn't be surprised if they mounted several cameras nearby and are observing from afar."

That actually made sense.

Why risk a face-to-face confrontation if the objective was only to find out who they were dealing with?

"The drone was a long shot," William said. "But we can learn something from there being nothing." He smiled at Kian. "If they wanted to flush us out by luring us into the canyon just to record who showed up, then they don't have a large force. Otherwise, they would have attempted to capture whoever was sent to investigate so they could interrogate them to learn what they need to know."

"My thoughts exactly," Kalugal said. "Except, I don't know what they hope to achieve by taking pictures or filming other than to satisfy their curiosity. What were they hoping to see? Whether the people showing up were Kra-ell or humans? I'm sure they weren't expecting gods or immortals. Unless these people came with a huge force, which, as William astutely noted, is doubtful, it would be stupid of them to reveal their presence just to gather intelligence."

Knowing that someone took over a large and well-defended Kra-ell settlement halfway around the world and also outmaneuvered and entrapped Igor must have worried the signal originators. They needed to find out who was behind such a complex, large-scale operation.

They had followed Igor's signal to Los Angeles, and when his tracker stopped broadcasting, they'd become desperate and announced their presence.

It was such a stupid move that Kalugal was sure he and the rest of their team were missing a big piece of the puzzle and that they had gotten the situation all wrong.

Could it be that the signals' owners were not adversaries?

For the move to be calculated rather than stupid, they had to want to establish contact without making a move that would seem aggressive, and the only possible form of communication they could establish with the Kra-ell liberators was the trackers.

They were being cautious and wanted the parley to be done on their terms and on their turf.

If Kalugal was in their shoes, and he wanted to make contact with a superior force, hoping for an amicable reception but not certain of it, he would have orchestrated a meeting at a place and time of his choosing, and in circumstances that negated the other side's strength and size advantage.

He turned to Kian. "Let's consider a different angle for a moment."

"Like what?" Kian asked.

"What if these people's objective is to seek our cooperation and help? If we assume that the signal broadcasters are aware of what we did in Karelia and that we captured Igor, then they are also aware of our operational capabilities. Why announce their arrival if they want to attack? And if their plan was to kidnap one or more of us for interrogation, that also would have been better accomplished covertly. If they tracked Igor and the Kra-ell, they would know all the locations that the trackers broadcasted from, including Safe Haven, the keep, and the clan's downtown warehouse. It would have been much easier for them to lie in wait for a clan member to appear at one of those locations and grab them."

Kian nodded. "It occurred to me that if I was in their position and had adversarial intentions, I would not have advertised my presence. But then that's my preferred modus operandi."

"Mine too," Kalugal said. "And we are both smart guys, right? We shouldn't assume that these people are stupid, and that's why I think they want to meet. But since they don't know what we are about and how we will respond, they want to control the circumstances of this meeting in a way that levels the playing field and negates our superior numbers, or what they think are our superior numbers. There could be more of them than there are of us."

SYSSI

"You should tell Kian about your vision," Amanda said. "What if it's connected to the signals?"

William had sent a text explaining that the lockdown was a precaution because the keep's location had been compromised, but he hadn't elaborated. Syssi had filled in the blanks for Annani, Alena, and Amanda as best she could, but she didn't know much herself.

"I don't want to bother him." Syssi handed Allegra a piece of bread to chew on. "You know what my visions are like. This could be something that happens hundreds of years from now or happened hundreds of years in the past. I don't even know if the vision was from a place on Earth."

It looked like Southern California, but it could have been an alien planet.

"What were they wearing?" Alena asked. "That could give us a clue."

Syssi frowned. "I don't remember. That's another thing about visions. Details that should be obvious are missing. They could have been wearing space suits or jeans. The only thing that was clearly visible to me was that weapon, and it didn't even look like a weapon. It looked like a monocular, not a gun, but I knew it was dangerous." She looked at Amanda. "Besides, we need to get busy. Alena came over to babysit Evie and Allegra so we could put in a few hours of work, and we are wasting her time."

Alena shrugged. "I don't mind just chatting with you two. It's not like I have anything more interesting to do."

"La-la," Allegra said.

Alena smiled. "Yes, sweetie?"

"We-we."

Syssi laughed. "She knows who she can bribe to let her watch her favorite show, *The Wiggles*."

When her phone rang with Kian's ringtone, she glanced at Alena. "Can you watch Allegra for a few minutes while I take this?"

"Of course." Alena waved her away. "Go, talk to Kian and get him to tell us what's going on."

"I'll do my best." Syssi pushed to her feet and walked over to the bedroom to talk in private.

Closing the door behind her, she accepted the call. "Hi, love. How is your day going?"

"Much better now that I hear your voice. It's a balm for my frayed nerves."

He'd said that so many times before that it shouldn't have affected her as much anymore, but she still loved hearing it.

"I'm glad I can help in some way." She sat on the couch. "Do you have time to talk now?"

"Yeah. I took a short break, and I'm out in the hallway, pacing back and forth. I need to compose a text to let everyone know what's really going on, and I thought that you could probably do a better job of phrasing it in a way that wouldn't induce panic but would be less vague than what William sent earlier."

"To do that, you need to tell me more. All I know is that the signals that previously came from China suddenly appeared nearby."

"They are coming from a location near Mount Baldy. We sent a team with a drone to investigate, but there was no one there. I'll have to summon the Odus again to check whether the signals are still coming from the same location. If they do, then our mystery visitors buried the trackers in the ground to lure us there, but we don't know for what purpose. The drone circled the entire area, so we knew that no one was there to ambush us, and it was not like there was anywhere to hide. It's pretty barren, and the bushes are only big enough to hide a gerbil, and probably not even that."

Syssi frowned. "The alien trackers need live hosts. So maybe they are inside a small animal, and the poor thing is tied to one of those bushes, or maybe in a cage that is covered in dirt."

"I didn't think of that, but I guess it's possible. It's also possible that the older model trackers were more versatile and could operate without a live host. They were also able to turn them on and off at will, which is not how the newer ones work."

"How did they know where to find us?"

"The keep's location was compromised when we brought Igor in without removing his tracker first. We thought he was the danger, and once we had him, we no longer needed to worry about the trackers. I'm just glad that I didn't allow any of them in the village."

"So, if the village location hasn't been compromised, there is no reason for a lockdown here. We are not in danger."

"I can't risk it before I know what and who we are dealing with. Especially not with my mother here."

Kian was always worried about Annani, but Syssi doubted that the goddess was his main concern this time.

"Right." She pushed a strand of hair behind her ear. "She's quite peeved at you for not telling her about the signals. After the text from William, I told your mother and sisters what I knew, but it wasn't much."

"I didn't have time to talk to her. All the usual suspects are in the war room, and we are trying to figure out what to do next. Can you tell my mother that I will call her as soon as I know more?"

"Of course."

"And can you also compose a message explaining the situation?"

"Sure. Amanda is here, and she can help me with that. Alena is babysitting Allegra and Evie, so we can do some remote work."

"Thank you. You are the best."

"Yeah, yeah." She laughed. "By the way, I had a strange vision that may or may not have something to do with your signals."

There was a long moment of silence before Kian spoke. "Did you force it?"

Syssi rolled her eyes. "I promised you that I wouldn't do that, and I didn't. I was anxious because you'd left before I woke up, and when I called you, you sounded stressed, so of course, I got stressed as well. I didn't want Allegra to pick up on those negative vibes, so I meditated, and the vision just came."

"Oh, so it's my fault."

Her mate sounded like he was chewing on gravel, which was sexy when they were playing their kinky games, but intimidating and annoying at other times.

"Will you stop and listen?"

"I'm all ears." He still sounded like he was chewing rocks.

"I was meditating and doing some breathing exercises to relax, and that actually helped. I felt calm and collected."

"When did the vision start, and what did you see?"

"Oh, so now you want to hear all about it when a moment ago you sounded like you wanted to spank me for being a naughty girl."

He chuckled. "Is that an invitation?"

"No. I'm upset with you, but since you are under a lot of pressure, I'll forgive you this time."

"You always forgive me," he said softly. "I don't deserve you."

64

KIAN

"You deserve everything, my love. Everything I have to give and more."

That hit Kian straight in the chest, and he lifted his hand to place it over his heart. "I'm so blessed, and I don't know what I did to deserve winning the lottery of life with you. You make it all worthwhile."

"We are both blessed," Syssi said. "Now, do you want to hear about my vision or not?"

"Yes, please. Although, frankly, I would rather come home and take you to bed."

He was still hard like a hammer from their little kinky exchange and thankful that he had stepped out of the war room to make the call, not just because his slacks sported a tent but also because he was over-whelmed with gratitude and love, and he probably looked like a sap right now.

Syssi laughed. "What is different about today? That's how you end every conversation with me."

He frowned. "Do I?"

Was he that predictable?

That unoriginal?

"Well, not every conversation, but most."

Kian sighed. "That's because I always want you, but since I can't have you right now, tell me about your vision."

"You said that the signals are coming from somewhere near Mount Baldy, right?"

"Yes."

"And you also said that you flew a drone over the area and didn't find anyone, right?"

"Well, technically, Charlie flew the drone, but yeah. There was nothing but rocks and dried-up bushes. Where are you going with this?"

Was he missing something that Syssi found obvious?

"Just bear with me for a moment. Are the signals coming from a canyon that's not near any paved road?"

Kian's blood chilled in his veins. "Is that a guess? Or do you know that for a fact?"

She laughed. "I'm a seer, darling. I've seen that canyon. You probably think that you are dealing with Kra-ell assassins, either from one of the pods or from another ship, and you are assuming that their sudden appearance here is related to either Igor's capture, the Kra-ell's move here, or both."

For some reason, Syssi was dragging it out. He would have thought that what she'd seen in her vision was so terrible that she needed to prepare him for it, but she sounded way too cheerful for that to be the case. In fact, she sounded as if she was almost amused and was trying not to offend him by revealing what she'd seen.

Could it be that William had miscalculated, and what they were getting from the canyon were the signals from escaped gerbils?

Did gerbils hibernate?

Maybe they had been in hibernation and had just awoken. Or maybe the gerbils had been eaten by a larger animal who had then gone into hibernation and had just woken up.

"I don't want to sound impatient, but just tell me already. I can't stand the suspense."

"Okay." She let out a breath as if she was disappointed that he hadn't given her the time to prepare her story for maximum impact. "While I was meditating, I found myself flying over a wilderness scored by deep canyons and ravines. The vegetation was sparse and seemed very similar to what we see in the mountains surrounding the village during the summer months. In one such canyon, I saw three men arguing about something. One of them held up what looked like a slim monocular, but I knew that it was a weapon, and I also knew that it was not manmade. Unless it was a movie prop made to look like an alien weapon, it was indeed of alien origins."

Kian stopped in his tracks. "Can you describe it in more detail?"

"It looked like a slim metal cylinder with a lens at the end. I didn't see telescoping parts, but it grew longer when the man held it up and aimed at an object that didn't register in my vision. For a moment, I thought that they could see me, but they were all looking at something behind me. I didn't know what it was, but it might have been your drone. When the one holding the weapon trained it on the thing that they saw that wasn't me, another one held onto his wrist and prevented him from shooting it."

"Hold on. I need to text Charlie to tell him to do another fly-by."

"But you said that the drone didn't see anything."

Kian finished typing the text. "I think that your vision was precognition, and you saw a couple of hours ahead. Three guys in a remote canyon not too far from the city, looking up at a drone and holding something that looked like an alien weapon, is too much of a coincidence. They have to be the ones we are looking for. When they all looked up towards you, were you close enough to see their faces? Any distinct features?"

There was a long moment of silence. "Hold on. I'm closing my eyes."

He frowned. "Did you see them or not?"

"Visions are funky, Kian. Sometimes they are clear, sometimes they are not, and sometimes details become clearer later on. I saw their faces when I was hovering above them, but they didn't register. But now that I close my eyes, I can see them clearly."

"Well?" he prompted.

"They were definitely not Kra-ell assassins." Syssi sounded very certain of that.

But who else could they be?

Their original suspicion had been that the signals originated from the scouts, but there would be no difference in appearance between them and the assassins. They both had to look the same as other pure-blooded Kra-ell, and they were hard to confuse for anyone else. They didn't look human, but then Jade and her consorts had traveled the world and had done business with humans using minimal disguises like dark sunglasses and clothing that had hidden their extremely narrow waists.

"Perhaps they were disguised to look more human? Who other than the Kra-ell could have had those alien trackers and emitted signals?"

All of a sudden, Kian knew the answer to his questions, but it was too outrageous to consider seriously.

"Well, weren't the trackers implanted in the Kra-ell by the gods?" Syssi asked rhetorically. "After all, the technology was developed by the gods and implemented by them as well. How else would the Odus know how to decipher the signals from those trackers?"

"Are you telling me that the three men you saw in the canyon were gods?"

"That is exactly what I am saying. I know a god when I see one, and the three men in the canyon were stunningly beautiful and inhumanly perfect. Also, I don't think that their intentions are nefarious. I am not sure what I am basing this on, and I might be biased because we are related, which kind of makes us on the same team, but I have a strong feeling that they are friendlies, not adversaries."

Syssi had never been wrong before, but she might be this time.

"We know that not all gods are nice people, but we have an innate bias towards beauty. We are programmed to perceive it as something good. We must proceed with extreme caution and assume a defensive position as if we are facing adversaries, including keeping the village locked down until we can confirm that these males are friendly and mean us no harm."

From all he had learned about the gods recently, Kian expected the worst rather than the best.

"I trust your instincts, my love, and I agree that we should proceed with extreme caution, but we should not be the aggressors unless we are forced to be."

"I can promise you that we won't shoot first and ask questions later,

247

but I can also promise you that we will be armed with everything we have and ready to use it if need be."

"That's smart. Perhaps you should bring the noise cannon to the canyon. I still remember what that thing did to a large group of immortals. If not for the drones and other precautions, those supposedly weak humans could have picked us off like flies and driven us away to their testing facility."

Kian felt his fangs punching over his lower lip. "I don't like to think about that evening, but you are absolutely right. The noise cannon could be a formidable weapon against gods with sensitive hearing. They heal incredibly fast, but a few seconds might make all the difference."

Syssi chuckled softly. "My intention wasn't to rile you up, just to offer one more defensive idea. I know that you need to get back to the war room, so I won't keep you. Keep me updated if you can and try to come home before Allegra goes to sleep tonight. She needs a hug from Daddy to have good dreams, and so do I."

And just like that, his fangs had receded, and a smile replaced his snarl. "I will do my best to get home in time to kiss Allegra goodnight and to take her mommy to bed. You might find it hard to believe, but I'm more excited about that than discovering three new gods, even friendly ones."

She laughed. "You're so bad."

"I know. But you love me anyway."

"I do."

65

GABI

Gabi read over the text she'd written to Uriel.

Something came up, and I won't be spending the day with my family after all. I also changed my return flight from Wednesday evening to Monday morning, and since I will be staying four days longer than I originally planned, I thought it would be nice if we could hang out together some more. You never told me how long you would be staying in L.A., but if you're going to be here over the weekend, we could go to the beach or visit The Huntington Library, and if you have a car, we can even drive up to Solvang and visit some wineries.

There was so much more she wanted to say to him, but first, she needed him to respond to her text so she would know that he was still interested.

She was already going out on a limb by contacting him, she wasn't also going to admit that he had rocked her world and probably ruined her for any other man.

Or male.

She doubted the immortals Darlene had gushed over could compete with Uriel. He was simply incomparable.

Her hand shook only a little as she pressed enter, and the text was sent.

Now it was only a matter of waiting, but as she looked at the screen, the three little dots didn't appear. He wasn't texting her back.

Perhaps he was in a meeting and couldn't answer.

The text was marked as delivered, but that didn't mean he'd read it, only that it was on his phone, tablet, or any other device capable of accepting texts.

When over two hours had passed with no return text, Gabi had to accept that Uriel was ghosting her.

But why?

Why was he acting like that?

After the two nights they had spent together, he could at least come up with a good lie to let her down easily. He could tell her that he had to fly back to Portugal because of an emergency back home, or that he'd heard of a hidden treasure in Nepal or some other exotic location and had to leave right away to chase it.

She would have known that he was lying, and he would have known that she knew, but it would have been better than this silence.

What if something had happened to him?

As images of car crashes and armed robberies zipped through her mind, her chest constricted with panic, and she had trouble catching her breath.

A brave warrior of God, my ass. She used anger to quash the panic.

Gabi was mad at herself for always imagining the worst, mad at Uriel for being a jerk, and mad at whatever circumstances had forced the immortals' village into lockdown.

How did they even do that? Was there a big wall around the village and a moat filled with hungry sharks, and a bridge that they could lift to prevent anyone from coming in or leaving?

She'd always had a vivid imagination, but most of the time, it didn't produce anything fun. It was mostly about imagining the worst thing that could happen and getting a panic attack.

Becky had said she should speak to a psychiatrist and get something to help with her anxiety, but Gabi hated the idea of chemicals altering her mind.

It wasn't logical since everything in the body was affected by hormones and by gut bacteria, and those were all chemicals, but they were naturally occurring, and they usually worked gradually. She didn't want to take a pill and become instantly carefree and cheerful.

That just wouldn't be her, and she didn't want to lose her identity, no matter how screwed up that identity was.

Would she still be so fearful when she became immortal?

Probably not.

Knowing that her brothers were immortal now and she wasn't going to lose them had already slashed her usual anxiety by at least half, probably more, and if she found an immortal male she could fall in love with, her fearfulness would be all gone.

What scared her more than anything was losing the people she loved.

Maybe Uriel was doing her a favor by ghosting her.

She didn't need to fall in love with a human and live in constant fear of losing him.

When her phone rang, she snatched it off the table and answered it without checking who it was.

She just knew it was Uriel.

"Hi," she said. "I thought you were ghosting me."

"I'm sorry I couldn't answer right away. What happened to your plans to spend the day with your family?"

"My brothers can't make it." She couldn't tell him the real reason because she was under compulsion to keep everything about immortals and their village a secret. Besides, the truth was more unbelievable than any lie she could make up. "They had a business emergency. I didn't ask for details because they wouldn't have told me. They still think of me as their baby sister who needs to be shielded."

He chuckled. "Yeah, you told me. What about the rest of your family? Your nieces and nephews? Don't you want to spend time with them?"

Damn, how could she possibly excuse that?

"I do, but it's not going to be the same without my brothers. I changed my return flight, so I could see all of them together once that emergency is over." She paused and took a deep breath. "And also, so I could spend time with you."

Gabi held her breath as she waited for him to say something, anything.

251

It seemed like long minutes had passed until he did. "I would love to spend more time with you, but right now, I don't know when I can. The business deal my partners and I are working on is very complicated and might involve travel."

Gabi swallowed.

It sounded just like the kind of polite excuse she would have devised to let a guy down easily.

"When will you know?"

"It could be by tonight, or it might take a few days. I'll call you as soon as I can."

"Okay." She swallowed the lump in her throat. "I just want you to know that I enjoyed being with you. Whatever happens, I'm glad that I met you, and I'm glad we had those two nights together. I will remember them fondly."

Again, there was a long moment of silence. "Is that a goodbye?"

"You tell me."

"Not if I can help it."

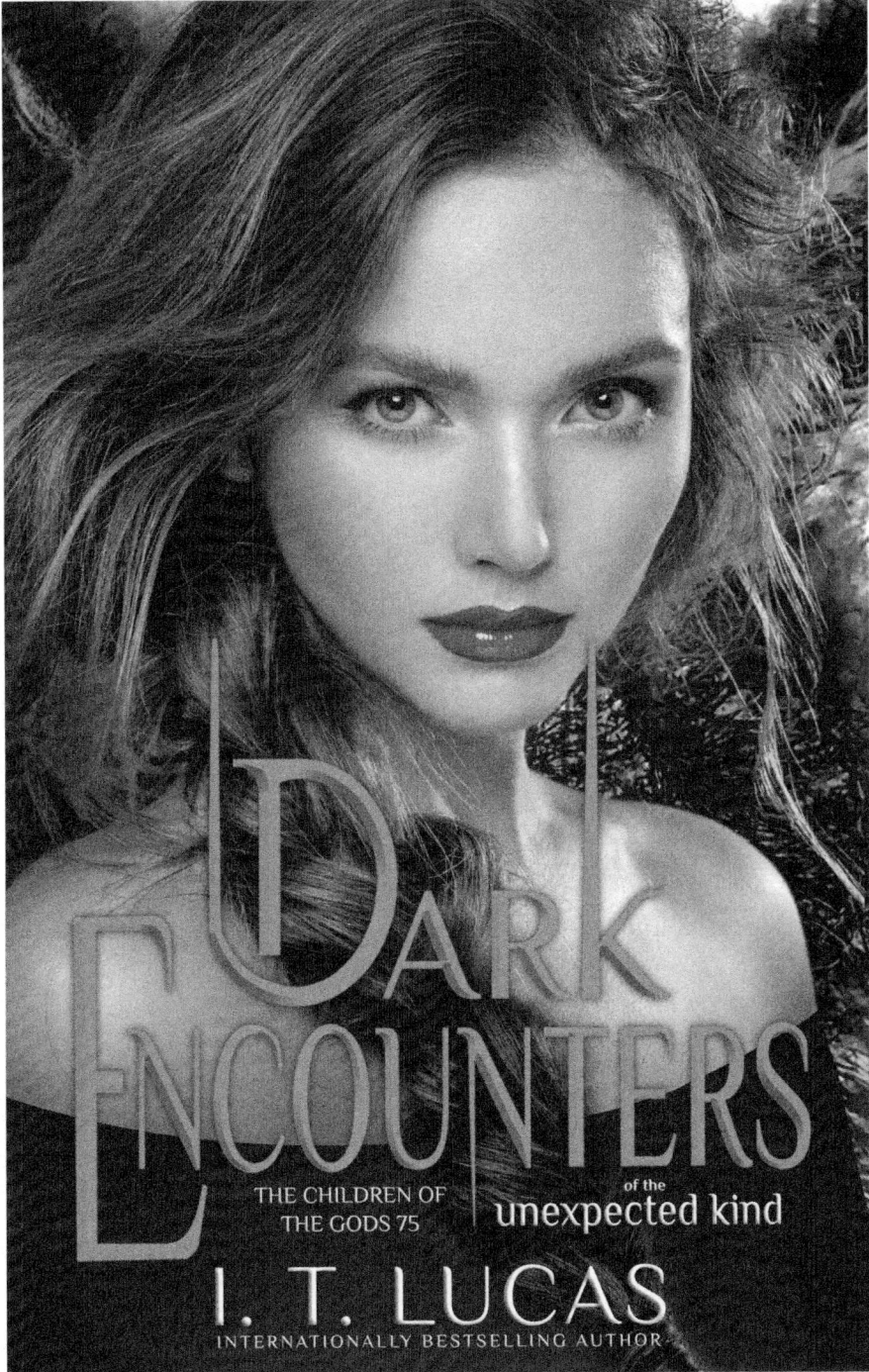

DARK ENCOUNTERS

THE CHILDREN OF
THE GODS 75

of the
unexpected kind

I. T. LUCAS

INTERNATIONALLY BESTSELLING AUTHOR

1

ARU

"This wasn't one of your smarter ideas." Dagor's voice was tinged with barely veiled annoyance.

"Really?" Aru arched a brow. "I thought it was quite clever."

Dagor swiveled his laptop toward him. "Instead of showing up in person, they sent a drone to scout the area, and now they know it was a ruse and that we are not there."

It had seemed like a great idea to plant the trackers in the remote canyon, put a couple of surveillance bugs in place, and watch who showed up.

Aru shrugged. "How was I supposed to know that they would do that?"

The mysterious abductors or perhaps rescuers of the Kra-ell had outsmarted him, but that didn't mean that the move had been a waste of time and effort. Getting a drone instead of people was disappointing, and he still didn't know who they were, but at least they had shown up in some form, which meant that the trackers had done their job.

"I told you they wouldn't fall for that." Dagor let out a breath. "If you were in their position, would you have rushed to investigate the sudden emergence of new signals without taking every precaution you could think of?"

"I wouldn't." Aru had to admit that he had wagered on the abductors or rescuers taking the bait, but he'd known it was a long shot. "It was a gamble, and it was worth a try. The good news is that we know much more about these people now than we did before the drone showed up."

"Like what?" Dagor asked.

"We know that they have the ability to decipher the location of the trackers, and we also know that humans don't have the technology to decrypt the signals they are emitting. Also, they came to investigate, just not in person."

Dagor didn't look satisfied. "All we really know is that they are too sophisticated to fall into our trap. We still don't know who they are, and we won't know how to proceed without determining whether they are Kra-ell or human. The two require very different approaches."

"I agree with Aru," Negal said in his usual monotone voice. "What's important is that they showed their hand. It was a smart gambit that prompted the opponent to make a counter move, which, in turn, will inform our next one. The fact that they can decipher the location of the signals means that they captured Gor and tortured the information out of him. He never would have volunteered it. We should assume that he's dead."

Surprised that the old trooper was backing him up, Aru nodded his thanks.

Usually, Negal grumbled about the rookie getting promoted because of damn politics or nepotism, and every time Aru made a wrong move, Negal smirked in satisfaction.

Still, despite the trooper's attitude and occasional snarky comments, Aru appreciated having the guy on his team and wouldn't swap him for someone more accommodating even if he could. Negal had the experience that Aru lacked, kept him on his toes, and would never sabotage the mission just to try to prove that their commander had been wrong to nominate Aru as their team leader.

Dagor leaned back in his chair. "The fact that Gor's tracker stopped broadcasting doesn't mean that he is dead. It only means they took the tracker out of him—like they did to the other settlers before him."

When nearly all the trackers embedded in the Kra-ell settlers had simultaneously stopped broadcasting, Aru had assumed the cause was interference. Not many things could disrupt signals produced by the sophisticated trackers, though, so he and his teammates had to assume that the interference hadn't been caused by a natural phenomenon or an accident.

Regrettably, they had been too far away to get to the compound in time to see what had gone wrong.

At the time, they had been investigating a possible pod landing in Tibet. The remote location was four days on foot from the nearest paved road and nowhere near any international or even local airport.

Getting to Karelia to investigate what had happened had taken a long time, and in the meantime, the signals had come back online from the Baltic Sea, not too far from the port of Helsinki.

When they had started winking out one after the other, Aru had feared for the lives of the Kra-ell.

Not that he would have been allowed to intervene even if he and his team could do anything about it. Their job was observing and reporting, which they had been doing since discovering the surviving Kra-ell in Gor's compound five years ago.

Nevertheless, they hadn't reported anything about the latest events in the compound yet, and if what Aru suspected was true, they wouldn't be submitting a report regarding the fate of the Kra-ell anytime soon.

Thankfully, they had one hundred and fifteen Earth years before anyone came to check on them. That left plenty of time to collect all the relevant information and come up with a compelling story to tell their commander about why they had failed to discover the others before they had taken over Gor's compound, or rather Igor's, which was the name he had chosen to be known by on Earth.

What they knew so far was that someone had blown huge holes in the wall surrounding the compound, taken out everyone who was still alive, and put them on a ship. Then, the invaders had either killed everyone or just taken out their trackers.

What gave Aru hope that the Kra-ell were still alive was that it didn't make sense for the invaders to storm the compound, kill only a small number of Kra-ell, capture the rest, put them on a ship, and then kill them all. The invaders had to be a formidable force to take the Kra-ell captive to begin with, and the prime suspects were other Kra-ell settlers

257

who had also woken up from stasis. But unlike those in Gor's compound, the others must have figured out that they had tracking devices implanted in their bodies and had taken them out before Aru and his team arrived on Earth and started tracking all the settlers whose devices were active.

It was a perfectly reasonable hypothesis, but Aru knew it wouldn't be good enough to appease their commander, who would view it as a failure. Their team's next mission would undoubtedly be in an even more godforsaken sector of the universe.

Hopefully, the other person Aru was secretly reporting to would intervene on their behalf and prevent their exile.

After all, Negal's rumblings about nepotism weren't entirely unfounded. In fact, they were spot on. Aru had earned the promotion not because of anything he had done in the service but because of his unique talent and its usefulness to that person whose name should not be mentioned even in thought.

Still, their commander could find other ways to make their lives miserable. Just the loss of favor would devastate Dagor and Negal. An unfavorable evaluation from the commander would ruin any chances of promotion for them, and no one wanted to spend hundreds of years in some wretched corner of the universe doing work that was of little importance to anyone back home.

In all fairness, though, Aru and his team had been instructed to stay away from the Kra-ell and not let their presence be known, so if the Kra-ell had gotten themselves free somehow, even with outside help, the commander couldn't blame Aru's team for being ignorant of what had been brewing inside the compound. That being said, if the rescuers were other settlers who had woken up from stasis, the commander wouldn't forgive their ignorance of that.

At the time of the attack, Gor and two other purebloods had been away, which suggested that the invaders had been waiting for just such an opportunity and had been helped by rebels from the inside, either with just intel or with active participation.

When Gor and his two companions had subsequently been captured and taken to Los Angeles, it had been the lucky break Aru had needed. It had given him a clue as to the whereabouts of the other settlers. But then their signals had winked out as well, and his team had been left in the dark.

Desperate for any thread or clue, Aru had come up with the idea to go to China and locate the trackers of the first Kra-ell who had arrived on Earth—the scouting team that the Kra-ell queen had sent ahead of the settler ship.

The location where the bodies of the dead scouts had been cremated was known, and since the trackers were impervious to fire, it was only a matter of finding them. It hadn't been easy, but they had found five, of which only three were still operational. They could have kept digging, but Aru had decided that three was just the right number to lure the invaders out of hiding and show their hand.

His gamble had paid off, and they had gotten a response from the invaders. The question was what to do next.

2

KIAN

Kian walked into the war room, pulled out a chair next to the conference table, and sat down. "Syssi had a vision earlier today," he said without bothering with a long preamble. "She saw three men in a canyon, which was sparsely covered in vegetation." He flicked his gaze to the screen mounted overhead, where footage from the canyon the signals were coming from was still playing on a loop.

Shifting his gaze to his war room team, Kian assessed their reactions. They all knew of Syssi's reputation, and he doubted any of them would be foolish enough to make light of her prophetic vision.

Turner nodded, but his expression remained impassive. It took a lot more than a foretelling to get the guy rattled.

William wasn't showing any reaction either. But since he was focused on scanning the footage from the drone and looking for anything he might have missed at the first pass-through, he might not have heard Kian.

Jade seemed nervous, which given the Kra-ell's esoteric beliefs was to be expected, and Kalugal looked curious and somewhat amused, which could've been perceived as him downplaying the importance of the vision or of Kian's regard for it, but Kian knew it wasn't so.

His cousin's mate also occasionally experienced visions, so he knew to give Syssi's foresight its due respect. Unlike Kian, though, Kalugal didn't mind Jacki having them, and he didn't fear their negative effect on her well-being.

Then again, Jacki probably wasn't as drained after having prophetic visions as Syssi. She was a resilient female and not nearly as sensitive as Syssi. Her visions were also mostly less intense in nature, but not always.

The one she'd had about Wonder's caravan had been quite shocking.

Jacki's gift worked by touch, and when she'd held an ancient figurine, she'd seen Wonder fighting to save the lives of her caravan companions. A powerful earthquake had opened a chasm in the desert floor, swallowing wagons, animals, and people alike, and eventually Wonder herself had fallen victim to it despite her heroic efforts.

The vision Jacki had been shown was of an event that had happened thousands of years in the past. If Syssi had seen something of such a catastrophic nature, she would have been shaken by it for weeks, or even months, but not Jacki.

Perhaps Kalugal's wife was tougher because her life had been less sheltered than Syssi's, or maybe she'd just been born different.

As a father, Kian often wondered whether nature or nurture had a more significant influence on his child's character, and he leaned toward nature. There was no doubt in his mind that Allegra had been born with a strong personality, which she'd most likely inherited from him. Hopefully, though, she'd also inherited her mother's empathy and emotional intelligence, which would make her a much better leader than he could ever be.

Onegus was the only one to actually respond to his proclamation. "I assume that the three men Syssi saw in her vision are the ones emitting the signals?"

The answer to that was complicated, and since there was no one in the canyon, Kian wasn't sure what exactly Syssi had seen, but he had a theory. "Since the drone footage from the canyon indicates that there is no one there, we have to assume that Syssi's vision was from the near future. On the next fly-by, we should switch to the high-altitude drone and hope they won't notice it."

"Why?" Jade asked. "They are not there, so they are not going to see it in either case. We can fly the smaller, low-altitude drone."

"They might have hidden cameras right next to the trackers," Kian said. "Since there is no one where the signals are coming from, we have to assume that they somehow managed to rig the trackers to transmit without the benefit of a live host. That means they could bury them in the ground or hide them in the bushes."

The alien trackers were the size of a grain of rice, so even if they weren't buried under the rocks, there was no way William could find them in the footage. Normally, the devices needed a live body to provide the energy for them to transmit the signal, so another possibility was that the men had implanted them in small animals. But to keep the critters from scurrying away, they would have needed to put them in cages, and that was probably what William was looking for as he scanned the zoomed-in footage in slow motion on his laptop.

"The vision could also be from the far future," Anandur said. "What were the men in the vision wearing?"

Kian lifted a hand. "Let me finish telling you about the vision first. When I'm done, you can ask your questions, and I'll answer them to the best of my ability."

Anandur nodded.

"When Syssi's consciousness flew over the men, they were arguing, and then something caught their attention, and they looked up. Naturally, Syssi's first thought was that they could see her floating overhead, but she quickly realized that it must have been something above or behind her. She couldn't see or hear what it was, but that's the dreamy nature of visions. Many of the details are missing, and others are unclear, and it's never obvious whether the vision is a window into the past or the future."

Kian took a sip from his bottle of water before continuing. "One of the men pointed a strange-looking weapon at what I assume was our drone, but then one of his companions stayed his hand, and their argument resumed." He put the bottle down. "Syssi didn't know that we were flying a drone or that the signals were coming from a canyon, so you can rest assured that her vision wasn't influenced by anything I told her."

"What exactly did you tell her?" Jade asked.

"All I told Syssi was that the signals were coming from a nearby location, and just like the rest of us, she assumed they were being emitted by the Kra-ell—either by members of the scouting team that had been sent ahead of the settler ship or some of the awakened settlers themselves. Most of the pods from the settler ship are still missing, so that's the most logical assumption, provided that they had learned of the trackers and how to manipulate them."

After more than seven thousand years, the Kra-ell scouts shouldn't be alive, but there was a small chance that they had gone back into their stasis pod to prolong their lives and stayed there for hundreds of years at a time.

It was the logical thing to do, and Kian still believed that at least some of the scouts had done that, but it no longer seemed like the signals were coming from them, and he had arrived at that conclusion even before Syssi had told him about what she'd seen in her vision.

His next suspicion had been that other settlers had come out of stasis before Igor had figured out how to track the signals, and since some of them were assassins who had been smuggled among the settlers to eliminate the Eternal King's direct descendants, they'd known about the trackers and had also known that they had to remove them from their bodies so they couldn't be found.

Those assassins must have been tracking Igor and had followed his signal to Los Angeles, which would explain the sudden appearance of the three signals in the clan's backyard.

But after Syssi's vision, he had to consider other options.

Perhaps the gods had left a sleeper cell on Earth?

Had members of that team been tracking Igor?

Had they been aware of what he had done to the members of each pod that had come online, and done nothing about it?

How could they have stood by while he'd murdered innocent males, adults and children alike, and subjugated the females?

Were they following a non-interference directive and were supposed to only observe?

If so, why were they interfering now?

Did they suspect the involvement of immortals? The hybrid descendants of the exiled gods they had been sent to eliminate?

Kian had so many questions and so few answers, and he hated relying on visions to form his strategy, but it seemed like he had no choice. Right now, Syssi's vision supplied the only clues they had.

3

KALUGAL

Before meeting Jacki, Kalugal would have been dismissive of Syssi's vision, in a polite manner of course, but he'd been shown the power of clairvoyance by his mate and was no longer a skeptic.

Regrettably, Jacki was not in the same league as Syssi. He wouldn't have traded his Jacki for anyone, but there was no denying that Syssi's abilities far surpassed hers.

What his mate typically saw was small-scale, localized, and individual, while Syssi got to foresee or past-view epic events—like the Odus's decommissioning, or rather attempted eradication, and the Kra-ell who had been put in charge of it.

Kalugal didn't know all the details, but he imagined the vision had been cryptic, as all postcognition and precognition tended to be. Nevertheless, Jade had confirmed what Syssi had seen happening to the Odus.

In fact, he'd been told that Syssi had envisioned the Kra-ell years before the clan had learned of their existence. At the time, she hadn't realized that the fictional people she'd created for one of the Perfect Match Virtual Studios environments were not the product of her imagination but a glimpse into the future or maybe the past. She hadn't gotten all the details right, though, so despite her visions being legendary, they couldn't be taken verbatim.

There was another problem with the story Kalugal had been told about Syssi and her Krall version of the Kra-ell. The one detail everyone seemed to overlook was that the original Krall adventure had been created by the Perfect Match programmers before Syssi had come on board. She'd elaborated on and changed it, but someone had thought of it before her.

Was one of the humans working for Perfect Match a seer?

It wasn't such a great leap of logic. Humans had been known to have prophetic visions, and some weren't even aware of their abilities. They didn't realize that their minds had not created what they envisioned.

It was also possible that Syssi had played around with designs for the different Perfect Match environments even before Kian had bought a majority stake in the company for her and made her a board member.

Kian's team had been involved with Perfect Match almost from its inception, which probably included Syssi. He'd been a silent investor and stock owner in the company during the development stage, and when the original founders had gotten stuck and couldn't finalize the product, Kian had asked William to help them overcome their difficulties.

William had been instrumental in debugging the software and giving it the edge the founders had envisioned but couldn't quite achieve.

"What else did Syssi see?" Onegus asked.

Kian leaned back. "Syssi said that the weapon one of the men aimed at the drone looked like a monocular, which is odd on two accounts. One is that it had no visible trigger, so it couldn't have been a projectile weapon, and so we have to assume that it was a laser-based weapon or something that operated in a similar way. The other is that one of the males aimed it at our drone." He looked at Turner. "Correct me if I'm wrong, but as far as I know, no manmade handheld weapons can shoot down a drone at the height we were flying it."

Turner nodded. "That's correct."

"I wish the alien-looking weapon was the most troubling part, but it's not." Kian leaned forward and put his hands on the table. "When the three looked up at the drone, Syssi got a good look at their faces, and she was positive that none were Kra-ell. She thinks that they were gods."

Jade gasped. "I'll be damned. How the hell did they get here so fast?"

"My thoughts exactly. They couldn't have. They had to be here already," Kian said. "Syssi's impression was that they were friendly, but as much as I trust her visions, I wouldn't base our strategy on them."

"We all know not to take Syssi's visions lightly," Onegus said. "But gods? We've been searching for other immortals for centuries and haven't found any. Do you want to tell me that gods were hiding among humans this whole time, and we didn't know? Wouldn't they have recognized the technology we were drip-feeding to the humans? All they had to do was follow the breadcrumbs to us."

"It depends on when they arrived on Earth," Turner said. "We know that they are not part of the original group."

"Why not?" Jade asked. "Maybe more have survived. Until recently, you didn't know about Toven, and he didn't know about you."

The cogs in Kalugal's mind started spinning.

If the three males were indeed gods, they couldn't be contemporaries of the original group of rebels. Annani might not have known about another group who had settled somewhere else on Earth, but Mortdh would have, and he wouldn't have bombed the assembly while knowing that other gods could find out about his crime.

These gods must have arrived long after the original ones had perished. In fact, they had likely arrived after the Kra-ell ship had exploded and the pods had landed on Earth, which had been thousands of years later. That meant they possessed more advanced technology and know-how, which were priceless.

If Syssi was right and they were friendly, they might have sought out the clan to get its help or cooperation, and if contact was established, he should seize the opportunity and become instrumental in the negotiations.

That would not only grant him access to what those gods would offer up as part of the negotiations, but it would also increase his influence in the clan and get him the second council seat that right now was looking even less likely than it had originally.

With Toven joining the council and possibly Jade as well, Kalugal would have no grounds to request another seat. Jade represented nearly half of the village population, so if he got two seats, she could ask for six, and Kian would never allow the majority of the council to be comprised of non-clan members.

Leaning back in his chair, Kalugal crossed his arms over his chest. "Syssi's vision reinforces my earlier assessment that the three activated the signals as a way to make contact with us and not to lure us into a trap and harm us. In fact, I'm so sure of their intentions that I volunteer to head to the canyon with a team of no more than two warriors to meet them on equal terms. I think that would be received better than showing up in force, which would signal that we are afraid of them." He smiled at Kian. "Not to toot my own horn, but I'm a much better negotiator than you are, so if you were thinking about heading to the canyon yourself, I would advise against it."

"I wasn't planning to." Kian regarded him with thinly veiled amusement. "Thank you for the offer, but let's not get ahead of ourselves." He braced his elbows on the table. "We must not forget who created Igor and the other assassins and who programmed them to dispose of all legitimate heirs to the Eternal King's throne. These three might be the assassins' handlers, or alternatively, they could be genetically modified gods who were sent to Earth to complete the mission that the original assassins had been tasked with but failed to complete because their ship exploded and their stasis pods were damaged."

Turner nodded. "I agree with Kian. For some, assuming the best in people is natural and safe, but it is not so for us." He scanned the faces of everyone present. "We don't have the luxury of being naive and trusting. We need to assume the worst and hope to be surprised for the better."

As much as Kalugal wished he could argue with that, he couldn't.

Too much was at stake, including the lives of his mate and son. He'd rather succumb to Kian's paranoia than make a rushed decision that might endanger everyone he loved and cared about.

After all, he was a descendant of the Eternal King as well. Ekin, his great-grandfather, had not been the official heir to the throne because he'd been born to a concubine and not the official wife, and the same was true for his mother, who Ahn had fathered with a concubine. Still, Ekin had been the Eternal King's son, and Areana was the Eternal King's granddaughter.

Kian regarded him with his intense eyes. "Even if we decide to send a small welcoming party with a massive backup in case things go wrong, you can't be a part of it. As a council member, you are privy to information we can't allow to fall into enemy hands."

Kalugal was immune to most compulsion, but not all, and if any of the three possessed Igor's ability, he wouldn't be able to resist the compulsion to reveal all of his secrets, and those included much more than the location of the village and how to get there.

"Unfortunately, you're right." Kalugal sighed. "As the saying goes, with great responsibility comes great sacrifice."

Kian chuckled. "Actually, the saying is 'With great power comes great responsibility, and with great responsibility comes great accountability,' but in your case, sacrifice and accountability are probably one and the same."

4

KIAN

It was apparent to Kian that Kalugal's motive for volunteering was the same one that had prompted him to offer assistance with the Kra-ell rescue mission.

His cousin wanted to be in the know.

Kian didn't mind, but what Kalugal had forgotten was that as a council member, he was already privy to nearly everything that was going on in the clan and that the price for that knowledge was certain restrictions.

"I should be the one to go," Jade said. "And my team should be comprised of only Kra-ell. If these gods are recent arrivals, they don't know about the exiled gods producing half-breed descendants with humans. If they did, they would have tried to make contact with you or the Doomers, either in a friendly or unfriendly manner. But we should assume they know about the Kra-ell or they wouldn't be here. They must have been tracking us, and once we got rid of the implanted trackers, they lost us and needed to find out what happened to us. That's why they are making contact."

Jade's reasoning was solid, but Kian still had trouble treating her like he would any other warrior and not trying to shield her because of her gender. His instincts rebelled against letting her walk into danger without Guardians to protect her.

Given how strong and well-trained Jade was, it was a ridiculous sentiment, but he couldn't just ignore two thousand years of conditioning.

"That might be so." He shifted in his chair. "But we don't know if their intentions toward you and your people are friendly or hostile."

Jade shrugged. "If they meant us harm, they would have already disposed of us. Since they didn't do that and kept their presence a secret, we have to assume their goal is not to eliminate us. They were probably sent to complete the mission the assassin on our ship failed to complete." She shifted her gaze to Kian. "After discovering that the gods were gone, their mission was probably to locate the other descendants of the Eternal King, meaning the twins."

Kian tilted his head. "Why would they think we can lead them to the twins?"

Jade took a deep breath. "Perhaps they need Igor back because he can find the other pods and the Eternal King's grandchildren. Regardless of their intentions, it is better to keep them ignorant of your existence until we know what they are after. That's why I should take a couple of purebloods with me when I meet them."

Kian wasn't convinced that Jade was right about the gods wanting Igor, but he agreed with her assessment that it was better to keep them in the dark about the clan. "I'd rather keep our existence from them as well."

"I'm glad we see eye to eye." Jade squared her shoulders. "There are additional benefits to sending a Kra-ell team. We are faster and stronger and stand a better chance in the event of a confrontation." She looked at William. "Naturally, we will need to be equipped with compulsion-filtering earpieces."

Compulsion was a rare ability even for the gods, but that was according to Annani, and her information was seven thousand years old. The gods had had a long time to improve their genetic know-how and breed more compellers.

"Of course." William waved a hand without lifting his eyes from the screen.

"I see two possibilities," Turner said. "And each requires a very different approach."

271

It was about time the guy voiced his opinion on the situation. "I've been waiting for you to come up with a new angle no one has considered yet." Kian cast him a smile. "Let's hear it."

"I'm not sure it's a new angle," Turner said. "I'm just clarifying things. The first possibility is that these gods—provided that we are indeed dealing with gods—were sent by the Eternal King to make sure no threat to his throne remains on Earth. The second one is that they were sent by his wife to protect her children and grandchildren from the Kra-ell assassins. If it's the former, walking up to them would be foolhardy because we do not know what capabilities were engineered into them and their weapons. If it's the second option, and these gods were sent by the queen, they might assume that the Kra-ell approaching them are the assassins, shoot first, and ask questions later."

"They left Igor alive and didn't touch the rest of us," Jade scoffed. "If they were sent by the queen, they would have taken him out long ago to prevent him from going after her son."

"Maybe they couldn't," Kian said. "We're assuming that the queen operates secretly and pretends to be loyal to the king. If Igor had a way to communicate with someone on Anumati and the queen was aware of that, she couldn't tell her people to launch a direct attack on him without showing her hand."

Turner nodded. "That's possible. Also, don't forget that if they were sent to eliminate Ahn and the other exiled gods or to find the twins, they had no reason to bother with Igor. But as soon as a new player appeared on the stage, they followed the trail in hopes of potentially finding the exiled gods. Who else could have liberated the Kra-ell? Humans? Not likely. And they should know it couldn't have been a different Kra-ell faction, because if it was, they could have tracked the signals they emitted."

"Not necessarily." Onegus crossed his arms over his chest. "Those other Kra-ell could have removed their trackers before the gods arrived. I'm sure that's a scenario they took into consideration."

"Why would they?" Jade asked. "We didn't know that we were implanted with trackers. Igor knew, and yet he didn't remove his. Knowing how the gods operate, I wouldn't be surprised if the assassins were programmed to keep their trackers."

Kian was losing patience. They could engage in what-ifs for hours and get nowhere.

He lifted his hand. "The way to address both possibilities is to send a mixed group. Two purebloaded females and two immortals. Igor claimed there were no female assassins because of the gods' attitudes toward females and their reluctance to involve them in military missions. Therefore, this new team would know that the female Kra-ell couldn't be assassins, and they would have no reason to shoot at them. The two immortals could pass for humans, so even if these gods were sent by the king, they would have no reason to shoot them either. Naturally, we will provide the team with an aerial defense of armed drones and a backup force nearby."

Jade nodded. "I wish Kagra was here. She's my best fighter, and she's good under pressure."

Kagra was currently in China with Yamanu and the rest of the team that had been sent to find the origin of the signals. But then the broadcast location had changed while they had been en route, and instead of it coming from China, it was coming from Mount Baldy.

Onegus swiveled his chair to face Kian. "Speaking of the China team, what do you want them to do? Do you want them to continue to Lugu Lake to assist the crew working on Kalugal's archeological dig?"

Kalugal suspected that a pod was buried on the site, but since the place was rigged with booby-traps, digging had been progressing at a snail's pace, and the assistance of several super-strong Kra-ell would be greatly beneficial to speeding it up.

The team was awaiting instructions in Chengdu, the capital of China's Sichuan province, but Kian hadn't decided yet whether he wanted to send them to Lugu Lake to help with the archaeological excavation of the suspected pod crash or to instruct them to return home.

"Not yet. Keep them on standby."

Nodding, Onegus turned to Jade. "Do you have anyone else you trust for a mission like that?"

"Borga is a good fighter, but she's not a diplomat, and I don't trust her. I prefer Morgada, but she hasn't kept up with her training. I'll have to give it some thought." Jade looked at Onegus. "I leave the selection of the immortals to you."

"Do you have a preference for anyone specific?" Kian asked.

She shrugged. "It makes no difference to me."

Kalugal regarded her with an arched brow. "Don't you want Phinas to go with you?"

She shook her head. "Phinas is an excellent fighter, but he's even better as a father figure for Drova. One of us needs to stay alive for her, and it's not a good plan to have us both face danger together. I wouldn't mind taking Rufsur, though, and if Dalhu is a choice, I wouldn't mind having him by my side either." She leaned back in her chair. "He claims that he can smell evil, and if that's true, I would like him to sniff those supposed gods to ascertain their intentions."

"Dalhu is not a Guardian," Onegus said. "He's also happily pursuing his art and prefers to stay out of conflicts. I don't think he would want to take part in this."

Onegus didn't know Dalhu as well as Kian did. His sister's mate would have enjoyed some action, but the problem was that Dalhu was mated to Amanda, who was a council member and therefore privy to too much information.

Rufsur couldn't be part of the team for the same reason.

"Neither Dalhu nor Rufsur can go because they are both mated to council members and know too much. I suspect that mates don't keep secrets from each other even when they are supposed to." He looked at Kalugal. "Do you have anyone else?"

Kalugal shook his head. "Perhaps Boleck. He's an excellent sniper, in case you need one. Greggory is also a good fighter, and he's coolheaded."

Greggory had been Eleanor's inducer, and the two hadn't parted on the best of terms, but that didn't mean he was not a good choice. Still, he wasn't the right man for the mission.

"Frankly, I prefer Guardians to accompany the Kra-ell females." Kian raked his fingers through his hair. "It's not that I have anything against your men, but other than Phinas and Rufsur, none of them is qualified to handle a delicate mission like this."

Jade let out a sigh. "Fine, I'll take Phinas with me."

Phinas had proven himself during the Kra-ell rescue, both as a fighter and diplomat, and Kian had no problem with him meeting the gods, but Jade had a point about both of them going on a risky mission together.

"What about Drova?" He looked into her eyes. "You were right to point out that one of you should stay behind to be with her."

"You just have to ensure that both Phinas and I return to her."

"I'll do everything I can to ensure your safety, but I can't guarantee it." He turned to Kalugal. "Are you okay with Phinas joining the team?"

Kalugal nodded. "Naturally. Phinas is an excellent choice. "

"He's also charming," Jade said. "And he can pass for a human. His godly genes are not as apparent as in some clan immortals. He's not as perfect."

That was true. Navuh had never been concerned with the looks of the immortal warriors he bred. Until recently, the men selected to father them were chosen based mostly on brawn and aggressive tendencies, and lately on brains, but never on looks. In contrast, the clan females were much more discriminating about the humans they chose to father their children, and looks played an important part in their selection process.

Jade squared her shoulders and pinned Kian with a stern look. "Just to be clear, Phinas's imperfections make him more attractive to me, not less. No offense to all of you pretty boys, but I prefer my man rugged and masculine."

Kian chuckled. "No offense taken."

Turner's face lit up in a rare grin. "I'm just flattered to be bundled with the pretty boys."

5

JADE

Jade held on to her impassive expression, but she was stunned Kian wanted her to lead the team.

Could she have misinterpreted his intentions, though?

He'd said that he preferred a Guardian to accompany her and a female Kra-ell of her choosing, and he would probably nominate that Guardian as head of their team.

Kian would never leave such an important mission in her hands even though, strategically, she was the best choice.

Frankly, if she were in his shoes, she would also choose a trusted Guardian. He needed someone to represent the clan, and Jade hadn't been a member long enough to do such a role justice.

Was she even a member?

The clan had welcomed her and her people, but as members of their community and not full-fledged members of the clan itself. The only way to join that inner circle was to mate a clan member, and that didn't include Kalugal and his men, so her mating Phinas hadn't earned her a clan membership.

The clan was comprised solely of Annani's descendants and their mates.

Leaving issues unresolved was not Jade's style, though, and she wasn't about to wait until Kian informed her of his decision. She needed to know whether she was leading the team or not. "What about the fourth member of our team?" She looked at Onegus and then shifted her gaze to Kian.

"I suggest Magnus," the chief said. "He is the most senior Guardian on the force after the head Guardians. He's also coolheaded and eloquent."

As Kian nodded in agreement, Jade asked, "Who will head the team?"

"That depends." Kian crossed his arms over his chest. "If Magnus and Phinas have to pretend to be human throughout the meeting, then you will naturally be in charge. But if they don't, then Magnus will take over the lead as the clan's representative."

"Makes sense." Jade wasn't surprised or even disappointed.

Kian trusted her enough to lead the meeting in at least one of the scenarios, and he did not give his trust easily, so she considered that an accomplishment.

Saving his life had probably earned her a spot on the list of those he trusted, but letting her lead the team meant that he also valued the skills she brought to the table.

That being said, he knew that her loyalties were split.

She was oath-bound to protect the twins, but even though Kian had refused to accept her offer of a life vow in gratitude for saving her people from Igor's tyranny, she owed him an immeasurable debt, and he knew she would do anything in her power to protect him and the clan.

Hopefully, she would never be faced with a situation where she had to choose between Kian and the clan, and the royal twins.

The irony was that the twins had more right to membership in the clan than she had. They were Annani's half-siblings and Kian's aunt and uncle, but even though they were his own flesh and blood, knowing that Jade might side with them probably didn't sit well with him.

The truth was that if she was forced to choose, Jade would probably select the clan, and she could even get away with that without losing her place in the fields of the brave.

Her vow to protect the queen and her family could be deemed invalid because it had been extorted under false pretenses, and that was a loophole Jade could use to her advantage. She hadn't known that she was vowing to protect what everyone on Anumati regarded as abominations, which was what both societies deemed children born to a god and a Kra-ell.

Not that she still believed that they were indeed abominations. Now, she suspected that the combination produced offspring so formidable that both societies feared them, which was the real reason for the prohibition.

Had the queen's consorts known that the Eternal King's heir had been the twins' father?

All Kra-ell males knew right away when their seed took and fertilization occurred, so the consorts had to know that none of them had fathered the twins, but they still might not have known that they had been sired by a god.

As was true for any Kra-ell, the queen wasn't obligated to restrict herself to her official consorts, and she could have invited whomever she pleased to her bed—from the palace guards to one of the gardeners. But people talked, and although no male was allowed to officially make a claim on the queen's children, it was difficult to keep such a thing a secret.

Perhaps Turner was right, and the queen had commanded one of her consorts to claim them in order to silence the talk.

"We need a contingency plan," Kian said. "Any thoughts?"

Jade had a few suggestions in mind, but Kian's question was directed at Onegus and Turner, and she preferred to hear their ideas first before offering hers.

Onegus swiveled his chair to face Kian. "No matter how well we prepare, our away team will be at risk, but we can take steps to even out the odds. Naturally, everyone on the team will wear the compulsion-filtering earpieces. They should also wear our specialty protective vests, although those are only good at stopping bullets, and we don't know what the gods' weapons can do." He looked at Jade. "Did you ever see the gods carry weapons like the one Syssi saw in her vision?"

She shook her head. "It must be something that was invented at a later time. The weapons they used during my time were much larger and looked like javelins, but they were not meant for throwing or piercing armor. They released an energy blast that I doubt your protective vests can stop. The blast stopped the heart. It was instant death."

The weapons were developed to combat Kra-ell, not humans, and they had been designed accordingly.

Kian grimaced. "The more I learn about my ancestors, the less I like them." He shifted his eyes to Onegus. "The vests are better than nothing, so I suggest the team members wear them just in case they can do any good. Our other option is exoskeletons, but those are not practical for a mission that is supposed to be diplomatic in nature."

"Actually, I think that's a great idea." Onegus smiled. "First of all, the gods won't know who's inside the suits, and secondly, those things provide a powerful advantage."

Jade snorted. "I've seen those suits, and they look super intimidating. If we wear them, I can guarantee that the gods will shoot first and ask questions later."

"True." Kian nodded. "Besides, Syssi said that we shouldn't come as aggressors. The vests will have to do."

"Reluctantly, I have to agree," Onegus said. "We will have to provide the team with aerial defense and ground reinforcements that will be on standby and they should have exoskeleton suits with them in case they need to engage. Our missile-armed drones will be in the air just beyond the canyon, and a large force of Guardians will be stationed as near to the meeting place as we can get them without detection." He glanced at William. "Can we retrofit the sound cannon onto one of the drones? That might be the most effective weapon we have against the gods."

Scratching his neck, William seemed unsure. "That is an interesting idea, and I regret not investigating it before. It would require some re-engineering and components that I will have to manufacture in our lab because we don't have enough time to buy or order anything, and I doubt I can make those parts in time for the mission."

"That's regrettable," Kian said. "Any other options?"

"We can retrofit a helicopter to carry the system we already have," William offered. "We can mount the speakers at the bottom of the bird, with the sound wave pointed away from the cabin. With the crew wearing protective gear, they should be fine operating it. I probably can manage to do that with what I have."

"Good. Get on it as soon as possible." Kian turned to the chief. "You and Turner need to figure out the logistics of getting the backup force to the canyon while avoiding detection."

"What about the village lockdown?" Onegus asked. "Does it stay in effect?"

"Nothing has changed in that regard. For now, let's keep it buttoned down." Kian turned to Jade. "Choose the female you want to take with you and report back here in two hours." He looked at Kalugal. "Send Phinas over as well. We need to work on the right approach and what to tell these gods and, more importantly, what not to tell them."

"Hold on." Jade lifted a hand. "There is no one in the canyon. We are basing all of this on Syssi's vision, and it's not that I doubt it, but we are basically going in blind. What if we get there, and no one comes to meet us?"

"They will come," Kian said. "We have to assume that they are watching the canyon, and as soon as the team shows up, they will join."

Jade frowned. "But how? The drone scanned the entire area, and I saw no paved roads for miles around. They will have to either walk there, parachute down, or fly in on angel wings." She flapped her arms. "That doesn't fit the way gods work. It's too haphazard."

"Maybe they are there but using some alien cloaking technology." William let out a breath. "I'm also worried that there could be many more than three out there."

That was a valid point, and Jade wasn't too keen on trusting Syssi's assertion that the gods' intentions were friendly. But then there was nothing to be done about it, and the backup Onegus was arranging should suffice.

"When do you want the team to head out?" the chief asked.

"Midday tomorrow, provided that we can be ready by then. If not, the evening should be fine as well. The longer they wait, the more they sweat, right?"

Jade shrugged. "I don't know what sweating has to do with it, but they might get nervous. The question is whether their nervousness is good for us or not."

Leaning back, Turner regarded her with his penetrating gaze. "The more important question is whether they are indeed gods. If William's suspicion about a cloaking device is correct, they could be anyone."

Kian chuckled. "A cloaking device wouldn't affect Syssi's vision. That's not how visions work."

Jade wasn't sure that he was right about the nature of foretelling, but she trusted her logic more than she trusted visions, and right now, gods were the most likely candidates.

Onegus leaned back in his chair and crossed his arms over his chest. "I sincerely hope they don't have a cloaking device, or flying high-altitude drones over the area will be a waste of time."

Kian mirrored the chief's pose. "Nevertheless, I want that canyon monitored twenty-four-seven. We don't know that they have a device like that, although it would make sense for them to be able to keep themselves hidden."

"How far is the canyon from the nearest road?" Jade asked. "I need to know how long it will take us to jog there." She was a fast runner, and the immortals could probably keep up, but she needed more precise information.

"It's about an hour and a half on foot for a human," Onegus said. "I assume it will take you a fraction of that time."

"Assuming that an average human's pace is three miles per hour, that's four and a half miles. I can cover such a distance in ten to fifteen minutes." Jade smiled. "The question is how fast can your immortals run."

"They can keep up," Onegus assured her.

6

GABI

With a sigh, Gabi put her book down and looked out the window of her hotel room. The romance novel was sweet, but it was predictable, and it didn't hold her interest. It was fine for reading in bed before falling asleep, but not as something to fill her day with.

Gabi was getting restless.

What was she going to do while waiting for the village situation to be resolved and for Uriel to let her know whether he could see her again?

He'd said that he would know by tonight whether he was staying in town or leaving because of the deal he was working on, but the whole story seemed iffy to her.

Flea-market flippers didn't negotiate huge deals that necessitated instant travel.

But then, what did she know about the flea-market flipping business?

Perhaps Uriel and his friends had found something truly amazing? Something even more valuable than the shoes of a Korean princess? And had several bidders they were negotiating with?

If the buyers in Los Angeles weren't offering them a price that was as good as or better than what the bidders from other places were willing to pay, then it would make sense for Uriel and his friends to fly over to where the better bidders were.

Another option was that the merchandise they were trying to find a buyer for was a contraband item that they were selling illegally.

Maybe Uriel suspected that the people they were negotiating with could sell them out?

That would necessitate a quick escape to avoid the authorities.

Nah, she was letting her imagination run wild again, and it was probably the fault of the book she was reading. It was about an international jewel thief trying to sell her loot to an undercover agent.

Uriel and his friends were probably actors, just as she'd suspected all along, and they were most likely working on a movie deal.

However, the problem with that assumption was that whether they got the movie deal or not, there was no reason for them to rush out of town—unless filming was about to start and the location was elsewhere.

Not a likely scenario.

Damn. It was so difficult to trust anyone. Life would be much simpler if everyone would just say what they meant.

It reminded Gabi of a movie that had had a profound effect on her. It was called *The Invention of Lying*, and it highlighted all the ways, big and small, that people used lies and platitudes to make life bearable.

It wasn't as if brutal truthfulness was desirable or practical, but she wished Uriel would be more straightforward with her.

When she'd asked him if it was a goodbye and his reply had been 'not if he could help it,' he'd sounded so sincere. But since he was probably an actor, it could have been a convincing act.

Well, it had been Uriel who had asked whether it was a goodbye, not her, and it was in response to her telling him that she'd enjoyed spending time with him and was glad that they'd gotten to spend two nights together, implying that she thought they wouldn't meet again.

Gabi had used Uriel's own tactics on him and thrown the question back at him, and that was when he'd said that it wasn't a goodbye if he could help it.

Ugh, it was pointless to guess what he would do, and staying cooped up in the hotel room was driving her nuts.

Reaching into her purse, she pulled out the phone Gilbert had given her and searched the contacts for Karen's number. Maybe she had an update about the lockdown and would be less cryptic than Gilbert.

The phone kept ringing for a long time before the call was finally answered.

"Hi, Gabi. What's up?" Karen sounded breathless, and the wailing babies in the background explained why it had taken her so long to answer.

"I just wanted to see if there was any news about the lockdown, but it seems like a bad time for a chat. You have your hands full."

"Yeah, Evan and Ryan are having a bad day, which is probably my fault because staying cooped up stresses me out, and they pick up on my moods. We are still in lockdown, and it doesn't look like they are going to lift it by tonight. I'm hoping for tomorrow morning." She sighed. "I need to get back to work so I can get a break from the little demons. I think they miss hanging out with Julia at the university, and that's why they are so cranky. They love their babysitter."

When another ear-piercing wail sounded in the background, Gabi winced. "I'd better let you get back to them. I'll call Darlene."

"Yeah, good idea. I'll call you later if I can."

As Karen ended the call, Gabi shook her head. "Poor Karen."

Gabi loved kids, and she loved her nephews, but she was very glad that she wasn't in Karen's shoes right now. Changing poopy diapers didn't faze her, but dual baby wailing was just intolerable.

Being a parent must be incredibly gratifying for people to be willing to suffer through that, not to mention the anxiety of raising little human beings while worrying about all the terrible things that could happen to them.

As Gabi scrolled through the list looking for Darlene's number, it occurred to her that Darlene worked in William's lab, so she probably knew more than Karen about the lockdown and when it might be lifted, but perhaps Kaia was even better informed. She was not only William's fiancée, but she was also privy to some secret project that the clan was working on, which meant that she had a high-security clearance and should know better than most what was going on.

Scrolling through the short contacts list on her clan phone, she quickly found Kaia's.

The phone rang a few times before her niece answered, "Hi, Gabi." She sounded rushed. "What's up?"

"I was wondering whether you knew anything about the lockdown and when it might end."

"Unfortunately, there is no news," she said breathlessly. "We are still in lockdown."

Kaia wasn't into sports, but she was young, not to mention immortal. She shouldn't sound so breathless unless—

Gabi sucked in a breath. "Am I interrupting something? I can call later."

Kaia chuckled. "Regrettably, you're not interrupting anything fun. I'm jogging home to get lunch for William and me. He's busy with the latest emergency project that Kian wants him to complete yesterday, and if I don't feed him something healthy, he's going to stuff himself with pastries from the café. When William is stressed, he's like a baby. Everything goes into his mouth. I'd rather he stuff it with healthy food that is good for him."

Gabi wanted to pat herself on the back. She'd been the one who had explained to Kaia about the importance of a balanced diet and how it affects the brain. Her niece had listened and adopted nearly all of it, but she'd refused to give up Coke, which was probably the worst offender.

Heck, even hamburgers and fries were better than that artificial junk. But hey, she was immortal now, and she could probably get away with a lot of unhealthy stuff before it negatively affected her.

"That's so nice of you, sweetie. I hope William appreciates how lucky he is to snag a rare gem like you."

Kaia chuckled. "Oh, he does, and I'm pretty lucky to have him, too. William is brilliant, kind, handsome, sweet, and caring, and it's an absolute joy to work with him every day in the lab, which is the best testament to how well we get along. We are together almost twenty-four-seven, and we love it."

Gabi could practically hear the love in Kaia's voice, and it made her so happy that she teared up a little.

"Indeed. Not many couples can spend so much time together without driving each other crazy. I can't imagine how wicked smart your kids are going to be, not to mention gorgeous and immortal."

"Well, our children won't be born immortal. They would have to be induced and go through transition like every other Dormant."

"About that. I'm still not clear on how it works."

Kaia laughed. "I thought that Cheryl had stated it bluntly enough. You have to have sex with an immortal male."

It had been so embarrassing to have her teenage niece explain how it was done. Well, technically, Kaia was still a teenager too, but at least she was legally an adult.

"I got that. But what about that mystical bond? I still don't know whether it's required for my transition."

She didn't remember who had said what, but she'd heard conflicting statements.

"Hold on. I just got home. I'll turn the speaker on so I can chop veggies while we talk." "Sounds like a plan."

7

KAREN

"I can't hear myself think," Gilbert grumbled. "Can't you take the boys to the playground or for a walk? I need to go over these inventory lists."

Karen dipped the tea bag in the hot water for the twentieth time. "They've already been to the playground, and it's getting too hot to be outside."

The boys were watching one of their kids' shows while playing with toy cars and trucks on the floor, and as long as they weren't screaming and wailing, she was happy to leave them be. Karen was a pro at tuning the noise out while taking a breather from taking care of the kids, but Gilbert had no practice. Before moving to the village, he would spend his days in the office, and on weekends they had usually taken the kids out so they wouldn't be bored and cranky.

If they were, Gilbert would find an excuse to disappear from sight.

Now that he was forced to work from home, it still hadn't been a problem because the kids were usually gone most of the day, Idina in daycare and the boys at the university, but the lockdown was messing up everyone's schedule, and that included her plans for organizing a way for her to transition.

"Can you at least lower the volume?"

She shook her head. "They like it loud. It's either that or them wailing."

"Yeah, I know." Gilbert leaned back in the dining room chair. "I was thinking about taking my work to the backyard, but the bugs are a nuisance. I think they like my immortal blood." He rubbed his arm. "At least their bites don't cause a reaction, but I keep wondering if they get to live longer or multiply even more thanks to my potent blood."

"Dada!" Evan lifted his toy train and chucked it at Gilbert.

He caught it and smiled. "Good throw."

"No throwing toys at people," Karen scolded her son before turning to her mate. "Don't encourage him. If not for your new immortal reflexes, the toy would have hit you square in the face."

"Send him to his room," Idina said. "He's not playing nice."

"Who should I send to his room, sweetie?" Karen stifled a smile. "Your daddy or your brother?"

Idina gave Gilbert one of her semi-evil looks. "Both. Daddy wants quiet, and Evan needs to learn not to throw his toys at people."

"From the mouths of toddlers," Gilbert murmured as he closed his laptop and put it in his briefcase. "I really don't want to, but I'm going to work in our bedroom."

"We need to get a desk in there." Karen cradled the teacup.

"I hope the lockdown will be lifted soon, and you can take the kids to daycare so I can work right here."

"You're working on the dining room table while sitting on a dining room chair. That's far from ideal. You need an office, but since we don't have room for one, our bedroom will have to do."

He joined her at the kitchen counter and wrapped his arms around her. "I don't want to bring work to our bedroom on a permanent basis. That room is a sacred temple for worshiping my goddess."

Her lips twitched with a smile. "You say the nicest things."

"Only the truth." He nuzzled her neck. "And nothing but the truth, so help me Karen, my goddess, who I worship." He trailed kisses down her neck.

She laughed. "Stop it. We have an audience."

Gilbert turned his head to look over his shoulder at their three children. "They know that Daddy loves Mommy. Right, kids?"

Idina frowned at them. "Daddy loves me."

"I love you, your brothers and sisters, and your mommy. I also love Uncle Eric and Aunt Gabi and Aunt Darlene and the rest of our family."

Idina was still frowning. "You forgot William."

Karen stifled a giggle. "Daddy is still working on it. William is a new addition to the family, and it will take Daddy time to learn to love him."

"He said that he loves Darlene, and she is newer than William."

"True," Gilbert said. "But Darlene is a girl, and William is a boy."

Idina's face brightened with a broad smile. "So, you love me more than Evan and Ryan?"

"Dear Fates," Gilbert groaned. "Our daughter is going to be a lawyer."

Karen shrugged. "You always said that every family needs one."

"I did, didn't I?" He walked over to the couch and sat next to Idina. "I love all of my children with the same ferocity, but in different ways. Does that make sense to you, munchkin?"

She nodded at him sagely. "You love the girls because they are like Mommy, and you love her, and you love the boys because they are like Uncle Eric, and you love him too, but not like you love Mommy."

Gilbert opened his mouth to say something but then changed his mind and lifted Idina onto his lap. "Yep, more or less." He kissed her on each of her chubby cheeks, which were the only part of her that still retained some of her babyhood.

The living room glass door slid open, and Cheryl walked in, heading straight for the fridge. "What's there to eat?"

"There is leftover chicken from yesterday." Karen waved a hand. "We can cut it up and make a Chinese chicken salad with it. Want to help make it?"

"Sure." Cheryl took out the dish with the leftover chicken. "Do we have wonton strips?"

"We do." Karen opened the drawer and pulled out a bag.

"I have an idea." Gilbert put Idina back on the couch and joined them in the kitchen. "How do you feel about sharing your cabana with me during the day?"

Cheryl cast him a horrified look. "Why?"

"I need a quiet place to work, and I don't want to do it in the bedroom. It's bad juju. I only need a couple of hours, and I can do that while you're not there." He smiled. "I'll pay you. Twenty bucks for each hour of use."

Those were the magic words Cheryl couldn't resist.

"You've got yourself a deal." She offered him her hand. "On one condition. I don't want to hear a word about the mess."

He took her hand. "As long as I have a stretch of table to use, I don't care about the condition of the rest of the place."

Karen frowned. Cheryl wasn't the messy type. "What happened to your cabana?"

Cheryl scrunched her nose. "I'm redecorating. With all due respect to Ingrid, her interior design is outdated, and it doesn't look cool in my product videos."

Her Instatock account was gaining followers, and brands were paying her to promote their products.

"Can't you use screens, or filters, or whatever it was that you were telling me about?"

It seemed like a new feature was being added every day, and Karen had too much on her mind to pay attention to all the Instatock wonders Cheryl had been gushing about.

Cheryl shook her head. "It needs to look authentic and age-appropriate, but the house and the cabana both look like they were decorated by the same person who did the Venetian hotel in Las Vegas. It's old."

"You should talk to Ingrid," Gilbert said. "Maybe she's open to making some changes. I will pay for the new furniture and whatever else you need there."

Cheryl's eyes widened. "You will?"

"Sure thing. I'm investing in my dau—." He stopped himself. "In your business."

"It's okay." She put her hand on his arm. "You can call me your step-daughter even though you and Mom are not married."

"I'd rather call you my daughter, but I know that you are not ready for that."

She patted his arm. "You can call me your daughter if you wish. But you will always be Gilbert to me."

8

GABI

G abi listened as Kaia opened and closed the fridge, ran water in the sink to wash the veggies, and then dropped the cutting board on the counter.

Those were such mundane sounds for such an extraordinary girl to make. But evidently even immortal geniuses needed to make food and eat it, clean up, and use the bathroom.

As the saying went, even a king puts his pants on one leg at a time.

In the grand scheme of things, people were slightly more evolved than their nearest relatives—the chimpanzees—and immortals were the next step in that evolution. It was a huge one, but at the end of the day, they were still just animals made of flesh, bones, and blood.

The question was whether people had something extra—an eternal soul that joined the universal consciousness once it was freed from the body.

In one of her deep dives down the YouTube rabbit hole, Gabi had stumbled upon a video of a near-death experience and had gone on to watch many more on the subject.

It had gotten her all philosophical.

Did consciousness emerge from the brain? Or did it exist prior to the brain's creation and continue after the brain's death?

Some claimed that it did, describing incredible encounters that, for some reason, tickled her memory.

Had she died in her sleep and revived without registering the event?

Could it be that her parents still existed in some form?

Were they following her life?

Did they approve of her and her life choices?

Why hadn't they contacted her?

A dream would have been nice, or a comforting whisper after she'd discovered that she'd been living a lie and that her husband had been cheating on her left and right while she'd been oblivious, believing that her life was going great.

Shaking the depressing thoughts off, Gabi forced a smile even though no one could see her. Sometimes, the act of smiling was enough to improve her mood, and lifting her head and squaring her shoulders could make her feel more confident when she was anything but.

It was a nifty trick of faking it until making it.

"So, what's that project that the boss wants William to complete yesterday?" she asked. "Does it have to do with the lockdown?"

"Of course," Kaia said. "How much did Gilbert tell you about it?"

"Only that another clan location was compromised and that Kian ordered lockdowns in both locations out of an abundance of caution."

"Yeah. That's more or less the reason, but there is much more that I don't want to get into at length because we would be on the phone for hours. The gist of it is that not too long ago, we welcomed into the village another group of long-lived people who are kind of related to us. They are a large group, and we took precautions when bringing them in, but we have reason to believe that another group of their kind followed them, and they are potentially hostile. We are not sure what their intentions are, and we are not taking any chances." She chuckled. "I'm saying 'we' and talking as if I'm in charge of the village security, but I'm just parroting what I've been told."

Kaia didn't sound concerned, but Gabi didn't think that a threat like that was trivial. "So those people who may or may not be hostile know where the other location is?"

"More or less. The place is located in downtown Los Angeles, but it's underneath an apartment building, and they wouldn't know how to get in even if it wasn't locked down. They can search the apartments, but all they will find are humans."

Gabi's hackles rose. "Would they harm the humans?"

"Not likely. They are searching for their people."

"I really hope you are right. Those innocent humans who live in that apartment building wouldn't know what hit them."

"We are watching the building, so it's not like they are being left without any defenses."

"Is that what William is working on? A way to defend that location?"

The truth was that Gabi had no idea what William's job description was.

Genius could describe many different things.

"He's working on outfitting a helicopter with a noise cannon. Immortals and other long-lived people have very sensitive ears, and a noise cannon can incapacitate them long enough for our people to slap handcuffs on them and bring them in for interrogation to find out what their intentions are."

Gabi had heard about noise cannons as an effective tool to disperse protestors and stop riots. It was a nonlethal weapon, and that made her feel better about the prospect of a possible confrontation.

She couldn't stand the thought of anyone getting hurt or dying.

"What about the humans in that building? Would they be hurt by the noise cannon?"

"We are not going to use the cannon there. These people seem to want to meet us in a remote location outside the city, and if they are friendly, we might not have to use it at all. It's just one more safety precaution to protect our team in case things go south."

"Good. I'm all for safety, and I'm worried about all the enemies the clan has. I assume that these people are not the Doomers that Onegus and Orion talked about in the restaurant?"

"No."

"So, two groups of immortals are enemies of the clan."

"Well, one that we know of. These new ones might be friendly."

Gabi sighed. "I have a feeling that the price of immortality will be more than just leaving everything I've worked for behind. I would be living in a constant state of anxiety. I don't like the idea of having known enemies who want me dead just because I belong to a group of people they disagree with. I hate it when humans do that, and I'm disappointed that immortals are just as bad."

"I don't live in fear," Kaia said as she closed a container with a loud pop. "And I don't regret it for a millisecond. I had to leave a career at Stanford behind and give up having articles written about me and by me in scientific journals, but I get to work on things I could have never even dreamt of, and I'm also less stressed than ever." She laughed. "That's probably thanks to all the great sex. Once you go immortal, you can never go mortal. The sex is just out of this world."

Gabi and Kaia had talked about intimate stuff in the past, and she loved being the cool aunt whom Kaia could ask for advice about boys. Except now the roles were reversed, she was the one doing the asking, and Kaia was the one supplying the information.

"In what way is it out of this world?" Gabi asked.

"Oh, boy. Where do I start? I need to put the containers in an insulated bag and then run to the bathroom. Can I call you back in a minute or two?"

"Sure. Take your time. It's not healthy to rush peeing. You need to relax and just let it flow."

Kaia chuckled. "Don't make me laugh, or I'll have an accident on the way to the bathroom."

"What's funny about keeping your bladder healthy? When you are stressed and rush things, the muscles in your pelvic floor tense up, which can lead to problems. Ask me how I know."

Whenever Gabi went through periods of stress, symptoms of bladder infection would send her running to the doctor, but most of the time the tests would come back negative. Eventually, she'd realized the connection between stress and the physical symptoms and had started making a conscious effort to relax her pelvic muscles.

The mind-body connection was more real than most people realized.

"I'm immortal," Kaia said. "I don't get infections, bacterial or viral, and everything heals fast. Got to go, Gabi. I'll call you in a bit."

9

SYSSI

"Time for lunch." Syssi closed her laptop and swiveled her chair to face Amanda. "Shall we adjourn to the kitchen and check on our daughters?"

Amanda lifted a pair of unfocused eyes to her. "Yeah. I was so absorbed in writing this paper that I didn't notice my stomach was growling." She stretched her arms over her head. "I have to admit that working from home has its advantages. I don't need to dress up. I have an excuse to wear my new Prada flats, and Okidu is in the kitchen making a tasty meal for us."

Syssi stifled an eye roll.

Amanda might be wearing flats, but that didn't mean she wasn't dressed in designer attire or that she looked any less than a million bucks. For someone so naturally stunning, it was odd that she felt the need to invest so much time and effort in perfecting her appearance, but perhaps it had something to do with her mother.

Annani's unearthly beauty was incomparable, so maybe the daughter felt as if she needed to work hard to measure up?

The mind was a strange and wondrous place, and each person had to navigate the landscape of their creation.

"Indeed." Syssi smiled at her sister-in-law. "But at home, you won't get the attention you're getting at the university."

Amanda waved a dismissive hand. "That used to be a factor, but it's not anymore. I'm happily mated."

"You are, but you still crave attention. Admit it."

Pursing her lips, Amanda shrugged. "It's much less important to me than it used to be. Still, as much as I'm enjoying this, working from home is not an option. We need test subjects, and we need the lab."

"How about a hybrid arrangement? We can work a couple of days a week at the university and the rest at home." Syssi pushed to her feet. "It would look less suspicious in cases like this when we both have to claim to be sick because we can't leave the village."

"It's the first time in the village's history that it's locked down. I don't expect it to happen often." Amanda leaned forward. "You should try to get another vision and clarify these gods' intentions."

Letting out a breath, Syssi plopped back down into her chair. "You have no idea how much I want to, but Kian doesn't want me to force them. He gets really upset when I do that."

Amanda arched one perfectly shaped dark brow. "It made sense to worry about the visions taking a toll on you while you were pregnant, but you're not pregnant anymore, and you need to set boundaries. My brother can be overbearing and intimidating, and I know that you don't like confrontation and love to appease him, but he shouldn't be the one deciding when you should or shouldn't use your Fates' given talent."

Syssi swallowed. "You're absolutely right, but you are also right about my aversion to conflict, and if I put my foot down on this, it will definitely lead to a major one. Besides, Kian is not entirely wrong. Sometimes, the visions take a lot out of me, and I faint or lose consciousness. I shouldn't attempt them alone, but the problem is that I can't concentrate and get in a receptive state when someone is with me in the room."

"It's not a difficult problem to solve." Amanda crossed her legs. "We can set up a camera in here, and I can watch you from another room. If something goes wrong, I will rush back in."

"That could be a solution, provided that I manage to forget that I'm being watched. Otherwise, I won't be able to reach the meditative state."

"Let's put it to the test." Amanda rose to her feet. "I'll go to the kitchen and call you from there on a video call. You'll put your phone on the coffee table facing you, sit down, and meditate."

"You'll need to be very quiet," Syssi said as Amanda opened the door.

Amanda made a gesture, zipping her lips. "I'll mute my side." She paused. "Do you want to eat lunch first?"

"No, I'd rather do it on an empty stomach. Sometimes, the visions make me nauseous."

"Don't try too hard." Amanda paused at the door. "If the vision doesn't come within minutes, let it go and come to eat lunch."

"Yes, ma'am." Syssi closed the door behind her.

Kian would be furious, especially since she was about to do it in his home office. Well, it didn't really matter where she did it. He would be mad regardless of where and how, but Amanda was right. She needed to put her foot down and stop being so accommodating.

Chuckling softly, Syssi sat on the couch and waited for the call.

She couldn't change who she was, and the truth was that Kian didn't need the additional worry when he was already dealing with so much, but it was also true that she might be able to find out valuable information that couldn't be obtained any other way.

10

GABI

Kaia's comment about immunity to infections got Gabi thinking. Since sexually transmitted diseases would no longer be an issue, condoms wouldn't be needed to protect against that either, so maybe she should consider going back on the pill.

After kicking Dylan out, she'd stopped taking contraceptives and had never gone back on them. At first, because there had been no point consuming chemicals that had undesirable side effects when she wasn't having sex. Then, when she'd become sexually active again, condoms had become a must, and since they did double duty, preventing disease and pregnancy, there was no need to consume extra chemicals.

While she'd still been married to Dylan, they had decided to wait for kids, and she had dutifully taken the pill, thinking there was no need for a married couple to use condoms. After all, they were supposed to be exclusive.

Right. Talk about naïveté.

Not only had Dylan been unfaithful, but he also hadn't been very discriminating, screwing every willing woman in his path. She'd been so lucky that he hadn't infected her with syphilis or some other cursed affliction.

Letting out a sigh, Gabi let her head drop back on the couch pillows.

She wasn't immortal yet, and until she turned, she should continue being careful and using protection, but she hadn't been careful with Uriel.

What had possessed her to decide that it was safe with him?

Why had she decided that she wouldn't mind getting pregnant with his child?

She'd believed him about being clean and about having a low sperm count, the same way she'd believed Dylan had been faithful to her.

Evidently, she hadn't learned from her mistakes, and she hadn't developed a healthy skepticism like she'd thought she had.

Healthy, yeah—what a joke.

Good nutrition and exercise might keep her body healthy, but her negative self-talk definitely didn't, and it was undoing all her other good work. After all, the body and the mind were interconnected, and one affected the other.

What she should do instead of berating herself was put a positive spin on the situation.

She was finally over Dylan's betrayal and was once again willing to take a risk and trust a man.

Yay, Gabi! You go, girl!

When her phone rang, she answered Kaia with a cheerful voice that was only slightly forced. "I see that you took my advice after all and didn't rush."

Kaia chuckled. "Yeah, but for a different reason. So, where were we?"

"You said that sex with an immortal is out of this world, and I asked you in what way."

"Right. Where do I start? I love William, so I guess it's not just about the mechanics and the chemistry but about how he makes me feel and the mystical bond we share. That probably amplifies the pleasure and takes it to a whole new level, but you are probably more interested in the other stuff."

"I'm interested in all of it. Hopefully, I'll find an immortal who will make me feel like William makes you feel."

The problem was that she kept seeing Uriel's gorgeous face whenever she thought of forever and mystical bonds, and that wasn't smart. She was setting herself up for heartbreak because he was human, and she would have to leave him even if he wanted more with her. The problem was that while she was with him, she didn't remember what she knew about immortals, and all the other obstacles to their relationship didn't seem so insurmountable.

"That's a good way to think about it." Kaia took a long breath. "I'm going to talk in generalities because it would feel awkward otherwise. Immortals are amazing lovers for several reasons. They are usually a lot older than they look, and they have a lot of experience pleasing women. It's also important to them to please the ladies even though they have to thrall them to forget the encounter. They pride themselves on being exceptional lovers, and they are totally focused on their partner, which takes some getting used to because it's intense and can reveal things you never suspected you were into. Their recuperating time is practically nothing. They are ready to go again in minutes, and they don't get tired even after the fourth or the fifth time." She chuckled. "That sounds like too much, and you might be thinking, ouch—that would be a lot of wear and tear on a human woman's intimate parts, but their venom and their saliva contain healing compounds, so instead of waking up sore and achy, you wake up feeling rejuvenated."

Instinctively, Gabi's hand went to a spot on her neck where Uriel had bitten her, or rather where she'd thought he had. She must have dreamt it because there was no sign of a hickey. Even if he had never broken her skin, what she remembered feeling should have left a mark.

"Tell me more about the bite. Does it hurt?"

Kaia snorted. "Of course, it does. The fangs slice into your skin and flesh, and there is only so much they can do to minimize the pain with their saliva. But their venom contains aphrodisiac and euphoric compounds, so as soon as it's released, the pain disappears, and it's replaced with the best orgasms you've ever had. Once you're done coming, you will float away into the best psychedelic trip you could have ever imagined having, and with zero negative side effects. You wake up feeling calm, satiated, and rejuvenated."

A pit of dread formed in Gabi's stomach.

That sounded a lot like what she'd felt this morning and the morning before that. Maybe Onegus and Orion had been right after all, and Uriel was an immortal?

But Darlene's son, who was a super hacker, had checked on him and found out where and when Uriel had been born, who his parents were, and plenty of other information that confirmed he was just a human living in Portugal and visiting the US frequently.

So why was she suddenly scared?

Wouldn't it be perfect if Uriel turned out to be immortal?

But what if he was one of those awful Doomers who kidnapped girls and sold them into sexual slavery?

Flea-market flipping could be a great cover for trafficking, and if the deal Uriel and the other two were working on involved buying women and transporting them somewhere to be sold again, that would also explain the need to fly out of town on a moment's notice.

Could the man she was falling for be a monster?

Gabi wanted to believe that she was a better judge of character than that, but she'd been proven wrong before.

"Are you there?" Kaia asked.

"Yeah, I'm here. I was just thinking."

"I bet." Kaia laughed. "You probably can't wait to finally visit the village and check out all the single guys. There are many hotties to choose from. It will be like a visit to a magical candy store. You can have as many as you want without rotting your teeth or making you nauseous, and the candy can make you immortal."

"Yeah." Gabi forced a chuckle. "I can't wait."

SYSSI

"Let's try again," Amanda said once they were done with lunch. "Allegra and Evie are napping, Alena is chatting with Orion on the phone, and Okidu is cleaning. You won't be distracted."

Trying to bring up a vision hadn't worked before. Syssi didn't know whether it was because she'd been hungry and her hunger pangs had been distracting or if it had been thoughts of her daughter waiting to eat lunch with Mommy.

Perhaps Amanda was right, and now that everything had been taken care of and there was nothing to divert her attention, she could do it.

Madame Salinka had always said that the mind needed to be calm to enter a meditative state. She'd even suggested taking a mild herbal relaxant, but Syssi didn't want to use chemical aids, especially since she didn't know what would work on her immortal body and how much of it was needed.

"Let's do it." She rose to her feet. "Are you going to stay here?"

Amanda nodded. "Call me from Kian's office."

"I will." Syssi picked up her phone and made her way down the corridor to Kian's home office.

Once there she called Amanda, propped her phone against her coffee cup, and settled on the couch. "Give me ten minutes. If nothing happens, come in, and we'll get back to work."

"Roger that," Amanda said. "I'll mute myself now."

Closing her eyes, Syssi started deep breathing as per Madame Salinka's instructions, but instead of emptying her mind, she thought about the three males she'd seen earlier in the day. The trick was not to force anything and let the information flow through her, but at the same time, direct it toward the desired outcome.

Easier said than done.

Soon, her mind was wandering in all directions, her thoughts floating in disorganized clusters that were becoming less and less cohesive the longer she was at it.

It felt a lot like the moments before falling asleep. It was a state of calm, a relief from the day's stress, and a portal into the dream world.

For a seer, it was also the portal into viewing events in the past or the future.

A female of otherworldly beauty appeared first, a goddess of such brilliant glow that Syssi had difficulty discerning her features. It was more of an impression of beauty. The female was tall and had long white hair that shimmered like diamonds. Her glowing skin made it impossible to see her eye color or the shape of her lips, but Syssi could make out her body shape from the parts covered by her silver gown.

She was exquisite.

There was another female with her, also a stunning goddess, but since she bowed as she entered the room, it was clear that she was the other goddess's servant.

Syssi couldn't understand what the servant was telling her mistress, but the impression was that she was delivering exciting news.

Who were they?

Could that be the past, and she was seeing Annani's mother and one of her servants?

The details of the room were fuzzy, but Syssi got the impression that it was a receiving room—a lady's salon.

As the vision started to fade, Syssi tried to catch some last details, but all she caught was a gleam of gold. She didn't know whether it was a vase or a statue, but the shape intrigued her. It looked like a modern piece, and it didn't match the goddess's dress or the rest of the room, with its delicate silks and ornate patterns and the dim light that added to the antiquated atmosphere. Was that a hint?

It was almost as if two worlds had collided in that singular vision.

Pulled back to reality, Syssi tried to dissect the fleeting moments she'd experienced. Why had she seen this? And what significance did the golden artifact hold?

Could it be a connection, a bridge between the present and the past?

The goddess and her servant surely held some importance to their current situation with the three gods, or perhaps it was a glimpse into the future. And that modern piece of golden art, was it an anchor to her time, a clue to aid her in deciphering the message the vision was trying to convey?

As the last vestiges of the vision evaporated, Syssi opened her eyes and let out a breath. "You can come in," she told Amanda.

A moment later, the door opened, and her sister-in-law walked in. "Well? What did you see?" She sat next to her on the couch.

"Nothing that's connected to our current crisis. I saw two goddesses, a lady, and her servant. I didn't hear them talking, and I don't know if the vision happened in the past or the future. The only clue I got was a gold vase or statue that looked like a piece of modern art." She shook her head. "I'm not even going to tell Kian about it because it's not going to help him with what he's dealing with now, and it will only stress him out that I forced a vision."

Amanda chuckled. "As if there is anything you can keep from him for longer than five minutes. How are you feeling? Are you okay?"

Syssi nodded. "I'm drained, but it's nothing a few minutes of rest won't fix." She leaned her head against the couch cushions and closed her eyes. "There was another clue. The goddess I saw shone so bright that I couldn't see her clearly. Do you know if your grandmother had a particularly strong glow?"

"My mother never mentioned it. She was very beautiful, though. More so than the other goddesses." Amanda smiled. "Nai was an insignificant goddess and underage when she seduced Ahn. Given that he was such a stickler for the rules and that every goddess vied for his attention, Nai must have been extraordinary to succeed in tempting him to break the law for her."

Syssi laughed. "Your grandfather was much naughtier than he made himself out to be. He was a rebel, had an illicit affair with the Kra-ell heir to the throne, got her pregnant with twins, and then later allowed the underage Nai to seduce him. I wonder how many other naughty things he did."

JADE

On her way home, Jade debated between the two candidates she had in mind for the mission. Borga was better trained, and she was also coolheaded and functioned well under pressure, but Jade didn't like the female, and she didn't fully trust her either.

It would have to be Morgada, even though she wouldn't be much help if things got dicey. She wasn't a great diplomat either, but she was a pleasant, non-threatening female, which was uncommon for pure-blooded Kra-ell.

Who knew? Maybe that was precisely what was needed for this odd situation.

The thing was, Jade didn't expect the meeting to turn violent. Whoever was broadcasting the signals wanted to find out who they were dealing with, and attacking the team sent out to meet them would be counterproductive to that goal.

Yeah, Morgada was probably the right choice.

Entering the house through the backyard, Jade found Drova in the area they had designated for training. For a long moment, she watched her daughter go through the stances, admiring the fluidity and accuracy of her movements. The girl was a born fighter.

Holding the staff horizontally behind her with both hands, Drova swung it overhead in a powerful arc, mimicking the dive of a hunting bird. The staff sliced through the air, creating a resonant hum. Transitioning smoothly, she twirled the staff deftly in front of her, the rotations tight and close to her body, making her a moving fortress.

It would be impossible for an adversary to get close without confronting the relentless rotations of her staff.

Next, using the staff as a vaulting pole, she kicked out both her feet in front of her, then landed and pivoted, sweeping the weapon around at ground level to target an imaginary opponent's legs. She fluidly shifted, twirling the staff above her head, creating a barrier and then striking diagonally.

With each movement, her feet danced in perfect synchronization, never missing a beat. She showcased not only power but also grace—each combat stance was a balance of strength and elegance.

To finish, she held the staff vertically in front of her, took a deep breath, and exhaled, pushing the staff in an upward motion. As it rose, she followed its trajectory with a leap, spinning in the air, and landing with the staff grounded beside her, standing tall and proud.

"Looking good," Jade complimented her daughter. "That was flawless."

Drova regarded her with a raised brow. "Thank you. Hearing praise from you is unexpected. Usually, you only bother to comment on my technique if it needs improvement."

"That's the traditional Kra-ell way. Excellence is expected, less than that is corrected. But even an old horse can learn a new trick, right?"

Drova chuckled. "I don't think that's how the saying goes, but I get what you're trying to say. You're learning many new things, and I guess giving out compliments is one of them?"

"More or less."

This was actually something Jade had picked up from Phinas. She'd seen him training with Drova and complimenting her left and right. The girl seemed to do much better with praise than with criticism, and Phinas had claimed that it was universally true and urged Jade to try it.

Drova leaned her staff against the fence. "So, what was the meeting about?"

"Come inside, and I'll tell you. Is Phinas home?"

"Yeah, he is." Drova followed her into the living room.

Jade found her mate sitting at the kitchen counter and eating a sandwich.

Poor guy didn't get to have dinners with his family. His mate and stepdaughter didn't eat the same things he did and never would.

He put the sandwich down and turned to her. "How did the meeting go?"

She pulled out a stool next to him and sat down. "It was surprising, to say the least. Kian wants me to lead the team, at least to start with. And if our immortal companions need to pretend to be human, I will lead the talk throughout the meeting."

Phinas grinned. "That's great. It means that he trusts you."

"It would seem so. He also let me choose who I want to take with me. The plan is to send two Kra-ell females and two immortals who can pass for humans. I didn't decide who the other female is going to be, but I chose one of the immortals." She smiled at him. "You."

"Me?" He put a hand on his chest. "And Kian is okay with that?"

"Kalugal suggested Rufsur, but since he's mated to Edna, who's a council member, that's not an option. Initially, I didn't want you to be part of the team in case things went wrong." She looked at her daughter. "I wanted at least one of us to be here for Drova, but I reconsidered. I'd rather have you by my side than a Guardian I don't know."

Frowning, Drova lifted her hand. "I assume that it has something to do with the village being locked down, but it seems like I'm missing crucial pieces of information. What's going on?"

When Jade was done explaining about Syssi's vision and who they suspected was sending the signals, Drova's eyes widened with excited determination.

"I want to be part of the mission, Mother."

It hadn't even occurred to Jade that Drova could be a candidate. Her daughter was a damn good fighter, but she was just a kid.

"You're too young."

Squaring her shoulders, Drova cast her a hard look. "I'm almost seventeen, and according to Kra-ell tradition, I am old enough to take part in defending our tribe. Besides, after you, I'm the best female fighter you have, and you know that."

Jade looked at her daughter with pride. "I appreciate your confidence and desire to help, but this mission requires diplomatic skills that you haven't mastered yet."

The stubborn expression on Drova's face wavered for a split second. "Who do you have in mind for the mission?"

"Borga or Morgada. Each has things going for and against her."

"Let me guess. You are considering Borga for her fighting ability and Morgada for her amiable nature."

"That's right."

"Neither of them has diplomatic skills, and you're not planning on letting them talk. You will do all the talking."

Jade had to smile. Her daughter knew her well. "That's right."

"Then you can take me." Drova cast Phinas a sugary smile. "It can be a family mission."

Phinas looked appalled. "You're too young, and this mission is full of uncertainties. I can't risk your safety, and even if I was okay with that, Kian would never let an underage girl join the mission. Don't waste his time even suggesting it."

Drova shifted her gaze to him. "Kian is not in charge of me or my mother. If Jade deems me ready, he can't say no."

Phinas snorted. "That's what you think. But go ahead and give it a try."

Drova returned her gaze to Jade. "It's up to you, and I hope you choose me. I won't be reckless. I promise to follow your guidance to the letter, and I'm a better choice than Borga or Morgada. Please, let me prove myself."

There was a very good chance that Kian would put his foot down and forbid Drova's participation, but even if he didn't, Jade couldn't deny that Drova was right. According to Kra-ell traditions, she was old enough, and she had the skills, and Jade had no right to keep her away from danger because she was her daughter.

"Fine. But if Kian refuses to let you go, I don't want you to argue with him. I need you to act professionally and accept whatever he says. We are forging an alliance with the clan, and this mission is a test. I don't want anything to screw it up."

Drova didn't look happy with that, but she nodded. "I'll be the picture of the obedient underling. Professional all the way. I won't let you down."

13

GILBERT

"Chocolate or vanilla?" Gilbert tugged on Idina's foot. She was sitting on his shoulders, her sandal-clad feet dangling over his chest and her small hands clasping his forehead.

He loved every freaking moment of it and dreaded the day she would no longer want to ride on top of her daddy's shoulders.

"Vanilla with sprinkles." She leaned her pointy chin on his head.

"They don't have sprinkles in the café."

"So tell them to bring some. Vanilla with no sprinkles is boring."

"The boys want chocolate," Karen said.

"I don't want ice cream." Cheryl turned the double stroller toward the playground.

"Wait." Karen caught her hand. "Look over there." She pointed with her chin. "Isn't that Ingrid?"

"It is," Gilbert said. "Go talk to her about decorating your cabana."

"She's busy." Cheryl chewed on her lower lip. "I don't want to bother her."

The designer was sitting at a table with a muscular guy who reminded Gilbert of the actor who played the military dude in *Avatar*. Cropped blond hair, a square jaw, and the aura of a drill sergeant.

"That's Atzil," Karen said. "He's Kalugal's cook."

Gilbert took another look. "That guy is a cook? Are you sure?"

She chuckled. "He looks like a bodybuilder, but he's the cook, and he's a very nice guy."

"How do you know that he's nice?" Gilbert narrowed his eyes at her.

"That's what I heard." She lightly slapped his bottom. "Go get the ice cream for the kids. I'll introduce Cheryl to Ingrid."

Half an hour later, Cheryl had an appointment at Ingrid's design studio for the next day, and she happily took her younger siblings to the playground, leaving the adults to talk in peace.

"So, Atzil," Gilbert started. "Karen tells me that you are Kalugal's chef."

"Cook," Atzil corrected. "I never studied in a fancy culinary school, but I can cook a hearty meal, and I hear no complaints from the men." He sighed. "I wish there was someone who could do my job, but there are no takers, and someone needs to cook for the men, or they will live off frozen pizzas and sandwiches from the café."

Ingrid put her hand on Atzil's massive shoulder. "Atzil has his eyes set on running the new bar, but there's more involved than just finding a replacement cook for Kalugal. Kian wouldn't allow a former Doomer in his secure section of the village, and that's where the bar is located. It's such an awesome place, and I put so much effort into decorating it authentically, but it stands empty, collecting dust because no one other than Atzil is interested in running it."

"The bar was built to look like a hobbit's home," Atzil said. "Ingrid decorated it with rustic furniture and earthy colors, and all it needs now is someone to pour the drinks and serve some food. It could be the new social gathering place for everyone in the village, but since it's located in Kian's secure enclave, that's a problem."

The wheels in Gilbert's head started spinning. "When you say that it's built to look like a hobbit's home, do you mean that it's hewed out of the earth?"

Ingrid nodded. "From a distance, it appears as a gentle hill with a circular door. It's made from dark wood and adorned with ornate iron hinges and a big rustic knob right in the center. Two round windows flank the door to let in some natural light to the entrance, which leads to a tunnel-like hallway with walls that are lined with earth and reclaimed timber beams. The floor is paved in rounded stones, made to look as if they were worn smooth by the footsteps of countless patrons." She smiled. "Not too comfortable for high heels, I'm afraid, so I covered them with hand-woven rugs in rich, earthy tones."

"The bar area has an arched ceiling that's supported by timber beams," Atzil said. "It gives the entire space a cave-like feeling. It's chilly even on a hot day."

Karen grimaced. "That sounds dark and dreary."

"Not at all," Atzil said. "Ingrid placed lanterns on the walls that fill the space with a soft glow, and the round windows at the front let some light in as well. The tables and chairs are crafted from polished wood, and each is uniquely shaped because they were handmade by a local craftsman."

"I added cushions and throws in deep reds and golds to make the place nice and cozy," Ingrid said. "But the real masterpiece is the bar counter. It's a single elongated slab of wood, polished to a gleam, show-casing its natural grain and knots. Behind it, I had shelves carved into the walls to display bottles." She cast Atzil a fond glance. "When I was coming up with the design, I had you in mind. Perhaps that's why you fell in love with the place at first glance."

The poor guy looked speechless, his Adam's apple bobbing in his throat. "You never told me that before."

Ingrid shrugged. "I didn't want it to go to your head."

Gilbert wasn't interested in all the decorating details or Ingrid and Atzil's sappy romance. He was concerned with more practical issues, like opening the bar doors to the public. "Since the bar is hewn from the hill, perhaps it's possible to dig a tunnel leading to it from another section of the village and block off the entrance from Kian's side. That way, everyone can use it. Once this latest mess is over, I can stop by the architect's office and review the plans with him to see what can be done." He leaned back in his chair. "Or I can have a word with Kian about the segregation of the village. I understand his concern with secu-rity, but everyone living in the village should be a trusted community member. If they are not, they shouldn't be here."

Ingrid snorted. "Good luck with that. The village might look like a democracy to you, but it's not. Kian has the final word, and the only one who can overrule him is Annani, but she never does because she doesn't want to undermine his authority. Besides, as much as I would like Atzil to have his bar, I don't think it's worth creating social unrest."

The interior designer was feistier than she looked, and Gilbert liked her. "So let me get this straight. Are you willing to accept every rule that Kian makes? How is that different from living in a dictatorship?"

"Kian doesn't make rules to benefit himself. He makes them to keep all of us safe."

"Really?" Gilbert cocked a brow. "So, the rest of us plebs are okay to intermingle with everyone else and live with the Kra-ell and the former Doomers, no offense meant, but Kian and the rest of the aristocracy are not?"

Ingrid opened her mouth, closed it, and then opened it again. "I guess there is something to that, but on the other hand, the rest of us are not important enough to merit threats. It's like the president. He or she needs to be protected twenty-four-seven because they are public figures, and some might wish them ill. The average Joe and Jane don't need to worry about safety because they are of no interest to anyone other than their family and friends."

Smiling, Gilbert lifted his soda bottle. "To the average Jane and Joe. We have it so much better than the aristocracy in many ways."

Karen clinked her bottle with his. "To being nobodies."

"To nobodies." Atzil and Ingrid joined the toast.

"I have an idea," Karen said. "How about the two of you come to our house for drinks? We can have a cheese and cocktails night."

Atzil grinned. "That's a wonderful idea, but I have a better one. Since you have a house full of kids, you should come to Ingrid's house, and I'll treat you to cocktails and appetizers Atzil style." He smiled apologetically. "I would have invited you to mine, but I live with a roommate."

Leaning forward, Ingrid whispered, "Atzil hasn't slept in his house for months. He's living with me, but we didn't make any official arrangements, so no one knows."

"Why not?" Gilbert asked.

Ingrid shrugged. "That's what works for us."

Under the table, Karen lightly kicked his shin. "It's like us," she said. "Everyone keeps asking why we are not married even though we have three kids together, and my answer is very similar to yours. That's what works for us."

Gilbert couldn't disagree more, but he was wise enough to keep his mouth shut.

Atzil and Ingrid weren't fated mates. That was the reason they were not making any official announcement. Both of them were still waiting for that special someone to show up.

He and Karen were a completely different story. There was no doubt in Gilbert's mind that they were truelove mates, and hopefully, there weren't any doubts in Karen's mind either.

14

KIAN

After a short break for lunch the team reassembled in the war room, and as everyone took their seats, Turner was the first to speak up. "I've thought about the situation, and I realized that we shouldn't just show up at that canyon and hope they will meet us there. We need to send a message to let them know that we are sending a team to talk to them and when we want to meet them."

"How do you propose to do that?" Onegus said. "Leave a big sign in the canyon saying meet us here tomorrow at two o'clock in the afternoon?"

Turner didn't even crack a smile. "Something along those lines. We know they are monitoring the canyon, either with cameras on the ground or a drone from above that our own drone can't detect. We can attach a banner to our drone with that information or drop a sign."

"Why not do a fly-by and announce it with a megaphone?" Kian asked.

"They might be using only video," Turner said. "Not that I think it's likely given the technology they possess, but just in case they are collecting visuals only, we should put down something in writing."

As a knock sounded on the door, Kian swiveled his chair to look at the monitor, and when he saw who was standing at the door, he shook his head. "Jade must have lost her mind," he murmured. "Let them in."

Onegus released the lock remotely, and the door swung open.

"Good afternoon." Jade walked in with Phinas and her daughter. "Meet my team members. Drova is the other Kra-ell female I chose to accompany me." She sat on the chair Phinas pulled out for her and motioned for her daughter to sit beside her.

Kian shook his head. "Not happening. How old are you?" he asked Drova.

The girl squared her shoulders and jutted her chin out. "I'm almost seventeen."

"Which means you are sixteen." He looked at Jade. "Whose idea was this?"

"Drova volunteered, but I approved. According to Kra-ell traditions, she's old enough to fight, and she's the best female fighter I have. If things go wrong, Drova will be more valuable to me than Borga or Morgada."

The Kra-ell were different, Kian was well aware of that, but only a couple of hours ago, Jade had been reluctant to take Phinas with her because she was worried about leaving her daughter with no parental figure. What had happened between now and then for her to do a one-eighty like this?

"Are you willing to risk your daughter's life?"

Jade winced. "I can't play favorites. I realized that if Drova was someone else's daughter, I would have considered her for the team based on her fighting skills and my level of trust in her. The only reason I didn't was that she was mine, and that's not fair. If I'm willing to risk other people's children, I have to be willing to risk mine."

Kian understood that all too well.

One day, Allegra would have to take up the mantle of leadership, and he wasn't looking forward to that day. He was torn between wishing that she would never develop the necessary traits to lead or the desire to become a leader and hoping that she would.

In the end, it wasn't up to him.

It was up to fate.

However, in Jade's case, he could play the role of fate and relieve her from the burden of having to either refuse her daughter or put her at risk when it was evident that she didn't want to.

"I'm sorry, but you represent the clan in this mission, and according to our traditions, Drova is too young. Choose someone else."

He could see the tension leave Jade's shoulders. "I understand." She turned to her daughter. "You'll have to be patient and wait until you are seventeen."

"Eighteen," Kian corrected. "Seventeen is the age of consent, but eighteen is the age of enlisting in the Guardian force." He smiled at Drova. "If you wish, you can join the training program as soon as you catch up on your general studies. I'm willing to bend the rules for you and allow you to join right now. If you are as skilled as your mother claims, then you might be ready for Guardian duty at eighteen, which would be unprecedented. It usually takes decades of training until a cadet is ready to be sworn in."

Drova glanced at her mother. "Can I join the training?"

"If you so wish. But you heard Kian. You have to pass your high school equivalency test first."

"I can do both. I can study and train at the same time." She turned a pair of defiant eyes at Kian. "It's not like I have anything better to do with my time, and I can't spend sixteen hours a day sitting in front of the computer and studying. I'll go insane."

He could understand that.

The Kra-ell were not made for stuffy classrooms. They needed fresh air and plenty of physical activity, but the problem was that most of the Guardian training happened underground.

"This is a discussion for a different time." Jade pulled out her phone. "I'm going to ask Morgada to join us. You can go back home, Drova."

Reluctantly, the girl rose to her feet and dipped her head in deference to Kian. "Thank you for the offer to join the Guardian training."

"You're welcome."

Onegus lifted his hand. "Come to my office after this crisis is over."

"Yes, sir." She turned on her heel and left the room.

"I'm sorry about that," Jade said after the door closed behind her daughter. "She is a good fighter, but I'm glad you didn't allow her to join the team."

"You're welcome." Kian smiled. "I just hope someday you will return the favor when my daughter demands to participate in a dangerous mission."

She cracked a smile. "I hope to still be here when Allegra is Drova's age, and I also hope to have a say in her decisions. I promise to do my best."

"Can we go back to the message issue?" Turner asked. "If we want to fly a banner, we should get to it before it gets too dark."

Kian looked at Jade. "Will you be ready to be at the canyon at noon?"

She nodded. "You still need to coach me on what you want me to say to those gods or whoever they are. But that shouldn't take too long, right?"

He nodded. "The list of things you can't tell them is much longer than the list of what you can."

"That's what I thought. We should be able to make it by noontime."

15

ARU

Negal stood next to the hotel room window with his hands tucked in the back pockets of his jeans. "It's getting dark. No one is going to show up at that canyon today."

"They flew the drone over the area again," Dagor said. "This time, it was a high-altitude military drone they thought we couldn't detect." He snorted. "Who do they think they are dealing with?"

Aru frowned. "Are you sure the military drone was theirs? Maybe there is an Air Force base nearby."

Dagor shook his head. "There isn't, and civilians don't have drones like that. It's another clue as to the military ability of our adversaries. In my humble opinion, we should take the drone down to show them that we are not to be messed with."

Dagor was young and hotheaded, but thankfully, Negal wasn't.

"We can't take their drone down," the old trooper said. "It would be considered a hostile act, and rightfully so. Our objective is to find out who took the Kra-ell and what they did with them. Not to start a war." He pinned Dagor with a hard look. "Above all, we need to keep our presence on the planet a secret. Humans can't be allowed to find out about us."

"We also don't want to get shot at by that drone." Dagor turned to

Aru. "We are hard to destroy, but if they blow us up, even we can die. I don't intend to end my life on this godforsaken planet."

"Clever." Aru snorted. "You couldn't have said it better if you tried."

Earth had indeed been forsaken by the gods. It had been erased from all historical records and all the astronomical maps. No gods were ever supposed to visit the cursed planet, and except for a select few, no one on Anumati knew that this sector was still being patrolled.

The remark didn't pull a smile out of Dagor like Aru had expected.

"We need to take that bird down. Whoever they are, they are not familiar with our technology and will not know that we were responsible for the drone's demise. They will think it malfunctioned."

Negal sat on one of the beds and leaned his elbows on his knees. "How many times do I need to tell you that we can't? Even if the cause of the drone's demise could be blamed on a malfunction, once the drone is disabled, it will crash, and it's a big bird that can cause a lot of damage. I don't want innocent human lives on my conscience."

"There is nothing to destroy on Mount Baldy," Dagor insisted.

Negal cast him an exasperated look. "It could start a brush fire, and given how dry everything is, it would spread so fast the humans wouldn't be able to contain it. Do you want to explain that to the commander?"

That got Dagor to finally nod in agreement. "Fine. I just hope that these people are other Kra-ell and not humans. I don't want to think what the commander would do to us if we reported that the Kra-ell from Gor's compound were taken by humans. The cleanup job would be massive."

"Yeah, and we would have to do it," Negal said. "But that's neither here nor there. I'm tired of sitting around and waiting, and since it's getting dark and no one is going to show up, I say we get out of here and get something to eat."

"Not yet." Aru pushed to his feet and opened the balcony door. "I need to make a phone call."

"To your human?" Negal asked.

Shrugging, Aru ignored the question and stepped outside.

Negal followed him. "You've been seeing her every night since we got here. You know that's irresponsible."

"It's not your place to lecture me about responsibility, Negal. I know what I'm doing."

"Do you? Are you thralling her to forget what you do to her every time you are with her? You know what repeated thralling can do to a human. If you care for the girl, you should stay away from her."

"We don't know that's true. It might have been part of the propaganda." Aru didn't sound convinced even to himself.

He could already see the damage his thralling was doing, even though it shouldn't have after only a couple of times. The female was getting headaches and often looked confused as if she couldn't remember the most basic things.

Perhaps she was already mentally compromised, and his thralling was exacerbating the problem?

"It's not propaganda, Aru. It's science. Human brains were designed to be susceptible to our manipulation, but we were warned that too much of it can fry them and to use our powers with caution."

"Not only humans," Aru murmured. "Every species our scientists created was designed to allow us to control it."

"All except for the Kra-ell." Negal smiled sadly. "They were the first, and the scientists didn't think to modify their genetics with a safety feature that would give us control over their minds. With that one simple modification, a lot of the bloody mess on Anumati would have been avoided. The Kra-ell wouldn't have sought equal rights, and there would have been no rebellion."

Aru waved a dismissive hand. "You know better than to believe everything they say, or anything for that matter. The propaganda machine is so massive that it's nearly impossible for commoners like us to know the truth."

Negal huffed. "Don't tell me that you believe the Kra-ell legends that claim they were the first people and that we are a modified version of them and not the other way around?"

"Why not? It's just as plausible as us creating them as our first modified species. What's recorded in history is what our rulers want us to believe, not the absolute truth."

322

16

GABI

After three hours of getting pampered in the hotel's spa, Gabi felt refreshed and much less irritable than she had been going in, and she had Karen to thank for the idea.

In fact, she should call her.

Once she exited the elevator on her floor, she pulled the phone out of her robe pocket and dialed her sister-in-law.

"Hi, Gabi," Karen answered right away. "Regrettably, I have no news. We are still in lockdown."

That wasn't a big surprise. If the lockdown had been lifted, Gilbert would have called her already to schedule a time to pick her up. Then again, she'd been around people, so everything pertaining to immortals, the village, and the lockdown had retracted to the recesses of her mind, and all she'd remembered was that her brothers were working on some big business deal and that was why they couldn't see her.

It was all very confusing, and it was a miracle she was still clinging to her sanity.

Uriel had a lot to do with that, no doubt. Without him to distract her, she would have gone nuts. But on the other hand, if it wasn't for him, she would have gone to the village when she'd arrived and would have been locked down together with her family, and her mind wouldn't be in danger of getting fried.

He was worth it, though.

Being with him was a once-in-a-lifetime experience, and she would cherish it for many years to come.

As sadness threatened to obliterate her good mood, Gabi took a deep breath and forced a smile. "I guessed as much. I'm just calling to tell you that I listened to your advice and splurged on a spa treatment. I got a massage, a pedicure, and a manicure and had my hair done. I feel like a new woman."

"Awesome. I'm glad you are not wasting your vacation by sitting around in your room and waiting for your brothers to call."

What Karen had probably meant by that was that Gabi wasn't waiting for Uriel to call her, not Gilbert or Eric, but the truth was that she'd held the phone in her hand throughout the spa treatments in case Uriel called.

She chuckled. "Hopefully, tomorrow I can finally come visit you in the village. I can't afford another spa treatment."

"Didn't they give you a discount?"

Karen had told her to say that she was Mr. MacBain's guest so she could get a discount, but when Gabi had gotten to the salon, she couldn't remember the name. It was part of the thralling or compulsion or whatever it was that Orion had done to her. She was only free to remember what she'd been told during the meeting with her family and their new friends when she was alone, and apparently, it included the names of those friends.

"I couldn't remember the name, so I didn't say anything. They charged it to my room."

"I'll take care of it," Karen said. "Don't worry about the bill."

"I don't want you to pay for it." Gabi pulled the room key out of her pocket and opened the door.

"I won't. I'll speak to Onegus and ask him to tell the front desk to give you a discount on the spa treatments."

"Don't bother him with that." Gabi sat down on the couch and lifted her feet onto the coffee table. "He needs to concentrate on solving the security issue and lifting the lockdown."

"That's okay. I won't mention it until the crisis is over."

"Good. Are the boys sleeping? I don't hear any ruckus in the background."

Karen chuckled. "That's because we are not home, and Cheryl took them to play in the sandbox. Gilbert and I are in the village café, sitting with a lovely couple and enjoying an adult conversation. You have no idea how great that feels after dealing with the little ones all day long."

Should she be offended that her brother was there and hadn't asked to speak with her? Evidently, Gilbert was enjoying the adult company as much as Karen and didn't want to be bothered by his sister.

"I'll let you go so you can enjoy your evening. Say hi to Gilbert for me, will you?"

"Of course. He sends his love."

Gabi rolled her eyes. Gilbert would never say something like that. Karen was just being nice. "Right back at him. Call me as soon as anything changes with the lockdown situation."

After ending the call, Gabi let out a sigh and wiggled her toes, admiring the bright red nail polish. She'd wanted dark green, but the beautician had convinced her to go with a traditional red, saying that it went better with her skin tone.

She was right, of course.

Her toes looked amazing, and it was a shame she didn't have open-toe sandals to show off the pedicure.

It would also be a shame if Uriel didn't call up and they didn't go out, and all that pampering went to waste.

Gabi wasn't the type who went out alone and picked up guys in bars, and she had no friends in Los Angeles whom she could call up and invite to a girls' night out. The only people she knew were her family, and they were stuck in the village.

When her phone rang a few minutes later, she knew it was Uriel, and not because she had any supernatural senses. The call came on her regular phone, not the one she had gotten from Onegus, and her clients and friends from Cleveland would text her first.

Onegus had offered to forward her calls to the new phone, but Gabi had declined, preferring to keep her old life separate from the one she was about to embark on.

Letting it ring several times before answering required a deliberate effort, but she didn't want Uriel to think that she was just sitting around and waiting for his call.

"Hi," she said as nonchalantly as she could. "Are you done with your meetings?"

"For today, I am. Did you hear anything from your brothers?"

"They are still not back. Their deal must be as complicated as yours."

"Their loss is my gain. I get to invite you to another dinner. We could go to the same restaurant or find something else in the city. What's your pleasure?"

"I'm in a mood for something more exciting. How about a nightclub? I can ask the concierge to recommend a classy place."

Looking at her painted toes, Gabi regretted again not having sandals. Perhaps she could go on a quick shopping run and get a pair. But that would be wasteful. She'd already bought a pair of new shoes on this trip.

"I don't like nightclubs," Uriel said. "They are too noisy."

She was so used to men agreeing to do everything she wanted that her first response to his answer was surprise.

The second was suspicion.

Uriel was too young and too hip to be bothered by the noise level in nightclubs—unless he had very sensitive ears—like the immortals.

Still, Onegus, or rather Roni, had checked Uriel's background, and everything had looked legit. Uriel was human.

Was he, though?

What if they were wrong?

It didn't make much sense that she could uncover something that the mighty clan hacker couldn't, but perhaps there were subtle hints she could pick up on?

What else gave immortals away?

Fangs, of course, and glowing eyes, which they got when they were aroused, but they could thrall their partners to forget seeing those things.

They were also super strong, but it wasn't as if she could tell Uriel to bench-press a car.

"We could go to a comedy club," Gabi suggested. "They are much less noisy."

"I'd rather go to dinner. I'm hungry, and not just for food."

Well, if he put it that way. "I'm hungry too. When can you get here?"

"Are you sure you want to eat in your hotel restaurant again?"

"Yeah, the food is okay, and the cocktails are great. But the best thing it has going for it is the convenient location. It's only two and a half minutes away from my room."

17

ARU

"I'll be damned." Dagor leaned closer to the screen. "They are sending us a message."

Aru put a hand on Dagor's shoulder and leaned over his head to look at the screen. A low-flying drone, the kind anyone could buy on the internet, was making passes over the canyon with a banner flying behind it.

On one end, there was a circle with a vertical line down the middle and an upside-down Y shape inside the circle. It was what the humans considered a universally accepted peace sign. On the other side, it had a dove holding an olive branch in its beak, which was another human peace sign. Between the two signs, written in bold letters and numbers, was 12:00 noon Wednesday.

"They want to meet us tomorrow at noon, and they come in peace," Negal translated the sign, as if it needed translation. "Or, more accurately, they want us to believe that they come in peace." He looked at Aru. "Should we send them a message back?"

"Not yet." He looked at the nearly dark sky. "They are not expecting an answer today anyway."

"They know we are watching the canyon." Dagor turned to look at Aru over his shoulder. "They expect some type of response."

"And they will get it. Just not today." He smiled. "Do they really expect us to accept that their intentions are peaceful and walk into a trap?"

"Maybe." Negal shrugged. "We expected them to rush in to check who was emitting the signals. They outsmarted us and sent a drone instead, and evidently, they also figured out that we must be monitoring the canyon."

Aru headed toward the door connecting Negal and Dagor's room to his. "They are not stupid, and once they realized that there was no one there, it was logical for them to assume that we were watching." He opened the door.

"Where are you going?" Negal asked. "We need to plan what to do tomorrow."

Aru smiled. "You know what to do. We talked about it. We will implement plan B, but we will wait until the last moment to do so."

"Smart but risky," Dagor said. "They might bolt."

"They won't." Aru stepped into his room and closed the door behind him.

They had rented a two-bedroom suite in the hotel, and although he usually didn't like pulling rank on his teammates, having a room to himself was the one exception.

Since the walls were thin and the doors provided no soundproofing at all, there was no real privacy to be had, but for this communication, he didn't need to say a word out loud.

Taking his boots off, he lay on the bed, closed his eyes, and opened a channel.

Can you talk?

Yes, Aria's voice sounded in his head. *Are you well, Aru?*

I am very well, thank you for asking. The plan worked, and the other party responded. They flew a banner that specified the day and time of the meeting. They also added two peace signs to reassure us that they meant no harm.

There was a long moment of silence on their mental connection. *What did they use to symbolize peace?*

She was always so literal. Even when they were children, Aria needed to know every detail. It was a wonder that she had not become a scientist, but then the Fates had decreed a different path for them, one that might be more pivotal to the future of Anumati than any new scientific or engineering marvel.

They used human symbolism. Luckily, we have been here long enough to be acquainted with them, so we knew what they meant.

It might be a trap, she said.

Aru smiled even though she could not see him. Hopefully, she could hear it in the tone of his mental voice. *It might be, but I am not going to walk into a trap. I have a plan.*

You always do. Aria sighed. *I miss you, and I miss your hugs. They are the only thing capable of bringing me peace. The years you've spent in stasis were the most difficult of my life. The silence in my head was depressing.*

Leaving Aria behind was the hardest part of joining the crew of the ship patrolling this sector, but it wasn't as if either of them had a choice. They had literally been born for this mission.

I miss you too, but now we get to talk whenever we please, and we can do it in complete privacy.

That was not something that Negal or Dagor could do. If they wanted to communicate with loved ones on Anumati, they had to route the call through the patrol ship, and even though the entire enormous interstellar vessel was staffed with people who supported their cause, everything they said on those calls had to be recorded and reported. It was protocol.

Semi-complete privacy, Aria chuckled. *The Supreme knows every word we exchange.*

Of course. Neither of us can keep secrets from the Supreme.

The Supreme could have several meanings in their language, and that was why they were using the term to describe their leader, even though it was probably an unnecessary precaution. No one had ever heard of anyone capable of eavesdropping on a telepathic communication, but he and Aria were not taking any chances.

No one knew that they possessed the ability to talk to each other telepathically, so no one had reason to penetrate their private channel. But if anyone was listening to their conversations, they could only accuse Aru of disclosing classified information to a loved one.

The one they called Supreme had to remain shielded at all costs, even if the cost was their lives.

18

GABI

Gabi put on lipstick, smacked her lips even though all the makeup tutorials said not to do that, and brushed her hair with her fingers.

"How am I going to trick Uriel into revealing whether he's immortal?"

Maybe she could whisper something scandalous from far away and watch his reaction?

She could go to the bathroom and, once she was out of his hearing range, say something about fondling his balls or licking him up and down like a popsicle. That would get a response out of him for sure. No guy, whether human or immortal, could keep a stoic expression when hearing a woman make a promise like that.

Not that she knew much about immortals, but since they looked like humans and had the same anatomy, it was safe to assume that what worked on regular men would work just as well on them.

Smiling, she took her purse, checked that her room key was in her wallet, and walked out. Uriel had offered to pick her up at her room, but Gabi knew that if they met there, they would never leave, which would have been fine with her if she wasn't hungry and didn't need to also talk to him and test whether he was immortal.

The problem was that she would forget her plans as soon as she entered a room full of people. Heck, she would forget it as soon as she saw him.

But maybe if she held the thought firmly in her mind, it wouldn't disappear, and she would remember to execute her plan. But then, if Uriel was indeed immortal, he could pluck those thoughts from her head, which was why Orion had messed with it to start with.

But what if she framed the test in her mind as a sexy game?

She could whisper naughty things to him and try to determine if he was actually hearing her or if he was guessing what she was saying just from her body language. She should be able to hold on to that thought.

The bullet elevator no longer made her nauseous, and as she exited on the restaurant level, she wasn't dizzy as she walked up to the hostess. "I'm meeting Uriel Delgado for dinner tonight. Is he here already?"

The hostess smiled. "He is. I'll take you to your table."

As Gabi followed the woman, something bothered her, but she couldn't put her finger on what it was. When had Uriel told her his last name?

She couldn't remember him actually saying it, but she knew it somehow. She also knew that there was something she needed to do later in the evening, but she couldn't remember what that was either.

When the hostess turned into the alcove and Uriel came into view, the bothersome thoughts flew out the window, and all Gabi could think about was how sexy he looked in the pale pink dress shirt and charcoal gray slacks.

The guy was magnificent no matter what he was wearing, and even more so when he had nothing on at all, but she liked seeing him in dress clothes that she would later peel off him one item at a time.

Standing with the chair pulled out for her, he leaned to kiss her cheek. "You look beautiful tonight."

"Thank you. So do you."

He grinned, flashing two rows of perfect white teeth. His canines were slightly longer than average, and in the back of her mind, Gabi knew that it was significant for some reason, but when she tried to remember why, a pulse of pain blasted through her head.

Wincing, she sat down and let Uriel push her chair in. "So, how did it go today? Did you close the deal?"

"Not yet." He sat across from her. "But we made significant progress. Tomorrow is going to be the pivotal day. How about you? Did you hear from your brothers?"

"No, not yet. I spoke with my sister-in-law earlier, but she had no news for me." Gabi could only remember telling Karen about the spa visit but not about when Gilbert and Eric were coming back.

"What about your nieces and nephews?"

To her shame, Gabi couldn't recall having asked Karen about them.

She shook her head. "I don't know what's wrong with me. I guess I forgot to ask her about them. But since she didn't mention anything, I assume that they are alright."

Uriel's eyes filled with worry. "Does forgetting things like that happen to you often?"

"Not normally, no, but since I got here, it happens a lot. At first, I thought that I was suffering from PTSD because I was so scared of flying across the continent, but thanks to you, the flight wasn't that traumatic. Besides, it has been days, and I shouldn't still be experiencing side effects." She rubbed her temples. "Maybe it's all the changes, and I will be okay once I return to my routine, and if not, I'll get my doctor to run some tests. I heard that thyroid imbalance can cause memory issues."

He seemed even more unsettled as he reached for her hand. "Regrettably, I'm ignorant about everything that has to do with medicine and what it takes to keep the body in balance. That being said, the main thing that has changed since you got here is me. I feel guilty because I keep you awake at night, and you might not be getting enough sleep."

This time, her smile wasn't forced. "If not for you, this trip would have been a complete disaster. With my family unable to meet me, I would have nothing to look forward to."

His worried expression turned into a guilty one. "Every night, I think it's going to be the last, and I prepare myself mentally not to see you again, but then you call me, or I call you, and I'm overjoyed that I will be seeing you again, even though I know that it will make parting from you so much harder."

It was nice of Uriel to say that, and he might have even meant it, but

Gabi knew as well as he did that there was no future for them. She had a life in Cleveland, and he had a life wherever it was he lived.

"I feel the same," she admitted. "You still didn't tell me where you are based or what you do when you are not hunting for treasures and making deals to sell them. For all I know, you might have a wife and six kids waiting for you to finalize your deal and bring home the bacon."

"Bacon?" He arched a brow. "Why would I be bringing home bacon?"

That was what had bothered him about what she'd said? Not the wife and six kids?

She narrowed her eyes at him. "When someone says they are bringing home the bacon, it's a reference to their role as a provider for their family, implying that they are earning a living and supporting their loved ones. Usually, their wife and kids."

19

URIEL

Gabriella Emerson was breaking his stupid heart.

He should have never allowed her to get under his skin like that, but there was something about her he just couldn't resist. She wasn't like any of the other women he had been with, not because she was more beautiful, or had softer skin, or a smile that was more alluring, and it wasn't that she was smarter, more charming, or a better lover, although to him she was all those things.

It was that she had that something extra he had never expected to find here or back at home.

"I'm not married, and I don't have children. You are the only woman in my life right now."

She arched a brow. "That's convenient. How about last week? Was there someone special back then?"

Answering truthfully wasn't the smartest move on his part, but he had never claimed to be particularly clever. Sometimes, he just had to follow his gut. "I never stay anywhere long enough to have someone special, but for some reason, you have become special to me in the short time we've had together, and that's why I know that saying goodbye to you will hurt like hell."

For a long moment, she just looked at him, seemingly debating what to say. "We are both single adults, and we get to decide what our future will look like. We could decide that giving this relationship a chance is more important than you chasing the next treasure or my nutrition practice. We could forge a future in which we can be together."

Her words were like a javelin to his heart. It was so gutsy of her to say them, but regrettably, nothing could be further from the truth.

She was human, and she could never find out that he was not, but to keep thralling her was irresponsible. The right thing to do would be to part ways with her tonight without taking her to bed, but he wasn't strong enough to just walk away.

He could refrain from biting her, but that wouldn't be helpful because he would have to thrall her to forget seeing his fangs and his glowing eyes.

Maybe he could blindfold her?

Would she trust him enough to allow him to tie her up?

He would never do that without her full consent.

Gabi let out a sigh. "Your silence is answer enough, and you're probably right. I don't know enough about you to fantasize about a shared future. For all I know, you might be a terrible person."

"I would like to think that I'm a good guy, but then no one thinks of themselves as evil, not even the most evil ones. They think that they are justified in their evil-doing."

She tilted her head. "Have you ever deliberately hurt someone?"

He was a soldier, but he was young, and he hadn't taken part in a violent conflict yet, so he was lucky enough to have never used force to hurt anyone, but there was no guarantee that he wouldn't in the future. In fact, it was almost a certainty.

But for now, he could answer her question truthfully. "I have not."

Her smile was radiant. "Then you are a good person. It's as simple as that."

"I wish it was." He sighed. "The truth is that I'm not free to do as I please, Gabi. In a perfect world, I would have been overjoyed by the chance of a relationship with you, but my world is far from perfect, and I can't really tell you much about it. My partners and I are involved in something pretty big, and I'm not in a position to walk away and do my own thing."

She nodded. "I understand. Is there anything at all that you can tell me about yourself?"

He could tell her his fake identity, but he didn't want to lie to her. Lies of omission were bad enough.

"I can't. I'm sorry." He leaned over the table and took her hand. "All I can tell you are anecdotes from my travels and the various finds my friends and I have discovered, if those are of any interest to you."

Looking defeated, Gabi nodded. "Maybe I'll get to know you a little better from those stories. I just wish I knew why you need to be so secretive. Are you a spy?"

In a way, he was, so he could admit it. "I am."

Her eyes widened. "For who?"

"No one you know, and I'm not spying on anyone you care about. I'm looking for a group of people that might be hiding somewhere around here."

That should be vague enough.

Her brows pulled down in a frown. "What are you going to do to them once you find them?"

"Nothing. My job is to observe and report. Nothing more."

Gabi was still frowning. "Okay. Let me ask it in another way. What are those you report to going to do to these people?"

"Nothing. They just want to know what they are up to."

"So, your treasure hunting is just a cover?"

"It is more than a cover. We actually make good money from it, and we enjoy doing it. It's like being part anthropologist and part archeologist."

Gabi was a smart woman, but there was no way she could guess from what he was telling her what he was up to or who he was, and yet he felt like he was saying too much.

Keeping his identity and that of his teammates a secret was of paramount importance to their security, and he should reach into Gabi's mind and erase the last few moments of conversation. The thralling would be minimal, and it wouldn't harm her, provided that he didn't thrall her again later.

20

GABI

As Uriel excused himself to use the restroom, Gabi smiled until he could no longer see her and then slumped in her chair.

Throughout the evening, she'd felt torn between the urge to get up and leave in a huff or drag Uriel back to her room to have her way with him. It was a miracle she had survived all the way through dessert.

He infuriated her with his refusal to tell her anything personal about himself, including his age, where he'd attended college, or even if he had attended. His answer to every question was that he couldn't tell her without lying to her, and he didn't want to lie. But why would he need to lie about the college he'd attended? Or where he'd been born? Or about his family?

He'd said that he was working on a project that required complete confidentiality, and he wasn't allowed to disclose any details, personal or otherwise. The only things he was willing to share with her were that he was single, childless, and didn't have anyone special in his life.

Did she believe him?

Given her experience with men, she shouldn't, but she did.

Why?

Maybe it was because he refused to lie to appease her curiosity, or perhaps it was the sincerity in his eyes and his tone of voice, but she didn't think he was lying about that.

Still, it didn't diminish her aggravation with him or the constrictive ache in her chest.

Tonight might be their last, and Gabi very much doubted Uriel would seek her out in Cleveland once his project was over.

He hadn't asked her any questions about her family except to inquire when her brothers would return from their emergency business trip, and those questions had been related to information she had volunteered.

He hadn't even asked her if she was married or had children, which was the clearest indication that he was only interested in the here and now.

On her part, Gabi hadn't volunteered the information either, and not just because he hadn't asked or because she was angry with him for insisting on remaining a mystery.

She didn't like talking about her parents dying when she was still a kid, or about the marriage that had failed so miserably, or about her turbulent relationship with food and why she'd become a nutritionist.

Who wanted to hear her depressing stories about loss and failure?

People were much more interested in success, which Gabi could now front with confidence. She was fully in charge of her life, and she was doing well—fear of flying and many other things notwithstanding.

"Ready to go?" Uriel startled her from her reveries.

"Yes." As Gabi's mind took a leap in a different direction, imagining Uriel's gloriously naked body moving against hers, she felt her cheeks warming, which was ridiculous given that she had no reason to feel embarrassed about her attraction to him.

Maybe the reason for the flash was the surge of desire and not shame for her lustful thoughts. Yeah, that was it.

Hiding a smile, Gabi lifted the small cappuccino cup, finished the last few drops, collected her purse, and pushed to her feet.

As he wrapped his arm around her middle, his large hand encircling nearly her entire waist, the heat in her body rose by several degrees, and as his hand traveled down her hip and then back again, it was all she could do to stifle a moan.

339

"What are you doing to me?" she murmured as they stood in front of the elevator doors, waiting for them to open.

"What do you mean?" he asked with mock innocence.

"I can't get enough of you. It's like you are an addiction that I never want to be weaned off."

"Same here." His hand on her waist tightened, and the moment the doors opened, he moved so fast Gabi didn't know how she found herself with her back pressed against the wall and the entire cabin shaking from the force of the impact as it lurched down.

"Uriel," she whispered against his lips.

"Gabriella." His hips pressed into her, and his mouth hovered a fraction of an inch away from hers.

Was he waiting for her to kiss him first?

She could do that.

Tilting her head, she drew his bottom lip between hers and gently nipped it with her teeth.

The growl that erupted from his chest sounded more like something coming out of an animal's throat than a man's. It belonged to a ferocious beast that was about to devour her, but instead of fear, all she could feel was a blast of lust.

As he took her mouth in a hard kiss, his hands landed on her ass and hauled her up, so she had no choice but to lift her legs and wrap them around his waist.

The friction was delicious even though his hard length and her moist center were separated by layers of fabric.

If she could just reach his zipper and free him, he could move her panties aside and be inside of her in a split second.

The annoying beep of the elevator reaching the lobby put an end to that fantasy.

"Gabi," Uriel whispered into her mouth as if her name was a prayer. "You need to let go."

The doors started opening as she finally dropped her feet to the floor, and it wasn't a moment too soon.

Two couples stared at them as they got out, and one of the women cleared her throat before getting into the elevator.

"She's just jealous," Gabi said before the doors closed.

Uriel chuckled. "I'd rather think that she's inspired. If there wasn't another couple with them, her husband would have been in for a treat." He led her to the other bank of elevators going to the hotel rooms on the top floors.

Holding on to his arm, Gabi smoothed a hand over her dress. "How do you know he was her husband? Maybe he was a boyfriend or a lover?"

"They both had wedding rings."

Gabi winced. "To some, that's meaningless. Some people have no problem cheating while wearing their wedding rings."

Some even thought it was sexy, which was really depraved, in her opinion. But then, who was she to judge? Actually, as a woman who had been cheated on, she had every right to pass judgment.

Had her husband worn his wedding ring while cheating on her? Had the women he'd picked up been turned on by it?

21

URIEL

The acrid scent of betrayal hung around Gabi like a fog, making him think that she hadn't been talking in generalities. It had been something she'd experienced. But it wasn't his place to ask. Since he couldn't tell her anything about himself, he had no right to inquire.

If she wanted to, she would tell him, and when she did, he would find the guy and avenge her.

Right now, all he could do was take her into his arms and comfort her, but as he reached for her hand to pull her to him, an older couple joined them, so handholding was all he could offer.

"Good evening," the older lady said. "Are you staying in the hotel?"

"Yes, we are," Gabi answered while squeezing his hand.

The lady smiled. "You make such a beautiful couple. Are you on your honeymoon?"

Gabi shook her head. "We are visiting my family." She leaned on his arm. "I'm going to introduce Uriel to my brothers." She lifted her head and smiled sweetly at him. "I hope they like him."

"What about your parents?" the lady asked as the four of them entered the elevator.

The smile slid off Gabi's face. "Regrettably, they are gone, so it's just my brothers and their families."

His heart clenched with sympathy, and he squeezed her hand.

"I'm so sorry to hear that," the lady said.

"Thank you. They passed a long time ago." Gabi pressed the button for her floor. "Which floor are you on?"

"The sixty-ninth," the man said. "Same as yours."

Thankfully, the lady refrained from asking any more questions, and they said their goodbyes as each couple headed to their room.

"I'm sorry," he said as he closed the door behind them.

Gabi put her purse on the entry table. "It's not your fault, and as I said, it happened a long time ago."

"How old were you?" He shouldn't have asked, but if Gabi's parents had passed away a long time ago, she must have been a kid when it happened.

"I don't want to talk about it now." She sauntered toward him. "We were in the middle of something, and we were interrupted." She pressed her body to his, pushing him against the door and lifting her head to trail moist kisses along his neck.

Smiling, he put his hands on her waist. "I can't remember where exactly we were interrupted. Can you remind me?"

"With pleasure." She covered his hands with hers and guided them to her ass. "You lifted me as you kissed me, and I wrapped my legs around your torso."

"Oh, yes." He hoisted her up so her center was at the exact spot where it could rub against his erection. "Now I remember. But you were kissing my mouth, not my neck." He tilted his head to allow her better access.

As she kissed and nibbled the column of his neck, he struggled to maintain the shroud that would mask his glowing eyes and elongating fangs. Under normal circumstances, it wasn't difficult to do, but Gabi evoked something so primal in him that he had trouble multitasking while being with her.

"God, how do you smell so good?" she murmured against his skin and then totally unexpectedly licked him. "Hmmm. You taste good, too." She lifted her head and looked at him with glazed-over eyes. "The question is whether you are good or poisonous to eat."

He laughed. "I'm probably both." His venom had healing properties, and his thrall was dangerous to her, but he wasn't going to do either tonight.

Her smile was brilliant. "I had a feeling you would say that," she teased.

"Do you feel brave tonight?" He carried her to the dresser, put her on top of it, and leaned over her. "Do you feel like the meaning of your name? A strong hero of God?" He pushed her hair over her shoulder and cupped the back of her neck.

"I do," she breathed with a challenge dancing in her blue-gray eyes. "You are intoxicating." She started humming a tune he didn't recognize. "You and I are in a twisted romance."

He covered her mouth before she had a chance to sing another verse, and when she tried to kiss him back, he tightened his hand on her nape to keep her from going in and nicking her tongue on his rapidly elongating fangs.

"Close your eyes," he commanded.

A crooked smile twisted her lips as she obeyed. "Are we playing that game again?"

"We are playing a new game." He opened the top drawer and pulled out a pair of skin-tone stockings. "These are perfect." He pulled out another pair that was black and silky to the touch.

"What is perfect?" Gabi opened her eyes.

Thankfully, his shroud was still holding, or she would have run out of the room screaming.

"These." He held the two pairs of stockings up. "One to blindfold you and the other one to tie your wrists together. Are you game?"

22

GABI

Was she?

If Uriel wanted to hurt her, he didn't need to blindfold her or tie her up. He was so much stronger that he could incapacitate her in a split second. This was just a sexy game, and she was curious to see where he took it.

Well, she wouldn't see anything because she would be blindfolded, but that was beside the point.

"I'm game," she whispered. "I've never done anything like this before."

"Neither have I." He wrapped the black stockings around her head, tying them in the back. "If it gets uncomfortable at any moment, tell me, and I'll take it off."

"Okay." Gabi opened her eyes to test whether she could see anything through the nylon.

She could see the general outline of Uriel's body as a dark silhouette, but that was only because the lights were on. If he turned them off, she wouldn't be able to see anything.

"Let's get you out of this dress first."

Excitement thrumming through her, Gabi lifted her arms as he pulled the dress off over her head.

The air conditioning vent was right across from her, and as her nipples pebbled, Uriel dipped his head and took one in his mouth through her flimsy lace bra.

"Yes." Moaning, she threaded her fingers in his hair and held him to her.

He kissed her other nipple, first through the fabric and then once more after releasing her breasts from the lace.

When he lifted her into his arms, she had only her panties on, but apparently, he planned on removing them once he got her where he wanted her, which was spread out on the bed.

"Hands up." He didn't wait for her to obey and lifted them over her head. "I'm going to secure them to the headboard. Is that okay?"

"Yes," she breathed.

This game was incredibly arousing.

Not being able to see and having to rely on hearing and touch alone added to the acuity of the sensations, and being at Uriel's mercy, even though it was only perceptibly more so than at other times, was exciting as well.

Were all women strange that way? Or was it just her messed-up mind that found this arousing rather than scary?

It was like the classic beauty and the beast scenario, not that Uriel resembled a beast in any way, but in that he could do anything he wanted to her, and yet she trusted him not to harm her. More than that, she trusted him to protect her.

If anyone chose that moment to burst into the room and attack her, she knew that Uriel would defend her, not because he loved her, but because that was who he was.

Her ex, the captain of the football team, would have run away and left her to die. That was who he was, only she hadn't seen it throughout the years they had been together. She'd only realized it when things had started to unravel.

"Are you okay?" Uriel asked. "You seem tense."

With her head going places it shouldn't, Gabi hadn't even noticed that he was done tying the pantyhose to the headboard.

After giving them a gentle tug, she knew that her hands could easily slide out from the loose knot he'd made, and that was reassuring.

"I'm perfect." She gave him a smile.

"I'm glad." He leaned over, the long strands of his hair brushing over her chest as he took her lips in a sweet kiss. "Now I'm going to remove the last barrier." He hooked his thumbs in the elastic of her panties and dragged them down her thighs.

When he kissed her belly button, she expected him to keep kissing down, but he surprised her by taking her mouth. Arching into him, she rubbed her aching nipples against his chest, melting into him.

Sliding his tongue into her mouth, he feathered his fingertips over her heated center, the touch too slight to give her what she needed.

"Touch me," she said as soon as he let go of her lips. "Don't tease me."

"Why?" There was a smile in his voice. "It's so much fun to tease you, to bring you to the edge and have you beg for more."

"You're cruel."

"Cruel to be kind," he sang before taking her lips again.

The sound of his singing had an unexpected effect on her. His speaking voice was beautiful, deep, and resonant, but when he sang, it was hypnotic, and even though he'd only sung those four words, the rest of the tune kept playing in her head over and over again.

Gabi had no idea how she remembered the lyrics of a song from the seventies that she hadn't heard more than once or twice throughout her lifetime. It was as if Uriel's voice had unlocked a hidden treasure inside her head.

Cruel to be kind in the right measure— Cruel to be kind in the right measure—

How appropriate for the game they were playing.

23

URIEL

Gabi was so damn beautiful, but it wasn't the sum of her features that made her so appealing to him. It was the personality that animated her, her expressions, her intelligence, the spark of mischief, and even her irrational fears. The sum of who she was, was unique, and for some inexplicable reason, a perfect fit for the sum of who he was.

The blindfold hid her eyes from him, which was regrettable, but it accentuated her delicate heart-shaped face and her lips, which were still covered in that hot red lipstick that didn't come off no matter how hard he kissed her.

And the rest of her body, Fates, it was perfection.

She was delicately built, not petite but close, with slender shoulders, a slim waist, and long, slim limbs. He could spend hours kissing every inch of smooth skin and map every freckle on her chest, her arms, her nose, and her cheeks. Even her imperfections were perfect to him, and he wanted to tell her not to cover them with makeup, but he knew better than to make such suggestions.

Beauty was indeed in the eyes of the beholder, and the more he got to know Gabriella Emerson, the more beautiful she appeared to him.

"Please," she whispered. "Pretty please with a cherry on top."

He chuckled. "Is that your version of begging?"

"That's the best I can come up with."

"Well, if you are asking so nicely."

Sliding down, he flicked his tongue over one nipple and then sucked it into his mouth while parting her moist folds with his fingers. As he slid one in, she moaned and arched her back, and as he slid in another, she tugged on the pantyhose restraint but didn't pull her hands out, even though she could have done so with minimal effort.

Gabi liked the game they were playing, which was fortunate for both of them. He could stop worrying about losing the shroud and about thralling her afterward to forget all the things that gave him away. He might even be able to bite her if he did that during a climax.

Sliding further down, he was transfixed for a moment by the sight of his fingers pumping in and out of her, but when she arched again, he treated the seat of her pleasure to a gentle lick that had her moaning his name.

As she lifted her legs and rested them on his shoulders, he cupped her round bottom and brushed kisses against the swollen nubbin. When he sucked it into his mouth, she undulated her hips against him with lewd abandon, and as she cried out, he shuddered with pleasure, his erection kicking up and demanding his attention.

Ignoring it, he kept licking and pumping until she came again.

"I love seeing you fall apart for me," he whispered against her pink, swollen petals and blew air over her heated flesh.

"I haven't even begun." Her lips lifted in a satisfied smile.

He was out of his clothes in a split second, and as he climbed on top of her, her smile widened.

"Can you release my hands? I want to touch you."

"Not yet, beautiful." He gripped her hips, angling her for his penetration and rubbing the head of his erection against her engorged clitoris.

"Uriel, please. No more teasing."

As he surged inside of her, they both groaned. It was a struggle to keep still until she stretched around him, and he took her mouth in a ravenous kiss to distract himself from the need to start moving. Only when he felt she was ready for more did he start to pound into her, but never while unleashing his full power.

No human female could survive that without major damage, and he would rather die than cause her harm, but it was damn hard when she was arching up to meet him thrust for thrust.

Needing to slow himself down, he reached between their bodies and stroked her, but when she exploded into another orgasm, he could no longer hold back both the intensity and the venom bite. One had to give, and it was better to bite her than to pound into her with the force he was capable of.

"Uriel," she groaned.

Clamping a hand over the back of her head, he tilted it to the side and sealed his mouth over the soft spot where her neck met her shoulder. A couple of seconds of sucking and licking was all the preparation he could afford to give her before his need overwhelmed him. He sank his fangs into her soft flesh, pumping his essence into her at the same time.

Gabi gasped, and her body tensed under him, but a moment later, she went lax.

As pain turned into pleasure, and pleasure turned into a climax, and then another, he retracted his fangs and licked the puncture wounds closed.

Long moments after her body had stopped shuddering, he braced his forearms and gazed at the blissful expression on her beautiful face.

Was he falling in love with his human?

He couldn't love Gabi. As wonderful as she was, there could never be anything more between them than these few moments of lust—these few moments of closeness that were more precious to him than all the other moments he'd collected so far.

24

GABI

The velvety cushion beneath Gabi's cheek lacked plushness, yet it radiated a comforting warmth and pulsed with a rhythmic heartbeat.

Now, that was a pleasant surprise.

She hadn't expected Uriel to be there in the morning, and for a moment she thought that it was still night, but a swift glance towards the window revealed a gleaming sliver of golden sunlight peeking through the gap where the heavy curtains met, hinting that the morning was well underway.

Being cocooned against the gentle rise and fall of Uriel's chest, reveling in the security of his arms encircling her and the warmth of his bare skin against her cheek, was a morning greeting more intimate and sweet than any words could offer.

If not for the insistent nudge of her bladder, Gabi would have relished this tranquil moment a little while longer. She was reluctant to break the embrace, but nature's call was not to be denied.

Perhaps she could make a dash for the bathroom, take care of business, and return to bed without waking Uriel?

However, the moment she shifted in his arms, his eyes popped open, and a smile bloomed on his gorgeous face. "Good morning." He leaned in and kissed her on the lips. "Did you sleep well?"

"Good morning. I slept splendidly, and finding you here in the morning was a nice surprise, but I really need to go to the bathroom. Wait for me?"

"Of course." He released her. "Hurry back."

"I will."

As she padded naked to the bathroom, the weight of his gaze was palpable, a gentle pressure against her skin. She wanted to treat him to a sultry saunter, but given how pressing her need had become, she probably looked like an ungainly duck, awkwardly hustling forward with her thighs clamped tight.

Having attended to her most immediate need, Gabi walked over to the vanity, and as she washed her hands, she lifted her gaze to the mirror and surveyed her reflection. Even with tousled hair cascading wildly over her shoulders and makeup slightly smudged from the night's escapades, a radiant glow emanated from her. It was the unmistakable sheen of satisfaction, the postcoital luminescence of a woman after a thoroughly satiating encounter between the sheets. A renewed energy coursed through her, a sense of well-being as though she had been revitalized by a deep, uninterrupted ten-hour sleep.

Had she slept that long?

Uriel had removed her wristwatch last night before tying her up, and her phone was in her purse, which was still on the entry table where she'd left it when they had entered the room, so she had no way to check what time it was, and the only clue Gabi had was how refreshed she felt.

As more memories of the evening surfaced, she brushed her hair aside and examined her neck. He'd bitten her just as he was climaxing, and it hadn't been a gentle nip, but somehow, there was no sign of it on her skin—not even a hickey.

Maybe she remembered it wrong, and he'd bitten her on the other side?

Tilting her head the other way, she moved her hair and examined her left side, but the skin there was just as unmarred as on her right side.

"What the heck? Did I dream it?"

It wouldn't be the first time she'd had an erotic dream, but none had ever felt so real. Well, she'd had that one dream a long time ago about a certain actor she'd been crushing on as a teenager, and that one had felt quite real, but it couldn't compare to the phantom bite. She could still feel the momentary slashing pain of his teeth breaking her skin and the panic she'd felt for a split second before it had been replaced by an indescribable pleasure.

Oh, goodness. The pleasure.

"If it could feel that good in dreams, I would never get anything done. I would just try to dream as much as I could."

"Gabi?" Uriel called out. "Were you saying something?"

Damn. She didn't even have the phone with her so she could pretend to have been talking with someone or listening to a podcast, and Uriel would think that she was a crazy woman talking to herself.

Oh, heck, whatever. Let him think whatever he wanted. It wasn't as if it would change his mind about wanting to stay with her.

He was leaving no matter what.

"Sorry about that. I was talking to myself." She reached for her toothbrush. "By the way, there is a hotel-provided spare toothbrush and a razor, so if you want to come in and freshen up, you are welcome."

The door opened a moment later and Uriel walked in, wearing his birthday suit, which included a very prominent erection.

Gabi's mouth watered. "Is that just a good morning greeting, or is he happy to see me?"

For a moment, Uriel looked confused, but as he followed her gaze, a laugh burst out of him.

What was it about the sound of his laughter that was like a switch on her libido?

"He's definitely happy to see you." He turned around, giving her a great view of his ass as he entered the toilet compartment.

As the door closed behind him, Gabi let out a sigh. It wasn't fair that he was so perfect in every way, yet she couldn't keep him. Hey, maybe that was why he could allow himself to be so great. He didn't need to push her away with jerky behavior because he'd just stated flat out that he couldn't share anything with her.

Then again, Gabi had dated plenty of men whom she'd informed right from the start that she only wanted to have fun and wasn't looking for a relationship, and that hadn't prevented some of them from exhibiting jerky behaviors.

When she was done brushing her teeth and applying her moisturizer, Uriel sauntered over to the vanity and turned on the faucet. "What are your plans for today?"

"I don't have any. Why?"

He grinned at her through the mirror. "It's only a few minutes after seven in the morning, and I don't need to leave until eleven, which gives us enough time for playtime and breakfast at the hotel restaurant."

25

URIEL

Gabi's cheeks pinked with what he knew was desire, not embarrassment. She was comfortable in her nudity, more than most of the human females he'd been with, and rightfully so.

He wouldn't have changed a single thing about her. She was perfect the way she was.

Lowering her lashes, she husked, "What do you have in mind?"

He glanced at the shower. "A way for us both to get ready for the day without wasting time."

She chuckled. "So, you are all about efficiency?"

"Today, I am." He lifted her by her waist and transferred her from the vanity into the shower.

"Hold on." She put her hand on his forearm when he reached for the faucet. "I don't want my hair to get wet. I had it done yesterday. We can use the handheld, so I don't get splashed from above."

"As you wish." He moved aside, transferring the command of the shower to her. "It's all yours."

Gabi cracked a smile. "Thank you." She twisted her hair in a bun and tucked the ends inside, securing it on the top of her head.

Pivoting on her bare heel, Gabi turned on the water in the handheld shower head, checked the temperature, and secured it on the long pole at the height of her breasts so her hair was safe from the water spray.

Perhaps the joint shower wasn't one of his brightest ideas. Already, he was being forced to shroud his glowing eyes and elongating fangs, but when things got heated, he would have to thrall Gabi not to see them.

After all, he couldn't blindfold her in the shower. As trusting as she was with him, that would surely make her suspicious.

Thankfully, she seemed mesmerized by the view of his straining erection, and he hoped it would provide enough distraction so only a minimal thrall would be needed to keep things under control.

"If you keep looking at me like that, it will be a very short shower." He gently pushed her against the shower wall and knelt before her.

The height difference between them meant that in this position, his mouth was aligned with those perky breasts that had him salivating from the moment he had woken up with them pressed against his skin.

Twirling his tongue over one nipple, he licked it into a stiff point, closed his lips around it, and sucked in hard.

"Yes," she groaned.

Smiling, he leaned over to her other nipple and nipped it lightly with his blunt front teeth.

Gabi jerked in surprise, but the scent of her desire intensified tenfold.

As he laved it with his tongue, soothing the small hurt away, she uttered an impatient sound that he could only interpret as frustration with the gentle treatment.

Interesting.

Evidently, the feisty human was into more than just bondage. She liked a little pain served with her pleasure.

Given his incredible strength, it would be tricky to control the precise level that would provide a little spice to her pleasure but no more.

Pushing to his feet, he spun her around. "Hands on the wall."

He could pull it off. For her, he would hold himself in check and delay his own gratification so he could give her precisely what she craved.

Doing as he'd ordered, she turned her head to look at him over her shoulder. "What are you going to do to me?"

"Cruel to be kind in the right measure," he sang before landing a light smack on her left cheek.

"Ow! What was that for?" She tried to sound indignant, but her voice was husky, and the scent of her arousal grew so overwhelming that he got lightheaded, probably because all his blood had traveled to his erection.

"Your pleasure." He massaged her bottom, spreading the heat, before delivering another smack to her other cheek.

She didn't contradict him. Instead, she pushed her butt out and spread her legs a little farther apart.

If that wasn't an invitation to continue the play, he didn't know what was.

Leaning down, he kissed the side of her neck and slid two fingers between her slick folds and then rubbed them around her entrance without penetrating her.

"What about you?" Her whisper would have been barely audible if he were human. "Do you enjoy this?"

"Very much so." He slid his fingers into her moist heat and pumped in and out slowly while his thumb circled the bundle of nerves at the apex of her thighs.

He could have told her that anything that heightened her pleasure was an aphrodisiac to him, but that might have diminished her enjoyment. She had to believe he was as much into the game as she was.

Two more light smacks had her sheath tightening around his fingers, and he had a feeling that she could have climaxed just from that play, but he needed to taste her again.

"Turn around." He went down to his knees and picked her leg up, resting her dainty foot on his shoulder and opening her glistening center to his ravenous gaze.

"Close your eyes," he commanded, afraid his shroud wouldn't hold.

"I want to watch." She threaded her fingers into his hair.

"Close your eyes," he reiterated with a featherlight slap to her wet folds.

"Ouch," she mewled. "You're not supposed to do that."

The outpouring of moisture said otherwise, but since she had closed her eyes, he didn't correct her. Instead, he licked the small hurt away and moved higher to suck her clit.

"Oh, yes." She thrust her hips forward and rocked them on his tongue while holding on to his head.

He breathed in her intoxicating scent and added his fingers to the play, penetrating her with two while still sucking on her clit.

"Please," Gabi pleaded. "I want you inside of me."

His plan had been to make her climax on his tongue and fingers, but he couldn't deny her anything.

"Well, since you asked so nicely." He planted one last kiss on her moist petals, lowered her leg down to the shower floor, and pushed up to his feet. "Turn around."

"So bossy," she whispered but did as he'd asked, planting her hands on the wall, pushing out her heart-shaped ass, and stretching up on her tiptoes to compensate for their height difference.

Bending at the knees, he wrapped an arm around her waist to brace her and positioned his erection at her entrance. With one swift surge, he was inside of her, pounding away, hard and fast, his thighs slapping against Gabi's upturned behind with each forward thrust.

He braced his other arm on the tile wall to cushion her head and let himself go a little faster, a little harder, but nowhere near the ferocity coursing through him. His fragile human couldn't take that force, meaning he couldn't bring it out even if he wanted to.

When her orgasm hit, and her muscles clamped around his arousal, his seed erupted, and he bit into his arm to refrain from biting her again, but he didn't release his venom.

He'd bitten her last night, so holding back wasn't as excruciatingly difficult as it would have been otherwise.

When the urge to bite subsided and his seed was spent, he kissed the spot where he'd bitten her the day before and inhaled the unique scent of her skin.

He needed to memorize every touch, every smell and every taste, and lock those memories in a treasure chest in his mind to revisit for moments when the world seemed too dark to bear, and he needed a ray of light to remind him that there were things worth fighting for.

26

GABI

As the server refilled Gabi's coffee cup, she lifted it to her lips and smiled behind the rim. "You know, I never liked bossy guys." She leaned closer to Uriel and whispered, "But I liked it very much when you got bossy in the shower."

She would have never admitted enjoying it to anyone other than Uriel, which was odd because he was the kind of guy that she wouldn't want to have such potent ammo to use against her.

Besides being too good-looking to be for real, he was the most evasive, relationship-averse guy she'd ever met, and she'd met her share of men with commitment issues, learning that there was a collection of various phobias under that umbrella. There were gamophobes—those who fear marriage, philophobes—those who fear love, and pistanthrophobes—those who fear trusting others, especially loved ones. She hadn't encountered any genophobes—those afraid of sex and intimacy—but that was a fear that was more prevalent among those born female and, therefore, physically weaker.

Thankfully, she no longer suffered from those particular fears.

Well, suffering less was a more accurate description of her mental state. Right after the divorce, she had carried all those phobias along with many others.

Reaching for her hand, Uriel lifted it to his lips and brushed them over her knuckles. "I aim to please."

She twisted their conjoined hands and kissed the back of his hand. "You please me very much." She didn't add the second half of her thought, that it was a shame he wouldn't be pleasing her for much longer, but then what was the point?

They both knew that they didn't like it and despite being single adults living in a free country, they couldn't do anything about it. Or maybe couldn't wasn't the right word. As her mother used to say, there was nothing a person couldn't accomplish once they put their mind to it. She was willing to move mountains to give their relationship a chance, but he either couldn't or simply didn't want to.

As her phone rang in her purse, Gabi frowned. It wasn't her regular phone, it was the other one Gilbert had given her, and she couldn't remember why he had done that. Something about a family plan?

Shaking her head, she pulled it out of her purse and looked at the caller's picture.

"It's my sister-in-law." She looked at Uriel. "Do you mind if I take it?"

"Not at all. Please, maybe she has news about your brothers."

Nodding, Gabi accepted the call.

"Hi, Karen. What's up? Any news from Gilbert and Eric?"

"Good morning, Gabi. No news. I just wanted to check how you are doing. I feel so bad about you being stuck in that hotel. Are you in the restaurant right now?"

"Yeah. How did you know?"

"The background noise of people talking and of clanking utensils."

"Oh, yeah. I'm having breakfast with Uriel, the guy I told you about. The one I met on the plane."

"Oh, right." Gabi could hear the smile in Karen's voice. "Did he come to meet you for breakfast, or did he spend the night?"

She smiled up at him. "A lady doesn't kiss and tell."

Karen chuckled. "Then it's the second one. I'm glad that you are at least having fun with your guy. Otherwise, I would have felt really bad about Eric and Gilbert being away."

"I know, right? But we should meet up like we did the other day. I can come to see you at the university, or we can go to that Italian restaurant, or I could visit your new house without the guys being there. It's Wednesday already, and I'm flying back on Monday. I can't extend my visit any longer."

Karen sighed. "I wish I could, but Evan came down with a bad case of the flu, and I think that Ryan is coming down with it, too. I'm staying home with them so they won't pass the germs on to anyone else, and I would hate for you to come over, catch what they have, and ruin the rest of your trip."

That was a bummer, and it also sounded off. It wasn't unusual for the twins to get sick occasionally, but Gabi couldn't shake the feeling that things were not as they seemed.

"What about Kaia and Cheryl? Were they exposed to the twins?"

"Kaia wasn't, but Cheryl was. It's good that it's summer vacation still, and she doesn't have school."

Well, perhaps she could at least meet Kaia and her fiancé. For some reason, she didn't remember much about him except for his intelligent blue eyes. Had he been silent through the dinner they had shared in the hotel restaurant?

No, it wasn't that. She'd drunk so much that day that she could remember almost nothing from that dinner. Kaia's fiancé might have talked up a storm, and she wouldn't have remembered it, just as she couldn't remember why she'd been given another phone. On the other hand, she remembered shopping with Darlene quite well.

The mind was indeed a mysterious place, with some pathways clear as day and others obscured by fog.

"I'll call Kaia later. Maybe she can meet me for coffee somewhere. If not for Uriel, this trip would have really sucked."

"I know." Karen affected an apologetic tone. "I'm so sorry about that, but you know how it is when running a business. Emergencies arise, and someone has to address them, and that's usually the owner."

"Yeah, I get it, but at this rate, you will all have to come visit me in Cleveland because I'm not flying in again to see you only to be stuck in a hotel waiting for my brothers to make themselves available. You know how much I hate flying. The only reason I survived this flight was that Uriel was holding my hand the entire time."

"It's so strange that you can tolerate short flights but not long ones. Any idea why that is?"

"I convince myself that a short flight is like a bus ride, but I can't keep up the illusion for long, and after an hour in the air, I start panicking."

Karen chuckled. "You're a strange lady, Gabi."

"Yeah, tell me something I don't know."

URIEL

It sounded like Gabi's family wasn't eager to meet with her. Maybe she'd been right all along, and there was something wrong with one of her brothers or nieces or nephews, which was why they didn't want her to come to their home.

He didn't know much about human medicine, but some treatments left people looking haggard, and maybe that was what they didn't want her to see.

When she ended the call, Gabi dropped the phone back in her purse. "I have a feeling that I won't see my family during this trip. Something is going on, and they are trying to hide it from me."

"My thoughts precisely. When you met your brothers the day you arrived, did they look okay?"

Gabi frowned. "They both looked great. Although Gilbert is still missing half of his hair, so my suspicion about him getting a hair transplant was a miss. His skin, though, looks amazing. He must have started seeing a dermatologist and getting some Botox and fillers or maybe laser treatments. Eric has had work done as well, which is strange. He's too young to do stuff like that." She leaned closer. "Tell me the truth, Uriel. Did you and your buddies have work done in Korea? You said that you didn't have plastic surgery, but they have fabulous creams and microneedling and laser treatments and a host of other things."

They hadn't even been to Korea, but the less she knew, the better.

"No, we didn't. So, what did Eric have done? Was it new hair?"

"Yeah. Eric definitely had a hair transplant." Gabi frowned. "Come to think of it, he didn't confirm that." She laughed nervously. "I had way too much to drink that day. I can't even remember what we talked about."

That didn't seem right. She'd been a little tipsy on the plane, but she'd been lucid and remembered everything they had talked about.

The story with her family was starting to creep him out. Humans got into some strange shit, and from what Gabi had told him about her brothers, their move to Los Angeles had been unexpected, and even more so was her niece's engagement to an older guy, who had recruited her for a secret project in bioinformatics.

Perhaps the entire family was involved in something illegal, and that was why they were keeping her away?

"What about the lunch you had with your sister-in-law? Was there something off about her or the fiancée of your other brother?"

Gabi frowned. "That's strange. I don't remember much from that lunch either. I remember playing with my nephews and gossiping about guys with the ladies, but that couldn't have accounted for the entire lunch." She smiled. "Although an hour can pass quite quickly when having fun. Later, I went shopping with Darlene."

That sounded innocent enough, and he was very interested in the gossip about men part.

"Did you talk about me?"

"Yeah." Gabi smirked. "They wanted to know about the hunk I met on my flight over. They all want to meet you. Maybe when Gilbert and Eric are finally back from their business trip, we could all go out to dinner. I want you to meet them."

He wanted to meet them and make sure they weren't doing something stupid that could get Gabi in trouble, but he wouldn't be around long enough to do that. After the mission, he and his partners were going to pull a disappearing act.

"I wish I could meet your family, but I don't think it will be possible this time. The deal my partners and I are working on might still require us to fly out on a moment's notice." He glanced at his watch. "I will probably know where things are heading after the meeting I'm supposed to attend in a couple of hours."

Nodding, Gabi lifted the coffee cup to her lips and took a sip. "I will keep my fingers crossed for you. I hope everything goes well and you won't have to leave town just yet. I hope to keep seeing you until I go back home." She put the cup down, leaned back in her chair, and closed her eyes.

She'd had a good night's sleep, he'd made sure of it, but she didn't look rested even though his venom bite from the night before should have given her a health boost.

"Are you tired?"

"A little." She opened her eyes and put a hand on her forehead. "I'm feeling a little under the weather. Maybe I caught the bug from my nephew when I played with him on Monday."

He'd heard her sister-in-law telling Gabi about her nephew coming down with the flu.

"Do you know a doctor in town you could see?"

Gabi waved a dismissive hand. "It's nothing, and I don't need to see a doctor for something as trivial as this. I'm very resistant to bugs, and even when I get the flu or a cold, I get over them quickly."

That was reassuring, but he felt terrible about leaving Gabi without anyone to care for her. "Can I get you something from the pharmacy?" He glanced at his watch. "I still have some time before I need to go."

"I don't need anything. I have my vitamins in my room. I always load up on vitamin C and zinc while going on trips, especially conventions when I'm around hundreds of people who bring in bugs from all over the country. Getting sick while traveling is the worst thing ever." She shook her head. "I shouldn't have said that. Getting sick on a trip is annoying. Losing a loved one is the worst thing that could happen."

As a wave of sadness followed her words, he remembered what she'd said to the lady in the elevator. Her parents had died a long time ago, which meant she must have been very young when that had happened.

He shouldn't ask her about it and get even closer to the woman he was about to leave, but he couldn't help himself. "I assume you are referring to your parents. I wouldn't have asked, but you told that lady in the elevator about them passing a long time ago."

28

GABI

"I don't like to talk about it." Avoiding Uriel's eyes, Gabi glanced around, looking for their server. "I need a coffee refill." Forcing a smile, she turned to him. "If I'm still craving coffee, I'm not sick. It's probably just an allergy, or it might even be the dry air in Los Angeles. I'm used to a more humid climate."

There was nothing like the weather to change the topic of conversation from personal to general.

"It's okay if you don't want to talk about your parents. I don't want to pry."

Of course, he didn't. If she revealed things about herself, he would have to reveal things about himself, and that was a big no-no for him.

As the server materialized with the coffee carafe in hand, Gabi lifted her cup for him to refill it. "Thank you." She smiled at the guy and waited until he refilled Uriel's as well.

"I'll make you a deal," she said after the server had left. "I'll tell you one thing about myself in exchange for you telling me one thing about yourself. It can be as small as your favorite book or as big as who was the most significant influence on your life growing up."

He hesitated for a split second. "Remember that you said it can be anything."

"Anything." She took a sip of the fresh coffee. "My father died when I was twelve. His heart just gave out with no warning. He wasn't sick, he didn't complain about chest pains or being tired, and he seemed perfectly healthy, only he wasn't." It still took effort to talk about it without getting teary-eyed or choked up, but she'd managed to deliver the information in a nearly flat tone. "Your turn."

"I'm not much of a reader," he admitted. "I like watching movies, and sometimes I can binge-watch an entire season in a couple of days."

She hadn't expected that—not from Uriel. Most of the men she'd dated hadn't been big on reading, but he seemed different, and it was a little disappointing to hear him say that.

"What attracts you to movies?" Gabi asked.

"The stories of human lives. I know it's fiction, but it provides me with a window to look through that I wouldn't have gotten otherwise. There is only so much that a person can experience himself."

Books were even better at that because they provided a window into the minds and souls of the protagonists and the antagonists, but some people were more visual than cerebral, and evidently, Uriel belonged to the visual group.

Except, he just didn't fit the profile.

"Fair enough." She took a sip from her coffee. "Why not books, though? You get so much more with books. You get into the characters' minds, their hearts. You don't get that with movies."

He shrugged. "We all have our preferences, and I prefer to guess what they are thinking from their facial expression and their body language. Also, I find that it's a great way to learn languages. I watch foreign films with subtitles."

"I've never heard of that method, but I can see how it can work for someone with a great ear and an even better memory."

"I have both."

"It's also great spy training," she said with a straight face.

He laughed. "Yeah, I guess it is. Your turn."

What he had told her wasn't earth-shattering, but she'd learned something about him that she hadn't known before, so it was well worth it.

"After our father died, our mother fell apart, and Gilbert basically took over running the household. Two years later, she died from an aneurysm, or what I call a broken heart. She just couldn't go on without our father. With time, I've forgiven her for giving up on life and abandoning us, but for a long while I was angry at her and feeling guilty for being angry. It was a very dark time in my life."

The choking sensation she'd expected arrived, but it wasn't as bad as it usually was, and a couple of deep breaths unclogged her throat.

"I bet." Uriel took her hand and gave it a light squeeze. "How old was Gilbert when your mother died?"

"Twenty-four. Eric was eighteen, and I was fourteen. Gilbert was already managing our household, including earning an income and supporting us, but after our mother died, he also had to deal with an emotionally broken kid sister and a young brother who was putting on a brave face but was as grief-stricken as I was." She forced a smile. "Your turn."

"I have a sister who I'm very close to but don't get to see."

That was another surprise. He hadn't mentioned any siblings.

A buzz started in the back of her mind, alerting her to some discrepancy she couldn't put her finger on. It was as if she had reason to believe that Uriel was an only child, but he hadn't told her that, so how could she know whether he had siblings or not?

"What about your parents? Are you close to them?"

He shook his head. "Not as close as I would like. They live far away."

For someone who was globe-trotting, visiting faraway places shouldn't be a problem, but there was probably more to his relationship with his parents than physical distance.

"Any other siblings?" she asked.

He shook his head. "Just one. Your turn. Have you ever been in love?"

"Yes."

She could swear that his eyes blazed with inner light for a moment, the dark brown turning a beautiful shade of amber. "What happened to him?"

"I divorced his cheating ass."

Uriel looked stunned, as if she'd slapped him across the face, and the sound he emitted was what she would have expected from a lion warning his prey.

"What kind of idiot could have cheated on an incredible woman like you?"

That was such a sweet thing to say. "A self-absorbed prick with an enormous ego that needed constant stroking. According to him, I didn't stroke it often enough." Gabi smiled sadly. "That was his opinion. I think that I stroked it too often, but I'm beyond the point of questioning myself about the failure of my marriage. It wasn't my fault. It was his. I'm just glad we didn't have children, or the divorce would have been much more difficult than it was."

29

URIEL

As Uriel's fangs punched out over his lip, he threw a quick shroud over himself, but that didn't do much to mask the growl that reverberated through his chest.

"How could you have fallen in love with someone like that?"

Gabi sighed. "I was young, and he was the guy every girl in the school wanted. When he became mine, I thought myself the luckiest girl on earth." She lifted the cup to her lips to hide the wave of embarrassment that washed through her.

Was she blaming herself for the mistake she'd made?

Humans had to rely on intuition and healthy skepticism to detect deceit, and Gabi had been a young girl who hadn't developed the skills yet.

"It wasn't your fault." He reached for her other hand.

"I was naive."

"Naïveté is a blessing, not a curse."

She arched a brow. "You're probably the only person I've ever heard say that. Normally, calling someone naive is a polite way of saying that they are stupid."

"Being naive is to judge others based on your own character. You were good and loyal, and you didn't expect him to be a lying scumbag. If you just tell me his name, I'll find him and avenge your honor."

To his surprise, Gabi laughed. "You are such a talented actor. You sounded so sincere, like a knight vowing to avenge the princess's broken heart."

"It wasn't acting. I meant every word."

"Sure you did." She patted his hand. "I appreciate the sentiment, but I divorced Dylan eleven years ago. It took me almost two years to mourn the end of the marriage, and during that time, I lost everything I had, but eventually I pulled myself up by the bootstraps, as they say. My brothers helped, of course."

He frowned. "What do you mean you lost everything? Was his betrayal financial as well as personal?"

Gabi briefly closed her eyes and let out a breath.

"I gained nearly as much weight after our divorce as I did after my parents died. Can you imagine what that did to my practice? I lost clients, couldn't get new ones, and couldn't support myself. I moved in with Gilbert and spent two years moping on his couch."

He'd seen enough movies to know that the cheating husband should have supported her. There was something called alimony that the former spouse was supposed to provide, but if her ex was a worthless loser in more ways than one, perhaps he hadn't earned enough to pay her alimony.

"What about the support he was supposed to pay you?"

"He wasn't. I was making more money than him when I started suspecting him. Gilbert hired a private investigator who provided proof of his cheating, but that had no bearing on the financial aspects of the divorce. I didn't need money from him, and I didn't want it. I just wanted to be rid of him." She closed her eyes again. "That's not true. I didn't want to be rid of him. I wanted the cheating to have never happened, and I wanted our fairytale life to continue. But wishing that was just as pointless as wishing my parents hadn't died, and the only solace I found in both cases was food.

"After my parents died, I gained nearly 100 lbs. A nutritionist helped me get that under control, and once I dropped the excess weight, I joined the cheerleading squad and boys started noticing me, including the captain of the football team. I fell in love with Dylan, and we were the prom king and queen. I felt on top of the world. I was finally over my grief and ready to start my enchanted life. We went to the same college, got married, and I started my own business. The nutritionist who had helped me get back in shape as a teenager inspired me to become a nutritionist myself. Life couldn't get better than that." She smiled sadly. "But, it was only downhill from there. "

"Not really. Look at you now. You have a successful practice, and you can have any man you want. You're gorgeous."

Her face brightened. "Thank you. I like to believe that fate had a different plan for me, and that Dylan was never meant to be the one for me. But I'm thirty-eight years old, and my clock is ticking. Soon, children will no longer be an option. Not that I'm convinced I want any, but having the possibility taken away is scary." She lifted her hand and wiped the back of it over her forehead. "I think I'm starting to develop a fever."

Uriel pushed to his feet. "Let me escort you back to your room so you can take those vitamins you mentioned."

"That's a good idea." She took his offered hand.

Dipping his head, he pressed his lips to her forehead. "You are only slightly warmer than normal. If you have a fever, it is very low."

She also didn't smell sick, which made it easier for him to leave her and head out to the meeting.

Still, it was a shame that he needed to go.

Gabi was finally opening up to him, and he wanted to keep talking to her and learn everything he could about her, but he'd run out of time.

3 0

KIAN

"The teams are in place," Onegus said. "But our guests are nowhere in sight. We are monitoring the nearest paved road, and there are no cars parked along the stretch that is closest to the canyon. There are also no hikers in a five-mile radius."

Kian glanced at his watch. It was twenty minutes to twelve, and if their so-called guests intended to show up on time, they should be entering the canyon. Then again, if they were Kra-ell or immortals, they could cover the distance from the road to the meeting in much less time, and if they intended to parachute from a helicopter, they wouldn't need any time at all.

They could also use dirt bikes.

They could be hiding in a cave and planning to emerge a few minutes before the meeting, but Kian couldn't see any advantage to that. Given how noisy those vehicles were, it wouldn't give their riders the element of surprise.

What worried him more was the possibility of them arriving in an aircraft.

"I don't like that our meeting team is exposed down there. They can't even take cover in case of an aerial attack."

Onegus cast him a look that had just a tinge of exasperation in it. "Stop being such a pessimist. They would not have gone to all this effort to lure our people into a trap just so they could kill them. They want information, and to get it, they need to show up."

"Fuck!" William exclaimed in a very uncharacteristic manner. "One signal winked out, and the other two are moving. How the hell are they doing that?" He looked at Onegus. "Do you see any movement on the feed from the drone?"

The chief shook his head. "If they are physically moving the trackers, they are using devices that are too small for us to see. But I suspect that they can manipulate where the signals are coming from. They are probably stationary and are only simulating movement."

"Not possible," William said. "Not with those trackers. The device is a solid piece that disintegrates if you try to crack it open. They can't do anything to them. I still think that they have some sort of cloaking device."

Kian arched a brow. "We know that they can activate and deactivate the signals, which is more than we have managed to do, so obviously they have superior technology, and if Syssi's vision is correct, which I believe it is, we are dealing with gods, not Kra-ell. They are very likely to have technology that we can't even imagine."

"Where are the signals moving to?" Turner asked. "That's more important than how. They obviously want us to follow them."

It made perfect sense. The gods didn't want to walk into a trap either, so changing the meeting place at the last moment was a brilliant move. In fact, Kian should have thought of that and done the same.

He turned to William. "They are being cautious, and that's a smart move. How fast are the signals traveling, and in what direction?"

William took a long moment to answer. "They are traveling at about sixty miles an hour, give or take a few, and they are heading west. It looks like they are flying."

Turner chuckled. "We were wrong about them implanting the trackers in gerbils. They must have implanted them inside carrier pigeons." He swiveled his chair toward Onegus. "Can you rewind the footage and check if a pigeon took flight in the canyon when the signals started moving?"

"What for? As you've said, it doesn't matter how they are doing it, only where they are going. I'm redirecting the drones to follow, and I pray to the merciful Fates that they don't run out of fuel before they reach their final destination."

Turner flipped his laptop open. "We need a new refueling station for the war bird. You also need to send the van with the replacement batteries for the smaller drones in the same direction."

"I'm already on it," the chief said.

Kian pulled out his phone. "I'm calling the Odus in here. We need to verify the direction and the exact location of the signal when the trackers become stationary."

Onegus nodded. "Do we tell the backup team and the meet-and-greet team to head west, or do we wait until the clock strikes noon?"

That was a good question. The gods might have moved the signals precisely for that reason—a bait-and-switch tactic—so he would show his hand by moving the backup forces out of their hiding spot across from the canyon.

Once the Odus arrived at the war room, the signals kept moving for another twenty minutes or so and then stopped.

After Okidu and Onidu had gone into their trance-like stance, Okidu pulled a folded piece of paper and a pencil out of his jacket pocket, wrote down a list of numbers, and handed them to William.

"It's in Simi Valley," William said while zooming in on the location. "It's another canyon, but it's not as isolated. There are residential neighborhoods a few miles away, but there is a new development going up right on top of the adjacent hill overlooking that canyon, and it's also easily accessible from the road."

The new location was only semi-secluded, which meant that they would have privacy for the meeting, but moving a large force into the area was problematic because they couldn't effectively shroud it without Yamanu, who was in China. Not even Toven possessed the ability to shroud a force that size.

"That's brilliant," Turner said. "They can pretend to be construction workers and hop down to the canyon when they feel it's safe to do so."

Kian turned to Onegus. "Is the drone on location?"

"The big war bird just got there, but it's keeping a high altitude. The small drones will be deployed when the van arrives."

"Have the camera zoom in on the canyon. I wonder if they left a message for us."

"On it." Onegus leaned over his screen. "I'll be damned. How did you know?"

Kian smiled. "I had a gut feeling. What did they leave for us?"

"There is a cardboard sign on the ground with 1:30 pm handwritten on it."

It was just enough time to get the people from Mount Baldy to the new location, provided that they headed there now, but since they had started as soon as the signals moved, they had about fifteen minutes to spare. Not that it was enough time to find a place for the backup force to hide, but at least they would be nearby.

31

JADE

"Simi Valley?" Phinas arched a brow. "Where is that?"

"It's due west," Magnus said. "Almost in a straight line."

Jade pulled out her phone and searched the map for the location. It was a long drive.

As soon as they had been told that the signals had started moving, they had jogged out of the canyon and gotten back into Magnus's car. It had taken them only fifteen minutes at a pace that allowed the immortals to keep up, which was about half the speed Jade was capable of, and yet Morgada had huffed and puffed as if she'd run a marathon. The female had become seriously out of shape, which she would have never been allowed to do if she'd remained on the home planet.

Jade had always believed that the Kra-ell were inherently physically active, but like many of the other beliefs she'd held, it was a misconception. Evidently, people acted in accordance with what was expected of them, and since Igor had thrown the tentpoles of their society out the window, Morgada had decided to forgo physical training, become soft, and concentrate on other pursuits, whatever they were.

"How long is it going to take us to get there?" Jade asked.

They had been driving in the direction the signals had been going, but as long as the trackers had kept moving, their team hadn't known where they were heading and how long it would take them. Hopefully,

Simi Valley was their final destination, and they weren't going on a wild chase.

"Another hour or so," Magnus said.

She didn't know the guy well, and she hadn't spoken more than a few words with him before the mission or during the ride to the canyon, but she trusted Onegus to choose the right person for the mission. Magnus could easily pass for a human, and he seemed levelheaded.

"I have more information about the location," the chief's computer-altered voice sounded in her earpiece.

William's team had redesigned the translation software to match an artificial narration with the tone and inflection of the speaker, so not everyone sounded the same, and in most cases, she could guess who the speaker was. It was a huge improvement, and it made the experience of listening to people through the specially-designed earpieces less disturbing.

"The good news is that there is a large construction site overlooking the location," Onegus said. "And that's also the bad news. There are multiple crews working on the subdivision, so there will be plenty of witnesses, which will limit what shenanigans either party can pull off. But that also means that our guests could be hiding among the construction workers and decide whether to show up based on who they see arriving at the meeting place. I'm glad that we decided to send two Kra-ell females and two immortal males who can pass for humans. Our guests will not perceive a small team of that composition as a threat."

"What about the backup?" Magnus asked.

"They are on their way, and I'm looking for the best place for them to hide. Our guests left us a cardboard sign invitation for one-thirty, so that doesn't leave us much time. Naturally, they did that on purpose."

"Smart," Phinas said. "I would have done the same."

Jade agreed. In fact, she was relieved. The new location was near humans, which meant that the gods didn't intend an armed confrontation. Even if one or more of them was a strong compeller, that couldn't protect them from an aerial assault, which was probably what they were worried about the most.

It was also what had worried her.

They had a military-grade drone providing aerial defense, but if the gods had more advanced weaponry, they might be able to take the drone out.

"I'm sending the location straight to your car navigation system," Onegus said. "You are about an hour away, which means you don't have time to make any stops on the way."

"Ugh." Morgada shifted in the seat. "I was hoping we could stop for a restroom break."

Jade cast her an incredulous look. "Are you unwell?"

The Kra-ell metabolism was such an efficient machine that using the restroom once a day was more than enough.

Morgada winced. "It happens when I get nervous. Other than Tom, I've never met a god face to face."

Magnus cast her a smile. "We don't know for sure that we are about to meet gods."

"Any more questions?" Onegus asked.

"Not for now," Jade said. "But I might think of something during the ride."

"I'm here. Onegus out."

Next to her, Phinas chuckled. "You know how in the old *Star Trek* show, the rookie crewman was always the one to die on away missions?" He shifted his eyes to Magnus. "Everyone knew that the one wearing a red uniform was not going to make it."

Magnus looked at his red Kevlar vest and grimaced. "I'm not a rookie, and you are not Captain Kirk." He looked at Jade through the rearview mirror. "But you remind me of Captain Kathryn Janeway."

The captain must have been a war hero, but Jade had never heard of her. "Who is Captain Janeway, and in what way do I resemble her?"

"Oh, lass." Magnus shook his head. "I've got to introduce you to *Voyager*."

32

GABI

"I'll call you as soon as I can." Uriel leaned to kiss Gabi's forehead, probably to check again how warm she was.

"I'm okay." She lifted on her toes and kissed him on his cheek. "Don't worry about me. Just finish this business deal already and come back to me."

The guilty look in his eyes was like a spear to her heart. "I'll do my best."

He didn't think he was coming back.

Then again, she'd felt the same way every time they had parted, so she wasn't going to agonize over it now only to have him call her later, saying that he was coming over.

As he walked away, Gabi's gaze followed Uriel, each step echoing louder in the hallway until he reached the elevator. She offered a lingering wave, catching his gaze for a fraction of a second as the metal doors were closing.

But even as her heart contracted with a familiar unease, somewhere deep within her, Gabi felt a grounding assurance. Despite the doubts, a gut feeling whispered that she would be seeing him again.

This isn't goodbye...

But then the lock on her memories sprang open, and she closed her eyes and groaned.

Oh, damn, maybe it is.

This split personality thing couldn't continue. She would lose her mind if it did.

Wait a minute, was Evan really sick? Or had Karen just provided a plausible excuse for why she couldn't meet Gabi?

Sitting on the couch, she pulled the clan phone out of her purse and dialed her sister-in-law.

"Gabi? Are you still with Uriel?"

"No, I'm back in my room. Is Evan really sick?"

"No, thank goodness, he's not. I hate pretending that one of my kids is sick, you know, bad luck and all that, but it was the first thing that popped into my head."

"I'm glad that he's okay." Gabi put a hand on her forehead. "I'm not feeling so great, and I thought that I might have gotten what Evan had, but if he's not sick, I must have gotten it from someone else."

"Maybe you caught something during the convention or on the plane. Bugs sometimes take a few days to multiply before you start showing symptoms."

Gabi winced. "Gross. Now I'm imagining an infestation growing in my body."

"In a way, it is. But you can't see it, so there is that. What are your symptoms? Do you have a fever? Runny nose? Sore throat?"

At the mention of her throat, Gabi lifted her hand to her neck where a bite mark should have been but wasn't. "I don't have a thermometer, but I'm a little warm, and I feel lethargic."

Karen snorted. "Since you spent the night and the morning with Uriel, you probably have a very legitimate reason for feeling tired."

Thinking of what had happened in the shower, warmth spread into Gabi's cheeks. "Yeah, you might be right. I think I'll crawl back into bed and take a nap."

"Good plan. Call me if you need anything."

Gabi rolled her eyes. "As if you could help me. Any news about the lockdown?"

"Nothing yet, but I don't think they can keep it up for much longer. People are starting to get antsy. But I was serious before. Call me, and I'll get you help. Our babysitter at the university has nothing to do as long as we are stuck here. I can ask her to babysit you instead. I can also order delivery of whatever you need."

"I'm fine, Karen. I've lived alone for the past nine years, and I survived with no help. I can manage this small inconvenience."

"I know, sweetie. But I can't help worrying about you. Promise me that you will call me if things take a turn for the worse."

"I promise."

After ending the call, Gabi opened her pill organizer, popped a packet of vitamin C and zinc into a tall glass, filled it with water, and drank the whole thing in one go.

Feeling a little nauseated, she pulled out a mint and popped it into her mouth, but instead of helping with the nausea, it irritated her throat and made her cough.

Some tea could help, but all the hotel supplied was coffee, and she was all caffeinated out after consuming three cups during breakfast. She could call the front desk and ask them to send up some teabags, or she could take a short walk to the drugstore around the corner and stock up on other remedies. She was out of Motrin, and in case her throat started to act up, she could use some lozenges.

Besides, the fresh air might do her good.

ARU

The midday sun bore down on the building site, the shimmering heat waves radiating from the rooftops.

Aru pulled a handkerchief from his back pocket and wiped the sweat from the back of his neck. "I hope they get here soon so we can get out of here."

Not that it was any cooler at the bottom of the ravine where the meeting was about to take place. The spot they had chosen was under the gnarled limbs of a tree that provided almost no shade, but that was the best they had found.

"This is kind of fun." Negal slapped a blob of cement over the previous layer of tile shingles and pressed another clay tile on top of it. "There is something to be said about building things with your own two hands."

"I'd rather be doing anything but that." Dagor adjusted his protective glasses with a gloved hand. "The sun is glaring, my hair is saturated with sweat under this hardhat, and my shirt is sticking to me."

Aru patted his back. "Stop complaining and be glad that this is not how I chose for us to make a living while we are stationed here."

Dagor executed an irreverent bow. "I'm forever grateful, oh great leader."

The roofers who had donated their hardhats, protective eye gear, and gloves were currently enjoying an afternoon at a local bar, drinking beers in an air-conditioned space.

Persuading them to make the switch had taken a minimal thrall and a couple of hundred dollars each. It was more than Aru had expected to pay for the privilege of laying roof shingles, but everything had gotten more expensive these days, including bribes.

"Here comes the drone," Negal said. "That was faster than I expected."

The humans working on the other roofs were oblivious to the warbird flying above their heads. They couldn't see it or hear it, and even if they did, they wouldn't think it posed them any danger.

"They are decisive." Dagor wiped the sweat off his brow with the back of his gloved hand. "I'll give them that."

"It's a pretty big bird, and it's armed," Negal said. "They say that they come in peace, and yet they are flying a military drone above our heads."

"They are being cautious." Aru collected cement on his trowel and smeared it over the first shingle layers.

The real roofers would have a lot of work just undoing the mess the three of them were making while pretending to be working. From above, those looking through the drone camera eye wouldn't be able to differentiate between them and the real roofers, so in a way, he was glad that their adversaries were flying the drone and getting reassurance that no one was waiting for them in the ravine below.

However, if he were in their shoes, he would suspect that their intended hosts were hiding among the construction workers. The beauty of his plan was that this was a large development with hundreds of workers milling around. It would be impossible for their adversaries to sift through all the humans to find the three who didn't belong.

"Damn," Dagor pulled out his disruptor. "How did they get the smaller drone here so quickly? There is no way they could have flown it here on one charge."

"Obviously, they drove it here." Aru put his tool down. "And they are flying the damn thing low enough to see our faces."

"I should disrupt both drones' navigation systems and bring them down." Dagor aimed the disruptor at the device.

"Don't." Aru put his hand on Dagor's arm, bringing it down. "It could

384

crash on the site, and people could get hurt. It could also start a fire, which might cause untold damage."

Dagor groaned. "Let me at least disturb the armed one. I can aim a weak blast and cause a malfunction that will only affect its navigation ability, so it won't crash here. If I do nothing, the moment we ditch our disguises, it could shoot us down."

Aru maintained his hold on Dagor's arm. "If we damage its navigation capabilities, it will eventually crash somewhere, and we can't risk innocent lives on the remote chance that our adversaries decide to fire upon us before hearing us out. They are no doubt just as curious about who we are as we are about them. They want to talk, not shoot. At least not at first. Besides, I hope that they are as concerned about staying under the humans' radar as we are."

Reluctantly, Dagor lowered the device. "You are the commander. If we die, it's on you."

Aru snorted out a laugh. "You've been watching too much television. We are not that easy to kill."

"Not true. If they blast us to smithereens, we can't be put together again. We are not Odu."

Aru couldn't help the shiver that ran through him at the mention of the disastrous creations. It didn't help that he knew now that what had been said about them had been a lie, just one more thread in the Eternal King's propaganda tapestry.

He'd grown up on horror stories about the Odus, a cautionary tale about creating soulless machines and the terrible unforeseen consequences.

"A car just pulled up to the curb," Negal announced.

That got Aru's attention. He watched as the four doors opened almost simultaneously, and the passengers got out. Two of them were tall, dark-haired females with sunglasses on their pert noses and tight-fitting clothes that didn't conceal their alien physiques.

"Kra-ell," Dagor stated the obvious. "Is the tall one Jade?"

"Given the swagger, it would seem so." Aru let out a breath. "I'm glad she's not dead. I think that the other one is Morgada. Both are original settlers."

"That's not good," Negal said. "They will immediately recognize who we are. And what the hell are they doing with two human males?"

Aru was wondering the same thing. "It would seem that humans helped liberate the Kra-ell from Gor's rule, which makes things much more complicated for us. If they are from the government, which they must be to possess such military might, we will have to abort the mission. We can't expose who we are, and the Kra-ell females will recognize us right away."

"Let's keep the hardhats and protective glasses on," Negal suggested. "They might suspect that we are not human, but they won't know for sure."

Dagor chuckled. "Does anyone want to bet how long it will take them to figure out who we are?" He looked from Aru to Negal and back to Aru. "My bet is ten minutes tops."

"I think we can do better than that." Aru adjusted his hardhat on his head. "Keep your heads down and try to walk with less fluidity."

A crease formed between Negal's eyebrows. "Do you want us to pretend to be human?"

Aru shrugged. "We can't pretend to be Kra-ell, so pretending to be humans is our only option."

34

GABI

The city seemed to be suffocating under a relentless summer sun, and as Gabi walked the streets of downtown, she felt the weight of that heat pressing down on her. The very air seemed thick, making every breath feel like a conscious effort.

The sidewalk stretched out ahead, appearing to emanate its own misty aura. She could see the heatwaves rising in delicate spirals like ghostly fingers. They distorted the air, making the world waver and dance in a dizzying mirage. The buildings, cars, and people seemed to ebb and flow in this heat-induced haze, their edges softening, blending, and occasionally disappearing altogether.

There weren't many people on the sidewalk, and the few who passed her hurried by with faces that glistened with sweat. Everyone was in silent agreement that the quicker they moved, the sooner they could find respite.

Gabi pulled out a tissue from her purse and dabbed it at her forehead. The paper came away damp. She knew she should quicken her pace, find shade, or enter one of the air-conditioned stores lining the street, but she couldn't.

She hadn't expected it to get so hot, and although she'd been walking for less than ten minutes, the exhaustion from being sick, combined with the oppressive heat, was slowing her steps to a near crawl.

If only there was a bench she could rest on for a couple of minutes and catch her breath.

But there were none in sight, and the drugstore was just around the corner. A few more minutes and she could rest in the air-conditioned space while shopping for her items, and if she still felt so bad after she was done, she would call a taxi back to the hotel.

Fifty feet never seemed so far away.

Forty feet.

Twenty.

She could make it.

Only a few more steps—

Her knees gave out, and then she was falling, but the impact never came. Sometime between being upright and hitting the sidewalk, everything went dark.

The next time Gabi opened her eyes, she was no longer outside in the hot sun. In fact, she was freezing cold despite having a blanket tucked around her.

It took her a moment to take in her surroundings and realize that she was on a hospital bed. A curtain separated her from the rest of the room, but given the sounds, she was in an emergency room. She felt a dull ache at the back of her head, her fingers instinctively reaching to touch the tender spot.

A moment later, the curtain was pushed aside, and a nurse came in. Or was she the doctor?

"I'd advise against that," the woman said.

"What happened?" Gabi asked. "Where am I?"

"You fainted, fell, and knocked your head," the nurse or the doctor said while typing on the keyboard. "Someone called the paramedics, and you were brought here."

The woman didn't bother to introduce herself, and since she was facing the computer screen, Gabi couldn't see the name tag.

"Where is here?"

"City Medical Center," the woman said.

Gabi's eyes widened in realization, and a rush of memories flooded back. The intense heat, the shimmering sidewalk, the weight of the sun pressing down on her. "I... I remember walking. It was so hot," she whispered, her voice shaky.

"Heatstroke, likely. It's been a scorching week. We've run some scans to make sure there's no internal bleeding. You have a mild concussion, and we'd like to observe you for a little while."

Gabi tried to sit up, a wave of dizziness making her wince. "I need to call... I have to let someone know."

Ignoring her, the nurse asked, "Do you have medical insurance?"

"Yes, of course. I hope the paramedics brought my purse. The card is in my wallet."

As the woman turned toward her, her name tag became visible. Cortney Duke was an R.N.

"They did." Cortney pulled a bag from under the hospital bed. "Everything you had on you when you were brought in is in here." She handed it to Gabi.

Gabi opened the bag, pulled out her purse, and took out her insurance card. "Here you go." She handed it to the nurse.

"Thank you." She took it and turned to her screen.

"When will I see the doctor?" Gabi asked.

"The doctor is making the rounds. You're not an urgent case."

She'd heard that hospitals were understaffed all over the country, but she hadn't known it had gotten so bad that emergency room patients did not get to see physicians and were taken care of by nurses.

"I fainted in the middle of the street. There is obviously something wrong with me, and I need to find out what it is."

Cortney looked at her over her shoulder. "The most likely causes are heatstroke, dehydration, or a stomach flu. We are running tests to rule out a bacterial infection, and the results should arrive shortly."

"I don't have an upset stomach, and I don't think I was dehydrated either." She'd drunk mostly coffee, which wasn't great for hydration, but it wasn't the first time she had done it, so she doubted that was the culprit. "I wasn't feeling well, and I was on my way to the drugstore to get some Motrin and other supplies. The heat must have exacerbated my symptoms, and that was why I fainted."

"It's possible, but we need to rule out other more critical possibilities. Bacterial infections can be very dangerous." The nurse finished typing. "The doctor will be with you shortly." She ducked behind the curtain.

Gabi was stunned. Was that how people were being treated in hospitals these days?

Pulling the white phone out of her purse, she called her brother.

"Hi, Gabi," Gilbert answered right away. "Can I call you back in a few minutes? I'm on another call."

"No, you can't. I'm in the hospital, and they are treating me like some vagabond that was found on the street." Which wasn't far from the truth, but she had insurance and could pay for the non-treatment she was getting. "I need you or Eric to come get me."

"What happened?" Gilbert sounded alarmed, as he should be.

"I was feeling a little under the weather and went to get some stuff from the drugstore. I fainted, and someone called the paramedics. They brought me to City Medical Center. I just woke up, and the nurse said that they were running some tests. I haven't even seen a doctor yet. Can you or Eric cut your business trip short and come get me?"

"I need to make a few phone calls to see what can be done, and I'll call you right back. Can you hang in there for a little bit longer?"

That wasn't the answer she'd expected, but what choice did she have? "Please hurry. I don't feel safe here."

"I will." He ended the call.

In case Gilbert and Eric couldn't get back to Los Angeles as quickly as she needed them, perhaps she should call Uriel as well. If she was lucky, he was done with his business deal and could come to her rescue.

Pulling out her old phone, she dialed his number, but the call went straight to voicemail.

Damn. It wasn't her day.

With a sigh, Gabi typed up a message to Uriel and hit send.

JADE

J ade lifted her dark sunglasses and looked at the construction site. At least thirty houses were being built, and many crews were doing different tasks. Some were still in the framing stage, while others were getting their roofs installed.

If she were in the gods' shoes, she would have chosen the roof for obvious reasons, preferably on one of the houses overlooking the canyon. There were six of them perched near the edge, and each had a roofing crew of three to four people, but since all of them were wearing hardhats and protective eye gear, it was difficult to discern differences between the humans and the non-humans.

Gods could suppress their glow which, other than their unnaturally perfect appearance, was the only other thing that could give them away. So, hiding their faces behind safety glasses was a smart move.

Shifting her gaze from one crew to the next, Jade smiled. "Got you." She nudged Phinas's arm. "Look at the footwear of the crew on the roof of the fourth house from the street, and then compare it to what the other roofers are wearing."

"They are all wearing boots," Magnus said. "But the others are wearing work boots, while those three are wearing regular walking boots."

Phinas shrugged. "It could be a different brand of work boots, but we should keep an eye on them." He tapped his earpiece to let Onegus know he was talking to him. "Did you get that?"

"Yes. We are zooming in. We've got you covered."

The knowledge that the drone could shoot them down if needed was reassuring. It wouldn't kill the gods, and it would scare the shit out of the real construction workers, but it might give them a chance to get away if necessary.

She still couldn't shake the feeling that they were walking into a trap, and Syssi's vision had made it worse instead of better. Jade could handle other Kra-ell as long as they weren't compellers like Igor, and even if they were, she had the protective earpieces to shield her from that. Gods, however, were a different breed, and it was impossible to know what capabilities they possessed. With how they manipulated nature, they could have discovered a way to create compellers that didn't need to use sound to carry their commands. They might be able to reach directly into the minds of their victims.

"So, are we going down there or not?" Morgada asked.

"Start the descent," Onegus sounded in their earpieces. "Double-check your gear and make sure that it fits properly. If the earpieces allow any untranslated speech through, they are useless against compulsion."

Jade checked to make sure hers were sucre in her ears. Since the earpieces didn't alter the ambient noise and it was passing through unfiltered, it was sometimes hard to determine whether they were working correctly.

"What's the status of the backup force?" Magnus asked.

"Getting in position. The ETA of the helicopter with the sound cannon is less than five minutes. By the time you get down to the canyon, it will be there."

The problem with the cannon was that the earpieces weren't designed to filter out the noise it was producing. If the need arose to use it, their team would be as affected as the gods, and the backup force would have to collect them all. The immortals would heal the injury to their inner ear quite fast, but she and Morgada would take much longer.

"Can I give you a hand?" Magnus offered his arm to Morgada.

She cast him an offended look. "I might be out of shape, but I'm still Kra-ell. I can jog down this canyon."

Jade doubted that, but Magnus nodded and retracted his hand. "No offense, eh? I was just trying to be a gentleman."

"No offense taken." Morgada took the first step down the steep slope.

"Careful," Magnus said. "If you break something, it's going to ruin the meeting. We will have to evacuate you."

Morgada was wearing dark sunglasses, so Magnus couldn't see the red glow that his words had no doubt produced, but given the tight line of Morgada's lips, she was glaring at the Guardian. "I'm not going to break anything."

As Jade shook her head, Phinas leaned closer to her and whispered in her ear, "Do you think they are flirting?"

"How should I know? Kra-ell don't flirt."

He chuckled. "I beg to differ. They might not have flirted in the past, but they are learning new ways."

"Look at that." Magnus pointed to the bottom of the canyon. "Our hosts have graciously prepared a meeting place."

Hidden under the scraggy limbs of a tree, a brown blanket was spread over the ground and secured with a large jug, presumably filled with water.

Jade looked at the metallic container with suspicion. "Like I'm going to drink anything they offer me." She glanced up to see whether the roofing crew had made a move.

They hadn't, and by the looks of things, they were still laying shingles.

Maybe Phinas was right, and that crew just happened to be wearing different work footwear. But if those roofers weren't their hosts, who were?

As Jade led the group down the steep slope towards the makeshift meeting place, the canyon walls loomed high above them, and the echoes of the construction work above them made it difficult to hear movement in time to react. Not that she expected any dangerous animals to leap at them, but there could be snakes and spiders, and some of them might be venomous.

The ravine was a labyrinth of rugged terrain strewn with loose gravel and rocky outcrops. Hardy plants dotted its walls, which rose like ancient fortresses, imposing and weathered, their colors ranging from deep russet to burnt sienna, and their gnarled forms providing only a modicum of shade.

Jade's hand searched for the pommel of her sword, but it wasn't there. They were unarmed save for the daggers they had hidden under their clothing and in their boots. The banner Kian had flown over the other canyon promised their hosts that they were coming in peace, so they had to maintain a peaceful appearance.

As they reached the tree with the brown blanket, Jade's eyes darted around, scanning for signs of traps or threats.

"They expect us to sit down." She motioned for the others to sit while keeping an eye on the roofing crew above, and then joined the others on the blanket.

The tension in the air was palpable, and everyone was on edge.

Morgada's eyes fixed on the jug of water. "I don't like this," she murmured.

Magnus nodded. "If they pass it around, just pretend to drink."

Phinas kept watch on the roofing crew. "Maybe they're just construction workers after all, and our hosts will approach from a different direction."

"That's why I'm watching the other slope," Magnus said.

Jade's gaze remained fixed on the crew above. "Gods are the masters of subterfuge. But sometimes, things are just the way they seem."

ARU

A ru watched as the two Kra-ell females and two human males carefully climbed down the rocky terrain.

The rock formations towered on either side, their jagged edges casting sharp shadows that seemed to deepen the canyon's barrenness, and the four people climbing down found temporary respite in those shadows as they made their way to the bottom, where Dagor had left a little surprise for them.

It was an exceptionally hot day, and the arid canyon was baking in the unyielding sun. The canyon floor was dry and cracked, marked by the imprints of long-gone streams, but now only the occasional scattered tumbleweeds and patches of dry grass clung to survival, their pale colors offering little relief from the desert's harshness.

Above, the cloudless sky stretched like an infinite blue canvas, offering no respite from the unrelenting sun, with only their adversaries' large drone hovering high above like a bird of prey.

"It's showtime." Dagor put his trowel down. "They got the hint and are sitting down."

It had been Dagor's idea to lay down a blanket with a jug of water as a symbolic gesture of hospitality. He believed it would promote a relaxed conversation. "People like to sit around while talking," he had said with a grin.

"Don't mistake that for complacence." Negal walked over to the edge of the roof and used the ladder to climb down, even though he could have just as easily jumped down.

They didn't want to attract attention, which was why they shrouded themselves as they started their descent down the canyon wall. It wouldn't fool the Kra-ell females, who wouldn't be affected by the shroud, but the humans with them would be taken by surprise when they got there because they wouldn't see them approaching. If they wanted to maintain the illusion of being human for a little longer, they would have to drop the shroud midway to the ravine floor.

As Aru followed Negal down the ladder, his phone rang, but by the time he reached the ground, the call went to voicemail.

"You were supposed to put your phone on airplane mode," Negal admonished. "Who is calling you?"

It could have been a number of people he had done business with, a random wrong number, or Gabi, but it wasn't as if he could respond right now, so he didn't even bother pulling the device from his pocket.

Except, a moment later, he heard a message come in and instinctively knew that it was from her. "Start down the ravine. I'll catch up with you in a moment." He lifted the phone and read the message.

The blood chilled in his veins.

Hi Uriel. I don't want to bother you during your important meeting, but I wanted to let you know that I'm in a hospital. I fainted on the way to the drugstore, and they brought me here. They suspect dehydration from sunstroke, but they are running some tests to be sure. I don't like it here, so I called Gilbert, and he promised to try to get me out. But in case you can make it here sooner, I would really appreciate it if you could help me get back to the hotel. They are probably not going to let me go without someone to take care of me, so I need someone to show up, but after that, I will be fine on my own. It was just too hot outside, and combined with my cold, it got to be too much. Let me know when you think your meeting will be over.

"She's in the hospital. I need to get to her."

"Have you lost your mind over that human?" Negal put a hand on his shoulder. "You can't go anywhere right now. Besides, what do you know about human medicine? If there is something wrong with her, she's at the right place and in the right hands. They will take care of her in the hospital."

Negal was right. Aru couldn't abandon the mission at this critical point to rush to the hospital.

"I need to text her back. Start on without me. I'll catch up."

"I'm not going anywhere without you," Negal said. "Dagor needs to stay back in case we are walking into a trap. You are our leader, and this was your idea. Just text her back quickly."

"This obsession with the human needs to stop," Dagor murmured.

Ignoring him, Aru typed. *I'm in the middle of something I can't get out of. I'll come as soon as I can. Which hospital are you in?*

Her answer came back immediately: *City Medical Center.*

That sounded like a generic term for a medical facility. There were probably several of them in every town.

Aru texted back, *which city?*

This time, there was no answer.

Had she gotten annoyed with him? Or perhaps the doctor walked in just then?

"Come on." Negal started walking. "We don't want to keep our guests waiting."

Aru pushed his worries aside and pocketed his phone. His heart was heavy, but he couldn't let his feelings jeopardize a critical mission. He had to believe that Gabi would be okay until he could reach her.

KIAN

s Kian's phone buzzed with an incoming message, he tore his eyes from the view of the canyon and his team at the bottom of it.

Seeing that it was from Gilbert he was tempted to ignore it, but since nothing was happening yet, he could allow himself a moment to read what the guy wanted.

Gabi called me from the hospital. She fainted in the middle of the street, and paramedics were called. I have to get out of the village and go see her. Is there any way you can lift the lockdown to allow me out? I'd like to bring her to the village, but if that's not an option at the moment, I will stay with her until she's discharged.

That was such bad timing, but Kian could empathize. If any of his sisters were in trouble, he would have moved mountains to get to them.

Instead of texting back, he called the guy. "Come to the war room. Do you know where it is?"

"Yes. I'm on my way."

Kian ended the call.

"What's going on?" Onegus asked.

"Gilbert's sister is in the hospital, and he wants me to let him out of the village."

The chief's brows furrowed. "What's wrong with her?"

"All I know is that she fainted on the street."

Onegus drummed his fingers on the table. "She's been seeing that Uriel Delgado guy. Maybe our initial suspicion was correct, and he is an immortal. He could have induced her transition, and that was what put her in the hospital. If that's the case, we need to get her out of there as soon as possible and do a thorough cleanup job to erase all records of her being there."

"You said that Roni had checked his background and that he seemed legit."

"Seemed is the operative word. I didn't think that Uriel Delgado's good looks were reason enough to spend time and money on researching him, but if Gabi is transitioning, then it's proof that he's an immortal."

A growl rose in Kian's throat. "He must be a Doomer."

Onegus shook his head. "Doomers wouldn't have done such a great job of creating a fake identity, so he might not be a Doomer." He chuckled. "Perhaps Gabi has stumbled upon one more of Toven's children. The dark hair and handsome face match, only the eye color doesn't, but maybe Uriel is wearing contact lenses to fool the facial recognition at airports."

It was an interesting hypothesis. Orion had created a fake identity for himself and had managed to survive on his own, believing that he was the only immortal until his chance meeting with his father. Uriel might have done the same after realizing that he was immortal.

They even had similar occupations. Orion dealt with antiques, and Uriel dealt with flea market finds that were just a cheaper version of the same thing. Someone who had lived through history had a better chance of recognizing valuable old finds and profiting from them.

"If Uriel is Toven's son, his meeting Gabi on the plane must have been fated."

Onegus regarded him with amusement in his eyes. "The heretic turned a believer."

The door to the war room was slightly ajar, and as a knock sounded on its other side, Kian called out for Gilbert to come in.

"So, this is the famous war room." Gilbert looked around. "I'm impressed. What's on the screen?"

"Take a seat." Kian motioned for the chair next to him. "What did Gabi tell you when she called?"

"What I texted you. She's not happy with the care they are giving her at the medical center, and she wants me to take her out of there. I would love to bring her to the village and deliver her into Bridget's capable hands, but if that's not possible, I'll just transfer her to another hospital. Gabi might sound like a spoiled princess, but she isn't. If she says that the level of care is subpar, it is."

Kian glanced at Onegus. "Should we tell him our suspicion?"

The chief nodded. "She's his sister. He should know."

"I should know what?" Gilbert asked.

"Remember how I suspected that the guy she'd met on the plane was an immortal? We didn't have a good enough reason to dig deeper, especially since his identity and backstory were convincing. But he might be an immortal after all, and he could have induced her transition. That might be why she ended up in the hospital, and if that's indeed the case, we have to get her out of there."

The color drained from Gilbert's face. "A Doomer induced my sister?"

"Not necessarily." Onegus smiled. "Uriel Delgado might be Toven's son. There is some remote familial resemblance."

"I'll be damned." Gilbert ran a hand over his spare hair. "It's a small world after all."

"It's just speculation," Kian said. "First, we need to get you out of here. If it looks like Gabi is transitioning, we will send out a team to retrieve her. If not, and it's just a bug or some other medical problem, you should prepare to stay with her."

"When can I leave?"

"As soon as you are packed," Onegus said. "I'll get a Guardian to escort you out."

ARU

As Aru and Negal made their way down to the canyon floor, their four guests waited patiently.

Amidst the harshness and aridity, there was a certain raw beauty to the canyon. The rugged rock formations, shaped by centuries of wind and water erosion, displayed nature's grandeur, and the colors of the rock, now intensified by the unrelenting sun, seemed to glow with an inner fire. Blessedly, the wind picked up a little, rustling the leaves of the gnarled bushes and trees and reducing the temperature by a few miserly degrees.

As Aru wiped the sweat from his forehead, he was tempted to take off the hardhat and let the breeze cool the top of his head, but he wanted to preserve the illusion of being human for a few more minutes.

If the Kra-ell females recognized him and Negal for who they were, they might attack first and ask questions later. There was no love lost between the gods and the Kra-ell, and for good reason.

What Jade and Morgada didn't know, though, was that the gods had evened out the playing field and that some of the young gods born after the settler ship had left had been enhanced to be just as strong as the Kra-ell. The Eternal King was closing every possible gap in his consolidated power, making every effort to prevent the possibility of future rebellions.

If Jade and Morgada decided to attack, they would be in for a surprise.

"We come in peace." He lifted his hands to show that he wasn't armed.

Negal did the same.

Dagor was on the roof of another building, and he had his disruptor, but it was not a weapon to be used against biological beings. It could disable equipment that was powered by anything other than muscle, and it could become useful if these people decided to use the drone to attack them.

"So do we." Jade removed her sunglasses, and Morgada did the same.

"Hello, Jade." He smiled. "I'm so glad to see that both you and Morgada are alive. We were very worried about you."

If looks could kill, her glare would have done him in. "How do you know who we are?"

"We've been watching you for a while." He motioned toward the blanket. "Let's sit down."

"First, tell me who you are and how you know my name."

Behind him, Negal cast a shrouding bubble around their group. Regrettably, it was only good for keeping human prying eyes from seeing them and ears from eavesdropping, but not for keeping the sun from baking their heads.

As the male standing next to Jade moved closer to her, the small hairs on the back of Aru's neck prickled, and he rubbed his hand over them. Usually, the sensation only happened when he met new, unfamiliar male gods, but not with humans. They were of no consequence to him, no threat, and there was no reason for his built-in alarm to go off.

The guy wasn't a god, that was obvious by his less-than-perfect features, and neither was the other one who was regarding him with surprising calm given the loaded situation.

Perhaps they were descendants of the gods?

There was a strong prohibition on gods procreating with the various species they had created, but the gods who had been sent to Earth had been rebels, so they might not have followed the rules in that as well.

The two males might possess a trace of godly genes, and that was why the hairs on the back of his neck were tingling.

To make sure, he turned to Negal. "Do you feel it, too?"

The trooper nodded. "Not as strongly as with others like us, but these males are not fully human."

"Who are you?" Aru asked the male wearing a strange red vest that didn't match the rest of his elegant clothing. "Or rather, what are you?"

The male smiled. "I would like to know the same about you, but let's start with simple introductions and continue from there. You already know Jade and Morgada. My name is Magnus." He offered Aru his hand.

"Aru." He shook what was offered. "And this is Negal."

"I'm Phinas." The other male offered his hand.

Once all the handshakes were exchanged, Aru lowered himself to the blanket and sat down cross-legged Kra-ell style.

With a look of approval in her big eyes, Jade followed suit and sat across from him, and Morgada did the same.

When Phinas sat on Jade's right, Aru noticed the earpieces he was wearing. A quick glance at Magnus revealed that he was wearing them, too. Jade and Morgada had their hair down, so he couldn't tell whether they were wearing them as well.

He pointed at the earpiece in Magnus's ear. "I assume that our conversation is not private."

"It's not," the guy confirmed. "My boss is listening in. For full transparency, we are also flying a drone overhead that is filming us and, if need be, can provide an aerial defense. In addition, a force of Guardians is on standby not far from here. Both are defensive measures in case you turn hostile. If you don't strike, we won't. We just want to talk and find out who you are and what you want."

Aru was sure that it was far from full disclosure, but admitting it was a step in the right direction.

"I assume that you expect a similar disclosure from me, but all I can say is that we want the same thing you do, and whatever measures we have in place are defensive and not offensive."

Magnus didn't look happy with his answer. "Is anyone listening to our conversation on your side?"

Aru could have lied and answered in the affirmative, but he preferred the truth whenever possible. Lies by omission were necessary, and in most cases, he could get by without crossing that line.

"No one is listening to our conversation, but we are not without backup. We are expected to report periodically. If we don't, a large force will come looking for us, and believe me, none of us want that."

Dagor was watching, but his only recourse was to summon the patrol ship, and it would take years for it to come back.

The truth was that if they had nothing of interest to report, years could pass without anyone checking in on them. Their commander had a large sector to patrol, and Earth was of little interest to anyone except for the two most powerful people on Anumati, each for their own reasons.

39

MAGNUS

hy me? Magnus thought while pinning the other group's leader with a hard look, which was hopefully not too threatening and not too soft either.

The only reason he'd been selected for this mission was his seniority. He was the highest-ranking non-head Guardian. That, however, didn't make him a good candidate for a diplomatic mission. In fact, he was probably one of the worst people Onegus and Kian could have chosen to represent the clan in a meeting with the gods.

Not that he was sure they were gods yet, but they weren't Kra-ell, and they weren't human, so the only option other than gods was that they were immortals like him.

"You're being vague," he told the leader. "Who are you, and who do you report to?"

"And how do you know our names?" Jade added.

The guy smiled. "Let's do things in their proper order and make it an equitable exchange of information. First, tell me who and what you are. You are definitely not human." He rubbed the back of his neck. "Do you also have this built-in alarm?" He glanced at Phinas, who neither confirmed nor denied.

Aru's admission, though, confirmed that he and his friend were either gods or immortals.

"You can tell him what we agreed on," Kian said in Magnus's earpiece.

"We are immortals," Magnus said. "We are the descendants of the gods. Your turn. Who are you?"

The guy arched a brow. "Fascinating. I assume that you are the product of dalliances between gods and humans?"

Magnus tilted his head. "I thought that was self-explanatory. How else could I be a descendant of the gods and not a god myself?"

"It is forbidden for gods to procreate with anyone other than their own, but your parents were known rule breakers."

Magnus's blood chilled in his veins. How did Aru know his mother? Had these beings been watching them as they had been obviously watching the Kra-ell?

No, that wasn't possible.

Aru didn't know who and what Magnus and Phinas were, and the only reason he'd figured they had godly genes in them was the built-in alarm system that male gods and immortals had—the prickling sensation when in the presence of possible male adversaries.

Perhaps Aru had misspoken.

"I assume that you meant our ancestors were known rule breakers. There is no way you know my mother, who is not a goddess but an immortal like me."

Aru's eyes widened. "I actually thought that one of your parents was a god. How many generations of immortals are there?"

The guy was either clueless or pretending to be.

"Many," Magnus said.

Negal leaned forward as if wanting a better look. "That's incredible. I had no idea that immortality could be hereditary. How does it work?"

Magnus shook his head. "Let's save the scientific explanations for later. I told you who we are, and it's your turn to tell us who you are."

"We are gods, of course. Who else could we be?" Aru removed his hardhat and his protective glasses, leaving behind only the dark sunglasses he'd worn under the shield. "It's way too hot out here."

Jade chuckled. "Your kind avoids the sun at all costs. You are not used to harsh sunlight."

"No, we are not, but we are better equipped to deal with it than

Magnus's ancestors. The heat and the harsh light must have been torturous for the exiled gods, which was no doubt the Eternal King's intent. After all, he wanted to punish them."

"It's getting interesting," Kian said in Magnus's earpieces. "Keep him talking, but don't reveal what we have agreed upon no matter what he tells you."

Magnus had no intention of mentioning the surviving gods, but since Aru and Negal were gods themselves, they could just reach into his mind and take the information from there. Kian should have sent Turner, who was immune, and Magnus had even suggested him, but both Onegus and Kian had rejected the suggestion.

"What do you know about the exiled gods?" Magnus asked.

Perhaps if he kept Aru talking, the god wouldn't be able to peek into his mind at the same time. Thralling required concentration, and if Magnus couldn't thrall humans while talking, the god shouldn't be able to thrall immortals while talking either.

Aru grimaced. "I know what our history records tell us, and it's nothing good, but my teammates and I are well aware that it's all propaganda meant to besmirch the heir's name. Now, it is blasphemous to even say his name out loud."

Jade cast the god a hard look. "That wasn't what we were told back in my day, but I don't really care about the lies the Eternal King spreads about his own people."

Magnus narrowed his eyes at the god. "You said, 'teammates.' That implies more than one."

Aru nodded. "The third member of our team is not here for security reasons. We didn't know what we were walking into, and bringing our entire team would have been foolish."

It was a valid concern. "Makes sense. Where is he now?"

Aru smiled. "Do you really think I will tell you that?"

Magnus lifted his head and looked at the roof the gods had been working on. The third member of their party was no longer there, but Magnus was willing to bet that he was on one of the other roofs, watching his teammates.

40

ARU

"We saw you on that roof," Jade said. "You overlooked one item of your disguise, and it gave you away."

"What is it?" He'd thought that they had blended in seamlessly.

She looked at his boots. "Those are not made for construction work. I knew all along that you left one of your teammates behind, but what I don't get is how you know who I am. You even know my adopted name. Have you been tapping into the compound's communications?"

"Something like that."

To answer Jade's question truthfully, Aru would have to reveal much more than he was comfortable with at the moment, but since he'd already shown his hand by recognizing her and Morgada, he had no choice.

The cloud that had provided a little respite from the sun had moved over, and the limbs of the tree they had spread the blanket under were so gnarled and devoid of leaves that it was like sitting out in the open.

"I wish we could have this meeting in an air-conditioned place." Aru put the hardhat back on his head.

Sweating was better than having his brain fry in the sun.

Jade rolled her eyes. "Stop stalling already and answer me. 'Something like that' is not an answer."

He nodded. "It's a long story that I don't want to get into detail with, but the gist of it is that we were sent to find you, see what you are up to, and report back. We periodically surveyed the compound to see what Igor was up to and whether he had captured more Kra-ell, but we were not allowed to intervene or to let our presence be known."

She arched a brow. "Really? So why are you here now, talking to us?"

Aru shifted his gaze to the two immortal males. "When we realized that new players had showed up on the scene, we had to find out what they were about."

As the implications sank in, the alarm in Magnus's eyes betrayed his thoughts even before he voiced them. "Where did you come from and why? Was it a nearby outpost or straight from Anumati?"

The immortal feared discovery by the Eternal King, and rightfully so.

"We left Anumati a hundred and one Earth years ago, and we've been here five years. Our arrival wasn't in response to any particular event. We are on a standard tour of duty in the sector."

"Where is your ship?" the other immortal asked.

"The ship dropped us off and continued on its tour. It will collect us on its way back and continue to the next sector."

"When will it come back for you?" Magnus asked.

Aru hesitated and then decided to go with the truth. As long as Magnus and whoever was listening to their conversation were afraid of an imminent strike by a superior force of gods, they wouldn't reveal anything about themselves. To gain the trust of the immortals and their Kra-ell charges, he needed to give them something else to focus on and show them that they were on the same side of the divide.

"Our ship will return in one hundred and fifteen years, give or take a few. The round trip from Anumati and back takes over seven hundred years, and the last time anyone checked on humanity was about six hundred years ago. Your world was very different back then, and the Eternal King had no reason to get involved in what was happening here. But things have changed dramatically since then. The human population has exploded, and its technological progress has advanced exponentially. Our primary task was to find out whether the settler ship had arrived, and we reported that it had and that only some of the settlers had survived. I didn't report what else we found on Earth even though it was much more important than the Kra-ell." He smiled. "It's also much more important than discovering that the descendants of the rebel gods are hiding among the humans." He sighed. "What I'm trying to say is that you don't need to be alarmed on account of us discovering you. There are much bigger concerns to worry about."

Beside him, Negal groaned in frustration, probably appalled by how much he was revealing.

Their four guests stared at him with wide eyes.

Jade was the first one to speak. "Aren't you a soldier in the king's army? Isn't it your duty to report everything?"

Aru nodded. "Officially, yes. The three of us were conscripted into service but not at the same time. Negal has been serving longer than the other teammate and me. But that doesn't mean that we are fully aligned with the Eternal King and his agenda."

Just to be safe, he'd worded it in a way that didn't sound like treasonous intentions but rather a difference in opinions.

"A lot longer," Negal grumbled. "And yet you got the command."

"Conscripted?" Magnus asked. "Service is not voluntary for gods?"

"For most, it is not. There are always the privileged ones who get exempt from duty under various guises of alternative service. But in my case, and in the case of my teammates and everyone on the ship patrolling this sector, we are here because we wanted to be stationed together. We are a ship of kindred people."

The new rebellion was thousands of years in the making, and it would take many thousands more. Ahn's mistake had been rushing in without enough support. This time around, they were building a solid foundation and waiting patiently for it to reach critical mass. When the time came to end the Eternal King's rule, what they were building would be so vast and powerful that no bloodshed would accompany the transition of power.

Hopefully.

"Why are you telling them all that?" Negal took his hardhat off and wiped the sweat off his forehead before putting it back on. "We don't know who they are or who they work for. You are endangering thousands of lives by revealing our most guarded secret as casually as describing the weather."

Aru shifted his eyes to him. "These people are obviously not working for the Eternal King, and they are in much more danger from him than we are. If we want them to trust us, we have to show them trust first." He shifted his gaze to Magnus. "In the eyes of the Eternal King, you and everyone like you is an abomination. You are not supposed to exist. He will exterminate you like bugs before listening to anything you have to say, and he will do that from afar so none of your blood will stain his pristine robes. He will also not allow humanity to keep growing. The last time a team reported from Earth, there were less than four hundred million humans. Now, there are more than eight billion people on Earth, and their technological progress has grown at an astounding rate. When the Eternal King learns of that, he will send a plague the likes of which Earth has never seen before, decimating the population and bringing it back to what he considers manageable, both in numbers and in technology. He might not act right away in human terms, and a couple of hundred years might pass before he makes his move, but once humanity gains interstellar travel capability, he will act swiftly. The king will not tolerate competition from what he views as inferior creatures."

"How do we stop him?" Magnus asked.

Aru smiled sadly. "The resistance is steadily gaining ground, but it is still far from being ready. Gods think in terms of thousands of Earth years. It will be a long time before we can do anything and hope to succeed. The best we can do for now is not report humanity's state until we are picked up in a hundred and some years."

Unless Aru came up with a brilliant excuse for failing to report that, he would be punished for the omission by exile to a rock at the end of the galaxy, but he wouldn't be executed. After all, his team's job was to find out whether the settler ship had arrived and if the twins had been found. He'd reported that some of the Kra-ell had survived and that the twins probably hadn't, so technically, he had fulfilled his duty.

41

KIAN

The weight of leadership had always rested heavily on Kian's shoulders, but he'd faced the many challenges with a resolve born of hope for a better future.

Aru's words had shattered that hope, bringing about a despondency that pressed down on Kian like a mountain of boulders. The walls of his war room, previously symbols of strength and resolve, felt like they were closing in on him.

All the work his mother and he and his sisters had put into helping humanity evolve could be undone in one swipe of the Eternal King's hand.

As the saying went, it wasn't the things he fretted over that would bring their downfall, but the unexpected that caught them off guard. His own great-grandfather would be the engineer of humanity's demise, and there was nothing Kian could do to stop him.

He let out a breath. "I really want someone else to take over my job." He leaned back in his chair and scanned the faces of his teammates. "Does anyone want it? Because I'm tired of the never-ending struggle."

He wasn't even joking. The only other time in his life he'd felt as helpless as this had been when he'd been forced to leave his first wife and their unborn child, but at least then, he could ensure that their future was as secure as he could make it.

That wasn't the case now.

What chance did he and his clan have against the might of the gods? How was he going to protect humanity from the Eternal King?

The immortals would not be affected by a plague, but they had spent their entire lives helping humanity, and none of them could even conceive of another global disaster wiping out most of the population.

It would be so devastating that it would break even his mother.

"I thought that the Doomers were our biggest problem," Onegus said. "I've been waiting for them to make their next big move, like start the third world war, but they are nothing compared to an army of gods and their biological weapons."

"Navuh would never be so reckless," Turner said. "He wants to control humanity, not destroy it, and the more humans there are, the bigger his empire would be."

The Eternal King had no such qualms, and the one thing he was determined to prevent was competition in any shape or form. If he suspected that humans presented a threat to his hegemony over the known universe, he would strike preemptively before they reached critical mass, and probably not for the first time. The flood described in Sumerian and other mythologies around the world might have been a natural disaster, but Kian believed that the gods would have intervened if the Eternal King had allowed it. The story of Noah's ark described one god's desperate attempt to save humanity from complete annihilation, but the other gods had obeyed the king's orders to do nothing and had watched with horror as their subjects drowned.

Birth rates were slowly declining all over the world, though, so the king might opt to just wait and see whether the trend continued. If it did, then no action was required. The human population would shrink in size, and its technological advancement would decline along with the shrinkage. There wouldn't be enough economic thrust to enable it, let alone propel it forward.

Trends were unpredictable, and intervention might reverse them, but it didn't always work. The Chinese were an excellent example of that. Even after the one-child policy had been lifted and having more children was encouraged, the populace refused to adopt the new policy.

Socio-economic factors were such that people preferred to have only one child so they could adequately provide for it.

Except for a few pockets where birth rates were still high, the same was happening all over the world.

The more advanced the nation, the fewer children it produced.

Turner gave Kian a sympathetic look. "Don't despair. We have a hundred years to find a solution. In godly terms, it might not be a long time, but it is in human terms. If introducing biological agents is how the Eternal King controls populations across the galaxy, we need to focus on finding a way to make everyone immune to them like we are. If we work with these rebel gods, they could help us understand the information in Okidu's journals, which might contain the blueprint for turning humanity immortal or at least immune to diseases."

Turner was the last person Kian had expected to provide words of encouragement, and coming from him, they weren't just platitudes to make him feel better.

"I never expected a pep talk from you. Thank you for your attempt to cheer me up."

"It wasn't a pep talk. I just stated the facts as they are."

Kian stifled a chuckle. That was such a Turner response. "The other factor we must consider is the steady global decline in birth rates. The Eternal King has nothing to worry about right now because humanity does not possess interstellar travel capabilities, and the population might significantly shrink before it does, if it ever gets there."

Turner arched a brow. "I've seen estimates of Earth's population halving in five hundred years and others predicting that it will shrink to below five hundred million. But keep in mind that those are highly speculative estimates based on simplistic assumptions. In reality, population trends are influenced by numerous factors like technological advancements, socio-economic changes, and unforeseen events. It's difficult to accurately predict the direction of global birth rates over such a long timeframe."

"Indeed, but all the factors you've mentioned point toward further decline, not reversal. The global economy is in trouble, and people know how to prevent pregnancies. My gut tells me that the more extreme estimates are the correct ones, but that could be a blessing in disguise. I'd much rather the human population shrink because fewer babies are born than to have them suffer another plague. I can only hope that the Eternal King is not in a rush and will wait and see what the next five hundred years will bring before making his move."

Onegus rubbed his jaw. "Do we even believe these gods? Introducing a mutual external threat is a perfect way for Aru to create rapport with us and gain our trust. He might have made up the prediction about what the Eternal King would do if he discovered how far humanity had advanced."

"That's possible." Kian wanted to believe that, but regrettably, Aru had probably told them the truth. "What their leader said was in line with what Jade has told us about the Eternal King and his politics."

Onegus nodded. "He also sounded sincere. Unless Negal is a superb actor, which he very well might be, his response reinforces the veracity of what Aru was saying. Negal sounded genuinely alarmed when his commander spoke about what could be perceived as treasonous intent, and his shoulders slumped in resignation."

Kian had been watching the same feed, and he hadn't seen the change in the god's posture.

The drone was flying high above, the camera feed was grainy, and the dried-out tree they were sitting under partially blocked the view, making it impossible to see the gods' facial expressions or even posture.

Kian had been relying on what had been said, and for long moments now, no one had said a thing. Magnus and the rest of them were stunned, and Aru was giving them time to process what he'd revealed.

Kian tapped his earpiece. "Ask Aru how often the Eternal King checks up on Earth and how come he doesn't just pick up transmissions from Earth's satellites to learn all he needs from there."

42

ARU

Aru waited patiently as Magnus and his team absorbed what he had told them. They were probably also listening to their boss in their earpieces.

Regrettably, the devices were very well-fitted, and he couldn't hear what was being said on the other side. He could've reached into Magnus's mind and gotten a good impression of what the guy was hearing, but he didn't know whether the gods had imparted their immunity to thralling to their immortal offspring or if the immortals were as susceptible as humans. He was itching to test it, but if the immortals could feel his mental probing, it would be considered a hostile move.

Most of the Kra-ell were immune, which was probably one of the reasons the old gods had made every effort to keep them in a disadvantaged state.

If they couldn't control their minds, they could control them economically.

The rebels had sought to correct that wrong and had paid with their lives for their effort.

"How often does the king check up on Earth?" Magnus asked.

Aru arched a brow. "Is that the only question your boss has for me?"

The guy listened for a moment and then smiled. "For now, he only has a few more questions. He says that we should meet again some-where more comfortable."

Aru wiped the sweat off his forehead with the sleeve of his shirt. "I agree wholeheartedly. This heat is unbearable."

Magnus nodded, but Aru had a feeling that it was in response to something his boss said. "We find it difficult to believe that a society as technologically advanced as the gods' needs boots on the ground to investigate. Aren't they monitoring Earth's broadcasts?"

"That's a good question, and it requires a long answer." Aru reached for the water jug, uncapped it, and took a long sip. "Anyone else thirsty?"

Magnus chuckled. "Now that you drank from it, I'm less apprehensive about it being drugged or poisoned." He took the jug from Aru, lifted it to his mouth, and poured the water into it without touching the rim.

"I could be immune to what's in it," Aru teased. "It could contain a drug that will loosen your tongue. Are you sure you want to risk it?"

Smiling, Magnus made a show of gulping down a substantial amount of water and then returned the jug to Aru. "If I start talking nonsense, my boss will have to send the backup force to extract me."

"Understood." Aru offered the jug to Jade. "It's not drugged."

Casting him a defiant look, she took it and drank.

"Signals from Earth can't be transmitted directly to Anumati, not with the technology available to humans. We used to have satellites that transmitted to a relay station, but they were destroyed. The official version was that the rebels blew them up to avoid answering questions from Anumati journalists about the so-called war crimes they were accused of, but a conspiracy theory claims that the Eternal King ordered the satellites destroyed."

"I've never heard that one," Negal said. "Where did you hear it?"

"From a reliable source." Aru would never reveal his source. Not even to his most trusted friends.

"Why would the king want to destroy communications with Earth?" Magnus asked.

Aru cast a quick look at his companion while formulating his answer. Some of what he was about to say was common knowledge, but some was not, and he needed to frame it accordingly. "Shortly after the settler ship went missing, the Eternal King had war-crime accusations trumped up against Ahn and the other rebels. Supposedly, new information had surfaced of crimes severe enough to warrant entombment. The Eternal King even brought up the flood that, in all likelihood, he had ordered himself. When reporters tried to get Ahn's response to the accusations, the communication satellites around Earth conveniently exploded. The king claimed that Ahn blew them up out of spite and to avoid being asked uncomfortable questions and being brought to justice."

Jade pursed her lips. "I assume you were not the only one who suspected the king was behind the destruction of the satellites. Anumati is ruled by a monarch, but it's supposed to be a semi-democratic monarchy, at least for the gods, if not for the Kra-ell. How come no one in the media investigated the allegations?"

The king's propaganda machine worked so well that even a Kra-ell like Jade, who was by no means a sympathizer of the gods and didn't support their king, believed in the lies as long as they had no bearing on her and her people. For some reason, people always found it easier to believe what they were told rather than use their critical thinking and analyze what information they were being fed and why.

Aru's rule of thumb had always been to look for who benefited from what. It wasn't always readily apparent, though, and in the past, he had often been left with no answers, but now that he was serving someone much smarter than himself, the web was much more transparent.

"The reporters knew what was good for them and their careers. They were afraid to push the envelope and lose their jobs or get sent to the farthest corner of the known universe to report on the seeding of a new planet." He leveled his gaze on Jade. "No one dares go directly against the king. Have you ever heard any reporter ask him an uncomfortable question that he didn't have a ready answer to? He always has the perfect answer to every question, and not because he's so brilliant, although he is. "

Jade shrugged. "He's the Eternal King for a reason."

"Yes. He's shrewd, and he knows how to manipulate public opinion. Every interview that you ever saw with him was scripted and rehearsed. He gets the questions before the interview and has time to prepare the answers. In fact, I'm sure that the answers are prepared by his army of assistants."

She let out a breath. "I always believed that the gods were deeply corrupt. I just didn't know the extent of it."

"The majority of people don't." Aru shifted a couple of inches to the right to move away from the rock that had been digging into his bottom ever since he sat down. "After the satellites were destroyed, the king made a mournful address to the nation, saying that he couldn't bring himself to entomb his children, but given the atrocious war crimes they had committed, he could not pardon them either. He would do the next best thing— they would be abandoned and forgotten on Earth forever. He ordered Earth's location expunged from all records and asked everyone to forget the rebels who were sent there as if they were never born. The Eternal King is a powerful compeller, but even he couldn't compel everyone through the televised event to forget the rebels and the location of the solar system they were exiled to, but many did nonetheless."

"Wait a moment." Jade lifted her hand. "The Kra-ell were supposed to arrive on Earth at some point. The Kra-ell queen would have never agreed to forget about her people."

"The queen who sent you here was dead by then. When the new Kra-ell queen protested, the king said that the prohibition to visit Earth was on gods, not the Kra-ell, and once they developed their own vessels, they could go visit their people on Earth whenever they pleased."

43

JADE

J ade grimaced. "Let me guess. The Kra-ell never got to develop their own interstellar ships."

Aru nodded. "They got to settle on many new planets, but they were brought there by the gods' ships. The gods never released their technology for building stasis pods, and without them, the Kra-ell couldn't travel to faraway places even if they managed to build the ships, which they didn't. The technology is closely guarded."

What else was new? The gods didn't part with any of their knowledge unless they were forced to.

"I've noticed you said it took you only a little over a hundred years to get to Earth. That's much faster than what was possible when we left."

"There are ships capable of even faster speeds than that, but they are much smaller. To this day, settlers' ships are slower than patrol ships."

"What happened to my queen? She was still a young female when we left."

The god cast her a sad smile. "She suffered an unfortunate accident forty-some years after your ship left. The official statement claimed that she fell off a cliff. Naturally, there were rumors about her daughter assassinating her to get the throne, but we both know that wasn't what happened."

"That's not the Kra-ell way." Despite the queen's duplicity, Jade felt a pang of sadness for her untimely death. "If the queen's daughter wanted to ascend to the throne before her mother was ready to step down, she would have challenged the queen to a duel, but that has only been done a couple of times throughout our history when the reigning queen was so terrible that she needed to be removed." Jade let out a breath. "The queen didn't have another daughter when I was still on Anumati. The new queen must have been born after our ship left."

Aru smiled apologetically. "I suppose so, but I'm not that well versed in Kra-ell history. For me, that happened a very long time ago."

Perhaps the queen had fallen to her death because the ship had been lost along with her children, and she'd been overcome with grief. It was a great sin to take one's own life, but maybe in her sorrow, the queen had not been as careful, and the fall was indeed accidental? Anumati's terrain was rugged, and losing footing on one of the narrow mountain passages was not uncommon.

"Do you know if our ship was already lost at the time of her death?"

"It was," Aru said. "After the Eternal King decreed that Earth was to be forgotten, the new queen pleaded with the Eternal King to turn the ship around. The answer from the command center was that they had lost contact with the computer running the ship."

"Hold on," Morgada said. "If Earth was to be forgotten, how did you learn about the queen's request? I assume that the king gave the order to forget Earth long before you were born."

"Only the location of Earth was expunged. The planet itself was not forgotten. It became a cautionary tale—the hell where sinners and evil doers dwell."

It was funny how that aligned with some of the human religious beliefs. Perhaps the Eternal King had found a way to drip-feed that into human mythology, or maybe it had arrived on the wings of some kind of cosmic awareness.

"What about the gold?" Magnus said. "The main reason the rebels were sent to Earth was to oversee the mining of it. Didn't they need it on Anumati?"

"We've been manufacturing a synthetic alternative that does everything gold was previously used for, for a very long time. No one uses gold for anything other than jewelry, which is quite expensive."

"Do they use money on Anumati?" Phinas asked.

Jade cut him a look. "Out of everything you've heard so far, that is what intrigues you?"

He shrugged. "That will be among the first things Kalugal will ask me."

"Who's Kalugal?" Aru asked.

"My boss."

The god frowned. "Isn't that the same person Magnus reports to?"

"No, but I also answer to that one. It's complicated."

Surprisingly, Aru smiled. "I get it. I know all about answering to several bosses. And to answer your question, we use credits, which is the equivalent of money. Generally, our society functions similarly to human societies, just on a much larger scale." He looked at Jade. "How are you enjoying living among humans?"

"I don't really live among them." She glared at him. "You said that you arrived only five years ago. How much did you learn about our history from observing us? You still didn't tell me how you were monitoring us. Was it through the compound's communication or by some other means?"

The god hesitated for a moment before answering. "We flew drones undetectable by human technology, so we had eyes and ears in the compound."

She cast him a glare. "So, you knew that we were subjugated, and yet you did nothing to help us."

"I'm sorry, but we couldn't. We were not allowed to intervene."

"Did you know what Igor's secret mission was?" Magnus asked.

The question seemed to take the god by surprise, but since his eyes were still hidden behind his sunglasses, the only indication was the tightening of his lips.

"How did you find out about his mission? I'm sure he didn't volunteer the information."

ARU

Neither Negal nor Dagor knew about Gor's primary directive. There had been no need for them to know, and Aru couldn't tell them without revealing his secret source of information.

The Eternal King believed in compartmentalization, and sending different teams to do the same thing without them knowing what the others were doing was a common tactic of his and others in his chain of command.

"We have our ways." Magnus looked at Jade. "She made a bargain with him. His life for information."

Aru shifted his gaze to Jade. "What did he tell you?"

When she hesitated and didn't respond right away, he wondered whether she was also listening to the immortals' boss. He still didn't know why and how they had liberated the Kra-ell and what their angle was, and so far, he had revealed much more than he had learned, and it was time to flip things around.

"He told us that he was sent to assassinate the royal twins. Was that your mission as well?"

"Our mission was to check whether the Kra-ell settler ship had arrived. When our patrol ship entered this sector, we started receiving signals from your trackers, but given that only a small number of them were broadcasting, we realized that not everyone had made it safely to

Earth. Our job was to find out whether the twins were among the survivors. After locating your compound, we reported that the twins were not there. Our next task was investigating the crash site and searching for the other pods. That was what we were doing when the trackers suddenly stopped broadcasting, came online again, and started winking out one at a time. We were afraid for your lives, but we couldn't get to you because we were too far away. We were investigating a potential lead to a pod location in Tibet, and getting to Karelia took us a long time."

"Right." Jade crossed her arms over her chest. "You cared so much about us that you left us under Igor's rule. But I get it. You followed orders until they no longer suited you, and you disobeyed them because you had a mystery to solve."

She wasn't wrong, and perhaps he owed her an apology. "The truth is that we had nothing to gain by helping you, and we had a job to do. But once you were taken by a superior force, we were obligated to investigate it." He shifted his eyes to Magnus. "I've told you many things I probably shouldn't have to gain your trust, but you haven't returned the favor. Tell me how and why you aided the Kra-ell."

"Hold on," Jade said. "Before Magnus answers your question, I need to know whether you were sent to kill the twins."

"We were not. We were only supposed to report whether they were alive, and we were forbidden to engage them if we found them."

Jade nodded. "You aren't powerful enough to deal with them. I wonder, though. When was it revealed that they were on the ship? I only discovered by chance that they were there, and I wasn't sure until Igor confirmed it."

"I didn't know that," Aru admitted. "I thought that everyone knew they were aboard the ship. The official story was that they were sent with the settlers as their spiritual leaders, and when the ship was lost in space, the Kra-ell queen mourned their loss. She was despondent, and there were rumors that her death wasn't an accident but a suicide."

"That possibility has crossed my mind," Jade said. "She wouldn't have committed suicide because that would have barred her from ever entering the fields of the brave, but she might have been less careful and more reckless with her life. It's difficult for a mother to keep on living after her children die."

After eavesdropping on several of her conversations with Kagra when they were still Gor's captives, Aru knew that Jade spoke from personal experience.

Dipping his head, he put his hand over his chest. "I'm sorry for your loss. I don't know all the details, but I know that you lost two sons."

She nodded. "The need for revenge kept me alive, but in the end, I gave it up for the greater good. Getting information out of Igor was more important than the satisfaction I would have felt from taking off his head."

"What did you do with him?"

Jade looked at Magnus, and when he nodded, she said, "We put him in stasis."

"I'm surprised that you didn't kill him."

Jade uncrossed her arms. "I gave him my word that he would not die by my hand. Besides, the things stored in his brain would have died with him, which would have been a waste. This way, we can wake him anytime we need to retrieve that information." She looked him in the eyes. "You know what I'm talking about."

He shook his head. "I suspect that you know more than I do."

45

JADE

id she believe him?

From what Aru had told them so far and from the little that his companion had said, Jade's impression was that he was a young god, not high on the totem pole of command and that he and his friends were part of some resistance. Except, he seemed to know a little more than Negal did, which made her suspicious.

Well, more suspicious. Gods were not trustworthy in the best of circumstances, especially not when they had something to gain by manipulating and lying.

"How did Igor know to decipher the signals?" she asked. "How did you know to do that?"

"We have a receiver."

As he reached into his pocket, Jade tensed, and so did Phinas, but what Aru pulled out was a phone.

"It's all in here." He tapped the device. "It can locate and identify the signals from the trackers."

Magnus leaned forward. "You can do that from your phone?"

Aru chuckled. "This is not an ordinary phone, but yes. It can do many more things, including communicate with our mother ship, but it's turned off right now."

She eyed the device with suspicion. "How do we know that? And besides, they could be listening to what you do without your knowledge, even when you think the thing is turned off. If human technology can do that, I'm sure the gods can do that as well."

"It can, but this one cannot. Everyone on Anumati, with even the most basic technical education, knows how to ensure privacy. Our society would have disintegrated without that ability. Even the Eternal King knows not to mess with that. He would lose support overnight."

Glancing at the other god, Jade noted that his expression and body language confirmed Aru's statement, but she would be a fool to forget even for a moment that gods were master manipulators.

Still, there was no harm in telling them about Igor's abilities. "Igor was not a regular Kra-ell. He was enhanced by the gods, and part of his enhancement was the ability to decipher where the signals were coming from. He needed a receiver to amplify the signals, but his mind supplied the location once he heard them. For some reason, he didn't have a receiver in his pod, and he had to wait for human technology to reach the stage where he could have one built to his specifications. Once he had it, he found every Kra-ell who woke up from stasis, and he came after us. He killed the males and took the females. He wanted to create a male-dominated Kra-ell community, and that was precisely what he did."

"We are aware of that part," Aru said. "I thought he told you more about the Kra-ell royal twins and how he planned to get rid of them."

As if she was going to tell him how Igor had planned to do that. She wouldn't risk Aru using the knowledge to take out the twins himself.

"He was an incredibly powerful compeller and had numerous enhancements. But what I can't understand is why the Eternal King thought that the queen's children were a threat to him. If they were as powerful as he believed, their mother wouldn't have felt the need to smuggle them off Anumati. They would have been safe where they were."

She didn't know whether Aru knew about the twins being the Eternal King's grandchildren, and her pretense of ignorance was a good way to find out.

"I don't know why he's so scared of them, but if they are so powerful, they are a threat to the king, and they might be helpful to our cause."

"Provided that they're still alive," Phinas said. "After so long, that's not very likely."

Aru nodded. "I share your opinion, but we will keep looking for the missing pods regardless, if only to put the occupants to rest and usher them on their journey to the other side of the veil." He looked at Jade. "It would be a good idea for you or another Kra-ell to accompany us to perform the ceremony. I know how to do it, but I doubt the souls of these Kra-ell would appreciate a god performing the ritual."

Surprised by the offer, Jade nodded. "There is much that still needs to be discussed, but once we all reach an agreement of cooperation of some sort, I will assign a couple of my people to assist you with the search and, if needed, the passing ritual. The custom calls for at least two adult Kra-ell to be present."

"Why not you?"

She lifted her chin. "I took it upon myself to lead our community, so I can't just leave them behind to go looking for what are most likely dead settlers."

"Understood." Aru shifted his eyes to Magnus. "I've waited patiently for you to explain why you aided Jade and her people and who you are aside from being the hybrid immortal descendants of the gods. You are obviously well organized and possess impressive military power, yet you let Jade govern her people independently. Not only that, she seems to trust you implicitly, which speaks volumes to the character of your organization." He turned to her. "Am I right?"

Jade nodded. "Despite being descendants of the gods, these immortals are honorable people, and they came to our aid without expecting anything in return. They did that because it was the right thing to do, and I owe them a debt of gratitude that I can never repay in my lifetime. My descendants will have to continue repaying the favor for many generations."

As she'd expected, Kian groaned in her ear. "I told you a hundred times. The only gratitude I expect is your people's loyalty and cooperation."

The young god smiled. "After such an enthusiastic endorsement of the immortals, I'm less apprehensive about trusting them with our secrets."

Jade had a feeling that he'd shared only a tiny portion of his secrets with them, but that was understandable. In time, he might feel more comfortable sharing more.

"Not too long ago, I was in your position," she said. "I'm not the trusting type, and I was very suspicious of my rescuers' motives, but after they proved time and again that they meant me and my people no harm and even welcomed us into their community, I laid my suspicions to rest and offered their leader my oath of loyalty. I wanted to give him a life vow, but he refused to accept it, which is another testament to his character."

"Indeed." Aru turned to Magnus. "The stage is yours, my friend. I want to hear your side of the story."

46

MAGNUS

"What do you want to know?"

Aru chuckled. "Everything. Who are you and what do you stand for, and how did you find Igor's compound? But I'll settle for whatever your boss is comfortable with you telling me."

"You can tell him about Emmett," Kian said in Magnus's ear. "They already know about Safe Haven because of Sofia's tracker. They might not make the connection right away, but I have no doubt that they will eventually get to investigate the place."

Magnus brushed his fingers over his short beard. "I'm not a good storyteller. Jade can tell you how we found her. She can also tell you about her capture by Igor."

She'd heard Kian's instructions and knew the backstory of what led them to her.

Aru arched a brow. "I'd rather hear that from you."

Magnus shook his head. "It's really not my story to tell. Once Jade is done, I'll answer your other questions."

Hopefully, Kian had gotten the hint and would instruct him on what he should and shouldn't say. They had covered the basics before the meeting and had agreed to keep things as vague as possible, but after Aru's revelations, they had to tell him more.

The god nodded. "Very well. While Jade tells me the story of her liberation, you can discuss with your boss what to tell me."

"You are a smart guy." Magnus chuckled. "No wonder you are in command even though you are less experienced than your teammates."

"One teammate. Dagor and I were drafted at the same time."

"Since you know what I'm about to do, there is no point in me whispering and talking in hints." Magnus pushed to his feet. "I'll walk over to that boulder over there to talk with my boss in private."

As Aru nodded again, Magnus turned and walked away. With how well these gods could hear, he would need to walk much farther than that, but he wasn't going to say anything that was of importance to them anyway.

"I'm about fifty feet away from the gods," he said quietly. "That's probably not far enough to keep them from hearing me, but it's enough not to interfere with Jade's story. What do you want me to tell them?"

"I want you to find out what they know about Ahn and what happened to the gods, and I have a feeling that he's not going to tell you anything unless you share some information with him. You can tell him about the Doomers, but keep the two people we discussed out of the story. Refrain from mentioning my ancestry, too. I'm just an immortal like you and Phinas."

"How am I going to explain the clan's origins?" Magnus lowered his voice to barely a whisper. "Or the animosity between us and the Doomers?"

"I'm sure you can think of something."

Magnus let out a breath. "I'm not good at things like that. I need guidance."

He heard Kian chuckle. "Talk slowly and pause frequently so we can feed the story to you."

"Thank you. That will be much appreciated. What else do you want me to ask?"

"I want to know whether he and his team were sent to discover if any of the gods survived and to finish the job, but there is no chance he will answer that truthfully. I also don't know how to ask it without revealing that we know Igor's mission was not only to eliminate the twins but also the gods."

431

"Neither do I," Magnus admitted. "Since we are going to schedule another meeting with them, you or Onegus should consider participating." He sighed. "After the initial exchange of information, the talk will move to diplomatic territory, and I'm really underqualified for such important negotiations. Also, where do you want to hold the meeting?"

"Agreed. They already know about the keep, so we can meet there. Not in the underground, I'd rather try to keep it a secret, but in my old penthouse. Let them think that's our alternative headquarters. Also, make sure that they know that most of the building is occupied by humans, just in case they get any ideas about blowing the place up."

"Why would they do that? They seem interested in cooperation. Besides, what makes you think that they care about humans getting hurt?"

"They seem to want to protect humanity at large, so I assume that they care. What I'm puzzled about is what they hope to gain by allying with us. They don't need us, and if they disclose our existence, we are toast."

Magnus swallowed. "I hate to suggest this, but maybe it's in our best interest to prevent that from happening?"

Hopefully, Kian would get the hint.

Eliminating the three gods was the safest way of preventing the information about humanity from getting to the Eternal King.

"Not really. The other god mentioned that thousands of lives were at stake, referring to the patrol ship. If something were to happen to Aru and his team, they would come to investigate, and I don't want to think what they might do to avenge their friends. Especially since they will most likely assume that humans were responsible."

47

ARU

"Exoskeletons?" Aru arched a brow. "Isn't that the external covering of animals without backbones? Like insects?"

Jade chuckled. "Where have you been during the five years you spent on Earth? Haven't you heard about power exoskeletons? They are in almost every science fiction movie."

"That would explain why I haven't heard of them. I don't watch science fiction movies." Aru preferred romantic comedies and historical dramas—the first because they were lighthearted and took his mind off depressing subjects, and the latter because they gave him an overview of human history without having to spend time reading about it. "But I can guess what exoskeletons are since you said the immortals wore them to enhance their strength. I'm just curious about the technology. As you know, we prefer to fix biological disadvantages biologically. We only have stasis pods because it took our scientists a long time to enhance our physiology so we could enter stasis without the aid of technology."

Jade's lips twisted in distaste. "I know all about your tampering with nature."

"Humans had to find other solutions," Phinas said. "But our exoskeletons are not the kind you can find in a store or order online. They were built for immortals and are too heavy and cumbersome for humans to wear."

That was a clue about the immortals he'd been curious about. Apparently, they had inherited the gods' strength. Not that it was a problem. Aru and his teammates were among the gods who had been enhanced to match the physical strength of the Kra-ell. After the revolution, it had taken their scientists several centuries to isolate the genetics and develop the enhancement without giving gods a Kra-ell appearance. Not all gods were given the trait because it came at the cost of others that parents might have valued more than physical strength.

"Interesting." He smiled. "I follow the news, and I haven't heard exoskeletons mentioned as being used in warfare. What do humans use them for?"

"You can look it up," Jade said. "Do you have a phone? I mean, something that connects to the internet?"

"Of course." He pulled the device from his pocket.

"Not now." She waved a dismissive hand. "You can do that after the meeting is over in the comfort of your hotel room." She looked at him from under lowered lashes. "You are staying in a hotel, right? You didn't thrall some poor human family into giving you their house?"

"What do you take us for? Amateurs? And even if that would not undermine our cover, we would never take what wasn't ours to take by force or mind manipulation."

Never was a strong word, and they had used their mind manipulation powers on multiple occasions, but never to cause harm to innocents.

Jade lifted her hands in the air. "Just checking. As you've learned from my story, I wasn't always very considerate of humans. Although, in my defense, their conditions outside my compound were even worse." She cast a quick look at Magnus. "The immortals were always much more mindful of human rights. Their mission is to elevate humanity, not enslave it or keep it from prospering, but that's Magnus's story to tell, and he's getting instructions from the boss. All I can do is continue the story of our rescue."

"Before you continue, will I ever learn the name of that mysterious boss you are referring to?"

She made a face. "Again, it's not my decision. My people and I are guests in their community, and we were given many more privileges than we've earned. The least I can do is honor their preferences regarding what I can tell you."

"I understand."

He was growing fond of Jade. She wasn't the same female he'd observed in Gor's compound, which could only be attributed to the immortals' influence. He also had a strong feeling that Phinas was her consort. She regarded him with a fondness that she did not accord to Magnus, and it wasn't because of deference to Magnus as their team leader.

"I have the definition for you." Phinas held his phone up. "Powered exoskeletons are used in healthcare, military, industrial, and entertainment applications. In the medical field, they can assist patients with mobility impairments or aid in physical therapy. In military applications, exoskeletons may be utilized to support soldiers in carrying heavy loads or enhance their capabilities on the battlefield. In industrial settings, they can improve worker safety and productivity in physically demanding jobs." He lifted his eyes from the screen. "Ours make us as strong as the Kra-ell and impervious to bullets, swords, daggers, and the like. They can even protect us from grenades."

"Impressive." Aru shifted his gaze to Magnus, who was heading back their way. "I think you will need to finish your story at a later time because your leader has received his orders and is ready to talk."

As Jade turned to look over her shoulder at Magnus, Aru peeked at his messages, but there were no new ones, and he didn't know whether it was a sign that Gabi was feeling better and not in a rush to leave the hospital, or that something was wrong and she couldn't communicate.

He hoped it was the former, and he wanted to wrap up the meeting so he could go to her.

48

MAGNUS

Magnus sat down on the blanket the gods had provided. "Before I tell you what my boss allowed me to share, he has one more question. If Earth's location has been expunged from the official records and visiting it was prohibited, how and why are you here?"

The god chuckled. "That's such a naive question. Your leader must be young."

"He's not." Magnus was offended on Kian's behalf.

"My apologies." The god dipped his head. "I've heard a clever human saying, but it was in Russian, and I can't do it justice by translating it because it wouldn't rhyme. The gist is that rules and laws do not apply equally to everyone. The king can prohibit citizens from visiting Earth and yet send patrols to monitor it, and no one will even question his right to do that. The public no longer has access to navigation charts that include the location of Earth, but the same is not true of the royal archives and interstellar fleet's records."

"Makes sense. My boss also wonders about the trumped-up war crimes. What exactly was Ahn accused of?"

Aru frowned. "The gods are gone, and you said that you are many generations removed from them. How do you know the heir's name?"

"You just made one hell of a slip of the tongue," Kian said in

Magnus's ear. "Tell him that the stories were passed down from one generation to the next, and remind him that he has referred to Ahn several times already, but as a leader of the rebels, not as the heir."

Magnus nodded even though Kian probably couldn't see him. He also had a question that Kian hadn't thought to ask.

"Legends about our godly ancestors were passed down through the generations. You yourself have mentioned Ahn several times as one of the rebel leaders. What I wonder, though, is how do you know with such certainty that the gods are gone?"

Aru smiled sadly. "The Kra-ell weren't the only ones who were implanted with trackers. All the rebels had them, too. When they died, the trackers stopped transmitting. We didn't know that until many years later when a patrol ship arrived at the sector and couldn't pick up their signals."

"Our bodies heal fast, which means they reject all foreign objects," Magnus said. "But I assume the gods found a way to overcome that problem."

"We did," Aru agreed. "Every god who leaves Anumati is implanted with a tracker. After all, the king wants to know where everyone is at all times. In the case of Earth, he lost that ability when he blew up the satellites, which is why the rebels' demise was only discovered many years later."

Luckily for them, the only surviving gods had been born on Earth and hadn't been implanted with trackers, so the Eternal King didn't know of them.

"So that means that you have trackers in you as well. How come we didn't pick up the signal?"

Aru shrugged. "Different technology. We figured out that you somehow knew how to decipher the signals from the old trackers, and in order to find you, we needed them. Luckily, we knew where the original Kra-ell scouting team had settled and where to find the resting place of its members—those who had died before the communication satellites were destroyed. We had to go to China to find them and return here, where the last of the still functioning Kra-ell trackers led us before winking out as well."

"Where in China?" Kian asked in Magnus's ear.

When Magnus repeated the question, Aru shook his head. "Enough. I've been very patient and accommodating, but this wasn't a fair exchange of information. I need some answers from you."

"Fair enough." Magnus took a deep breath and recited the speech Kian had given him. "There are two known groups of immortals, and by known, I mean to each other, not to humans. Our group calls itself Annani's clan, and we are named after one of our godly ancestors. The leader of our clan is named Kian, or the boss, as we've been referring to him so far. The other group calls itself the brotherhood of the Devout Order of Mortdh, with Mortdh being their godly ancestor, and their leader's name is Navuh. We are adversaries. Our clan works to elevate the human condition, perpetuating the work that our godly ancestors began when they got to Earth. The other group wants to rule humanity and enslave it, and they hate us for enabling human progress. The feud between us has been going on ever since the gods perished. Sometimes, we gain the upper hand, and sometimes they do. If one of your patrol ships visited during the Dark Ages or before that, during Sumer's decline, it would have witnessed the fruits of their success."

Aru smiled. "From what we have seen so far, you seem to be winning the war. Humanity is doing much better than it has ever done."

"Thank you, but it's a never-ending struggle, and we've learned not to celebrate our triumphs. Regrettably, more often than not, they are temporary."

49

GABI

Gabi was having the most delicious dream. She and Uriel were on a beach, walking along the shore and eating ice cream, and he looked so dreamy that she wanted to throw the ice cream away and lick him all over instead.

Why was she so cold, though?

The sun was shining bright, and the sky was cloudless. Maybe it was the ice cream dripping over the back of her hand?

It was so cold.

"What's the matter?" Uriel asked. "You're shivering."

"My hand is cold." She lifted it and examined the back.

Nothing had dripped. Dreams were so strange. And how the hell did she know that she was dreaming? Maybe it wasn't a dream, because if it was, she wouldn't be so cold when the sun was shining so bright.

"I'll warm it up for you." Uriel took her hand between his. "Better?"

"Much." She smiled.

"Gabi."

"Yes?" She looked up at him.

"Gabi. Please wake up." Uriel's mouth was moving, but the voice coming out wasn't his.

"Uriel?"

"It's Gilbert, sweetheart."

Gilbert? What was he doing in her dream?

Gabi's eyes popped open. "Gilbert. How did you get here so quickly?"

"You were unconscious for hours. It's after five o'clock in the afternoon."

She tried to calculate the time in her head, but everything was fuzzy, and she just wanted to go back to sleep and dream about Uriel and a sunny beach.

"Why is it so cold in here?"

"I'll ask the nurse to bring you another blanket."

As he let go of her hand and pushed to his feet, she noticed the IV line and the needle in the back of her hand. That was why it felt so cold.

When Gilbert returned, he had the nurse with him and a warm blanket, which she tucked around her.

"Thank you." Gabi felt the ache in her muscles subside.

She must have been clenching all over from the cold. What kind of crappy operation was this hospital running? Were they trying to freeze their patients to death?

"What's wrong with my sister, doctor?"

So that wasn't the nurse. It was the doctor. Why the hell didn't she wear a white coat and eliminate the guesswork? How were the patients supposed to tell the difference?

"We didn't find any evidence of bacterial or viral infection, and her CAT scans are normal, so it's not a brain tumor or stroke, and we have no idea why she's been losing consciousness. At this point, all we can do is observe her for the next twenty-four hours and hope she pulls through."

Gabi reached for Gilbert's hand. "I don't want to stay here. Please don't leave me here overnight. I might never wake up."

"Don't worry." He gave her hand a light squeeze. "I'm not going to leave your side."

"Perhaps she needs something to calm her down," the doctor said. "I'll send the nurse with a sedative."

"That won't be necessary." Gilbert used his boss voice. "Gabi gets a little anxious sometimes, and the last thing she needs is a sedative."

The doctor looked at him as if he was a bug she'd squashed with her orthopedic shoe. "As you wish."

"I wish to transfer my sister to a different hospital. Are there forms that I need to sign?"

"Are you your sister's legal guardian?"

"She's an adult. She doesn't need a guardian."

The doctor's cold smile would have petrified anyone other than Gilbert. "Then you can't sign her out. Only she can do that, and if she's unconscious, her spouse."

"Gabi is not married."

"Oh, for Pete's sake. I'm right here, and I'm conscious. Bring me the paperwork, and I'll sign it."

"Very well." The doctor looked down her nose at her and then turned to Gilbert. "You need to arrange medical transport to the hospital to which you want to transfer your sister. I can't just discharge her when she's going in and out of a coma. Once you are done making the arrangements, you can tell the nurse that you are ready to leave, and she will double-check that there is indeed a hospital bed for Gabriella in another hospital and that you've secured an ambulance to transfer her. Once that is done, Gabi can sign herself out."

"I'll get right on it." Gilbert cast Gabi a reassuring look. "I'll just step outside and make the arrangements."

"Thank you." Gabi closed her eyes and let herself relax for the first time since waking up in a hospital bed.

Gilbert was with her, and she had nothing to worry about. He would take care of her as he had always done.

50

KIAN

Kian silenced his earpiece and turned to Onegus. "Them having trackers is bad news. Should we try to grab them and remove the trackers? We know that the third one is on the construction site, and as soon as the meeting is over, the three of them will get into a car, which we can follow with the drone and send the backup forces after."

Onegus shook his head. "We have to consider that they might have superior weapons and also that they can communicate with the patrol ship that is supposedly staffed with thousands of gods. I think we should tread very carefully with them."

Kian shifted his eyes to Turner. "What do you think?"

Turner regarded him for a long moment before answering. "I agree with Onegus. Since the three were dropped off five years ago, it would take the patrol ship about the same time to get back here, so Aru was bluffing when he implied that they could get here immediately. Our best bet is befriending these gods and getting to the bottom of what they want from us while keeping them at arm's length. I can't see how we can be of any help in their rebellion."

"We are not on the map," Onegus muttered. "We are not important. The patrol ship cruises by Earth twice in the span of seven hundred years, and the size of the crew they send down to investigate indicates that Earth is not of much interest to the king. It's almost perfunctory. That means Aru and his friends can build a base here that can fly under the radar. Earth's status as a forbidden planet provides a unique opportunity. Perhaps that's also the reason humanity was allowed to spread to such an extent. Other planets that the gods have seeded apparently get visited frequently or are even governed by the gods, and the growth of their populations and what they are allowed to do is restricted."

That was a very insightful observation, and Kian was surprised that it hadn't occurred to him before. If what Aru had told them was true, Earth was the perfect place for the rebellion headquarters, but if that was the gods' angle, he would not agree to help them. Humanity was at risk from the Eternal King just for thriving. If they were to assist the rebels in any form, Earth's annihilation was guaranteed.

On the other hand, if the clan couldn't come up with a way to make all humans immune to diseases in the next century or so, the rebels might be the only thing standing between humanity and the Eternal King.

Turner nodded. "I hadn't thought of that angle. That's a very good point." He shifted his gaze to Kian. "Perhaps you and I should attend the next meeting with them. Magnus is obviously out of his element and can't continue representing us."

"I intended to do that even before you suggested it."

Onegus shook his head. "I don't like exposing you. I should go."

The chief was a great diplomat, but Kian wanted to meet those gods in person. He would be taking a risk, but in this case, it was worth taking. Too much was at stake for him to sit on the sidelines and act like a puppeteer, telling Onegus what to say.

"If they agree to meet in the keep, we can have sufficient backup in place. I'll even take a couple of Odus with me."

Onegus uncapped his bottle and took a sip. "That would be one hell of a surprise for them. They are going to freak out."

"I don't know why," Kian said. "The gods used the Odus to fight the Kra-ell, and if the Kra-ell didn't react strongly to them, the gods shouldn't either."

Turner chuckled. "The Kra-ell who joined our village weren't subjected to seven thousand years of propaganda. If the Eternal King decided to vilify the Odus, which he obviously did, since they were decommissioned and the technology to create them was destroyed, he has made sure to reinforce that message until it became indisputable in the mind of the populace."

When Kian's phone buzzed with an incoming message, he knew who it was from even before looking at it.

"Gilbert's sister seems to be transitioning." He lifted his gaze to Onegus. "She is slipping in and out of consciousness, and they can't find what is causing it. We need to get her to the village and erase all traces of her ever being admitted to the hospital, and the tests they ran on her."

Onegus's forehead furrowed. "I'll be damned. That guy she was with was a Doomer, after all. How did I miss it?"

Turner didn't look surprised. "Evidently, the Doomers have gotten much better at creating their fake identities. From now on, we will have to investigate any suspect much more thoroughly."

"I don't think the guy is a Doomer." Kian got to his feet and walked over to the big screen where the feed from the drone's camera was broadcasting. "Is there a way to zoom in further?" He turned to Onegus. "Do you still have the passport picture of Gabi's guy?"

Onegus had reported Roni's findings to him, and Syssi had told him about the lunch she'd had with Gilbert's sister and what she'd told them about her lover.

The guy didn't sound like a Doomer.

That being said, Phinas and Rufsur were former Doomers, and yet they were as attentive and devoted to their mates as any clan immortal, so it wasn't as if all Doomers were misogynistic bastards. But it was safe to assume that most of them were.

"It's no use zooming in," William said. "The gods are still wearing their hard hats; the leader has dark sunglasses on, and the other is still wearing the construction protective glasses. Unless they lift their heads and look in the drone's direction, we can't even see the structure of their faces or the shape of their lips."

"Here is Uriel Delgado's passport picture." Onegus swiveled his laptop for Kian to see. "He's a handsome dude, but he's not a god."

Kian had to agree, but the picture could have been Photoshopped to make the guy's face less attractive but still recognizable. Besides, most people's mugshots looked terrible.

"We can fly the drone lower," Onegus said. "That will force them to look up."

"It might scare them off," Turner said. "If one of them is indeed Gabi's guy, we don't want him rushing to the hospital and bumping into our people while they are getting her out and erasing all traces of her presence there. We need to keep the gods talking until our people are out of the hospital and Gabi is in a safe location."

"Good point." Kian shifted his eyes to Onegus. "Take care of Gabriella's extraction. We missed a whole chunk of conversation, and Magnus might need our help."

"He's doing fine," William said. "I've been listening the entire time."

"Good." Kian turned to the chief again. "When choosing the extraction crew, don't include head Guardians or council members. I don't want Arwel or Bridget in the hospital. Julian is in the downtown warehouse anyway, so he can go." The young doctor was waiting for the team to be done to check them for bugs before they could return to the village. "And choose Guardians who are good with thralling and shrouding."

"Naturally." Onegus pushed to his feet. "I'll make the calls from my office."

51

MAGNUS

The silence in Magnus's earpieces was starting to worry him. He wasn't sure whether the answers he'd provided to Aru's questions were approved, because Kian wasn't guiding him. While he was telling Aru about Navuh and his band of hoodlums, the war room team was probably talking about strategy, and he should give them as much time as they needed, but Aru seemed to be overly interested in the Brotherhood, and Magnus couldn't blame him.

As a god, Aru might be able to take control of the Doomer army, and if he needed soldiers for his rebellion, the Brotherhood had many more than the clan.

"You say that your strategy is to hide," Aru said. "Is that because your enemies are stronger and more numerous or because your clan prefers to avoid armed conflict?"

Damn, Magnus really needed Kian to tell him how to answer that.

When the familiar hum sounded in the earpieces, signaling that the war room crew was back online, Magnus sighed in relief. "Could you please repeat the question?" he asked the god.

Aru tilted his head. "Is it for the benefit of your boss?"

"Yes," Magnus admitted. "He went offline for a few minutes, and I'm not sure how he wants me to answer this question."

The god's lips narrowed into a tight line. "Your boss should have met us, but I understand his caution. Perhaps we should meet again with him present this time?"

"I need you to keep the conversation going," Kian said in Magnus's ear. "Drag it out as much as you can. Gabi, Gilbert's sister, is transitioning, and I suspect the guy she's been seeing is one of these gods, and he induced her transition. We need to get her out of the human hospital and bring her here, and I don't want to chance the gods showing up at the hospital in the middle of the extraction."

"What did your boss say?" Aru asked.

Magnus let out a sigh. "I'll repeat your question."

"You can tell him the truth," Kian said. "Explain in detail why the Doomers are horrible, and why aligning with them would be a colossal mistake."

It was maddening to conduct two parallel conversations, especially out in the open, where the sun was still baking their heads and the hard ground was flattening his ass. So yeah, he'd become spoiled, but right now he would pay a king's ransom for an air-conditioned room and a cup of coffee.

"The Doomers are a far superior force, and they have no problem playing dirty. They thrall and shroud indiscriminately, and human lives mean nothing to them. They have instigated countless wars, causing the death of millions."

Aru's brow furrowed. "How did they become so powerful? Were there more of them to start with than you?"

"Yes, and they are also not choosy about who produces their next generation. Our clan members are much more discriminating, and we procreate at a much slower pace."

These gods seemed not to know about Dormants and their activation, and Magnus was not about to volunteer the information, especially not in light of what Kian had told him. Aru was an intelligent guy, and he would put the puzzle pieces together just as quickly as Kian had.

The less he knew, the better.

"I can see how that's a problem." Aru smiled. "Hiding is also the resistance's way, but we are building up our foundation so one day we will become so powerful that no one will dare oppose us. The idea is to win without a fight."

Was that even possible?

Magnus wasn't sure, but a philosophical discussion about the merits and pitfalls of revolutions would be just the thing for dragging out the time.

"What starts as a need for reform, a wish to correct a wrong, often results in a much greater harm. The rebellion led by Ahn and the young gods had all the best intentions. They saw the suffering of the Kra-ell and wanted to end it. The result was a bloody war with countless casualties on both sides. Do you think it was worth it?"

"No," Aru admitted. "But doing nothing would have been wrong. Your clan did the same thing, just on a much smaller scale. You found out about the Kra-ell, welcomed a few members into your clan, and when you learned about Jade's plight, you assembled your forces and flew across the globe to free her and her people."

Magnus smiled. "But we were smart about it. We suffered no casualties and managed not to kill any innocent Kra-ell either, so it was definitely worth it. We also seized the money Igor had stolen from the tribes he'd attacked and reimbursed ourselves for the expense. It was a definite win-win for all except Igor and his cronies."

52

ARU

"You made a good plan and didn't rush into it, which was why you succeeded." Aru reached for the jug, uncapped it, and took a long gulp of water. "We should continue our talk tomorrow. We've been here for hours, and Negal is tired of keeping the shroud up. I'm sure you are all as tired of sitting on the hard ground and baking in the sun as I am."

"Yes, we should definitely reconvene," Magnus agreed, "but I have a couple more questions." He smiled. "I answered many of yours, so now it's your turn again."

That was true. He hadn't expected Magnus's candid answers about the clan enemies. They didn't seem like the kind of people Aru wanted to associate with, but they were a formidable force that merited a closer look. The thing that bothered him was that in the five years since his arrival, he hadn't gotten even a whiff of a rumor about immortals still roaming the planet. Human mythology was rife with gods and their shenanigans, and it also talked about the many children born half-god and half-human. The thing was, even mythology didn't claim that the descendants of those hybrids were immortal. They were supposed to be humans with a godly pedigree.

"Fine, but try to keep it short."

"I'll do my best." Magnus smiled politely. "When you first noticed what was going on with the signals and then discovered that the compound had been invaded and vacated, who did you suspect had done it?"

That was a fair question. "We considered two options. The most likely one was that some of the pods had come online before Igor found a way to build a transmitter and that those Kra-ell discovered that they had trackers and removed them, which was why we didn't pick them up. The other option was that the compound was liberated by humans, which was the more troubling scenario. I'm glad that wasn't the case."

"So, you didn't expect immortals or other gods?" Phinas asked.

"Not at all. We knew that the rebel gods were dead, and we assumed that the myths about the gods taking human lovers and having hybrid children with them were not based on reality because it was such a strong taboo in our home world. We assumed that it was the humans' way to aggrandize themselves. Did any of these mythological children of the gods really exist? Were they based on people like you?"

Magnus shrugged. "Our own mythology confirms the existence of gods, and we are proof that the stories about them taking human lovers were true, so perhaps there was a Hercules. Immortals are much stronger than humans. I'm curious, though. What happened after the king was informed that his children and all the other gods were dead?"

"That's actually funny if it wasn't so tragic. After ordering everyone to forget about these gods, the king couldn't admit that he was still checking on them. What he did instead was to say that the oracles told him about the rebel gods' demise, and he declared a day of mourning. When reporters asked him how these gods perished, he said the oracle didn't specify. It could have been a natural disaster, or perhaps the savage humans turned on them and killed them."

Jade nodded. "Sometimes that happened on the gods' remote settlements. The people would rebel against the tyrants and kill them."

Aru chuckled. "That was what everyone was told. What was more likely was that the Eternal King got rid of meddlesome gods that didn't toe the official line or were born with undesirable traits."

That got Magnus's attention, or perhaps his boss's. "I thought that the gods determined all traits with genetic manipulation?"

"Not every trait can be pre-programmed." Aru looked at Jade. "Mother Nature does not reveal all of her secrets."

"What are the undesirable traits?" she asked.

"Immunity. The Eternal King does not want gods who are immune to his compulsion to remain on Anumati. They usually get shipped off to faraway places, and many fall victim to the so-called savages."

"My sister was an immune," Negal said. "She was sent to one of those hellholes and was murdered by the locals, or so her family was told."

"Was she a soldier like you?" Morgada asked with surprising kindness in her voice.

"Goddesses are not conscripted into military service. They are sent to outposts as doctors, nurses, and scientists. It's a civil duty."

"Interesting," Magnus said. "So, everyone gets drafted on Anumati, but for different tasks. Is it only the young gods or everyone?"

"It's mostly the young children of gods who are less influential. After the rebellion, the king realized the problem was the young gods who wanted to change how things were done. His power base is the old gods, so he keeps them close while sending the young on missions of seeding and developing other civilizations."

"That's a great tactic," Phinas said. "The young are by nature more adventurous, and they probably look forward to traveling to remote locations and living in the wild, so to speak."

Aru nodded. "Very few bother to look under the thin veneer of the Eternal King's fake benevolence."

"He's evil." Jade crossed her arms over her chest. "All he cares about is preserving his power. I bet he didn't feel an ounce of remorse or real grief when he learned that his own children died in exile. He was glad to be rid of the troublemakers."

"I wonder if he views himself as evil," Magnus said. "Or whether he makes excuses for himself for why he must do those things."

Aru had a feeling that Magnus and the others were dragging the meeting out for some reason.

Were they amassing forces?

What for?

The two immortal males and two Kra-ell females could overpower two unenhanced gods, and they had no way of knowing that Aru and Negal were as strong as the Kra-ell males.

"We really should be going." He pushed to his feet and offered Magnus his hand.

Reluctantly, Magnus got up and took the hand he offered. "It was a pleasure to meet you, and I'm not just being polite. I've learned a lot today." He looked at his companions. "We all did. Thank you for sharing your knowledge with us."

"It was our pleasure as well." He pulled Magnus closer and clapped him on the back, attaching a tiny drone to the back of his shirt.

The device was smaller than a mosquito and undetectable by human technology. Even the Kra-ell hadn't been aware of the tiny things attaching themselves to their clothing and hitching a ride into the compound to preserve their limited energy.

He'd told Jade about the drones, but he had intentionally omitted supplying any details. The tiny things had very limited independent flying capability. That's why they usually attached them to the people they wanted to spy on. To infiltrate the compound, they attached it to the guards at the first tunnel entrance. The things were so small and made so little sound that even the Kra-ell hadn't noticed them.

After repeating the embrace with Phinas and only shaking hands with the ladies, Aru turned to Magnus. "When are we meeting again to continue our talk? Preferably indoors, in an air-conditioned room."

"My boss suggests a building we own in downtown Los Angeles for our next meeting."

"Perfect. Will your boss be there?"

Magnus nodded. "My boss plans to attend, provided nothing else comes up."

"What time?"

"Same time as today," Magnus said. "One-thirty in the afternoon. "

Aru chuckled. "Something bigger than three gods showing up on his doorstep?"

"About that." Magnus looked in the direction of the construction project. "Will the third member of your team attend the meeting? You really have nothing to worry about. We mean you no harm as long as you don't mean us harm. We are honorable and peaceful people."

Jade put her hand over her chest. "I vow that no harm will come to you from the clan immortals or me and my people. You know that I wouldn't have given you my vow if I believed differently."

He nodded. "I know how seriously the Kra-ell take their vows, but are you sure you know what your new friends plan?"

"I do, and I vouch for them."

"I will take your word and bring the third member of our team to the meeting, provided that nothing else comes up."

Shortly after Magnus and his team left, believing they were out of Aru's earshot and talking freely, he would find out exactly what they had in mind.

"Excellent," Magnus said. "Give me your phone number, and I'll send you a pin to the precise location along with a text with instructions."

If they thought they could track him by his phone, they were mistaken. It was a burner phone, but he'd had it modified by an expert who promised it would be untraceable.

Hopefully, the guy was worth the outrageous payment he had demanded in exchange for his services.

As Magnus pulled out his phone, it looked like the same model Gabi had. It resembled a popular brand but wasn't. Aru had thought it was a cheap knockoff, but the immortals didn't seem like the kind of people who needed to save money and purchase cheap equipment. Perhaps the knockoffs were easier to modify.

"Thank you." Magnus finished inputting the information. "How far is your hotel from downtown?"

"It's right there. The location is very convenient."

"Excellent. I'll send you the pin twenty minutes before the meeting."

So, they didn't want him to know where it was ahead of time. He could understand that. Jade's vow reassured him that these people were trustworthy, but they had nothing to reassure themselves about his intentions, and although those were good, he had just done something underhanded.

That being said, Aru would be very surprised if Magnus's boss didn't do the same. He was willing to bet the drone would follow them after they left, or at least try to.

Naturally, he had a plan to ditch it.

"Until tomorrow." He waved as their guests turned to leave.

"Let's clean up here," he told Negal.

They folded the blanket, and once their guests were no longer in view, they removed their hardhats and glasses.

The sunlight was no longer as harsh, and the sky transformed into a canvas of vibrant hues as the sun began its descent.

The colors differed from the reddish hues in Anumati's sky. The symphony of shades transitioned from a warm and fiery orange to a soft, delicate pink that gradually melded into serene blues. Wisps of clouds caught fire, their edges igniting with hues of magenta and lavender and then deepening into shades of indigo and violet.

"Are you looking for the drone?" Dagor asked.

Absorbed in the beauty above them, Aru hadn't even noticed his teammate joining them. "I can't see it."

"Neither can I, but I can hear it, and it's getting closer."

"We knew that they would try to follow us." Negal put the blanket over his shoulder and handed Aru the jug.

"Yeah." Dagor took up his monitor. "They drove away. Let's hear what they are saying."

"Don't activate the spy drone yet," Aru said.

"Why? It's soundless."

"Fine." For some reason, he felt uncomfortable activating it while the immortals and the Kra-ell were still in the car. It was safer to wait until they got out, but on the other hand, the drone was utterly soundless when stationary, and since it was on Magnus's back, which was pressed against the back of the seat, it was well hidden.

"Here we go," Dagor said.

Surprisingly, no one was talking, but given the sound of the car engine, Aru knew that the audio transmission was working just fine.

Negal chuckled. "We must have stunned them into silence."

"The drone is getting closer." Dagor pulled out his disruptor and aimed it at the bird as it came into view. "Why are they flying it so low? Do they want us to know that they are following us?"

"Their boss is curious about what we look like." Aru smiled at the drone and waved.

"Are you crazy?" Dagor removed the safety from the disrupter. "That thing is filming us."

"So what? We are meeting them tomorrow in their stronghold." He put his hand on Dagor's arm and lowered it. "I'm sure that they are going to record the meeting."

"Not if I fry their equipment. We shouldn't let them have proof against us."

"That's okay." Aru patted his back. "Jade gave me her vow that we have nothing to fear from these people. She seems to trust them implicitly, and she's not someone who trusts easily. These immortals have earned her trust. They are not going to betray us, and even if they wanted to, who are they going to tell?"

KIAN

"I'll be damned." Kian got up and walked over to the large screen on the wall in the back of the war room. "I was right. That's the guy." He turned to Onegus, who was watching the screen with an annoyed expression on his face.

"The passport picture was doctored," the chief said. "He didn't look half as good in it. I thought that Gabi was exaggerating, but evidently she wasn't. What do we do now?"

"Good question." Kian glanced at Turner, who just shrugged.

The guy wasn't interested in the romance part of the story and wasn't concerned with the Fates and the intricate tapestry they were weaving. To him, it was probably mumbo-jumbo, as it had been for Kian until not too long ago.

Aru and Gabi's encounter wasn't accidental. It was a sign, just as Syssi's vision was, and they pointed toward a future collaboration between the clan and these gods, but Kian couldn't risk his people's safety based on superstition.

Pulling out his phone, he dialed Julian's number. "What's your status?"

"We are in the hospital. We are wheeling the gurney out."

"Good. Get her out of there as soon as you can. The guy who induced her transition was one of the two who met with our team, and

I'm sure he will head that way as soon as he leaves the canyon. Luckily, it's an hour's drive, so you have plenty of time. Just don't delay unnecessarily."

"We won't. Can I tell Gilbert?" Julian asked.

"Of course. He's going to get a kick out of that."

Julian chuckled. "I'm not so sure. He's going insane with worry, and it won't matter to him who induced Gabi, only that she's transitioning and intermittently losing consciousness."

"Make sure you don't miss any of the staff that need to be thralled. Check if there were any shift changes."

"Theo and Jay will take care of the hospital staff. I'm here to take care of Gabi."

"Naturally. Let me know when you are out of there."

"I'll call you from the van." Julian terminated the call.

Roni had already erased Gabi's record from the firm employing the paramedics who had brought her to the hospital, and he was on standby, waiting for Onegus's signal to erase her from the hospital records as well.

Julian and the two Guardians were not great thrallers or shrouders, but between the three of them, they were good enough.

"Do we lift the lockdown and bring her in?" Onegus asked. "Or do we take her to the keep?"

"I'm not ready to lift the lockdown yet." Kian walked over to the fridge and pulled out a bottle of Snake Venom. "Anyone want a beer?"

When there were no takers, he returned to his seat, removed the cap, and took a long swig from the bottle. "Syssi's vision and the so-called chance meeting between Gabi and Aru indicate that the gods are here for a reason, and it is not to harm us, but I don't like to rely on signs and visions when the safety of my people is involved. I'm just wondering whether we should tell Aru about Gabi when we see him tomorrow."

Leaning back in his chair, Onegus crossed his arms over his chest. "The gods are not supposed to procreate with humans or other created species. Aru seemed very surprised by the existence of immortals, and yet he had sex with Gabi and probably many human females before her. How does he reconcile the two?"

Turner swiveled his chair to face the chief. "Maybe the rules are different for gods who are stationed on remote outposts without female companions? Surely, they don't expect them to remain celibate."

"Maybe they do," Kian said. "Aru and his teammates are part of the resistance, so maybe they enjoy breaking the rules. Or maybe the prohibition is only on actually procreating and not the sex part."

"I'm sure the prohibition includes sex," William said. "Do you remember what Jade said about the gods and the Kra-ell? Both societies deemed mixing the two species a taboo."

"Gabi was quite taken with the guy." Kian cradled the cold bottle between his hands. "I think we should tell him. Maybe he feels as strongly about her. After all, Toven mated a Dormant and is as happy as can be with her. Maybe Gabi and Aru can also have their happily ever after."

Onegus chuckled. "I never took you for a romantic. Aru can be with Gabi for the next one hundred or so years, but then he will be picked up by the patrol ship. It's not like he can decide to end his tour of duty without consequences. If he goes AWOL, his people will come looking for him."

Kian didn't think of himself as a romantic either, but Syssi said he was, and his wife was always right. "A hundred years is a long time." He took another swig from his beer. "A lot can happen between now and then."

54

GABI

An abrupt jolt pulled Gabi out of a deep sleep. Disoriented, she felt as though her bed had suddenly gone airborne. "What's going on?" she murmured, blinking her eyes open.

The surroundings seemed to suggest the interior of a van, or more accurately, an ambulance, given the array of medical equipment. She clutched the guard rails and attempted to hoist herself up. Relief washed over her at the sight of her brother's face smiling at her from the ambulance's open doors.

"Gilbert?"

"It's okay." He climbed after her into the ambulance. "We are transferring you to another clinic."

"Hi." A striking man leaned over her. "I'm Doctor Julian, and I will be taking care of you from now on."

"I'm Theo," said one of the paramedics.

"I'm Jay," said the other.

Gabi's eyes danced between their too-handsome faces. "I must have died and gone to hunk heaven," she murmured. "But since you are here," she smiled at Gilbert, "I know that I'm not dead, or at least I hope that I'm not because I don't want you to be dead."

He leaned over and kissed her cheek. "You are not dying, Gabi. It's the exact opposite."

"What do you mean?"

He hesitated for a moment. "Let's get out of here first, and I'll explain on the way. I just hope you will stay awake long enough so I can do it all in one go."

That sounded very mysterious, but she was too spaced out to try to guess what he'd meant by the opposite of dying. Usually, it implied thriving, but she was definitely not doing that. In fact, she felt miserable and longed for the respite from the aches and pains that sleep provided.

Her body knew when to knock her out to minimize her discomfort, and there was nothing wrong with that.

Gabi just wanted to know what was causing the aches and pains and disorientation, but despite Gilbert's previous comment about the opposite of dying, he wasn't looking or acting like his usual jovial self, and that worried her.

Had he learned something new while she'd been out? Perhaps they had found something, and she was dying from some little-known disease? She'd read about deadly bacteria and viruses that weren't diagnosed in time. And given how incompetent everyone in that hospital had seemed, she wouldn't be surprised if they had overlooked something.

"Did any of my test results come back while I was asleep?"

"They all came back negative."

"That's good, I think." She lifted her head once more. "Did you get my things? My phone in particular?"

"I have everything right here." Her brother lifted a large plastic bag that hopefully contained her clothes, her purse, and all its contents.

"We need to get rid of the phone," the doctor said.

"Right." Gilbert reached into the plastic bag.

Gabi pulled herself up again and glared at the guy who claimed to be a doctor. "Why would you want to get rid of my phone?" If not for Gilbert being right there, she would have panicked that someone had kidnapped her from the hospital to cut her up and sell her organs on the black market, but Gilbert would never allow that. "I need to tell Uriel that I'm no longer in the hospital and the name of the new one you are taking me to."

The doctor and Gilbert exchanged loaded looks, and then the doctor leaned toward the driver. "I made a mistake. Her phone is still here, and it's active. We need to employ Turner's evasive techniques."

"What's going on, Gilbert? Who are these people, and where are they taking me?"

"Everything is okay." He took her hand and gave it a gentle squeeze. "You know I will never let anything bad happen to you if I can prevent it, right?"

Gabi nodded even though she didn't like the caveat he'd added.

"I will explain in a little bit." He looked at the doctor, who Gabi was pretty sure wasn't a doctor at all. "Do you think he put a bug in her phone?"

"Why would he? He thought that she was just a human."

Just a human? What else could she be?

"I don't want to risk it," Gilbert said. "Maybe he suspected something and bugged her phone."

Gabi's eyes were closing again, and she felt herself slipping away, but she had to know what was going on.

"Who is he?" she murmured. "Who are you talking about?"

"Get some rest, sweetheart." Gilbert lifted their conjoined hands and kissed her knuckles.

"Promise me that you won't get rid of my phone, or at least write down Uriel's phone number so I can call him from another phone."

"I promise."

It was so difficult to hang on, but she had to make sure her wishes were obeyed. "Swear it on our parents' souls."

"I swear," Gilbert said.

Letting out a breath, Gabi closed her eyes and let herself drift away.

55

GILBERT

"She is out again." Gilbert stroked his sister's hair like he had done so many times when she was a kid.

"Gabi is doing well," Julian reassured him. "The fact that she's waking up quite often is an excellent sign. All the Dormants who exhibited this pattern transitioned easily."

"That's reassuring," Gilbert said while continuing to stroke Gabi's soft hair. "What do we do about her phone?"

"Maybe we can use it to set up a trap?" Jay asked.

Gilbert arched a brow. "For the god? What for?"

"I don't know." The doctor shrugged. "Maybe Kian wants to catch them. I wasn't in the war room, so I don't know what the status is."

"Weren't you in the warehouse? Waiting for the team to put them through your detecting machines?"

"I was, but I wasn't getting live updates."

Julian pulled out his phone and placed a call. "We have her."

"Good," Kian's gruff voice sounded loud and clear as Julian activated the speaker. "Did you get everyone who had any contact with Gabi?"

"We did," Theo said from the front of the van. "One obstinate doctor took more work than the others, but I got her memories of Gabi shoved deep. For some reason, she really didn't like Gabriella."

Julian shook his head. "Doctors shouldn't let their personal preferences affect their attitudes towards patients."

Gilbert chuckled. "Gabi was very vocal about how she didn't like the way they were treating her in that hospital, and knowing my sister, she voiced that opinion to everyone who cared or didn't care to listen. I can't really blame that poor overworked doctor who had probably been on her feet for the past twelve hours."

"Is the meeting over?" Julian asked Kian.

"It is. Our team drove away first, and the gods followed several minutes later. We were lucky that they chose Simi Valley for the meeting. It will take them about an hour to get to the hospital, and by then, all traces of Gabi will be gone. Roni is hacking her hospitalization records as we speak."

"Did you decide where we should take her?" Julian asked. "I vote for the village, but then the team will have to wait for me to get back to take care of the scanning. If we take her to the old clinic at the keep, I can make it in time to the warehouse, but I will have to leave Gabi with no medical supervision. Gilbert and the Guardians can watch her while I'm gone, but it's not ideal."

"Nothing is ever ideal," Kian said. "Take her to the keep. We are meeting Aru and his friends at the penthouse tomorrow, and I thought that Gilbert might want to meet his future brother-in-law."

Gilbert nearly choked on his own tongue. "Are you serious? You will let me meet the new gods?"

"I'm only semi-serious. I wonder how he will react to the news that the human woman he's been seeing is a Dormant transitioning into immortality. We've learned today that the gods consider procreation with all other species a taboo—not just with the Kra-ell. It's beneath them. They also have no idea about Dormants or how immortals create other immortals."

Gilbert's baby fangs started itching despite his venom glands being inactive. "So, it's okay for them to have sex with what they consider lesser species, but just not to make children with them?"

"That's how it would appear," Kian said. "Throughout history humans weren't much better, and they were discriminating based on nonsensical differences like social status or skin color."

463

"Let us make men in our image, after our likeness, and let them have dominion over the fish of the sea, and over the fowl of the air, and over the cattle, and over all the earth, and over every creeping thing that creepeth upon the earth," Julian quoted. "I guess that likeness is in all things, for better and for worse."

Gilbert rolled his eyes. "Never mind that. I don't care about meeting the damn god. What I care about is getting my sister the best medical care, and that's not going to happen in the damn keep. I want her in the village, where Bridget and the nurses can watch her twenty-four-seven. If Fates forbid something happens to Gabi while Julian is gone, I wouldn't know what to do, and neither would the Guardians."

"We have basic emergency medical training," Jay said.

"And the warehouse is less than ten minutes away," Julian added. "I can be back right away."

Gilbert looked at the young doctor. "If we bring Gabi to the keep, all of us will have to stay in the keep until the village is no longer in lock-down. Are you okay with being away from your mate for several days or a week? Because I'm not."

Julian's mood soured. "Right. I didn't think of that. Can you let Ella out? And maybe one of the nurses?"

"Let's see how tomorrow goes," Kian said. "You can survive one night without your mates." He ended the call.

Gilbert sighed. "I'd better call Karen. She won't be happy about having no help with the kids."

"I can ask Ella to lend her a hand," Julian offered. "She studies and works online, but she can spare a couple of hours, and she loves kids." He grimaced. "Other people's kids. She's not ready to have some of her own yet."

"Are we going back to the hotel?" Gabi mumbled with her eyes closed.

"No, we are not." Gilbert cupped her cheek. "Do you need anything from there?"

"All my things are there. You need to get them."

"I can go later and collect them." He lifted his gaze to Julian. "But it will have to wait until the doctor returns, and I know you are in good hands. I won't leave you before then."

464

"Good." She gave him a faint smile. "I'm so glad that you came."

"Of course." He leaned over and kissed her forehead. "I would move mountains and fight dragons to get to my baby sister."

Her smile widened. "How big?"

It was a game he'd played with her when she was little. He would say he would fight dragons for her, but only if they were really small.

"This big." He spread his arms wide.

Gabi's eyes twinkled, a hint of the playfulness they used to share as children lighting up her pale face. "That's a pretty big dragon," she teased.

Julian watched their interaction with a fond smile. "It's nice to see a brother and sister as close as you are."

Gilbert's expression sobered. "For a long while, all we had was each other."

Gabi's hand found Gilbert's. "Tell me more stories," she whispered. "Like the ones you used to tell me when I couldn't sleep."

He chuckled, brushing a stray strand of hair behind her ear. "Alright, do you remember the one about the mischievous fairy who stole the moon's light?"

She nestled deeper into the pillow and closed her eyes. "I love that one."

56

MAGNUS

"I still don't trust them," Jade said. "Gods are master manipulators."

Magnus cast her a warning look.

Kian had instructed them not to say anything they thought that the gods shouldn't know until Julian put them through the scanner and they changed clothing. The third god could have attached a tracking device to their car, and Aru and Negal could have attached miniature listening devices to their clothing or their hair when they all shook hands.

The instructions they had gotten were to discuss what they had learned from the gods and not say anything negative about them or anything that could betray things Kian didn't want the gods to know, Gabriella's transition being one of them. Kian suspected that one of the gods was responsible for inducing her, and he didn't want them to learn about it just yet.

Jade winked at him and continued. "Aru was full of smiles, and he said all the right things, but he kept the hardhat and dark sunglasses on. I don't like talking to people whose eyes I cannot see. Besides, I gave him my vow, and he didn't give me one in return."

"Gods don't take their vows as seriously," Phinas said. "Aru knew that it wouldn't affect your judgment of him."

"He was sincere," Morgada said. "But he was hiding things even from Negal."

Magnus put a finger on his lips, reminding her that she shouldn't be saying things like that.

"He's the team leader," he said out loud. "In most organizations, the leader knows more than the others."

Given Jade's frown, she wasn't happy with his explanation. She turned to Morgada. "What makes you say that? I've known you for a very long time, and you were never any more intuitive than others."

Morgada shrugged. "When you were engaged in the conversation, I was observing, and Negal wasn't very guarded with his expressions. He seemed like a simple guy, for a god, that is, and he often looked surprised when Aru spoke. So, it might have been because Aru wasn't supposed to reveal those things to us or that they were news to Negal as well. I might be wrong, though. It was just my impression."

"Hello, team." Kian's voice sounded in Magnus's ear, and given the startled expressions on the others' faces, he was speaking to them as well.

He must have heard the exchange and was about to reprimand them for not following his instructions to the letter.

"I don't want you to react verbally to what I'm about to tell you," Kian said. "We know now that Aru was the guy Gabi has been seeing. After you left, we flew the drone low enough for the gods to lift their heads and look at it, and the resemblance to the guy Gabi was seeing was unmistakable. He called himself Uriel Delgado and had an excellent fake identity that was based on a real person. Roni tells me that sometimes American citizens living abroad sell their identity to foreigners so they can enter the United States. He thinks that's what the real Uriel Delgado did, and Aru bought the identity through a broker dealing in those things."

"Okay," Jade said. "What does it have to do with us?"

"I'm just giving you an update. Julian has brought Gabi to the keep, and he's going to meet you in the warehouse as scheduled. As for the gods, they used the same technique as we usually employ to ditch the drone. They got into the parking lot of a mall, and they either switched cars or went shopping. My bet is on the first option."

"So is mine," Phinas said. "I have a question. Given the news, is it wise to have a meeting in the penthouse?"

The four of them were going to spend the night in the other penthouse, which used to belong to Amanda, and Magnus thought that it was very convenient. He would have preferred to spend the night at home with Vivian, but this wouldn't be the first time they had been separated, nor would it be the last. He was a Guardian, and although Onegus tried to make accommodations for the mated Guardians, it wasn't always possible.

"It's fine," Kian said. "The entrance to the underground facility is well hidden, and they won't have time to snoop around because we will give them the address only twenty minutes before the meeting. When they get to the building, someone will be waiting for them to escort them straight to the penthouse. "

Magnus wanted to ask whether Kian still planned to attend the meeting, but the question would have to wait for after they'd changed clothing and gone through the scanner.

"Thanks for the update, boss," he said.

ARU

As soon as Negal pulled up to the hospital, Aru threw the vehicle door open and rushed in through the sliding doors.

Where to go from here?

He stopped the first person he passed. "How can I find a patient who was admitted to the hospital today?"

The woman smiled. "Labor and delivery is on the third floor. Is this your first?"

He frowned. "Is it obvious that this is my first time in a hospital?"

"I meant, is this your first child?"

Finally, her previous words about labor and delivery registered. "Oh, no, I'm not having a baby. I mean, my girlfriend is not having a baby. She fainted earlier today and was brought here."

"Aha." The woman nodded. "Check the ER. You can't get in, but you can ask the nurse at the admissions window. It's down the hall where it says Emergency Room."

"Thank you." He dipped his head. "Have a wonderful day." He dashed in the direction she'd pointed.

"Such a charming and polite young man," he heard the woman murmur. "If only I was thirty years younger."

Aru couldn't help but smile. He was a young god, but he was at least that woman's age, if not older. She looked to be in her mid-fifties, and he was sixty-eight years old, not counting the years he'd spent in stasis en route to this sector.

There was a line in front of the window of the Emergency Room, which was strange since emergency implied urgency, and yet no one seemed in a rush to assist the people standing in line.

When he finally got to the window, he leaned to look at the nurse and used a slight thrall just to make her more cooperative. "I'm looking for Gabriella Emerson. She was admitted earlier today. She fainted on the street."

The nurse pursed her lips. "I don't remember anyone by that name." She typed on her keyboard and frowned at her screen. "How does she spell her name? Is it with one L or two? An E or an A at the end?"

"I'm not sure." He pulled out his phone and checked Gabi's contact. "It's with two Ls and an A at the end."

"We don't have anyone by that name. In fact, we don't have anyone with the last name Emerson. Are you sure she was brought into this hospital?"

"She texted me the name." He turned the phone so the woman could see Gabi's text. "City Medical Center."

"Maybe she meant City Clinic. People often confuse the two. City Clinic is only ten minutes away. You should check there."

"Can you call them and ask whether they have her?"

The nurse tilted her head and looked behind him. "I wish I could help, but there are people in line who need help."

Aru looked over his shoulder and winced. The guy behind him was cradling an arm that looked broken, and the woman in the wheelchair behind the guy looked like she was about to throw up.

"Yeah. You're right. I can call them myself."

When he got back to the car, Negal asked, "Well? Did you find her?"

"She's not here." Aru closed the passenger door and turned to Dagor. "I need to call other hospitals in the area. Can you find the numbers for me?"

The guy didn't look happy to do it, but he did it anyway, and then it was time to make the calls.

They divided the seven possible hospitals and clinics between them.

Fifteen minutes later, they had exhausted the list without finding Gabi in any of them.

"I don't understand it." Aru raked the fingers of both hands through his hair. "Where can she be?"

"Maybe she used a different name," Negal said. "She might have given you a fake name like you gave her. Did you see her driver's license or her passport?"

"Why would she do that? She doesn't have to hide who she is."

"She could be married," Dagor said. "Humans are very possessive of their mates, and she didn't want her husband to find out."

Letting out a frustrated groan, Aru lifted a hand to stop them from suggesting any more absurd ideas. "You are not helping. What's going on with our new friends? Did they reach their destination?"

"They are still driving, but you'll be glad to know that they are close by. They also talked about us. Jade doesn't trust you, and Morgada thinks you are hiding things from us."

Morgada wasn't wrong. Aru was hiding things from his teammates, but he didn't have a choice, and it was better for them not to know. Humans called it plausible deniability, and it was a very apt term.

"They have no reason to trust us." He shifted in his seat. "What radius did you specify when searching for hospitals and clinics?"

"Five miles. Do you want me to expand the perimeter?"

"Yes, please. In the meantime, let's go to her hotel. Perhaps she was discharged and is back in her room."

"Did you try calling her?" Negal asked.

Aru nodded. "She's not answering. Calls go straight to voicemail, and texts don't get delivered. I suspect that her phone has run out of charge."

She'd texted him from the hospital, so he knew she had it with her, but he didn't know whether it had just run out of charge or something was very wrong with Gabi.

58

MAGNUS

When the team got to the warehouse, Julian wasn't there yet, but there was plenty to do before the doctor ran them through the more advanced scanners after they changed clothing to make sure that nothing was attached to their skin and hair.

Regrettably, there was no shower, so they would have to put clean clothes on their sweaty bodies.

The first step, though, was running the handheld bug detector over each of them, and Magnus performed the scan as soon as they entered.

"You are all clear." He handed the bug detector to Phinas. "Can you check me?"

"Sure." The guy did a thorough job of it, scanning every inch of Magnus's clothing, but the device hadn't beeped even once.

"You're clear as well, but we won't know for sure until Julian performs his body scans, and maybe not even then."

"Morgada and I will change over there." Jade pointed to the large scanner. "So don't look that way."

Magnus lifted the duffle bag with his change of clothes and slung the strap over his shoulder. "Don't forget to brush your hair, rub disinfectant on your skin, and then moisturize everywhere your skin was exposed."

Later, when they got to the keep, Magnus planned on taking a long shower, scrubbing his skin, and changing his clothing again. He would advise the others to do the same.

"I remember Julian's instructions." Jade took her own duffle bag and followed Morgada behind the scanner.

The problem was that all of their precautions were based on known technology, but the gods possessed technology that was far superior to anything humans and immortals had. They could have bugs made from materials that were undetectable by the scanner and so small that Julian couldn't see them on the screen even if detected. Heck, they could have created biological bugs that were indistinguishable from real flies or even mosquitos.

After all, they were genetic experts.

William had said that they might have spy nanos that transferred through contact and advised them not to shake hands with the gods, but when Aru offered Magnus his hand, he knew that refusing to shake it would undermine the negotiations.

Jade's vow had done a lot to make the gods trust them, but it wasn't enough.

The truth was that the meeting had left him unnerved despite Aru being perfectly polite and seemingly mellow. The gods' might was terrifying, and the prospect of the Eternal King turning his attention to Earth was enough to induce a panic attack even in a hardened Guardian like Magnus.

Perhaps having a family had softened him, but Magnus couldn't remember ever feeling as out of sorts as he felt now.

"Here." Phinas dropped an empty cardboard box at his feet. "You can put your old clothing in here." He had a similar box for his belongings.

"Thank you."

Removing his Kevlar vest, Magnus folded it in two and put it inside the box. Next went his shirt, then his pants, socks, and shoes. There was no need to change underwear since the gods couldn't have touched it.

He brushed his hair thoroughly, put an oily moisturizer over the parts of his skin that had been exposed, including his face, and then got dressed in fresh clothing.

"I feel like a new man." He looked at Phinas, who was pushing his feet into a new pair of short leather boots. "Nice soles. What brand are they?"

"Blundstone. They are from Australia." He glanced in the direction of the scanner. "Jade and I got matching pairs."

Magnus's lips twitched with a smile.

It was such a couples' thing to do, and to think that only a short time ago, Jade had not believed in monogamous relationships.

As the warehouse door opened and Julian walked in with Jay, Magnus asked, "How is Gilbert's sister doing?"

"Given the circumstances, she's doing very well. I've left her in the keep clinic with Theo and her brother. He is freaking out, but I told him that I can be back there in less than ten minutes and that nothing can happen to her in such a short time."

Magnus arched a brow. "Is that true? Or did you just say that to reassure him?"

"It's mostly true." Julian smiled at Jade and Morgada, as they emerged from behind the scanner. "Who would have thought that one of those naughty gods would induce Gilbert's sister? I still don't know whether it's a good thing or bad."

"Good for her," Jade said. "She saved herself a lot of trouble looking for an immortal to induce her, and her transition will probably go smoother. Other than that, I doubt it's a good thing. She might be enamored with him, but he will think of her as nothing more than a temporary plaything. By and large, his people do not mingle with what they consider lesser beings."

"I don't like that term," Julian said. "It's derogatory."

Jade shrugged. "It's true, though. They are superior, and they are the creators."

"But they are not more intelligent," Julian said. "That's why I don't feel superior to humans even though physically I am. There are so many people who are smarter than me and knowing that keeps me humble." He pushed his shoulder-length hair behind his ear. "Frankly, it surprises me that the gods didn't breed for intelligence. With their genetic manipulation ability, they could have easily done that."

"Maybe they didn't want to," Jade said. "And by 'they' I mean the Eternal King. He wouldn't have wanted young gods to be born who

474

could be smarter than him." She braided the ends of her long hair. "That would also explain why compulsion ability is so rare among the gods. The king doesn't want competition."

Julian nodded. "That's a good observation and one more question to ask the gods tomorrow, but I shouldn't waste time talking and delay my return to the keep. Let's get the scanning over so we can get out of here. Who wants to go first?"

"I do." Jade toed off her boots, which were indeed identical to Phinas's. "I want to be done with it. I can't put my weapons back on before I go through the scanner, and I feel naked without them."

59

ARU

The good news was that Gabi's things were still in her hotel room, and she hadn't checked out, but that was the only good news.

Aru and his teammates had called every hospital and clinic in downtown Los Angeles and its periphery, and none had any record of her ever being there.

It just didn't make sense.

Had Gabi invented the whole hospital thing to get his attention?

She had some dramatic tendencies, but she was mostly reasonable, and she wouldn't have scared him like that for nothing. Besides, where could she be if she wasn't in her room?

The receptionist downstairs hadn't seen her coming in since she'd left earlier.

Could she have been kidnapped?

Perhaps her brothers had finally returned from their business meeting, and she was spending time with them?

But then she would have called him or sent him a message.

Unless her phone was out of charge, and she hadn't noticed.

With a sigh, Aru lifted one of the pillows and buried his nose in it. Gabi's scent still lingered on the fabric, providing a momentary relief from the aching void in his chest.

He was so worried about her.

Yeah, it was worry, nothing else.

He couldn't have feelings for the feisty human with intelligent eyes and pouty lips. The gods' taboo on relationships with created species was obviously bogus and needed to go, but a relationship between them was still impossible because of the long-term mission he had undertaken. He couldn't get attached to anyone.

Except, a small voice in the back of his head whispered that he was about to spend more than one hundred years on Earth, and Gabi wouldn't even live that long.

Damn, why did it hurt so badly to think of her inevitable mortality?

Shaking himself off, Aru dropped the pillow and left the room.

Down on the street, he opened the car's passenger door and got in. "She wasn't there, but her things were. I don't know what to think."

Dagor wasn't paying him any attention. Instead, he was looking at his laptop screen and smiling like he knew something that Aru didn't.

Nudging his arm, Aru got his attention. "What's going on?"

"They are onto us," Dagor said. "They didn't go back home as we thought they would. They stopped by a warehouse, changed clothing, and are about to enter a scanner. Jade is going first, and as soon as the machine starts making a noise, I'll fly our little spy out of the box."

So that's why there were no visuals, and since Dagor had his earbuds on, there was no sound either.

"What is the drone doing in the box?" Aru asked.

"I told you they are onto us. They took off the clothes they were wearing and put them in boxes. Thankfully, Magnus didn't close the box, or that would have been the end of our little spy."

"Take the earbuds off so I can hear what's going on."

"Yes, sir." Dagor plucked the devices from his ears and put them in their little container. "Here we go," he said as the scanner was turned on. "Fly little birdie, fly."

As the device flew out of the box, the warehouse came into view, and Dagor directed it toward a wall where it had a good view of the scanner and the people standing around it.

As Magnus lifted his head and looked in the direction of the drone, the three of them held their breath, but he must have assumed it was a mosquito and turned back to the scanner.

Aru let out a relieved breath. "This thing works better in open spaces."

Dagor nodded as he directed the drone to attach to the wall. "Landing was successful."

"Indeed." Aru clapped him on the back. "Good job."

On the screen, Phinas shook his head. "I still can't wrap my head around Gilbert's sister hooking up with Aru."

The words hit Aru in the chest like a ballistic rocket.

He had hooked up with only one female recently, and she had a brother named Gilbert. How the hell had these people found out about Gabi, and how were they connected to her brother?

"The Fates' fingerprints are all over this." Magnus crossed his arms over his chest. "What are the chances of a random encounter between Gilbert's sister, who doesn't even live here, and one of the gods? And what the hell was she thinking about, having unprotected sex with a stranger?"

Morgada frowned. "Why do you think she did that?"

"Maybe she wanted to get pregnant," Phinas said. "She's nearing forty, and childless human females start getting desperate at that age. Aru is an exceptionally good-looking, smart guy. If I were a human female looking for a daddy for my kid, I would have chosen him too."

Chuckling, Morgada slapped Phinas's arm. "I wasn't referring to why she didn't use protection. The question was how do you know that she didn't?"

"Condoms would have prevented her entering transition," Magnus said. "To induce an adult female Dormant, both a venom bite and insemination are required."

What were they talking about?

What did they mean by dormant and inducing an adult female?

Inducing to do what?

"Oh, I see." Morgada pursed her lips. "I didn't know that. I thought that an immortal male's venom bite was enough to induce a Dormant into immortality."

"What would be the fun in that?" Phinas nudged her with his elbow.

"The Fates are interested in love matches, and according to the immortals' beliefs, they are three mischievous female spirits. They want to ensure that their pawns have fun while fulfilling their objectives."

"They belong in your tradition as well," Magnus said. "The fact that Doomers weren't taught anything about the Fates doesn't mean they don't govern your life. After all, do you really think you and Jade met by chance?"

"It was by chance," Phinas insisted. "Kalugal could have chosen Rufsur for the mission. I just happened to be in the right place at the right time, and Jade and I are kindred spirits."

Magnus regarded him with an amused expression. "If that's what you want to believe, it's your choice, but I don't think that you truly believe the Fates had nothing to do with it."

Phinas smiled slyly. "I didn't say that. Who am I to doubt the all-powerful Fates?"

"I don't understand," Aru murmured. "If Phinas is a Doomer, what is he doing with his enemies? And how did they find out about Gabi and me?"

Negal shook his head. "I told you that you shouldn't get involved with her. I had a feeling that nothing good would come out of it."

Nothing good?

How could what he and Gabi had together be described as nothing good?

It had been the best experience Aru ever had, and he couldn't tolerate the thought of anything bad happening to Gabi.

But what was happening to her was good.

She was turning immortal.

60

GABI

As Gabi's mind stirred into wakefulness, groggily pulling her out of a deep sleep, she blinked, struggling to focus in the unfamiliar room. The soft beeping of machines buzzed in her ears, indicating that she was in a medical facility, but none she recognized.

She took in her surroundings.

The room wasn't big, with walls that were painted off-white and dim lighting that was soft and calm. Machines with green and blue displays were scattered in the periphery of her gaze, with tubes and wires connecting her to them.

Her body felt heavy, and as she tried to lift her hand, she realized she was connected to an IV bag hanging above her. Confusion crept in, mixing with her grogginess.

Where was she?

Why was she there?

Turning her head slightly, she tried to see more of the room. Cabinets lined the walls, and there was a desk with a computer on it. The screen displayed data that didn't make much sense to her. Everything was so quiet, almost eerie, making the sound of her breathing seem loud in comparison.

Her fingers twitched as she attempted to reach for the call button on the side of the bed. It was harder than she expected, as if her body was moving through thick fog. She sighed in frustration. She knew she needed to figure out what was happening, but her memories were like puzzle pieces that just wouldn't fit together.

Closing her eyes briefly, she took a breath and tried to gather her thoughts. The beeping of the machines kept up a steady rhythm, distracting her and preventing her scattered thoughts from coalescing.

Had she been drugged?

She sure felt like it. Perhaps she should pull out the IV?

But what if she was sick and the bag contained necessary medication?

Taking a steadying breath, Gabi willed herself to grasp the fragments of her memory and recall how she had arrived here. But the events leading up to this moment remained elusive, a collage of pictures that didn't make sense. She remembered getting out of the hotel, then she remembered the face of a rude nurse, or was it a doctor?

Wait a moment. Gilbert was there. Had she dreamt him up?

As a door she hadn't noticed before opened, and her brother stepped in, the relief washing over her would have made her feel faint if she wasn't already feeling like passing out.

"Gilbert," she murmured.

He rushed to her side. "I'm here, sweetheart." He took her hand and clasped it between his large ones. "How are you feeling?"

"Terrible. I can't remember anything. How did I get here? What's wrong with me? Am I being drugged? What's in the IV bag?"

Chuckling, Gilbert bent over her and kissed her forehead. "You might be thirty-eight, but you haven't changed a bit. You still ask a million questions without waiting for an answer." Holding on to her hand with one of his, he climbed on the bed and sat next to her. "Do you remember fainting?"

"No. But I remember feeling sick and going to the drugstore. I don't remember getting there, though."

"That's because you never got there. You fainted on your way to the store. Someone called the paramedics, and they took you to a hospital. You called me, and I came as soon as I could. I got you out of there and brought you to the clan's clinic."

The clan.

Something about that sounded familiar, but her thoughts were still jumbled.

Lifting her hand, Gabi rubbed her temple. "Something is really wrong with me, Gilbert. My mind feels like it's stuffed with cotton candy. I feel like I should remember things, like they are on the edge of my conscious mind, but I can't bring them to the forefront. Tell me the truth. Do I have a brain tumor? Am I going to die?"

He frowned. "There is nothing physically wrong with you, Gabi. Orion's compulsion must have jumbled up your mind. Remembering things one moment and forgetting them the next, and then going through that cycle over and over again, while at the same time entering transition, must have been too much." He pulled out his phone. "I'm not a doctor, but that's just common sense. I'm calling Orion."

Who was Orion?

The name sounded familiar, but it was like everything else she was trying to remember. The end of the thread appeared to be within reach, but when she tried to grasp it, it slipped farther away, and she was getting a headache.

With a sigh, she closed her eyes and let her mind wander aimlessly. The headache subsided, and Uriel's handsome face appeared behind her closed lids. "Did anyone tell Uriel where I am?" she murmured. "He's going to be so worried about me."

Gilbert just patted her hand.

"Orion, this is Gilbert. I'm with Gabi, and she's transitioning."

That word again.

Transition.

It should mean something to her, but what?

61

ARU

Gabi was transitioning into immortality.

That was what had been wrong with her.

Was it dangerous?

"Your turn." Jade tapped Morgada on the shoulder. "We need to hurry up so Julian can return to Gilbert's sister. She needs to be supervised by a doctor."

Aru's blood chilled in his veins. If she needed medical supervision, the transition into immortality was dangerous.

"Getting induced by a god is a definite plus," Magnus said. "But I expect many immortal bachelors will be disappointed about not being given a chance with her."

"It's for the best." Jade waved a dismissive hand. "The competition would have been stiff, and the males would have gotten too aggressive."

"Immortals are not like the Kra-ell," Magnus said in an indignant tone. "We don't fight each other to impress females."

"Maybe not physically, but even humor can be a form of aggression." Jade cast Phinas a fond look. "Males compete by amusing females, and I, for one, am more impressed by that than physical prowess."

"Oh really?" Phinas pulled her into his arms. "So, me saving Kagra had nothing to do with it? I thought you were pretty impressed with my leap."

"I was." She pushed on his chest. "But your wit and your humor impressed me more."

As the group kept talking and the doctor ran everyone through the scanner, Aru tried to decipher what he'd heard so far.

Phinas was a former enemy of the clan, and as Aru had suspected, he and Jade were a couple. These immortals had formed the utopian community he and others like him were hoping to one day have on Anumati, and he couldn't wait to meet their leader, who had made this dream a reality, albeit on a small scale.

Right now, though, he needed to find a way to get to Gabi. They kept mentioning the keep as the place she'd been taken to, and the doctor was going to her.

They needed to attach the drone to Doctor Julian and have him lead them to Gabi.

Aru tapped Dagor's arm. "I need you to attach the drone to the doctor."

Dagor nodded. "I can do that, but what do you want to do? Force yourself into their stronghold? That wouldn't be helpful in finding out more about them and getting them to cooperate with us if we deem them worthy. I still don't think a bunch of immortals and Kra-ell would be helpful to us."

"I think they would. But I have to see her." He rubbed his hand over his chest. "It's like there is a void inside of me that only she can fill."

In the backseat, Negal sighed. "The young are so impetuous. Think about it, Aru. You don't know what transition into immortality entails, you don't know how to help her, and all you are going to achieve by barging in there is to reveal that we were spying on them."

"They were also trying to spy on us, but we outsmarted them. It's part of the game, and we won. They will understand that." He turned to face the front of the car. "If Gabi is transitioning into immortality, she will no longer be a human, and I can have a life with her."

"Really?" Negal scoffed. "You are a soldier. In a hundred years or so, you will have to return to the patrol ship and then back home. If you disappear, we will pay the price, and if we all disappear, our families will pay it."

For Aru, it was worse than that. He had an obligation to return that had nothing to do with his draft. "I don't intend to let you get punished because I want to stay behind. I have to return the same way you do. But in the meantime, I can enjoy Gabi's company. A hundred years is a blink of an eye for a god, and it won't be enough, but I can't turn my back on her." He shook his head. "I just can't."

Dagor sighed. "Maybe we can use it to our advantage. If these immortals know how strong the bond is between love mates, they will know that they can trust you will never do anything to endanger Gabi or those she cares for or her family."

Negal snorted. "He doesn't have a love bond with her. She was just a human while they were together, and gods cannot form bonds with lesser creations. I doubt a bond can form between a god and an immortal either, but at least there is a small chance of that."

Aru turned to look at his teammate. "You know that most of what we were taught about the horrible consequences of procreating with the created species was propaganda, right? These immortals are far from monstrosities. Jade bonded with an immortal and seems happier than I thought she was capable of. Also, a Kra-ell and god union did not create abominations. We know about the royal twins."

"We don't know that for sure," Negal said. "We suspect that."

"The twins are why we are here. Do you really think that the Eternal King would have bothered patrolling this planet to find out the fate of the Kra-ell queen's children? His interest alone indicates that he knows that they are his grandchildren."

Negal swallowed. "It's blasphemy to suggest that, but by now, everyone knows that the king's heir and the Kra-ell heir had a dalliance. They just don't know that the twins were the result."

"It was more than a dalliance." Aru sighed. "They were in love, and they dreamt of a better future for both of their people, but their dream turned into a nightmare."

GABI

Gabi's consciousness fluttered drowsily, slowly emerging from the warm cocoon of pleasant dreams.

As her senses gradually came online, the soft, steady beeping of medical equipment reminded her that she was in a hospital room or a clinic, and she even remembered that Gilbert had brought her there for some reason.

Oh, yeah, she'd called him and asked him to get her out of that horrible hospital.

But where was she now?

Had he answered her questions, and she'd forgotten already?

Lifting her eyelids with effort, she was greeted with the view of Gilbert's broad back. He was holding a phone to his ear and speaking with someone.

"Gilbert?" she murmured.

He turned around. "Oh, good. You're awake. I thought I would have to call Orion again. Let me transfer the call to video."

Panicking, she lifted her hand. "Don't. I probably look like roadkill. I don't want anyone to see me like this."

Gilbert smiled. "You look lovely even when you are disheveled. Besides, you are transitioning, and no one expects you to look your best."

There it was again, that word.

"You keep saying that I'm transitioning. What does that mean?"

"Talk to Orion. Hopefully, things will make more sense after he does his thing." Gilbert unceremoniously turned the phone around.

The face on the small screen was strikingly handsome and familiar. "Hello, Gabi. I'm sorry about the mess my compulsion created in your head. In hindsight, it wasn't a good idea."

"I know you. You were at the dinner in the hotel."

"That's right. You were told things that needed to be kept a secret, but since you were seeing a guy who we suspected of possessing a certain ability, we couldn't let you remember what you were told when you had company. That was what created the confusion and eventually made you forget everything, even when there were no strangers around. I will remove the compulsion now, and hopefully, that will clear the confusion."

At the edges of her consciousness, Gabi knew what he was talking about, but the information was like a slippery noodle that refused to stay on her mental fork.

"How are you going to do that?"

"Simple. Look into my eyes and focus on the sound of my voice. You will remember everything you've learned about immortals, and you can speak freely about them with anyone. You are not restricted in any way."

For a brief moment, her head felt like it was going to explode. But then the sensation subsided, and she could feel things organizing themselves in her mind, until the pressure lifted, and she felt a refreshing lightness combined with clarity.

"Immortality. That's what I'm transitioning into. But how? I didn't have sex with an immortal, did I? Or did you make me forget that as well, and the memory just didn't come back yet?"

Orion chuckled. "I'll let Gilbert explain. This is one hell of an incredible story. I wish you the best of luck with your transition."

"Thank you." She rubbed her aching temples.

"I'll see you in the village soon," Orion said. "Or so I hope. Goodbye, Gabi."

"Goodbye, and thank you again."

Gilbert ended the call, put the phone on the table beside her hospital bed, and took a deep breath. "There is no easy way to do this. Your lover boy is not a human, after all. He's a god, and he induced your transition. What I want to know is, what the hell were you thinking having unprotected sex with a guy you'd only just met?"

She arched a brow. "Are you serious? That's what bothers you about this situation? And what do you mean by a god? Do you mean immortal, a descendant of the gods?"

"You were induced by a god. Not an immortal, not a demigod, but a pureblooded god." He surprised her with a grin. "And so was I. You don't have exclusive bragging rights."

"Wait a moment." She lifted a hand. "You said that all the gods were dead, and only their immortal descendants remained."

He arched both brows in mock innocence. "I didn't say that all the gods were dead."

Gabi tried to remember what exactly she'd been told, but evidently her memory was still a little fuzzy. Not that it was surprising, given what she was going through.

"I don't remember what you and the others said, but it was implied that there were no gods left on Earth and that only their immortal descendants remained."

He sighed. "The gods living in the village are our most guarded secret, even more so than the existence of immortals. It's like the Holy of Holies of secrets. They were supposed to be the only ones, but then Aru and his friends showed up, getting our attention by activating trackers that we knew were of godly origins."

"How did you know that they were of godly origins?"

"The history of those trackers is a long story for another day. When we identified the signals, we panicked, and the village went into lockdown. Do you remember that?"

She nodded. "It got so confusing. When I was alone, I remembered what you told me about a clan's location that got compromised and that the lockdown was a security measure. Was all of that because of Uriel?"

Gilbert nodded. "His real name is Aru, and he's not from Portugal. It's just a fake identity he bought. Anyway, a team of our people met with him today, and it seems like his intentions are not hostile, but further talks are needed to ascertain that. He and his friends are very dangerous."

"Why?"

"Because gods to immortals are like immortals to humans. We are powerless against them. They can get into our minds and thrall us, and some of them can even compel us. Also, they come from a planet of gods who don't hold humans in the highest regard. I don't know all the details of what Aru told the team, but it seems like he is on our side."

"Good." Gabi rubbed her temple. "I think. Will I be able to see him again?"

"It depends on how the talks are going. If Kian is convinced that Aru's intentions are good, he will not stand in fate's way."

"Fate?"

"The Fates, fate, it's all the same thing." He smiled. "Do you really think that your flight getting canceled and you getting a first-class ticket and sitting next to a god was coincidental?"

"No, I guess it wasn't."

Gabi's heart did a happy little flip.

Uriel was a god, and his secret mission had been to meet with the clan and negotiate something with them. Whatever it was, it had nothing to do with flea-market flipping or illegal activities, and since he had no reason to return to Portugal, they could be together.

On top of that, he had induced her immortality, meaning they could be together forever.

The question was whether he wanted to have forever with her.

After all, he was a god, and she wasn't.

"When can I see Uriel?" She murmured. "I mean, Aru."

"I don't know." Gilbert took her hand and gave it a gentle squeeze. "I guess it's up to Kian. It depends on how the negotiations go."

Fear accumulated in the pit of her stomach. "When will I know?"

He gave her an apologetic smile. "Your guess is as good as mine."

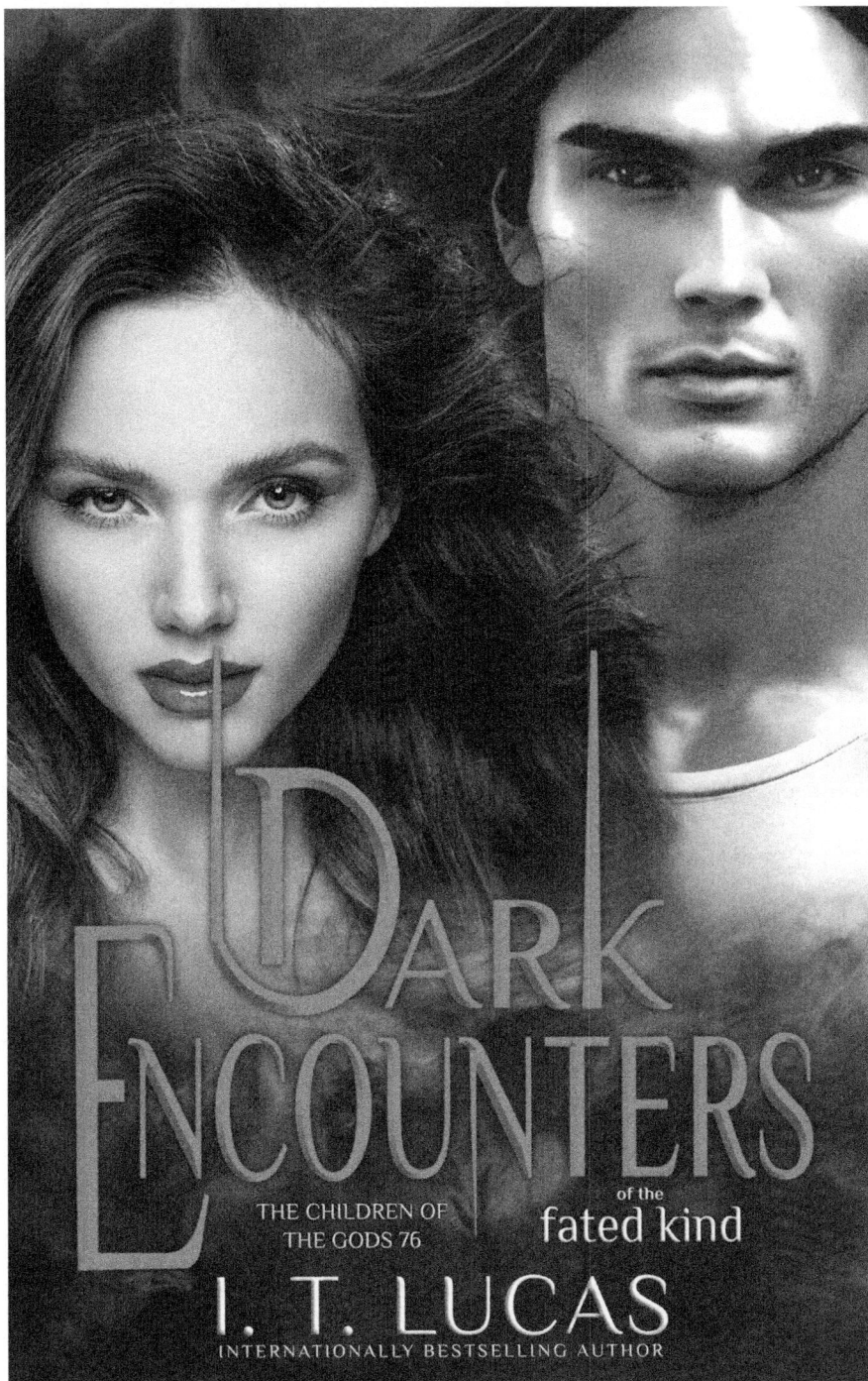

DARK

ENCOUNTERS

of the
fated kind

I. T. LUCAS

1

ARU

Aru stood motionless and silent behind Dagor's chair, watching the laptop screen. The video quality of the bug perched on Doctor Julian's shoulder was remarkably clear, and what Aru saw twisted his gut with worry.

Gabi looked drained, so pale and gaunt that she seemed almost ethereal. Her once vibrant and animated face was drawn, and her small frame barely made a rise under the blanket.

The contrast between the woman he'd known intimately over the last few days and the vulnerable figure in the hospital bed was jarring. In his memories she'd seemed like a force, a spirit that filled his heart and any space she occupied with her quirky personality and vivacious energy.

He was a damn god, and yet he was completely helpless to do anything about it. What were all his godly powers good for if he couldn't help her? Make her better?

Worse, Aru couldn't even hold the hand of the woman he cared for in her time of need, and putting his faith in the doctor was not something he was even remotely comfortable with.

Julian was the immortal descendant of the rebel gods, and Aru didn't know where he had gotten his education. Did he even know how to take care of Gabi?

As the urge to go to her became overwhelming, his grip on the back of Dagor's chair tightened to the point of the wood groaning in protest.

"Cut it out." Dagor looked at him over his shoulder. "You're going to break the chair."

"She doesn't look good," Aru murmured.

"On the contrary." Dagor turned back to the laptop screen. "She's a looker. I can understand now why you are so obsessed with her."

Over on the couch, Negal chuckled. "A human female's beauty can't compare to that of a goddess. It shouldn't affect you."

That was true. Gabi lacked the perfection of the goddesses back home, but her imperfections, her uniqueness, only made her more beautiful to Aru.

"Beauty is in the eye of the beholder," Aru said without sparing Negal a glance. "And there is much more to it than physicality. It's the bright soul animating Gabi's body that makes her beautiful."

"If you say so," was the trooper's sarcastic response.

"Your sister is doing very well." On the screen, the doctor turned to look at Gabi's brother, who appeared to be standing, given the angle of the bug's camera. "Her vitals are strong, and her bouts of unconsciousness don't last more than a few hours at a time. You should get some rest, Gilbert."

As relief flooded Aru, he let out a breath. That was good news.

That was excellent news.

"I told you so," Negal murmured from the couch. "She's in good hands."

"I'm not leaving her side." Gabi's brother looked around the room. "Is there a cot I can put in here? I plan on sleeping next to Gabi tonight."

"There should be one somewhere in the clinic. I'll get it for you."

"Thank you," Gilbert said.

As the doctor turned toward the door, Aru leaned over Dagor's shoulder. "Move the bug from the doctor to the brother."

"Are you sure? It's a small room. They might notice it flying over."

The outdated medical equipment in the room was making enough noise to mask the barely perceptible buzz the tiny drone would make as it crossed the short distance between the doctor's shoulder and Gilbert's. The device was smaller than a mosquito, made less noise than one, and was undetectable by human technology because it was mostly biological rather than mechanical.

"Do it," Aru commanded in a tone that brooked no argument.

"Yes, sir." Dagor moved his finger on the laptop pad, and the spy's viewpoint moved accordingly.

The doctor paused at the door. "Did you eat?"

"I didn't." Gilbert put his hand on his stomach. "But that's okay. I could lose an inch or two around the middle."

The doctor cast him an amused look. "I'll tell the guys in security to order us something. Anything in particular you're in the mood for?"

"Whatever you get is fine." The vantage point changed as Gilbert sat back down. "I want to call Orion and ask him to remove the compulsion from Gabi. It wasn't a smart idea to have her remember and forget things depending on where she was. Now, her mind is all scrambled, and she's confused. I hope that no damage was done, and she will go back to normal as soon as Orion removes his compulsion."

That explained so much—the memory lapses and the headaches. But why had they compelled her to forget things?

What were the secrets she held in her mind that she was allowed to remember in some circumstances and not others?

And who was Orion?

Was he a god?

Compulsion was a rare ability, and Aru doubted the immortal descendants of the rebel gods could have inherited that trait. Then again, the Eternal King's children could have gotten it from him and transferred it to their offspring, making these immortal descendants both dangerous and useful. There weren't many compellers left on Anumati, and those who had been sent to remote corners of the galaxy had usually met with one calamity or another.

The doctor frowned. "That worries me. The compulsion should be removed as soon as possible. Call Orion, explain the situation, and have him on standby for when Gabi wakes up again."

"That's precisely what I intend to do."

2

ARU

"I'm taking the laptop to my bedroom." Aru closed the device and lifted it over Dagor's head. "You two can take a rest."

Dagor cast him an amused look. "Are you planning on watching your human in the privacy of your bedroom?"

"You bet." Ignoring the innuendo, Aru tucked the laptop under his arm and headed to his room.

He didn't want his teammates watching Gabi in her vulnerable state, especially when the doctor was doing things that required exposing her.

Besides, he wanted to hear Gilbert's conversation with the mysterious Orion without them present. If Gabi knew important secrets pertaining to the gods and immortals, he wanted to hear them first and then decide whether to share them with Negal and Dagor.

"How is it going, Orion?" Gilbert asked when his call was answered.

Regrettably, Aru couldn't hear what Orion's reply was. The spy bug's receiver was not sensitive enough for that.

"Yeah, I know. The lockdown is maddening. But I'm not in the village. Kian let me out because Gabi is transitioning, and I begged him to let me be with her."

There was a short pause. "She wasn't feeling well and decided to walk over to the pharmacy around the corner from her hotel, but she never made it. She fainted on the way and was taken to a human hospital. Kian sent an extraction team to get her out of there, and we brought her to the keep."

After another short pause, Gilbert continued, "Yeah, we know who induced her, but I don't know if I can tell you. Since you're mated to Alena, and you are also Toven's son, you probably know what's going on, and I don't need to spell it out for you." Gilbert turned around to look at Gabi, giving Aru another glimpse of her before turning his back to her again. "Yeah, that's right. It was one of the gods. Anyway, the reason I'm calling you is your compulsion. It's messing with Gabi's head, and since she's no longer exposed to him and isn't going to be anytime soon or at all, you can release her, at least until she's out of the critical stage of her transition."

Critical stage sounded ominous, and Aru's gut clenched with worry. The doctor had said that she was doing fine, though, and he'd sounded sincere. So perhaps the critical stage didn't refer to how dangerous it was but to how important it was?

"Gilbert?" The sweet sound of Gabi's voice had Aru's heart flutter.

Her brother turned around, giving Aru the gift of seeing her with her eyes open. "Oh, good. You're awake. I thought I would have to call Orion again. Let me transfer the call to video."

Her beautiful eyes widening, Gabi feebly lifted a hand to shield her face. "Don't! I probably look like roadkill. I don't want anyone to see me like this."

Aru laughed. This was so like Gabi. Everyone was worried about her transition while she was fussing about looking presentable on the screen for Orion. Thankfully, Gilbert had said that the guy was mated, or Aru would have gotten jealous, thinking that Gabi wanted to look pretty for the guy.

But wait, did she know that Orion was taken? Perhaps she thought he was single?

"You look lovely even when you're disheveled." Gilbert echoed Aru's thoughts. "Besides, you are transitioning, and no one expects you to look your best."

Gabi frowned. "You keep saying that I'm transitioning. What does that mean?"

She didn't know?

So, Aru wasn't the only one who hadn't heard about Dormants and their ability to transition into immortality with the help of an immortal or a god's essence.

"Talk to Orion. Hopefully, things will make more sense after he does his thing." Gilbert turned his phone screen toward Gabi and activated the speaker.

Regrettably, Aru couldn't see Orion.

"Hello, Gabi," he heard the guy's voice. "I'm sorry about the mess my compulsion created in your head. In hindsight, it wasn't a good idea."

"I know you." She frowned at him. "You were at the dinner in the hotel."

Feeling like an idiot, Aru let out a relieved breath. Gabi could barely remember the guy, and she didn't sound interested in him.

"That's right. You were told things that needed to be kept a secret, but since you were seeing a guy who we suspected of possessing a certain ability, we couldn't let you remember what you'd been told when you had company. That was what created the confusion and eventually made you forget everything, even when there were no strangers around. I'm going to remove the compulsion now, and hopefully, that will clear up the confusion."

If they had suspected that the man Gabi was seeing was not human and could enter her mind, why hadn't they set a trap for him and caught him?

It would have been so easy.

He'd had no idea that she wasn't fully human or that she was related to the people he was searching for.

As it dawned on him that their encounter must have been destined, Aru lifted a hand to his chest. No wonder he felt so strongly about Gabi.

They were fated to be together.

"How are you going to fix that?" Gabi asked Orion.

"Simple. Look into my eyes and focus on the sound of my voice. You can remember everything you've learned about immortals, and you can speak freely about them with anyone. You are not restricted in any way."

Scrunching her nose, Gabi squinted as if she was in pain, but then her eyes grew large, and she lifted a hand to her temple. "Immortality. That's what I'm transitioning into. But how? I didn't have sex with an immortal, did I? Or did you make me forget that as well, and the memory just hasn't come back yet?"

Orion chuckled. "I'll let Gilbert explain. It's one hell of an incredible story, and he has more details than I do. I wish you the best of luck on your transition."

"Thank you." Gabi kept rubbing her temples.

"I'll see you in the village soon," Orion said. "Or so I hope. Goodbye, Gabi."

"Goodbye, and thank you again." She lifted a pair of questioning eyes to her brother.

He put the phone aside. "There is no easy way to do this. Your lover boy is not a human after all. He's a god, and he induced your transition. What I want to know is, what the hell were you thinking having unprotected sex with a guy you'd only just met?"

She arched an indignant brow. "Are you serious? That's what bothers you about this situation? And what do you mean by a god? Do you mean immortal, a descendant of the gods?"

"You were induced by a god. Not an immortal, not a demigod, but a pureblooded god. So was I, though, so you don't have exclusive bragging rights."

What in purgatory's name?

Who had induced Gabi's brother? Other than Aru and his teammates, there were no other gods on Earth.

"Wait a minute." Gabi lifted her hand. "You said that all the gods were dead, and only their immortal descendants remained."

That was precisely what Aru had believed up until a moment ago.

"I didn't say that all the gods were dead." Gilbert waved a hand.

Gabi cast him an accusing look. "I don't remember what you and the others said, but it was implied that there were no gods left on Earth and that only their immortal descendants remained."

Gilbert sighed. "The gods living in the village are our most guarded secret, even more so than the existence of immortals. It's like the Holiest of Holies of secrets. They were supposed to be the only ones, but then Aru and his friends showed up, getting our attention by activating trackers that we knew were of godly origins."

So, there were still gods left on Earth.

But how?

Had they removed their trackers?

Could the heir still be alive?

Hope surged in Aru's chest and then quickly winked out. Perhaps some gods had managed to survive, but it wasn't likely that the heir was one of them.

"How did you know that they were of godly origins?" Gabi asked.

"The history of those trackers is a long story for another day. When we identified the signals, we panicked, and the village went into lockdown. Do you remember that?"

She nodded. "It got so confusing. When I was alone, I remembered what you told me about a clan location that got compromised and that the lockdown was a security measure. Was all of that because of Uriel?" She asked in a whisper that carried a betrayed tone.

"His real name is Aru, and he's not from Portugal. It's just a fake identity he bought. Anyway, a team of our people met with him today, and it seems like his intentions are not hostile, but further talks are needed to ascertain that. He and his friends are very dangerous."

"Why?"

"Because gods are to immortals like immortals are to humans. We are powerless against them. They can get into our minds and thrall us or compel us. Also, they come from a planet of gods who don't hold humans in the highest regard."

"He wasn't condescending with me."

Gabi defending him to her brother brought Aru hope. Perhaps she wasn't angry about the deception and understood why it had been necessary.

"I don't know all the details of what the gods told the team that was sent to meet them, but from what I've heard so far, it seems like they are on our side."

"Good." Gabi rubbed her temple. "I think. Will I be able to see him again?"

She sounded hopeful, which reinforced Aru's belief that she didn't hate him for lying to her. There was still a chance he could salvage what they had.

To what end, though?

He couldn't stay. In a hundred and fifteen years, give or take a few, the patrol ship would return for him, and he would have to leave. But even before that, he couldn't be with her and endanger her and her community by his mere presence.

The tracker in his body made him into a beacon, a pointer, and Gabi's people had to hide not only from their terrestrial enemies but also from the Eternal King.

"It depends on how the talks go," Gilbert said. "If Kian is convinced that Aru's intentions are good, he will not stand in the way of fate."

Gabi arched a brow. "Fate?"

"The Fates, fate, it's all the same thing." Gilbert waved a dismissive hand again. "Do you really think that your flight getting canceled and you getting a first-class ticket and sitting next to a god was all a coincidence?"

She frowned. "No, I guess it wasn't. When do you think I will be allowed to see Uriel? I mean, Aru."

"I don't know." Gilbert took Gabi's hand. "As I said, it's up to Kian and how well the negotiations go."

3

GABI

The cycle of slipping away into unconsciousness, waking up, and then slipping away again wasn't so much scary as it was annoying.

Mostly, it was the unpredictability of it that got to her. She could be in the middle of a sentence and then find herself in the dream world or just drifting away into nothing.

Still, Gabi was grateful to be waking up at all.

According to the doctor, she was luckier than most, and other transitioning Dormants hadn't been as fortunate, spending the entire process unconscious.

Come to think of it, it shouldn't have been too difficult for them because they had been unaware of what was going on, but it must have been hard for those who cared for them and were helpless to do anything other than wait for the process to run its course.

Usually, though, the transitioning Dormants were accompanied by a mate, who worried about them and stayed by their side, sleeping on a cot in their hospital room.

Gabi had Gilbert.

Her eldest brother was the rock in her life, and he would probably remain the only male she could rely on, with her other brother being the runner-up. As far as a romantic partner, though, Gabi had never had one she could rely on.

Dylan was a self-absorbed cheater, others she'd dated hadn't clicked, and Uriel was a damned god who lied to her and whom she would most likely never see again.

"I miss you too," Gilbert whispered into his phone. "Where are you now?"

Gabi tuned him out, giving him privacy to talk to Karen the only way she could, which was by turning inward to the place where her heart ached from Uriel's betrayal.

He'd told her so very little about himself, claiming that he couldn't reveal more because he didn't want to lie to her, but even the little he'd told her had been a lie, including his name.

Why had he lied about that?

He could have told her that his name was Aru. What would it have mattered to her whether he was named Uriel or Aru?

It's not like everyone on the planet knew that there was a god named Aru roaming around, and she would have immediately recognized him by his name.

He wasn't a flea-market flipper either.

What did gods do for a living? Could they conjure gold from thin air?

The gods she'd read about had been worshiped and attended by the humans who revered them, so they didn't need to do anything other than look godly.

The same went for contemporary monarchs. They were figureheads, symbols, and, in a way, modern myths. The British didn't need their monarchs for anything, but the royal family was worshiped almost like deities.

Ugh, her mind was drifting again, and she couldn't even blame the transition for that. Or maybe she could?

Gabi lifted her eyes to the IV bag hanging over her bed. Perhaps they were feeding her relaxants in the IV, and that was why she was feeling so unfocused and scatterbrained.

Bringing her focus back to Uriel, she remembered fondly his offer to avenge her honor. He sounded so sincere when he'd offered to beat up Dylan. In retrospect, though, he'd probably had a different retribution in mind.

What did gods do to humans they didn't like?

Could Uriel summon lightning from the sky like Thor and smite those who incurred his wrath?

Nah, probably not.

Obviously, Uriel and his friends were just aliens who called themselves gods, the same as her ancestors, but she didn't know what powers they had other than mind manipulation.

Perhaps she could ask Gilbert to tell her what he knew about gods after he was done talking to Karen. He'd said that a god had induced his transition, so he must know a thing or two about these aliens.

Oh, crap. Why had he told her that?

That was so bad. If he felt free to tell her about the gods, he didn't expect her to ever see Uriel again.

Now that she was free of Orion's compulsion to forget what she'd been told about immortals, her mind was open to infiltration by immortals and gods, and she would never be allowed to see Aru again.

Hell, she would probably never be allowed to return to Cleveland.

The knowledge she'd gained was too valuable to risk infiltration by aliens or humans who could read minds.

Suddenly, the world seemed like an even scarier place than before. She had to worry not only about bodily harm but also about thought thieves.

Would they at least let her talk to Aru on the phone?

From what she understood about thralling, he couldn't peek into her mind unless he was physically next to her. But would they trust her to keep her mouth shut about what she knew?

Probably not.

So that was it. Instead of a child, Uriel's parting gift to her had been immortality. Not bad as a consolation prize, except Gabi didn't feel like a winner.

Too weak to fight the tears, she let them stream down her cheeks.

Gabi wasn't a pretty crier, but down in the clan's underground clinic, there was no one to see her and pass judgment.

Gilbert was there, but it wouldn't be the first time he'd seen her falling apart. In fact, he'd seen her in a much worse condition after she'd gotten proof of Dylan's infidelity.

Somehow sensing that she was distressed, Gilbert turned around and looked at her. "I gotta go," he told Karen. "I'll call you later." He ended the call and got up. "What's wrong? Why are you crying?"

"It's nothing. I hate being weak and sick, and that's how I feel now."

He arched a brow. "You know that I can always tell when you're lying. Out with it, Gabi."

There was no point in resisting because he would just keep on pushing.

"Now that you've told me about the gods, I can never see Uriel again. I can't even say goodbye to him over the phone because I might inadvertently blurt something out."

"Oh, sweetheart." He sat on the bed beside her and took her hand. "Orion is available whenever you need him, at least as long as the lockdown is in effect, and if you ask him, he can compel you again to forget what you've learned."

She lifted her hand to her temple. "But his compulsion is messing with my head. I don't want my brain to turn to mush."

Gilbert smiled. "And yet I can see that your mood has improved, which means that you like having the option, and you're considering it."

"Well, yes, of course. It's a door that was closed before and is now open if I wish to step through it. But I hope it can be done better so it's less bothersome to my mind. Maybe Orion can just make me forget about the gods. Uriel already knows about immortals, right? So that's no longer a secret, and I don't mind not knowing about the gods at all."

"I guess so." Gilbert shifted his position to get more comfortable on the sliver of space he'd claimed on her bed. "I'm not privy to the details of their talks. You and I will have to wait until we are told, and I don't know when that will be."

"Can't you ask? Perhaps Julian knows more?"

Gilbert leaned closer and kissed Gabi's forehead. "You can ask him yourself the next time he checks on you."

She shifted sideways to make more room for her brother. "Can you do me a favor and call Orion now? I want to forget about the gods."

Gilbert patted her hand. "There is no rush. We will worry about it when meeting Orion in person becomes an option."

4

ANNANI

Annani surveyed the somber faces of her family and let out a sigh. "We are gathered around the dining table, surrounded by our loved ones, and being served a delicious dinner by our dear Odus. We should treasure these precious moments with family and friends and not let outside worries ruin them, or we will never get to enjoy ourselves." She smiled. "Life is full of challenges, and that is never going to change."

The news Kian had delivered about the Eternal King and the future of Earth was far from encouraging, but nothing was imminent, and they had plenty of time to prepare. The grace period of one hundred and fifteen years might be a blink of an eye for the gods, but it was an eternity for humans. The technological advancements of the last century were staggering, and with the help of artificial intelligence, progress would be exponential. By the time the team of newly arrived gods had to report their findings, a solution might present itself.

Her grandfather might send a new plague to cull the number of humans and halt their technological progress, but Annani believed that Kian was right about their ability to make humans immune to disease and maybe even make them immortal. Doing so might introduce new problems that would have to be solved, but that was a worry for another day.

Amanda's lips twisted in a grimace. "It's hard to be joyful after hearing that Earth's population is in danger from none other than my great-grandfather." She shivered. "I always believed myself to be good, but with his genes inside of me, I'm no longer sure that I am." She turned to Dalhu. "I felt the call of darkness once, the need to rage and destroy. Fortunately, I didn't have the means to do damage, but what if I had? Would I have destroyed the world in my grief and anger? What if that darkness is still hiding inside of me, waiting to emerge in response to a strong enough trigger?"

When Amanda had lost her young son to a tragic horseback-riding accident, Annani had sensed that darkness threatening to consume her daughter—its toxic allure sadly all too familiar. But she knew that she had raised Amanda and her other children to resist the lure of darkness and cling to the light with all their might, and she had trusted that her teachings would hold even in the face of such incredible tragedy and pain.

As sweet as the call of the dark side was, it was a trap, and one step too many into its hot embrace could be the point of no return.

Dalhu put his hand on Amanda's shoulder. "Your great-grandfather is not necessarily evil. He's brilliant and pragmatic and does what he thinks is best for his people. I wouldn't have minded having his blood running in my veins instead of the blood of the hoodlum my mother was forced to breed with."

Amanda's eyes softened. "Oh, darling. Thank you for reminding me that we are more than our genetics and that we always have a choice."

Toven, however, did not look encouraged by Dalhu's words, and his somber expression had not abated. "Even if we manage to make all humans immune to disease or immortal, we won't be able to save humankind. Once the Eternal King realizes that a pathogen his scientists have introduced hasn't worked, and humans haven't been infected by his plague, he will order a different way of culling the population, which will be no less devastating. Probably more so."

As silence stretched across the table, Annani searched for a rebuttal to Toven's grim prediction, but nothing came to mind. Humans, along with the immortals living alongside them, were no match for the might of the gods.

"Our only hope is the rebellion," Syssi said. "The king needs to be replaced with someone who sympathizes with the created species." She turned her gaze to Annani. "I happen to know his legitimate heir, and she is a big-time sympathizer."

Annani laughed. "Are you suggesting that I take the throne and become the queen of the gods?"

"Why not? The original rebels wanted to make your father the king. If they knew of your existence, the new rebels would choose you. You'll make a wonderful queen."

Annani had been groomed to take the throne, and as a young goddess, she had been ready to ascend if and when her father chose to step down, but she was not the same goddess she had been then, and she had no wish to rule anyone—not even her clan. She would not mind being a figurehead and being worshiped and admired, but she would leave the day-to-day affairs of the throne to others who were better suited for the job.

"I do not wish to rule the planet of the gods, but even if I did, it is not feasible. Not now, not in the near future, and probably not ever." She turned to Kian. "Aru said that the rebellion is thousands of years in the making and has many more thousands to go before it is ready. We do not have that long. We need to come up with a solution and implement it within the next century."

Kian shrugged. "Maybe we don't. As long as humans do not possess interstellar travel capability, the Eternal King will not deem them a threat. Perhaps all we need to do is ensure that they never get to that point. Besides, the Eternal King is not in a rush to do anything. He moves in godly time, and until he turns his sights on Earth, the natural shrinkage in human population due to declining birthrates might be enough for him to leave humans alone."

Toven reached for Mia's hand. "If the Perfect Match adventure the AI designed for us was a hint from the Fates, then in five hundred years, the human population will have shrunk in size to what it was when the original rebels were exiled to Earth, and a new crop of gods will arrive to once again rule over humans."

5

ARU

"Have you learned anything new?" Dagor asked as Aru handed him the laptop.

He'd spent the evening of the day before, most of the prior night, and into the early morning watching Gabi through the little spy's eyes. She'd been unconscious for many hours, but when she'd woken up, she'd talked with her brother and the doctor, and Aru had gotten to eavesdrop on their conversations.

He'd learned quite a lot, but he wasn't about to share it with his teammates.

"I've learned a few things, but none of them are of much use to us. There were several mentions of a village, which is what they call the place they live in, and along with it, talk about a lockdown, which was done in response to our arrival. As soon as they identified the signals, they panicked."

As Negal unlocked their car, the three of them got in, with Negal behind the wheel, Aru on the passenger side, and Dagor in the back.

Magnus hadn't sent them the location pin yet, but thanks to the spy drone and what they had learned from listening to the feed, they knew where Gabi had been taken and that the meeting with the immortals' leader would take place in the same downtown location.

Scoping the area and the building itself was standard protocol.

They couldn't get inside, though, because thralling and shrouding were not going to work on the security cameras or the people watching the feed, but their little drone spies could be their eyes and ears and get into places they probably couldn't.

Most standard doors were not precisely fitted, and the bugs could pass under or above them. Anywhere a mosquito or an ant could go, their spy drones could go as well.

"I wonder if Jade and the other Kra-ell reside in the same village," Negal said.

"It would seem so." Aru turned around to look at Dagor. "Do you need the laptop, or can I use it until we get to the building?"

Rolling his eyes, Dagor closed the device. "You checked on her less than five minutes ago. Nothing has changed since then."

"You never know." Aru flipped the laptop open and brought up the feed from the clinic.

True to his promise, Gilbert hadn't left Gabi's side except to use the bathroom. During those brief breaks, Aru had muted the feed and busied himself with watching television to respect the brother's privacy until the guy was done with his business.

Thankfully, Gilbert hadn't showered or changed his clothing, so there had been no need to maneuver the bug. By now, the drone was running low on energy, and having it fly would drain what was left.

Aru would be lucky if the thing kept transmitting for a couple more hours.

They could attach new drones to their hosts, but Aru didn't want to push his luck. Security around the leader would be much tighter than it had been during the meeting in the canyon, and he wouldn't be surprised if they got strip-searched.

It hadn't been an easy decision to forgo bringing more bugs to the meeting with the leader, and as Aru had debated the pros and cons, he was well aware of what would happen if he lost contact with Gabi.

It was much worse than attaching spy drones to these immortals.

He was a god, and if pushed, he would use his mind powers over them.

No, diplomacy was always a better solution, and he would have to negotiate something with the clan's leader. The problem with that was having to admit that he knew they had Gabi. It would force him to also reveal the truth about the spy drone he'd attached to Magnus.

As hard as Aru tried to come up with a convincing lie about how he'd learned about Gabi's transition, he couldn't come up with one.

It had occurred to him that he could claim to have attached the drone to Gabi to make sure that she was unharmed when he wasn't with her, but in a way, it was worse than admitting he had attached the spy bug to Magnus.

The leader would be more understanding about the bug than she would, and rightfully so. Attaching the drone to Magnus wasn't personal. It was a strategically smart move. Attaching it to Gabi would have been an invasion of her privacy.

Come to think of it, Aru was crossing the line by monitoring her as it was.

"You still didn't tell us what you hope to get from them," Negal said. "We know now that the Kra-ell are not dead, and we know who took them. The question is what we tell the commander. We can't tell him about the immortals because our communications with the ship are recorded, and he will have no choice but to report our findings to head-quarters."

"I'm glad that you arrived at the same conclusion I did." Just then, Gilbert turned to look at Gabi, and Aru got a glimpse of her sleeping face. "We will report that there was an uprising and that Gor and some of his males were taken out by the others."

Negal nodded. "You know what the problem with that is. We will need to report their new location, and that's where the immortals live. The Kra-ell will have to find a different place to settle."

"I know." Aru sighed. "Which is a shame. I love the idea of the Kra-ell and the immortal descendants of the gods living together in harmony and mutual respect. Also, Jade has an immortal mate, and she might not be the only one. Separating the two groups is going to be tough even though they haven't been integrated for long."

Aru hadn't told Dagor and Negal about the gods who also resided in the same location, and he didn't intend to, not because he didn't trust them, but because the less they knew, the safer the secret was.

6

KIAN

"Thank the merciful Fates for air conditioning." Anandur patted his light suit jacket. "Covering up the arsenal I have on me would have been miserable without it." He opened the limo door for Kian.

Surprisingly, Brundar nodded in agreement. Like his brother, he was armed to the teeth and covered it with a suit jacket.

Okidu was behind the wheel, and Turner followed Kian into the back of the limo. "Wasn't Onidu supposed to join us as well?" he asked.

"I decided against it." Kian leaned back in the seat. "I don't want the gods to think I'm bringing the Odus as part of my security detail. I want them to see Okidu in his primary function as my butler. If I brought Onidu as well, it would be obvious that their presence is about providing protection." He smiled at the brothers. "With Brundar and Anandur assuming their tough guy personas, they will be my obvious and only bodyguards."

Turner was former special ops, and if needed, Kian had no doubt the guy would rise to the occasion and fight alongside him and the brothers, but he was short and didn't look physically intimidating, so the gods would accept that he wasn't part of Kian's security detail.

Turner shrugged. "We could have pretended that Onidu is my butler."

"We could have," Kian agreed. "But I really don't expect any trouble from these gods. What worries me is the might they represent."

Turner cast him a questioning look. "Aren't you concerned with how easily they agreed to meet you on your turf? They will be walking into a building that they know is under your control, and the fact that they are okay with that troubles me. They might have something up their proverbial sleeve."

That had occurred to Kian, and he had taken all the necessary precautions. Guardians had been in place since morning, fortified by a group of young Kra-ell males who had already received basic training and had been vetted by Bhathian as ready to assist.

"The gods owe us. The first meeting was on their turf, and we assumed the risk by walking in without knowing what to expect. On the other hand, they have already met our people and can be reasonably assured that we mean them no harm."

"These gods have trackers in them." Forgetting about all the weapons he had strapped on, Anandur crossed his arms over his chest. That must have made him uncomfortable because he winced and uncrossed his arms. "Which means that their shipmates and the Eternal King know where they are at all times, and after this meeting, they will all know where the keep is as well."

"Regrettably, the keep is already lost to us as a strategic location," Kian said. "It's compromised beyond salvation, so meeting the gods there will not make it any worse."

"I wonder if we can remove the trackers from these gods." Turner crossed his legs at the ankles.

Kian cast him a curious look. "Don't you think they would have done it themselves if they could?"

"They probably can't, and I wonder whether they'll be interested in getting rid of them. How are they supposed to start an uprising when their location is always known?"

Kian shook his head. "If the king knows everyone's movements and whereabouts, it's next to impossible. I can't imagine living with no privacy like that. They can't do anything without someone knowing about it. They can't meet people in secret because everyone is being tracked, and they can't make contraband purchases because they use credits for transactions. It's so easy to program artificial intelligence to analyze the data from the trackers and from the purchase history and flag anything that might indicate rebellious behavior."

Turner nodded. "I have no idea how they manage the resistance and recruit new people."

"You've heard Aru." Kian let out a sigh. "Snail's pace is fast compared to how they are progressing. The rebellion is thousands of years in the making, and it will take many thousands more until they are ready to act. The problem is that we might not have that long until the Eternal King learns about the progress of humans and decides to curtail it."

Yesterday, Kian had told his mother and the rest of the family that the king was likely to move slowly and that he might wait patiently for the size of the human population to shrink naturally. It hadn't been a lie, but it was one of many possible scenarios, and Kian had given it voice mainly to ease their minds.

"Aru could have made it up," Anandur said. "Humans don't pose a threat to the Eternal King's hegemony, and they won't even once they gain interstellar travel capability. I don't see any reason for him to bother with them."

It was no surprise that Anandur had echoed Kian's thoughts. After being his bodyguard for millennia, the guy had learned a thing or two about how Kian's mind worked. But Anandur was an optimist, while Kian was a pessimist.

The best scenario did not always play out, and they needed to be ready for the more pessimistic possibilities.

If eleven thousand years ago the king had thought that the few hundred thousand humans on Earth were a threat, he would surely deem the eight billion of them a threat now.

Kian had no proof that the Eternal King had been responsible for the flood, but if the myths surrounding the disaster were true, then the king was definitely the prime suspect.

The gods had seeded Earth and jumpstarted the human population. They had been involved in human affairs long before the group of rebels had been exiled to Earth. It wasn't a stretch to assume that the vengeful god of myths who had ordered the flood had been none other than the Eternal King or his heir, whom the king had sent to implement the culling.

Reaching into his pocket, Kian pulled out a pair of new earpieces and offered them to Turner. "I want you to put them on."

"Why? I'm immune, and these gods don't seem to have compulsion ability."

"We don't know that for sure." Kian put the devices in Turner's hand. "We don't know if these gods are compellers because they didn't try to compel our teammates. And if they are compellers, or one of them is, we don't know whether or not you are immune to that particular compulsion style. We have plenty of examples that immunity is not universally applicable, nor is compulsion. Some people can be immune to one compeller but not the other, and I always prefer to err on the side of caution."

The truth was that the earpieces were most likely useless because the gods could thrall them, and thralling didn't require sound. The gods could reach straight into immortals' minds.

"I was thinking," Anandur said. "If we take the trackers out of Aru and his teammates, we will have to implant them in animals. Otherwise, their comrades on the patrol ship will think that they are dead and come to investigate. But those animals have to be long-lived, or we will have to keep transplanting them. Large turtles can live for up to five hundred years, so they would be perfect for that." He looked at Turner. "Any idea where we can get some? Other than the zoo, that is." He chuckled. "Imagine the headlines." Anandur lifted his hands, shaping quotation marks. "Three Large Turtles Escape From the Zoo. Authorities in a Slow-Motion Pursuit! Or how about this one? Three Massive Turtles Make a Slow Getaway."

Kian laughed. "I have one. Three Turtles Execute Slowest Zoo Heist in History. Security Two Steps Behind!"

Anandur lifted a finger. "I have a winner. Zoo Turtles Make a 'Speedy' Getaway. Authorities Hope to Catch Up by Next Friday!"

Clearing his throat, Turner offered with a straight face, "Breaking news: Three Turtles Escape a High-Security Zoo. Expected to Cross State Line in Six Months."

As the three of them laughed, Kian was thankful to Anandur for defusing the stressful atmosphere and lifting their spirits. Turning to Brundar, he asked, "Any headlines come to mind?"

The Guardian turned around and treated Kian to an icy look. "No."

The answer only made the three of them laugh harder, and even Okidu emitted a few chortles from behind the wheel.

7

ARU

"So far, everyone seems to be human." Dagor watched the six squares representing the six drones they had sent flying into the building. "We should collect them when we get in."

They had to be frugal with the little spies.

The case of drones they had arrived with was down to sixty-seven out of the original one hundred, and since they couldn't replenish their supplies, they had to be careful with how they used the remainder of the drones and reuse as many as they could.

Once the little bugs ran out of juice, there was no way to retrieve them. They just stopped broadcasting, and their location was lost.

Aru nodded. "There are too many floors with too many apartments in the building for us to check each one. We know that they have it well monitored, and the security guards in the lobby look like they know what they are doing. Other than that, we will have to trust that their intentions are as peaceful as ours and that they mean us no harm."

Negal snorted. "Even if they are wonderful people with the best intentions at heart, it's in their best interest to get rid of us. Naturally, that would prompt an investigation from our ship, but thanks to you, they now know that it will be a long time before that happens."

The accusation was not completely baseless, but it didn't have as much merit as Negal believed it had. It wasn't a big deal that Aru had told the immortals about the patrol ship's schedule. Their time horizon was not human, and it didn't make much difference to them if the expected retribution was in a year or a hundred years. They would still take it into consideration.

"We are safe." Aru's phone pinged with the pin Magnus had sent him. "These immortals are not stupid, and they are still going to be around when the patrol ship returns. They know that if we are gone, teams will land on Earth to investigate, and they would be much less friendly than we are, especially if they have reason to believe that we were murdered. Also, we have valuable information that they want about Anumati and the Eternal King's motives and machinations. In addition, I will come up with more reasons for why they need to not only keep us alive but also to stay in our good graces."

"How?" Dagor closed the laptop.

"I don't know yet," Aru admitted. "I'll think of something."

Dagor groaned. "We are doomed."

"Should I drive up to the valet?" Negal asked. "Or should I wait a few minutes to make it seem like we weren't parked a block away from the building?"

"We are expected to show up in twenty minutes, and I don't want us to arrive more than five minutes ahead of time. When we get there, stop a few meters from the building. We need to collect the six drones and leave them in the car before we pull up to the valet."

The only spy drone remaining would be the one monitoring Gabi.

"Got it." Negal checked the time. "That gives us ten minutes to brainstorm what we are going to tell these descendants to incentivize them to keep us alive."

"Your human might be useful," Dagor said. "Since she's apparently a descendant, once she transitions, she will become part of their community. She can claim you as her mate, and therefore guarantee your safety. The problem is that it doesn't help Negal and me."

"As long as one of us is alive, the descendants are in danger, so if Gabi claims me as hers and that offers me immunity, they will have no reason to eliminate you. But I really don't think that we need any additional guarantees. I also don't think that Gabi claiming me as her mate protects me."

519

Besides, she might not want to have anything to do with him, let alone claim him as hers.

"It's an old Kra-ell custom," Negal said. "And it might be our old custom as well, so the descendants might have adopted it from their godly ancestors."

"Even if they do, I will not use Gabi like that. She has enough reasons to resent me as it is. I don't want to add fuel to her ire and guarantee that she never chooses me as her mate."

"Don't worry." Negal waved a dismissive hand. "Females are more forgiving than males. You can sweet talk her into accepting you with open arms."

"I wish I shared your confidence."

In the backseat, Dagor sighed. "Nothing stands in the way of the Fates' plans, and if they decree that you belong with each other, you do."

Negal snorted. "Since when do you believe in that romantic nonsense? I thought you were smarter than that. The fated mates story is a classic example of the Eternal King's propaganda."

Even Aru had to raise a brow at that. "How could the king benefit from promoting a story like that?"

"Simple." Negal crossed his arms over his chest. "It's so self-explanatory that I wonder how the two of you haven't figured it out yet. Fated mates are supposed to be rare, and finding your one and only is supposed to be the greatest gift imaginable, and it's offered only to those who have suffered great hardship or sacrificed a lot for others. That's the perfect combination to incentivize young gods to journey to faraway crappy settlements in the hopes of being rewarded with a truelove mate."

Aru shook his head. "The king doesn't need to incentivize that because we don't have much choice in the matter. We are drafted, and we go where we are sent. Searching for truelove mates might be a nice perk, but it's not like the king needs to sell us on the service. It's mandatory."

"Oh, but he does." Negal smiled. "That's precisely how the king operates. There is always a carrot along with the whip, a perk to soften the hardship so he can maintain his benevolent façade of the almighty father, the shepherd of us all."

Aru had to admit that Negal was onto something, but the myths about fated mates were so old that they even predated the king.

"I have no love lost for the Eternal King, but in this case, I don't think he invented that story. I personally know couples who are truelove mates."

Negal arched a brow. "Give me one example?"

"My parents."

The trooper laughed. "Is that what they told you?"

"They did, but I would have known that even if they hadn't. Their love is evident in every word and look they exchange, and they are loyal to each other. Gods in arranged marriages play around, and they don't even try to hide it. Having multiple lovers is not only common practice, but it is a reason to brag."

"And you know for sure that your parents don't play around?" Negal chuckled. "The young are so naive. Your parents are stationed on a faraway outpost, and your only contact with them is via holo-calls. You haven't visited them in many cycles, and you have no idea what they are up to."

"That's true, but I know what I know, and you are not going to make me doubt it. Once you see true love, you can't mistake it for anything else."

Looking amused, Negal shrugged. "If you say so. So, tell me, is your transitioning human your truelove mate?"

"She might be."

8

KIAN

On the laptop screen, Kian watched his three guests shaking hands with Magnus in the lobby.

Without the hardhats and the glasses, they looked like gods, and yet they didn't. They were not luminous, but they could be suppressing their natural glow. Still, their features, although perfect, were not as striking as Annani's or Toven's.

Could it be that the royal family had been gifted with rare genes to make them more beautiful than the common gods?

In a society of genetic experts, it made sense that the more prominent members ensured better genetics for their offspring. Then again, if the Eternal King didn't wish to create competition for himself, he shouldn't have ensured his offspring's superiority. Although, given the way he operated and his keen awareness of public opinion, he would make them as beautiful and as physically perfect as Anumati's scientists could craft them, but he wouldn't enhance their intelligence or their leadership skills.

Except, it didn't look like he had done that either.

Toven, who was the king's grandson, wasn't a leader, but he was smart, and Annani lacked neither smarts nor leadership skills.

What she lacked was the will to lead. She was satisfied with being loved and worshiped, and she was perfectly content to let Kian and Sari lead in all the ways that mattered.

Her father, though, had been smart, politically savvy, and hadn't shied away from leadership, so either the Eternal King hadn't thought to alter those genes in his heir, or maybe those weren't the types of things that genes could be coded for.

Not everything was biological. Free will had to play a role.

"I'm a little underwhelmed." Turner looked at the laptop screen. "I expected to be awed."

"Maybe they are more impressive in person." Kian got to his feet and walked over to the bar. "Anyone care for a drink?"

"I'll wait for our guests." Turner glanced at Okidu. "Is your butler going to open the door?"

Kian smirked. "That's the plan. I can't wait to see their expressions when they encounter him for the first time." He poured himself a shot of whiskey and returned to the couch.

On the screen of his laptop, he watched as the elevator doors opened on the penthouse level, and the three gods followed Magnus out.

"You can open the door, Okidu. Our guests have arrived."

"Yes, master." The Odu bowed before rushing to the door.

Behind Kian, Anandur and Brundar got in position.

Turner leaned over to look at the screen. "Do you think they will be disappointed that Jade and Morgada are not here?"

Kian shook his head. "They want to see me, not the Kra-ell."

"Good afternoon, masters." Okidu bowed at the open door.

"Impossible," he heard one of the gods hiss. "You are not supposed to exist."

"My apologies for existing, master," Okidu said. "Please, come in. Master Kian is awaiting you."

"Thank you." Aru earned points with Kian for thanking Okidu and not treating him like a machine.

He rose to his feet and offered the god his hand. "Welcome to my home, Aru. My name is Kian."

"Nice place you've got here."

The god's handshake was firm but not overly so, and he was much more impressive in person than on the screen. His face was the sculpted

523

perfection of male beauty, but he still wasn't in the same league as Annani or Toven.

"These are my teammates. Negal and Dagor," Aru introduced his friends, who were each model-perfect in their own way, but again, not in the same league as his mother and her cousin.

It kind of made sense that in a society of millions, or perhaps billions, not everyone was as perfectly made as the elite. Variation was needed, and Kian wondered whether they had artists who specialized in creating perfect genetic models.

"It's a pleasure to meet you." Kian motioned for Turner to come forward. "This is my good friend and advisor, Victor Turner."

Surrounded by four tall males, Turner had to look up, but that didn't affect his confidence. The power of his personality and his intelligence more than compensated for that.

After shaking Turner's hand, Aru shifted his gaze to the brothers. "Hello." He smiled at them.

Anandur returned his smile. "I'm Anandur, and this is my brother, Brundar."

Brundar nodded.

Aru's eyes darted around the room until they landed on Okidu. "How did you obtain an Odu? I thought that all of them were decommissioned. Did the rebels smuggle it onboard their ship?"

Aru had just lost points for calling Okidu 'it.'

"Okidu is a 'he' and sometimes a 'she,' but never an 'it,' and the rebels didn't bring any Odus with them. Someone sent the Odus to Earth. They crash landed and wandered the desert until they were found by one of the gods. They have served my family through many generations."

Aru's eyes widened. "So, there are more of them on Earth?"

"Yes." Kian didn't provide a number. "Regrettably, their memories were either wiped or lost because of the crash landing, and they couldn't tell us anything about their creators. We only learned about their fate when we rescued Jade, and she told us their story. They were used, abused, and then used again as scapegoats."

9

ARU

It was obvious to Aru that the leader of the immortals cared for the Odu, even though he treated him as a servant, and Aru had made a mistake by referring to the Odu as 'it.'

Could he blame it on faulty translation?

Pronouns in his native language were different, and there were many ways to refer to a person, some gender-specific and some gender-neutral. The gender-neutral ones were actually considered more formal and respectful, and gender-specific addresses were reserved for one's close friends and family.

Except, Aru had referred to the Odu as 'it' precisely for the reason Kian had thought he had, and lying about it would only make him uncomfortable.

Aru nodded. "I couldn't agree more, but just so you know, most people on Anumati were brainwashed to believe that the Odus were monstrosities. That was what I was taught, and that was what the historical records claim. So even now, knowing that most of what we were told did not happen the way it was presented, I can't help the instinctive, negative, fearful response that was programmed into me."

Kian's harsh expression softened. "I understand. Jade told us about the pervasive propaganda that is meant to show the Eternal King in the best light possible and explain his actions as necessary no matter how monstrous they might be." He motioned toward the couch. "Please, take a seat."

The gesture implied that he wanted all three of them on the couch, which was fine with Aru. Taking the middle seat, he waited for Negal and Dagor to flank him.

"Can I offer you gentlemen a drink? I have many fine whiskeys to choose from."

Aru smiled. "I'd prefer beer if you don't mind."

"Of course." The twinkle in Kian's eyes didn't bode well, and Aru wondered what the leader was plotting.

Poisoning by beer?

"I'll join you." Kian sat on one of the armchairs and waved the Odu over. "Beers all around, please."

The advisor sat on the other armchair, and Magnus pulled up a chair that he'd removed from the dining table. The two bodyguards remained standing.

The Odu bowed. "Of course, master. Should I bring a plate of appetizers along with the beers?"

"That's a great idea. Beers first, though. I don't want our guests to be thirsty."

"Right away, master." The Odu bowed again, turned on his heel, and walked over to the bar.

As Aru contemplated how to start the conversation, a long moment of awkward silence ensued. He hadn't formed an opinion about Kian yet or his silent advisor. He had taken an immediate liking to the big redheaded bodyguard and was wary of his blond brother.

The blond with the icy eyes had a lethal aura that was like a big warning sign—'don't mess with my boss, or you'll regret it.'

Aru had a feeling that the guy would be a challenge even for an enhanced god's strength and agility.

When the Odu returned with a case of six beers, Aru arched a brow. "Only six?"

"Anandur and Brundar are on duty," Kian said. "And they don't drink while guarding me. Okidu doesn't drink either."

"Okidu? Do you mean the Odu?"

"That's his name." Kian waved at the beer Aru was holding. "Go ahead. Take a sip. This is a very special beer. It packs a punch."

"Snake Venom," Aru read the label. "67.5% ABV. No wonder it packs a punch."

The drink tasted awful, and Aru did his best not to grimace. Putting the bottle down, he glanced in the direction of the kitchen, hoping the Odu would hurry up with the appetizer plate so he could bite into something that would wash away the taste.

Kian arched a brow. "What's the matter? You don't like the beer?"

"I don't wish to offend, but I'm not a fan."

"It's not bad," Negal said. "After the first few gulps, you get used to the taste. It reminds me of some of the beers back home." He sighed. "It makes me nostalgic."

Kian was still watching Aru with interest in his penetrating blue eyes. "What do you usually drink?"

"I prefer light beers and cocktails that are favored by the ladies." What was the drink that Gabi had introduced him to? It was delicious. Aru smiled sheepishly. "I drink for the taste, not for the alcohol. I don't like being inebriated."

"You like being in control." Kian was still staring him in the eyes.

Was it a competition? Was he supposed to look away?

Some cultures deemed it disrespectful to look a high-ranking person in the eyes.

"I like my mind to operate on all cylinders, as the humans like to say. I'm out of my element here, and I need all my faculties. I'm not much of a diplomat, and I don't know your customs, so if I do or say something that you consider offensive, please let me know so I don't repeat it."

Kian frowned. "Other than referring to Okidu as an object, you were perfectly polite. I don't consider you not liking my beer offensive."

"That's good to know." Aru let out a breath. "How about this staring competition? Am I supposed to look away? What are the rules?"

Kian laughed. "No, you aren't. It might have appeared as if I was staring you down, and I apologize if it made you uncomfortable, but I was just fascinated by you. You look more like an immortal than a god."

That was a fantastic slip of the tongue that Aru could have used to confront Kian about the gods living in his village of immortals, but he didn't want to do that in front of Negal and Dagor.

"And you look more like a god than an immortal."

Kian chuckled. "I'm far from perfect."

"You look quite perfect to me. I can't point out even one imperfection."

"Oh, gosh," said the redhead standing guard behind Kian's chair, in a mocking tone. "Do you two want to continue your bromance in private?"

Kian turned around. "Really, Anandur? You couldn't help yourself for once?"

The redhead affected an apologetic expression and shrugged. "Sorry, boss. I'll keep my mouth shut from now on."

"Right." Kian let out a long-suffering sigh. "I apologize for my associate. He enjoys turning everything into a joke."

"No apologies needed." Aru looked up at the guard. "We were practically asking for it, and I welcome a joke or a humorous comment whenever the situation calls for it." He smiled at the redhead, who didn't seem apologetic at all. "You have a gift, Anandur. You make people smile."

10

KIAN

Anandur beamed at the god. "That's a male with a good sense of humor. You are my kind of guy, Aru."

Brundar groaned. "There will be no stopping him now. We will have to suffer through his infantile jokes for the rest of the afternoon."

Kian rolled his eyes. "Way to impress our guests, guys. Now they think that we are running a clown operation."

Across from him, Aru grinned. "On the contrary. Seeing how free your men feel to goof around with you tells me a lot about your leadership style. It reinforces Jade's favorable impression. Her vouching for you means that she trusts you, and after what she's been through, I bet that it's not been easy to earn her trust."

Aru claimed not to be much of a diplomat, but he was better at it than Kian. Despite Kian's wariness and mistrust of his three guests, he couldn't help but like Aru, and it had a lot to do with the compliments the guy was showering on him.

Also, he didn't act like a god.

The only two examples of godly behavior Kian had been exposed to were Annani and Toven. His mother was a diva with a personality a hundred times bigger than her petite frame, and Toven was aloof and condescending without meaning to be. It was just the way he was.

Aru, on the other hand, was a nice guy without the inflated ego Kian had expected a god to have. Appearances might be misleading, but Kian's gut was rarely wrong. It might be off a little, but he'd never completely misjudged a person.

Aru's companions weren't afraid of him, and they afforded him only the barest of deference, which meant that his style of leadership was similar to Kian's.

No wonder Aru appreciated it. It echoed his own.

"I have to admit that Jade has grown on me." Kian took a swig of his beer. "Listening to her former tribe members' descriptions of her, I had expected a tyrant with no regard for her people's feelings, but when I met her, I changed my mind. She's made mistakes in the past, of which she's aware, and she is doing her best to guide the future of her people. She's honorable, capable, and trustworthy."

"How about the rest of the Kra-ell?" Aru asked. "How are they getting along with your people?"

"We are still learning to live with each other, and we are all making an effort to accommodate our differences. The Kra-ell are doing their best to assimilate the social etiquette that is accepted in the West, and my people are learning to be patient and accept that it's going to take a while. So far, the integration is going better than I expected." He smiled. "People are people no matter where they come from and what their customs are. We all want the same things in life, and the same is true for the Kra-ell."

"You give me hope." Aru put a hand over his chest. "If the descendants of the gods can coexist with the Kra-ell in peace and harmony and collaboration, then there is hope for Anumati to one day achieve that utopian state as well."

Kian tilted his head. "It's not the same. My people and I did not have preconceived notions about the Kra-ell's inferiority or an ingrained mistrust and animosity towards them. Also, the vast majority of the Kra-ell we welcomed into our community were born on Earth, either to two purebloooded parents or a pureblood and a human." He observed the change in Aru's expression and was glad to see surprise but not horror. "Igor was a vile creature, and I hesitate to attribute anything good to him, but thanks to his resolve to create a new kind of Kra-ell community, they weren't exposed to negative talk about the gods and what happened on Anumati. In a way, it was a fresh start for both of our peoples with only a handful of preconceived notions. That's not the case on the gods' home planet, especially for the old gods who had held on to those beliefs forever."

Aru frowned. "Are you suggesting that we shouldn't try to change things on our home world and should start anew somewhere else in the galaxy?"

Kian shook his head. "I know next to nothing about the politics and socioeconomics of Anumati, so I'm not qualified to make suggestions. It was just a thought."

He wondered whether he should bring up Gabi and her transition. The god had no way of knowing that his lover was a Dormant and that he had inadvertently induced her transition. If he knew, he would have seemed much more worried. Then again, perhaps Aru didn't care about Gabi as much as she cared about him.

"I appreciate your candor." Aru took a cube of cheese off the tray Okidu had brought and popped it into his mouth. When he was done chewing, he looked at Kian. "It's food for thought, but the people of Anumati deserve better, and the grassroots movement that started there is growing by the day. Eventually, there will be so many of us that the king will have no choice but to bow to our demands and become nothing more than a figurehead, step down, or be removed."

"How populous is Anumati?" Kian asked.

For some reason, he hadn't asked Jade that question. Maybe because it had never occurred to him that his ancestral world could become a threat to him and his people.

"It's very populous compared to Earth. There are over three trillion gods residing on Anumati and about one trillion Kra-ell. And then there are the colonies, which probably quadruple that number, and that does not include all the created species."

Kian couldn't comprehend a planet with such a vast population. How could they produce enough food to feed everyone?

"How large is Anumati?" he asked.

"Large." Negal spoke his first word since they had exchanged greetings. "It's about a thousand times larger than Earth."

"That explains it." Kian took a long swig of his beer. "I wondered how they fed all those people."

Aru nodded. "Many gods choose to go into stasis for prolonged periods. We have a labyrinth of deep underground structures that are built under the cities. They are filled with pods that are preprogrammed to wake their occupants at predetermined times."

What Aru had described evoked thoughts of the clan's crypt and human cemeteries. The gods' stasis structures were the equivalent of those.

"Fascinating," Turner said. "What percentage of your population chooses to hibernate?"

"Currently, the rate is about fifteen percent at any given time, but demand for pods is growing. The Kra-ell don't take part in this trend, though, in part because the service is costly and most cannot afford it, and in part because their lifespans are short. They don't get bored with their lives like we do."

"I wish there was a documentary about Anumati we could watch," Anandur said. "It would be easier for me to absorb all the strangeness if I thought of it as a science fiction movie."

Aru smiled up at him. "That's why I love watching human television. This method, more than any other, allows me to learn much faster about human societies. I don't need the deep understanding that comes from reading philosophy and history, and I hate trying to understand all those stuffy words that the authors use to aggrandize themselves. Movies convey the essence of the human condition, and I don't mind that the storylines are oversimplified. They are good enough for me."

ARU

So far, the meeting was going exceedingly well. Kian seemed like a decent guy, and the big bodyguard provided some much-needed comic relief, given the somber theme of the meeting. Magnus, whom Aru had gotten to know the day before, was contented to remain silent today and just listen to the talk.

Aru still hadn't formed an opinion about the advisor, and the other guard was a killer, but since he was the redhead's brother and tolerated the guy's quirky humor, he couldn't be too bad.

"Tea is served, masters." The Odu placed a tray with a teapot and several teacups on the table and offered a fake smile to Aru. "Would master like me to pour for him?"

"Yes, please." Anything was better than the horrible beer, and Aru was thirsty.

Watching the Odu pour the tea, he was fascinated by how closely the cyborg mimicked a human butler.

The representations in the historical records always portrayed the Odus with ugly faces, mean expressions, and a stocky, muscular build.

Up close, Okidu wasn't ugly. He resembled an older human male, and his expression was kind. He was stocky, but he didn't look overly muscular.

Still, Aru and his teammates had easily recognized the Odu for what he was, and it wasn't just his scent that was not fully biological. He resembled the depictions in the historical records, but not completely. It was amazing how slight changes had been enough to portray the Odus in a completely different light.

It always surprised Aru anew how easy it was to manipulate public opinion, especially since the gods were not designed to be easily manipulated like the species they created.

When the Odu handed him the teacup, Aru thanked him, and as Okidu continued pouring tea for the rest of the group, he sipped slowly and watched the interplay between the Odu and the immortals.

They were all fond of him, even the cold blond and the calculating advisor.

Interesting. The Odu might not be the creature of horror Aru had learned about, but he was still an artificial intelligence dressed in a butler suit. He wasn't a person, and as long as he was programmed to be a servant and not a killing machine, he shouldn't evoke any feelings, positive or negative.

"So, Aru," Kian said. "You wanted to meet me, so I assume that you want something from me and my people. Let's hear your proposition."

"I don't have one. Not yet, anyway. I wanted to see who you were and maybe bounce a few ideas around." He smiled. "Don't forget that until yesterday, I didn't know of your existence. Since my teammates and I couldn't find any contemporary mentions of gods or people with extraordinary abilities, we assumed that the rebels and all of their offspring had perished."

Kian regarded him with a raised brow. "You told the team I sent to meet you that it was a known fact that the rebel gods were gone. Their trackers stopped transmitting, and the Eternal King told the public that he had been informed by the oracle that they were gone. That contradicts what you just said about searching for contemporary mentions of gods. You knew there shouldn't be any."

The leader of the immortals was a suspicious guy, and he seemed eager to poke holes in Aru's story. The truth was that Aru happened to know more details about what had actually happened to the rebels, but he couldn't reveal that without casting suspicion on himself. Negal and

Dagor weren't privy to the information, and they would wonder how he had come by that knowledge.

"You are right and wrong at the same time. We knew that the original rebels were gone, but they had over two thousand Earth years to produce offspring, who wouldn't have been implanted with trackers and therefore were not accounted for. Some of those gods could have survived, and that was who we were searching for. We assumed that the rebels honored the prohibition on procreating with created species, so we didn't expect to find any hybrid offspring, just young, pureblooded gods. Naturally, we were aware of the human myths surrounding the gods' dalliances with humans, but we didn't take them too seriously. We did a precautionary search for enhanced humans, but when all the leads we investigated proved to be bogus, we stopped searching."

Kian's expression softened. "We are very good at hiding. The Doomers are less so, but they also know to stay under the humans' radar. Your king is right about one thing. Humans might be weak as individuals, but they are formidable when organized. Still, given that there are trillions of gods and only billions of humans, your king has nothing to worry about."

Aru lifted a hand. "First of all, he's not my king. I don't belong to him, although he would like to think that all the gods are his to do with as he pleases. And secondly, he doesn't share his goals with the population. Well, he does, but it's all pretty lies about the beauty of creation and other platitudes. I don't understand why we create intelligent species all over the galaxy but curtail their proliferation and their advancement."

The Supreme probably knew the answer to that, but Aru wasn't in a position where he could ask the Supreme questions, and neither was Aria.

Kian's advisor rubbed his fingers over his clean-shaven jaw. "The king needs to keep his people busy. Seeding new planets and creating new intelligent species seem like exciting endeavors that gods would be glad to partake in. Besides, I'm sure he uses these created species to do work for the gods. Whether it is mining for materials, producing food, or making things. Am I right?"

Aru nodded. "The spin is that we, the benevolent gods, give these people knowledge and the tools necessary to build a civilization, and in their gratitude, they pay us tribute."

"In other words, taxes." Kian put his teacup down. "The more intelligent and productive species the gods create, the more riches they produce for Anumati in the form of taxes, or tribute as they call it. That keeps Anumati's citizens happy and loyal to the king, who makes it all happen. That being said, the gods, or rather the Eternal King and his government, don't want those species to become too numerous, too strong, and too advanced and feel emboldened enough to refuse to pay tribute to the gods. Of course, since Earth was declared a forbidden planet and no taxes are collected here, that doesn't apply to humans, but it's probably a general policy that is implemented universally."

Aru regarded Kian with new appreciation. "You are very astute, Kian. I guess it takes an outsider to see things so clearly. It should have been obvious to me, and yet I once again allowed myself to believe the propaganda."

"I have had the advantage of witnessing human history unfold and empires rise and fall. Instead of creating new species to exploit, humans have conquered and subjugated other humans. The history of Anumati probably was similar in its early days, and different groups of gods fought for dominance. At some point, the Eternal King or his predecessor united all the gods on Anumati and subjugated the only other intelligent species on the planet. When that proved successful, the operation was expanded to other planets in the galaxy."

"We were not taught that," Dagor said. "But Anumati's civilization is very old, and since we suspect that we were not always immortal, it's possible that in our early days, we were not all that different from humans and fought among ourselves."

"There is a saying I once heard," Anandur said, "about a fly in a dung heap who thinks he's in paradise because he's warm and well fed."

Aru tried to decipher what the saying tried to convey, but Anandur must have forgotten the punchline.

Brundar turned an icy stare on his brother. "You have just insulted our guests."

"I'm not offended," Aru said. "Just puzzled. What does the dung fly have to do with what we are talking about?"

KIAN

"Nothing." Kian lifted a hand to stop Anandur from elaborating. "It has nothing to do with our discussion."

They could probably keep talking for hours, and although Kian wanted to learn as much as he could about Anumati, the Eternal King, the rebellion, and how it all affected Earth and humanity, it couldn't all be done in one afternoon. He needed to establish a working relationship with the gods, reach a general understanding regarding future collaboration, and create a platform for future talks.

He couldn't invite them into the village, but he could offer them the penthouse as accommodation during their stay so he could have access to them whenever he pleased.

Under normal circumstances, the gods would not accept his invitation. They wouldn't want to give him so much control. But he had an ace up his proverbial sleeve.

Gabi was in the keep, and if Aru wanted to see her and have access to her, he would have to agree to be the clan's guest with all the limitations on his freedom and privacy that it implied.

The question was how to broach the subject.

"Do the gods still believe in the Fates?" Kian asked. "And in truelove mates?"

"We do." Aru frowned. "Why do you ask?"

"Our ancestors passed the belief in the Fates to us, but I was a skeptic up until not too long ago. Now I'm a believer, especially when it applies to finding one's truelove mate. I've witnessed it happening time and again, first when my own fated love appeared in my life under the most unlikely circumstances, and then when many more were found in similarly strange situations by my clan members. Dormant carriers of godly genes are nearly impossible to identify, and they are very rare, and yet the Fates found a way to make those unions happen, for us and for you."

He expected Aru to look surprised or puzzled, but given the gleam in the god's eyes, he knew precisely what Kian was talking about.

The only way he could have known about Gabi's transition was if he had managed to attach a bug to one of the team members despite all the precautions they had taken.

Once again, Kian's paranoia had prevented a disaster. His insistence on the team staying in the keep had saved them from compromising the village's location.

"What are you talking about?" Aru said in a tone that attempted to sound puzzled but didn't.

The god should never play poker.

"You know what I'm talking about. Or rather, who."

"How should I know that?" Aru was still trying to keep up the pretense. "I didn't thrall you. That would have been a hostile act on my part."

It was possible that Aru or one of his teammates had entered Magnus's mind and plucked the information about Gabi's transition from there, but since they hadn't had enough time with the Guardian to do it stealthily, Magnus would have felt it.

A bug was the more likely method.

There was a slight chance that the god might be a powerful thraller who could enter their minds without them feeling a thing, but Kian was willing to bet it was a spy bug.

"You couldn't have thralled Magnus or me without us feeling the intrusion. You planted a bug on one of the team members you met with yesterday, and that's a hostile act as much as thralling would have been."

Aru swallowed. "Did you find it? If you didn't, you have no proof."

"I don't need proof." Kian leaned forward. "You don't have a poker face, Aru, so I suggest you never play the game, or you'll lose all your money."

For some reason, that seemed to upset Aru more than anything else that had been said so far, including Anandur's inappropriate comment about the happy dung fly.

Kian continued before things could further escalate between them. "I bet that you are dying to see Gabi, and if you drop the charade, I will take you to see her."

Aru let out a breath. "I guess that the cat is out of the hat, or the rabbit is out of the cage, or whatever the saying is. I would very much like to see Gabriella. I've been very worried about her."

The truth was that Kian wasn't even upset about Aru's subterfuge. He would have done the same thing if he was in the god's shoes. What made him angry was that they had somehow missed the spy bug, which meant that the team and Julian had been sloppy.

Who knows what they had talked about after they were convinced that they were bug-free? They could have talked about Annani for all he knew. He would have to question them thoroughly about every word they'd said.

"How much do you know about Gabi's condition?" Turner asked Aru.

"I know that she's transitioning into immortality, but I don't know what that entails. Is she in danger?"

"The transition is not without risks, but Gabi is doing better than most." Kian pushed to his feet. "Come. I'll take you to her."

As Negal and Dagor rose to join Aru, Kian put up a hand. "Only Aru can come. You need to stay here."

Negal looked at his team leader with worry in his eyes. "We shouldn't separate."

"It's okay." Aru motioned for him to sit back down. "If they wanted to harm us, they would have done it already. They need us as much as we need them."

Kian wasn't sure what the gods could do for him and the clan, but evidently Aru had something to offer.

As Anandur and Brundar followed them out of the penthouse, Aru raised a brow. "Why do they get to come? I trusted you not to harm me, and you should have trusted me in return."

Right, as if he was any match for the god. The guy could thrall him to do whatever he pleased, and Kian would happily comply.

"It's protocol." He put his thumb on the elevator button. "Their job is to protect me at all times."

"Aren't you the boss?" Aru asked. "Don't you make the rules?"

The guy was sharp, and Kian made a mental note to be more careful with what he said to him from now on.

"I answer to a council. The clan is not an autocracy."

"Is it a democracy?" The god followed him into the elevator, and the brothers entered after him.

"It is, and it is not. All major decisions have to be put to a vote. Some do not merit the full assembly, and the council vote is enough, but some require the vote of every clan member. Still, I have a lot of autonomy to run things as I see fit."

"But not regarding the twenty-four-seven guards," Aru said.

"No. I can't defy the rules on that."

13

ARU

Aru's heart was thrumming with excitement mixed with trepidation. He would finally meet Gabi as himself, not as Uriel—his borrowed identity.

He'd been lucky that a name close to his real one had been available for purchase, and it had made it a little easier to use it and hear it on Gabi's lips, especially when she was climaxing.

He'd never expected her to learn that he was a god, and the fact that the Fates had made it so spoke volumes about their plans.

Was Gabriella Emerson his one and only?

Would she forgive him for the lies?

He had no choice; surely she would understand that?

"How did you smuggle the bug past all of our precautions?" Kian asked. "Were my people sloppy?"

They had been, but it wouldn't have made a difference if they had been more diligent.

"It's very small, undetectable by human devices, and we can control it remotely. We just kept moving it from person to person."

Kian frowned. "Our hearing and eyesight are nearly as good as yours. How is it possible that they didn't hear or see it? How small is that thing? The size of a mote of dust?"

"A little larger than that." Aru watched the numbers on the elevator display change from positive to negative. "How deep into the ground are we going?"

"Pretty deep. After this episode is over, we are going to collapse the passages and block all entrances to the underground. Regrettably, this location is compromised beyond salvation."

As the elevator doors opened, Kian motioned for Aru to step out first; his bodyguards followed, and he was the last to exit, but as they started walking, the brothers fell a few steps behind to give them privacy.

Aru could feel the cold gaze of the blond guard, freezing a hole in his back.

"What's wrong?" Kian asked.

He must have shivered. "I like Anandur." Aru glanced over his shoulder, and sure enough, the blond's hard eyes were boring holes into him. "But the other one gives me the creeps, as the humans like to say." He'd spoken quietly enough so only Kian could hear him.

Kian laughed and clapped him on the back. "You've got good instincts, Aru. Brundar is the one you should be wary of."

Surprised by the familiar gesture, Aru realized that Kian's presence hadn't evoked the prickly response that encountering an unfamiliar god or immortal usually did. "I wonder why the back of my neck didn't prickle even once. It should have."

Kian shrugged. "Not necessarily. You knew that you were meeting an immortal. In my experience, the prickling gives you a warning when you don't realize that you are in the presence of a competing immortal, or in your case, a god."

"That wasn't my experience, but then we are separated by seven thousand years of genetic tinkering, so things might be different for me."

"Yeah, I guess so. Is that why you and your friends don't glow?"

Aru stopped walking. "Only members of the royal family glow."

Were the gods living among the immortal descendants of Ahn or his two siblings? Otherwise, how would Kian know about the glow?

"Oh, really?" Kian affected a surprised tone. "Jade must have mentioned something about the gods glowing. Perhaps she didn't know that commoner gods didn't glow."

"Perhaps." Aru resumed walking.

Kian had remarked about Aru's lack of a poker face, but Kian wasn't a good liar either. If he'd learned about the gods having a glow from Jade and the ones living in his community didn't have it, he would have wondered why they didn't. But since he wondered why Aru and his teammates didn't glow, the ones in his village most likely did.

Should he reveal that he already knew about the surviving gods?

Kian would find out soon enough, so perhaps it was a good idea to build a better rapport with him before it happened and reassure him that he had nothing to fear from Aru and his teammates.

"You shouldn't abandon this great building and its underground compound just because my teammates and I followed the signals here. We will never disclose this location. Your secret is safe with us."

"Even if you mean what you say, you and your friends have implanted trackers, and your movements are recorded. Your commander and his superiors will know that you were here."

Aru shrugged. "So what? We've visited thousands of locations, and we will visit many more over the next century. No one will pay attention to our short sojourn here."

"What about the old trackers? The ones we took out of Igor and several others when we thought that he was the only threat? Their movements were recorded as well."

"Don't worry about that. No one other than us follows those."

Kian sighed. "Even if I trusted you and your friends to keep quiet about us and this location, which I don't, because I'm too paranoid to trust strangers, especially gods, the information could be compelled out of you, right?"

"Yeah, but why would anyone bother? We are not important. We are just what the humans refer to as foot soldiers."

He happened to be more than that, but it was thanks to his unique talent, which was a secret he and Aria guarded zealously.

Kian stopped and turned to him. "The only way the information will be safe is if they can't find you. We can take the trackers out of you the same way we did for the Kra-ell, and we can stage a plane crash to explain your demise." He grimaced. "My wife won't like the idea, but we could put your trackers inside gerbils and put those gerbils on a private plane that will crash into the ocean. It would be very convincing, especially if you notify your commander that you are chartering a private jet for some important mission."

Kian must have spent some time thinking about that, or else he had staged someone's fake death before. In either case, it was a tempting proposition, and Aru wished he could accept it.

"Thank you for the offer, but we can't do that. We have families that depend on us, and if we disappear, they will suffer."

"If you and your friends die in an accident, there will be no retribution against your loved ones back home. Are there financial consequences?"

"Not really, but we wouldn't want to cause our families the anguish of believing we've died." He smiled. "Eternal life is a blessing and a curse, and living forever with the pain of losing a child is not something I want to subject my parents to."

Kian nodded. "I can understand that."

"I'm not dismissing your idea out of hand, though. Let's revisit it in a hundred years. In a century, our circumstances might change dramatically."

"Indeed." Kian stopped in front of a door marked as a clinic. "Where is your bug now? I assume that when you heard about Gabi, you attached it to Julian?"

"Correct. And then we moved it to Gilbert because he promised Gabi that he wouldn't leave her side."

"Does your bug need a live host like the trackers?"

"No, but it's easiest to hide it on a person. It has a very limited range, and its charge doesn't last long. The less we move it around, the longer it can broadcast."

"I appreciate your candor." Kian put his hand on the door handle. "I would also appreciate you removing it from Gilbert and handing it over to me."

14

KIAN

"I'm sorry, but I can't do that," the god said.

Kian removed his hand from the handle. "Perhaps you would like to rethink your answer?"

Aru was taken aback. "What I meant was that I couldn't hand the bug over because we are running low on the spy drones, and we can't resupply, but if you allow me free access to Gabi, I'll gladly remove the bug and show it to you if you'd like. The technology is so far superior to anything humans can currently produce that it won't do you any good to take it apart."

After William's unsuccessful experience with trying to take apart the trackers, which were supposed to be old technology, it hadn't even crossed Kian's mind to suggest that William try to reverse engineer the bug. What he was concerned with was that there was more than one, and more specifically, where the others were deployed.

Thankfully, no one who had been in contact with the gods had returned to the village, so the location hadn't been compromised, but Kian had no desire to spend the night in the keep, especially since he planned to offer Aru and his friends the penthouse.

"How many more bugs did you attach to my people?"

"That's the only one."

"I doubt it."

As Kian put his hand back on the door handle, he could hear Aru's heart thundering in his chest. The god was anxious to get inside the clinic and see Gabi, which meant that he was primed to make concessions to make it happen, especially since the object of his desire was right there behind the door, and Kian was the only thing stopping him from entering.

"I swear on my honor, that's the only one," Aru said. "Well, the only one left. Before entering the building, we swept it with several bugs, but we didn't make it all the way to the penthouse or down to the underground levels, so we didn't find anything of use and retrieved them before they ran out of power. We are very frugal with how we use the drones we have left. They need to last us over a hundred years, and we've already used up a third monitoring the Kra-ell."

Kian believed him, but he wasn't done with his interrogation. "You no longer need to monitor the Kra-ell, and human technology will catch up at some point, so you will be able to replenish your supplies."

Aru groaned. "There is only one drone in here, and it's perched on Gilbert's shoulder. I would like to take it back, but if you want it that much, you can have it."

Kian still didn't depress the handle. "I'll make you a deal. You'll tell me how I can locate and identify these drones, and I'll let you have it back."

"You don't have the necessary technology."

Kian smiled. "Then you'll have to provide it."

If Aru was human, he would have popped a vein by now. "I can't. If I do, you will be able to see everything our drones see."

Kian's smile broadened. "I don't see a problem with that. For the next hundred years or so, all you can spy on is us, the Kra-ell, and various humans. Sharing the information with us does not present a conflict of interest for you."

Letting out a breath, Aru closed his eyes. "If I agree, Dagor and Negal will remove me from my post and keep me under house arrest until the ship returns for us."

"So, it's a yes?"

"You don't leave me much choice."

"No, I don't, but I'll sweeten the deal for you. For as long as Gabi is transitioning, you can stay in the penthouse we've just come from and see her whenever you want. I'll add your thumbprint to the elevator's database so you can use it to travel freely between the penthouse and the clinic."

Aru looked surprised. "Isn't that your place?"

"It belongs to me, and I used to live there, but I live elsewhere now, and I rent out the penthouse. The previous renter moved out not long ago, and I haven't found a replacement yet, so you and your friends can use it. There are three bedrooms, each with its own bathroom, and a gorgeous terrace that includes a swimming pool. It even comes with a concierge service. Whenever you are hungry, you can call the security desk downstairs, and they will arrange for a delivery."

The god regarded him with amusement in his dark eyes. "Are you sweetening the deal for me or for you?"

"I think it's a win-win, which is what great deals are all about. I get to keep an eye on you, and you get to see Gabi whenever you want."

"Not to mention Jade and Morgada and the two immortal males who are staying in the penthouse across the vestibule."

"Indeed."

Aru must have learned that from eavesdropping on the team's conversations through the spy drone, but the team wasn't going to stay in the other penthouse for long.

Once the god showed him how to identify and locate the bugs and agreed to stay in the keep, Kian was going to lift the lockdown and allow the team to return home.

His main motivation was that he wanted to return to the village, and it wouldn't be fair to do so while the others were stranded in the keep.

"How long is Gabi's transition going to last?" Aru asked.

"About six months." When the god's face fell, Kian chuckled. "But she's not going to be in the clinic for the entire time. The first stage is the most difficult, and it lasts anywhere between a few days and several weeks."

"You scared me." Aru let out a breath. "I thought that Gabi would be bedridden for half a year."

15

ARU

If Kian didn't open the door in the next two seconds, Aru was going to shove him aside and barge in, consequences be damned.

The invitation to enjoy the penthouse was a honey trap, but he had a feeling that if he declined, he wouldn't get to see Gabi at all. Especially after Kian learned what he'd heard thanks to the spy drone.

Aru had no doubt that Kian would interrogate every member of the team he had sent the day before, the doctor and Gilbert, and when they recounted everything that had been said, he would realize that the genie was out of the bottle or the lamp, or whatever it was that genies were usually trapped in, and that Aru knew about the gods living in Kian's community.

"We can continue our talk later." Kian finally opened the door to the waiting room.

The doctor greeted them with a smile. "Hello, Aru. Can I call you Aru?" He offered his hand.

"What else would you call me?" He shook the immortal's hand.

The doctor was another example of an immortal who could have passed for a god.

It made sense to him now. Some of these immortals were the descendants of the royals, and therefore possessed a more godly appearance than those who were the descendants of commoner gods.

"Do gods have last names?" Julian asked.

Kian chuckled. "Given that there are three trillion of them on Anumati, I'm sure they do. How many individual names could they have come up with?"

"We are usually referred to as the son or daughter of, fill in the mother and father's name. And if that's not enough to distinguish who we are, we can include the maternal and paternal grandparents' names. Familial connections are more important to us than our ancestors' place of origin or their occupation, which is what most human surnames are based on."

"We are the same," the doctor said. "But we have to adopt fake last names when dealing with humans. You did so as well."

"I did." Aru darted his eyes toward the door standing between him and Gabi. "Can I please see Gabriella now?"

"Regrettably, she's not awake at the moment." The doctor walked over to the door. "But given her pattern so far, she will wake up soon. In the meantime, you can chat with her brother."

Aru wasn't looking forward to that. Gilbert was not his fan at the moment, and Aru expected some posturing on the brother's part.

Julian opened the door and poked his head inside. "Can we come in? Aru and Kian are here." He glanced at them over his shoulder. "Brundar and Anandur will have to stay in the waiting room."

Anandur nodded. "That's okay as long as the door stays open."

"That's doable." Julian stepped aside. "You can go in."

Aru didn't wait for Kian to let him pass. Instead, he surged forward, entered the room, and went straight to the hospital bed.

"Oh, Gabi." He took hold of her small limp hand and brought it to his cheek. "I'm so sorry."

"Sorry for what?" her brother asked. "For inducing her transition? For lying to her? For planning to abandon her? You need to be more specific."

"All of the above," Aru murmured against Gabi's soft palm.

"That's not what I want to hear," Gilbert said.

Kian cleared his throat. "Since Gabi is asleep, we can take care of the spy drone business. Where is it?"

With a sigh, Aru put Gabi's hand down and turned around to look at her brother. There was some familial resemblance, but even though the brother had claimed to have been induced by a god, he still looked human.

"What are you talking about?" Gilbert frowned. "What spy drone? Ours?"

"No, his." Kian pointed with a tilt of his head.

So much of what had bothered Gabi about her family's uncharacteristic behavior made sense to Aru now, but he didn't have time to think about it. Perhaps later, they would leave him alone with her so he could gather his thoughts.

Pushing away from the bed, he walked over to Gilbert and extended his hand. "May I touch your shoulder? You have a little something there."

"What is it?" Gilbert turned his head, trying to see what was there, but the bug was too close to his neck for him to see.

Aru gently lifted the tiny device and put it on his fingertip. "This is it. The mighty spy."

Gilbert's eyes bugged out. "That's a drone? It's the size of a flea."

"It's a little larger than that." Kian leaned over to take a closer look. "But not by much. It's the size of a small mosquito. How does that thing see and hear and transmit information?"

"How does a real mosquito do that?" Aru retorted. "Much of our technology is based on genetics and is built from biological components." He smiled. "That's the extent of my technical acumen, so don't expect me to explain more."

"How long has this thing been on my shoulder?" Gilbert asked.

"It arrived with Julian," Kian said. "And since Aru was mostly interested in how Gabi was doing, he kept the drone in this room."

"Crap," Gilbert muttered. "I might have said things to Gabi that he shouldn't know."

Kian frowned. "Like what?"

"I'd rather not repeat them in case he missed it."

"I didn't miss it." Aru turned to Kian. "Let's step outside. I don't want any negative energy around Gabi."

16

KIAN

Anger mixed with worry had Kian flexing his hands. "Why should the energy turn negative? We are all civilized people here. What have you heard?"

Aru cast the brother an apologetic look. "Gilbert told Gabi that she doesn't have exclusive bragging rights to having been induced by a god because he had been induced by one as well."

Kian swallowed a vile curse. "What else?"

"Gabi said that she was under the impression that all the gods were gone and only their immortal descendants remained. Gilbert told her that the surviving gods are the clan's most guarded secret."

Fuck! If Gilbert had said anything about Annani, he was going to throttle him.

"What else?" Kian demanded.

"That's it." Aru shrugged as if he hadn't just learned the clan's most guarded secret. "Then he talked about me and what I was supposedly capable of and why I was dangerous to immortals."

"Was I wrong?" Gilbert asked.

"I don't know." Aru rubbed the back of his neck. "I've never tried to thrall any of you, so I don't know if I can. I know that the Kra-ell's minds are not susceptible to manipulation, but human minds are, so perhaps I can thrall those who are half human and half something else."

Thank the merciful Fates Gilbert hadn't said more. Perhaps the situation was still salvageable.

Kian liked Aru, and he really didn't want to kill him and the other two or force them into stasis, but if they learned about Annani, he would have no choice. Toven was less problematic because he wasn't a direct heir to the Anumati throne, but it was better if the gods didn't know who the survivors were.

It would be a damn shame to have to get rid of them, because the clan and humans needed them.

If taking down the Eternal King was the only way to save the human race, Kian would need access to the resistance, and that meant he needed the three rebel gods alive and well and not in stasis.

Aru took a deep breath and then looked at Kian. "Gilbert didn't say more, but I've deduced a few things from clues you provided."

Kian was afraid of that. "That's not a conversation we should have while standing in the waiting room of the clinic. We should move it to my office." He started toward the door.

Aru didn't follow. "I want to stay with Gabi."

"She's asleep. You'll get to talk to her when she's awake."

The god arched a brow. "Will I?"

Evidently, he was afraid that after learning what he had deduced, Kian would retract his offer to stay in the penthouse and see Gabi whenever he pleased.

"Don't worry. Everything I promised you still stands. I'm not the kind of guy who goes back on his word. I want us to go to my office because this is not the kind of conversation that should be conducted while standing next to a woman in a hospital bed who needs peace and tranquility."

Aru cracked a smile. "Wasn't that what I said a moment ago?"

"Come on, wise guy. My old office is just around the corner."

"Is it really?"

"No, it's one level up."

When Aru still hesitated, Kian shook his head. "I give you my word that you'll get to spend as much time with Gabi as she will allow you, which might not be much after she learns of your deceit. But in my experience, women are merciful, and if you grovel enough, she might forgive you. My offer of free use of the penthouse still stands as well."

Casting one more longing look behind him, Aru let out a sigh and followed him out of the clinic.

Thankfully, Gilbert got the hint that he wasn't invited and stayed behind, or maybe he just didn't want to leave his sister.

Kian waited with his questions until the four of them reached his old office and took seats around the conference table. It wasn't that he feared someone might overhear them on the way, but the subject was too grave to discuss casually.

He also needed time to think, but the short walk hadn't been long enough to come up with a solution for the conundrum he found himself faced with.

"So, what did you deduce from what I've told you?" he asked.

Aru cast a glance at Anandur and Brundar. "My teammates don't know any of this. I watched the feed from the drone alone in my room, and I deleted the relevant footage. If they ask about the missing time, I'll say that the doctor was examining Gabi and that I didn't want them to see that."

Obviously, Aru was hinting that the confidential nature of what he was about to reveal might not be appropriate for the ears of Kian's bodyguards.

"You can say anything in front of Anandur and Brundar. I have no secrets from them. "

The god nodded. "You asked me why my teammates and I don't have a glow. I concluded from your question that the gods living in your village have it. Since only those of royal descent glow, your gods are the descendants of the Eternal King's children."

The blood chilled in Kian's veins.

If Aru was not who he claimed to be, and he was one more assassin the Eternal King had sent to eliminate any potential heirs, Kian would really have no choice but to kill him or force him into stasis.

Then again, if Aru was an assassin, he wouldn't have revealed what he'd figured out.

Why was he doing that? Was it an attempt to gain Kian's trust?

And how come his mother had never mentioned gods with no glow?

Could it be that Aru was fishing for information?

That would be a clever way to get Kian to admit that descendants of the Eternal King were living in his community.

He wasn't going to fall into that trap.

"According to our legends, all gods were luminous. That was how humans identified them. Some might have been brighter than others, and there were stories about gods who had lost their glow after losing a truelove mate or suffering some other calamity, but there was no mention of any gods that were born without a glow."

17

ARU

W as Kian weaving tales of radiant gods to conceal the presence of the Eternal King's descendants in his community?

Or were his tales true, and all the exiled gods had been luminous?

Much had changed over the seven millennia since the rebels had been exiled. Gods born post-rebellion might have been designed without the radiant glow. Yet, the majority of Anumati's population was ancient, predating the rebellion, and save for those with royal lineage, they were not luminous.

It wasn't likely that they had all undergone procedures to remove their glow, but perhaps there was an elixir that could create or enhance luminosity or, conversely, one that muted it.

Was it possible that the rebels had striven to equalize things in more ways than anyone had suspected?

In their quest for equality, they might have found a way to make everyone in their community glow, at least a little. It could have been achieved with simple measures like rubbing oil infused with gold on their skin or by more complicated methods that involved genetic alterations.

As far as Aru knew, the rebels hadn't been equipped with what was needed to conduct genetic experiments and alterations, but it was possible that some equipment and instructions had survived from the original creation of humans, which had happened two million years ago.

It was hard to believe that any tools had remained hidden for so long, and the technology must have been primitive compared to what the gods could do now, but perhaps it had been enough to make everyone luminous to some degree.

"The division is very clear on Anumati," he said. "Those of royal descent glow, and everyone else does not. There are several royal lines, their descendants are numerous, and they possess different degrees of radiance. Those closest to the original royals naturally are the brightest. It makes it very easy to differentiate between the aristocracy and the commoners."

"How do you explain our legends then?" Anandur asked. "They were very clear about all the gods being luminous creatures. That's how they appear in human legends as well."

Aru shrugged. "It's just a thought, but maybe there was a way to enhance or subdue the glow with chemicals. The rebels were all about equality, so they might have wanted every god in their new utopia to be equally luminous."

Kian looked skeptical. "I doubt that's what happened. The gods could suppress their glow at will. Maybe the Eternal King decreed at some point that all the non-royals had to stop glowing. The old gods were forced to suppress it, and the young gods were genetically altered so they no longer had the ability."

Again, Kian surprised Aru with insight into the way the Eternal King might have thought and operated that would have never occurred to him. "You might be right about that. When I get back to Anumati, I'll try to find some old gods who are not the Eternal King's supporters and who are willing to tell me the truth."

Perhaps the Supreme would answer that question if he asked very politely and explained what had prompted his inquiry.

Tonight, Aru would contact Aria and tell her what he had found out. He had no doubt that the Supreme would be delighted by his discovery and would want him to find out more.

He might have no choice but to enter one of the immortals' minds to get the answers the Supreme would demand.

Kian regarded him with a frown. "Do you still think that you are going back to Anumati? With what you know, I can't let you leave."

"I'm on your side, Kian. I'm not a threat to you, your people, or the gods living among you, whether they are the descendants of the Eternal King's rebellious children or just common gods. I'm part of the resistance, and admitting that to you was a risk I took because I knew that you needed me as much as I needed you."

Kian leaned back in his chair. "What exactly do you need me for? What can a bunch of immortals do to help free a trillion gods from the rule of the Eternal King? We are utterly insignificant."

18

KIAN

Did Kian even want to help free the gods?

The Eternal King was a piece of work, but he kept the gods in check, and he at least cared about public opinion, which limited to some extent what he could get away with.

Whoever replaced him might be worse.

"Of course, you are significant," Aru said. "Every person, every mind is important, and every day more minds join the resistance. Your advantage is that you don't exist as far as the king is concerned. He doesn't know about you, and I would like to keep it that way. The problem is that I need to keep reporting about the Kra-ell. I can say that they rebelled against Igor, overthrew him, and took out their trackers, but then I will have to supply their new location, and that's where you live. I hate to say it, but your communities will have to separate, and it's better to do it now than to wait a century, when the integration will be so complete that it would be too painful to do so."

Kian had no intention of doing that, and not only because he now felt like he needed the might of the Kra-ell more than ever. He liked the idea of their integrated community.

The worst thing for immortals was stagnation and boredom, and the Kra-ell infused the village with new interest—even if not all of it was positive.

Kian shook his head. "There is no need for that. You can claim to have lost track of them because they removed the trackers. What else are you supposed to do during your tour of duty on Earth?"

"After we found out about the settler ship's arrival and we discovered the surviving Kra-ell, we were tasked with finding the missing pods and either verifying that their occupants had perished or reviving those who are still in stasis."

"Your job was to find the royal twins," Kian stated.

He had no doubt that he was right, and Aru didn't try to deny it.

The god nodded. "Yes, that too."

It hadn't occurred to Kian before, but it was likely that the twins were also luminous, which might explain why they had always been veiled. Maybe they couldn't manage their glow as adeptly as his mother and Toven could. The ability to control it might come with age, and they had been young when their mother had smuggled them onto the settler ship.

It was a question he should address to Annani and perhaps also Toven.

Toven had been so good at suppressing his glow and had done it for so long that he had lost the ability, and according to Annani, her half-sister's luminosity had also been lost or greatly diminished after her first mate had been killed.

Come to think of it, Areana and Toven had both been suffering from depression when they lost their glow, and Toven had regained his after finding happiness with Mia, so perhaps there was a connection.

Bridget would say that a test sample of two was not good science, but Kian didn't need to prove anything to anyone, and two was good enough for a hunch.

Leaning back, he crossed his arms over his chest and leveled his gaze at Aru. "What exactly are you expecting us to help you with?"

"I'm not sure yet." Aru mimicked Kian's pose. "But if you believe in the Fates, then you must suspect that they brought us together for a reason."

"I knew it," Anandur muttered under his breath. "This is a bad bromance."

Shaking his head, Kian ignored the fatuous comment. "My belief in the Fates does not influence my decision-making, especially when the safety of my people is at stake. The Fates might have orchestrated your meeting with Gabi, but that's as far as my belief in supernatural forces can stretch. Even those who believe in them wholeheartedly accept that the Fates are not supposed to get involved in the greater design of nations."

Aru nodded. "You are right. Forget I said that. We can't rely on supernatural beings who are known to be capricious to guide us, but everything else I said about the Eternal King and the resistance is true. A cooperation could be beneficial to both of us." He smiled. "We have similar goals, but the most important one for now is staying alive and protecting the lives of those we care about."

"Who am I supposed to cooperate with? I can accept that you are a member of the resistance, but you are not its leader, nor do you even have access to whoever is running the show."

"You don't know much about me. What are you basing your assumptions on?"

Could he have been wrong about the god? Was there more to him than being the leader of an insignificant team investigating an insignificant planet?

Perhaps he was the son or nephew of someone who was close to the resistance leadership?

"All I can base my assumptions on is what you have told me. Did you lie about who you are?"

"I did not." Aru uncrossed his arms and leaned forward. "This information has to stay between us." He looked at Brundar and Anandur and then back at Kian. "I need the three of you to vow that what I'm about to tell you doesn't leave this room."

Kian uncrossed his arms as well. "I can give you my vow, but since I'm not Kra-ell, how can you trust it? The same is true for Anandur and Brundar. I can vouch for their trustworthiness and honor, but how can you be sure that I'm not lying?"

"Sometimes, a gut feeling is all we have." The god's eyes bored into Kian's. "If we want to move this to the next level, I have to trust my instincts about you and take a risk, and the same is true for you. Otherwise, we will just keep dancing around each other and make no progress."

That was true, and they each had leverage over the other. Kian had Gabi, who seemed to be Aru's truelove mate, even if the god hadn't realized that yet, and that made her the most precious person in the universe to him. He would never do anything to endanger her, her family, or anyone she cared about.

Also, Aru and his teammates were currently isolated on Earth, and Kian had the means to force them into stasis or kill them. Other than inborn immunity, there was no defense against the gods' thrall, but he was lucky to have the Kra-ell on his side. The purebloods were immune to thralling and could easily overtake the gods.

Aru's leverage was obvious. He knew about the immortal community, and now he also knew about the gods being part of it and suspected they were of royal descent.

"I give you my word that what you are about to tell us will not leave this room unless you later give me permission to share it with my council and the leaders of the other branches of our community when the time comes for decision-making. I'm not an absolute ruler, and important decisions have to be approved by the council." And also by his mother.

"That's acceptable." Aru shifted his gaze to the brothers. "I need to hear you say it."

After both of them gave him their word, Aru let out a breath. "I have a way to communicate with the resistance leadership. My teammates don't know about it, and neither does anyone on the patrol ship, and I need it to stay that way. That's why it can't leave this room."

Kian frowned. "How? You said that you can't communicate with Anumati unless the signal goes to the patrol ship first and is then redirected from there."

"I have a way, but I'm not going to disclose it."

Kian had an inkling about the method Aru was using to communicate with Anumati, and it was the same one he had suspected Igor of employing but couldn't prove.

"Fair enough. So, what's the next step?"

"I have to ask for instructions. I suspect that the resistance will find

561

it very advantageous to have a base of operation on the forbidden planet, and they will appreciate your help establishing it."

"I'm not sure that's something I want." Kian leaned back. "As you have said, the human race might already be a target for the Eternal King just because of how populous it has become and how technologically advanced it is. Why would I want to add rebel sympathizers to that and ensure this planet's annihilation?"

His words didn't seem to have the impact he'd hoped for.

The god regarded him with his dark, focused gaze. "The resistance can give you and your people a fighting chance. The alternative is to submit and helplessly watch the end. The Eternal King will not stop at culling the human population. He deems hybrids of all kinds abominations, which is ironic because all the created species have some godly genes in them, but he would order your annihilation nonetheless."

19

TURNER

Ever since Aru had left with Kian and the brothers, Turner had been trying to get information out of Negal and Dagor, but so far, they hadn't said much about anything of consequence. If they weren't stuffing their mouths with the little sandwiches Okidu kept bringing out or sipping on their coffee, they were expertly avoiding answering his questions about the resistance.

Turner suspected that they had centuries' worth of experience talking in circles about important issues and not saying much. They were supposedly young gods, but what was considered young on Anumati?

Anyone under a thousand years old?

These two were either born politicians or had been trained to avoid answering questions without appearing rude.

Usually Turner was a great interrogator, walking a fine line between befriending his subjects and intimidating them, but evidently gods were not easily intimidated by immortals, and rightly so.

The two seemed more wary of the Odu than of him or Magnus, so maybe he should let Okidu conduct the interrogation.

Well, that was an idea. Perhaps the subject of the Odus would be a good one to get them talking. The Odus were ancient history to these gods, so discussing them shouldn't be a problem, and once Negal and Dagor loosened up, they might reveal a thing or two that was useful.

After Okidu had refilled their coffee cups and returned to the kitchen, Turner leaned back. "So, there are no more Odus on Anumati?"

Jade had told them that they had been replaced with simpler versions of household robots, but he could pretend not to know that.

"Not this model," Negal said. "The new models look more like machines, and their learning ability is greatly curtailed." He glanced in the direction of the kitchen. "The old model is so lifelike that it's disturbing. It's difficult to think of him as anything other than a person, but that wasn't why they were banned."

"It was because of the back door to their programming," Dagor said. "They could easily be turned into killing machines. The new ones have brains that are solid core. You can't tamper with those without destroying them, so the way they come out of the assembly line is the way they stay. All our technology is like that now, and it's a pain in the ass because we can't fix anything. Once it's broken, it has to be discarded."

That was progress. He might have just learned something useful.

"It makes sense." Turner rubbed a hand over his jaw. "I assume that production is closely monitored and regulated, and when the product leaves the factory, it can't be altered in any way. That ensures that no new monstrosities can be built."

Dagor grimaced. "Everything that's made on Anumati has to have the king's stamp of approval. Which makes it very difficult for the resistance to come up with creative solutions for encrypted communication. The only way to transfer information so it doesn't fall into the wrong hands is in person, and even that is problematic because the king employs telepaths. They can't read what you are thinking, but they can sense that you are not happy and plotting something, and then they send the interrogators after you."

"No wonder the resistance has to work at a cosmic snail's pace," Magnus said.

That was so terrifying and disturbing that Turner had to suppress a shiver, which was rare for him. He'd seen and experienced too much to get easily rattled, but what Dagor described was hell disguised as utopia.

Turner suspected that drug use was rampant on Anumati. If people had to be happy to avoid interrogation, they needed something to help them achieve that state. Happiness was doable in short bursts but wasn't sustainable over time.

"Are any of the products used by the gods manufactured in the colonies?"

Negal shook his head. "The colonies supply raw materials. Whatever they make is for internal consumption."

"Yeah, because it's crap," Dagor said. "Even if it was allowed, no one would buy stuff made off planet."

"What about food?" Magnus asked. "Is that brought into Anumati from the colonies?"

Negal cast him a condescending look. "It makes absolutely no sense to use interstellar ships to transport food. It makes much more sense to transport those who need the food to the colonies than the other way around."

So that was why the gods were colonizing. It wasn't only to collect raw materials and experiment with creating new species. They needed to offload chunks of their population repeatedly, but since gods didn't like to work hard, they created servants from local species. It was much cheaper and less complicated than building factories and producing robots or cyborgs to do the work.

Not a bad system.

Turner took a sip from his coffee and put the cup down on the table. "The Eternal King might be a cold bastard, but he's found a way to keep the population well fed and occupied. Boredom is probably the most difficult problem for gods. If they are not kept busy with interesting and creative endeavors, they will go insane or choose to go into stasis."

Negal nodded. "Many of the wealthy old gods choose to sleep for thousands of years. It solves both of the problems you mentioned. Food and boredom."

"That's a clever solution," Magnus said. "It seems like the king has everything running as well as can be expected, and I wonder why people are rebelling. Is it still about the Kra-ell and their quest for equal rights?"

"It started with the Kra-ell struggle for equality," Negal said. "But it didn't end there. The rebellion gave the king the perfect excuse to tighten his control over the population and further reduce individual freedoms. Most people accepted the new reality, but some didn't. Every day, more and more realize how little freedom they really have and that everything in their lives is predetermined, including what traits they and their children possess. Those born with traits the king doesn't want and can't control are discriminated against. Immunes, in particular, have been targeted until there are practically none left on Anumati. Those unlucky enough to be born like that do their best to hide their immunity to compulsion. Getting off planet and settling in one of the colonies is usually their best option. That way, they can at least choose where to go and not get sent to a dangerous place."

Turner lifted his coffee cup. "Not to mention that being off planet means that they can allow themselves the luxury of not feeling happy every minute of the day."

"What other traits are discriminated against?" Magnus asked.

"Telepaths, seers, remote viewers," Negal said. "All of them threaten the Eternal King's control because they can pierce the veil of his propaganda."

Turner tilted his head. "Aru mentioned something about the king pretending to have learned about his children's demise from the oracle. Isn't the oracle a seer?"

Negal snorted. "He doesn't kill them off. He gathers them around him so he can control which of their predictions see the light of day. Seers are either employed in the service of the crown or sent away to remote planets with volatile populations where they are not likely to survive."

"Clever bastard," Turner muttered. "I just wonder what will happen once he's removed. Whoever replaces him might not be as capable and cause more harm than good."

Turner had seen that happen too many times on Earth. Eliminating despicable rulers did not guarantee a better life for their populations. More often than not, the replacement turned out even worse.

Negal surprised him by nodding. "That's why the resistance is not in a rush to remove him anytime soon. We are taking it slow, so when the time comes, we will not ruin our civilization while trying to make it better."

20

ARU

Aru had hyperbolized the consequences of Kian and his clan refusing to assist the resistance, but he had a good reason.

He had done it to drive the point home.

Nothing was immediate. They had one hundred and fifteen years before his team could no longer hide what they had found, and when they did and the news got to the king, he wouldn't respond right away. When he finally turned his sights on Earth, it would take a ship another hundred years or so to get there, or perhaps a little less if the king only sent a group of scientists with a pathogen on a small ship that was faster.

According to this calculation, Kian had between three to five hundred years to come up with a solution. Hopefully, humans would not develop interstellar travel ability in the interim, or the grace period would be severely shortened.

But even if they had the full five centuries until the arrival of the Eternal King's forces, the resistance might not yet be ready to help.

Humans were most likely doomed with or without the resistance, and Kian probably knew it.

What Aru was offering him was a sliver of hope.

There was nothing worse than hopelessness and helplessness, and those could only be alleviated with action. Waiting for the inevitable disaster without doing anything to prevent it, even if the chances of success were low, would destroy Kian and everyone he shared the dire news with.

That was no way to live, and Aru was sure that despite Kian's reservations, he would grasp at the proverbial straw he'd been offered.

Briefly closing his eyes, Kian took a deep breath and nodded. "You are right. I'd rather go down fighting. In a hundred years or so, we might be able to make all humans immune to disease or even turn them immortal, but that won't save them, nor would it save us. The king will just use some different means to decimate or annihilate the population. It could be done by introducing a pathogen that will kill crops worldwide and cause mass starvation or by detonating EMPs in Earth's atmosphere and frying our electrical grids and means of transportation. Our existence is so fragile, so perilous, and so easily extinguished." He waved his hand. "We live with a false sense of security that is born of ignorance, or maybe the ostrich syndrome. We bury our heads in the sand and convince ourselves that nothing is going to happen to us."

Aru was still stuck on Kian's remark about his clan's ability to turn humans immune to disease or even immortal.

Was the clan privy to the gods' secrets of genetic engineering?

"I don't know what ostrich syndrome is, and I'm not well versed in the state of human scientific research, but I was under the impression that they are far from being able to eradicate all diseases. Does your clan have proprietary knowledge that the rest of your world does not?"

Kian's pinched expression relaxed. "A hundred years is a long time, and scientific research has gotten a boost from artificial intelligence. I'm told that experiments that would have taken years to run can be simulated in minutes. AI even makes suggestions for new treatments."

Aru doubted Kian was telling him the entire truth.

He had said 'we' might be able to make humans immune to disease, and Kian didn't bundle his people together with humans. He definitely had been referring to his clan's ability to do so, and not to human science.

Aru smiled. "Nice try, but I know that you are not relying on humans to find the solution."

Kian didn't deny it, but the small lift of one corner of his mouth indicated that he wasn't angry about Aru being able to deduce the truth once again.

"I need to watch myself with you, Aru. You are cleverer than you appear. No wonder you were chosen to lead the team and to communicate with the resistance."

"Thank you." Aru dipped his head.

He had been chosen because of his ability to telepathically communicate with his sister regardless of distance, but he also needed to watch what he said to Kian. The guy was watchful, intelligent, and paranoid. He didn't miss much.

Pushing his chair back, Kian got to his feet. "Since you need to get instructions before we can continue our talks, let's get back to the clinic and see whether Gabriella is awake."

Finally.

Aru was out of his chair so fast that the thing toppled on its back.

Anandur chuckled as he lifted the chair. "Someone is anxious to get to his mate."

Glaring at Aru, Brundar re-sheathed the dagger he'd pulled out. "No more sudden movements, please."

"Noted."

GABI

G abi was lost.

She'd been walking for hours, searching the deserted streets of downtown Los Angeles, but she didn't know what she was looking for.

Perhaps when she saw it, she would recognize it.

Night was falling, and her legs were hurting badly, but she couldn't stop. If it was the normal pinching of shoes that got too tight after a long day, she wouldn't have been worried, but it was an all-over ache, the type she usually experienced when having the flu, just ten times worse.

She had to keep going, though. She couldn't stop.

What was she searching for?

Was she trying to find her way home?

Where was home?

She had a vague memory of a contemporary-looking townhouse, but she hadn't been there in so long that it couldn't be her home.

Gilbert would know where she needed to be.

She should call him. He would come to get her and drive her home, wherever it was. Her brother was always there for her when she needed him, and she needed him now.

"Gilbert," she murmured. "Come get me."

As a large hand clasped hers, she smiled, thinking that her wish was answered, but there was no one with her on the street. She was still alone. Was it a phantom touch?

"It's me, Gabi. Can you open your eyes?"

The voice sounded familiar, but it didn't belong to her brother. She had mixed feelings about it. She was excited to hear it and also aggravated by it, but she didn't know why.

"Can you wake up, Gabi?" the voice insisted. "I don't know how long they will let me stay here. Gilbert agreed to leave you alone with me, but he is in the waiting room, so if you wish, I can ask him to come in."

Was the voice part of the dream?

If she was sleeping and dreaming, then walking on the streets of Los Angeles didn't make sense, so that part belonged in the dream world, and the phantom voice was real.

She also realized that she knew whom the voice belonged to.

Uriel.

The guy who hadn't answered her text and left her stranded in that horrible hospital.

"Good of you to finally show up. Are you going to get me out of here?" She still didn't open her eyes, not because she didn't want to, but because her eyelids refused to obey her command. "Why can't I open my eyes?"

"I'll get the doctor." Sounding alarmed, he let go of her hand.

"No. Stay." She lifted her hand, hoping he would take it again because she missed his touch. "Just give me a moment."

She heard him exhale, and then he took her hand, lifted it, and kissed her palm. "I'm so sorry. I should have been there for you."

"Why weren't you?" She finally managed to force her eyelids to part, but her vision was blurry. "Did you get my text?"

"I did, but I was in the middle of something very important that I couldn't get out of, and I couldn't come to you." He chuckled. "In the end, it's good that I didn't because I wouldn't have been able to find you if I hadn't sent a spy drone after Magnus, who talked about you with Julian, who said that he was going to take care of you. I moved the spy from Magnus's shoulder to Julian's, and that's how I knew that your brother was with you and that you were taken care of. I also knew where they had taken you, so if Kian hadn't offered to bring me to you, I would have infiltrated the place no matter what it would have cost me."

Her vision finally clearing, Gabi narrowed her eyes at Uriel. "I have no idea what you are talking about. Who is Magnus? And who is Julian? And where am I?"

He frowned. "You shouldn't be so confused. Orion released you from the compulsion to forget things around me, and you should remember everything you were told. I need to get the doctor in here. "

The door opened a moment later, and the handsome doctor walked in. "I heard you through the camera." He pointed at a cylinder that was attached to the wall near the ceiling and then looked at her. "Do you remember me?"

She smiled. "How could I forget a face like yours? You are the doctor."

"What's my name?"

"Julian?"

Uriel had said that someone named Magnus had talked with Julian, who had said that he was going to take care of her, so it was logical to assume that the doctor's name was Julian.

"What's wrong with Gabi?" Uriel asked. "Is it my presence that's causing the memory problem?"

"It might be." The doctor checked her pupils. "Let's put it to the test. Can you step outside for a moment?"

"Of course." Uriel cast her one more worried look before letting go of her hand. "I'm not going anywhere. I'll be just outside the door."

Lifting a feeble hand, Gabi pointed a finger at him. "Don't you dare disappear on me again."

"I won't. I promise."

When the door closed behind Uriel, the doctor asked, "Do you know why you are here?"

"I'm transitioning into immortality," she said quietly as the memories rushed back in. "I was in a hospital. Gilbert came to get me with you and a couple of other guys. Then you brought me here." She looked at the closed door and shook her head. "I must have dreamt the part about Uriel being a god and his real name being Aru." A snort escaped her throat. "He's a god in bed, that's for sure. That was probably what prompted the crazy dream."

"It wasn't a dream." Julian didn't look amused. "I hope the confusion is temporary and that it will clear up. Otherwise, we might have a problem."

"What do you mean? What problem?"

"Your mind might have been permanently affected by the yo-yoing of memories. I hope it wasn't, and that the transition will clear it up, but you might need rehabilitation after the critical stage of your transition is over."

22

ARU

"What's going on?" Gilbert asked as Aru walked out of Gabi's room.

"She has issues with her memory. It seems that my presence triggers Orion's compulsion to forget what she knows about immortals. She thought that she was still in the human hospital and didn't remember that you took her out of there."

"That's not good." Gilbert rubbed a hand over his mouth. "What does Julian think?"

"He's checking whether her memories will return in my absence."

"What if they don't?"

"I don't know. I know nothing about any of this, and I feel so damn helpless. There is nothing worse than the inability to do anything."

Gilbert regarded him with curiosity in his eyes. "You really care about her."

"Of course, I do."

"It's not at all obvious. You two had a fling, you accidentally induced her transition, and now she's becoming immortal. You have no obligation to her. You can walk away, and Gabi will find a nice immortal dude to settle down with. There are plenty of them in the village who would do anything for a chance to score an immortal mate."

The growl that rose from deep in Aru's throat had Gilbert take a step back.

He lifted his hands. "No need to growl, buddy. I was just checking to see how serious you are about my baby sister. She's been hurt before, and I vowed to do everything in my power to never let it happen again."

"I understand." Aru let out a breath. "I have a sister, too, and if anyone ever hurt her, I would tear his insides out with my fangs."

The look Gilbert gave him was far from horrified. In fact, he seemed satisfied. "I assume that your sister is still single?"

"Yes."

"Younger? Older?"

Aru had never told anyone that Aria was his twin. He'd emerged from their mother's womb first so he could claim to be older.

"Aria is younger. We are very close, or we used to be, before I was drafted to the service."

"Drafted?" Gilbert raised a brow. "Is that a thing in your world?"

"Yes. All young gods have to serve in one capacity or another."

"Do the gods have enemies?"

Aru smiled. "Not officially, but occasionally, there are uprisings or revolts on planets controlled by the gods. Some of the created species are not as grateful as others for being created and shaped in the image of the gods. That's what the official statements usually say, but I assume that they are particularly opposed to paying tribute. They want to do their own thing, and they don't want to part with a large chunk of their resources. One of the tasks of the patrol ships is collecting a portion of the tributes for Anumati. Most of it is symbolic, though, and useless to us. I guess it's meant to habituate the created species to the custom, so when they have something of real value, they will know that some of it should be put aside for the gods."

Gilbert nodded. "Gold used to be a tribute to the gods."

"Precisely."

"So, you are tax collectors?"

Surprisingly, Gilbert had arrived at the same conclusion as Kian. Perhaps it had to do with the way humans interacted and governed themselves. Taxes were an integral part of their lives, while the concept didn't exist on Anumati.

Gods did not pay tribute or taxes, and massive projects were funded by crowd-sourcing that was supposedly voluntary. The prominent families had pet projects that they supported. The rest was financed by the tribute collected from all over the galaxy.

"Only some of us are involved in collecting tribute," Aru said. "Most of the drafted gods are tasked with seeding planets, creating new species, and helping them evolve. A small portion is trained in weapons and assigned patrol duties."

Gilbert opened his mouth, no doubt to ask more questions about life on Anumati, but as the door opened and Julian stepped out of Gabi's room, he turned to the doctor. "What's going on with my sister?"

"After Aru left the room, Gabi's recall improved, so there is definitely a connection. The vestiges of Orion's compulsion are probably the culprit, and I believe that they will clear up in time. Don't forget that she's spending more time unconscious than conscious, and each time she wakes up, she has to reconstruct what she'd learned before. That on its own can create confusion."

Gilbert bobbed his head, accepting the doctor's authority, and Aru should have done the same, but he'd always had trouble with accepting things at face value.

"Don't you think that Orion needs to come over and reinforce the undoing of what he has done in person?"

Julian shook his head. "I don't think his compulsion is still in effect. At this point, Gabi's mind is working autonomously, but it's following the rules it has been given by Orion. It will take time to reset itself." He looked at Gilbert. "I'll call Vanessa and ask her opinion. She's better equipped than me to deal with problems that have to do with the mind."

So, the doctor was not as sure as he'd pretended to be about Gabi's mind returning to normal without assistance.

That helpless feeling washed over Aru again, making him suddenly sweat even though the clinic's air conditioning was working just fine.

"Who's Vanessa?" he asked.

"The clan psychologist." Julian quirked a smile. "She's mated to one of the Kra-ell purebloods."

The lack of concern in the doctor's voice eased some of Aru's worry.

Perhaps Julian had decided to consult with the psychologist just as an afterthought.

"Which Kra-ell is she mated to?" Aru asked.

"Mo-red."

"He's a good guy."

Listening to the spy drones, Aru had never heard Mo-red being rude or berating anyone, which wasn't true of most of the purebloods.

"Yeah. Surprisingly so," Julian said. "He was one of Igor's pod members, and he stood trial with the others, but Vanessa and Lusha got him and the others off with just community service." He chuckled. "With how bloodthirsty the Kra-ell are, the outcome of the trial surprised me."

That was a fascinating story, and Aru wanted to hear more about the trial, but right now, he wanted to see Gabi more than he wanted anything else.

"Can I go back in there?" He waved a hand at the door.

Hopefully, the doctor wouldn't tell him that she needed to rest and he couldn't see her.

Could he thrall the guy to let him in?

Perhaps he could do that like he did with humans, and Julian wouldn't even know that he'd been thralled.

"Yes. Definitely. She will wring my neck if I don't get you back in there." He smiled at Gilbert. "I thought that you were overbearing, but you're easy compared to your sister. She's a ballbuster."

A proud grin spread over Gilbert's face. "I taught her not to take shit from anyone."

If Aru wasn't confusing idioms, calling a person a ballbuster, especially a woman, was not a compliment. Why would Gilbert be proud of that?

"Excuse me, but Gabi is nothing of the sort. She's kind, accommodating, and sweet. She's a lovely lady any male would be proud to call his mate."

Julian and Gilbert exchanged amused glances.

"I applaud women who are assertive and don't take bull from anyone, so it wasn't meant as an insult." Julian put his hand on Aru's shoulder. "It was a compliment. Come on. We don't want to keep your lovely lady waiting."

Aru frowned at him. "Why do I have a feeling that you are mocking me?"

"I'm not. If I look amused, it is because I know what it's like to fall in love, and it makes me happy to see another male as besotted as I was. Still am." He paused at the door. "I'm not embarrassed to admit that I fell for my mate just from gazing at her picture."

"Is she a ballbuster?"

The doctor chuckled. "Ella can definitely rise to the occasion."

23

GABI

The doctor had promised to keep Uriel in the waiting room for a few minutes so Gabi could sort herself out, not that she could do much while confined to the hospital bed and attached to a catheter and an IV bag.

She wished she could take a shower, do her hair, and put on makeup, but none of that was an option.

For some reason, when she'd asked Julian for her bag, he had given her a half-mumbled excuse and left the room, so she didn't have a brush or a mirror and had to untangle her hair with her fingers. He had left some mints on her bedside table, though, so at least she wouldn't have a stinky mouth when she berated Uriel.

Aru. His name is Aru.

Why was it so difficult to hold on to her memories? They were like beads and pebbles in a kaleidoscope, creating different random patterns every time she woke up, and her mind went into another mental spin.

As the door opened and Julian ushered Aru in, Gabi couldn't decide whether she should smile or glare at him. She was happy he was there, but she was also mad at him.

"Look who's back," Julian said. "Do you know who he is?"

She nodded.

"Do you remember his name?"

"Which one? Uriel Delgado or Aru?"

"Fantastic." Julian clapped Aru on his back. "I told you that Gabi's mind will sort itself out. I'll leave the two of you alone now." He glanced at the camera and winked. "I promise not to peek."

Gabi rolled her eyes. "As if. Why are males so obtuse? You're a doctor. You should know better."

Grinning, he looked at Aru. "What did I say? She's a ballbuster."

"I'm not." Gabi groaned.

Even if she was willing to forgive Aru, and even if she was in the mood for some hanky-panky, which she wasn't, she was too weak to move, every bone and muscle in her body ached, and she was hooked up to a catheter and an IV.

When the door closed behind Julian, Aru pulled the rolling stool Gilbert had used out from under the counter and rolled it over to her bedside. "Julian is a strange guy." He straddled the small stool, dwarfing it with his bulk. "Are all doctors like that?"

She frowned at him. "I don't want to do small talk. I want to know who you are, why you lied to me, and what you were thinking having unprotected sex with me when you knew you could induce me?"

"I didn't know that I could do that, and since disease and pregnancy were not an issue, I had no reason to be concerned. I had no idea that you were a Dormant or even what Dormants were, and I didn't know that I could induce a Dormant's transition. The world of the immortals is as new to me as it is to you."

Well, that took care of at least half of her ire. He hadn't known.

"What does it mean to be a god? Do you have special powers?"

"I have mind control powers that work on most species but not on other gods. I can thrall, which is a form of hypnosis, for lack of a better description. It's not what Orion did to you. That was compulsion, and it works differently." He raked his fingers through his hair. "Compulsion is supposed to be less dangerous than thralling, but perhaps my information was wrong. Or maybe the combination of my thralling with Orion's compulsion was what got you in trouble. But I used so little. It shouldn't have had an adverse effect on you."

Aru was rambling, which was kind of cute. He was nervous and unsure, which meant that he cared about her and wanted her to think well of him, but he'd also admitted that he'd hypnotized her, and that wasn't okay.

"When did you thrall me?"

He lifted his eyes to her. "I thought you knew. The fact that you are transitioning should be clue enough. You wouldn't be if I hadn't bitten you. Do you remember me doing that?"

"I don't." She lifted her hand to her neck. "I thought that you bit me here, but there was no mark the next morning, so I thought that I dreamt it."

"My saliva has healing properties, and so does the venom. That's why there was no mark. But if I hadn't thralled you to forget the bite, you would have remembered it." He took a deep breath. "I also thralled you to ignore my fangs and glowing eyes. They would have terrified you and given me away. I couldn't allow that to happen."

Gabi nodded. "That makes sense."

If she hadn't fainted on sight, she would have definitely run away screaming. Eric had shown her his fangs during the welcome dinner, and they were monstrous. Later, she'd learned that his fangs weren't even fully grown yet, so Aru's were probably the size of a saber-toothed tiger's.

"Am I forgiven?" Aru's eyes pleaded with her to say yes.

"For what exactly should I forgive you?"

"For not telling you the truth about who I was, for inadvertently inducing your transition, and for not rushing to your side when you asked me to come get you from the hospital."

Yeah, it was all of the above, and it didn't help that she understood why he had done all those things. It hurt that she hadn't been his first priority.

Gilbert had begged Kian to let him out of the locked-down village to come to her aid. That was what people who cared for each other did.

But to Aru, she had been just another inconsequential human female he was having a good time with.

Gabi sighed. "Tell me the truth, Aru. Throughout our time together, did you think of me as just another random hookup? Or did you feel that there was something different about me? Something more?"

24

ARU

Aru rose to his feet, sat on the bed next to Gabi, and took her hand. "You were not a random hookup." When she arched an eyebrow, he chuckled. "Well, maybe at first. But no, not even then. From the first moment I saw you in the airport lounge, I knew that there was something special about you. Something that called to me, but I didn't know what it was. I just assumed that I was attracted to a beautiful, intriguing woman. But then we were seated next to each other on the plane, and I got to know you a little, and you enchanted me. "

Gabi snorted. "You were enamored by my irrational fear of flying?"

"I was impressed with your bravery. You were worried about your family, and you overcame your crippling fear of flying to check on them. I think I started falling for you right then."

Her eyes widened. "Don't say the L word."

He lifted her hand and kissed the tips of her fingers with their dainty, red-painted nails. "I'll save it for last, then."

"Don't make false promises just because you feel sorry or guilty or anything like that. It's not fair to me or to you."

"I'm not making any promises because I'm not talking about the future. I'm still talking about the past."

"Fine." She gave him a half-hearted smile. "So, what else did you like so much about me on the plane? Was it how I was crushing your hand the entire five hours? Or was it my endless prattle about my family?"

"Both." He smiled behind her fingers. "I loved it that you found solace in my touch." He closed his eyes. "I'm sorry. I forgot that the L-word is disallowed. It made me feel good that you relied on me for comfort, and it felt good to hold your hand and distract you from your fear. It was also nice to hear about your family and how close you were to your brothers and your nieces and nephews. The way a person interacts with their family says a lot about them, and your heart is full of the L-word for your brothers, their children, and their mates." He glanced toward the door. "I like Gilbert. He's very protective of you."

Gabi's eyes misted with tears. "Gilbert is my rock. I don't know what I would have done without him."

Damn, hearing her say that chafed.

He wanted to be Gabi's rock, the one she could count on to come to her aid whenever she needed anything, be it rescue from a clinic where she didn't feel comfortable or emotional support when she felt overwhelmed or scared and needed someone's hand to hold on to.

Except, he couldn't be that male for her, not in the long run, so it was good that she had Gilbert, and they were both immortal. Well, Gilbert was, but Gabi was on her way to becoming so as well.

Come to think of it, Gilbert hadn't triggered Aru's alarm. He must already consider him family because he was Gabi's protector.

"Yeah, your brother is a good guy. He's also smart and insightful."

The mist evaporated from Gabi's eyes. "I'm glad that was the impression he left on you. He's such a goofball that sometimes people don't take him seriously, but on the inside, he's a very serious guy. After our parents died, he had to support two depressed teenagers financially and emotionally. I guess that's when he developed his sarcastic humor. It was a survival mechanism." She stopped and pursed her lips. "You wouldn't know anything about it, would you?"

"About sarcasm? I think I do."

"I mean about dealing with death. You're a god. Your loved ones don't die."

"Hopefully, they don't, but there are many things that can kill gods and immortals. Anything that is flesh and blood can be killed. It's just harder to do."

Her cheeks pinked. "Thank goodness. When Gilbert told me that you were a god, I thought that maybe you could become incorporeal or corporeal on demand." She lifted her other hand and rubbed her temple. "I might have had a few creative dreams about it."

Her words, combined with the deepening color of her cheeks, made him harden in an instant. "Might have? You either did or didn't."

"I did." She looked at him from under lowered lashes. "They were very…interesting."

"I would love to hear all about them." He glanced at the camera mounted on the wall. "But perhaps not here."

She laughed. "Julian said that he muted the sound, but since I'm not in a state to do anything other than talk, perhaps I should save my sexy dreams for when we can actually do something about the side effects of my storytelling."

Unable to help himself, he leaned over and kissed her cheek. "I can't wait."

"Yeah, neither can I." She lowered her eyes. "Are you going to stick around? Or do you still plan on leaving as soon as your negotiations are done?"

"You know that I wasn't negotiating flea-market finds, right?"

Gabi nodded. "You were negotiating with Kian, but I don't know what about or why. Gilbert doesn't know what's going on. He knows you and your friends are gods, but he doesn't know why you are here or what you want. Or maybe I just haven't been awake long enough for him to tell me."

He stroked her hair. "I want to tell you everything, but Julian warned me not to overtax you. How are you feeling?"

She smiled. "Not sleepy. I think I'm getting better." She glanced at the IV bag. "I told Julian that I was aching all over, so he put something in the bag to help with the pain, and it was such a wonderful relief. I think that the aches sapped my energy and made me sleepy, and now that it's gone, I can stay awake longer."

There was a difference between falling asleep and losing consciousness, but Aru wasn't sure what it was. That being said, he suspected that bodily aches didn't cause the loss of consciousness.

"Is it normal for the transition to be painful?"

Gabi smiled sheepishly. "Julian said that I might be growing taller. He didn't take my measurements before it started, so he can't say for sure, but he says that all the transitioning Dormants who had similar complaints grew a little taller. I wouldn't mind gaining an inch or two."

"You are perfect the way you are. I don't want you to change."

She pouted. "A couple of inches wouldn't change what I look like or my personality but becoming immortal might. I already feel different."

25

GABI

Aru or Uriel, god or human, it didn't really change anything. He was still the same guy, and the more they talked, the more comfortable Gabi was with him.

It was like nothing had changed when everything had.

She was turning immortal, and he was a god, and she didn't really know what it meant for their future. They had so much to talk about, but she would probably slip away again, and the fear that he wouldn't be there when she woke up was enough for her to cling to consciousness for as long as she could.

Aru frowned. "In what way does turning immortal make you feel different? Is your eyesight better or your hearing?"

Males were so literal.

"I think that the biggest change is knowing that Gilbert and Eric and the rest of my family are immortals or on the way to becoming immortal. It makes me less fearful, so maybe the next time I need to fly across the country, I won't be as terrified."

Aru kissed the tips of her fingers again, which she really liked. It was as if he couldn't keep his hands and lips off her, but since she wasn't well, he only allowed himself to touch and kiss her fingertips.

It was so sweet.

His dark brows turned down in a deep V. "If immortals possess the same healing abilities as gods, surviving a plane crash is possible, but it's not guaranteed. That being said, commercial flights are extremely safe, much safer than driving a car or taking the train."

She rolled her eyes. "I know that. But phobias are not rational. Knowing that my family is more resilient than ever and that I don't need to stay awake at night worrying about them eases me in ways I couldn't imagine. It's such a liberating feeling."

"I'm glad." He turned her hand palm up and kissed it.

Gabi chuckled. "Do the gods practice Vulcan lovemaking customs? For them, it's all about touching hands."

"I've never heard of the Vulcans. Is there a country or a people by that name?"

"Yes, but they are fictional." She glanced at the television screen across from her bed. "If you stay with me, we can watch old episodes of *Star Trek* together. It was such a fun show, and I know how much you like watching television."

"What is it about?"

"It's about humans going where no one has gone before, meaning the stars, and meeting all kinds of interesting aliens. Hey, maybe the creator was one of your people who somehow got stranded on Earth and fed the imaginations of millions, preparing us for possible future contact with extraterrestrials."

"Not likely. The previous team was picked up in its entirety, and none of the other teams reported missing a member."

"It was just a joke, Uriel. I mean Aru." Gabi shook her head. "It's all so confusing, but it shouldn't be. I knew very little about you before, and now I know a little bit more than just your last name and that you are from Portugal, but then that's all fake." She shook her head. "Now that you don't have to go anywhere, and you don't need to keep secrets from me either, you can finally open up and tell me everything."

Given his frown, that was a no.

"How did you know that my fake last name was Delgado? Or that I was supposedly from Portugal. I never told you that."

"Oops." She lifted a hand to her lips. "I thought you knew that we knew. Well, I didn't remember that when I was with you, but I remembered it when I was alone. I thought that Delgado sounded sexy, and it suited you so well. It's a shame that it was fake."

He shook his head. "Was there an answer somewhere in there that I missed?"

Gabi smiled sheepishly. "On the day of my arrival, when I had dinner with my family, they introduced me to Orion and Onegus—two gorgeous immortal males. I told them that the guy I met on the plane was just as gorgeous as they were, and Onegus got suspicious, so he asked the clan's hacker to check your background. The hacker found out your name and that you were living in Portugal. Your fake identity must have been really good, because they concluded that you were just a handsome human who didn't warrant further investigation. They probably didn't bother to dig too deeply because I wasn't anyone important, so it didn't matter who I was dating. But just in case, Orion compelled me to forget everything I was told when I was around strangers, including you."

Gabi had expected Aru to be angry about the hacker investigating him, but the only part of her story that seemed to bother him was Onegus's decision not to continue the investigation.

"I haven't met Onegus yet, and I don't know who he is, but he should have done a better job checking up on my fake background. The guy who sold me the fake identity promised that it was a hundred percent legit and that it would pass every inspection, but I was sure he exaggerated just so he could charge the obscene amount that he did."

"So, you're not mad that they investigated you?"

"Why would I be mad? I'm just stunned that a series of coincidences could have potentially derailed my mission. I don't know what would have happened if the clan had trapped me while I was with you. Dagor and Negal would have tried to free me, the clan would have retaliated, and things might have ended badly." He let out a breath. "I'm so glad that I decided to splurge on the best fake identity money could buy. It helped us avoid a disaster."

That didn't sound good. What the heck was Aru's deal, and what did he want from the clan?

Gabi pulled her hand out of Aru's grasp. "Tell me why you are here and what you hope to achieve from your negotiations with the clan."

He sighed. "It's a long story."

"Are you in a big rush to leave?"

"No. I'm staying with you even if I have to sleep on the floor. Your brother might have an issue with that, but I'll just have to explain that from now on, I am your rock and that he can return to his family."

26

ARU

As soon as Aru had uttered the words, he regretted saying them. He wanted them to be true. He wanted to be Gabi's rock, the one she turned to when she needed anything, big or small. Not her brother.

Except, he hadn't told her the truth.

In a perfect world, nothing would have made him happier than becoming Gabi's rock, but the world was far from perfect, and he was committed to a cause that had the fate of trillions on the line. He had to go wherever the Supreme sent him to be the eyes and ears of the rebellion and report his findings.

Gabi regarded him with a penetrating look. "Can you be my rock, Aru? Because you don't look sure about it."

"I want to be with you." He squeezed her hand.

"But you can't."

"I can, but not forever."

"How long?"

"A hundred and fifteen years, give or take a couple. That's when my patrol ship returns."

She laughed. "That's long enough. Let's see if you can survive one month with me first, and then we can talk about a century."

It was a relief to realize that Gabi didn't think of him in the same terms he thought of her. If she did, she would be talking about forever.

Aru forced a smile. "Is that a challenge?"

Did she even know about truelove mates?

If she didn't, he wasn't going to tell her. His feelings for her ran deeper than any he'd had for any female before her, but that didn't mean that she was his one and only.

Could she even be his truelove mate?

Gabi was a hybrid, half human and half goddess, or rather mostly human, with just a little bit of godly genes, making her immortal.

According to the lore, she couldn't be his truelove mate, but then the lore was as much part of the propaganda as everything else on Anumati.

Her smile turned into a frown. "No, it's not a challenge. I would never want you to stay even a minute longer than you want to. If you stay, it will be because you want to be with me and not because you want to win a bet. That's a terrible reason to be with someone. We should be together only as long as we make each other happy, whether it's a week, a month, or a year. I don't want to be stuck in a relationship that doesn't work."

It was such a human thing to say that it pained him.

Even gods who had their mating arranged by their families, and did it out of convenience and not love, stayed together. They might have enjoyed scores of paramours, but the family unit stayed intact. The union was sacred whether they loved each other or not and whether they had children together or not.

So yeah, it was mostly about politics, forging alliances, and uniting with other families, but the system worked. Separations were incredibly rare, and when they happened, it was usually because one of the partners found his or her truelove mate, and no one dared to stand in the way of Fate.

It was considered bad luck.

Gabi's forehead furrowed. "You don't seem to agree with me."

"I don't agree with the way humans take their mating commitments lightly. Things are different on Anumati."

"Of course, they are." She waved a dismissive hand. "If they are anything like the immortals, they are all mated to their truelove mates and can't think of being with anyone else."

So, Gabi knew about that and apparently didn't consider him a worthy candidate for being her one and only.

Aru laughed without mirth. "Nothing could be farther from the truth. Truelove matches are extremely rare, and arranged matings are the norm, as is sleeping around. We are a promiscuous bunch."

She recoiled as if he had slapped her. "I will never tolerate infidelity, not even in a casual relationship. If that's how you are, how you conduct yourself, you'd better leave now. There is no future for us. Not even for a day."

Damn, he should have remembered that she'd been badly hurt by her ex's infidelity. Hell, he should have remembered how angry hearing about it had made him.

"I apologize. That was incredibly insensitive of me." He reached for her hand, but she pulled it away, and his heart squeezed painfully. "I was just describing things as they are for Anumati's upper class, but that doesn't mean that everyone is like that. I am not. I'm not interested in sleeping around. In fact, being a commoner affords me the freedom of not having my mating arranged, and I promised myself that I would not mate anyone unless she was my one and only. I just never expected to find her, and certainly not on Earth, so I resolved to remain a bachelor, which is very upsetting to my parents. Especially my mother. She hopes for a grandchild."

GABI

Aru's words reverberated in Gabi's head—"I promised myself that I would not mate anyone unless she was my one and only. I've just never expected to find her, and certainly not on Earth."

Her heart thundered in her chest, and it was a wonder that Aru didn't hear it with his godly ears, or maybe he did, and he thought that the sound was coming from the medical equipment.

Thank goodness for that.

Had he just told her, in so many words, that she was his truelove mate?

Maybe she misunderstood?

No, she couldn't have.

"Aru." She touched his hand. "Look at me."

He lifted a pair of haunted eyes to her. "I'm sorry. I must make no sense to you."

"You just said that you didn't expect to find your truelove mate on Earth. Does that mean that you found her?"

A small smile bloomed on his handsome face. "Did I?"

"Don't do that." She wanted to slap his arm but regrettably wasn't strong enough to do that. "Don't you dare answer my question with a question. Is it yes or no?"

"Maybe? I've never felt this way before about anyone. Does wanting to be with you every minute of the day mean that you are my truelove mate? Does the fact that seeing you makes my heart soar mean that you are my one and only?"

She shook her head. "That's how I felt when I was dating Dylan, but that could be simple love or infatuation, and there is nothing mystical about it. I don't know how a truelove mate is different from someone you just love."

His eyes looked tormented. "Do you feel for me the same way you felt for your ex? Do you love me?"

She swallowed. "I don't feel about you the same way I did about Dylan. I was a kid when I fell for the most popular guy in school, and it might not have been real love. I'm older and smarter now, and I acknowledge that I don't know you well enough to love you. But I do want to be with you every minute of the day, and seeing you does make me happy, at least most of the time. Does that mean that you are my one and only?"

He arched a brow. "Most of the time, but not all?"

"Sometimes I'm mad at you or frustrated with you, but I'm still happy to see you."

His smile was brilliant. "Then you love me."

Damn, it was so difficult to admit it, and it made no sense to be in love with a guy that she'd just met, but he was a god, and the rules were different with him. Heck, there were no rules.

"I might be in love with you," she admitted. "But who wouldn't be?" She waved a hand over his face. "You are a god. So gorgeous that you're blinding. And you're also charming and attentive. What's not to love except for your fear of commitment and your evasiveness?"

"I don't have a fear of commitment. I just can't commit for more than a hundred and fifteen years."

He'd said that before, and she'd laughed, but that was before he'd told her that he had found his truelove on Earth.

"Why do you need to go? Can't you quit?"

Aru shook his head. "I wish I could, but the fate of Anumati is more important than what I want, and I made a commitment I can't back out of no matter what it costs me."

"Then can I come with you?"

Aru's eyes widened. "You can't. No one back home knows that there are immortals on Earth—" He stopped mid-sentence. "But I'll have to report it so they will know." He swallowed. "I can't report it." He raked his fingers through his hair. "I don't know what to do."

He looked so lost, and she didn't know what to say to make it better for him. The only comfort she could offer him was the warmth of her embrace.

"Come here." She scooted aside to make room for him. "Lie down next to me."

He looked with longing in his eyes at the sliver of space she'd created. "Are you sure it's okay? You have wires and tubes attached to you."

"Then you will have to be careful around them."

Moving with the speed of a god, he kicked his boots off and climbed on the bed so carefully that it barely moved under his weight.

Lying on his side, most of his body must have been hanging over the side of the bed because it wasn't touching hers, but Gabi would have none of that. "Come closer." She also turned on her side and put her hand on his shoulder, which was as far as it would go, given the limitations.

Aru scooted a little closer, his chest lightly touching hers, and put his arm gently around her. He kept the bulk of his body away from hers, which was probably smart given all the wires attached to her chest and other things she didn't want to think about, like the fact that there was no female nurse on site, which meant that Julian had put the catheter in.

Talk about embarrassing.

Whatever. He was a doctor, and he had probably done that a thousand times to scores of female patients.

Aru closed his eyes. "It pains me to see you like this. I want you out of the hospital bed, out of the clinic, and out of the underground."

She snorted. "You and me both. But on the bright side, I haven't lost consciousness yet, which is probably the longest stretch since I started transitioning. That's a good sign." She lifted her hand off his shoulder and cupped his cheek. "Maybe your presence makes me stronger."

He leaned into her hand and closed his eyes. "I hope so. I only want to bring you happiness and joy, but instead, I'm the harbinger of doom."

"What are you talking about? My transition? It's not a bad thing. It's a good thing. You turned on my immortal genes, and I'm grateful for that."

"Thank the merciful Fates for that and for making your transition relatively easy. I was told that it's much tougher for some." He turned his face, so his lips were at her palm, and he kissed it. "If you'll have me, I will gladly spend the next hundred and fifteen years with you. That's more than I ever hoped for."

28

ARU

When Gabi fell asleep, Aru wasn't sure whether she'd lost consciousness or was just dozing off, but since no alarms went off and the doctor hadn't rushed in, he assumed that everything was okay.

Sliding his arm gently off her, he shifted back and lowered his feet to the floor.

The effort at stealth was probably unnecessary, but Gabi needed her rest, and if she was sleeping, not unconscious, he didn't want to wake her up.

Aru would have loved nothing more than to stay with her and hold her until the next time she opened her eyes so they could talk some more, but he had promised Kian to tell him how to identify the spy bugs, and the immortal was probably waiting for him to do so before going home.

They had only touched the tip of the iceberg, and there was so much more Aru could learn from the immortals, provided that they agreed to share things with him.

Holding his boots in his hand, he tiptoed to the door and opened it.

Outside, he found Gilbert in the waiting room, but Kian was gone. Not that it surprised him. The leader of the immortals had better things to do than wait around for him. What did surprise him was that no one had knocked on the door to remind him that Kian was waiting.

"Where is Kian?" he asked Gilbert after closing the door.

"Got tired of waiting for you and went back upstairs. He said to send you up when you emerge."

Aru dropped his boots on the floor and pushed his feet into them.

"I hope you don't mind." Gilbert didn't wait for Aru to answer before pulling out his phone and snapping a picture of him. "My better half wants to see what you look like."

Aru shrugged. "You could have asked the security people to supply you with a portrait from the surveillance feed."

"Nah, I doubt the surveillance cameras caught your best side. By the way, what do the gods wear on Anumati? I keep imagining them in white togas and gold sandals."

"You're not that far off. Anumati is hot and humid despite being dark, and clothing tends to be airy."

Gilbert grinned. "I'll be damned. So, the Greeks and the Romans were imitating godly fashion?"

"Perhaps." Aru headed for the door. "Or maybe similar climates prompted similar fashion." He opened the door and then stopped. "How does Kian expect me to get back to the penthouse when I can't activate the elevator?"

"Anandur is on his way to get you," the doctor called from the open door to his office. "I notified Kian as soon as you came out."

That made sense. Neither Gilbert nor Julian had asked him how Gabi was doing because they didn't need to. The doctor could see everything that was happening in her room, as well as the readouts from the monitoring equipment.

Turning around, Aru walked into the tiny office. "Gabi said that it was the longest stretch of wakefulness she'd had since her transition started. That's a good sign, right?"

Julian nodded. "She's doing remarkably well. You have nothing to worry about."

"She also said that my presence makes her feel stronger. Do you think it's true, or did she imagine it because my presence lifted her mood?"

The doctor lifted his hands. "The mind and body are interconnected, and positive feelings have a positive impact on the body. That's one explanation. The other could be that you release some pheromones that are beneficial to your mate. There isn't much known about the gods' physiology." He chuckled. "Contrary to popular belief, doctors don't know everything, and we are often stumped by what human bodies can do, let alone the bodies of gods."

"What popular belief?" Anandur poked his head into Julian's office. "No one thinks that doctors know everything other than the doctors themselves. You are the only doctor I know who admits to being stumped."

Far from looking offended, Julian lifted one brow. "How many doctors do you know that you are entitled to an opinion about my entire profession?"

"I know three." Anandur smiled. "Four, if you include Vanessa. She's my favorite, by the way." He turned to Aru. "Let's go, buddy. Kian is impatiently waiting."

With a nod goodbye to Julian and Gilbert, Aru walked out of the doctor's office. "Someone should have knocked on the door to remind me that Kian was waiting. I forgot all about it until Gabi fell asleep."

"And interrupt a mates' reunion?" The big redhead draped his muscular arm around Aru's shoulders. "Even the mighty Kian wouldn't dare to intrude on that. The Fates wouldn't be happy."

It was reassuring to find out that the immortals shared the gods' belief in the Fates. Any commonality was welcome, making conversations flow more naturally without having to explain the foundation of their belief system and how it affected their actions. So much of the gods' culture was influenced by their belief in the Fates, the oracles, and the one force in charge of everything.

"I don't know whether Gabi and I are fated to be together," Aru said, even though deep down he knew that they were. "Everything happened so fast. We barely know each other."

The guard summoned the elevator, which must have been idling at the clinic level because its doors opened immediately.

"After you." He motioned for Aru to go in. "I have a little test that might help you determine whether or not Gabriella is your one and only."

"You do?"

Anandur frowned. "I wouldn't have said that I have it if I didn't. So here is the test. Think of the sexiest, most desirable movie star or celebrity on Anumati or here on Earth, someone whom you fantasized about hooking up with. Is there someone like that?"

"There is," Aru admitted with a sheepish smile. "There is a famous singer on Anumati who is one of the most beautiful goddesses ever born, but that's not why I was attracted to her. It was that damn voice. I got hard every time I heard her sing."

"Excellent." Anandur rubbed his hands in glee. "Try to recreate her singing voice in your head."

Closing his eyes, Aru imagined listening to one of his favorite songs by Alva, and he felt his lips curving in a smile.

"Are you thinking about the song?" Anandur asked.

Aru opened his eyes. "I'm already on the third verse."

"Congratulations." Anandur clapped him on the back. "You passed the test. You didn't get aroused, which means that no one other than Gabi can elicit a sexual response from you, which means that she's your one and only."

29

KIAN

"I'm so glad it's finally over that I'm going to invite the family for dinner tonight." Syssi's grinning face filled Kian's laptop screen. "That way, you can tell everyone at once about the gods."

"You don't have Okidu."

"I don't mind cooking for a change." She let out a breath. "I didn't expect to feel so cooped up after only a few days, but I can't wait to be back at the university." She leaned on her elbows and looked into the camera of her phone, which she'd propped on her cappuccino cup. "Hanging around the students makes me feel young."

He chuckled. "You are young."

Kian rarely left the village, and he had no problem with that. In fact, he avoided mingling with humans as much as possible. He hated the attention he got—the looks, some ogling, some envious, and some hostile, but rarely friendly.

His godly heritage had gifted him with nearly godly looks, and humans were attracted to beauty regardless of sexual interest. Even small children liked the pretty teachers better. Come to think of it, perhaps humans had been preprogrammed by the gods to give beautiful people preferential treatment to enhance willing compliance. But despite their preference for beauty, they resented those whom they considered better looking than themselves.

Syssi smiled. "Compared to you, nearly everyone is young. So, when are you lifting the lockdown?"

"You want out of the village, and I can't wait to be back, which is my main motivation for lifting it this evening. I can't return to the village while the others are stuck here, so I need to allow everyone aside from the Guardians stationed at the keep to return home. In the meantime, though, I'm stuck in the penthouse, waiting for Aru to finish snuggling with Gabi. I can't lift the lockdown until I'm assured that there are no more spy drones following our people back to the village."

Syssi groaned. "I thought that it was a done deal. Don't tell me that you might not lift the lockdown after all. What if Aru can't prove to you that there are no more bugs? We can't stay locked down forever. I'm getting island fever."

"Don't worry. I'm holding the female he loves. Aru will bend over backward to please me so I will allow him to keep seeing her."

"The Fates are amazing." Syssi sighed. "Who could have ever imagined an encounter like Gabi and Aru's? And the consequences are just mind-boggling. Gabi was the necessary ingredient to make this cooperation work."

"Indeed. From all the pairings the Fates have orchestrated so far, this one must be the most daring. They might get in trouble for that."

"Why? And from whom? Aren't they the ultimate force in the universe?"

"According to our lore, even the Fates have to obey the rules governing them. Their job is to help individuals fulfill their potential and to arrange love matings for the worthy, but they have to do it in a way that seems plausibly coincidental. If they break the rules, they are sent to purgatory by some larger force."

"God?"

Kian snorted. "We have a good reason not to use the term God in reference to the unspecified all-encompassing universal law that has no name."

"How about the Architect? I like that one."

"Of course, you do. You are an architect."

"That's what my diploma says, but the only thing I've designed in recent years was the addition to our old home. I also offered a few suggestions to Gavin when he was designing phase three."

"You forget the Perfect Match environments. Yours are the most imaginative."

She chuckled. "That's because they probably don't come from my imagination but from precognition, like the Krall environment. Perhaps there is an underwater city somewhere like the one I created for the Mer adventure. Maybe even on Earth. We still don't have access to the deepest parts of the oceans."

"That would be nice." Kian got distracted as he saw the elevator door open on the small window in the corner of his laptop screen. A moment later, Anandur walked out with Aru at his side. "Aru is back. I'll call you later."

"Take a picture of him and his friends for me. I'm curious to see how closely they resemble my vision."

"Will do. Goodbye, my love." He blew her a kiss before ending the call.

Turner was in the living room, getting as much information out of the two other gods as he could, but they were well trained and said very little.

Kian closed the laptop, lifted it off the desk, and tucked it under his arm. Using the room that used to be his old office evoked some nostalgic feelings, but the truth was that he didn't miss the penthouse. The only fond memories he had from the place had been after Syssi moved in with him. All the years he had lived there as a bachelor were one big blur of days indistinguishable from one another.

Being alone sucked.

With a sigh, he opened the door and walked to the living room.

Aru nodded in greeting. "I apologize for keeping you waiting. I was so immersed in my reunion with Gabi that all other thoughts and considerations were pushed aside."

Kian cast him what he hoped was an understanding look. "I know how precious it is to find your one and only. Nothing in the world seems to matter apart from her."

Aru's face fell. "I wish I had the luxury of dedicating the rest of my life to Gabi, but I have duties that I cannot abdicate." He glanced at his two teammates. "Are you okay?"

Negal nodded. "Turner gave us what the humans call the third degree, but we didn't tell him anything that he wasn't supposed to know." He smiled at Turner. "But you got some insight into life on Anumati and the reasons for the unrest, right?"

Turner nodded. "It was a fascinating conversation. The Eternal King is a genius, and I doubt the rebels can find someone to replace him who's as capable but is honest and transparent. No one can hold so much power and be in charge of so many people and not become corrupt."

"Power corrupts, and absolute power corrupts absolutely," Kian quoted.

"We will find a suitable replacement." Aru walked over to Dagor and took his laptop. "As part of our negotiations, I promised Kian access to the software that's monitoring our spy drones so he can be assured that we have no more drones following his people."

Dagor's fangs punched out over his lower lip. "Why would you do that? What is he giving you in exchange other than access to your human?"

"My human is turning immortal, and as important as she is to me, there is much more at stake here." He shifted his gaze to Kian's laptop. "I see that you come suitably equipped. You can download the software we are using to monitor the drones. Do you have my little spy?"

Kian pulled a ring box out of his pocket. He had placed the tiny thing in an old box the previous renters had left behind so it wouldn't get squashed. He'd also sent pictures to William, but that had been an exercise in futility because looking at the device told William nothing about how it worked.

"Let's do this in my office." Kian turned back toward the hallway.

"How many offices do you have?" Aru asked.

"Too many. I have one in every residence, past or current, and in every office building my clan owns."

"I think you work too hard."

Kian snorted. "Tell me something I don't know."

"There are many things I can tell you that you don't know." Aru waited for Kian to open the door.

"I can't wait to hear them." Kian motioned for the god to go in. "But we both have mates we are eager to return to, and I also have a young daughter who wants her daddy to play with her before her bedtime, so we will have to continue our talks tomorrow."

Also, the family was coming over for dinner so he could give everybody an update in one go, but that wasn't something he wanted to share with the god.

He would still need to update the council, but they could wait until he had something more concrete to tell them.

ARU

"How old is your daughter?" Aru asked Kian.

It was difficult to reconcile the gruff leader with a loving mate and the father of a small child, but the way his harsh face softened and the crease between his brows smoothed out told a story of a very different male when he was off the clock, as the humans referred to leisure time.

Aru had a feeling that Kian didn't get to spend much time with his family and that he had to fight for every minute he could salvage to be with them.

"Allegra is almost ten months old going on twenty."

"That must be one of those idioms I haven't grasped yet. What does it mean that she's going on twenty?"

Kian smiled, his whole face brightening. "It means that she acts much older than her actual age. Allegra is very smart, and she knows how to communicate with us even when she doesn't have the words to express herself yet. Slight changes in tonality convey her meaning as well as if she articulated it, or better. All parents think that their child is special, but I know that mine is."

"Of course. I would love to meet her."

Kian regarded him with a guarded look. "Perhaps one day we can meet up in a restaurant in the city or here, but I can't invite you to my home if that is what you were suggesting."

"It wasn't. I would rather not know where your village is so no one can compel me to reveal your location. I'm just curious to meet your wife and daughter."

Kian nodded. "Let's leave the social interactions for the future. Right now, I need to make sure that no spy drone is following me or my people home."

"Naturally." Aru put the laptop on the desk and flipped it open. "This is the software that monitors the drones." He opened the ring box and gently picked up the miniature device. "It's low on energy, so I can't fly it. I'm just going to put it on your shoulder and show you what it sees."

"How do you charge it?"

"I have a charger back in my hotel room."

"I can have someone pick up your things and bring them over."

Nice try. As if he was going to let the immortals go through his stuff and discover the other gadgets his team had. The landing pod didn't have much space, so they could bring only a limited number of things with them, and they couldn't afford to part with any of it.

"I'll send Negal to do that later." Aru opened the application and showed the screen to Kian. "All these squares represent spy drones. The ones that are grayed out are those we've lost. They ran out of juice before we could collect them, and there was no way to find them. When they stop emitting, that's it."

"It seems to me like a flawed design."

"As with everything else, something had to be sacrificed to make the drones nearly soundless and invisible. What we used them for in Gor's compound was not what they were designed for, but it worked great for our purposes. We would get the drone to land on the clothing of one of the guards that were stationed at the entrances to the tunnels, and it would hitch a ride with him into the compound. That's how we got to see and hear what was going on. If we were lucky, we managed to move the spy to the guard that was stationed outside the compound the next day so the spy could hitch a ride back with him, and we could fly it a few meters out and collect it from a branch or a bush. But most times, that wasn't possible, and we just collected the information it transmitted until it died, and that was it."

"I see." Kian leaned toward the screen. "I guess the yellow squares represent the active drones."

"They represent the drones that are fully charged and ready to deploy, but look what happens when I click on one of these squares. The crossed-out eye means that they are not active." He moved the cursor to the only green square. "That's the one on your shoulder."

As he clicked it, the office and his face filled the screen. He smiled and waved.

Kian still looked skeptical. "Can I click on all the yellow squares?"

"Go ahead." Aru slid the laptop toward him.

Kian clicked through twenty or so before he was reassured that the rest would show him the same thing.

"How do you activate the other drones?"

"They need to be out of their box, and then I double-click on the yellow square until it turns green. It's not going to turn green unless the drone is detached from its carrier case."

The case was in the car, but Kian didn't need to know that. As far as he was concerned, it was in their hotel room.

"I want you to activate the other drones for a few seconds each. I want to see their squares turn green when they are on. I want to see what they see."

"But I don't have them with me."

"Then send Negal to collect your things. I'll wait until he returns with the drones."

The guy was paranoid, but Aru could understand that. If he was protecting his mate and daughter, he would have been just as diligent.

"Very well. Our hotel is not far from here, so it shouldn't take long, but before he goes, I need some reassurances from you."

Kian nodded. "What do you need?"

"We didn't bring a lot of equipment with us, but we can't allow what we have to fall into the wrong hands. I want your word that our things won't be searched and that we are not under surveillance while we are your guests in this penthouse."

It was a leap of faith to trust Kian to answer him truthfully, but Aru's gut said to trust the guy, and it wasn't as if he had much choice. Either way, Kian's answer would reveal what kind of person he was and if there was a future for their cooperation.

"There is one surveillance camera outside the door, so security knows when everyone who stays here comes and goes. There are also two cameras on the terrace, and their job is to warn against burglars and assassins. There are no cameras or listening devices inside the penthouse, and I'm willing to bring in a bug detector to prove it to you. As to your things, I need to know that none of them are weapons that could be used against my people. If you have defensive weapons, I can understand your need for them, but I don't want them up here in the penthouse. You will have to leave them in one of the lockers downstairs. You'll have the code, and I can give you access to the security camera feed that monitors the locker room so you'll know that no one is taking your things out, but you should know that security will alert me the moment you take them out."

Aru shook his head. "You could alter the feed so it will run in a loop, showing that there is no one in the locker room. We need to come up with another solution."

Kian rubbed his chin. "What if we put one of your bugs in there? I don't know how to tamper with your technology, so you'll know when and if anyone tries to get your stuff, and my surveillance will tell me if you are attempting to get your weapons out without notifying me."

"The spy drones are not built for long-term surveillance. It will run out of juice in a couple of days, and I don't know how long it will take Gabi to transition. I'm not leaving until she is out of the clinic."

"I get it. Can you put the bug there along with its charger, so it doesn't run out of juice?"

"That's not a bad idea. If the bug doesn't need to be hidden, that's not an issue. And you will know that I'm not using it or any of the others to spy on you or your people because I'm giving you access to the monitoring software."

KIAN

K ian frowned. "It just occurred to me that you are using a human-made laptop. If your bosses back home didn't know about the progress humans have made, they couldn't have expected you to get what you needed to monitor the spy drones on Earth."

"That's very astute of you, Kian, and you are absolutely right." Aru reached into his pocket and pulled out a device that looked like a cell phone. "This is the device we use to communicate between ourselves and to monitor the drones and many other things. For some reason, that specific application doesn't work, and the way our devices are built, it's impossible to fix a problem. Luckily, Dagor knows a thing or two about programming, and he found a way to duplicate the application using human-made resources."

That sounded way too convenient, but Kian couldn't detect deceit in Aru's scent or tone. "I find it hard to believe that all of your devices malfunctioned at the same time and with the same application. Also, our programming language is not compatible with yours. I'm not an expert on those kinds of things, but if the same apps need different programming to run on an Apple or an Android device, I assume that god-made devices and their applications cannot run on human-made laptops."

"Our devices are synchronized, so if there was a problem with one, the others get it too, but I'm not an expert, and we should ask Dagor. He will probably be able to explain this better than I can, and in the meantime, Negal can bring our things from the hotel. Where is that locker room you were talking about?"

"It's in the lobby." Kian pushed his laptop closer to Aru. "First, though, load the application onto my laptop."

Despite Aru's reassurances, Kian had an uncomfortable feeling in the pit of his stomach. His paranoia didn't need much fuel to flare up, and now it was burning hot.

He'd given Aru a clean laptop that wasn't connected to any of the clan servers. The god might have a bug capable of decrypting even William's state-of-the-art encryption.

It took longer than he'd expected to copy the application, and when it was done, Aru checked that everything was working correctly. "Here you go." He pushed the laptop over to Kian. "We've just made one more step in our complicated courtship dance."

Kian chuckled. "Which one of us is the skittish bride?"

"You, of course. I'm the one doing the courting, and you are the one pushing back."

"Simple," Dagor said. "I had to write the program from scratch, using an application that can write other applications. I can show you the YouTube video that taught me how to do it. It's easy when you know the basics."

Kian still wasn't convinced. "What went wrong with your devices? Why couldn't they monitor the drones?"

Dagor grimaced. "Do you think that only humans produce subpar glitchy products? Someone in acquisitions must have gotten a hefty kickback from the supplier of these spy drones. They are cheap garbage."

If that was garbage, Kian wondered what quality products looked like on Anumati.

"They are not that bad," Aru said. "But you are probably right about the kickback. The Borvod conglomerate got the contract for all the military surveillance equipment, and they are big supporters of the Eternal King, so of course they get the lucrative contract even though their products are not as good as their competitors'. That's how things work on Anumati."

"It would seem that's the way things work everywhere." Kian chuckled. "If the gods only knew how similar they are to the humans they created, they would think twice before looking down their noses at humans and referring to them as a lesser species."

"Created species," Aru corrected him. "It's considered rude to call them lesser."

"Of course." Kian smiled. "I wouldn't want to be rude. I just hope that nepotism isn't used when building interstellar ships. That could be dangerous."

"The king is not stupid," Dagor said. "Although he might have realized that it was a bad idea to award ship-building contracts to his supporters only after the settler ship got lost. Maybe it had a subpar onboard computer and communication system."

"Possibly." Aru rose to his feet. "Can we wait for Negal in the lobby? I want to store our things in the locker and go back to the clinic. I don't want Gabi to wake up without me there. I promised that I would stay with her so her brother could go back to his family."

"What about the demonstration?" Kian asked. "I want you to activate the drones so I can make sure that I can monitor their activity on my laptop."

"Dagor can probably do a better job with that than I can."

Turner followed the god up. "I don't know about you, but I want to head back home. Is that okay with you?"

Kian stifled a snort. "You are the security expert. You tell me if that's okay."

"I think it is." He looked at Aru. "You really want this alliance, don't you? And not just because you found your mate among our people."

Kian had a feeling that Turner was asking the question for his benefit and not because he expected an answer from Aru. He had already arrived at the conclusion that Aru wanted to establish cooperation.

The god nodded. "I do."

"And you are not going to do anything to jeopardize it, right?"

Again, this was meant for Kian's ears.

"Not if I can help it." Aru shifted his gaze to Kian. "But if you try to stop me from seeing Gabi, I will not be as agreeable as I am now."

"As long as we are on friendly terms, and I don't deem you a threat to her or any of my people, I will never use your visiting privileges for leverage."

He'd planned on doing that before, but Aru was honorable and making good on every promise, so it would be uncalled for.

"Good." Aru offered him his hand. "Thank you for being reasonable."

Kian shook what he'd been offered. "Thank you for being reasonable as well. Today, we've planted the first seeds of future cooperation. I hope they will grow into a mighty tree."

Beside him, Turner murmured, "Let's hope that the Eternal King doesn't discover it and chop it down."

32

ARU

"Gabi hasn't woken up since you left." The doctor's expression was indulgent as he regarded Aru. "She fought hard for every waking moment with you, and it has taken a toll on her body. She's compensating for the lost hours of rest."

"So, she's well?"

"Yes." Julian waved him off. "Go on. She's bound to wake up soon."

"Thank you."

Aru turned around and headed to Gabi's room. If she was still out, there was no point in knocking, so he just opened the door and walked in, startling her brother.

"You could've knocked." Gilbert held a hand to his chest in a dramatic parody of fright. "You scared me."

Ignoring the theatrics, Aru walked over to the bed and moved a stray curl away from Gabi's forehead. "My apologies. I didn't know that you were still here."

The guy lifted a brow. "Where else would I be?"

"You should've gone home to your family. I told you that I will be staying with Gabi from now on."

"Oh yeah? Where have you been for the past three and a half hours?"

Gilbert was right about that.

"Kian needed lots of assurances that I don't have any more spy drones following his people. Your leader is very thorough, and he doesn't take shortcuts or trust anyone's word when it comes to his clan's safety."

"That's good. I appreciate him keeping my family safe." Gilbert didn't get up from the stool, forcing Aru to remain standing.

His only other option was to sit on Gabi's bed, and he didn't want to do that with her brother in the room.

"But sometimes his paranoia is a pain in the rear," Gilbert continued. "I have a business to run, and from time to time, I need to visit it in person, but even if that wasn't an issue, I work from home, which is really a pain when my three little ones are there because my mate can't take them to preschool or the babysitter's."

"Well, I'm here now, so you can go home."

"Oh yeah? What if you need to leave again? Who is going to keep an eye on Gabi?"

"I'm done for tonight. My teammate brought our things here, and we are staying in Kian's old penthouse, so if I need to grab a quick shower or change clothes, it's only going to take me a few minutes. I also have access to the elevator now, so I don't need to wait for one of the guards to escort me."

Gilbert didn't look convinced and remained seated. "Are your friends going to come down here to visit Gabi as well?"

Aru shook his head. "Kian only allows me to come down here."

That was actually good because it had given him an opportunity to talk to Kian privately without Negal and Dagor around, and tomorrow, they would probably continue their talk away from others as well. The problem would be leaving Gabi alone. When she was asleep or unconscious, the doctor was good enough, but when she was awake, she should have someone who cared about her for company.

"Smart guy," Gilbert said. "I don't want strangers around my sister."

"I'm a stranger to you as much as my teammates."

That got a smile out of the guy. "But you are not a stranger to Gabi, and she likes having you around. Your buddies, on the other hand, are not welcome here. She wouldn't appreciate them coming in and out of her room." Gilbert cast a fond smile at his sister. "Gabi has always hated being sick, and she would absolutely hate it if strange men saw her in this weakened state. She can barely tolerate Julian taking care of her. She would much prefer a female doctor. Although to be fair to Julian, Gabi likes him much more than the female doctor who took care of her in the human hospital." When Aru bared his fangs, Gilbert lifted his hands. "Julian is happily mated, and he's giving Gabi all of his attention because she's his only patient. The doctor in the hospital was probably overworked and had no time for Gabi. Just keep your buddies away from her until she's back to her normal self."

"That's a given. I would never allow anyone in this room other than the doctor or a family member."

"Good." Gilbert rose to his feet. "I'll take a break for a few hours, visit the family, help Karen put the little ones to sleep, and I'll come back. I don't want Gabi to be alone even for a moment."

"She's never alone. The doctor is here, and when she's asleep, she doesn't need anyone to keep her company."

"Maybe." Gilbert stopped at the door. "But there is a change of guard. Julian is going home, and Merlin is taking the night shift."

The way Gilbert had said the other doctor's name raised Aru's hackles. "What's wrong with the other doctor?"

"He's a bit strange. You'll see what I mean when he gets here."

That was unacceptable. "Does he know how to take care of Gabi?"

"He's a real doctor with the right schooling and a degree, but he's eccentric. He makes fertility potions in his house. Who does that in the twenty-first century?"

That didn't sound so bad.

Aru didn't have a problem with someone experimenting with things, especially since he came from a place that regulated everything and didn't allow private innovation.

As a knock sounded on the open door, Aru and Gilbert both turned their heads toward the sound.

"Hi there." A male with white hair and a long white beard walked into the room. "I'm Doctor Merlin." He offered his hand to Aru. "And you must be the god who induced Gabriella."

The guy's eyes were smart, with a hint of mischief crinkling their corners, but the rest of his appearance didn't inspire confidence. His white coat was stained, and he was wearing red sports shoes with purple pants.

"My name is Aru." He shook the guy's slender hand. "I understand that you are replacing Julian."

"Only for tonight. The young man misses his mate, and he asked me to take over for him. Caring for transitioning Dormants is not my usual thing, but I'm doing him a favor." The doctor must have caught Aru's appraising look because he waved a hand over his colorful attire. "Excuse my unprofessional appearance. I was supposed to be here earlier, but as usual, I lost track of time working on an experiment, and when I realized how late it was, I didn't have time to change. I hope Julian has a clean coat I can borrow."

Great. Someone with an iffy grasp on the concept of time and no experience caring for transitioning Dormants was going to be in charge of Gabi's life for the next twelve hours or so.

"Excuse me for a moment." Aru rushed out of the room and walked into the doctor's office.

Thankfully, Julian was still there, collecting his things into a brown leather satchel.

"Are you sure it's okay to leave Gabi in the hands of a doctor who has no experience with transitioning Dormants?"

"I'm sure." Julian cast him a smile. "And not just because I can't spend another night away from my mate. Gabi is not in danger, and Merlin is a capable and experienced doctor. He was treating humans a century before I was born." Julian slung the strap of his satchel over his shoulder. "Don't let Merlin's clownish appearance fool you. He's a far more accomplished physician than I am."

SYSSI

"Let me help you." Alena walked into the kitchen. "You've been slaving in here for hours."

"I underestimated how long everything takes." Syssi handed Alena a bowl of potato salad. "But I'm so glad that the lockdown is finally over. Kian thinks that I'm organizing this dinner so he can give the entire family an update about the new gods all at once, but the truth is that I'm celebrating the end of being stuck in the village."

Okidu had been with Kian the entire afternoon, and Syssi hadn't wanted to ask Amanda or Alena to loan her their Odus. But it had been a long time since she'd cooked anything elaborate, and she'd forgotten how much work went into preparing a meal for a large family.

She'd thought it would be fun to have the kitchen at her disposal without Okidu wringing his hands and telling her to be careful because the kitchen was full of dangers, but halfway through it, she'd wished he was there to do the cleanup.

Alena had been watching Allegra and couldn't help in the kitchen until Annani had arrived and taken over babysitting her granddaughter.

"When is it officially happening?" Alena returned to take another dish to the dining room. "Can we leave now?"

"I'm not sure, but I think so. In any case, Kian's return to the village will signal the end of the lockdown." She cast her sister-in-law a smile. "Can't wait to get out, can you?"

Alena shrugged. "I'm used to being cooped up in the sanctuary for weeks and sometimes months at a time. The village is much larger than the sanctuary, and there are more people to interact with, so I'm good, but Orion is going nuts. He can't wait to get out."

Syssi glanced in the direction of the playroom, where Annani was entertaining Allegra, or perhaps the other way around. "Are you planning on going back there?"

"To visit, for sure. To live, I'm not so sure. I'm working on convincing my mother to permanently relocate to the village and have the sanctuary residents elect a council to run the place."

"Maybe some of them will want to join us in the village as well?" Syssi finished arranging the imitation-meat pie slices on the tray and handed it to Alena. "Can you put this in the warming drawer?"

Would anyone notice that the meat inside the pie wasn't real?

She could have made two separate dishes, one with the imitation ground beef and one with the real thing, but she had no real ground beef in the freezer and no time to get some.

Alena looked around the kitchen until she found the bank of warming drawers. "Most will probably want to stay in the sanctuary, but perhaps some will want to leave and settle here or in Scotland. I also expect some of the village and castle residents to join the Alaskan community. It's a great place for recluses who don't enjoy interacting with humans. I think we should open the sanctuary to whoever wants time out from the world."

"That's not a new idea." Syssi handed her another tray to put away. "Turning the sanctuary into a retreat for clan members has come up several times, but somehow it never gets done."

"It won't happen until Annani officially declares her intentions." Alena put the tray of sliced potatoes in one of the drawers. "As long as the sanctuary is her home, it's going to remain restricted to members by invitation only."

Syssi gasped. "Why didn't I think of it before? I should have asked Gerard to cater this dinner. He wasn't stuck in the village, and he could have delivered it ready."

"As if that was an option. First of all, you decided to have this dinner a few hours ago, and if you called Gerard about it, he would have laughed in your ear and hung up on you. Secondly, I offered to help, and you said that you were looking forward to cooking because you never get the chance with Okidu around."

Syssi sighed. "I forgot how much work it is. I'm just glad that Okidu is returning home with Kian so he can serve dinner and clean up afterward."

"Indeed." Alena laughed, the sound nearly as ethereal as her mother's, only several decibels louder. "What would we do without our Odus?"

Wiping her hand on a dish towel, Syssi turned around and leaned against the counter. "Pretty soon, we will have an Odu for every household. Kaia and William say that they have deciphered enough of the journals to build a basic house servant who can perform all the simple tasks of cleaning, cooking, gardening, etc. It's not going to be an Odu, and it won't be able to babysit or look human, but perhaps it's for the better."

"I don't know." Alena scrunched her nose. "I'm very fond of my Odu, and he's a lot more to me than a servant, even though he hasn't been rebooted yet, so he doesn't exhibit the same sentience as Okidu and Onidu. I don't want a glorified Roomba cooking in my kitchen. I want someone I can talk to."

"If we can talk to Siri and the Google Assistant, I'm sure we will be able to talk to the new breed of servants."

"Not a new breed," Alena corrected. "A new model."

"Right."

As the front door opened and Allegra squealed in happiness, Syssi pushed away from the counter. "Kian is home, and so is Okidu. My kitchen duty is over."

34

KIAN

As the family gathered around the dining table, Kian took Syssi's hand and kissed her knuckles. "Thank you for preparing this amazing meal for us."

"That's sweet of you to say, but dinner hasn't been served yet, so you can't comment on it being amazing. I'll settle for edible." Syssi smiled apologetically at his mother. "I'm so out of practice that I had forgotten the recipes I used to make all the time. I had to look them up online."

Kian didn't let go of her hand. "It must have been difficult without Okidu's help."

"It was, and it reminded me how much I appreciate having him around. By the way, how did the gods react to him?"

"They recoiled," Kian said. "Aru quickly got over his initial reaction, though. He explained that they were taught the Odus were monsters, or rather that they were turned into monsters, but what was not written in the history books was that they were altered at the command of the Eternal King. Since then, the king has gone as far as changing the entire manufacturing process on Anumati. Everything they make is solid state, meaning that they can't take things apart to fix them or alter them in any way. The official position is that it was done to prevent turning devices into weapons, which they were never intended to be. What it means for the resistance is that they cannot alter communication devices, and the only way they can transmit information is in person, which severely limits what they can do."

Aru hadn't revealed his secret communication method, and Kian wasn't expecting him to ever disclose it, but he had guessed it. He was communicating telepathically with someone on Anumati, and that person was either part of the resistance leadership or had personal contact with someone who was.

Kian was betting on the sister Aru had mentioned.

The sample he was basing his assumptions on was too small and had only two members, Vivian and Ella, but since they were mother and daughter and the only ones in the clan who could actually converse with each other in their minds, it made sense to him that only people who were closely related could communicate that way.

He'd promised Aru to keep it a secret, so he wasn't going to say anything about it to his family, not even to Syssi. Although, for once, he was actually hoping that she could get into her receptive state and see who Aru's contact was on Anumati.

Could it be the brightly luminous goddess Syssi had seen in a vision? Or maybe the servant?

Syssi hadn't planned on telling him about the vision but had thankfully changed her mind and had also asserted her will about inducing future visions.

She was right about him having no right to limit her access to her Fates' given talent. Now that she wasn't pregnant, passing out or losing consciousness for a few moments wasn't dangerous to her.

After all, she was an immortal.

Still, he was uncomfortable with her doing it while alone because she often passed out, and he got her to promise him that she wouldn't induce visions unless there was someone in the house with her who was aware of what she was doing and when and could rush in to help her if needed.

"What about the other two gods?" Orion asked. "How did they react to Okidu?"

"More or less the same as Aru. They didn't run away screaming, but they were uncomfortable around him." Kian chuckled. "That didn't stop them from consuming the appetizers he served them. When I took Aru to see Gabi, Turner managed to get them to talk a little about life on Anumati and tell him why people were unhappy."

Annani put down her glass of sparkling water. "I would like to hear what they said."

On the way back to the village, Turner had updated him about his conversation with the two gods, and Kian did his best to recount what Negal and Dagor had told Turner, as well as what he had learned from Aru.

When he was done, silence stretched across the dining table.

"This is a major conundrum," Annani said. "It must be terrible for those who do not agree with the king. I cannot imagine needing to censor my thoughts for fear of someone invading my mind, deciding that I am up to no good, and calling in the inquisitors. But taking down the king might do more damage than good. I do not know how the resistance is going to achieve that, and I cannot concern myself with the future of Anumati's monarchy when humanity's fate and our clan's fate are at stake. We need to find a way to protect Earth." She turned a pair of worried eyes on Kian. "After all the talk of me moving to your village, I think we need to consider moving the entire clan to my sanctuary. Naturally, it will need to be expanded to accommodate so many people, but it is the most secure location we have. It is the best hidden."

Kian leaned over and patted his mother's hand. "Nothing is imminent. We have many years to build a new shelter if we so desire. Most of our people will not want to live in Alaska under a glass dome that is buried deep under the snow."

"Survival is paramount, my son. Personal preferences are secondary. Until now, we were worried about the Doomers doing away with us. Now we are facing a much bigger threat." She rearranged the folds of her silk gown. "I need to tell Areana about the Eternal King. The Brotherhood needs to prepare as well."

Amanda huffed out a breath. "The Eternal King can have Navuh and his bunch of hoodlums. But we need to get Areana out. We also need to get Sari on a video call so she can be part of this discussion. This affects all of us."

"Good idea." Kian pushed to his feet. "I can cast the call on the television screen so we can all see her."

"We can't let the king get Navuh and his so-called hoodlums," Kalugal said. "If the king finds any of the hybrid descendants of the rebel gods, he will either destroy the entire planet to make sure that all the abominations are gone, or he will comb Earth until the last one of us is hunted down." He turned to Amanda. "Like it or not, we need to warn the Brotherhood."

She arched a brow. "How do you propose to do that? Expose Areana or Lokan? Or maybe we should just send Navuh a letter?"

"We can figure out the logistics later," Kalugal said. "First, we need to decide whether to do it and when. As Kian said, nothing is happening anytime soon, but we need to prepare."

"Hello, family." Sari appeared on the screen. "What a nice surprise."

35

ANNANI

At first, when Aru had told them about the Eternal King's possible displeasure with the rapid increase in the number of Earth's inhabitants and their technological advancement, Annani had not been overly worried.

The growth rate was slowing, and as far as she knew, no one had come up with a way for humans to travel faster than light even in theory, so the king's two major concerns were taken care of.

If he still wanted to cull the human population by introducing a pathogen, though, finding a way to make every person on the planet immune to disease seemed to be more easily achievable than interstellar travel, and a hundred or so years was probably long enough to make that a reality.

But Aru had delivered another warning, which Kian had either failed to mention before or only found out about today.

The Eternal King deemed all hybrids abominations, and if he ever found out about their existence, he would destroy them. That threat hit much closer to home, and Annani's worry intensified tenfold.

They all had to hide, and a secret village in the Malibu mountains was not a good enough hiding place from the might of the Eternal King.

"Good evening, Mother," Sari said from the television screen, and as

David joined her on the couch, he dipped his head and repeated the greeting.

Annani forced a smile. "I do not know whether I should greet you with goodnight or good morning. It is three o'clock in the morning in Scotland. Did we wake you up?"

"We were both awake," Sari said. "We were watching the telly."

"So, that's what it's called in Scotland," Amanda said. "TV watching."

Sari glared at her sister while David blushed, proving Amanda right.

As everyone waved their hellos, she smiled. "I wish I was there with you. It's not Friday yet in Los Angeles, though, so this is not a Friday night family dinner. Have I missed someone's birthday or anniversary? What are you celebrating?"

"Regrettably, this is not a celebration," Kian said.

"So, what is it about? Are the three new gods causing trouble?"

"They aren't," Kian said. "But what they have to say about our dear great-grandfather is most troubling. He's a threat to humanity and to us, and the resistance is not ready to take him down, nor will they be ready a hundred years from now or even a thousand. They are very limited in what they can do." He recounted what he had told the family for Sari and David's benefit. "Mother is so worried that she's suggesting we all move into her sanctuary."

Sari's eyes darted to Annani. "Seriously? You are usually the most optimistic among us. What prompted this extreme concern?"

"A gut feeling." Annani smoothed her hand over the folds of her silk gown. "It is similar to what prompted me to get into my plane and escape before Mortdh's attack. I knew that I had to act quickly or things would not end well for me. I was right then, and I am right now, but with a little less sense of urgency. We have time, but we need to use it wisely."

"I agree," Kian said. "But I don't want us to make hasty decisions born of fear either, and moving everyone into your sanctuary is exactly that."

Annani lifted her chin and looked down her nose at her son. "When Mortdh started amassing an army in the north, the council of gods deliberated for days on end on what to do about the threat. Perhaps if they had talked less and done more, they would not have all died."

"Maybe we need a new sanctuary," Syssi said. "I don't know where, though. We have a difficult time hiding from the Doomers and from humans, and their technology is nowhere near as sophisticated as what the gods have at their disposal." She chuckled. "Perhaps the underwater city I created for the mer's Perfect Match adventure was a premonition of where we are going to live in the future."

"What about the ship?" Alena asked. "The king would never think to search for us on a cruise ship."

"Not a bad idea," Amanda said. "But first, we need to get that wedding cruise underway, or you are going to deliver your baby out of wedlock just like I did." She smiled sweetly at her sister.

Alena chuckled. "I've had thirteen children without the benefit of marriage or a mate, so I win." She rubbed her protruding belly. "I can have this baby without a wedding, but Orion wants us to be married by the time it arrives. I still think we can have a modest ceremony at the village square and get it over with."

Annani glanced at Orion, who had not responded verbally to Alena's comment, but his face revealed how disappointed he was with her dismissive attitude toward their wedding.

"We should still have the wedding cruise as planned." Annani turned to Kian. "Alena and Orion are not the only ones who are waiting. The other couples are just as disappointed."

"I know." Kian sighed. "But what can I do? When we came up with the idea, and I purchased the ship, we didn't know that we would be sharing the village with the Kra-ell or that we would be visited by three gods from Anumati."

Annani put her delicate hand over his. "You have a knack for over-complicating things because you seek perfection. Things become much easier when you are willing to compromise. As much as I would have liked every resident of the village to join the celebration, that is not possible. The Kra-ell will have to stay behind to safeguard it, and Kalugal's men will remain with them." She smiled at her nephew. "You can bring Shamash to help with Darius, and Rufsur will want to accompany Edna, but Phinas can stay behind and help Jade hold the fort, so to speak. Also, Vrog and Aliya should come because Vlad and Wendy are one of the couples who want me to marry them on the cruise ship."

"What about the new gods?" Toven asked. "What will we do with them while we are merrily sailing on the boat?"

"They can continue to be our guests at the penthouse," Annani said. "Aru will be busy taking care of Gabriella following her transition, and we will be back before she is well enough to be moved."

"I want to meet these gods." Toven turned to Kian. "Can you arrange a meeting?"

Kian shook his head. "I don't want them to see you or Annani. As it is, they already suspect that you are the descendants of the Eternal King's children."

Annani frowned. "How and why? Did anyone say something they should not have?"

Kian grimaced. "I did."

KIAN

"I asked Aru why he and his friends didn't glow."

Kian hadn't wanted to bring up the glow question in front of the entire family, and he would have preferred to do that privately with his mother and Toven, but he couldn't explain why Aru suspected that without telling them the entire sequence of blunders, first with the spy drone that had gotten past all of their careful prep work, to Gilbert telling Gabi what he shouldn't have, and then Kian's own slip-up.

"They do not glow at all?" Annani looked surprised. "They must be suppressing their luminescence."

"They aren't," Kian said.

"Oh," Syssi exclaimed. "You promised me a picture of Aru and his friends. I bet everyone wants to see what he looks like."

"I've sent it to you already." Kian waved a hand. "Check your messages."

Syssi's cheeks pinked. "Oops. I was cooking and didn't check my messages. I don't have my phone with me either."

She started to rise when Okidu rushed over. "Here is your phone, mistress."

"Thank you, Okidu." Syssi opened the messages application. "Oh, wow. He's even more handsome than he was in my vision." She handed the phone to Annani. "Right? Look at those cheekbones. So chiseled."

Kian gritted his teeth. "Aru doesn't look like a god. In fact, he looks like he has Kra-ell blood in him, but that's not possible given the taboo they have on intermixing."

His mother was still looking at the photo. "Not all gods were fair skinned like me." She lifted her eyes to Toven. "Toven and Mortdh were darker, and so was Ekin. My father was very fair, though, and his hair was nearly white. My mother was a redhead like me."

"I wonder what the Eternal King looks like." Alena took the phone from Amanda.

"Very luminous," Kian said. "According to Aru, royals glow and commoners do not, but there are thousands of royals. Not that thousands out of three trillion is a lot, but it's still pretty rare." He turned to Toven. "Do you remember any gods who had no glow?"

Toven shook his head. "Some were more radiant than others, and I remember Ahn as being very luminous, but I can't think of anyone who had none whatsoever." He tilted his head. "As you know, with practice, gods can control their glow. We can diminish it, extinguish it, or enhance it. Maybe commoners on Anumati are not allowed to be luminous and are taught at a young age to stifle it."

"That's another issue I wanted to address with you," Kian said. "Since Ahn was the father of the Kra-ell royal twins, they probably were radiant as well, and that might have been another reason for them to be veiled at all times. Maybe their control over their glow wasn't good. At what age do the gods start to glow, and at what age can they control the level of luminosity?"

"That's a good question." Amanda looked at their mother. "Did you glow as a child? Or did you develop it later?"

Annani pursed her lips. "I do not remember ever being without it. Even some of the immortal children were born luminous, and as to the issue of control, it takes practice. I was able to control it by the time I was eleven years old, but only for short periods of time. I did not gain full control of it until I was sixteen, and even then, I had slip-ups when I got emotional." She smiled wistfully. "I was willful and impulsive, so that happened quite often."

"Well, that sucks." Amanda crossed her arms over her chest. "Why have none of us inherited your glow?"

"I do not know." Annani smiled apologetically. "I was never good at science. Maybe luminosity is a recessive gene."

"It probably is," Amanda said. "It's also not beneficial to earthlings who don't live underground. Being luminous makes it difficult to hide."

"That is why it is important to learn to suppress it." Annani waved a hand. "If only the royals glow, I do not understand how all the gods I remember were luminous to at least some degree. I know for a fact that not all of them were of royal blood." She looked at Toven. "Am I right?"

He nodded. "Your mother was a commoner before she mated your father, and she was quite luminous."

"Aru could have been lying," Sari suggested via the video feed. "He might have made up the claim that only gods of royal descent glow, knowing that it would trick you into revealing that you had seen gods and knew that they were radiant."

Kian shook his head. "He already knew that gods were living among us. Gilbert told Gabi that she didn't have exclusive bragging rights for being induced by a god and that he had been induced by a god as well. He didn't know that he had a tiny spy drone on him and that everything he was saying to his sister was being heard by her inducer."

"That's most unfortunate," Kalugal said with a smug smile. "Someone got sloppy and allowed a bug to infiltrate the keep."

"It's not detectable by our technology," Kian defended the team.

"How big is it?" Alena asked.

"A little larger than a flea and smaller than a mosquito."

Kalugal snorted. "That's still big enough to see with the naked eye. If your people were more diligent about security, they would have noticed it."

Kian narrowed his eyes at his cousin. "Is that how you learned about all the things you were not supposed to? Did one of your startups develop a tiny spy drone?"

Kalugal lifted his hands in mock surrender. "I don't have tiny spy drones, and I never did."

Behind him, Darius uttered a little whimper in his stroller, and Kalugal turned to pick up his son. "Hey, sweetie. There is no reason to get upset." He kissed the baby's cheek before cradling him in his arms. "No one is angry at anyone. Uncle Kian and your daddy just enjoy teasing each other, but we are the best of friends."

As the baby settled in his arms, Jacki let out a breath. "Kalugal has the magic touch. Somehow, he always manages to calm Darius down."

Annani regarded Kalugal and his infant son fondly. "He is a sensitive little fellow."

"I know," Kalugal murmured. "He doesn't like it when people argue." He kissed the top of Darius's head.

"So, what's the verdict?" Amanda said. "Was Aru lying, or is there another explanation for the discrepancy?"

"Maybe there was a way to create the glow artificially," Kian said. "The rebels were all about equality, and they didn't want to recreate Anumati's class system in their community. Perhaps one of their doctors came up with a way to chemically induce luminescence, or maybe they stumbled upon a way to activate the gene responsible for it."

"It might not have been about equality," Annani said quietly. "It might have been about hiding the royal descendants by making everyone luminous. Perhaps my father knew that the Eternal King would one day send assassins to kill him, his siblings, and their children, and he wanted to protect the next generation by making them indistinguishable from the other gods."

Alena shook her head. "Forgive me, Mother, but that doesn't make sense. You all knew how to suppress your glow. All your father had to do was to decree that glowing was disallowed, and everyone needed to suppress it."

"That is true," Annani conceded. "But the young gods could not have obeyed his command. They did not have the control needed to do that."

"Perhaps we should consult Okidu's journals," Syssi suggested. "Maybe the answer to this riddle is hidden between their pages."

ARU

Aru sat on the little swivel stool that Gilbert had vacated and looked at the bed longingly. He wanted to lie down next to Gabi, but the bed was narrow, and he was afraid she wouldn't be comfortable.

Julian had said that she needed her rest, and Merlin had repeated the same instructions, so it was best if Aru didn't disturb her regenerative sleep for his own selfish reasons. He worried about her despite both doctors reassuring him that she was doing splendidly.

Through the eyes of the spy drone, he'd seen Gilbert lying down on a field cot last night, but he must have removed it from the room in the morning.

It wasn't important. He could lean his head on the bed and catch a few minutes of sleep until Gabi woke up, which would hopefully be soon.

With a sigh, Aru put his arm on the bed and rested his forehead on it. From this angle, he spotted something that he hadn't noticed before. A little corner of a canvas fabric that was the same color as the clinic's floor protruded from under the hospital bed, and as he dropped down to his knees and leaned down to pull it out, he was happy to discover a folded bundle of tubes that were connected to the cream-colored canvas fabric with cords threaded through loops.

So, that was where the cot disappeared to during the day.

As Aru spread it out next to Gabi's bed, he made a mental note to purchase three of those for his team. The cot wasn't heavy, so it wouldn't add too much weight to their backpacks as they hiked through Tibet in search of more Kra-ell pods, but it would make camping during the night much more comfortable.

But wait, what about Gabi?

Would she want to join them on their quest?

He had to convince her to come with them because he couldn't conceive of leaving her, and he couldn't just stay idle for the next century until the patrol ship arrived.

Fates, what a mess.

Lying down on the cot, Aru let his booted feet dangle over the end and draped an arm over his eyes.

"How am I going to solve this puzzle?" he murmured quietly. "Is there a solution?"

If anyone could figure it out, it would be Aria. His sister was brilliant and an expert solver of complicated puzzles. She was the reason that he'd joined the resistance, but even before that, she'd always been a source of guidance and advice.

Taking a few long breaths, Aru quieted his mind and reached through the ether to his sister.

Can you talk?

Yes. Her mental voice sounded joyful. *How have you been, Aru?*

I'm well. I've met the leader of the immortals, and I think we can rely on him and his people. But before we talk about that, there is something more important I want to tell you about.

What can be more important than the rebellion?

My truelove mate. I found her, Aria.

There was a long moment of silence on their mental connection before Aria's mental voice sounded in his head. *You said that there are no gods left on Earth.*

I was mistaken. I have reason to believe that some are living among the immortals. Perhaps they are the children of the rebel gods who were born on Earth, so they have no trackers in them and don't show up on our tracking systems.

Did you meet those gods or not?

I did not.

So, who is your truelove mate? Did you fall in love with a human?

The incredulity in her tone was ironic. Aria was a rebel through and through, and she abhorred the discrimination against the Kra-ell and the other created species, and yet she sounded shocked that he might have fallen in love with one of them.

Gabriella is not human. She is immortal or about to become one. She is in the process of transitioning into immortality. He explained the what and the how as best he could, given the limited knowledge he had received on dormant carriers of godly genes and the way they were activated.

When he was done explaining, Aria asked, *How do you know that she is the one?*

I feel no desire for anyone else, not even for Alva. And you know how obsessed I am with her. I want to be with Gabi, and I can't imagine being without her. I just don't know how I'm going to accomplish the tasks I still have to complete while being with her. She will be nearly as strong and as resilient as a goddess when her transition is complete, but I do not know whether she would want to travel with me and my team to remote corners of this planet. Most of our travels involve long hikes and sleeping on the hard ground in the cold and in the heat. That is not the lifestyle I want for my mate. I want her to be comfortable, pampered, and have all the luxuries this planet has to offer.

The sound of Aria's laugh stopped his ramblings. *What is so funny?*

When you informed me and our parents that you would never take a mate unless she was your one and only, I lost hope of you ever finding happiness with a worthy female. But here you are, completely besotted with a hybrid, half-human half-goddess. When Mother and Father learn of your choice, they will don their mourning garb.

Their parents were not part of the resistance, and even though they had been shipped off planet to one of the less hospitable colonies, they still believed in most of the propaganda. They would consider Gabi an abomination.

I do not intend to tell them.

The only way he could communicate with his parents was through the patrol ship, and anyone who thought the connection was private was a fool.

Neither would I, Aria said.

She couldn't even if she was so inclined. Their parents did not know about his and Aria's mental connection, and they could never find out.

But you will have to tell them when you return with your mate.

Aru let out a mental sigh. *Think about what you just said. How can I return with my hybrid mate? I cannot take her with me on the ship.*

That is right. You cannot. Aria sounded as despondent as he felt.

I need you to use that brilliant brain of yours and come up with a solution.

You ask too much of me, Aru. This is a puzzle that even I cannot solve.

Give it a try. Perhaps the Supreme will inspire you with an idea.

Aru entertained a slim hope that the Supreme would relieve him from his duties and arrange for a permanent posting on Earth for him. But the truth was that his and Aria's connection was too valuable to waste, and although the Supreme might be sympathetic, a discharge was not in the cards.

Do you really want me to tell the Supreme about your half-human mate?

We hide nothing from the Supreme. He sighed. *Genetically, my mate is mostly human and has only a little bit of godly genes in her, but she is more perfect to me than any goddess could ever be.*

3 8

ANNANI

While the discussion about Okidu's journals and the possibility of future robotic servants continued throughout dinner, Amanda did not take part in it. Instead, she leaned back with a contemplative look on her lovely face and barely touched her food.

Annani waited for a lull in the conversation to ask, "What is on your mind, daughter of mine?"

Amanda shrugged. "Nothing that's important to what we were talking about, although it is related."

"Let's hear it," Kian said. "You have a knack for thinking outside the box."

Amanda rewarded her brother with a brilliant smile. "Thank you, Kian. Usually, you refer to my unorthodox ideas in less complimentary terms."

He let out a long-suffering sigh. "Because many of them are harebrained and don't bring the results we hoped for, like the paranormal conventions you and Syssi organized or publishing Eva's book in the hopes of the story attracting Dormants, but once in a while, you have a good one."

She rolled her eyes. "That's how it works, Kian. If you try a hundred things and one of them pans out, consider yourself lucky, but if you don't try any, you won't get the one that does."

Kian cast her a fond look. "With that out of the way, please share your thoughts with us." There had been only a trace of sarcasm in his tone.

"Fine. I was thinking about Aru's claim that only the gods with royal blood glow and commoners do not, and it occurred to me that the gods might have experimented with the created species, using royal genetics to enhance some and commoner genetics to enhance others. There might be created species out there who glow. Then, another thought crossed my mind. What if the glow was connected to metabolic function? What if the food on Earth activated the glow gene for all the gods and not just the royals? What if that was one of the reasons Earth was declared a forbidden planet?"

"Oh, wow." Syssi put a hand on her chest. "That could totally be the reason. The royals on Anumati wouldn't have wanted the commoners to discover how to get the glow and lose their exclusive luminous status as a result."

"I find it hard to believe," Annani said. "If the food on Earth enabled common gods to have a glow, it would have been discovered eons before the rebels were exiled to Earth. According to the myths, the gods created humans, and we know that humans existed on Earth long before the rebels were forced to make Earth their permanent residence. The information would have found its way back to Anumati."

"Not necessarily." Amanda tapped her lower lip with her finger. "It might have been a more recent development. Perhaps a new food was introduced. Beer, for example, was created by the goddess Ninkasi. It didn't exist on Earth prior to the rebels' arrival. It could have activated the glow gene."

"Then how come we don't glow?" Kian waved a hand over himself. "With how much beer I consume, I should be as luminous as Mother, and Anandur should glow like a supernova."

As everyone laughed, Amanda pouted. "I used beer only as an example of a newly introduced dietary consumable. It was one of many new foods that were introduced during that era. The rebel gods jumpstarted human civilization, and one of the ways they did it was by introducing innovative agricultural systems and cultivation of plants."

Annani smiled. "I remember learning about that. My father hired Khiann to teach me about commerce, trade, and the different methods of shipping goods from faraway places." She chuckled. "Now I wish I had paid more attention to what he was actually trying to teach me rather than flirting with my future husband."

She had done more than flirting during those precious days, but even though her children were all adults and immortals were not shy about their sexuality, there were some things a mother did not discuss with her children.

Amanda smiled at her sadly. "I'm glad that you enjoyed every moment you had with Khiann. Your time was better spent flirting than learning about commerce."

Taking a fortifying breath, Annani nodded. "I agree. But back to our discussion. Let us assume that you are right, and a certain food activated the commoner gods' glow genes. We need to find out what it was. Perhaps Bridget and Kaia can take a sample from me or Toven and find the gene responsible for our glow."

Next to her, Kian stiffened. "We have not analyzed your blood for a reason, Mother. This needs to remain a mystery."

Annani shook her head. "We had our reasons before, but perhaps it is time to take the next step in our quest for answers."

Kian glared at her. "We are not going to learn anything helpful from analyzing your blood, Mother. I can tell Aru that we suspect Earth's food is the activator and send him on a quest to find which one it is." He chuckled. "Maybe that was what Gilgamesh was trying to find."

"Grapes?" Syssi suggested. "How old are they?"

"We can easily find out." Amanda pulled out her phone and looked to Annani for permission. "May I?"

The dinner table was not the place for phones or tablets. It was a time for family and friends to come together and enjoy each other's company, face to face with lively conversation. But dinner was over, coffee and tea had been served along with dessert, and the evening was winding down.

Annani nodded. "Yes, you may, but please read to us what you find out so we are all part of your discovery."

"Thank you, Mother." Amanda got busy typing on the screen.

39

ARU

fter Aru had exhausted all the amorous words that he knew in his native language to sing Gabi's praises, he hoped he would be able to translate them into English so he could tell her all the things he'd told Aria about her.

His sister had patiently listened to him describing the way he and Gabi had met, and how he was convinced that their encounter had been fated, and how Gabi's connection to the clan of immortals couldn't have been coincidental either.

Oh, Aru. It gladdens my heart that you are so deeply in love, and that your connection to Gabriella opened up an opportunity for the resistance to establish a base on the forgotten planet, but I worry about your mate's perilous condition. Perhaps you should aid her transformation to ensure her survival.

Aru frowned. *How can I aid her? I'm not a healer.*

His sister laughed. *You do not need to be a healer to aid one of the created species. Your blood is a potent medicine to them, and your mate can benefit from a small transfusion.*

Aria had studied to become a healer before she had been offered a position in the service of the Supreme, so he didn't doubt her knowledge, but he had to wonder why none of the troopers tasked with monitoring the created species had been told about such an important remedy.

That should have been a crucial piece of information in the Watchers' training. Why have we not been told about our blood's curative abilities? Is it a closely guarded secret that only healers are privy to?

Most of the gods on Anumati will never encounter a member of the created species, so there is no need for this to be common knowledge, and the Watcher troops are supposed to watch and squash uprisings when needed, not to interact with the locals. The healers, on the other hand, are expected to be shipped off to distant colonies and help the ruling gods there. Can you think of a better way to gain the population's gratitude than to offer miraculous healings to its leaders? Mostly, it is achieved with our genetics-altering equipment, but in an emergency, when nothing else is available, our blood can be used instead.

That makes sense, but it would have been good to know, nonetheless. Aru opened his eyes and glanced at Gabi, who was still sleeping soundly. *How much should I administer, and are you sure it is safe?*

Very little, Aria said. *The quantity should be the size of the tip of your little finger, and it is perfectly safe. A good spot to take the blood from is the bend of your arm, and to administer, use the vein on the back of your mate's hand. If you lick the spot first, it is not going to hurt when you put the needle in. Do you know where you can find a syringe?*

I am in a well-equipped clinic. They have syringes here.

He had been updating Aria about the state of human progress ever since he had landed on Earth five years ago, including what he had learned from watching shows about doctors and hospitals. She knew it wasn't the primitive place it used to be only a few centuries ago, and so did the Supreme, who had informed him through Aria that he should not report the full extent of human progress to his commander even though the god was part of the resistance.

Still, it was not possible to report nothing. The patrol ship had noted the human-made satellites and other signs of progress, and some of it must have already reached the Eternal King.

Excellent, Aria said. *So, it should not be a problem. Do you know how to use it?*

I can find an instruction vid, but I'm afraid of administering the transfusion and doing something wrong. Perhaps I should thrall the doctor to do it for me.

That might be a good idea. But make sure that the healer doesn't remember it. The created species shouldn't know about this method, or the gods among them will be in danger.

These are immortals. They don't get sick, and they don't need our blood's help. The transition is a rare occurrence for adults. Usually, the induction is done at puberty when the risks are so minimal that they are negligible.

It took a moment for Aria to respond, and Aru imagined her looking up as she examined the information from all angles.

The question is how good these immortals are at keeping secrets. If they are closely involved with humans whom they care about, they might reveal your secret.

Could their blood work as well as ours? Aru asked.

Not likely. You should proceed with caution. Have you thralled any of the immortals yet?

Not yet. Thralling the doctor will serve two purposes. I will find out whether I can thrall immortals, and I will get a trained healer to administer the transfusion instead of doing it myself and risking hurting Gabi.

Good luck, Aru. Tell me how it goes.

Hold on, we are not done yet. I also need you to consult with the Supreme about what I should tell the leader of the immortals.

He could sense the tension coming from Aria even without her verbalizing it.

What did you tell the leader? she asked.

I didn't tell him about our method of communication, only that I have a way to get in touch with the resistance leaders.

What if he figures out how you are doing it?

Aru turned on his side and propped his head on his hand. *He won't. Not unless he knows someone who can do what we can, and that is impossible. Our ability is extremely rare.*

Aria sighed. *It is rare now, but it might not have been over seven thousand Earth years ago when the original rebels were exiled to Earth. Some of them might have been strong telepaths.*

Not much was known about the group of the original rebels. The three known names were the king's children—his two sons and a daughter. The rest were only mentioned as rebels, and no names were provided, supposedly to save their families the shame.

However, the problem with a society of people who live forever was

643

that someone always remembered what really happened and who had been involved, but the king knew how to deal with that as well. Not everyone choosing to enter stasis and sleep through several hundreds or thousands of years did so because they were going insane from boredom. Some were coerced, some were bribed, and some did it to save themselves the trouble of dealing with the king's secret army of informants.

Turning on his back, Aru stared at the ceiling. *It would be a very unlikely coincidence if there were telepaths like us among the immortals, especially given their diluted godly genes.*

Aria sighed. *I hope that you get invited to their community soon so you can find out what talents these immortals have.*

That wasn't going to happen. He and Kian had both agreed on that, but Aru could find out about the different talents from Merlin. The doctor was a talkative fellow, and it wouldn't be difficult to get him to list all the various talents the immortals had.

I might have another way of finding out that does not involve visiting their secret location. I have a tracker embedded in my flesh, and I don't want to expose them unnecessarily.

I forgot about that, Aria said. *Luckily, I got recruited for this job before I was implanted with a tracker. However, given how paranoid our ruler is, he will soon have every god implanted even if they have no plans of ever leaving the planet. He just wants to know where everyone is and what they are doing.*

Aru let out a mental breath. *On Anumati, he does not need trackers to follow every citizen. Surveillance is everywhere.* Supposedly, it was to prevent unlawful or unkind behavior, but it was about so much more than that.

That is why we are building the resistance, Aru. We are fighting for our freedom while the noose is tightening around our necks. Tell me all you have learned about these immortals so far, so I can give the Supreme all the pertinent information about them. We should welcome any help we can get in moving the rebellion forward.

40

SYSSI

G rapes had turned out to be older than they had suspected. They'd been cultivated for over eight thousand years, and other crops had conflicting cultivating times on the web.

Syssi had been ecstatic to discover that coffee had been used to brew beverages in Ethiopia over five thousand years ago, but the date was quoted only by one website, and its claim was disputed by several others that reported a much later date.

That was very disappointing. She would have loved for coffee to be the gods' glow activator.

"It seems that Amanda's first guess about beer was the most likely," Kian said. "But the problem with that hypothesis is that Aru likes beer, which means that he drank it during his five years on Earth. If that was the activator, he would have developed a glow by now. That being said, he's not much of a drinker, so maybe larger quantities and a more prolonged consumption are needed to make a difference."

"I wonder if they make beer on Anumati," Annani said. "Ninkasi must have brought the knowledge of how to brew beer from home. Otherwise, how would she have come up with the idea?"

"Beer can be produced from more than just barley," Syssi remembered Jacob telling her about it.

He'd wanted to start a home brewery and had done all the research, but then his life had ended needlessly.

He could have lived forever.

As a wave of sadness threatened to swallow her, she shook her head and continued, "Wheat, corn, rice, and oats can also be used to make beer. The fermentation of the starch sugars in the wort produces ethanol and carbonation to make beer. What I'm trying to say is that beer on Anumati could be made from other grains that don't have the same effect as the one made from barley."

"It's very unlikely that beer is the activator," Kian said. "It was just a shot in the dark."

"It was an idea." Amanda shrugged and went back to reading on her phone. "Listen to this. Bioluminescence is not exclusive to sea creatures that glow in the dark. According to research that was done at the Tohoku Institute of Technology in Japan, humans have it as well, just at very low levels, and it has to do with metabolism. Free radicals interact with lipids and proteins, which sometimes contain fluorophores, a fluorescent chemical compound that can produce photons of light." She lifted her eyes to their mother. "It looks like I was right, and humans were created with the help of royal godly genes." She smiled. "I wonder if they were someone's pet project."

Kian chuckled. "Perhaps humans are the Eternal King's pet project, and he has a soft spot for his creations, so he will not do away with them when he finds out how successful his experiment has become."

"You might be onto something. Maybe humans were the king's pets," Annani said. "Maybe we have misinterpreted everything, and he sent his rebellious children to Earth to make a new start away from Anumati. Perhaps he made Earth a forbidden planet so no one could interfere with their new world."

Amanda leaned over and took their mother's hand. "That's wishful thinking, Mother, and you know that. I would like to believe that great granddaddy is a nice guy too, but we've heard enough to know better."

Annani sighed. "Spreading propaganda can go both ways. What if his enemies are spreading lies about him?"

Kian had a feeling that their mother knew very well that her grandfather was not a good guy and was just entertaining what-if thoughts to lift everyone's mood.

"There is more." Amanda went back to her phone. "The glow is most pronounced in the early afternoon when human metabolism is the most active. The glow is mainly concentrated in the cheeks, forehead, and neck." She looked up and grinned. "Those are precisely the spots that get red when someone gets drunk. Coincidence? Maybe not."

"As fascinating as this is, that is not how my glow works." Annani intensified her luminance until it was difficult to look at her. "We glow all over, and we don't need to eat a big meal to do so." She looked at Toven. "Am I right?"

He dipped his head. "Naturally, but I can't make mine as bright as yours. I couldn't do that even when I was in my prime."

Mia elbowed him. "Don't talk like that was in the past. You are still very much in your prime."

"Thanks to you." He leaned toward her and kissed her cheek.

It suddenly dawned on Syssi that her vision of a brightly shining goddess must have been of a royal, and since it seemed like the more royal blood one had, the more intense the glow, perhaps the goddess she'd seen in her vision was the queen? Annani's grandmother?

As a shiver ran down her spine at the thought, she resolved to induce another vision about the goddess.

Turning to Kian, she reached for his hand. "Aru told you that there are many royals, right?"

"Yes, thousands. There is more than one royal family."

"Then the Eternal King is not really eternal," Dalhu said. "For there to be other royal families, there must have been other monarchs before him."

"Good observation," Kian said. "I should make a list of questions for Aru and his friends. As long as Gabi is transitioning, he will be more inclined to answer them."

Dalhu's comment must have distracted Kian because he hadn't noticed Syssi squeezing his hand. Usually, she and Kian were so in tune that he could guess her intent from the subtlest clues, but not this time. He hadn't gotten the hint when she'd asked him about the royals on Anumati.

Amanda knew about the vision as well, but she hadn't connected the dots either.

Perhaps it was better that way.

Syssi wasn't ready to share her vision with Annani before she knew more. Her mother-in-law might get excited for nothing.

"I have a question," Jacki said. "Is what causes humans to glow the same as what makes bioluminescent creatures emit light?"

Amanda shook her head. "Deep-sea fish, fireflies, and most other light emitting creatures have luciferin, which means light bringer in Latin."

Jacki's eyes widened. "Is that what Lucifer means? A light bringer? Why would the devil bring light?"

Amanda laughed. "Religions have a way of distorting the meaning of words for no good reason. Lucifer is the Latin name for Venus, as it appears in the morning. Therefore, it is the light bringer. Since Venus is also the goddess of love, my take on it is that it was a malicious attempt to attribute carnal love to the devil and, by association, portray all women as devilish."

41

ARU

As Aru's mental conversation with Aria continued, he kept glancing at Gabi, hoping to see her make the slightest of moves or sounds, anything to indicate that she wasn't unconscious and only resting, but so far, she hadn't stirred even once.

Was it normal?

Would Merlin know?

Despite Julian's assurances about Merlin's competence as a healer, Aru still didn't trust the guy.

Thank you for all the information, Aria said. *I will relay it to the Supreme at the first opportunity I have.*

Aru put his legs over the side of the cot and sat up. *Please let me know as soon as you have instructions for me.*

I will. Good luck with the transfusion operation.

Thank you. Be well, Aria.

You too, Aru.

As the mental channel closed, Aru pushed to his feet and walked over to Gabi. Her breathing seemed normal, and so was her heartbeat, and the monitors were humming away as they had been doing when he'd returned.

There had been no change.

Turning around, he walked to the door, opened it only as much as he needed to slip through so the bright light of the waiting room didn't disturb Gabi, and stepped out while leaving the door slightly ajar.

The office door on the other side of the waiting room was open, and through it, Aru could see Merlin sitting in the swivel chair with his back to the desk, his red-clad feet propped on the file cabinet that stood against the wall, and a phone pressed to his ear.

"Don't you go baking in the middle of the night, love," Merlin said. "I know you miss me, but you don't need to make me cookies for when I return tomorrow morning. You should take a relaxing bubble bath or watch a movie with Lisa."

"She's not home," the woman on the other side said. "Supposedly, she's studying for a test with Parker."

"Oh, so that's what they are calling it these days, studying."

The woman laughed. "Cheryl is with them as well as Jade's daughter. Parker is an immortal with the stamina to match, but I doubt he has the chutzpah to flirt with three girls at once."

"Not with Drova, he doesn't, that's for sure. That girl is almost as intimidating as her mother."

Aru smiled, happy to hear that Drova had made friends among the young immortals. From what he'd learned while spying from afar on the Kra-ell in Gor's compound, he was under the impression that the relationship between Jade and Drova was strained, and Drova hadn't had many friends.

Not wanting to eavesdrop further on Merlin's private conversation, he tiptoed down the hallway in search of the supply room.

After finding a syringe, he could wait for the doctor to be done with his phone call and thrall him to administer the transfusion, or he could do it himself.

Perhaps it was better not to chance thralling Merlin.

The immortal might be resistant, and Aru wasn't sure whether it was wise to let him in on the secret of the curative effects of the gods' blood.

Aria's warning was sound, but if these immortals had stayed hidden from humans, gods, and even other immortals, they were very good at keeping secrets, and they could probably handle this one as well.

Perhaps he could use it as leverage in future negotiations.

The gods living among them probably didn't know about it, and it was too useful a trick to leave unknown. One day, a human leader who was essential to the immortals might be dying, and it might be that the only way to save that leader was with a god's blood.

For now, though, it would be better to do the transfusion himself and save the information for when it would come in handy in future negotiations with Kian.

Surely, there was an instructional video on YouTube on how to use syringes.

After opening a few doors Aru finally found the supply closet, but looking at the assortment of syringes, he didn't know which one to choose. Aria had said that the quantity of blood should be the size of the tip of his smallest finger, so the syringe needed for that was probably the smallest size.

Pocketing three syringes just in case he messed up the first two, he walked out of the supply room, closed the door, and tiptoed back.

Merlin was still talking to his lady, but much more quietly than before, and given his throaty chuckles, they were talking about intimate stuff.

Smiling, Aru shook his head and continued to Gabi's room.

He closed the door behind him, toed off his boots, and climbed into bed with her.

Moving her just a little to make room for himself, he lifted the additional blanket from the foot of the bed and covered them both. Anyone watching the footage from the surveillance camera would only see him cuddling with his mate, and no one would see what he was doing under the blanket.

The problem was that Aru didn't know what he was doing either.

Pulling out his phone, he brought up the YouTube application and first searched how to extract the blood from his own vein.

When he was sure that he could handle that part, he searched for how to administer the blood infusion, which was more difficult to find than the first part, but eventually, he found an instructional video from India. Fortunately, he understood enough Hindi to follow it.

Extracting his blood was surprisingly easy, but when it was time to find the vein in Gabi's hand, he got nervous. Bringing it to his lips, he kissed the spot and then laved it with his tongue to provide the healing agent, and he stopped breathing as he inserted the needle.

Thank the merciful Fates, Gabi didn't react in any way, which he took to mean that she was unconscious rather than asleep, and when all of his blood was gone from the syringe, he pulled the needle out and licked the insertion point once more.

In moments, there was no trace of what he had done.

For the next hour, Aru lay next to Gabi, enjoying her closeness and listening to her steady heartbeat and even breathing, but eventually, he got restless and decided it was time to check on Merlin again.

By now, the doctor had most likely finished his phone call, and he could answer questions about the various talents the immortals possessed. Aru needed to find out whether any of them had a telepathic connection like the one he shared with his sister.

42

MERLIN

The god emerged once more from Gabi's room and walked over to the office. Stopping at the doorway, he leaned in. "Are you busy?"

Merlin had noticed Aru skulking around the clinic while he'd been on the phone with Ronja, probably looking for a pillow or a blanket for his cot or perhaps for something else that wasn't as innocuous as that.

Did gods do drugs?

No morphine or any of the other drugs in that class were missing, though, so perhaps Aru was just the curious type and liked to check things out.

Merlin had intended to ask him what he needed after he was done chatting with Ronja, but a glance at the monitor in Gabi's room revealed that Aru was snuggling with her, and he seemed to be asleep.

Merlin arched a brow. "Do I look busy to you?"

"You were an hour ago. How are things at home?"

"They are splendid. What can I help you with?"

The god walked in, pulled out a chair, and sat down. "I'm worried about Gabi. She's been unconscious for long hours now, and that's not the pattern she's been following previously of waking up every couple of hours and staying awake for a little while before slipping under again. Is that normal?"

Merlin shrugged. "There is no normal with transitioning Dormants. Each case is unique, but I can tell you that Gabi is doing very well, and you have nothing to worry about. Of all the cases we've seen so far, hers is one of the easiest. Eric, her other brother, took a long time to transition. Her niece breezed through it, but her actual transition took a long time, which was very frustrating to her."

Aru frowned. "What do you mean by the actual transition? What Gabi is going through is not the actual thing?"

Merlin lifted a hand with three fingers up. "There are three stages to the transition. The first one is the most traumatic because it is fast. The body is undergoing dramatic changes, so the long bouts of sleeping and even unconsciousness are good because they let the body direct all its energy toward the change. Once the initial stage is done, the Dormant is already immortal, which translates into rapid healing, better hearing and eyesight, a more acute sense of smell, etc., but the changes continue at a slower pace for about six months, sometimes longer. For males, in particular, it's a difficult time because they grow fangs and venom glands, and that's painful. Nowadays, we have painkillers that can ease them, but in the not-too-distant past, the only remedy was getting drunk." Merlin grinned. "The amounts of whiskey the lads consumed were staggering. As you know, it takes much more alcohol to get an immortal or a god drunk than it takes a human."

Aru didn't smile, which wasn't the response Merlin had been hoping for. The guy was too serious.

"I wouldn't know because I don't drink to get drunk. But back to what you said before about Gabi's niece. What did you mean by actual transition?"

"Oh, yes." Merlin smoothed his hand over his long beard. The thing needed trimming, but Ronja did not allow him to do it himself and demanded that he go to a barber, and he simply didn't have time for that.

"Merlin?" Aru reminded him that he was still waiting for an answer.

Merlin's mind tended to wander, and it often did that, even in the middle of a conversation. "Yes, yes. Where was I? Oh yes. We usually run a test once the initial stage is completed to see how fast the newly transitioned immortal heals. We make a small cut on the palm of their hand,

and we time how fast it closes. Initially, Kaia took over four minutes to heal, which is considered very long. It took weeks for her healing time to go down to under a minute, which is what it should have been when she was tested the first time. That didn't happen to any of the other transitioning Dormants. I'm telling you all this so you know to expect the unexpected. Gabi still might slip into a deeper coma and not wake up for days or even weeks, but the chances of that are small."

The god shook his head. "My mind is still stuck on the barbaric test you perform. I'm sure there is a more advanced method of testing healing speed than inflicting an injury on the Dormants right after they suffered through the transition."

Merlin pursed his lips. "When you put it that way, yeah, you have a point. But you know what? They all want to do the test even if there is no need for it. It became a tradition, a rite of passage of sorts."

"Not all customs are good, and some are better done away with. I'm not allowing anyone to cut Gabi's palm."

Merlin smiled indulgently. "It's not your decision to make. It is Gabi's, and I'll bet you that she will want the test with all the pomp and ceremony that's involved."

"How do you know? You haven't even talked to her."

"That's true, but I know her brothers. And if she's anything like them, she will want exactly what they got." Merlin leaned forward. "I have a lovely mate who transitioned not too long ago, and she came with a daughter whom I adore. My mate is a very delicate lady, and yet, she wanted to do the test, and when the time comes for Lisa, I have no doubt she will want it as well."

The god leaned back in the chair and crossed his arms over his chest. "If Gabi wants to do the test, I will not stand in her way. It's not my place to make decisions for her. But I will express my opinion about the barbarity of it."

"Suit yourself. But if you want my advice, you will keep your mouth shut and say nothing. Your most important job as a mate is to support your lady in whatever she chooses to do."

43

ARU

The healer had turned out to be not as nutty as he appeared, and he had some strong opinions. The good news was that he didn't have a clue about the clandestine blood transfusion Aru had performed an hour ago.

If everything went well and Gabi's transition progressed faster and easier, Aru would use the knowledge in his negotiations with Kian. The immortals didn't get sick, but other transitioning Dormants could benefit from the blood of the gods residing in the immortals' village, especially those who didn't have an easy transition like Gabi's. Hopefully, she would have it even easier going forward.

"I'll take your advice under consideration." Aru unfolded his arms. "Perhaps we should move ahead and talk about what happens after the transition is complete. At what stage do the specific talents manifest, if there are any?"

Merlin frowned. "I assume that you refer to thralling and the like?"

"Thralling, compulsion, telepathy, foresight, remote viewing, and all that. Those are the most common traits for gods."

Hopefully, he had phrased it generically enough not to raise the doctor's suspicion.

"Let's see." Merlin leaned back and smoothed a hand over his white beard. "Those who transition at puberty learn to thrall with relative ease. That applies to all the clan children and also those born in the Brotherhood. Older transitioned Dormants, like Gabi and my beautiful mate, seem to have great difficulty learning to do that, and most don't bother to make the effort. The other talents you've mentioned usually manifest even before the transition, but not always. Kian's mate has had visions of the future since she was a little girl. She even predicted the discovery of the Kra-ell. Kalugal, who is Kian's cousin, is a compeller, and he had the ability since he was a little boy as well. Magnus's wife can communicate telepathically with her daughter, who is Julian's mate, and they could do that as humans years before they joined the clan and were induced. Aside from the ones I mentioned, we also have telepaths, empaths, seers, remote viewers, immunes, and compellers, all with varying degrees of ability. In addition, many clan members are creatives, and I'm sure that some of those artistic talents are supernatural as well."

Aru was only interested in the mother and daughter telepaths, and since the daughter was mated to Julian, he could ask him about her when he replaced Merlin tomorrow morning, but he couldn't wait so long to find out whether her talent was like his and Aria's, which was the ability to actually talk in each other's heads. The more common type of telepathy was receiving or transmitting limited information to anyone in the vicinity with some level of telepathic sensitivity.

"Can Julian's mate communicate with anyone other than her mother?" he asked.

Merlin lifted both white brows and pursed his lips at the same time, looking comical. "I'm not sure whether Ella can communicate with anyone other than Vivian, but I know that Vivian can only communicate with Ella. The daughter is the stronger telepath."

Aru closed his eyes and opened a channel to his sister, who surprised him by opening it on her side and letting him in. *You were right*, he said. *They have a pair like us in their village.*

Aria's answer came in the form of a laugh. *I cannot talk right now, but I am always right. Make sure the leader of the immortals doesn't connect the dots.*

"You should get some sleep, Aru," Merlin said. "You can't even keep your eyes open. Make use of the cot, though." He smiled indulgently. "I saw that you climbed in bed with Gabi before, and I didn't say anything because it was fine for a little while, but she needs her rest, and you crowding her in bed makes her sleep less restful."

"You are right." Aru pushed to his feet. "Thank you for the talk. I think I'm going to catch a couple hours of sleep. Goodnight, Merlin."

"It was nice talking to you. Goodnight, Aru."

Later, when Aru lay awake on the too-short cot in Gabi's room, he thought about ways to salvage the situation.

Perhaps he could make up a story about an illegal secret communicator that his teammates didn't know about and throw hints about communicating with a resistance base somewhere in a direct line of sight of Earth.

From there, the messages could be transmitted to the resistance leadership on Anumati.

However, he and his teammates had already told Kian and Turner about the way things were manufactured on Anumati and that devices were made in a way that didn't allow for modifications.

But then things could have been made off planet, where manufacturing was a little less regulated, especially if the products were meant for the local market and internal consumption. Dagor had said that they were crap, which was true in most cases, but even a crappy device was better than none.

Kian could demand to see the communicator, but Aru would refuse, and that would be the end of it.

Yeah, that was what he had to do.

No one other than the Supreme knew about his and Aria's ability, and it was crucial that it stay that way.

44

KIAN

When all the guests had left, Kian pulled Syssi into his arms. "Thank you for preparing dinner. Now that I've eaten all the dishes you made, I can honestly say that it was wonderful."

"Thank you. I'm glad you liked it, even though everything tasted a little off. I'm so out of practice."

"I savored every bite." He kissed her lightly on the lips. "Now let me make it up to you for taking Okidu away when you needed him." He swung her into his arms and carried her to their bedroom—princess-style.

Winding her arms around his neck, she rested her cheek on his chest and sighed. "I'm so tired."

That was disappointing. "Too tired for bedroom fun?"

She laughed. "Not if I get to be lazy and you do all the work."

"It's a deal, and I'll even throw in a foot massage."

Leaning up, she kissed his cheek. "That's why you are such a good businessman. You make the best deals."

"Damn right, I do." Kian sat on their bedroom couch with his mate in his lap. "It's called closing." He arranged her so her back was resting against the plush arm and her feet were in his lap. "Throwing in a treat to sweeten the deal almost always leads to a signature on the dotted line."

Her short-heeled mules were easy to take off and toss on the floor, and as he started kneading the arch of one foot, Syssi closed her eyes and let out a throaty groan that went straight to his groin.

He chuckled. "Sometimes it sounds as if you are having more fun when I'm massaging your feet than when I'm making love to you."

Syssi cracked one eye open and smiled. "Do I hear a note of insecurity in the voice of the most confident male on the planet?"

He shook his head in mock affront. "And now you are insinuating that I have an overinflated ego. I get no respect in this house."

Syssi knew he was joking, and she chose to ignore his banter and submit to the pleasure his fingers were wringing out of her foot instead.

"Do you remember the vision I told you about the other day?" she murmured.

"The one you were not supposed to induce? Yeah, I remember."

She opened her eyes and glared at him. "We talked about this, Kian. I'm not carrying a baby, so even though the visions take a lot out of me, I can handle them. I promised you that I would not induce them without telling someone what I'm about to do so they could check in on me if needed, but we agreed that I would have them whenever I wanted, and you would not give me the stink eye for that."

He lifted a brow. "Stink eye, eh? A stinging bottom is more my style."

She pouted, but there was a gleam of mischief in her eyes. "You gave me both. I don't mind the second, but I do mind the first, and you promised not to do that." She lifted a finger and tapped his nose with it. "We've made a deal."

"Oh, lass, you've got me there. I can't go back on a deal, now, can I?" He let his Scottish accent come through, knowing how much it turned her on.

"No, you can't, and stop distracting me. Back to my vision. The goddess I saw must have been a royal, and if the intensity of the glow was an indicator of royal blood, she was a queen. Do you think she could have been your great-grandmother?"

"You said that her glow was so bright that you couldn't see her face, so you don't know if she looked anything like my mother or one of my sisters, which would have been a clue."

Syssi sighed. "True. The only vivid clue was that gold vase that didn't fit with the rest of the room's decor. It looked like modern art." She frowned. "That was actually a good clue. It should have made me realize that what I was seeing wasn't ancient Sumer but somewhere else entirely—like an alien planet."

Kian moved to massage Syssi's dainty toes, which she always found ticklish, but he did that gently this time so as not to distract her again. "What else do you remember from the room? Perhaps the face of the other goddess, the servant, was clearer?"

Closing her eyes tightly, Syssi let out a breath. "Nope. I don't think that I saw her face clearly either, but I noticed her dress and also the dress of the other goddess. They were both made from a silk-like fabric like the gowns your mother favors, but the royal goddess's was much more elaborate. I mean, the pattern of the fabric was. The dress itself was simple. It was like a Greek toga, and she also wore a gold necklace." Syssi frowned. "It had a medallion, and I think it had some design on it." She opened her eyes. "I need to induce another vision."

Kian had been afraid of that, but he'd made a deal with her, and he wasn't going back on his word. "Do you want to do it now?"

Syssi gaped at him. "Now? Do you want me to do it with you in the room?"

"Well, yes. That way, I can take care of you if you faint."

"I can't do it with you here because I won't be able to concentrate. Besides, I'm too tired. I will do it on Saturday."

That was in two days, and it wasn't like Syssi to postpone something she was determined to do.

"Are you going to the university tomorrow?"

She had been complaining about being cooped up in the village, so even though it was Friday tomorrow, and it would have made more sense for her to return to work on Monday, she probably couldn't wait to get out of the house.

"No. Amanda wants us to start on Monday. She convinced me to go shopping with her tomorrow instead. After that, I'll probably be too exhausted to induce a vision, which is why I'm planning to do it on Saturday."

That explained why Syssi didn't want to induce the vision tomorrow. Shopping with Amanda was probably more exhausting than running a marathon.

He was glad that she was taking time off for herself, but shopping was one of her least favorite activities. "What prompted you to humor Amanda? You order everything online."

"I do, but Amanda has been on my case for a while now to give my wardrobe a serious update. We are going to Joann's. She's reserving the entire morning just for the two of us."

Kian grinned. "I'm glad that you are finally going to splurge on yourself a little. Are you taking Allegra with you?"

"Your mother and Alena are babysitting Evie and Allegra so Amanda and I can enjoy our shopping spree." She let out a sigh. "The last time Amanda took me to Joann's, the visit cost a small fortune. I told her that I was never going to do it again, but the truth is that I'm not the same woman I was then. I'm a little less frugal these days."

"Thank the merciful Fates." Kian lifted one small foot and kissed its arch. "You are a major stockholder in a successful enterprise, and you can afford a fancy wardrobe."

"Right." Syssi smiled. "I keep forgetting that I own a large chunk of Perfect Match. With all that has been happening lately, Toven and I have neglected the company. We are lucky to have Hunter and Gabriel still running things for us."

"Indeed." He kissed her toes. "You are better at managing your business than I am. You have capable people running it for you."

"That's because I bought an existing enterprise and hired the founders. This is their baby, and they won't let it fail if they can help it. You, on the other hand, are running numerous enterprises for the clan, some that you bought and some that you've built from the ground up. Frankly, I don't know how you manage all of them while dealing with the seemingly perpetual emergencies that threaten the clan. I would have lost my mind from anxiety."

Leaning, he kissed her forehead. "You are my counterbalance. You bring me peace, and when it seems like the giant house of cards is going to collapse, all I have to do is think of you and Allegra and I know that everything is going to be all right."

45

ARU

Come morning, Gabi was still asleep, or at least Aru was pretty sure that she was sleeping and not unconscious.

Throughout the night, she'd moved her hands a few times and had even tried to turn on her side but had given up, probably because of all the wires tethered to her. He'd wanted to assist her but had been afraid to wake her up.

Both healers had emphasized how important it was for Gabi to rest as much as possible. Her body was working hard on the transition, and every unnecessary movement put a strain on her limited resources and slowed the process.

As much as Aru craved the sight of her open eyes and smiling lips, he'd refrained from doing anything that might have interfered with the speedy progression of her transition.

The sacrifice was worth it if it helped speed things up.

Once Gabi was done with the first stage of her transition, she would be out of the damn hospital bed, feeling great and having the resilient body of an immortal.

Were immortals as strong as gods, though?

Last night, he'd learned from Merlin that they didn't heal as fast. If a minute was considered the average time for an immortal's body to heal a cut, then it was significantly slower than it took a god. Aru's scrapes and other small injuries healed within seconds, and if he and an immortal both sustained the same serious injury, his fast healing might save him, while the slower rate of an immortal's healing might not repair crucial organs in time to prevent them from permanently failing.

A minute could mean the difference between life and death.

Still, immortals healed much faster than humans, and Aru was grateful that Gabi would no longer be that fragile.

If he was to be her protector from now on, which he hoped to be for the next one hundred and fifteen years, he had to learn more about immortal physiology and which injuries could be catastrophic to Gabi.

Julian could probably provide him with a basic overview, and he also needed to ask the doctor about his mate's telepathic abilities.

Pushing to his feet, he leaned over the bed and kissed Gabi's cheek. "I'll be right back, my love."

Was it his imagination, or did her lips curve up a little?

Aru hadn't told her he loved her yet, and he couldn't drop the news on her as soon as she woke up, but he was going to do that as soon as he thought she could hear it and not faint from stress.

As he'd expected, Julian had returned sometime during the early morning hours, replacing Merlin.

"Good morning," the doctor welcomed him into his office. "If you want coffee, I brewed a pot in the kitchen. It's to the left of the clinic down the hallway all the way to the end."

The smell of coffee was enticing, and Aru would have loved a cup, but he didn't want to wander too far away from the clinic in case Gabi woke up.

"I'll get some later, thank you." He pulled out a chair and eyed the bowl of candy on the healer's desk. "May I?"

Aru was hungry, and candy was better than nothing.

Julian followed his gaze and chuckled. "Suit yourself, but I would check the expiration date. I don't know how long these have been out here."

"I'll chance it." Aru dipped his hand in the bowl and scooped up as many as he could. "I'm starved."

Julian frowned. "Of course, you are. You haven't eaten anything since yesterday afternoon." He picked up the receiver of his desk phone and pressed the square that had security written over it. "Hi, it's Julian. Can you get coffee and something to eat from the café for our guest? And make sure that his buddies in the penthouse are not starving either."

"They went out to eat," the guy on the other side said.

Aru shook his head. Dagor and Negal should have notified him that they were leaving, even if it was for a short excursion to get food.

"Good. I forgot that they have a car." Julian smiled at Aru.

"I'll send someone with a tray downstairs," the guy said. "Do you want anything?"

"I'm good. I ate at home. Thank you." Julian put the receiver down. "I'm so used to relying only on my mobile phone that having a desk phone feels strange." He tilted his head. "Do they have phones on Anumati, or is all communication telepathic out there?"

Aru smiled. "Funny you should ask."

"Why is that?"

"Because I wanted to ask you about your mate's telepathic ability."

Julian's mellow expression turned menacing so quickly that it startled Aru. "How do you know about my mate?"

"Merlin told me about the various talents immortals have, and he mentioned that your mate and her mother can communicate in their heads. It's a very rare ability. In fact, there hasn't been a case of a telepathic duo on Anumati for thousands of years."

4 6

GABI

"I'll be right back, my love."

It must have been part of the dream, and Gabi didn't want to wake up and discover that Uriel hadn't said those words to her. The problem was that she was itching to get up, go to the bathroom, and take a shower.

Oh, and drink coffee.

The wonderful smell was making her mouth water. How long had it been since she'd last had anything to drink or eat?

It seemed like she'd been in a hospital bed forever. It must have been days, maybe even weeks, but it was worth it. She'd never felt so good in her life.

Lifting her hand effortlessly, she smoothed it over her hair, wondering at how silky it felt despite not having been washed in a while.

But wait, had it really been that long?

Gabi had difficulty assessing the passage of time, but if every awakening marked a new morning, then she'd been here for many sunrises she hadn't gotten to see because there were no windows in the room.

Finally opening her eyes, she glanced at the monitoring equipment to see if any of the devices displayed a date or at least what day it was.

It was truly amazing how much detail she could see now. There was no date, but next to the time, it said Friday. It was Wednesday when she'd fainted on the street, so did it mean that her entire transition had taken only two days? Or was it a week and two days? Two weeks?

And where was Uriel?

Had she dreamt about him lying next to her in the hospital bed and talking with her for hours?

And had he really called her his love?

Nah, that must have been a dream.

They had talked about many things, including truelove mates and what it meant. He'd said that he had fallen for her, and she'd told him not to say the L word, and he'd said that he would save it for last, but she must have fallen asleep, and he hadn't gotten the chance to tell her that he loved her.

Warmth spreading from her heart outwards, Gabi let herself feel all the love she'd been suppressing out of fear. It was like a balloon was inflating inside of her and making her buoyant.

What a wonderful feeling it was to love, even better than being loved, but only if it was safe to do so, and for the first time in forever, Gabi felt that it was.

She could love this male, this god, without fear of rejection, of betrayal, of abandonment—

Then she suddenly remembered the other things Aru had said that she'd conveniently forgotten because they didn't make her happy.

His time on Earth was limited, and in one hundred and fifteen years, the ship patrolling this sector of the galaxy would return to pick him up, and he couldn't take her with him because she was a hybrid—mostly human and only a little bit goddess.

Her eyes misting with tears, she draped her arm over them and sniffled. A century was a long time, longer than any humans got to enjoy their partners no matter how much in love they were. They had an expiration date, and there was nothing they could do about it.

She was lucky to get something amazing that would last so long. Besides, a lot can happen in a century, and there was no reason to mourn Aru's future departure when it might never happen.

So yeah, she was an optimist, and that had gotten her in trouble before, but it was better to live with hope than with despair. It was better to be an optimist than a pessimist.

Letting out a breath, Gabi lifted her arm off her face and patted the stand next to her for a tissue. When she found none, she lifted a corner of the sheet covering her and wiped the tears away.

The rest would have to wait until the doctor came in and gave her a tissue to blow her nose in. She had a call button she could press, and the doctor would rush in right away, but she wasn't ready to face anyone yet. She needed a few more moments to herself to calm down and put on a brave face.

ARU

"Is that so?" Julian was still glaring daggers at Aru. "I assume that there is a story associated with that last famous pair of telepaths."

Aru couldn't understand the healer's hostility.

If Merlin had talked about it so freely, his mate's ability couldn't have been such a great secret. Why was he so angry at Aru for asking about it?

His mate and her mother's situation was very different from Aru and Aria's. They didn't expect to be persecuted or exploited because of their ability.

Or maybe they did?

"There were several famous pairs of telepaths," Aru said. "There are many stories about them, most probably fictional. As you can imagine, the possible scenarios are endless."

"Oh yeah, I'm well aware of the possibilities. My mate and her mother escaped sexual slavery by a hair's breadth. If not for Turner's quick thinking and connections in the military, I would have lost my Ella, and Magnus would have lost Vivian."

Sexual slavery was a travesty that Aru couldn't comprehend. He'd heard about the abhorrent trade that some sub-humans engaged in, abducting females and forcing them into sexual slavery by means of coercion, whether drugs, threat of physical harm, or threats to their families.

"That's terrible, but how did your mate and her mother's special talent get them involved in that?"

Julian was still aggravated, but he was making an effort to calm down. "That's a long story that I'm not sure I can tell you. The gist of it was that someone wanted to kidnap them so he could use one of them to infiltrate a harem and report to the other what she saw there. In his defense, he was trying to save his mother, who was trapped there, but that didn't justify what he attempted to do."

Aru could easily conceive of people who would use a talent like his and Aria's for spying. They were perfect for the job, so limiting who knew about the ability was smart.

"How did that individual find out about your mate and her mother's telepathic ability?"

Julian grimaced. "He's a very talented guy too. He's a compeller and a dream walker. He first met Ella when she was still human, and he thralled his way into her mind. That was how he knew about her talent. Then, he pursued her by using his dream-walking ability and lured her and her mother into a trap. We knew that he was up to no good, and we planned to trap him ourselves, but he was very clever and almost outsmarted us." Julian shivered. "I can't even think of what would have happened if he had succeeded."

"Did you get the chance to avenge your mate?"

The doctor shook his head. "I don't believe in vengeance. That person apologized and repented, and that's all I'm going to say about the subject." He pinned Aru with a hard stare. "Whatever you planned on using my mate and her mother for, you can forget about it. They are never using their talent for anything other than enjoying each other's mental company."

Aru nodded. "I agree with you a hundred percent. There are too many people out there who would love to put their hands on a pair of perfect spies. My respect and appreciation for Kian increased significantly knowing that he doesn't force people in his community to use their talents for the greater good and leaves the decision up to them."

That got Julian to deflate a little, and he slumped in his chair. "Vivian and Ella will do anything for the clan, even if it means endangering themselves. But Kian doesn't like to use civilians for military operations, and especially not females." The doctor smiled. "The ladies accuse him of being a chauvinist, but as a mated guy, I applaud him. I don't want my mate recruited for dangerous tasks."

Aru reflected on his sister's recruitment and service to the Supreme. In Aria's case, she was probably the safest where she was right now. People in the service of the Supreme were untouchable.

"I agree with you, but we don't get to make decisions for our mates. All we can do is advise, right? And the same is true the other way around."

Julian laughed. "I don't dare to do anything that Ella disapproves of. Mated bliss means avoiding strife at all costs. Fortunately, we see eye to eye on most things."

"That's good." Aru raked his fingers through his messy hair. "I hope Gabi and I will get along as splendidly as you do when we are together for a while." He let out a breath. "I haven't even told her that I love her yet."

"So, what are you waiting for? Do it! We are immortal, but life is still too short to waste on insecurities."

Aru hoped that Julian would impart more advice on achieving mated bliss, but their conversation was interrupted when the clinic door opened, and a guard walked in with a cardboard tray with four coffees and a large paper bag. "I didn't know what you like to eat, so I got one of each of the sandwiches they offer. Enjoy."

"Who did you bring all these coffees for?" Julian asked.

The guard shrugged. "I ordered two, and they gave me four by mistake."

"Then why don't you take one?" Aru pulled one of the paper cups out of the tray.

"Thank you for the offer, but I'm all coffeed out." He waved a hand. "Save it for later."

"I want coffee!" Gabi called out from her room. "Please and thank you!"

Julian and Aru exchanged looks, and a moment later, they were both out of their chairs and rushing to Gabi's room.

GABI

s Aru and Julian burst into the room, Gabi chuckled. "Hello,
boys. Where is my coffee?"

She'd managed to lift the back of her bed so she was semi-reclined, and she'd popped into her mouth one of the tiny mints Julian had left on her bedside table.

"You're awake," Aru stated the obvious and turned to Julian. "How come we didn't see it on the monitors?"

The doctor smiled sheepishly. "I was distracted by what we were talking about, so I wasn't paying attention."

Aru frowned at him. "What if something went wrong?"

"The alarm would have gone off." He walked up to Gabi. "How are you feeling?"

"Wonderful." She lifted the hand with the needle stuck on the back of it. "I want this out, and also the other one." She looked down and felt herself blush. "Is there a chance you can get a female doctor or nurse to do that?"

"If it's important to you, I can ask one of the nurses to come from the village, but what makes you think that you won't slip away again?"

"I'm over the first stage. I just know it. Is there a test you can run?"

Aru stiffened, and Julian grinned.

"Yes, there is. I can make a small cut on the palm of your hand, and if the incision closes in minutes instead of how long it would have taken a human to heal it, then you are out of the first stage, and that's a reason for celebration."

"Then do it." Gabi offered him her palm.

The doctor chuckled. "Not so fast. Most transitioning Dormants prefer to have their family and friends around them when the test is performed. It's become a tradition in the village. It's like a rite of passage, but instead of passage into adulthood, it's into immortality. As I said, it's a reason for celebration."

Gabi chewed on her lower lip. "Did Gilbert and Eric have the family and their friends watch the test performed?"

Julian nodded. "The clinic was bursting at the seams with your lovely, large family."

Gabi smiled. "I would love for them to be here. But on the other hand, I don't want to wait for the removal of the IV and the other thing. I want to shower, change into something clean, do my hair, etc. Knowing Gilbert, he's going to record the testing ceremony, and I want to look good, so when I show it to our kids one day, they won't think that their mom was a mess when she transitioned." She glanced at Aru, hoping for a smile but getting a frown.

Well, so much for what she'd thought was the infamous L word and all the talk about one and only and truelove and all that.

"Oops." She lifted a hand to her lips. "Did I say too much and scare you away?"

He shook his head. "Forgive me. I'm just not on board with the test. It's primitive and unnecessary."

That was what bothered him? Not her mention of the future kids she hoped to have with him one day?

Perhaps he was still thinking about the limited time he had with her and that it was unlikely that they could conceive in that relatively short period.

One thing at a time.

First, she needed those tubes out, then she wanted the test to confirm that she was out of the first stage of transition and could get out of the clinic, and third, they needed to have THE TALK.

"I want the test, so I know for sure that I'm out of stage one, and I want my family to be here when it is done. It's a wonderful opportunity for the rest of them to meet you. Kaia and Karen are dying to see the hunk I've been telling them about, and now that they know you are a god, I bet they're triply curious." She looked around, searching for her purse. "Where is my phone? I need to start making phone calls."

Julian put a hand on Aru's shoulder. "I need to perform a few tests that do not involve cuts. Would you mind stepping out of the room for a few moments?"

Aru's frown deepened. "What are you going to do to my mate?"

"Nothing dangerous or unsavory. Given the level of energy Gabi is exhibiting, I don't think she's going to pass out again, and I can remove the tubes that are bothering her." He glanced at her. "If you don't mind me doing that. If you want to wait for the nurse to get here, that's perfectly fine with me."

Gabi was still stuck on Aru calling her his mate. Did it mean what she thought it did?

"I don't want to wait," she said before she could change her mind. "I'll just close my eyes and pretend you're a female."

"I can live with that." Julian smoothed a hand over his stubble. "The long rest must have been very beneficial to you. Yesterday, I was convinced that you would spend at least three more days in the clinic, if not more, before you were ready for the test, and look at you now. You seem to be bouncing off the walls with energy."

"I can also see from much farther away, hear better, and also smell more things, which reminds me that you have coffee in the other room. Can I please have it? I woke up dying for coffee."

Julian sighed. "Just a sip. You are not supposed to have anything other than water after waking up from a coma, and not much of it either, but I can't say no to such a heartfelt request."

"Thank you." She rewarded him with a bright smile. "You're an angel."

675

49

ARU

Aru paced the small waiting area, replaying in his head what Gabi had said.

Their future children.

He had never dreamt about being a father. He still didn't. Why bring children into a world that might get destroyed?

The threat of the Eternal King wasn't imminent in human terms, which was how these immortals perceived the passage of time, but it was real, and it was coming.

Even if the resistance managed to topple the king much sooner than estimated, it would be a disaster if they didn't have someone better to replace him with, and that was a tall order. Things could get much worse than they were, and the Eternal King wasn't the ultimate evil.

An enormous bureaucracy implemented the king's policies, and it was old and corrupt. Not to say that it was evil either, just self-serving.

Aru wasn't a brilliant strategist or a gifted philosopher. He was just a simple god who wanted to be free to choose the way he lived his life, where and how he chose to live it, and he wanted to be free to say what he wanted to say as long as it didn't incite anyone to violence against another.

He wanted freedom, and that was the one thing that the common gods on Anumati no longer had. The erosion had been so gradual that most hadn't even realized how restricted their lives had become. His parents were the perfect example of that.

Frankly, he couldn't imagine how the resistance was going to cure the bureaucracy of corruption, build a system that prevented future corruption from forming, and replace the king with someone just as capable but of better character.

Perhaps Anumati should abolish its constitutional monarchy and become a full democracy, but that was also an unrealistic goal.

He just wasn't smart enough to think of solutions to all of Anumati's problems and had to trust in the Supreme and the Fates to lead the resistance toward it.

As the door to Gabi's room opened and Julian walked out, Aru wanted to rush back in, but Julian stopped him with a hand on his chest.

"Gabi is showering, and she specifically asked that you do not come into the bathroom. I told her that you would be in the room, listening, and if she needed help, you would come in."

Aru nodded. "I'll stand guard by the door."

"Good." Julian clapped him on the back. "I really don't understand how she's doing so well. She walked to the bathroom without my aid." He started toward his office and then turned around. "I forgot to mention, but Gabi grew half an inch in the two days since her transition started."

That wasn't a big change. "Anything else?"

"Gabi says that her skin is smoother, and her eyes are brighter, but I have to take her word for it. I failed to take a close-up photo of her when we picked her up from the hospital."

"Her skin was smooth before she got here."

The doctor shrugged. "If you notice any more changes, let me know, and I will write them down. We keep records of every transition."

"Of course." Aru walked into the room and closed the door behind him.

In the bathroom, the water was running, and Gabi was humming a tune he didn't recognize. Leaning his back against the door, he crossed his arms over his chest and tried to sing along. Perhaps Gabi's jubilant mood would improve his own.

He should be happy that his blood transfusion had worked, and he was. The melancholy he felt was related to the children Gabi wanted that he didn't wish to bring into an unstable world.

Opening a channel to Aria, he wanted to tell her about Gabi's miraculous improvement, but she didn't open the channel on her end, so he couldn't share the good news with her.

Aria was probably busy at some official function with the Supreme, and she never communicated with Aru unless she was alone. He was supposed to do the same, but sometimes he cheated a little when what he needed to tell her was brief.

When Gabi turned the water off, he pushed away from the door, and when she didn't come out right away, he got worried.

"Are you okay in there?" he asked.

"Yeah, I'm great. The sticky pads left a residue that refuses to come off. I'm trying to rub it off."

"I can help. Can I come in?"

There was a moment of hesitation. "Not yet. Give me a few minutes to sort things out."

He didn't know what things she needed to sort out, but it wasn't as if he could argue. "I'm right here if you need me."

"I know. Thank you, Aru."

50

GABI

Gabi scrubbed off the last of the sticky residue and then stood naked in front of the bathroom mirror.

Not much had changed about her, but Julian reassured her that this was only the beginning and that her appearance would become more youthful as her transition kept progressing at a slower pace.

Her breasts were still a little saggy, but the color of her nipples was brighter, and she hadn't shed as much hair as she usually did while showering.

Supposedly, she'd grown half an inch over the past two and a half days, which was a lot for a body to do in such a short time, but she hoped she would grow some more. She'd always wanted to be taller, but that was in her silly teenage days when she'd dreamt of being a fashion model.

Now that she was older and smarter, she knew better. The world of fashion was not as glamorous as it appeared, and she wanted no part of it.

Gabi chuckled at her reflection.

Even if she wanted to become a model, she couldn't. Immortals couldn't be in the limelight. They had to disappear.

"Oh, crap. I can't go back to Cleveland."

"Gabi? Are you talking to me?"

Crappity crap, she had to stop talking to herself. "No, I just remembered that I'm supposed to be back in Cleveland on Monday, and Julian said that I can't go anywhere because he wants to keep an eye on me for a couple of weeks."

When there was silence on the other side of the door, Gabi wrapped a fluffy white towel around herself and stepped out of the bathroom.

Aru stood with a hand on his hip, the other on his jaw, looking despondent.

"What's wrong?" She lifted a hand to his unshaven cheek and cupped it.

"I thought that I could take you out of here. Are you telling me that you need to stay in this room for two more weeks?"

She laughed. "No way. After the test is done, I'm out of here. Julian said that I can stay in the penthouse with you, and he will come every other day to check up on me."

Letting out a breath, he pulled her into his arms. "I love you. I just wanted to say that before something else interfered, but if that freaks you out, forget that I said it, or put it aside for when you are ready to hear it."

Her heart melted a little just from how sweet he was.

"I love you too." She wrapped her arms around his neck and stretched on her toes to kiss him on the lips. "I am Gabriella Emerson, the brave warrior of God. I will forever stand by your side with my sword drawn and my dagger in my other hand, ready to fight off your enemies, large and small." She smiled. "Well, maybe not the large ones, but the small ones for sure." She made a slashing gesture with her hand before returning it to his nape.

He gaped at her, his eyes searching hers in an effort to understand her silly declaration.

"I spoke metaphorically, Aru. I've never held a sword in my hand, and if I picked up a dagger, I would probably injure myself with it. What I was trying to convey was that I would always have your back or that I'll have it for as long as we can be together, which I hope is forever, but I know that you can't promise me that."

Looking lost for words, Aru did the next best thing and smashed his lips over hers.

The kiss quickly turned heated, and Gabi was ready to drop the towel and have her way with Aru on the narrow hospital bed, but a knock on the door put an end to those plans.

"Is everyone decent in there?" Julian's voice sounded from the other side.

"Don't come in," Aru called back. "Gabi is getting dressed." He reached under the bed and pulled out the plastic bag with her belongings. "You can get dressed in the bathroom while I see what he wants."

Gabi was about to mention that Julian had seen everything already, so there was no point in acting modestly around him, but she had a feeling that Aru would not appreciate her honesty on that subject.

"If he needs to run any more tests on me, let me know. He said something about taking blood samples."

Aru nodded, and as she took the plastic bag and sashayed back into the bathroom, she caught sight of his arousal and licked her lips. "Soon, Aru. Very, very soon."

51

ARU

"This better be important," Aru murmured as he opened the door, not caring if the doctor heard him. "What is it?"

He sounded annoyed even though he'd tried to go for matter-of-fact. After Gabi's sexy taunt, a polite tone would have been too difficult to muster.

"Kian is here to continue your talks."

Talk about bad timing. "Did you tell him about Gabi being ready for the test?"

"I didn't have a chance. I got a call from Anandur asking for you to come up to the penthouse. I need to take some blood samples and measurements, but after I'm done, I can escort Gabi up to the penthouse to join you."

"Okay, that's good." He rubbed a hand over his jaw. "Let me just tell her that I have to leave."

Julian nodded. "I'll wait out here."

Smart guy.

Aru closed the door, walked up to the bathroom, and knocked on the door. "Gabi?"

"Yeah?"

"Kian is back in the penthouse and wants me to come up."

"Oh." She opened the door, wearing jeans and a tight-fitting T-shirt that barely covered her midriff. "How long will you be gone?"

His eyes were riveted to the sliver of flesh showing above her waistband. "I don't think I'm coming back." When she gasped, and her hand flew to her heart, he realized how it had sounded and reached for her. "You are coming to stay with me in the penthouse as soon as Julian is done taking blood samples and some other tests. Neither of us is coming back down here."

Gabi put her hand on his chest and leaned her forehead on his clavicle. "You scared me. Don't ever do that again."

"I won't. I promise." He rubbed soothing circles on her back. "Well, I'll try, but I can't promise I'll never again say something without thinking how it sounds."

"Good enough." She patted his chest. "Go. Don't keep Kian waiting. I've heard that he can be a grouch."

"Oh, right. You haven't met him yet. This will be your first time meeting the clan's leader."

"Supposedly, Kian's bark is worse than his bite, but I'm a scaredy cat."

"No, you're not. You are my brave warrior."

She smiled. "Nevertheless, I'm glad you will be there, so I don't have to face him alone. I've gotten the impression that he's intimidating. But his wife and his sister are very nice, so he can't be too bad, right?"

"Kian is not bad. He's intense, but I didn't find him intimidating. I actually like him. He seems like a good guy doing his best for his people or trying to."

"Is he as beautiful as his sister? I mean, Amanda is so stunning that I couldn't take my eyes off her, and I've met models and actresses before."

"Kian is very good-looking. His godly genes are probably less diluted, and so are his sister's. They are most likely direct descendants."

Gabi shrugged. "It makes sense for the direct son of a god or a goddess to be the clan's leader, right? I mean, that's how society usually works. Those at the top of the food chain get to lead, and gods are definitely up there, then the immortals, then humans, and then the rest of the animal kingdom, right?"

He chuckled. Gabi always talked up a storm when she was nervous. "There are endless varieties of species in the known universe, and gods are definitely at the top of the food chain. That's why we call ourselves gods. But there is also a hierarchy among us, with some at the top and some at the bottom."

Gabi frowned. "Where are you on that scale?"

"Somewhere in the middle. If I were human, I would call myself middle class."

"That's a good place to be." She leaned into him and kissed his neck. "I'm glad that we have this in common. We are both middle class. Other than that, though, we are literally worlds apart."

"I disagree. We have a lot in common, and I would love to stay here and show you all the ways we are alike, but I need to go." He planted a gentle kiss on her forehead. "See you in a bit."

"Yes."

It was difficult to extract himself from her arms, and Aru wished they could go up to the penthouse together, but Julian needed to run more tests on Gabi, and Kian probably wanted to talk in private.

52

KIAN

Kian stood in front of the wall of glass that formed the entire front of his former penthouse and looked at the high rise across the street, which also belonged to the clan. In fact, most of the buildings on the block belonged to the clan, and there was a network of hidden passages beneath them.

The keep was compromised, so he would have to block all the entrances to the underground from this building, but it would still be accessible through the tunnels from the other buildings.

After all, the place also housed the crypt, and it wasn't as if he could relocate it. He'd lost count of how many Doomers were in stasis down there, their bodies preserved in the meticulously controlled environment, awaiting potential revival should the need ever arise.

Moving them was too complicated to consider.

As several cars honked at once down below, Kian stepped onto the terrace and peeked over the railing to see if anyone was hurt and needed help. When everything seemed fine, he returned to the air-conditioned interior and closed the sliding door behind him.

This time of year, downtown Los Angeles was too hot and bright for him to be comfortable outside. Perhaps he should consider his mother's suggestion to move everyone to Alaska.

At least he wouldn't have to deal with the blasted heat and glare.

Except, the weather was much nicer in the mountains of Malibu, with the elevation and the ocean breeze cooling things down and the marine layer overhead providing a reprieve from the glare. Besides, Kian really liked the location, remote and yet in the center of one of the largest metropolises in the country.

Where could they possibly hide from the Eternal King?

Even the Doomers' island wasn't safe. With the technology the gods possessed, no place was, not even Syssi's imagined underwater Poseidon City.

"Did you locate the other two stooges?" Kian sat on the couch across from Anandur.

Aru was down in the clinic, but his two friends hadn't been in the penthouse when Kian and his entourage had gotten there. The guy in security had said that they were out for breakfast, but it didn't take that long to grab a coffee and a sandwich.

"You didn't tell me that you wanted to find out where they were." Anandur opened the locations application on his phone. "Their car is still in the Starbucks parking lot." He looked up. "They might have left the car there and continued on foot or called a taxi. If I were them, I would have assumed we attached a tracker to their car."

Kian leaned back and crossed his legs at the ankles. "I get that, but what else is there for them to do? Their mission is to find the Kra-ell. They found the ones who went missing from the compound, and they still have to find the other pods. They won't find them in downtown Los Angeles."

"Maybe they went shopping?" Anandur looked at his impassive brother. "Or maybe they are searching for Dormants?"

Brundar cast him an incredulous look and went back to watching the front door of the penthouse as if he were expecting assassins to burst through it at any moment.

Kian didn't expect any trouble from the gods or anyone else, but he had brought Okidu with him just in case.

The Odu was in the kitchen, preparing assorted canapés and brewing coffee.

When the door opened, and Aru walked in, Okidu rushed forward with an affronted expression on his face. "Master Aru. You should have waited for me to open the door for you."

The god arched a brow at Kian. "I thought these were our living quarters for as long as Gabi needed to stay in the clinic. Should I knock every time I return to my temporary lodging?"

It was a polite way to tell Kian that he shouldn't have just come in and made himself at home without Aru's invitation, even though the place belonged to him, but he was going to ignore it. He was doing the guy a favor, and they both knew it had nothing to do with hospitality.

"No, you don't need to knock." He motioned for the couch. "Please, sit down. We have a lot to discuss, and the day is short. I would like to avoid Friday afternoon traffic if possible."

Aru nodded. "I would like to keep it short as well. Gabi is out of the initial stage of transition, and once Julian is done administering some tests, he will escort her here. He says that he needs to monitor her for the next two weeks. If it's okay with you, I would like to stay here until he clears Gabi to go. If it's not, I can rent another place that's conveniently located for Julian to visit. He said that he would do that every other day."

"Of course, you can stay here," Kian said absentmindedly.

He hadn't talked with Julian this morning, but he had yesterday evening, and it hadn't looked like Gabi was anywhere near ready to be done with the first stage.

Had Aru aided her transition in the same way Annani and Toven had been aiding other Dormants?

Was the knowledge about the curative properties of gods' blood common on Anumati?

"That's fantastic," Anandur said. "I thought it would take her much longer to transition. Has anyone called her family to let them know? I'm sure they all will want to be here for the test."

Kian wanted to find out whether Aru had given Gabi his blood, but he didn't want to ask him about her miraculous transition in the presence of the brothers.

"Not yet," Aru said. "Gabi will start making the calls after Julian is done taking blood samples and measurements." He looked at Kian. "Is it okay if Julian performs the test here? The clinic is too small to accommodate Gabi's large family."

Reluctantly, Kian nodded. "We can load everyone on the bus and get them here this evening after rush hour traffic is over."

Aru dipped his head. "Thank you. It will make this primitive custom more tolerable. I don't like the idea of an injury being inflicted on Gabi even if her body can heal it in seconds."

Kian smiled. "I felt the same way when my mate was tested, but it's the fastest way, and it's very visually effective. That's why it lends itself to a ceremony. Everyone can see that the Dormant has transitioned. Besides, the cut is really small." He pushed to his feet. "Let's go to my office."

When Anandur followed him up, Kian motioned for him to sit back down. "I need a few words with Aru alone, and you need to stay here for when Negal and Dagor return."

The brothers didn't look happy, but they obeyed his command without an argument for a change.

At least they knew to behave in company.

ARU

Aru followed Kian to the office and waited until the immortal closed the door behind them.

"I thought that you didn't hide anything from your body-guards. Are you concerned about the Odu overhearing our conversation?"

The truth was that right now, Aru would have preferred to be in the living room, eating whatever the Odu was serving and drinking coffee. He hadn't gotten a chance to consume the sandwiches the security guard had brought for him because he'd been too nervous to eat while waiting for Julian to finish removing all the wires and tubes from Gabi's body, and then he'd been summoned to the penthouse.

It still irked him that Kian had just made himself at home in the penthouse, even though it belonged to him. One did not enter the guest quarters in one's home when guests occupied them, even if those guests were not there at the moment.

Meeting in Kian's old office in the underground would have been much more appropriate.

"I'm not concerned about Okidu overhearing anything. He's like a vault." Kian motioned to one of the chairs in front of the massive desk and pulled the other one out for himself. "I need to ask you about Gabi, and I assumed you would prefer privacy for that."

Aru frowned. "What can I tell you about her that you don't already know?"

Kian's smile was suspiciously knowing. "I just find it curious how Gabi managed to leapfrog through her transition. She was unconscious through most of yesterday and the night, and then this morning, she wakes up full of energy and ready to leave the clinic?"

Aru shrugged. "Julian seemed surprised as well, but he told me that every transition is different. Some remain unconscious for weeks, while others are over it in just a couple of days. But if you think Gabi's transition is unusual, you should direct your questions to the doctor."

Kian had said that Aru shouldn't play card games because he had a terrible poker face, but he hoped he had done well enough to pass Kian's bullshit detector.

For some inexplicable reason, the immortal's smile got even broader. "As long as you keep it to yourself, it's fine with me. Don't ever reveal the truth to anyone, though, including Gabi herself."

Did he know?

Damn, there must have been a camera in the supply closet. The fact that he hadn't seen any didn't mean that there wasn't. It could have been miniature and well hidden.

Kian or Julian must have seen him take the syringes, and Kian had guessed what he'd used them for.

"How do you know about it?" he asked.

"It has been handed down through the generations, but it's a secret that only a select few are privy to. If it fell into the wrong hands, you and your friends would be hunted down, and not even your godly powers would save you. Humans can be very determined when they covet something so valuable, and they will sacrifice many to get their hands on a miracle cure."

Kian hadn't mentioned the gods' blood explicitly, but it was obvious that he knew. Still, Aru wouldn't be the first to spell it out.

"The same is true for the gods living among you. Did they use this method to aid other transitioning Dormants?"

Kian hesitated for a long moment before nodding. "Don't tell Julian or anyone else. They don't know."

Aru frowned. "You don't trust your own people?"

"It's not about trust. We have powerful enemies, and if they capture one of ours, they could torture or compel the information out of them. That's why only a few in our community know how to get into our hidden village. Most of our members use self-driving cars that are programmed to turn their windows opaque within several miles of the entrance."

"Clever." Aru approved. "Do your enemies have compellers?"

"Their leader is a powerful compeller. That's how he controls his army of immortals."

"Is he a god?" Aru asked.

"Navuh is an immortal like me, but he inherited his power of compulsion from his godly ancestor."

Aru chuckled. "Are we back to dancing, Kian? Was one of Navuh's parents a god? Perhaps a direct descendant of the Eternal King? The most powerful compeller ever born?"

54

KIAN

Kian considered an evasive answer or an outright lie, but he was tired of the dance as well, and it was no skin off his nose if Aru knew who Navuh's father was.

Mortdh was dead.

"His father was a god, and his mother was a human. How much do you know about the exiled gods?"

"I know about the main players. The others remained nameless, supposedly to save their families the shame."

"So, you know the names of the Eternal King's three direct descendants. The heir and his half-brother and half-sister."

Aru nodded. "Ahn was the heir, the only son of the Eternal King from his official wife. Ekin was an older son born to a concubine, and Athor was a daughter born to a concubine as well."

"Correct. Ekin didn't inherit the Eternal King's compulsion ability, but he did inherit the womanizing. He had two sons. His firstborn was a very strong compeller and a powerful god all around. Mortdh was also somewhat unhinged and had delusions of grandeur. Long story short, he fathered Navuh with a human female, and for a long time, he didn't acknowledge him as his heir because he was hoping for a pureblooded son from one of the goddesses he bedded, but after many centuries of trying, he reluctantly declared Navuh as his successor."

Aru frowned. "Why was he hoping to get a son? He could have nominated his firstborn daughter as his heir."

Kian smiled. "I don't know if he managed to produce a daughter with a goddess either, but Mortdh was the quintessential misogynist, and he wouldn't have wanted a daughter to be his successor. I don't know whether he hated women because his mother was rumored to be unhinged or maybe because a goddess had rejected him, but he detested the matrilineal ways of the gods and wanted to establish patriarchy. I don't think that he planned to ever step down, but he wanted a second-in-command, and he apparently preferred a half-breed male to a daughter. To be fair, though, even as a young immortal Navuh was more powerful than many of the gods, and his power only increased with age. If you ever find yourself in a position where you need to fight him, don't assume that you will win because you are a god."

Aru's lips curved in a barely-there smile. "What about you? Should I be worried about you besting me in a one-on-one fight for power?"

Kian didn't like the smugness on Aru's face, but regrettably, he was physically no match for a god. He could outmaneuver a bunch of them in business dealings and perhaps even in strategizing, but that was probably all.

"Regrettably, my special talent is spotting great business deals and closing them for my clan. I'm not a compeller, and Anandur can best me on the wrestling mat without even breaking a sweat."

Aru leaned back with a calculating look in his eyes. "Then why are you alone with me? I'm not a compeller either, but I can most likely thrall you, and you wouldn't even know that I was in your mind. It would definitely save me a lot of dance moves."

Kian laughed. "That is true, but you are smarter than that. You could probably overpower me either with a thrall or with your bare hands and fangs, but to what end? You can't overpower my entire clan and the Kra-ell who swore alliance to us. They are immune to your thralling and physically stronger than you."

Evidently Syssi and Turner had been right all along, and the Kra-ell were a valuable addition to the village, providing protection against powerful foes Kian couldn't have conceived of only weeks ago.

The Fates must have been at work again, and not only to arrange for

Jade and Phinas's pairing. The threat of the Eternal King had been looming over humanity ever since the Industrial Revolution, and if Kian had chosen not to respond to Jade's call for help, he would have never learned about it.

The god nodded. "You are very fortunate to have gained the Kra-ell's loyalty. Your clan is better off for it."

"I know." He leveled his eyes on Aru. "Since we've got one step closer in our dance, and I told you about Mortdh's son, you need to tell me something in return."

"What would you like to know?"

"How do you communicate with the resistance?"

The god smiled. "Ask me another question."

"Have you gotten instructions from your bosses in the resistance?"

"Not yet. I will inform you as soon as I do. By the way, how did Navuh survive when his father did not? Wasn't he with him when it happened?"

Kian's hackles rose. "When what happened?"

Aru hadn't been told about the fate of the rebel gods, only that they were gone.

"Whatever it was that killed the gods."

Kian narrowed his eyes at him. "What do you know about it?"

"Not much. I assume that the Eternal King was somehow involved."

Kian grimaced. "I wish we could pin it on him, but the most likely candidate for the bombing of the assembly was Mortdh."

"Really? Why would he do such a thing?"

There was no harm in telling Aru about how the gods perished. Kian would just omit details about his mother's role in what had started the chain of events that had resulted in the eradication of the rebel gods and most of their offspring.

55

GABI

"Thank you." Gabi leaned over and kissed Julian's cheek. "You've gone above and beyond the doctor's duty."

"It was my pleasure."

He'd insisted on rolling her carry-on and carrying her duffle bag to the elevator even though she was perfectly capable of doing it herself.

Heck, she was ready to do some bench presses and run a couple of miles on the treadmill, but Julian had advised against strenuous physical activities in the next couple of weeks.

We shall see about that.

She followed him inside the elevator.

There were some strenuous activities that Gabi was not going to wait two weeks for or even two hours.

Hopefully, Aru's meeting with Kian was over, or it would be soon, so she could drag him into the bedroom and tell him about the naughty dreams she'd had.

Perhaps he could re-enact some of them with his mind tricks. After all, he was a god, so even though she was an immortal now, he could still thrall her, and the best part was that it wouldn't cause her any damage.

Ah, the fun she was going to have.

Aru didn't know what he was getting himself into. He might think that gods and goddesses were a lustful bunch, but Gabi was going to prove to him that newly transitioned immortals could be just as amorous or even more so.

Julian looked at her with amusement in his eyes. "What's that smile for?"

Gabi searched her mind for a quick answer that didn't include carnal activities. "I'm so glad that my clock is no longer ticking. I can have babies whenever I want." The elevator doors opening saved her from having to say more.

"Well, that's a bit optimistic." Julian motioned for her to exit first. "As I explained, immortals have a very low fertility rate, and gods even more so. Merlin might be able to assist with his fertility potions, but you need to talk with Aru first. As gods go, he's a baby, and he's probably not ready to have kids yet."

Her eyes widened. "I didn't even ask him how old he is. Or maybe I did, and I can't remember? Do you know how old he is?"

Julian stopped at one of the double doors flanking the gorgeous vestibule. "You should ask him. I only know that he's very young. I don't know his exact age."

Was he telling her the truth?

"It doesn't matter." Gabi scanned the vestibule again, taking in the elaborate details. "This is beautiful. How much is it to buy a penthouse apartment in this building? Must be a fortune."

"It is."

As Julian lifted his hand to knock, the door opened, and an enormous redhead grinned down at her.

"Gabriella Emerson." He offered her his huge paw. "It's a pleasure to finally make your acquaintance. I'm Anandur."

"Nice to meet you, too." Hesitantly, she put her hand in his, but his grip was surprisingly gentle, and he gave it a light shake.

"Come in." He threw the door open. "Aru is still with Kian in the office, but you are more than welcome to hang out with us. Okidu made delicious canapés, and there are a few left."

"I shall make more expeditiously, mistress." An older gentleman in full butler regalia rushed out of the kitchen and bowed. "Would mistress like tea or coffee with her canapés?"

"Coffee, please." She offered him her hand. "And please, call me Gabi."

Looking horrified, the butler didn't take her hand. "Oh, no, mistress. It is most improper for me to address you by your given name." He bowed again.

Anandur leaned down, bending nearly in half to whisper in her ear. "Resistance is futile. Just go with it."

"Got it." She smiled back at the butler. "Thank you so much for the canapés. I can't wait to taste them."

His bright smile confirmed that it had been the right thing to say. "Please take a seat on the sofa, mistress. I shall bring out fresh offerings momentarily."

As she headed toward where he'd indicated, a blond angel rose to his feet and gave her the slightest of nods but didn't say a thing.

"That's my brother Brundar," Anandur said. "He's not a mute, but he pretends to be. Engaging him in conversation is as futile as trying to get Okidu to call you Gabi or to stop bowing."

She caught a barely there smile on the blond brother's lips before it disappeared, and he sat back down.

It seemed like the two enjoyed playing the good cop, bad cop game, with Anandur being the friendly, jovial one and Brundar the intimidating one. They weren't fooling her, though. The jackets they wore bulged in strategic places, indicating that they were both armed, and she had no doubt that if their boss was in danger, Anandur would drop his friendly act in the blink of an eye and become as deadly as his brother.

"Are Negal and Dagor still not back from their Starbucks excursion?" Julian asked.

"They are on their way back," Anandur said. "I asked a couple of Guardians to check whether they were actually there or gave us the slip, but they found them sitting in the coffee shop and flirting with a couple of lawyer ladies on their lunch break."

"Good for them." Julian chuckled. "Even when I was still single, I wasn't that gutsy."

"Right." Anandur nodded in agreement. "I prefer ladies that don't talk circles around me."

Julian shook his head. "I would have never thought that you would be intimidated by lawyers. Not with what your mate can do."

That got Gabi curious. "What can she do?"

"Kick mine and Brundar's butts," Anandur said with pride.

"I don't believe it." Gabi glanced at the blond brother. "Is that true?"

The guy nodded.

"Well, I'll be damned. She must be a superwoman."

Anandur grinned. "My lovely mate's name is Wonder, and it's totally a tribute to Wonder Woman."

ARU

Aru would have loved to tell Kian that Mortdh hadn't been the one who had bombed the assembly hall, but then he would have to disclose how he had found out who had probably done it, and that would blow his cover.

Besides, there was no proof, only circumstantial evidence and speculation.

Perhaps the gods had indeed been killed by Mortdh, who in a fit of rage had decided to launch a bomb from a civilian aircraft, which was all the rebel gods had been allowed to bring with them.

Had no one wondered why and how he had managed to smuggle a bomb of that kind to Earth?

It surely wasn't part of the standard equipment that had been routinely provided for gold mining or to colonists who were establishing a permanent base on a planet.

Still, it was possible that Mortdh had managed to either smuggle the weapon or make it. Ekin's elder son had been born on Anumati, and he was an adult when his father had been exiled, so he might have planned ahead and managed to smuggle some contraband, or he might have used his father's technical know-how to build a bomb from components that had been used to launch crafts with cargo and personnel from Earth to the orbiting ships.

Kian arched a brow. "No questions, Aru? I was sure you would have a thousand of them by the time I was done talking."

"I was just wondering how Mortdh got his hands on that kind of a bomb. Could it be that he built it himself? Ekin was known as a brilliant scientist, so he might have imparted some of his knowledge to his sons."

"From what I know about Mortdh, he wasn't interested in science. He wanted power." Kian crossed his arms over his chest. "The thing is, no one knows what really happened because all the witnesses died. We will probably never know for sure."

"Mortdh's son might know," Aru said. "Is there a way to ask him? Perhaps you know someone who is close to him?"

Kian regarded him with suspicion in his eyes. "That's not the kind of information I'm comfortable sharing with you. But if Navuh knew anything, he would have told the people close to him, and my spies in his camp would have brought the information to me."

Evidently, they were back to dancing around each other.

Not that he could blame Kian. They were both withholding information to protect others, and it wasn't as if Aru could even promise Kian that the information would remain between them. Everything he learned, he would report to Aria, who would report it to the Supreme, and it wasn't up to him to even know what the Supreme would do with the information.

He could share what he knew about the healing properties of gods' blood, but it seemed that Kian knew that already, so that wouldn't serve as a bargaining chip in their negotiations.

Hopefully, Aria would get back to him soon with instructions from the Supreme or the other resistance leaders.

As Aru's stomach rumbled, he put a hand over it to silence it. "Gabi should be here already." He glanced at the door. "You have very good soundproofing in here. Everywhere else I've stayed, I could hear what was going on in the adjacent rooms, but not in this building."

Kian smiled. "This place was built for immortals, and I always include the best soundproofing for our dwellings." He pushed to his feet. "It's time I was introduced to Gilbert and Eric's sister, and you need to put something in your belly. Have you eaten anything today?"

Aru shook his head. "I only had a few sips of coffee. It's been an eventful morning."

"I bet." Kian walked over to the door. "I still remember vividly how I felt when Syssi was discharged from the clinic. My sister was missing, abducted by a Doomer, so I was still frantic with worry, but I was grateful to the Fates that my mate survived the transition." Kian opened the door.

Aru followed him out of the room. "What happened to your sister?"

Chuckling, Kian stopped and turned to Aru. "That's a long story for another time, but just so you don't worry about her fate, it all ended well. My sister and the Doomer turned out to be truelove mates, he left the Brotherhood and joined the clan, and they have a little baby girl. It took me a while to get accustomed to the idea that my sister chose to mate a Doomer, but once I got my head out of my ass, I realized that he was perfect for her."

"That's one hell of a story." Aru regarded Kian with even more appreciation than before. "I don't know if I would have been able to accept a former enemy as my sister's mate. I'm very protective of her."

He would have probably shot first and asked questions later, and his sister would have hated him for the rest of their days.

Perhaps the Fates were trying to tell him something, and he should take Kian's story to heart?

"It wasn't easy." Kian cast him a wry smile. "I'm just glad that my sister is not a pushover and that she didn't let me ruin the relationship for her. She fought me tooth and nail until I had no choice but to accept that she and Dalhu were fated to be together and that I should stop trying to keep them apart or suffer the consequences."

"Like losing your sister?"

Kian nodded. "And angering the Fates."

GABI

"Should I bring out more canapés, mistress?" The butler bowed at the waist.

Gabi looked at the half-empty tray and wondered how much of it she had demolished. The Guardian brothers had helped, but she'd consumed her fair share, devouring the small sandwiches one after the other and ignoring Julian's instructions to take it easy with food for at least twenty-four hours.

She'd been famished, Julian had left, and the brothers hadn't said a word about her not following the doctor's instructions.

"Not for me, but Aru and Kian might be hungry when they are done with their meeting."

The butler looked like she'd just given him a great gift.

"Right away, mistress." He turned on his heel and walked back into the kitchen.

"He's such a sweet old guy." Gabi snatched another tiny triangular slice covered in a delicious sauce and a slice of cucumber.

Anandur chuckled, and he looked like he was about to say something when he froze, and a smile bloomed on his handsome face. "Your mate's friends are back." He got to his feet and walked over to the front door.

She remembered Aru's friends from the lounge in the airport and the flight itself, but the truth was that she'd been so absorbed with Aru that she hadn't paid them much attention and didn't remember what they looked like other than being very handsome but not as gorgeous as Aru.

When Anandur opened the door and the two came in, she got a good look at them and had to reassess her previous opinion. They weren't as gorgeous as Aru, but they were still too beautiful to be real, like mannequins in a department store or the Ken dolls she'd played with as a kid.

What were their names? Had Uriel introduced them to her?

Gabi still wasn't sure about the soundness of her memories and what she should remember but didn't.

"Negal." Anandur offered his hand to the one with the sandy hair and blue eyes. "That was one hell of a long breakfast."

"Anandur." The guy shook what he was offered. "We didn't know that you were waiting for us." His eyes darted to her and widened. "Gabriella. Are you well?"

"I'm very well, thank you." Gabi pushed to her feet and waited for the males to approach her. "How are you doing?"

"Excellent." He shook her hand as if she was made from breakable glass.

The other guy with dark brown hair and golden eyes regarded her with a less friendly look, but he offered his hand as well. "I'm Dagor. It's my pleasure to make your acquaintance, Gabriella Emerson."

They were so formal for guys who looked so young.

She gave Dagor a bright smile. "A word of advice for when you are trying to score a hookup. Don't be so formal. You sound like someone from a previous century."

He frowned. "How should I have greeted you?"

"Hi, I'm Dagor. Nice to meet you, Gabi. I've heard a lot about you. Aru couldn't stop talking about you."

Dagor's frown deepened. "Aru didn't talk much about you at all."

"He didn't have to," Negal said. "His frantic worry for you said it all."

"Masters." Okidu emerged from the kitchen with an enormous tray. "You have returned just in time for a fresh batch of canapés."

Dagor's lips twisted in distaste. "We ate." He walked toward the sitting area without giving Okidu a second glance.

"That was rude," Gabi murmured under her breath. Out loud, she said, "Thank you, Okidu. It is so kind of you to prepare snacks for us. I can't believe how fast you are making such beautiful and precisely cut little sandwiches that are also delicious. You must show me your technique."

"With pleasure, mistress."

As he bowed to her while holding the huge tray, Gabi was sure the little sandwiches were going to slide off and fall on the floor, but the butler performed an admirable balancing act, and the tray hadn't changed its angle even by one degree.

"Wow. I'm impressed."

"Gabi!" A familiar voice diverted her attention from the butler.

"Aru!" She rushed toward him, happiness filling her heart as if she hadn't seen him in months and she missed him terribly.

She skidded to a halt when she noticed the gorgeous hunk standing next to him.

For a moment, she thought that it was another god, but then she remembered that Aru had been secluded with the clan leader in the office, so the hunk was Syssi's husband.

"Hi. You must be Kian." She offered him her hand. "I'm Gabi. Gabriella Emerson."

"I know." He took her hand and shook it firmly but gently. "Welcome to immortality, Gabi."

"She didn't have the test done yet," Anandur said from the couch. "You can't welcome her until the cut on her hand closes. That's how it's done."

Kian cast him a mock glare. "I can do whatever I please." He turned back to her. "I understand that you want your family to be here for the test."

"Of course."

He smiled. "That's quite a crowd. They won't all fit in the clinic. I told Aru that you could have it done here instead. It's not a hundred percent according to the custom, but it will be more comfortable for everyone."

That was such a generous offer.

As it turned out, Kian was generous and kind, and he wasn't intimidating at all.

"Are you sure?" Gabi looked around. "I mean, Julian will have to cut my hand, and I don't want to stain any of this beautiful furniture or carpets."

"Don't worry about it. Julian won't let a drop escape, and if he did, Okidu would take care of it." He turned to the butler. "Am I right, Okidu?"

"Yes, master." The guy dipped his head. "It would not be the first time I cleaned up blood. I remember that time outside Mistress Amanda's laboratory. That was a lot of blood to clean up. I believe that it was—"

Kian lifted a hand to stop him. "Gabi does not want to hear all the gory details. She's just left the hospital bed, and she's new to our world."

"Actually, I would love to hear that." She leaned against Aru, absorbing strength from his solid body. "I want to learn everything there is about the immortals."

Kian laughed. "It's not going to happen today, so you'd better start making a list." He looked at Aru. "I'm heading home, but I'll be back later tonight for the ceremony."

That was another pleasant surprise.

Did Kian attend every ceremony, or was he giving her special treatment because Aru was her inducer?

In either case, she was deeply honored.

"Thank you, Kian." Gabi dipped her head. "I really appreciate everything you have done for my family and me, including sending a team to get me out of the hospital and sending Julian and Merlin to take care of me. I don't want you to think that I'm taking any of that for granted. You didn't have to do any of that."

"Yes, I did. Your family is part of the clan, and so are you. We take care of our own."

58

ARU

Kian had gone, but he'd left the butler behind to prepare the place for the ceremony or maybe to keep an eye on Aru and his teammates. Gabi had offered to help and the Odu had declined, but she'd somehow managed to convince the cyborg to let her work with him in the kitchen.

Evidently, she didn't know that he wasn't human or immortal, but since he looked like an older human, she must have wondered what he was doing working as a butler for the leader of the immortals.

Aru wondered that as well, but for a different reason. Kian had said that the Odus had been sent to Earth by someone, crash-landed, and wandered the desert until they were found by one of the gods. He also had said that they had been in his family for many generations.

Kian hadn't told him how many Odus there were even though Aru had asked, but there couldn't be too many of them.

Had someone from the resistance sent them?

Would the Supreme know anything about it?

Was there anything the Supreme didn't know?

Aru smiled at the thought. No one made from flesh and blood was all-knowing, but the Supreme came pretty close.

Aru had forgotten to tell Aria about the Odus, and since he still had time before the guests arrived and the ceremony commenced, he could steal a few moments alone in the master bedroom.

It would have been better if he could have tempted Gabi to join him, but she was adamant about lending a hand with the preparations. The Odu had tried his best to dissuade her by pointing out the dangers of the kitchen, his worry for the safety of her delicate hands, and Julian's instruction for her to rest, but Gabi had stubbornly insisted on staying.

If the Odu couldn't convince her to get out of the kitchen, then Aru had no chance.

Well, perhaps it was worth another try.

He walked into the kitchen and wrapped his arms around her from behind. "I'm going to lie down for a few minutes." He kissed her neck. "Care to join me?"

Turning to look at him over her shoulder, she gave him a brilliant smile. "Give me five minutes to finish what I'm doing, and I'll be there. I haven't seen the master bedroom yet."

That had been surprisingly easy.

Five minutes should be enough to communicate what he needed to Aria unless the Supreme was ready to give him instructions, in which case it wouldn't be a good time. But a male had his priorities, and right now, it was getting Gabi in bed with him, even if all they did was share a few kisses.

She wasn't supposed to engage in any vigorous activity, but he could think of a few things that involved very little exertion on her part.

He would gladly do all the work.

"Hurry up, and I'll give you the grand tour." He kissed her neck again and then nibbled at it a little, making her shiver deliciously in his arms.

"You're not playing fair." She pushed her bottom out in an attempt to bump him off.

"And you are?" He gave her lush bottom a little squeeze before leaving.

"Five minutes," she called after him.

With a smile lifting his lips and a hard length filling his pants, he made his way to the primary bedroom.

Aru had already showered and changed before, so he didn't feel guilty about lying on the pristine bed fully dressed, but on second thought, perhaps he could get rid of a few items of clothing and entice Gabi with some exposed skin when she arrived in the bedroom.

In less than two seconds, he was down to his boxer briefs, and the only reason he had left them on was that he didn't feel comfortable communicating with his sister in the nude.

Closing his eyes, Aru opened the channel and asked the usual question, *Can you talk?*

I have a minute, but no more. Aria's mental voice held a note of urgency.

Is everything all right? Aru asked.

Yes, the Supreme is receiving petitioners, and I am supposed to take notes. I am doing so while talking to you.

They shouldn't communicate when in public, but this was important as it could affect the Supreme's instructions for him.

I will make it quick. Several Odus made their way to Earth and were found by one of the rebel gods. They are now the property of the immortals. I do not know how many of them there are. The leader of the immortals refused to say. I thought that the Supreme might want to know that. Perhaps they are significant in some way.

What are you thinking, Aru?

Perhaps their creator sent them to Earth to save the technology. Perhaps the Supreme would be interested in this information.

These Odus had been made before everything manufactured on Anumati was made as solid-state, so they could be used by the resistance to reverse engineer them and create more. If they were used as weapons before, they could be used as weapons again, only this time, they would work for the rebels and not against them.

I shall inform the Supreme, Aria said. *I need to go.*

Before you do, tell me, did you have a chance to discuss what I told you with the Supreme? I am still waiting for directions.

Not yet. I was only summoned now to assist with the petitioners. I hope I will have the opportunity to talk with the Supreme in private once it is done and the doors close for the night.

I hope so, too. Be well, Aria.

You too, Aru. Take care of yourself.

59

GABI

Gabi wiped her hands with the dish towel and removed the apron Okidu had loaned her. "Are you going to be okay on your own?"

"Oh, yes, mistress. It was most pleasant working side by side with you in the kitchen, but I have to confess that I prefer to work alone." He smiled apologetically.

She'd had to guilt the butler into letting her help, but most of the food was ready, the kitchen was clean, and all that was left to do was to watch over the few items that were still in the ovens.

Okidu could definitely handle that on his own.

Heck, he hadn't needed her help and hadn't wanted it, but Gabi wasn't the type of person who let others prepare a party for her while she idled.

Leaning closer to the squat man, she kissed his leathery cheek. "Thank you. It's very nice of you to do all of this for me. I appreciate your hard work and your dedication to culinary excellence."

The butler froze in place as if she'd unplugged him from the wall. Had she overstepped a boundary?

"Are you okay?" she said as she tried to look into his eyes. "I'm sorry if that offended you."

"I am not offended, mistress." He lifted a hand to his cheek. "No one has ever kissed me before. It is a strange sensation."

The poor guy had never been kissed? What kind of a mother had he had?

Perhaps he was an orphan?

"That's a travesty that needs to be corrected, and if you allow me, I will kiss your cheek every time I say hello and goodbye. Is that okay with you?"

A bright smile illuminated his face, and for a moment, he looked much younger than before. "I would like that very much. Can I kiss your cheek in return?"

"Of course." She turned her cheek toward him and tapped it with her finger. "Right here."

He hesitated for a split second before touching his oddly cold lips to her cheek and quickly retreating. "Thank you, mistress."

"You're welcome." She gave him a smile before walking out of the kitchen.

"Such an odd guy," she murmured on her way to the bedroom. "But sweet nonetheless. How could he have never been kissed?"

Shaking her head, Gabi opened the door to the bedroom and froze in her tracks.

The room was large, with a massive bed that sat on a raised platform and faced a fireplace with a big screen hanging over it. There was also a sitting area with a couch and two armchairs, and two bookcases filled with well-used books. But the most impressive thing in the room was the male spread out on top of the covers, wearing nothing but a pair of tight-fitting boxer shorts.

"No one ever deserved the name god more than you." She kicked off her shoes, shimmied out of her jeans, tossed them aside, and climbed on the bed in her tight T-shirt and underwear.

"Gabi." Aru wrapped his arms around her and pulled her under him. "You took longer than five minutes."

Staring up into his impossibly gorgeous face, Gabi forgot for a moment why she'd delayed. "I'll tell you about it later. Now, kiss me."

"Yes, mistress," he imitated the butler's voice.

"You're so bad." She laughed, but then his lips were on hers, and all she could do was feel.

Closing her eyes, she moaned into his mouth.

When he let go of her lips, she tried to chase his by lifting her head, but he was out of reach.

"Open your eyes and look at me," Aru said.

She did as he asked and gasped. "Your eyes are glowing."

It wasn't a subtle glow either. It was so strong that his eyes looked like they had flashlights inside of them, and instead of the dark chocolate ring and the black iris, all she could see was white light.

"My fangs are also elongated." He bared them. "Do they look scary to you?"

"A little." She lifted her hand and brought a finger to his mouth. "May I?"

"Yes, you may, but be careful. They are very sharp, and you could nick your finger."

Gabi smiled. "Now, that's a way to conduct the immortality test. Do you think we can forgo Julian's scalpel and use your fangs instead? It can be a new tradition, but I'm not sure whether it's any less barbaric. Probably more so, but it's also sexier."

Aru chuckled. "Just do it. But be careful."

"I don't want to be careful." She touched the sharp point with her finger, and a moment later, a drop of blood welled up on the tip.

Aru swiped it away with his tongue, and the tiny sting was gone.

"Now look what you have done. Your saliva has healing properties, so we won't know whether you healed me, or my body did that all on its own."

"No, we won't." He scraped those sharp fangs over her neck, somehow managing to do it with their blunt side and without drawing blood. "Let's save the testing for later. What I'm more interested in now is tasting rather than testing."

"Are you now." She lifted her pelvis and rubbed her mound over his delicious bulge. "Maybe I'm interested in some tasting myself."

"That can be arranged." He licked a spot on her neck. "As long as you don't exert yourself."

"Of course." Her eyes rolled back in her head. "We wouldn't want that."

60

ARU

Gabi's proposition was too good to turn down, but it would have to wait for another time. She'd already exerted herself in the kitchen, and Aru's plan had been to pleasure her until she screamed his name in ecstasy, but without her moving a muscle.

Thankfully, the penthouse had amazing soundproofing, so Gabi could be as loud as she pleased without his teammates or the Odu hearing her.

It was a great plan, but after seeing how Gabi had convinced the Odu to let her help him, he knew it would be a battle of wills.

Gabi was stubborn, and she overestimated what she could and should do right after her transition. The only way to ensure her compliance would be to tie her up.

The problem was that he had nothing to tie her with. His socks were not long enough, and twisting his T-shirts into ropes would produce uncomfortable restraints.

But wait a moment. Gabi had what he needed.

The Odu had put her carry-on in the bedroom, and if everything she'd had at the hotel was in there, he knew what he could use.

Dipping his head, Aru took Gabi's lips in a scorching kiss, his hands roaming all over her half-clad body. When he finally let go of her mouth, she was left flushed and panting.

"I'll take a rain check on your proposal." He kissed the tip of her nose. "This time is going to be all about you."

A mischievous smile curled her lips. "I know that you are new to Earth, but you must have heard the term sixty-nine."

He knew very well what she was referring to, and declining her offer was torturous.

"Not today, my love. The doctor said you shouldn't do anything physically strenuous, and I'm adamant about following his orders. In fact, I want to secure you to the bed to ensure compliance."

"Do you, now?" The scent of her arousal intensified. "I'm game for that, but no blindfold. I want to see you in all of your godly glory."

"Good. Do I have permission to open your luggage and take out a pair of stockings?"

She nodded and then giggled. "How many pairs are you going to use?"

He glanced at the ornate headboard and smiled. "One should do. I'm only going to secure your wrists to one of those iron swirls."

Lifting her head, she looked at the headboard above her. "How convenient."

"Indeed." He moved with his godly speed to get the stockings out of her carry-on and get back in bed.

Her eyes had stayed on him. "I'll never get tired of looking at you, and the thought that this magnificent body is never going to age is just mind-boggling. How lucky can a girl get?"

"I hope that was a rhetorical question." He tugged her shirt over her head and disposed of her bra almost at the same time.

Gabi laughed. "I've never been undressed so quickly."

He looped the stocking around the iron swirl and then slowed down to wrap the nylon around her wrists. "Comfortable?"

As she tugged on the restraints, her slender hands nearly slid through, but Gabi didn't want to get free. She liked the game they were playing as much as he did, and maybe more.

Straddling her upper thighs, he hooked his thumbs in the elastic of her panties, and as he pulled them down, the sweet scent of her arousal hit his nostrils, making him dizzy with desire.

"I forgot to lock the door," Gabi said. "Can you lock it with your mind?"

He chuckled. "I'm not a vampire, my love."

"You sure look like one from here."

She'd meant it as a joke, but Aru could detect a slight note of fear in her tone, and that wouldn't do. "I'm not going to bite you down there if that was what has gotten you thinking about vampires. At least not today."

Aru had no plans of biting Gabi anywhere before the ceremony. He didn't know whether immortal females blacked out from the bliss like human females did, and he couldn't risk having the star of the festivities passed out for the night.

Gabi's eyes widened. "Are you planning to do it some other day? Because if you are, I'm not on board with that at all." She tugged on the loose restraints, changing her mind about freeing herself when her hands were halfway through the loops.

Gripping them in her hands, she looked as if she was hanging from the headboard by nylons.

"Noted." He pressed a soft kiss to her inner thigh. "I will not do it unless you ask me."

Gabi frowned. "Not going to happen, and don't even think of thralling me to agree to that."

That was another thing that wouldn't do. "I will never thrall you, Gabi. The only reason I did that before was because I couldn't let you see my fangs and glowing eyes." It was a strange conversation to have while he was between his female's thighs, the enticing aroma of her arousal making him salivate, but these things had to be said. "I will never do anything to you without your explicit consent."

61

GABI

Well, that wouldn't do.

Gabi had planned on asking Aru to use his thralling in a very specific way. She wanted him to bring to life the naughty dreams she'd had while at the clinic, and that required granting him access to her mind.

"I didn't say that you can never thrall me. I want you to thrall me when I ask you to." She smiled. "Remember those dreams I told you about?"

He arched a brow, which looked comical with his head peeking from between her spread legs. "You never told me what they were about." He kissed her other inner thigh, so close and yet so far from where she wanted him.

"In my dream, you created phantom limbs and tongues in addition to the real ones to touch me all over. It was incredible."

His eyes, which had been glowing already, looked like they were burning, or rather, emitting fire.

"It never occurred to me that I could do that." He grinned at her with those enormous fangs on display, and yet, he didn't scare her. "But that's an incredible idea. May I give it a try?"

Gabi sucked in a breath. "Yes, please."

If it was even half as good as in her dreams, she was in for one hell of an orgasm.

When two phantom tongues wrapped around her nipples at the same time, it was so much more intense than what she'd dreamt about that she nearly climaxed. But when he penetrated her with his fingers, real or phantom, and licked at her most sensitive spot, Gabi exploded like a firecracker.

"Incredible." Aru kissed her quivering flesh. "That took less than thirty seconds." He looked up at her with a satisfied expression on his handsome face.

He should have been terrifying to her with the fangs and glowing eyes, but he wasn't.

She was still panting, trying to catch her breath after the explosion. "Give me a moment to recuperate," she managed to say between one panting breath and the next. "I'm sorry that I didn't last longer."

"Nonsense." He smirked. "That was just the first of many more to come." His words were coming out slurred, probably because of the fangs that didn't allow his mouth to close. "Thank you for giving me the idea."

She glared at him. "Only with me. No one else."

"Oh, sweetheart. There will never be anyone else. You are it for me." His hands caressed her sides as he moved on top of her and propped his arms on the mattress on both sides of her.

Pulling her hands out of the restraints, she put her arms around his shoulders. "I promise to lie as still as I can."

He hesitated only for a moment before aligning himself with her entrance and surging all the way in.

Gabi gasped, the fullness of their joining so perfect that it brought tears to her eyes.

Aru dipped his head and kissed her eyelids one at a time while rocking gently into her.

It was just perfect, but one thought prevented her from surrendering to the bliss.

Was he going to bite her with those huge fangs?

She didn't remember the other bites because he'd thralled her to forget them, so she didn't know how painful they had been or, conversely, how pleasurable.

"What's the matter?" he murmured against her ear, still rocking gently inside her.

He was such an accommodating and thoughtful lover. Who would have ever thought a god could be so kind?

The thought amused her.

Who would have ever thought that she would be making love with a god?

"Everything is perfect." She rubbed her hands over the strong muscles of his back. "It's just surreal that you are here, making love to me, and about to bite me again, but I can't remember what it felt like the other times you bit me, so I don't know if I should be afraid or not. Kaia said—"

He stopped her tirade by claiming her mouth, and it was a claiming. His sinfully talented tongue thrust between her lips, mimicking the action below, and tasting herself on him only added to the erotic moment.

When he'd gotten his fill, or maybe when he ran out of air, Aru lifted his head and smiled down at her. "I'm not going to bite you this time, but I'm going to release your memories of the other times."

She was relieved but also disappointed. "Don't you need to bite me?"

"Oh, I do, but you have a ceremony coming up, and I don't want to have to explain to your family why you passed out and can't attend."

"Oh."

He laughed. "Yeah, oh. Now look into my eyes."

"Where else am I going to look?"

"Concentrate for just a moment."

She did, and as Aru's luminous gaze bored into her eyes, it felt as if a door was cracked open, letting the wind rush in. It carried with it memories of pleasure so indescribable that they were enough to trigger another orgasm and snap Aru's control.

As his thrusting turned urgent, she had to hold on to the ironwork of the headboard for purchase, and when he found his release, she climaxed again and called his name.

"Aru." She let go of the headboard and wrapped her arms around his trembling body. "I love you," she murmured into the crook of his neck.

He groaned. "I love you more than words can describe, but I need a cold shower."

Gabi frowned.

She could feel his essence dripping out of her, so she knew that he had found release. Why did he need a cold shower?

"Aru?" She stroked his hair. "Are you okay?"

He lifted his head, and as she saw his pained expression coupled with the enormity of his fangs, she got her answer. "You need to bite me."

He nodded. "I do, but I can't."

She cupped his cheeks. "Later tonight, after everyone leaves, we are doing this properly. The memories of your bites were awesome, but I want to experience the bliss in real time."

62

ARU

After Aru and Gabi had both showered, not together because he had been serious about taking a cold shower, he had convinced Gabi to lie down on the couch until her guests arrived.

"We can watch a show together." He sat next to her and clicked the giant screen on. "What are you in the mood for?"

"I'm not much of a television watcher. I prefer to read." She eyed the overfilled bookcases.

He remembered her telling him that during one of their dinners together, but he'd hoped to seduce her into watching something with him. "It doesn't have to be a show. We can watch a movie." He clicked on the menu. "A comedy, perhaps?"

She waved a feeble hand. "As long as it is not a war movie or horror, you can choose whatever you want, and I'll watch it with you. A comedy is fine."

He had a feeling that Gabi was going to fall asleep during the first few minutes, but that was fine. They had two and a half hours until their guests started arriving, and it would be great if she napped for most of it.

"It has been a long day. You can take a nap. Do you want to get in bed?"

She shook her head. "But it would be wonderful if you bring me one of those fluffy pillows." She glanced at the bed that she had put back in order before they had headed to the shower. "It's such a beautiful bed. Do you think Kian will let us live here?"

They hadn't discussed the future yet, and even though Aru had given it some thought, he wasn't sure how they would make it work.

"Kian said that we can stay here, but he didn't specify for how long. He usually rents the penthouse out, so he might be amenable to renting it to us if we decide to stay here. Do you mind rooming with Negal and Dagor?"

Gabi turned to look at him. "I don't mind. This primary bedroom is nearly the size of my entire condo in Cleveland. We can have privacy here, and when we want to hang out with our friends, we can be in the living room. My family will surely visit a lot too, and this place is gorgeous, but can you afford it? I can pitch in after I rent out my condo. I'll probably get at least three thousand a month for it, but this place is probably in the tens of thousands. Do you think Kian will give us a discount?"

As usual, Gabi talked a lot when she was nervous. It seemed like she'd made some life-altering decisions, so it was no wonder that she was anxious, but when had she had time to think and arrive at those decisions? Had she done it while working in the kitchen alongside the Odu?

"Don't worry about the cost. I can afford to pay whatever Kian charges for this place, and I don't need you to pitch in. But what about your clientele and your life in Cleveland?"

Gabi turned on her side and propped her head on her hand. "I'm immortal now, which means that I don't age, and sooner or later, my friends and clients will start to notice. I can probably stretch this out for a decade or so, excusing my appearance with extensive plastic surgery, but to what end? You are here, my family is here, and I can probably keep most of my clients even if I switch to virtual counseling. I'm already partnering with a laboratory that I send all my clients to. They do all the necessary blood work and urinalysis, and they email me the results. The only thing I won't be able to do are the in-person weigh-ins, and I can do without them." She closed her eyes for a moment and then opened them and leveled her blue gaze at him. "The big question is, what are your plans, and what part do I play in them?"

Aru took her hand and put it on his chest. "I want to spend every moment with you, but part of my mission is searching for the missing Kra-ell pods, and that involves travel. Sometimes, we have to hike for miles to get to a potential pod location, and we camp out, sleeping on the ground in sleeping bags and most times not even bothering with a tent. Would you be up for that?"

She smiled brilliantly. "I would love that. I love camping, and I love traveling to exotic locales." Her smile wilted a little. "I don't think I will be as terrified of flying as I was before my transition, so that shouldn't be an obstacle, but if it is, you can thrall me. But if I want to keep my practice while traveling, I will need a connection to the internet, so a satellite phone is a must."

"Of course." He lifted her hand to his lips and kissed her knuckles. "I love you, Gabriella Emerson. You are just as courageous as your name implies, and I'm so grateful that you are willing to accompany me on my travels. In fact, I'm overjoyed." He leaned down and took her lips in a gentle kiss. "The Fates have given me a perfect mate. I should offer them a prayer of thanks."

GABI

"Oh, Aru." Gabi cupped his cheek. "I will add my thanks as well."

Gabi had had a few minutes to think about her future while helping Okidu in the kitchen.

Regrettably, the butler wasn't the talkative kind who shared juicy gossip about his employer, and she hadn't been able to coerce him into disclosing anything other than his recipes, which she had written down for when she and Aru lived together.

Okidu's steadfastness in the face of her questioning hadn't been a total waste of time, though, and since she'd had nothing better to do than think while washing dishes and chopping vegetables, Gabi had made some major decisions.

The most important one was that she was not going back to Cleveland. Her friends could help her wrap things up, and the truth was that not much was needed. Her condo was perfectly furnished and decorated and would be really easy to rent out. All she needed from there was her wardrobe, but since she'd grown half an inch in three days and was still growing, she would probably need new clothes anyway.

The biggest question had been Aru and his plans for the future. She knew that he had to return to the patrol ship in one hundred and fifteen years, but until then, they could spend all of their time together, provided that he wanted that.

She hadn't been sure about that until now, and she couldn't be happier about what Aru saw for their future. The next one hundred and fifteen years would be wonderful, full of love and adventure, and Fates willing, a solution would present itself that would allow Aru to stay.

"Here is your pillow, love." He gently lifted her head and placed the pillow under her cheek.

She loved it when he called her his love.

"I didn't even notice that you moved." She reached for his hand. Perhaps if she held on to it, he wouldn't be able to sneak out as stealthily as he did.

"You dozed off." Aru leaned down and kissed her cheek. "Sleep, my love. You need it."

She tightened her hold on his hand. "Don't leave me. You can watch television while I nap."

He looked conflicted. "I need to check up on Dagor and Negal and see if the butler needs anything."

"Then do it quickly and come back." Gabi brought Aru's hand to her cheek and rubbed his palm over her skin. "I promise that I'm not usually this needy and clingy. It's just that everything is in flux, and every time I wake up, I'm faced with a new reality. You are my anchor, Aru." She smiled. "You wanted to be my rock, and that comes with certain responsibilities and limitations."

"I love being your rock." He toed off his boots and lay next to her. "Dagor and Negal can wait. I'll hold you in my arms until you fall asleep."

"That's truly lovely." Gabi closed her eyes and let Aru's warmth envelop her.

They hadn't had moments like this before. It had been about pleasure and satisfaction, and they had cuddled only once and only after sex.

This was different.

This was about affection, not attraction, and about love, not lust.

Not that there was anything wrong with attraction and lust, but it was nice to have the softer side of togetherness as well.

Thinking back, she hadn't had many moments like this with Dylan.

They'd had passion, they'd had all the outward expressions of love like words and gifts and grand gestures, but she couldn't remember them ever cuddling on the couch just for the sake of being together and not as a prelude to sex.

"You're not sleeping." Aru brushed his lips over her forehead. "What are you thinking about?"

She didn't want to bring Dylan into this precious moment between them.

"The different languages of love. I think mine is time. To show me love, you need to spend time with me."

He chuckled. "I have no problem with that. Isn't that a universal expression of love, though? Don't all lovers want to spend time with each other?"

"It depends how they want to spend that time. Some just want to have sex all the time, and when sex is not on the table, they lose interest and walk away. I'm glad you are not like that. It means a lot to me that you are content to just be with me without expecting anything other than closeness."

64

ARU

Aru waited until Gabi was fast asleep before reluctantly sliding off the couch.

He would have loved nothing more than to keep holding her in his arms until it was time for her to wake up, but he didn't like the idea of his teammates alone with the Odu.

Aru knew what the thing was capable of. He was fully aware that the propaganda painted a false picture, but he didn't know what the true picture was.

The Odu appeared as the dutiful servant he had been originally designed to be, but there was more to him, and that was what worried Aru.

The cyborg was so human-like that it appeared sentient, and sentient beings were even less trustworthy than machines. That being said, machines were made and programmed by unreliable sentient beings, so there was that.

Aru was about to push his feet into his boots when he felt Aria tug on their communication channel.

As he opened it on his end and let her in, her voice sounded in his head, *Can you talk?*

Yes. Leaving the boots by the couch, he walked over to the bed and lay down. *Do you have news?*

I do. I spoke with the Supreme, and I have instructions for you. You are to stay as close as you can to the immortals, learn as much as you can about them, and report back.

If only he could do that, it would solve many of his problems, but he served more than one master, and the commander expected Aru and his team to produce results.

My mission is to follow the Kra-ell and find the other pods. I cannot do both.

Yes, you can. Make your base of operation among the immortals or in their vicinity if they still do not welcome you into their secret village, and from time to time, go on excursions or send your teammates to search for the pods alone. The Supreme suggested that you involve the Kra-ell from Gor's compound in the search. They can accompany Negal and Dagor while you stay behind. Do the minimum required to fulfill your official duties or just a little more. You are to be our liaison to the immortals.

That wasn't going to be simple. How would he explain to his teammates why he was neglecting his duties? He couldn't tell them that he was following the Supreme's instructions. Besides, his clock was ticking, as the humans liked to say.

What about when I get picked up in one hundred and fifteen years? Who is going to be the liaison then?

Aru held his breath as he waited for Aria's response.

I do not have an answer for you at the ready, but I am sure the Supreme will find a way for you to stay on Earth and continue this most important task. Aria sighed. *I am going to miss you terribly, Aru, but I am happy for you. You will get to stay with your truelove mate. That is more important than a sister's loneliness.*

Aru's heart, which had soared to the stratosphere just a moment ago, sank down to the pit of his stomach.

One day, you will meet your truelove mate, Aria, and he will banish your loneliness. You will not miss me as much when you are in the arms of your mate.

Her laugh went through him like bubbles of champagne. *I do not need a truelove mate to enjoy the solace of strong arms around me. Do not worry about me, Aru. I keep myself entertained. One day, when our objectives are achieved, we will be reunited. Until then, we are blessed with this mental connection that allows us to talk with each other whenever we please. That is more than most gods get.*

He had said the same words to her many times, but it was the first time she had said them back to him.

It seemed that Aria viewed his connection to the immortals as the top priority, which must have reflected the way the Supreme viewed it. But why? What could these immortals do for the resistance?

The only thing he could think of was providing a secret base that could fly under the radar of the Eternal King, but the truth was that the resistance could do that without the immortals' help.

Can you find out what the Supreme has in mind in regard to these immortals?

Aria sighed again. *You know how the Supreme operates. Stealth and secrecy are the ways of the wise.*

Indeed. If you find out anything more concrete, let me know.

Of course. Be well, Aru.

You too, Aria.

As he closed the channel, Aru got up and walked over to the couch where he had left Gabi sleeping.

Crouching next to her on the floor, he looked at her beautiful face, and his heart swelled with love and hope. If the Supreme wanted him to be the resistance's liaison to the immortals and remain on Earth indefinitely, one way or another, it would be done. The Supreme always found a way. The question was how to tell Gabi about it without revealing his telepathic connection to his sister or lying about some other secret method of communication.

He would have to wait until the Supreme's machinations found their way down the chain of command and he received a notice from his commander that he would not be picked up in one hundred and fifteen years.

What about Negal and Dagor, though?

They wouldn't want to be stuck on Earth with him. They had loved ones they wanted to return to as much as he had wanted to return to his sister and their parents until he found his truelove, fated mate.

The Supreme wouldn't care about that, and if he stayed, his teammates would probably have to stay as well.

They wouldn't like it.

The good thing was that he wouldn't be the one to have to tell them that they were staying on Earth. The order would come from the patrol ship after their commander received it from Anumati.

Perhaps he should use the same excuse with Kian and tell him that the order included a coded message.

Except, that would only work if the Supreme moved fast and the commander contacted him soon, which wasn't likely. It also occurred to him that the Supreme hadn't commented on the Odus. Perhaps Aria hadn't had the chance to mention them yet or had forgotten what he had told her.

65

GABI

"It's time to wake up, love." Aru kissed Gabi's cheek. "Your family will be here in fifteen minutes."

Gabi sat bolt upright. "Why did you let me sleep so long? You said that you would wake me up half an hour before the ceremony."

"I did." He smiled apologetically, but the apology wasn't genuine. "You murmured something about a few more minutes, so I let you sleep a little longer."

For some reason, Aru seemed to be in a much better mood than he'd been before she'd fallen asleep, and given that they had made love shortly before that, he should have been in the best mood then.

Was he excited about meeting the rest of her family?

That wasn't likely. Most people were intimidated by large families with small children, and as a god, Aru probably had zero experience with kids.

But wait, perhaps he hadn't been in such a great mood after their lovemaking because he hadn't bitten her? It was such an integral part of sex for his kind that it must have been very difficult for him to refrain.

But what had changed since then?

It wasn't as if he could have taken care of that himself. Biting his own arm probably wasn't fun.

Whatever the reason, she needed to hurry up and get ready. Aru was wearing jeans and a T-shirt and looking like the god he was, but she would have liked it if he put on a dress shirt and slacks for the ceremony.

Then again, the one person she wanted to approve of Aru had already met him, so perhaps he didn't need to change.

Gabi, on the other hand, needed to put on makeup and fix her hair so she wouldn't look like Cinderella before the fairy godmother sprinkled her magic dust over her. The dark circles under her eyes and the unexpected weight loss that had made her cheeks look hollow was not an attractive look.

Dashing to her carry-on, Gabi flipped it open and started taking things out.

"Do you want coffee while you are getting ready?" Aru asked.

She turned to look at him over her shoulder. "Did I tell you already how much I love you?"

His grin could have illuminated a football stadium. "I will never tire of hearing you say that." He crouched next to her and wrapped his arms around her. "I love you."

Given how his eyes were glowing, Gabi had a good idea where this was going, and if she wasn't pressed for time, she would have been a hundred percent on board, but the clock was ticking—not the biological one, though, thank goodness. That one was taken care of.

"Stop." She put her hand on his chest. "Save it for after the party."

"Right." He dropped his arms and pushed to his feet. "I'll get the coffee."

Gabi smiled. "You are an angel. Oh, wait, that's a downgrade for you. You are a god."

"You can call me anything you want, and I will love it." He opened the door, walked out, and closed it behind him.

"I must be the luckiest girl on Earth to score a guy like Aru." She lifted her face to the ceiling. "I don't know what I did to deserve such a gift. Thank you for giving Aru to me, and please, never take him away."

As usual, no one answered her plea, but perhaps this time it had been heard.

Looking back at her modest selection of clothing, Gabi chose a short-sleeved blue dress that wasn't too short so it wouldn't ride up if Julian demanded that she lie down while he administered his test.

The truth was that she wasn't scared of the cut, and she didn't care if it took her palm a minute to heal or five, as long as it healed faster than it would have while she'd been fully human.

"Here is your coffee, love." Aru handed her the cup.

"Thank you." Gabi took a sip and closed her eyes. "This is so good. What brand do they use?"

"I'll ask Okidu. He made it for you." He chuckled. "He was so happy when I told him that you wanted coffee. If I didn't know better, I would have thought that he was in love with you."

It must have been the kiss.

Poor guy. How could someone go through life without being kissed?

"I was nice to him. That's all."

Aru frowned, looking like he wanted to tell her something, but then shook his head. "I'll leave you to get ready and see if Okidu needs help." He straightened up and walked out of the room again.

Something must have gotten lost in translation, but Gabi wasn't sure what it was.

In the bathroom, she brushed her teeth and her hair and applied moisturizer. She was pale, but her skin looked smooth, and other than the dark circles under her eyes and the hollow cheeks, she looked great.

"The model look." She chuckled. "And I might even grow tall enough."

After applying concealer under her eyes, she dusted a little bronzer over her cheeks, did her eyes with eyeliner and mascara, and finished with the bright red lipstick that had Aru mesmerized every time she put it on.

Her hair was no longer as smooth and well-behaved as it had been when she'd stepped out of the salon, but it still looked good enough to leave loose around her shoulders instead of braiding it.

When she walked out of the bathroom, her eyes darted to the nylons that were still tied to the headboard, and she contemplated taking them down and putting them on.

She had other pairs in her carry-on, but wearing those particular ones would keep her smile turned on throughout the ceremony and drive Aru crazy.

By the time her guests went home, Aru would be wild with desire for her, and she would finally get to experience the bite in real time and not as a retrieved memory.

ARU

"I have everything under control, Master Aru." The Odu stood in the entrance to the kitchen. He smiled his fake smile. "Is there anything you require? Perhaps a little snack before the guests arrive?"

The Odu was appropriately accommodating and subservient, but Aru detected an undercurrent of hostility that the cyborg shouldn't be capable of, and even if he was, he had no reason to direct it at Aru.

Unless the Odu was jealous over Gabi, but that was even less likely than him being hostile. Then again, his face had lit up upon hearing her name.

He needed to speak with Kian and ask him whether the Odu had been modified in any way because it was giving him the creeps.

Come to think of it, he'd forgotten to ask Aria whether she'd mentioned the Odus to the Supreme. He was curious to hear whether the Supreme had a theory regarding their appearance on Earth.

"No, thank you." Aru returned the butler's fake smile. "The coffee will do for now." He reached for the cup he'd left on the counter.

The Odu bowed. "Very well, master."

Coffee cup in hand, Aru walked over to the living room couch and sat down next to Negal. "You know that Gabi's family will be here shortly, the doctor, of course, and Kian might show up either alone or with his wife and daughter. If you want to avoid meeting them, you should go to your rooms."

"I want to stay." Negal put down the magazine he'd been leafing through. "Are all the members of Gabi's family immortal?"

"The young ones are not, and neither is Gilbert's mate. Gabi told me that Gilbert's fangs and venom won't be operational for another five months, and until they are, he can't induce his mate."

"How do they induce men?" Dagor asked. "I hope it's not the same way that females are induced."

"I have no idea." Aru put his coffee cup on the table. "There is much more that we need to find out about these people. The question is whether you want to hang around all these immortals and try to get some answers."

Dagor lifted a brow. "Is that part of our mission?"

"It is now."

Dagor nodded. "Then it is our duty to mingle with the immortals and find out as much as we can."

"It would appear so."

Aru would have preferred this evening to be about Gabi and only Gabi, but his friends were right.

Her family of immortals and humans lived in the secret village, but they were civilians and, therefore, less guarded. They might reveal things that Kian and his advisor wouldn't.

"They are all arriving at the same time," Aru said. "Kian said he would arrange for a bus." He looked at his teammates. "They will ask a lot of questions as well, so be on your guard and don't say anything that you are not a hundred percent sure is okay. When you are not certain or just want to avoid answering, send them to me."

"Good deal." Negal lifted the magazine off the table and opened it to the page he'd earmarked.

"What are you reading?" Aru asked.

"Nothing important." Negal showed him the page. "It's an article on interior design and how to choose complementary colors."

"He's bored," Dagor said. "You need to find him something to do."

Aru raised a brow. "What about you?"

"I'm not bored." Dagor looked in the direction of the kitchen. "I'm studying the Odu," he whispered. "He's acting very strange for a cyborg. Have you noticed?"

Aru nodded. "He seems to have clear preferences for some people. He adores Gabi and is slightly hostile toward me."

Dagor cast another quick glance toward the kitchen before lowering his head and whispering, "He also hums as he works."

"Hums?" Aru asked. "Like in a machine noise? Maybe there is something wrong with him."

"He hums melodies of songs I recognize, and sometimes he sways to the music. That's not something cyborgs do."

"How do you know?" Negal asked. "The models we are familiar with don't sing, but maybe the old models were programmed to learn songs and repeat them? It's not like the technology is available to study. We don't know what they were capable of."

"True," Dagor admitted. "But I don't think the old Odus were programmed to enjoy and appreciate music. It would have been a waste."

As the bedroom door opened down the corridor and a moment later Gabi walked into the living room, Aru's heartbeat accelerated.

She looked beautiful in a blue dress and black heels, but what got his throat to go dry was the pair of pantyhose she'd put on. He recognized the pair he'd used to tie her to the headboard.

Pushing to his feet, Aru walked up to Gabi and wrapped one arm around her narrow waist. "That was a very naughty move, love," he whispered in her ear.

"Not at all." She lifted a pair of mockingly innocent eyes to him. "It's just a reminder of the unfinished business we need to attend to after the ceremony."

"Umm," Dagor cleared his throat. "I hope Aru told you that we have exceptionally good hearing. Same goes for eyesight and sense of smell."

He was going to throttle Dagor.

Unperturbed by the comment, Gabi leaned sideways to peer at Dagor and smiled. "I'm well aware of that, but I was told that gods and immortals are not shy about certain matters. Besides, we are going to be roommates for a couple of weeks, if not more, so we'd better get used to hearing things we shouldn't and pretending that we didn't."

67

GABI

"I'm so glad that you brought the little ones." Gabi hugged Karen. "I just hope that they won't get scared when Julian makes the cut."

Karen squeezed her tight. "I'll keep the boys in their stroller so they won't see over the crowd, and Idina is not easily spooked." Karen let go of Gabi and patted her daughter's head. "I don't know whether she will grow up to be a surgeon or a general."

The girl gave her mother a wicked smile. "I don't want to be either. I want to be a witch."

"You already are." Kaia picked her sister up and planted a sloppy kiss on her cheek. "The question is whether you are a good witch or an evil one."

"Good one." Looking offended, Idina pulled out a pink wand from her pocket and waved it at Kaia. "Evil witches don't have pink wands. You can only do good magic with a pink wand. The silver wand is for dark magic."

"You are absolutely right." Kaia let the girl down and pulled Gabi into her arms. "Where is Aru?" she whispered in Gabi's ear. "I've seen the picture, and he's gorgeous, but I want to see him in person."

Gabi turned around and stretched up on her toes. "Gilbert and Eric cornered him. Come, I'll introduce you." She took Kaia's hand and led her to where Aru stood talking with her brothers.

The penthouse elevator could transport only so many people at a time, which was a good thing because not everyone had arrived at once. It gave Aru a few minutes to recuperate between the groups of people who wanted to meet him.

"Make room." She patted Eric's arm. "Kaia wants me to introduce her to Aru."

"Hi." Kaia extended her hand to him. "I'm Gabi's niece."

Smiling, Aru shook her hand. "The genius who gave up a position at Stanford to move in with an older guy."

"That's me." Kaia looked over her shoulder and waved William over. "And that's my mate, who is the greater genius in the family."

"I'm not." William offered Aru his hand. "Kaia is much smarter than me." He leaned closer to whisper loudly, "Young brain and all that."

"I'm sure," Aru laughed.

Cheryl shook her head. "Imagine living with those two around." She offered him her hand. "I'm Cheryl, Gabi's other niece, who is not a science genius but who has a good head for business."

"So I've heard." He shook her hand. "Gabi told me that you are conquering social media."

"That's a slight exaggeration, but not for long."

As the door opened again and Kian walked in with Syssi, Allegra, and his bodyguards, Gabi reached for Aru's hand. "Come. We need to say hello to Syssi and Kian."

He followed her gaze, and his smile widened. "Look at that baby girl. She's adorable."

"I know, right? And she's wicked smart."

"How do you know?"

"I told you. I met Syssi and her daughter in a restaurant when I met Karen and Darlene. Syssi and Kian's sister work in the same university as Karen, and they organized a little daycare for all the little ones."

Allegra's too-smart eyes were focused on Aru, and she lifted her hand and waved at him.

He waved back, and the baby's smile grew bigger.

"Hello." Syssi gave Gabi a warm smile. "I know that I'm not supposed to say congratulations until the test is done, but I'll say it anyway." She pulled Gabi into a one-armed embrace. "Congratulations." She let go of her and turned to Aru. "It's nice to finally meet you in person, Aru. I'm Syssi. Kian's wife."

"It's my honor to make your acquaintance." He dipped his head as he took her hand.

"The honor is all mine." Syssi held on to his hand. "By the way, I've seen you and your friends in a vision."

ARU

A cold shiver rushed down Aru's spine.

That was very bad news. Visions could reveal things that should remain hidden, and there was no way to shield himself or Aria from them.

"Are you an Oracle?" he asked hesitantly.

If she was, wouldn't the Supreme have known that she had a sister on Earth?

Syssi laughed. "Thank the Fates, I am not. I don't give divine counsel on things big or small, and Kian doesn't seek answers from me on strategy or the outcomes of battles. My visions are sporadic, unpredictable, and often too enigmatic to make any sense of. Once in a while, though, I get a glimpse of something useful. I believe that the Fates sent me a vision of you and your friends so I could tell Kian that your intentions were peaceful and that he shouldn't shoot first and ask questions later."

Aru dipped his head again. "Thank you for your intervention."

Thank the merciful Fates that Syssi was only a seer and not an Oracle. Nevertheless, he would inform Aria as soon as he got the chance. Perhaps the Supreme might be able to shield the telepathic connection between him and Aria from the seer.

"You are most welcome," Syssi said.

"Aro." The baby girl stretched her arm and reached for his cheek. "Ari."

This time, the shiver was so powerful that he was sure Syssi and Kian had noticed.

Was the child a more powerful seer than her mother?

Foresight ran in families.

Perhaps he was reading too much into the baby's babbling.

Swallowing hard, he plastered a smile on his face. "Hello, Allegra."

The child's regal, satisfied smile reminded him of someone, but thankfully it wasn't the Supreme. Was it similar to Kian's?

Perhaps when he was younger and less reserved, Kian had a smile like his daughter's, but right now, it was very different than that.

Behind Syssi and Kian, Julian lifted his hand high in the air. "Can I get everyone's attention, please?" When the chatter quieted, he continued, "I need you all to sit down wherever you can find a place. Gabi's had a long day, and she needs her rest."

"I'm okay," she assured her guests. "But I'm curious to see how fast I heal, so let's do it."

"Hop on the counter," Julian instructed. "So everyone can see."

Gabi looked at the counter and frowned. "Can someone bring me a chair? Actually, I'm immortal now, so maybe I can try hoisting myself to sit up there."

Before she could do that, Aru put his hands on her waist, lifted her, and deposited her on the counter next to the surgical tray that Julian had left there.

"Thanks." She smiled at him.

No one had followed Julian's request to sit down, and they were all standing next to the kitchen counter, crowding Gabi.

"Everyone, please take several steps back," Julian commanded.

When his command was obeyed, he picked up a stopwatch from the tray. "Who wants to time how fast Gabi is healing?"

"I do." Cheryl took the timer.

"Next, we need someone to film the test for posterity."

"I'll do that." Eric pulled out his phone.

"Aru." Julian looked at him. "You can hold Gabi's other hand."

Glad to be given a task, Aru clasped her hand in his while she extended the other one to the doctor.

Julian cleaned her palm with something that smelled bad and then lifted a tiny blade from his tray. "Eric, start filming. Cheryl, start the timer when I say now."

Gabi looked away but then changed her mind and looked at her palm. "I'm ready. Do it."

"Now!"

As Julian made the cut, Gabi didn't jerk or try to pull her hand away. Instead, she watched as blood welled over the incision.

It seemed like everyone in the penthouse was holding their collective breath as the stopwatch kept running, including the two little boys in the stroller and their toddler sister, whom Gilbert was holding so she could also watch.

As Julian took another square of white gauze and wiped the blood off, and Aru saw that the skin underneath was already knitting itself together, he let out a relieved breath. "Thank the merciful Fates. You are immortal."

"It's not healed yet," Gabi murmured. "The stopwatch is still running."

"One minute and forty-seven seconds," Cheryl said when the cut had disappeared completely.

"Congratulations," Julian said. "Welcome to immortality, Gabi."

69

GABI

"Thank you." Gabi kissed Eric's cheek. "Can you send me the video of the test?"

"Sure. I'll also send you all the other pictures and videos I shot today. You can create a transition album." He lifted a finger and tapped it on his lips. "Here is an idea. You can ask Julian to send you the footage from the clinic. You can pick a few clips to add to the album so you'll have the whole experience." He turned to Darlene. "Come to think of it, we should do it for our own transition as well."

Darlene cleared her throat. "I'd rather forget all about it and pretend that I was born immortal." She offered Aru her hand. "It was nice meeting you. Welcome to the family."

Gabi tensed, expecting him to say that he didn't belong with her family, but he surprised her by taking Darlene's hand and saying thank you.

"I have a question." Aru looked at Eric's phone. "Isn't it dangerous to keep moments like that on the web where everyone can access them?"

Eric smiled indulgently. "This is a clan phone, and it's connected to a private satellite network. I don't understand much about encryption, so I can't tell you what kind of protocol William deployed, but we can communicate with each other without worrying about Big Brother watching."

"That explains a lot." Aru wrapped his arm around Gabi's waist. "I wondered why Kian and the rest of you were using a cheap knockoff of a popular brand."

"Not cheap at all." Kian stopped by their group and clapped Aru on his back. "We make them in-house, so they don't cost us a fortune, but they have the best components money can buy." He turned to Gabi. "Congratulations again, and welcome to the clan. Regrettably, I can't invite your mate to visit the village, but you are invited." He glanced at Aru. "Don't even think about attaching a bug to her. I'll have her searched with a magnifying glass, a millimeter at a time."

Aru put his hand over his chest. "I vow on my honor that I will never try to find out the village's location. Even if I find a way to stay on Earth and never return to Anumati, I don't want to know where it is. I don't want to risk it." He pulled Gabi closer against his side. "I was meaning to ask you if I can rent this penthouse. Gabi likes it here, and it's a convenient location for her family to visit, but I don't want to take advantage of your hospitality for more than the couple of weeks that you offered."

Hope surged in Gabi's chest. Aru had just implied that there might be a chance he wouldn't have to return to his home world.

Kian eyed him with a small smile. "The first month is on me. After that, we will figure out something." He cast a glance at Negal and Dagor, who were hanging back but listening to everything that was being said. "Are they going to live with you?"

Aru nodded. "Gabi doesn't mind."

When Syssi arched a brow, Gabi confirmed, "I really don't. The master bedroom alone is nearly the size of my condo in Cleveland, so I will have all the privacy I need." She leaned to whisper in Syssi's ear, "With how good the soundproofing here is, I really don't have to worry about a thing."

Given Negal's chuckle, he'd heard, but it didn't bother Gabi.

Aru's teammates were nearly as gorgeous as he was, and they seemed like decent guys, so she expected them to bring ladies over to spend the night quite often.

Turning around, she mock-glared at the duo. "As long as you behave and don't turn the place into a disgusting bachelor pad. No empty pizza boxes, beer bottles, and articles of clothing strewn around. Also, if you bring your lady friends to stay the night, I don't want to see anyone parading around the living room in their underwear or birthday suits. If any of these rules are broken, I'm kicking you out."

"Understood." Negal saluted her. "But you don't need to worry about any of that. We are soldiers, and we are trained to keep things tidy."

"What about the underwear rule?" Dagor asked. "Is that negotiable? What if I want to swim in that lap pool on the terrace?"

"You can buy a pair of swimming trunks." Kian took the sleeping baby from Syssi's arms. "Goodnight, and good luck." He wrapped his other arm around Syssi's waist and motioned with his head for his guards and the butler to follow.

"Goodbye, Mistress Gabi." Okidu bowed. "It was a pleasure serving you and your family tonight."

"Thank you, Okidu." Gabi pulled out of Aru's arm and embraced the butler. "You are a priceless asset to your employer." She kissed his cheek. "Goodnight."

This time, he didn't look as stunned as the first time she'd done it, but she could tell it made him happy.

70

ARU

As totally uncalled-for jealousy washed over Aru, he wondered whether he should tell Gabi that Okidu wasn't a real man. Perhaps she would be less inclined to kiss his cheeks when she realized that she'd kissed a robot.

The Odu had looked decidedly smug, too.

When the door closed behind the last of their guests, Gabi looked at him with a sheepish smile. "Congratulations. You survived your first encounter of the fifth kind with my family."

Aru frowned. "The fifth kind? It was the first time I met them."

Gabi put a hand on her hip and struck a pose. "You're an alien, so you should know the alien encounters terminology scale." She lifted one finger. "Encounters of the first kind are visual sightings of unidentified flying objects. I didn't see the ship you arrived on, so I can't claim that one." She lifted a second finger. "The second kind is some form of physical impact from those vessels, like crop circles or chemical traces, etc. Again, can't claim that." Gabi lifted a third finger. "The third kind is meeting an actual alien." She smiled. "That's me and you, and the fourth kind is an abduction by an alien, but I can't claim that one either. The fifth kind is when people are actually communicating with aliens. That's us, and that's you and my family, but the joke was that they were the aliens you encountered."

He smiled. "I can't do anything about the first and second kinds of encounters, but I can rectify the fourth." He picked her up by her waist and threw her over his shoulder. "Consider yourself abducted."

Laughing, she banged on his back. "Put me down, you oaf. Negal and Dagor will see you carry me off." She was kicking her legs up, and her shoes went flying.

"They are out on the terrace relaxing with a couple of beers, and the less commotion you make, the less chance there is of you attracting their attention."

"Oof." She tried to slap his butt but reached only the upper part.

It was the perfect excuse to respond in kind, and as his hand landed on her upturned bottom, she uttered a little squeak that sounded more like an invitation than a protest.

Walking into the primary bedroom, Aru closed the door with his foot and continued to the bed. He lowered Gabi gently on top of the comforter and sat next to her. He smoothed his hand over her nylon-covered legs. "I've been fantasizing about taking these off the entire evening."

"Then what are you waiting for?" She lifted her arms, folded them, and tucked her hands under her head. "You have my permission."

He bowed his head. "Thank you, oh kind mistress." He mimicked the Odu's fake British accent.

"It's not nice to make fun of Okidu. He worked very hard today."

"That's his job, love." Aru snaked his hands under the hem of her dress and pulled the pantyhose down her hips, dragging her tiny panties along with them.

Just the feel of her bare skin on his knuckles was enough to make him hard enough to hammer nails.

"He went above and beyond his job description," Gabi said. "I doubt Kian paid him overtime."

There was no gentle way to say it.

With a sigh, Aru dropped his head. "It might come as a shock to you, but Okidu is a cyborg. He doesn't get paid, and he doesn't get tired."

Gabi's eyes widened and, a moment later, narrowed. "You are toying with me."

"I'm not, and if you don't believe me, call your niece, the scientist.

She knows what Kian's butler is. They were made on my home world, but the technology was banned."

Fear sparked in her eyes. "Why?"

That was not what Aru wanted Gabi to feel right now, and the cyborg was not what he wanted to talk about, but he had started it, so he needed to finish it.

"The Odus were created to be house servants, but there was a flaw in their design. They could be reprogrammed by unscrupulous individuals to become weapons. But I assume that Okidu is safe if Kian lets him around his daughter."

"Does he know?"

"He knows." Aru smoothed his hands over her outer thighs, going up. "No more talk about Odus. We have unfinished business to take care of, but only if you feel up to it. If you're tired, we can cuddle naked in bed instead."

It would be torture, but he'd rather suffer than cause her discomfort.

A mischievous gleam sparked in her eyes. "I am a little tired, but I have no problem repeating what we did this afternoon. You don't even have to tie me up. I'll just keep my hands right under my head and let you do all the work. I only have one condition."

Here it comes.

"What is it?"

"I want you to strip for me, slowly, so I can enjoy watching you getting naked."

He could do that.

Smiling, Aru rose to his feet. "Your wish is my command, Mistress Gabi."

GABI

The room was dim, illuminated only by the moonlight streaming through the windows, which had been thankfully left uncovered, but it wasn't enough for Gabi to see Aru clearly.

Her eyesight had improved after her transition, but not sufficiently for her to see well in the dark. Julian had told her that it would come and that her healing time would improve as well, but that wasn't helping her at the moment.

Regrettably, Aru wasn't in the direct path of the moon's gentle glow, and Gabi had to make do with the ambient light.

A playful smirk lifted his lips as he reached for the button of his jeans, and as he leaned down to toe off his boots, his dark hair cascaded over his forehead.

"Shirt first," Gabi instructed.

He arched a brow. "Do you want to choreograph my striptease?"

Some men had a problem with following directions from a woman, but Aru was so confident that he probably wouldn't. Still, customs might be different where he'd grown up, and it was better not to assume but to ask.

"Would it bother you if I do?"

"Not at all. It turns me on."

She gifted him with a brilliant smile. "I thought it would, but I wasn't sure. It's better to ask, right?"

"Always." He reached for the hem of his T-shirt and tugged it up with the fluidity she now associated with gods and immortals. He paused with the fabric covering his beautiful face. "Am I going too fast?"

A little, but although Gabi could stare at the sculpted muscles of Aru's chest and his defined abs forever, she wanted to see his face, and she also wanted him to feel comfortable going at his own pace.

"You're doing great, my sexy god. Take the shirt off."

Aru tugged it over his head and tossed it all the way to the couch.

"Now, the bottom part," she breathed.

As Aru pushed his jeans down his muscular thighs, he tried to go slow, but he was either unable to slow down much or was impatient to get going.

When he turned around to push his boxer briefs down and gifted her with the sight of his ass, Gabi swallowed.

She'd seen his erection before, and it was impressive, but just like the rest of him, it was a sight to behold that she would never get tired of watching.

Never before had she considered that part of male anatomy as visually appealing. It was useful, and it served a function, but she would never say it was beautiful.

Until Aru.

Everything about him was perfect.

When he finally spun around, and she got a full frontal view, Gabi licked her lips. "Come here, my love." She beckoned with a finger.

"Tsk, tsk. You were supposed to keep your hands behind your head."

"Okay." She shifted to her knees and put her hands behind her neck. "I guess that you will have to feed me."

Aru's eyes, which had been luminous before, turned blazing, and his fangs punched over his lower lip, but he still hesitated.

The lack of panties underneath her dress only added to Gabi's arousal. She undulated her hips, trying to create some friction to relieve the ache, and her inner thighs got moistened with her juices.

Aru's nostrils flared.

"This dress is pretty, but it needs to go." He grabbed the hem and pulled it over her head.

Her bra was gone in the next split second.

When she mock-glared at him, he shrugged. "You didn't ask me to go slow while undressing you."

She hadn't, but with how fast he had done that, he could have torn her dress or damaged her bra. Besides being fast, he was also incredibly strong. She opened her mouth to tell him so, but he took the opportunity to fulfill her previous request and fed her his erection.

Only the tip at first, but then he wrapped his hand over hers at the back of her nape to hold her in place and started to shallowly pump in and out of her mouth.

Had he done it to shut her up?

The truth was that she didn't care why he had done it, only that he had. His body was so responsive, shuddering with pleasure as she took him deeper.

It was so arousing to be at his mercy like this, with her hands behind her head and him using her mouth as he pleased.

ARU

With her nipples peaked, her inner thighs glistening, and her mouth stretched over his girth, Gabi was a vision of lust.

Aru combed his fingers into her hair and fisted it, holding her head in place as he fed her his erection a fraction of an inch more with every forward thrust. When he got as deep as she could take him, he cupped her jaw and withdrew almost all the way before pushing back in, but not as deep as before. Gabi was struggling, but given the strong scent of arousal she was emitting, she enjoyed the game no less than he did.

Her hands were still behind her head, and seeing her like that was sexy as hell, but it couldn't be comfortable in this position.

"You don't have to keep your hands behind your head," he told her. "You can do with them as you please."

Anyway, there wasn't much she could do while on her knees, with him feeding her his shaft.

He relaxed his hold and let her hands fall, but they didn't stay down for long.

Groaning around his length, she lifted them to grip the back of his thighs for purchase.

He planned to give her a few more moments of this before flipping her on her back and devouring that nectar that was being wasted on coating her inner thighs instead of his tongue.

But Gabi had other plans, and as her hand closed around his balls from behind and kneaded, he growled a deep-throated groan and jerked deeper into her mouth.

She must have liked his response because her fingers tightened around his balls.

If this continued for another minute, he was going to climax, and that wouldn't do. His venom glands were full to bursting, and his fangs itched, but this position didn't lend itself to a proper bite that would bring them both pleasure.

Pulling out of the wet heat of her mouth required a herculean effort, especially since she didn't want him to go. Groaning in protest, she gripped his butt cheeks to keep him in place.

"Some other time, my love." He removed her hands from his ass and, in one swift move, repositioned her so she was on her back.

When he spread her thighs and dived between them, she moaned but didn't protest, and when he licked into her, she cried out and shuddered with pleasure.

"Nectar of the gods," he murmured against her slick folds before lapping it up.

Gabi stretched her arms above her head without him having to say a thing, and as he covered her entire cleft with his mouth, she arched up to get more.

"So greedy." He fluttered his tongue over her swollen nub and then rimmed it before applying gentle pressure again.

Adding his fingers to the action, he thralled her to feel two phantom mouths sucking on her nipples, and as her body started quaking, he added two more phantom mouths with fangs that gently scraped along the sides of her breasts.

The quaking became violent, and Gabi erupted with a scream. Through the tremors, he kept sucking and licking gently until the trembling subsided, and she pushed on his head.

"No more. I'm too sensitive."

73

GABI

As Aru climbed on top of Gabi, her eyes were riveted to his beautiful face. His eyes were blazing white light, his fangs were fully elongated, and his skin was stretched over his high cheekbones and strong jaw. He was power and lust and love tied together with a ribbon and offered to her like a gift.

"I love you." She cupped his cheek.

"Gabi." He eased into her much more gently than she'd expected.

He was a big male, and she was slightly smaller than the average female, but after her climax, she had no trouble sheathing him comfortably. The fit was a little tight but not painfully so, and as he remained wedged deep inside of her without moving, her body adjusted to his size.

Reading her responses, he started moving the moment she was ready. His hands gripping her hips and pinning them to the mattress, he started a punishing tempo. Thrusting hard and fast, it took only moments for her to climb all the way to the edge, and as he released her hip to palm the back of her head, the anticipation of what was coming next was enough to trigger an explosive climax that had her screaming his name.

As he grew impossibly big inside of her, she knew that he was close, and from the retrieved memories of the other times he'd bitten her, she knew the bite was coming.

The anticipation was both terrifying and carnal, and her body flooded with another wave of heat.

As Aru moved her head, tilting it sideways and elongating her neck, Gabi fought the urge to close her eyes. She was terrified but also curious, and she wanted to see those monstrous fangs sinking into her flesh.

When he pressed his fangs against her throat, she thought he would bite right away, but he kissed and licked the spot before uttering a snake-like hiss and striking.

The searing pain was enough to make her black out, and if not for the hand clamped on the back of her head, she would have jerked away and torn her neck on those instruments of torture. But then the initial heat was replaced with the cooling sensation of the venom entering her bloodstream, and the pain was gone as if it had never existed.

A tsunami of lust was next, triggering a chain of orgasms or maybe one long one, and when that ended a lifetime later, a wave of euphoria washed over her.

The sense of peace and buoyancy was incredible, and soon she was soaring on a fluffy cloud and passing over psychedelic landscapes rich with colors that didn't exist on Earth.

Perhaps she was seeing Aru's home planet?

Or maybe she'd been catapulted into another dimension?

The second one seemed more likely because the people waving at her from below didn't resemble humans, immortals, or gods. They were translucent and glowing and, at the same time, substantial.

Perhaps they were ghosts?

Willing the cloud to glide down did not work, so she couldn't ask them who they were, and all she could do was wave back.

It was so beautiful and peaceful that Gabi was in no hurry to return, but in the back of her mind, she remembered that Aru was down there on Earth, waiting for her to float down to him and that this trip was just one of many she would go on throughout her life with him.

She would be back soon and could explore this strange world at leisure, but right now, she needed to get back.

This time, when she willed the cloud to turn around and float back to where it had picked her up, the little puff obeyed, zipping through the psychedelic landscape much faster than it had on the way there.

With a gasp, Gabi opened her eyes and gazed into Aru's relaxed face. "Hello."

He smiled. "Welcome back. Did you have a nice trip?"

"The best. How long was I gone?"

"About an hour. Why did you come back so quickly? Weren't you having fun?"

"It was amazing, but I remembered that you were waiting for me, and I knew that I would have many other opportunities to travel through the alien fields and cities, so I willed the cloud to take me back."

He grinned happily. "You must really love me to shorten your euphoric trip to return to me."

"Duh." Gabi rolled her eyes. "Isn't that obvious? I love you more than anyone and anything."

The glow returned in full force to Aru's eyes. "I love you more than anything, too. You are my truelove mate."

"I know." She cupped his cheek. "And you are mine, and no force in the universe can keep us apart."

74

SYSSI

"That's the last of it," Syssi murmured as she walked out of the closet in a simple, comfortable summer dress.

Then again, calling it simple might be an affront to the designer. The cut was perfect, the fabric so luxurious that she couldn't stop touching it, and the color was gorgeous. The only two things that were simple about it were the loose fit and that it was machine washable.

All the other outfits she'd gotten on her shopping excursion with Amanda were the kind that required dry cleaning, which was not practical for a mother of a nine-month-old baby. Still, there were many occasions that required a dressed-up look, like Perfect Match board meetings, celebrations of all kinds, and the occasional date night with Kian.

Lately, all they could manage was dinner at Callie's, which was fine with her. The food was excellent, and the company was even better.

Who needed to schlep to the city for an outing?

"I love it," Kian said quietly, not to wake up Allegra, who had fallen asleep in his arms. "It looks chic and comfortable."

Kian and Allegra had enthusiastically complimented all the new outfits she'd modeled for them, with Allegra showing her appreciation by clapping her hands and Kian by giving her sultry, glowing looks.

"Thank you." Syssi turned in a circle, trying to imitate Amanda's model moves but failing. "It's supposed to be an everyday dress, but given how much it costs, it will feel decadent wearing it around the house."

Kian glared at her. "I don't want to hear how much it cost. If you like it, wear it. In fact, I'll ask Amanda to order six more for you, one in every color."

Chuckling, she sat down next to him. "It only comes in three colors, and charcoal was the nicest."

"Then I'll order you six more of the same color. You'll have to wear them then because if you don't, it would be a waste."

He knew her too well. "Don't. I promise I'll wear this one until you are sick of seeing me in it. I might get the light gray, too, though."

"That's my girl." He wrapped his arm around her.

Leaning down, she kissed Allegra's tawny head. "Let's put her in her crib."

Kian sighed. "I love holding her, but she'll be more comfortable in her bed and sleep better."

When their daughter had a good afternoon nap, she was an angel for the rest of the day. If she didn't, she was grumpier than her father on his worst days.

As Kian pushed to his feet with Allegra in his arms, Syssi got up as well and joined him.

In the baby's room, she lifted the blanket and moved the mobile aside so he could gently lay their daughter down and then covered her. For a long moment, they just stood there, looking at their sleeping bundle of joy.

Kian moved first to activate the baby monitor, which gave Syssi an idea.

"Remember that I wanted to summon a vision today?"

Kian's shoulders immediately tensed, and he turned toward her. "I do. Where do you want to do it?"

She was glad he was standing by the deal he'd made with her and wasn't trying to dissuade her from attempting it.

"I can do it here, and you can watch over me through the baby monitor."

He arched a brow. "I thought that you couldn't concentrate and get into the special headspace when someone was with you in the room."

"That's true for everyone except for Allegra when she's asleep. The sounds of her breathing are so soothing to me that I can reach the meditative state effortlessly."

He hesitated for another split second before leaning down and kissing her cheek. "Good luck, and don't try too hard. If the vision doesn't come, don't try to force it."

"I won't."

Syssi waited until Kian left the room and closed the door behind him.

Her options for sitting were the rocking chair or the carpet on the floor, and given that she was wearing a dress, the rocking chair won.

For the first couple of minutes, she thought about Aru and his friends, then her previous vision of the brightly glowing goddess and her servant, and then took several long breaths.

As she'd told Kian, listening to Allegra's breathing made finding the receptive headspace effortless, and soon, a vision started playing in her head, clearer and more vivid than any she'd had before.

75

KIAN

It was nerve-wracking watching Syssi looking comatose in the rocking chair. Kian had cranked the baby monitor volume up so he could hear them both breathing, which was reassuring up to a point.

The fact that Syssi was breathing didn't mean that she was conscious, and he never wanted to see her unconscious again.

He would lose his shit.

It would remind him of her fighting for her life during her transition. If not for his mother's timely intervention, Syssi might not have made it, and the thought of that possibility still haunted him years later.

Stop it. She is fine. Kian walked over to the wet bar in the master bedroom and poured himself a shot of whiskey even though it wasn't one in the afternoon yet. *Syssi is immortal now. A vision can't kill her.*

The glass of whiskey in hand, Kian paced their sizable master suite while darting glances at the monitor and hoping to see Syssi with her eyes open.

How long was she going to be in a trance state?

He hated not having anything to do.

Well, that wasn't true. He had a pile of files to go through over the weekend, but he hadn't been in a rush to retire to his home office and hadn't made a dent in that pile yet. Spending time with his wife and daughter took priority.

As a deep inhale followed by a loud exhale announced the end of Syssi's vision, he didn't wait for her to open her eyes and rushed to Allegra's room.

Opening the door as quietly as he could despite the urgency, he walked into the room and was greeted by his wife's smiling face.

"It was incredible, and I didn't suffer any ill effects." She turned her head and looked at their sleeping daughter. "Do you think being near her enhanced my vision? I've never had one that was so clear."

"It's possible." He crouched in front of the rocking chair and put his hands on her thighs. "We know she has your gift. Are you sure you are okay?"

"I'm great." She took his hands in hers and used them for leverage to get out of the chair. "Let's go to our room, and I'll tell you what I saw."

"Did you see the goddess?" Kian asked as they sat on the couch in their bedroom with another shot of whiskey for him and a glass of sparkling water for Syssi.

"I saw a goddess, but I don't think it was the same one as before. I couldn't see her face this time either because of the intense glow she was emitting. Her bearing was different, though, also regal but not as rigid." Syssi took a sip of water. "You know how my visions are. It's not just about the visuals. It's also about the impression they leave, the feelings they evoke, etc., although the visuals in this one were stunning. The cavernous room was illuminated by torches, so I assumed it was a glimpse into the past. Massive pillars held the domed ceiling, but their capitals weren't done in any style I could recognize." She smiled. "And I should know since I studied the different architectural styles of various epochs and civilizations."

"I didn't know that they taught history in architecture school."

"Of course, they do. Everything we know is built on top of previous knowledge. History is important."

"Naturally." Kian took another sip from his whiskey. "So, there was nothing modern at all in the room this time?"

In her previous vision, Syssi had seen a contemporary-looking gold vase.

She shook her head. "The goddess wore a toga-style outfit that was pure white with a gold clasp holding it gathered at her shoulder, so maybe the vision was from Greece or Rome, but given the capitals, maybe it was from somewhere else." She chuckled. "Like the lost world of Atlantis."

"Or Mount Olympus," Kian offered.

"Could be." Syssi laughed. "The glowing goddess sat on a throne-like chair on top of a dais that was less than a foot tall. A couple of petitioners knelt at the foot of the dais."

"How do you know they were petitioners? Your visions are mostly soundless. Did you hear them talking?"

"I did, but I couldn't understand their language. The tone, however, was easy to interpret. They were pleading for something. The goddess rose to her sandal-clad feet, walked over to them, and put her hands on their heads. For long moments, no one said anything, and then she spoke in a deep and resonant voice that almost sounded like she was singing. The female petitioner clasped the goddess's hand and kissed the ring on her finger, and her mate did the same with the goddess's other hand."

"How did the couple look?" Kian asked. "Maybe that will give us a clue as to the location."

Syssi frowned. "They were both beautiful, but they didn't glow, and they were so grateful to the goddess. The female started crying, they embraced each other, and then thanked the goddess with a deep obeisance."

"Wait." Kian lifted his hand. "You said that they didn't glow. Are you implying that they were gods, just not luminous?"

Her eyes widened. "Yes, they were gods. They must have been commoners. Once they thanked the goddess again, they rose to their feet, and that was when I noticed a scribe sitting next to one of the massive columns. She didn't have a glow either, but since she was in the shadows, I couldn't see her face." Syssi shook her head. "Strangely, she sat on a pillow on the floor, and she had a small table in front of her with a big book open on it, and she was writing in it with something that looked like a stylus. When the couple left the chamber, the goddess told her something, and she wrote that in the book as well."

"If not for the lack of technology, I would have thought that the vision was from Anumati. It couldn't have been from Earth in the era of the gods because all of those on Earth had a glow. Maybe the vision showed you one of the gods' colonies, and the supplicants were members of the resistance."

Syssi regarded him from under lowered lashes. "Are you seriously suggesting that, or are you joking?"

He'd been serious. But apparently, Syssi found his suggestion ludicrous. "Why are you dismissive of the possibility?"

"I'm not. But nothing in the vision indicated that it was taking place on Anumati or some other planet the gods had colonized."

"I'm just speculating. What else did you see? Maybe the clue is still to come."

Syssi shrugged. "After the couple, a lone male god entered, and he had a little bit of a glow. He also knelt in front of the goddess and lowered his forehead to the floor in obeisance. He spent a few minutes talking and pleading, but the goddess didn't rise from her throne-like chair and didn't put her hand on his head. The answer she gave him didn't bring him joy either. He thanked her and left the same way the couple did, and then the vision ended."

Kian leaned back, taking Syssi with him. "So, what is your vision trying to tell us? Who was that goddess, and why was she glowing so intensely that you couldn't see her face?"

"She must have been a royal like the other one, and it must have been Anumati despite the lack of technology. I don't think that beautiful reception hall was in one of the colonies."

Kian arched a brow. "A moment ago, you dismissed my suggestion that it had to do with Anumati or one of its colonies."

"I know, but there was a clue in my previous vision that I didn't pay attention to at the time. In today's vision, torches illuminated the goddess's reception hall, but there were none in the previous one. The room was well illuminated and not because of the glowing goddess. I remember seeing a light fixture directly over the golden abstract-shaped vase. You know, like the spotlights we use to illuminate art pieces."

"Now, I'm confused."

Syssi nodded. "Perhaps what I was shown was a temple, and for some reason, technology was not allowed inside."

"That could be. Perhaps it is time to tell my mother about your visions. She might be able to help us interpret them and solve the mystery of what they are trying to tell us."

COMING UP NEXT
DARK VOYAGE TRILOGY
Children of the Gods Series Books 77-79

INCLUDES
77: DARK VOYAGE MATTERS OF THE HEART
78: DARK VOYAGE MATTERS OF THE MIND
79: DARK VOYAGE MATTERS OF THE SOUL

As Annani and Syssi set out to unravel the mysteries of Syssi's visions about the gods' home world, the long-awaited wedding cruise sets sail with Aru, Gabi, and Aru's teammates on board.

While the gods find themselves surrounded by immortal clan ladies eager for their affections, they soon discover that destiny has a different plan for them.

TURN THE PAGE TO READ THE EXCERPT—>

JOIN THE VIP CLUB
To find out what's included in your free membership, flip to the last page.

DARK VOYAGE EXERPT

1

FRANKIE

Frankie regarded her boss with a wide-eyed stare and a sinking sensation in the pit of her stomach. "Are you serious? You're not even giving me two weeks' notice? You want me to leave right now?"

Who fired people on a Monday afternoon, right after the lunch break?

Scumbags like Vernon. That's who.

He nodded. "I've found that it's best to make a clean cut and not drag things out. I will pay you for the next two weeks, of course." He gave her one of the fake smiles he usually reserved for customers. "Consider it a paid vacation."

The finality in his tone didn't leave room for argument.

"Can I at least know the reason for my termination?"

Frankie had a feeling it had to do with the 'niece' he'd brought to the office the other day and paraded around like a prize horse, introducing her to everyone. What was her name?

Was it Ashley?

Frankie couldn't remember and didn't care.

The thing was, no one's niece looked like that or clung to her uncle's arm like a panda to a tree branch.

Did Vernon need to set his mistress up with a job?

The guy was so cheap that he couldn't even be a proper sugar daddy.

Vernon sighed dramatically. "Where should I start?" He braced his elbows on the desk and steepled his fingers. "Let's see. You are often late, you make typos in the emails I dictate to you, and you don't bother to run them through a spellchecker. Do you know how embarrassing that is for me? People assume that I wrote those emails myself."

Frankie squirmed in the uncomfortable chair. Everything he'd said was true, but it didn't happen as often as he'd made it sound. Everyone was late once in a while, and everyone misspelled a word here and there, and the spellchecker didn't catch every mistake.

His 'niece' wouldn't do any better, that was for sure.

Well, at least Vernon hadn't told her that she had a big mouth and an attitude. That was the reason Frankie had been fired from her previous job.

The problem was that if he fired her for a cause, she wouldn't get unemployment benefits, especially if he exaggerated her supposed misconduct, which the scumbag would certainly do.

"What if I promise to do better?" She was fighting tears. The money in her bank account wouldn't cover next month's rent. "Can you give me another chance?"

"It's not conducive to a good office environment to have a disgruntled employee spreading discord." Vernon leaned forward, giving her a surprisingly earnest look. "You are not happy here, Francesca, and you let everyone know that. You might be happier somewhere else."

So, that was supposed to be the reason for her sudden and totally unprovoked termination?

But, no one working for Vernon was happy. He and his partners expected each of their employees to do the work of two or three people, and on top of that, the pay sucked. Still, the others might have been better at keeping their discontent to themselves, while Frankie had a big mouth and no filter.

She might have blabbed to the wrong person.

Was it the barista at the coffee shop across the street?

Or maybe someone had overheard her talking shit on her lunch break about Vernon and his sleazy partners?

At least he was going to pay her for the next two weeks. That might be enough time to find another job with less stress and better pay.

Heck, she could probably make more money taking care of kids and cleaning houses, and she might even enjoy that, but Frankie had a college degree for Pete's sake. Her parents would be mortified if she didn't use it after all the effort and sacrifice they had made so she could get the education they never had.

Besides, Frankie liked dressing elegantly and working in an office.

That said, the office attire at the dream job Mia had promised her was probably super casual. Beta testers for the Perfect Match Virtual Fantasy Studios couldn't wear anything form-fitting while performing their duties, and they had to take their shoes off.

Mia had promised her the job months ago, but nothing had come out of it so far. Supposedly, the machines weren't ready because of production delays, but Frankie had a feeling that Mia might have promised something that she couldn't deliver.

"Will you at least write me a reference letter?" she pleaded, hating herself for having to beg Vernon for anything.

But what else could she do?

If he wrote her a reference, he couldn't later claim that she was a horrible employee and wasn't entitled to unemployment benefits.

"Of course." Vernon Hoffesommer III looked relieved. "In fact, you can write whatever you want, and I'll sign it."

That was better than Frankie had expected, but knowing Vernon, she'd better write it and get his signature before she left, or he would later claim he'd never promised to do it. Right now, he obviously wanted to get rid of her as fast as possible, and she needed to take advantage of that.

"Thank you." She gave him a dazzling smile. "I'll type it up right now, so I don't need to return for it."

Vernon's expression soured, confirming her suspicion that he was desperate to get rid of her, but he nodded. "Make it short."

Was his 'niece' in the waiting room? Ready to jump into Frankie's seat or onto Vernon's lap?

Probably.

"I'll be right back." She rose to her high-heeled feet and walked out of his office holding her chin up, even though she was faking it big time.

After typing up a glowing reference letter, she actually checked it for spelling mistakes before printing it out and striding back into Vernon's office.

He read through the letter with a grimace, twisting his fleshy lips, and when he shook his head, Frankie held her breath, but then he reached for his pen and signed it.

"Good luck, Francesca."

Unbelievable.

Frankie hadn't thought he would actually sign the thing. She'd made herself sound like the best assistant an executive could ever hope for.

To sign that, Vernon must have felt guilty for kicking her out to make room for his 'niece.'

Relief washing over her, she took the printed page from his hairy fingers and offered him her hand. "Thank you, Mr. Hoffesommer."

In exchange for his signature on the letter, she was willing to suffer his gross touch one last time.

Vernon had never done anything more than put his sweaty paw on her shoulder or her upper arm while passing by her desk, so it wasn't enough to sue his ass for sexual harassment, but to say that it had been unwelcome was to put it mildly.

Dreading his slimy touch, she'd stopped wearing outfits that exposed her shoulders or arms to the office.

Back at her desk, Frankie collected the one picture of her family and the tiny cactus she'd brought to decorate her space. Lifting her eyes, she scanned the rest of the staff working in the office's main room. She searched for one face that she would miss, but none of them even bothered to look up.

Hell, she'd made some friends during the eighteen months she'd worked there. They could at least wish her luck.

Turning around, she saw why no one dared to lift their heads.

Vernon stood at the doorway with his arms crossed over his chest and resting on his large belly.

Was he worried that she would steal a pen? Or maybe a book of stamps?

Plastering on a smile, she waved at her former coworkers. "Goodbye, everyone." She turned to Vernon with that smile still affixed to her face. "Goodbye, Mr. Hoffesommer. I hope your 'niece' will like it here better than I did."

2

DAGOR

"What do you think?" Negal pointed with his chin at the two women walking through the door of the coffee shop that had become their refuge over the weekend.

The females were pretty, for young humans that is, but neither had the poise, elegance, and self-assurance that Dagor appreciated in his companions.

Sneakers and jeans just did not do it for him, and neither did all the skin decorations that were so fashionable among the young humans in this city.

Gods couldn't get tattoos because their bodies healed the punctures faster than the artists could make them, and Dagor was thankful for that. Who wanted to be stuck with crappy artwork for eternity?

Or even great artwork, for that matter?

"Not my type." He closed his lips around the paper straw and drew up more of the delicious Frappuccino that had become his favorite drink since he'd discovered it.

"You are too picky." Negal leaned closer to him. "You won't find goddesses here, and you need to compromise. For humans, those two are not bad."

"I'm not picky." Dagor put the Frappuccino down. After spending five years on Earth with him, Negal should have known what type of females interested him. "The attorneys the other day were very pleasant company."

Neither had been beautiful or even pretty, but the conversation was stimulating, and they had been immaculately dressed.

Negal grinned. "Yeah, those two were superb in more ways than one, or at least the one I picked. It's a shame we can't see them again."

After spending the night with them in the hotel, the ladies had been more than eager to provide their phone numbers, but Dagor and Negal had a rule about being with human companions more than once.

Before meeting Gabi, Aru had obeyed the same rule, but he'd broken it for her without giving it a second thought. At the time, Dagor couldn't understand their commander's odd behavior and his fascination with the human, but as it had turned out, Gabi had not been fully human. She had godly genes in her, which explained the attraction.

Still, Gabi was not a goddess, only an immortal—a hybrid who was considered an abomination in their home world.

Not that Dagor believed in that nonsense. Gabriella was a lovely female, but even more importantly, she was Aru's fated mate. Nevertheless, the union was problematic in the sense that Aru could never take her back to Anumati with him and could never introduce her to his family and friends back home. The resistance would have welcomed her, but there was no way to smuggle her onto the patrol ship, or any other ship for that matter. All the stasis pods were accounted for, and their occupants' biometrics were monitored from Anumati.

If only the resistance could build its own ships somewhere away from Anumati's watchful eyes, but that was impossible. Humans thought their privacy was being eroded, but they had no idea how much worse it could get.

The one good thing about being on Earth was the freedom to do and say whatever he wanted without worrying about the censorship that possibly extended even to thoughts. There was no proof, but there were rumors about the king employing telepaths. Most of them couldn't read actual thoughts, but they could sense intentions, which was dangerous for the resistance.

Rebels had learned how to shield their thoughts and emotions.

The problem was that it didn't mean much when there was so little that he could do with this planet's primitive technology.

Leaning back in his chair, Dagor groaned. "I need something to do that involves using my head for more than people-watching. I'm bored out of my mind, and I'm not even a century old yet."

A guy sitting at the table next to theirs turned to him and nodded. "I get it, bro. Sometimes I feel ancient, too."

Forcing a smile, Dagor lifted the plastic cup and saluted the guy.

He'd found out that humans responded well to noncommittal gestures that could mean many different things.

Negal glared at him. "You need to keep your voice down."

"I know. My bad."

That was another human expression Dagor had adopted that worked very well for a variety of situations.

Leaning even closer to him, Negal whispered in his ear, "You are too young to suffer from the affliction of boredom. Perhaps you should contact the ship's counselor."

Dagor wasn't losing his mind, and he had no intention of talking to the counselor, but to get Negal off his back, he had to acquiesce.

"Perhaps I will go to see her after this mission is over. You know that empaths need skin-to-skin contact to be able to provide real help. She can't do much for me through the communicator."

"By the time we get picked up, it might be too late," Negal said in their native tongue. "A hundred and fifteen years is not long in the life of a god, but if you are already showing signs of mental fatigue, you should not delay seeking help. Even talking with the counselor might be beneficial. She might give you advice on how to combat these early signs of decline."

Dagor didn't wish to offend Negal, but he'd had enough of the insinuations that he was going insane. It was a major concern for Anumatians, but he was too young to be showing even early symptoms.

"My mental faculties are intact. It's just that we are stuck here doing nothing while Aru takes care of his mate. I am tired of sitting in this blasted coffee shop and watching humans come and go." He lifted the venti Frappuccino cup. "That's the only saving grace of this place."

Arching a brow, Negal leaned back. "I quite enjoy the respite we have been given. Sitting here and hunting for suitable bed companions is far more enjoyable than trekking through Tibet and sleeping on the cold ground. I am not looking forward to the day Aru decides that Gabriella is strong enough to travel, and we will be back on the road, searching for the missing Kra-ell pods."

Sometimes, Dagor wondered whether Negal's linear way of thinking was an inborn tendency or a product of his many years in the service.

"The pods are not the only thing we should be searching for."

The immortals were hiding gods among them, and Aru knew about it. He just didn't seem to think that his teammates were trustworthy enough to tell them about what he had discovered.

No matter how Dagor tried to excuse his leader's motives, the insult stung.

The smirk slid off Negal's face. "We are not supposed to know about the gods, and I feel conflicted about not telling Aru that we do."

The guy at the other table looked at them with curiosity in his eyes. "What language are you two speaking?"

"It's a dialect of Hungarian," Dagor said. "We are from a small village high up in the mountains, and our people are the only ones who speak this particular form of the language."

The guy nodded sagely. "I thought that it sounded European."

Dagor wasn't sure whether Hungarian sounded like their native tongue or even if the country had mountains, but this explanation had worked before, so he used it again.

Negal shook his head. "If you want to keep talking, we should get out of here."

"And go where? To the penthouse where Gabi and Aru might be frolicking amorously on every available surface?"

He didn't begrudge Aru his happiness, but he wished the guy would get over the honeymoon phase so they could get moving again.

They had a mission to complete.

Negal released a sigh. "We could go to a museum or to a library. There is so much we still don't know about these humans, and we can use this idle time to learn more about them."

"The humans are of no interest to me. I want to find out who the gods are that Gabi's brother talked about. Perhaps we should just confront Aru and tell him that we know."

The conversation between Gabi and her brother had been recorded by the spy bug they had attached to the brother, and Aru had later erased it. Their leader wasn't familiar enough with human tech and didn't realize how primitive it still was. He couldn't have guessed that deleting the recording wouldn't do the trick.

Dagor's intention hadn't been to spy on their leader when he'd checked the trash folder. Suspecting that Aru had messed with the laptop, he had checked it just to make sure that nothing important had been deleted by mistake.

Listening to the recording, he'd realized what Aru had been trying to hide, but not why he had done it. They were supposed to be a team, and they were all members of the resistance.

Aru should have trusted him and Negal with the information, and it was disturbing that he hadn't.

What else was he hiding from them?

3

ANNANI

After spending the weekend in atypical solitary contemplation, Annani had a little more clarity about the information they had learned from the three gods who claimed to belong to the resistance. Regrettably, it was not enough to help Kian form a strategy regarding the threat of the Eternal King.

Her paternal grandfather.

Her greatest nemesis.

It was funny how inconsequential Mortdh and Navuh seemed in comparison.

Mortdh had been a bully with delusions of grandeur, a powerful compeller, but a mediocre politician at best. He had not been difficult to outmaneuver, but in the end the law of unintended consequences had prevailed, resulting in a disaster that had eclipsed anything Mortdh had in mind for her and the future of the gods.

Perhaps things would have ended the same way regardless of her role in shaping the events, but Annani would always carry the guilt of inadvertently being responsible for her people's demise.

For Khiann's death.

His murder at the hands of Mortdh.

If she could have seen the future, she would never have pursued him.

It would have been better to have never known the great love they had shared than to mourn his death.

Mortdh was dead, and his successor, her current arch-nemesis, was not as delusional and not as powerful as his father, but Navuh was smarter and a better politician. It took more than his incredible compulsion ability to lead an army of immortal warriors dedicated to the cause and eager to do his bidding.

Her clan could deal with Navuh and his Brotherhood of murderers, but just barely so, while the Eternal King was in a league of his own.

He had been ruling over the gods, the rulers of the galaxy, for hundreds of thousands of years, and according to Aru, a large number of his subjects were not opposed to his rule. They were satisfied with their lives on Anumati.

Her grandfather was brilliant, a true master of propaganda, but then even the gods were easy to manipulate. As long as there was prosperity and something to strive for, people were willing to overlook things like the gradual erosion of their personal freedoms, especially when such things took place ever so slowly over eons.

So what if saying things that did not agree with the official line could get them in trouble?

Remaining silent was easier than becoming part of the resistance and actively doing something against the censorship.

Not everyone had what it took to be a rebel, but she must have inherited her father's rebellious character because no one could accuse her of being complicit.

Annani was an idealist and a fighter.

Or had been.

Now that she had a clan comprised of her descendants, their chosen mates, and two other groups of people to protect, she was much less hasty to rise to the challenge than she had been in her youth.

Still, she was keenly aware that Earth was uniquely positioned to host the rebellion against her grandfather. Come to think of it, her father had laid the groundwork, either anticipating this or just as a result of following his moral compass and building a community based on the ideals he had pursued on Anumati.

Had Ahn envisioned Earth becoming the place where gods, immortals, humans, and Kra-ell, both purebloods and hybrids, could coexist in harmony and equality?

Had he foreseen that Kra-ell and immortals could someday form fated bonds and produce uniquely gifted hybrid children?

The tapestry the Fates had woven on Earth was unlike anything else in the universe. Had they done it to show the gods a model of a civilization that did not discriminate between the different species?

A society that did not place taboos on mating between gods and Kra-ell, immortals and humans?

Had they foreseen the new species of hybrid children that would be unlike anything the galaxy had seen before?

Right now, Earth was far from utopia, and humans overwhelmingly outnumbered all the other alien species living among them, but that was just the beginning. It could become the crown jewel of the resistance, the place they could point to for people to see what was possible.

The problem was protecting this precious jewel from the Eternal King and also from self-destruction.

Thanks to technology, the world's economy was so interconnected that it did not make sense for one superpower to launch a military attack against another, but humans did not always do what made sense, and the threat of a third world war was not as far outside the realm of probability as many believed.

Regrettably, the vast majority of the world's leadership was not concerned with the well-being of its citizenry. The elites looked after their own, filling both their pockets and those of their associates, while the young died in senseless wars and families died of plagues and famines that could have been avoided.

There was nothing new under the sun. Generations came and went, but the dynamic never changed.

With a sigh, Annani walked over to her favorite armchair and sat down.

Would things ever get better?

She had spent her entire life, over five thousand years, working on improving the human condition, and the fruits of her labors were evident, but there was still so much to do, and now it seemed like she was running out of time.

Lifting her arm, she examined her luminous skin and wondered whether it looked dimmer because of her melancholy mood or if it was her imagination.

The mystery of the commoner gods on Anumati lacking glow still had not been satisfactorily answered, and perhaps the simplest and easiest explanation was lack of energy. Perhaps they lacked luminosity because they were suppressed and their freedoms were limited. Maybe positive energy was needed to fuel the glow, and the commoner gods on Anumati did not have enough of it, while all the gods she had known on Earth had a healthy glow, and not all of them had been nobility.

Annani shook her head.

That could not be the explanation.

She had not met Aru and his friends yet, but if finding his fated mate did not make Aru burst with positive energy and activate his glow, then he did not have the ability.

When her phone rang, Annani pulled it out of the pocket of her gown and smiled at Kian's handsome face filling the screen.

"Hello, my darling son," she answered.

"Good evening, Mother. Are you busy?"

"Not at all."

"Are you in the mood for receiving guests?"

Annani chuckled. "That will depend on who the guests are."

"Syssi and I would like to share a vision that Syssi had and ask your opinion about it."

Excitement bubbled in Annani's chest, and as she lifted her arm to look at her glow, it was much brighter than before. Perhaps there was a connection between mood and luminosity after all.

"I would love a visit from you whatever the reason." She had to admit that the vision added a level of excitement. "Are you bringing Allegra along?"

"She is asleep. I'll leave Okidu to watch her, and if she gets fussy, he can bring her over."

Annani laughed. "Am I a bad grandmother for wishing her to get fussy just so I can see her?"

"You are the best grandma," Syssi said in the background. "We will put her in the stroller and bring her over."

"She is sleeping!" Kian protested. "You know what happens when we wake her when she doesn't want to be up. She becomes a terror."

"I'll be careful," Syssi said. "Perhaps she should be there when I share my vision."

To Annani's great surprise, Kian agreed.

"Yeah, you might be right."

She could not stifle her curiosity. "Why would you need Allegra with you to tell me about your vision?"

"Syssi will explain when we get there," Kian said. "We will be on our way shortly."

4

KIAN

"You're incredible," Kian whispered after Syssi had somehow managed the impossible and transferred Allegra from the crib to the stroller without waking her up.

"I know." Smiling smugly, Syssi packed several bottles and pacifiers in the baby bag.

Allegra wasn't a great fan of pacifiers, mostly using them as projectiles to throw at people when she wanted their attention, but occasionally they helped her fall asleep.

The soft pink blanket she had gotten from Anita was also a necessary sleeping aid. It was surprising that Syssi's mother even knew how to knit, let alone found the time to knit a blanket for her granddaughter.

Which reminded Kian. "Did you talk to your parents about the cruise?"

"I did." Syssi transferred the command of the stroller to him. "Surprisingly, my mother was excited about joining and said that she would try to get a replacement. If she finds a doctor to take over for her, she'll let me know so we can make the flight arrangements." She smiled. "It's not like we are giving my parents ample notice to plan. You only decided to go ahead with the cruise yesterday, and we are sailing in two and a half weeks."

It wouldn't have mattered if her parents had months to prepare. Most of the time, Anita just didn't want to leave her clinic, and not being able to find a replacement was always a convenient excuse for why she couldn't come to this or that event.

And yet, Syssi never made a fuss about it or showed her disappointment, and it wasn't because she didn't want to see her parents. She was just selfless and accepted that her mother's work always came first.

His wife was the most understanding person on the planet, and he was the luckiest guy to have her.

"Let's take a little stroll up the street," Syssi said.

It was only a few paces to his mother's house, and it was a pleasant evening for a stroll, but he had promised that they would be there shortly.

"Just for a few minutes." He passed his mother's house and kept walking. "Are you excited?"

Syssi shrugged. "I'm excited about Alena and Orion finally getting married and all the other weddings that will take place on the cruise. As for my parents, I will hold off my excitement until their flight is booked, and even then, I won't allow myself to celebrate until I see them boarding the ship."

"That's a wise attitude." He wrapped his arm around her and pushed the stroller with his free hand. "But then everything you do is wise."

She arched a brow. "Really? Says the guy who was upset about me chasing visions."

"In your infinite wisdom, you convinced me of the futility of my worries."

Syssi's frown deepened. "Who are you, and what did you do with my husband?"

"I am a reformed man." Kian winked. "Most of the time."

"Oh, yeah? And what are you at other times?"

He chuckled. "Sometimes I'm still the alpha-hole you fell in love with and married."

She didn't smile. "I've never called you that. Where did you even hear that expression?" She narrowed her eyes at him. "Have you been reading my romance novels again?"

He pretended to look guilty. "You leave your books in my office, and it's easy to pick one up and start reading a paragraph or two." He smiled. "I need to know how to keep things fresh, and those books are a great source of inspiration." And also a few laughs, but he kept that part to himself.

Sometimes, when he had to work late into the night, Syssi sat on the couch in their home office and read while he worked. He loved having her there and seeing the relaxed expression on her face while she was immersed in the story. She read romance novels to relax at the end of her day, and those types of books guaranteed happily-ever-afters, where nothing truly terrible ever happened to spoil her mood.

There was enough of that in the real world.

Letting out an exasperated sigh, Syssi put her hand on his arm. "Please don't. Those are someone else's fantasies, not mine. If you want inspiration, my Perfect Match scenarios are a better source."

"You haven't written anything new in a while."

"I know." She sighed. "Between taking care of Allegra, working at the university, and dealing with one crisis after another, I don't have the bandwidth left to think creatively." She lifted a hand to her temple. "I used to be able to tune everything out and concentrate on the scenarios, but lately, I can't even bring myself to read through the Perfect Match financial reports or do anything productive at the end of the day."

"You need a vacation." He kissed the top of her head. "That's one of the reasons I accepted my mother's suggestion and made compromises regarding the cruise. The Kra-ell will stay behind with most of Kalugal's men."

Syssi tilted her head. "I hope Jade doesn't feel left out."

He snorted. "I would love to reenact her response for you, but I'm not a good enough actor to do it justice. The gist was that she called me nuts for thinking that her people would ever want to get on that ship again. The Kra-ell hate deep water, and some are still traumatized by the swimming lessons Phinas forced them to take in the ship's freezing pool."

"Yeah, it occurred to me that they might not be overly enthusiastic about going on the cruise. Your mother will be disappointed, though.

Knowing her, she thought seeing her presiding over the weddings would be the best way to introduce her to the Kra-ell without making it formal."

Annani had met with Jade and several of the other main Kra-ell players, but there hadn't been a formal meeting with all the newcomers.

Kian trusted Jade, but he didn't yet trust all of the Kra-ell. That was one of the reasons he hadn't lowered the security alert level even after the crisis with the new gods had been resolved. A team of Guardians watched over his mother twenty-four seven.

"I just hope she won't demand a formal meeting with the Kra-ell before we sail."

Syssi arched a brow. "I thought you trusted Jade."

"I do, and she also vowed to protect the village to her last breath, but I'm not sure about all the others, and I need more time to get to know them."

"Did she give you the life vow? You said that you didn't want her to do that."

"It wasn't the life vow per se, and I tried to stop her, but it was no use. Jade is an incredibly stubborn female."

"And yet you like her."

He nodded. "I see a lot of myself in her."

"I'm okay with you admiring Jade, but don't overdo it." Syssi pouted. "You are making me jealous."

Kian stopped and turned to his mate. "You are the person I admire most in the world. You are everything to me." He took her hand and brought it to his lips. "You and our daughter own my heart."

Perhaps he could have come up with something more eloquent, but that was how he felt.

"I know." Syssi smiled. "I was just kidding about Jade. But you can't admire me more than your mother. That's just not right. She's the Clan Mother, the only legitimate heir of the Eternal King, and therefore, the second most important person in the galaxy, or perhaps even the most important one if the resistance takes the Eternal King down."

DARK VOYAGE TRILOGY

INCLUDES

Also by I. T. Lucas

PERFECT MATCH

Vampire's Consort
King's Chosen
Captain's Conquest
The Thief Who Loved Me
My Merman Prince
The Dragon King
My Werewolf Romeo
The Channeler's Companion
The Valkyrie & The Witch
Adina and the Magic Lamp

TRANSLATIONS

DIE ERBEN DER GÖTTER
Dark Stranger
1- Dark Stranger Der Traum
2- Dark Stranger Die Offenbarung
3- Dark Stranger Unsterblich

Dark Enemy
4- Dark Enemy Entführt
5- Dark Enemy Gefangen
6- Dark Enemy Erlöst

Dark Warrior
7- Dark Warrior Meine Sehnsucht
8- Dark Warrior – Dein Versprechen
9- Dark Warrior - Unser Schicksal

LOS HIJOS DE LOS DIOSES

EL OSCURO DESCONOCIDO
1: EL OSCURO DESCONOCIDO EL SUEÑO
2: EL OSCURO DESCONOCIDO REVELADO
3: EL OSCURO DESCONOCIDO INMORTAL
EL OSCURO ENEMIGO
4- EL OSCURO ENEMIGO CAPTURADO
5 - EL OSCURO ENEMIGO CAUTIVO
6- EL OSCURO ENEMIGO REDIMIDO

LES ENFANTS DES DIEUX
DARK STRANGER
1- DARK STRANGER LE RÊVE
2- DARK STRANGER LA RÉVÉLATION
3- DARK STRANGER L'IMMORTELLE

THE CHILDREN OF THE GODS SERIES SETS

BOOKS 1-3: DARK STRANGER TRILOGY—INCLUDES A BONUS SHORT STORY: THE FATES TAKE A VACATION

BOOKS 4-6: DARK ENEMY TRILOGY —INCLUDES A BONUS SHORT STORY—THE FATES' POST-WEDDING CELEBRATION

BOOKS 7-10: DARK WARRIOR TETRALOGY
BOOKS 11-13: DARK GUARDIAN TRILOGY
BOOKS 14-16: DARK ANGEL TRILOGY
BOOKS 17-19: DARK OPERATIVE TRILOGY
BOOKS 20-22: DARK SURVIVOR TRILOGY
BOOKS 23-25: DARK WIDOW TRILOGY

Books 26-28: Dark Dream Trilogy

Books 29-31: Dark Prince Trilogy

Books 32-34: Dark Queen Trilogy

Books 35-37: Dark Spy Trilogy

Books 38-40: Dark Overlord Trilogy

Books 41-43: Dark Choices Trilogy

Books 44-46: Dark Secrets Trilogy

Books 47-49: Dark Haven Trilogy

Books 50-52: Dark Power Trilogy

Books 53-55: Dark Memories Trilogy

Books 56-58: Dark Hunter Trilogy

Books 59-61: Dark God Trilogy

Books 62-64: Dark Whispers Trilogy

Books 65-67: Dark Gambit Trilogy

Books 68-70: Dark Alliance Trilogy

Books 71-73: Dark Healing Trilogy

Books 74-76: Dark Encounters Trilogy

MEGA SETS

The Children of the Gods: Books 1-6

INCLUDES CHARACTER LISTS

The Children of the Gods: Books 6.5-10

Perfect Match Bundle 1

CHECK OUT THE SPECIALS ON
ITLUCAS.COM
(https://itlucas.com/specials)

FOR EXCLUSIVE PEEKS AT UPCOMING RELEASES & A FREE I. T. LUCAS COMPANION BOOK

FOR EXCLUSIVE PEEKS AT UPCOMING RELEASES & A FREE I. T. LUCAS COMPANION BOOK

JOIN MY *VIP CLUB* AND GAIN ACCESS TO THE VIP PORTAL AT ITLUCAS.COM
TO JOIN, GO TO:
http://eepurl.com/blMTpD

INCLUDED IN YOUR FREE MEMBERSHIP:

YOUR VIP PORTAL

- READ PREVIEW CHAPTERS OF UPCOMING RELEASES.
- LISTEN TO GODDESS'S CHOICE NARRATION BY CHARLES LAWRENCE
- EXCLUSIVE CONTENT OFFERED ONLY TO MY VIPs.

FREE I.T. LUCAS COMPANION INCLUDES:

- GODDESS'S CHOICE PART 1
- PERFECT MATCH: VAMPIRE'S CONSORT (A STANDALONE NOVELLA)
- INTERVIEW Q & A
- CHARACTER CHARTS

IF YOU'RE ALREADY A SUBSCRIBER, AND YOU ARE NOT GETTING MY EMAILS, YOUR PROVIDER IS SENDING THEM TO YOUR JUNK FOLDER, AND YOU ARE MISSING OUT ON IMPORTANT UPDATES, SIDE CHARACTERS' PORTRAITS, ADDITIONAL CONTENT, AND OTHER GOODIES. TO FIX THAT, ADD isabell@ itlucas.com TO YOUR EMAIL CONTACTS OR YOUR EMAIL VIP LIST.

**Check out the specials at
https://www.itlucas.com/specials**

Printed in Great Britain
by Amazon

57096434R00443